SURFACE DETAIL

BY IAIN M. BANKS

Consider Phlebas
The Player of Games
Use of Weapons
The State of the Art
Against a Dark Background
Feersum Endjinn
Excession
Inversions
Look to Windward
The Algebraist
Matter
Surface Detail

BY IAIN BANKS

The Wasp Factory
Walking on Glass
The Bridge
Espedair Street
Canal Dreams
The Crow Road
Complicity
Whit
A Song of Stone
The Business
Dead Air
The Steep Approach to Garbadale
Transition

IAIN M. BANKS

SURFACE DETAIL

www.orbitbooks.net

ORBIT

First published in Great Britain in 2010 by Orbit

All characters and events in this publication, other than those clearly in the public domain, are fictitious and any resemblance to real persons, living or dead, is purely coincidental.

A CIP catalogue record for this book is available from the British Library.

ISBN 978-1-84149-893-5
C FORMAT 978-1-84149-894-2

Typeset in Stempel Garamond by
Palimpsest Book Production Limited, Falkirk, Stirlingshire
Printed and bound in Great Britain by Clays Ltd, St Ives plc

Papers used by Orbit are natural, renewable and recyclable products sourced from well-managed forests and certified in accordance with the rules of the Forest Stewardship Council.

Orbit
An imprint of
Little, Brown Book Group
100 Victoria Embankment
London EC4Y 0DY

An Hachette UK Company
www.hachette.co.uk

www.orbitbooks.net

For Seth and Lara

With thanks to Adèle

One

"This one might be trouble."

She heard one of them say this, only ten or so metres away in the darkness. Even over her fear, the sheer naked terror of being hunted, she felt a shiver of excitement, of something like triumph, when she realised they were talking about her. Yes, she thought, she would be trouble, she already was trouble. And they were worried too; the hunters experienced their own fears during the chase. Well, at least one of them did. The man who'd spoken was Jasken; Veppers' principal bodyguard and chief of security. Jasken. Of course; who else?

"You think so . . . do you?" said a second man. That was Veppers himself. It felt as though something curdled inside her when she heard his deep, perfectly modulated voice, right now attenuated to something just above a whisper. "But then . . . they're all trouble." He sounded out of breath. "Can't you see . . . *anything* with those?" He must be talking about Jasken's Enhancing Oculenses; a fabulously expensive piece of hardware like heavy-duty sunglasses. They turned night to day, made heat visible and could see radio waves, allegedly. Jasken tended to wear them all the time, which she had always thought was just showing off, or betrayed some deep insecurity. Wonderful though they might be, they had yet to deliver her into Veppers' exquisitely manicured hands.

She was standing, flattened, against a flat scenery. In the gloom, a moment before she had spread herself against the enormous backdrop, she had been able to make out that it was just painted canvas with great sweeps of dark and light paint, but she had been too close to it to see what it actually portrayed. She angled her head out a little and risked a quick look down and to the left, to where the two men were, standing on a gantry cantilevered out from the side of the fly tower's north wall. She glimpsed a pair of shadowy figures, one holding something that might have been a rifle. She couldn't be sure. Unlike Jasken, she had only her own eyes to see with.

She brought her head back in again, quickly but smoothly, scared that she might be seen, and tried to breathe deeply, evenly, silently. She twisted her neck this way and that, clenched and unclenched her fists, flexed her already aching legs. She was standing on a narrow wooden ledge at the bottom of the flat. It was slightly narrower than her shoes; she had to keep her feet splayed, toes pointing outwards in opposite directions, to stop herself from falling. Beneath, unseen in the darkness, the wide rear stage of the opera house was twenty metres further down. If she fell, there were probably other cross-gantries or scenery towers in the way for her to hit on the way down.

Above her, unseen in the gloom, was the rest of the fly tower and the gigantic carousel that sat over the rear of the opera house's stage and stored all the multifarious sets its elaborate productions required. She started to edge very slowly along the ledge, away from where the two men stood on the wall gantry. Her left heel still hurt where she'd dug out a tracer device, days earlier.

"Sulbazghi?" she heard Veppers say, voice low. He and Jasken had been talking quietly to each other; now they were probably using a radio or something similar. She didn't hear any answer from Dr. Sulbazghi; probably Jasken was wearing an earpiece. Maybe Veppers too, though he rarely carried a phone or any other comms gear.

Veppers, Jasken and Dr. S. She wondered how many were chasing her as well as these three. Veppers had guards to command, a whole retinue of servants, aides, helpers and other employees who might be pressed into service to help in a pursuit like this. The opera house's own security would help too, if called on; the place belonged to Veppers, after all. And no doubt Veppers' good friend, the city Chief of Police would lend any forces requested of him, in the highly unlikely event Veppers couldn't muster enough of his own. She kept on sliding her way along the ledge.

"On the north side wall," she heard Veppers say after a few moments. "Gazing up at varied bucolic backdrops and scenic scenes. No sign of our little illustrated girl." He sighed. Theatrically, she thought, which was at least appropriate. "Lededje?" he called out suddenly.

She was startled to hear her own name; she trembled and felt the painted flat at her back wobble. Her left hand flew to one of the two knives she'd stolen, the double sheath looped onto the belt of the workman's trousers she was wearing. She started to tip forward, felt herself about to fall; she brought her hand back, steadied herself again.

"Lededje?" His voice, her name, echoed inside the great dark depths of the fly carousel. She shuffled further along the narrow ledge. Was it starting to bend? She thought she felt it flexing beneath her feet.

"*Lededje?*" Veppers called again. "Come on now, this is becoming boring. I have a terribly important reception to attend in a couple of hours and you know how long it takes to get me properly dressed and ready. You'll have Astil fretting. You wouldn't want that now, would you?"

She indulged a sneer. She didn't give a damn what Astil, Veppers' pompous butler, thought or felt.

"You've had your few days of freedom but that's over now, accept it," Veppers' deep voice said, echoing. "Come out like a good girl and I promise you won't be hurt. Not much anyway. A slap, perhaps. A minor addition to your bodymark, just possibly. Small; a detail, obviously. And exquisitely done, of course. I'd have it no other way." She thought she could hear him smiling as he spoke. "But no more. I swear. Seriously, dear child. Come out now while I can still persuade myself this is merely charming high spirits and attractive rebelliousness rather than gross treachery and outright insult."

"Fuck you," Lededje said, very, very quietly. She took another couple of shuffling, sliding steps along the thin wooden band at the foot of the flat. She heard what might have been a creak beneath her. She swallowed and kept on going.

"Lededje, come on!" Veppers' voice boomed out. "I'm trying terribly hard to be reasonable here! I *am* being reasonable, aren't I, Jasken?" She heard Jasken mutter something, then Veppers' voice pealed out again: "Yes, indeed. There you are; even Jasken thinks I'm being reasonable, and he's been making so many excuses for you he's practically on your side. What more can you ask for? So, now it's your turn. This is your last chance. Show yourself, young lady. I'm becoming impatient. This is no longer funny. Do you hear me?"

Oh, very clearly, she thought. How he liked the sound of his own voice. Joiler Veppers had never been one to fight shy of letting the world know exactly what he thought about anything, and, thanks to his wealth, influence and extensive media interests, the world – indeed the system, the entire Enablement – had never really had much choice but to listen.

"I am serious, Lededje. This is not a game. This stops now, by your choice if you've any sense, or I make it stop. And trust me, scribble-child, you do not want me to make it stop."

Another sliding step, another creak from beneath her feet. Well, at least his voice might cover any noise she might be making.

"Five beats, Lededje," he called. "Then we do it the hard way." Her feet slid slowly along the thin strip of wood. "All right," Veppers said. She could hear the anger in his voice, and despite her hate, her utter contempt for him, something about that tone still had the effect of sending a chill of fear through her. Suddenly there was a noise like a slap, and for an instant she thought he'd struck Jasken across the face, then realised it was just a handclap. "One!" he shouted. A pause, then another clap. "Two!"

Her right hand, tightly gloved, was extended as far as she could reach, feeling for the thin strip of wood that formed the edge of the scenery flat. Beyond that should lie the wall, and ladders, steps, gantries; even just ropes – anything to let her make her escape. Another, even louder clap, echoing in the dark, lost spaces of the carousel fly tower. "Three!"

She tried to remember the size of the opera stage. She had been here a handful of times with Veppers and the rest of his extended entourage, brought along as a trophy, a walking medal denoting his commercial victories; she ought to be able to remember. All she could recall was being sourly impressed by the scale of everything: the brightness, depth and working complexity of the scenery; the physical effects produced by trapdoors, hidden wires, smoke machines and fireworks; the sheer amount of noise the hidden orchestra and the strutting, overdressed singers and their embedded microphones could create.

It had been like watching a very convincing super-size holoscreen, but one comically limited to just this particular width and depth and height of set, and incapable of the sudden cuts and instant changes of scene and scale possible in a screen. There were hidden cameras focused on the principal players, and side screens at the edge of the stage showing them in 3D close-up, but it was still – perhaps just because of the obviously prodigious amount of effort, time and money spent on it all – a bit pathetic really. It was as though being fabulously rich and powerful meant not being able to enjoy a film – or at least not being able to admit to enjoying one – but still you had to try to re-create films on stage. She hadn't seen the point. Veppers had loved it. "Four!"

Only afterwards – mingling, paraded, socialising, exhibited – had she realised it was really just an excuse and the opera itself a side-show; the true spectacle of the evening was always played out inside the sumptuous foyer, upon the glittering staircases, within the curved sweep of dazzlingly lit, high-ceilinged corridors, beneath the towering chandeliers in the palatial anterooms, around fabulously laden tables in resplendently decorated saloons, in the absurdly grand rest rooms and in the boxes, front rows and elected seats of the auditorium rather than on the stage itself. The super-rich and ultra-powerful regarded themselves as the true stars, and their entrances and exits, gossip, approaches, advances, suggestions, proposals and prompts within the public spaces of this massive building constituted the proper business of the event.

"Enough of this melodrama, lady!" Veppers shouted.

If it was just the three of them – Veppers, Jasken and Sulbazghi – and if it stayed just the three of them, she might have a chance. She had embarrassed Veppers and he wouldn't want any more people to know about that than absolutely had to. Jasken and Dr. S didn't count; they could be relied upon, they would never talk. Others might, others would. If outsiders had to be involved they would surely know she had disobeyed him and bested him even temporarily. He would feel the shame of that, magnified by his grotesque vanity. It was that overweening self-regard, that inability to suffer even the thought of shame, that might let her get away.

"Five!"

She paused, felt herself swallow as the final clap resounded in the darkness around her.

"So! That's what you want?" Veppers shouted. Again, she could hear the anger in his voice. "You had your chance, Lededje. Now we—"

"Sir!" she shouted, not too loudly, still looking away from him, in the direction she was shuffling.

"What?"

"Was that her?"

"Led?" Jasken shouted.

"Sir!" she yelled, keeping her voice lower than a full shout but trying to make it sound as though she was putting all her effort into it. "I'm here! I'm done with this. My apologies, sir. I'll accept whatever punishment you choose."

"Indeed you will," she heard Veppers mutter. Then he raised his voice, "Where is 'here'?" he called. "Where are you?"

She raised her head, projecting her voice into the great dark spaces above, where vast sets like stacked cards loomed. "In the tower, sir. Near the top, I think."

"She's up there?" Jasken said, sounding incredulous.

"Can you see her?"

"No, sir."

"Can you show yourself, little Lededje?" Veppers shouted. "Let us see where you are! Have you a light?"

"Um, ah, wait a moment, sir," she said in her half-shout, angling her head upwards again.

She shuffled a little faster along the ledge now. She had an image in her head of the size of the stage, the sets and flats that came down to produce backgrounds for the action. They were vast, enormously wide. She probably wasn't halfway across yet. "I have . . ." she began, then let her voice fade away. This might buy her a little extra time, might keep Veppers from going crazy.

"The general manager is with Dr. Sulbazghi now, sir," she heard Jasken say.

"Is he now?" Veppers sounded exasperated.

"The general manager is upset, sir. Apparently he wishes to know what is going on in his opera house."

"It's *my* fucking opera house!" Veppers said, loudly. "Oh, all right. Tell him we're looking for a stray. And have Sulbazghi turn on the lights; we might as well, now." There was a pause, then he said, testily, "Yes, of *course* all the lights!"

"Shit!" Lededje breathed. She tried to move even faster, felt the wooden ledge beneath her feet bounce.

"Lededje," Veppers shouted, "can you hear me?" She didn't reply. "Lededje, stay where you are; don't risk moving. We're going to turn on the lights."

The lights came on. There were fewer than she'd expected and it became dimly lit around her rather than dazzlingly bright. Of course; most of the lights would be directed at the stage itself, not up into the scenery inside the fly tower carousel. Still, there was enough light to gain a better impression of her surroundings. She could see the greys, blues, blacks and whites of the painted flat she was pressed against – though she still had no idea what the enormous painting represented – and could see the dozens of massive hanging backgrounds – some three-dimensional, metres thick, sculpted to resemble port scenes, town squares, peasant villages, mountain crags, forest canopies – hanging above her. They bowed out as they ascended, held inside the barrel depths of the carousel like vast pages in some colossal illustrated book. She was about halfway along the flat, almost directly above the middle of the stage. Fifteen metres or more still to go. It was too far. She would never make it. She could see down, too. The brightly shining stage was over twenty metres below. She tore her gaze away. The creaking sound beneath her desperately shuffling feet had taken on a rhythm now. What could she do? What other way out was there? She thought of the knives.

"I still can't—" Veppers said.

"Sir! That bit of scenery; it's moving. Look."

"Shit shit shit!" she breathed, trying to move still faster.

"Lededje, are you—"

She heard steps, then, "Sir! She's there! I can see her!"

"Buggering fuck," she had time to say, then heard the creaking noise beneath her turn into a splitting, splintering sound, and felt herself sinking, being lowered, gently at first. She brought her hands in, unsheathed both knives. Then there was a noise like a gunshot; the wooden ledge beneath her gave way and she started to fall.

She heard Jasken shout something.

She twisted, turned, stabbed both knives into the plasticised canvas of the flat, holding on grimly to each handle as she pulled herself in as close as she could, her gloved fists at her shoulders, hearing the canvas tear and watching it split in front of her eyes, the twin blades slicing quickly down to the foot of the enormous painting where the jagged remains of the wooden ledge sagged and fell.

The knives were going to cut right through the bottom of the canvas! She was sure she'd seen something like this done in a film and it had all looked a lot easier. Hissing, she twisted both knives, turning each blade from vertical to horizontal. She stopped falling and hung there, bouncing gently on the torn, straining canvas. Her legs swung in space beneath her. Shit, this wasn't going to work. Her arms were getting sore and starting to shake already.

"What's she—?" she heard Veppers say, then, "Oh my God! She's—"

"Have them rotate the carousel, sir," Jasken said quickly. "Once it's in the right position they can lower her to the stage."

"Of course! Sulbazghi!"

She could hardly hear what they were saying, she was breathing so hard and her blood was pounding in her ears. She glanced to one side. The now broken length of wood she'd been sidling along had been attached to the bottom of the scenery flat by big staples sunk into the double-folded hem of the giant painting; to her right, just under a body-length away from her, some of these still held. She started swinging herself from side to side, her breath whooshing and hissing out of her as she forced her arms to stay locked in position while her legs and lower body pendulumed. She thought she heard the two men shouting at her but she couldn't be sure. She swung wildly to and fro, moving the whole rippling extent of the scenery flat. Nearly there . . .

She hooked her right leg onto the ledge, found purchase and detached one knife, hooking and stabbing at the canvas above her, keeping the blade horizontal. Flat, angled down behind the canvas, the knife held; she hauled herself up until she was about midway between prone and upright. She brought the other knife out and swung it up too, still higher.

"Now what's she—?"

"Lededje!" Jasken yelled. "Stop! You'll kill yourself!"

She was upright, hanging by the two embedded knives. She swung up and out, stuck a blade in still further up. Her arm muscles felt as though they were on fire, but she was pulling herself upwards. She'd had no idea that she possessed such strength. Her pursuers controlled the machinery, of course; they could rotate the whole vast apparatus and could lower her as they wished, but she'd resist them to the last. Veppers had no idea. He was the one who still thought this was a game; she knew it was to the death.

Then there was a deep humming sound, and with a low, moaning noise, the whole scenery flat, and all the others around, above and below it, started to move. Upwards; hauling the scenery flat up into the dim heights of the enormous carousel. Upwards! She wanted to laugh, but had no breath for it. She was feeling for the knife holes beneath with her feet now, finding them, using them as footholds, taking some of the strain off her protesting arm muscles.

"That's the wrong fucking way!" Veppers screamed. She heard Jasken shouting something too. "That's the wrong fucking way!" Veppers bellowed again. "Make it stop. Other way! Other way! Sulbazghi! What are you playing at? *Sulbazghi!*"

The gigantic carousel continued to turn, rotating the sets and flats like a vast spit-roast. She glanced over her shoulder and saw that, as the whole assemblage rotated, lifting the backdrop that she was climbing away from above the stage itself, it was getting closer to the next flat, all of the stacked sets pressing in towards each other as they came to the horizontal limit of the space. The set closing in on her back looked plain and smooth and lacking in features; just another painted scene with a few thin supporting cross-beams and as hard to climb as this one. Above, she could see more complicated, three-dimensional sets, some boasting lights that must have come on when they'd turned on all the rest. She put her face against the canvas, stared through the knife hole she'd just made.

A very convincing olde-worlde rooftop scene greeted her; oddly angled gutters, quaintly tiny dormer windows, steep-pitched slate roofs, wonky chimney pots – some with real pretend smoke just starting to come out of them – and a net, a tracery of tiny blue lights strung right across the width of the set and for twenty metres or more above the chimneys and ridge tiles, impersonating stars. The whole thing was sliding gradually closer, edging slowly downwards as the carousel continued to revolve.

She ignored the still-shouting men, slit a hole in the canvas big enough for her to slip through and once on the far side launched herself at the rooftop set. The canvas flat she'd thrown herself from moved away as she kicked back at it; she started to fall, heard herself scream, then half her body from the waist up thudded into the fake slates. Winded, she found both her knives had gone and she was holding on with both hands to a set of flimsy-feeling railings in front of a tall set of windows. Something clattered far beneath her; the knives, she guessed.

The two men below were still shouting; it sounded like half at her and half at Dr. Sulbazghi. She wasn't listening to either of them. Veppers and Jasken couldn't see her now; part of the rooftop set was hiding her from them. She hauled herself up on the phoney wrought-iron railings, the plastic bending in her grip and threatening to break. She found more handholds on hoax gutters, dummy window ledges and counterfeit chimneys.

She was at the top, trying to make her way along the ridge through the cold fake smoke issuing from the chimney pots, when the carousel came grinding to a stop, making the whole set judder. She lost her footing, slipped and fell down the far side, screaming.

The tracery of tiny lights, the pretend star field of a clear night sky, caught her, entangling her in their chilly blue embrace, the net bowing and stretching but not breaking, the hard wires conjoining the lights seeming to wrap themselves around her and tighten as she struggled.

"Now!" she heard Veppers shout.

There was a single crack of rifle fire. An instant later she felt a blindingly sharp pain on her right hip, and then, moments after that, the little fake blue stars and the drifting smoke that wasn't real smoke and the whole insane edifice all just drifted away from her.

Manhandled. She was being manhandled.

Now she was being laid down on a hard surface.

Her limbs flopped around her, feeling somehow disconnected. If she'd had to guess, she'd have hazarded that she had been gently placed here rather than just thrown down; that was a good sign.

She hoped it was, anyway. Her head felt okay; not nearly as sore as the last occasion.

She wondered how much time had passed. They had probably taken her back to the town house, just a few city segments away from the opera house. She might even be back in Espersium; runaways were usually returned to the great estate to await Veppers' pleasure. Sometimes you had to wait days or even weeks to discover the full extent of your punishment. One of Jasken's tranquilliser rounds usually knocked you out for a good few hours; there would have been time to get her anywhere on the planet, or off it.

It struck her, as she lay there hearing muffled words spoken around her, that she was thinking a lot more clearly than she'd have expected. She found she could control her eyes, and opened them as narrowly as she could, peering through the lashes to see whatever was around her. Town house? The estate? Interesting to find out.

The surroundings were dim. Veppers was standing over her, all perfect teeth, radiantly elegant face, white mane, golden skin, wide shoulders and dramatic cloak. There was somebody else there, more felt than seen, doing something at her hip.

Dr. Sulbazghi – grizzled, brown, square of face and frame – walked into view, handing Veppers something. "Your knives, sir," he said.

Veppers took them, inspected them. He shook his head. "Little bitch," he breathed. "Taking these! They were—"

"Your grandfather's," Sulbazghi said, voice rumbling. "Yes, we know."

"Little bitch," Veppers said, and almost chuckled. "Mind you, they were her great grandfather's before that, so you can see . . . But, still." He slid both knives into his waistband.

Dr. Sulbazghi was squatting down now, to her left, looking at her. He put a hand to her face, wiping away some of the pale, millimetre-thick makeup she'd applied. He wiped the hand on his jacket, leaving a pale streak. It was very dim around her, dim above Dr. S, too. And their voices hardly echoed at all, as though they were standing in some enormous space.

Something didn't feel right. There was a tug at her hip; no pain at all. Jasken's pale, lean face came into view, made insectile by the Oculenses. He was squatting by her right side, still holding the rifle, the tranq dart in his other hand. It was hard to tell in the dim light with the lenses obscuring half the man's face, but it looked like he was frowning at the dart. Behind him, a scaffolding tower reached up to an enormous roofscape hanging in the dimness, its roofs oddly angled and foreshortened, its comically askew chimneys still leaking pretend smoke.

Great God, she was still in the opera house! And quickly coming to, almost undrugged, by some miracle.

"I think her eye just flickered," Veppers said, and started to lower himself towards her, cloak belling out around him. She closed her eyes quickly, shutting out the view. She felt a tremor run through her body, she half-flexed her hand and fingers and sensed that she would be able to move now if she wanted to.

"Can't have," the doctor said. "She ought to be out for hours, shouldn't she, Jasken?"

"Wait," Jasken said. "This round hit the bone. Might not have fully . . ."

"What absurd beauty," Veppers said quietly, his deep, infinitely seductive voice very, very near to her. She felt him wipe at her face as well, removing the makeup she had applied to hide her markings. "Isn't it odd. I rarely just . . . look at her this close, as a rule." *That is because*, she thought calmly, *when you rape me, sir, you choose to take me from behind.* She sensed his breath; a wave of warmth on her cheek.

Sulbazghi took her wrist in his chubby hand, gently probing for a pulse.

"Sir, she might not—" Jasken began.

Her eyes flicked open. She was staring into Veppers' face, immediately over hers, filling her field of vision. His eyes started to widen and an expression of alarm began to form on his fabulously smooth and perfect features. She pushed herself up and twisted her head, opening her mouth, baring her teeth and aiming for his throat.

She must have closed her eyes at the last instant but sensed him pulling up and away; her teeth crunched closed on something and Veppers shrieked. Her head was shaken back and forth as her teeth remained tight around whatever she had bitten and he tried desperately to pull himself free. "Get her off me!" he screeched, his voice strangled and nasal. She bit harder with the last of her strength and forced another anguished scream from Veppers as something tore free. Then her jaw was clamped from beneath, an iron grip causing astounding pain, and she had to let go. She could taste blood. Her head was forced back down to the floor with a painful thud and she opened her eyes to see Veppers staggering away clutching his nose and mouth; blood coursed down over his chin and shirt. Jasken was holding her head down, hands still clamped round her jaw and neck. Dr. Sulbazghi was rising from her side to go to his master.

There was something hard and grisly in her mouth, something almost too big to swallow. She forced it down all the same, gagging and sputtering; whatever it was it hesitated as it passed down her throat beneath Jasken's clamping hands, and he might have thought to stop her swallowing, but didn't. She grabbed a tight, wheezing breath.

"Has she—" Veppers sobbed as Sulbazghi came up to him, teasing the taller man's hands away from his face. Veppers, staring down, cross-eyed, took a sudden breath too. "She fucking has! She's bitten my fucking *nose* off!" he howled. Veppers pushed Sulbazghi away, sending the older man staggering, then took two steps to where she lay, held down by Jasken. She saw the knives in Veppers' hands.

"Sir—!" Jasken said, taking one hand away from her throat and raising it towards his master. Veppers kicked Jasken aside and straddled Lededje before she could even start to rise, pinning her arms to the floor. Blood was flowing freely from his nose and spattering all over her face, neck and shirt.

Oh, not even the whole nose, she had time to think. *Just the tip. A fine, ragged mess, though. Try laughing that off at your next diplomatic reception, Prime Executive Veppers.*

He plunged the first knife into her throat and slashed sideways, the second into her chest. The second knife hit off a rib, bouncing away. Upper arms trapped, she tried as best she could to put her hands up as her breath bubbled out of her neck. The taste of blood was very strong and she needed to breathe and to cough, but could do neither. Veppers batted her hands away as he looked down and carefully aimed his next thrust a finger-width further down from the one that had been deflected. He briefly lowered his face to hers. "You little *cunt*!" he screamed. Some of his blood fell into her slackly open mouth. "I was supposed to appear in *public* this evening!"

He pushed hard and the blade slid between her ribs and into her heart.

She looked up into the darkness as her heart thrashed and jerked around the blade, as though trying to clutch it. Then her heart spasmed one last time and fell back to a sort of faintly trembling, pulseless calm for a moment. When Veppers jerked the knife out, even that ceased. A weight infinitely greater than that of just one man seemed to settle on her. She felt too tired to breathe now; her last breath fluttered from her torn-open windpipe like a departing lover. Somehow everything seemed to have gone very quiet and still around her, even though she was aware of shouting and could feel Veppers rise up and off her – though not without giving her a final slap across the face, just for good measure. She could sense the other two men were moving quickly to her side once again, touching, feeling, trying to staunch, to find a pulse, to plug her wounds.

Too late now, she thought, . . . *Meant nothing* . . .

The darkness was moving in remorselessly from the edges of her field of vision. She stared up into it, unable even to blink. She waited for some profound insight or thought, but none came.

High above her, the simulated sceneries and architectures stacked within the giant carousel swung slowly back and forth, all slowly going dim. In front of the hanging roofscape above her she could see a flat, tattered-looking mountain scene; all soaring, snowy peaks and ruggedly romantic crags beneath a cloud-dotted sky of blue, the effect somewhat spoiled by rips and tears in the fabric and a broken lower frame.

So that was what she'd been pressed up against. Mountains. Sky.

Perspective, she thought woozily, slowly, as she died; what a wonderful thing.

Two

Conscript Vatueil, late of Their Highnesses' First Cavalry, now reduced to the Third Expeditionary Sappers, wiped his sweating brow with a grimy, calloused hand. He worked his knees forward a few centimetres across the stony floor of the tunnel, sending fresh darts of pain up his legs, and plunged the short-handle spade into the shadowy face of the pebble-dotted wall of dirt immediately ahead of him. The exertion set off further stabs of pain, which ran up his back and across his straining shoulders. The worn spade bit into the compacted earth and stones, its tip connecting with a larger rock hidden within.

The collision jarred his hands, arms and shoulders, setting his teeth on edge and ringing his aching back as though it was a bell. He almost cried out, but instead just sucked in a breath of stale, warm, humid air, pungently scented with his own bodily odours and those of the other sweating, straining miners around him. He worked the embedded spade to one side within the dirt and tried to sense the edge of the buried rock, pulling the spade out and heaving it back in again a little to the side in an attempt to find the edge of the obstruction and lever it out. The spade bit into solidity on both sides, making his arms and back ache again each time. He let the breath out, putting the spade down by his right thigh and feeling behind him for his pickaxe. He had moved too far forward since he'd last used it and had to look round, back muscles protesting, to find it.

He turned carefully, anxious not to get in the way of the man to his right, who was already swinging hard with his own pickaxe, cursing under his breath all the time. The new kid on his other side, whose name he'd already forgotten, was still stabbing weakly at the face with his spade, producing little. He was a big, powerful-looking lad, but still face-weak. He'd need to be relieved soon if they were to keep up to target, though he'd pay for such deemed lack of application.

Behind Vatueil, in the flickering, lamp-lit gloom, the tunnel stretched back into darkness; half-naked men, on their knees or walking bent over at the waist, shuffled about the confined space, loaded with spades and shovels, picks and pry bars. Somewhere behind them, over their coughs and wheezed, bitten-off exchanges, he heard the irregular hollow rumble of an empty rubble wagon approaching. He saw it thud into the buffers at the end of the line.

"Feeling delicate again, Vatueil?" the junior captain said, walking over to him, back bent. The junior captain was the only man at the face still wearing the top half of his uniform. He was sneering, and had tried to put some sarcasm into his voice, though he was so young Vatueil still thought of him as a child and found it hard to take him seriously. The delicacy the junior captain was referring to had occurred an hour earlier just after the start of Vatueil's shift when he'd felt and then been sick, sending an extra unwanted shovelful of waste back to the surface in a rubble wagon.

He'd felt ill since just after breakfast back at the surface and on the walk to the face. The last part especially, doubled over, had been a nightmarish slog of increasing nausea. That was always a bad bit for him anyway; he was tall and his back hit more of the roof support beams than the other men's. He was developing what the long-serving sappers called back buttons; raised welts of hardened skin above each bone in his spine like giant warts. Ever since he'd thrown up, his stomach had been rumbling and he'd had a raging thirst that the single meagre hourly water ration had done little to alleviate.

There was a chorus of shouting starting further back in the tunnel and another rumbling sound. For a moment he thought it was the start of a cave-in, and felt a sickening pulse of fear run through him, even as another part of his mind thought, *At least it might be quick, and that would be an end to it*. Then another rubble wagon came hurtling out of the darkness and slammed into the rear of the first one, sending dust bursting out from both wagons and knocking the leading wheels of the front wagon off the track just in front of the buffers. There was much more shouting and swearing as the track layers were blamed for unsettling the track behind, the surface wagon emptiers were cursed for not fully emptying the wagon in the first place and everybody else further up was shouted at for not giving them more warning. The junior captain ordered everybody away from the face to help get the wagon back on the rails, then added, "Not you, Vatueil; keep working."

"Sir," he said, lifting the pickaxe. At least with nobody around him he could get a proper swing at the obstruction. He turned back and heaved the pick at a spot to the side of where the spade had baulked, briefly imagining that he was swinging it at the back of the young captain's head. He hauled the pick out, twisted it to present the flat blade rather than the spike towards the face, found a slightly different position and swung hard again.

You developed a feel for what was going on at the end of a shovel or a pick, you started to gain an insight into the just-hidden depths in front of you, after a while. There was another jarring strike to add to all the others that had run up through his hands into his arms and back over the year he'd been down here, but he sensed the slightly flattened blade make a sort of double strike inside the face, sliding between two rocks, or into a cleft in a single more massive rock. That felt hollow, he thought, but dismissed the idea.

He had leverage now, a degree of purchase. He strained at the worn-smooth handle of the pick. Something grated inside the face and the weak light from his helmet lamp showed a stretch of dirt face as long as his forearm and tall as his head hinging out towards him. Dirt and pebbles slumped about his knees. What fell out of the hole was a piece of dressed stonework, and beyond was a rectangular hole and a damp darkness, a dirt-free inky absence from which a thin cold wind issued, smelling of old, cold stone.

The great castle, the besieged fortress, stood over the broad plain on a carpet of ground-hugging mist, like something unreal.

Vatueil remembered his dreams. In his dreams the castle truly was not real, or not there, or genuinely did float above the plain, by magic or some technology unknown to him, and so they burrowed on for ever, never finding its base, tunnelling on without cease through the killing muggy warmth and sweat-mist of their own exhalations in an eternal agony of purposeless striving. He had never mentioned these dreams to anybody, unsure who amongst his comrades he could really trust and judging that if word of these nightmares got back to his superiors they might be deemed treacherous, implying that their labours were pointless, doomed to failure.

The castle sat on a spur of rock, an island of stone jutting above the flood plain of the great meandering river. The castle itself was formidable enough; the cliffs that surrounded it made it close to impregnable. Still, it had to be taken, they'd been told. After nearly a year of trying to starve the garrison into surrender, it had been judged, two years or more ago, that the only way to take the stronghold was to get a great siege engine close in to the rocky outcrop. Enormous machines had been constructed of wood and metal and manoeuvred towards the castle on a specially built road. The machines could hurl rocks or fizzing metal bombs the weight of ten men many hundreds of strides across the plain, but there was a problem: to get them close enough to the castle meant coming within range of the fortress's own great war machine, a giant trebuchet mounted on the single massive circular tower dominating the citadel.

With its own range increased by virtue of its elevation, the castle's engine dominated the plain for nearly two thousand strides about the base of the rock; all attempts to move siege engines to within range had been met with a hail of rocks from the fortress's trebuchet, resulting in smashed machines and dead men. The engineers had been forced to concede that constructing a machine of their own powerful enough to remain out of range of the castle's war engine while still being able to hit the fortress was probably impossible.

So they would tunnel to near the castle rock, open a pit and construct a small but powerful siege engine there under the noses of the castle's garrison, and, supposedly, under the angle at which the castle's trebuchet could fire. There were rumours that this absurd machine would be a sort of self-firing bomb device, some sort of explosive contraption that would throw itself into the air, up past the cliff and against the castle walls, detonating there. Nobody really believed these rumours, though the slightly more plausible idea of constructing a sufficiently powerful wooden catapult or trebuchet in a pit excavated at the end of a tunnel seemed just as fanciful and idiotic.

Perhaps they were expected to tunnel up inside the castle rock when they got to it, burrowing up through solid stone, or maybe they were meant to place a gigantic bomb against the base of the rock; these seemed no less absurd and pointless as tactics. Maybe the high command, immeasurably distant from this far (and, if rumour was to believed, increasingly irrelevant) front, had been misinformed regarding the nature of the castle's foundations, and – thinking that the fortress's walls rested on the plain itself – had ordered the mining as a matter of course, imagining that the walls could be sapped conventionally, and nobody nearer to the reality of the situation had thought, or dared, to tell them that this was impossible. But then who knew how the high commanders thought?

Vatueil put one fist to the small of his back as he stood looking out to the distant fortress. He was trying to stand up straight. It was getting harder to do so each day, which was unfortunate, as slouching was looked on unfavourably by officers, especially by the young junior captain who seemed to have taken such a dislike to him.

Vatueil looked about at the litter of grey-brown tents which made up the camp. Above, the clouds looked washed out, the sun hidden behind a grey, dully glowing patch over the more distant of the two ranges of hills that defined the broad plain.

"Stand up straight, Vatueil," the junior captain told him, emerging from the major's tent. The junior captain was dressed in his best uniform. He'd had Vatueil put on his best gear too, not that his best was very good. "Well, don't malinger here all day; get in there and don't take for ever about it. This doesn't get you off anything, you know; don't go thinking that. You've still got a shift to finish. Hurry up!" The junior captain clouted Vatueil about the ear, dislodging his forage cap. Vatueil bent to retrieve it and the young captain kicked his behind, propelling him through the flap and into the tent.

Inside, he collected himself, straightened, and was shown where to stand in front of the board of officers.

"Conscript Vatueil, number—" he began.

"We don't need to know your number, conscript," one of the two majors told him. There were three senior captains and a colonel present too; an important gathering. "Just tell us what happened."

He briefly related prising the rock away from the face, sticking his head through the hole and smelling that strange, cave-like darkness, hearing and seeing the water running in the channel beneath, then wriggling back to tell the junior captain and the others. He kept his gaze fixed somewhere above the colonel's head, looking down only once. The officers nodded, looked bored. A subaltern took notes on a writing pad. "Dismissed," the more senior major told Vatueil.

He half turned to go, then turned back. "Permission to speak further, sir," he said, glancing at the colonel and then the major who'd just spoken.

The major looked at him. "What?"

He straightened as best he could, stared above the colonel's head again. "It occurred to me the conduit might contribute to the castle's water supply, sir."

"You're not here to think, conscript," the major said, though not unkindly.

"No," the colonel said, speaking for the first time. "That occurred to me, too."

"It's still a long way, sir," the junior major said.

"We've poisoned all the nearer sources," the colonel told him. "To no obvious effect. And it is from the direction of the nearer hills." Vatueil risked nodding at this, to show he had thought this too.

"With their many springs," the senior major said to the colonel, apparently sharing some private joke.

The colonel looked at Vatueil through narrowed eyes. "You were with the Cavalry once, weren't you, conscript?"

"Yes, sir."

"Rank?"

"Captain of Mount, sir."

There was a pause. The colonel filled it himself. "And?"

"Insubordination, sir."

"Down to conscript tunneller? You must have been spectacularly insubordinate."

"So it was adjudged, sir."

There was a grunt that might have been laughter. At the colonel's instigation the offisorial heads were brought together. There was some muttering, then the more senior major said, "There will shortly be a small exploratory force sent along the water tunnel, conscript. Perhaps you might care to be on it."

"I'll do as ordered, sir."

"The men will be hand-picked, though volunteers."

Vatueil drew himself up as straight as he could, his back complaining. "I volunteer, sir."

"Good man. You might need a crossbow as well as a shovel."

"I can handle both, sir."

"Report to the senior duty officer. Dismissed."

The calf-deep water was cold, swirling round his boots and seeping into them. He was fourth man back from the lead, lamp extinguished. Only the lead man had a lit lamp, and that was turned down as low as it would go. The water tunnel was oval shaped, just too broad to touch both sides at the same time with outstretched arms. It was nearly as tall as a man; you had to walk with head lowered but it was easy enough after so long being bent double.

The air was good; better than in the mining tunnel. It had flowed gently into their faces as they'd stood in the water, ready to move off from the breach leading from the mining tunnel. The twenty men in the detail moved down the partially filled pipe as quietly as they could, wary of traps or guards. They were led by a fairly old, sensible-seeming captain and a very keen young subaltern. There were two other tunnellers as well as himself, both more powerful than he though with less combat experience. Like him they carried picks, spades, bows and short swords; the larger of the two also carried a pry bar slung across his broad back.

These two men had been chosen by the young junior captain. He had not been happy that Vatueil was being allowed to go on the exploration of the water tunnel while he himself was not. Vatueil expected further unsubtle persecution when he returned. If he returned.

They came to a place where the tunnel narrowed and horizontal iron bars ran across the channel, set at heights that meant they had to clamber over them one at a time. Then came a section where the floor of the tunnel angled down, and they had to brace themselves two-by-two, each with a hand on one wall, to stop themselves from slipping on the slimy surface under the water. The tunnel all but levelled out again after that, then another set of bars in a narrow section appeared out of the gloom, again followed by another downward sloped section.

He had not dreamed this, he realised as he walked. This was easier than anything he had imagined in his nightmares, or – as it felt – that they had imagined for him. They might stroll all the rest of the way to the castle without having to dig another spadeful. Though, of course, the way might be blocked, or guarded, or might not lead to the castle after all. And yet the water was here, in this carefully constructed tunnel, and where else would it be going on this otherwise near deserted plain if not to the castle? Guards or traps were more likely, though even then the castle was so old that perhaps those within just drew the water unthinkingly from a deep, seemingly unpoisonable well and knew nothing of the system that brought it to them. Better to assume that they did know, though, and that they or the water tunnel's original designers and builders would have set up some sort of defence against enemies making their way down it. He started to think about what he would put in place if he had been in charge of such matters.

His thoughts were interrupted when he collided softly with the back of the man in front. The man behind him piled into his back, too, and so on down the line as they came to a halt, almost without a sound.

"A gate?" the subaltern whispered. Looking ahead, over the shoulder of the man in front, Vatueil could just make out a broad grating filling the tunnel ahead. The single lamp was turned up a little. The water sieved itself between thick bars of what appeared to be iron. There was more whispering between the captain and the subaltern.

The tunnellers were called forward and were confronted by the grating. It was locked shut against a stout, vertical iron stanchion immediately behind. It looked like it was designed to hinge back towards them and then up towards the ceiling. A strange arrangement, Vatueil thought. All three tunnellers were ordered to light their lamps, the better to inspect the lock. It was about the size of a clenched fist, the chain securing it made of links thick as a little finger. It looked rusted, but only slightly.

One of the other tunnellers lifted his pickaxe, testing his swing and where the point might strike to break the lock.

"That will be noisy, sir," Vatueil whispered. "The sound will travel a long way down the tunnel."

"What do you suggest, bite it?" the younger officer asked him.

"Try to lever it off with the pry bar, sir," he said.

The senior officer nodded. "All right."

The tunneller with the pry bar brought it over his shoulder and wedged it under the lock while Vatueil and the other miner held it out from the grating, angling it just so to increase the effect, then, once their comrade had taken the strain, joining him to pull hard on the end of the bar. They strained for a few moments to no effect beyond a faint creaking sound. They relaxed, then pulled again. With a dull snap and a loud clank the lock gave way, sending the three of them falling backwards into the water in a clattering tangle. The chain rattled down into the water to join them.

"Scarcely *quiet*," the subaltern muttered.

They picked themselves up, sorted themselves out. "No sticks or branches or anything against it," one of the other men said, nodding at the foot of the grating.

"Settling pool further back," another suggested.

Through the grating, Vatueil could see what looked like stony blocks in the path the water took beyond, like square narrow stepping stones filling the base of the tunnel. *Why would you put those there*, he wondered.

"Ready to raise it?" the captain said.

"Sir," the two tunnellers said together, taking a side each, arms thrust into the dark water to pull at the foot of the grating.

"Heave, lads," the officer told them.

They pulled, and with a dull scraping noise the grating hinged slowly up. They shifted their grip as it rose and pushed it towards the ceiling.

Vatueil saw something move on the ceiling, just behind the slowly moving grille. "Wait a moment," he said, perhaps too quietly. In any event, nobody seemed to take any notice.

Something – some things, each big as a man's head – fell, one glinting in the lamp light, from the ceiling. They smashed on the edges of the raised blocks beneath and dark liquid came pouring out of them as their jagged remains vanished into the moving water. It was only then that the men hauling up the grating stopped; too late. "What was that?" somebody asked. The water around the blocks, where the liquid had entered, was bubbling and fuming, sending great grey bubbles of gas to the surface of the water, where they burst, producing thick white fumes. The gas was rising quickly into the air, starting to obscure what view there might have been down the tunnel beyond.

"It's just . . ." somebody started, then their voice trailed away.

"Back, lads," the captain said as the fumes drifted closer.

"That might be—"

"Back, lads, back."

Vatueil heard water sloshing as some of them started to move away.

The pale fog now almost filled the place where the grating had been. The men nearest it, the two tunnellers, stood back, letting go of the grille; it crashed down into the water. One of them took a step back. The other seemed transfixed by the sight, remaining close enough to sniff the milky grey cloud; he started coughing immediately, doubling up, hands on knees. His lowered head met a long silky strand of the gas at waist level, and he wheezed suddenly, standing up and coughing again and again. He turned and waved down the tunnel, then seemed to have a seizure. He fell to his knees, clutching at his throat, eyes wide. His breath rattled in his throat. The other tunneller moved towards him but was waved away. The fellow slumped back against the wall of the tunnel, eyes closing. A couple of the other men, also now near to the advancing cloud, started to cough as well.

Almost as one, they started to run, suddenly pounding down the tunnel, slipping and sliding and falling, the surface underfoot that had supported slow and steady steps with barely a slip turning to something like ice as they tried to run through the calf-deep water; a couple of them pushed past Vatueil, who had not yet moved.

We will never get past the narrow places with the bars, he thought. *We won't even make it up the slopes before them*, he realised. The cloud was flowing up the tunnel at a moderate walking pace. It was already at his knees, rising to his groin. He had taken a deep breath as soon as he'd seen the dirty looking bubbles rising out of the water. He let it out, took another one now.

Some of the others were shouting and screaming as they ran away up the tunnel, though the principal noise was a frenzied splashing. The cloud of gas enveloped Vatueil. He clamped his hand over his mouth and nose. Even so, he could smell something sharp, choking. His eyes began to sting, his nose to run.

The grating would be too heavy, he thought. He stooped, felt for it, then with an effort he would not have believed himself capable of, lifted it in one movement and swung himself beneath it, stumbling through the water beyond as he let the grille go. His boots crunched on shattered pieces of glass under the surface of the water. He remembered to lift his feet for the blocks the bottles had smashed on.

The grey cloud was all around him like a cloak, his eyes were stinging and starting to close up seemingly of their own volition. He stepped quickly over the blocks, staggered into the water on the far side, then ran as fast as he could into clear air beyond, his lungs feeling as though they were about to burst.

Somehow he managed to delay breathing until he could see no trace of the grey mist either in the air or rising in bubbles from the water. He could hardly see, and the first deep, heaving breath he took stung first his mouth and then his throat all the way down to his lungs. Even the exhalation seemed to sting his nose. He took more deep, deep breaths, standing doubled over with his hands on his knees. Each breath hurt, but stung less than the one before. From up the tunnel, he could hear nothing.

Eventually he was able to breathe sufficiently freely to move without gasping. He looked back into the darkness and tried to imagine the scenes he might find walking back to the breach, once the gas had cleared. He wondered how long that would take. He turned and made his way in the other direction, towards the castle.

*

Guards found him hollering at the far end, where a vertical well shaft descended to a deep pool. Taken before the castle authorities, he informed them that he would tell them anything they wanted to know. He was just a humble tunneller who'd been lucky and resourceful enough to evade the trap which had claimed the lives of his fellows, but he knew of the scheme to tunnel to near the castle and set up some sort of compact but powerful siege engine, and additionally he would tell all that he could about the little he knew of the disposition, numbers and quality of the forces besieging the castle if they would but spare his life.

They took him away and asked him many questions, all of which he answered truthfully. Then they tortured him to make sure he'd been telling the truth. Finally, uncertain where his loyalties might lie, unwilling to support yet another mouth to feed and judging his torment-broken body of little practical use, they trussed him and fired him from the giant trebuchet in the great tower.

By chance he fell to earth not far from the tunnel he had helped dig, landing with a thump that some of his old comrades heard above them as they tramped back to camp after another back-breaking shift stopping up one tunnel and continuing with their own.

His last thought was that he had once dreamed of flying.

Three

It was some time before Yime Nsokyi realised she was the last one left firing.

The Orbital's Hub had been the first thing to go, blitzed in an instant by a staggeringly bright CAM burst before there had been any warning whatsoever. Then the hundred or so major ships moored beneath the O's outer surface, contained within Bulkhead Range docks or approaching or leaving the Orbital, had been destroyed in a single synchronised scatter-gun blaze, Minds precisely obliterated by exquisitely focused Line-gun loci, their already cram-packed substrates collapsing into particles more dense than neutron star material, all that prized wit, intelligence and knowledge-almost-beyond-measuring snuffed in every case to a barely visible ultra-dense cinder almost before they had time to realise what was happening to them.

While the shock waves from the gravity-point collapses were

still propagating through the victim vessels' internal structures and hulls, they were slammed with meticulously graded degrees of further destruction, the craft within or very close to the O targeted with small nukes and thermonuclear charges sufficient to destroy the ships themselves without compromising the strategic structure of the Orbital itself, while those further out were simply smithereened with anti-matter warheads, their megatonne bodies slashed across the outboard skies in blinding pulses of energy that threw jagged shadows across the vast internal surfaces of the world.

All of this in a handful of seconds. A heartbeat later the independent high-AI Defensive Nodes overseeing each of the O's original Plates had been knocked out with pinpoint plasma displacements and simultaneously the few thousand nearby Interstellar-class ships were attacked, meeting their fates in a grotesque parody of size seniority; first the larger, more capable craft vanishing in nuclear or thermonuclear explosions, then the second-rank ships moments later, followed by smaller and smaller vessels until all those were gone and the blossoming waves of annihilation moved on to target the slowest, in-system craft.

Finally the semi-slaved AIs, dotted at random throughout the fabric of the entire bracelet world, had stopped communicating all at once, the weapon systems that they had fallen heir to as the higher-level control processes had been destroyed either subsiding to dormancy or actively starting to attack whatever defensive capability there was left.

Drones and humans taking command of independently controllable weapon and munition delivery systems made up what was left, the few machines and people in the right place at the right time scrabbling to take over from the blitzed machines even as they were struggling to comprehend what was happening to their world. *Its end*, Yime Nsokyi thought as she'd careened down a drop shaft from the traveltube interchange she'd been in as the attack began. She'd bounced into the little blown-diamond bubble of the ancient plasma cannon's back-up control blister in time to be almost blinded by a detonating in-system clipper ship less than a millisecond away, the diamond's outer protective film barely having time to switch to mirror and her own eyes reacting late, leaving her with dots dancing in her eyes as well as the blush of an instant radiation tan warming her face.

Not the end of the world, though, she thought as she settled into the seat and felt the restraints close around her. *Not destroying the O itself, just everything about it. Probably the end of my world, though; this doesn't look survivable*. She tried to remember when she'd last backed up. Months ago? She wasn't even sure. Sloppy. She kicked the gun's systems out of network and into local control, dumbing its systems down to minimally interferable-with hardened optic communication with atomechanical back-up readied and mirroring, then flicked antiquely solid switches on a control panel, creating a great hum and buzz all around her as the thirty-metre turret woke up, screens bright, controls alive.

She brought the bulky helmet over her head, checked it was working on visual and audio and that there was air in the mask component, then left it in place for added protection as much as anything while the gun's ancient control comms established direct links with her neural lace; systems designed and code written millennia apart met, made sense and established rules and parameters. It was a strange, invasively unpleasant feeling, like a spreading itch inside her skull she could not scratch. She felt the lace using her drug glands to jink her already quickened senses and reactions up to one of her pre-agreed maxima. Felt like the setting was deterioration within minutes and burn-out in less than a quarter of an hour. Ah, the very quickest, the all-out emergency mode. That wasn't encouraging; her own lace was giving her just a handful of minutes to be of use as a fully functioning component of the Orbital's last-ditch defence.

Outside, grippings and pressings all over her body, like being nuzzled by a few dozen small but powerful animals, confirmed that the gun control blister's protective armour had enfolded her. She and the gun were as ready as they'd ever be for what came next.

She stared out into the darkness, senses enhanced to the point of nearly painful distraction as she searched for anything that wasn't basically Culture stuff getting wasted. Nothing visible, appreciable at all. She established hardened comms links with a few other people and drones, all of them within the limit of this section's original plate boundary. Her fellow warriors were shown as a line of blue tell-tale lights on a screen at the lower limit of her field of vision. They quickly determined that none of them knew what was happening and nobody could see anything to fire at. Almost immediately, there was a hoarse scream, quickly cut off, and one light turned from blue to red as a compromised high-kinetic cannon picked off another plasma turret a thousand kilometres away. Five hundred klicks spinward a drone controlling a Line-gun with links to a skein-sensing field reported nothing happening on the skein either, save for the fallback waves following the initial pulses that had wrecked the ship Minds.

"Whoever it is they want the O," one of the humans said as they watched the spread of detonating sparks that were just a few of the nearby in-system craft meeting their ends. The ships' deaths outshone the stars, replacing the familiar constellations with bright but fading patterns of their own. Her lace stepped her awareness speed down to a level where something like normal speech was possible.

"Grunts on the ground," another agreed.

"Maybe they'll just drop into the surface, displace onto the interior," Yime suggested.

"Maybe. Edgewall stuff emplaced for that."

"Anybody in touch with any Edgewall firepower?"

Nobody was. They had no contact with the O's interior at all, or with any independent craft or with anybody manning the defences anywhere else. They busied themselves with scanning with what senses they had access to, checking and readying their own weaponry and trying to establish contact with survivors further afield. In the darkness, the wrecks of the last in-system craft winked out, brief fires exhausted. Around Yime's position a few traveltube cars dropped away into the night as people tried to save themselves by using the cars as lifeboats. On average they got about ten klicks out before they were picked off too, quick tiny eruptions of light pinpricking the black.

"Anything—" somebody began.

—Got something, the drone with the skein sense sent, too quick for speech. Her lace kicked her awareness speed up to maximum so quickly the last syllable of the previous speaker's word went on for many seconds, providing an impromptu soundtrack to what was happening in the skies beyond.

The ships were popping into existence just a few thousand klicks out, travelling at between one and eight per cent of lightspeed. No beaconry, IFF or any signal at all; not even trying to pretend they were anything else but hostile.

—Thinking these are targets, somebody communicated. Over the still-open voice comm channels came a high-pitched whine like something charging.

A first glance indicated hundreds of the ships, a second thousands. They filled the sky, darting like demented fireworks in as many different directions as there were craft. Some accelerated hard, some slowed to almost stationary seemingly within seconds; those incoming zipped in and were a few tens of klicks out and closing fast before there was time to get more than a few shots off. *The drones*, Yime thought. *The drones will be reacting fastest, firing first*. She swung the ancient plasma turret directly outwards, found a target and felt the antique machine's senses and hers agree, lock and fire in the same instant. The old turret trembled and twin pulses of light lanced out, missing whatever it was they were aiming at. Plenty more targets, she thought, as she and the gun swung fractionally, retargeted, set for a wider beamspread and fired again. Something blazed within the cone of beam filaments but there was no time to celebrate as she and the gun swung again and again, flicking minutely from side to side and up and down like something trembling, uncertain.

There were more bursts of fire within the targeting focus and there was a certain desperate exultation in just firing, firing, firing, but in some still-calm part of her mind she knew they weren't getting more than a per cent of the attacking craft, and the rest were still closing or had arrived.

Something at the lower limit of her vision attracted her attention;

she watched the last of the little blue tell-tale lights turn red. All gone? So quickly? She was the last one, she realised; the last one left firing.

The view hazed, quivered, started to die. She killed the link systems, swept the helmet back over her head as its screens went blank and – staring out into the night through her own eyes and the invisible diamond blister – yanked the manual controls from the arm squabs and hauled the turret round to fire at a fast-approaching bright dot just starting to take on substance.

There was a thump that somehow felt nearby, back here by the turret, not out there where she was aiming, and the impression of something just outside the diamond bubble. She clicked a switch to let the gun's atomechanical brain do its own targeting and turned her head.

The things scrabbling towards the turret across the O's outer surface looked like metallic versions of a human ribcage plus skull, running and bouncing on six multiply jointed legs. Bizarrely, they appeared to be racing across the surface as though they were experiencing the equivalent of gravity drawing them down against it, rather than its exact opposite. She was still reaching for the control seat's hand weapon when one of the creatures launched itself at the bubble, smashed through it and landed where her lap would have been had she not been swaddled in the turret's control blister armour. The air in the diamond bubble left in a burst of white vapour that disappeared almost instantly as the skull-faced creature – a machine, she saw – stuck its face up to hers and, despite the lack of atmosphere and no visible method of producing the sound, said very clearly, "Drill over!"

She sighed, sat back, somewhere else entirely, as the shattered control blister, the crippled plasma turret itself and the doomed Orbital dissipated like mist around her.

"It was unpleasant, distressing and of little practical use," Yime Nsokyi told her drill supervisor sternly. "It was a punishment drill, a simulation for masochists. I saw little point to it."

"Granted it is about as extreme as they get," her supervisor said cheerfully. "All-out equiv-tech complete surprise attack just short of total Orbital destruction." Hvel Costrile was an elderly-looking gent with dark skin, long blond hair and a bare chest. He was talking to her in her apartment via a wall screen; it looked like he was on a sea vessel somewhere, as there was a large expanse of water in the background and his immediate surroundings – a plush seat, some railings – kept tipping slightly this way and that. The screen display was in 2D, by her choice; Yime Nsokyi didn't hold with things looking too much like whatever they were not. "Instructive, though, don't you think?"

"No," she told him. "I fail to see the instructional element implicit in being subject to a completely unstoppable attack and thus being utterly overwhelmed in a matter of minutes."

"Worse things happen in real wars, Yime," Costrile told her with a grin. "Faster, more complete destruction."

"I imagine simulations of those would have even less to teach, apart from the wisdom of avoiding such initial condition sets in the first place," she told him. "And I might add that I also fail to see the utility of causing me to experience a simulation in which I harbour a neural lace, given that I have never possessed one and have no intentions of ever having one."

Costrile nodded. "That was propaganda. Neural laces are just useful in that sort of extremity."

"Until they too are corrupted, and possibly the person invested by the device as well."

He shrugged. "By that time the game's pretty much up anyway, you'd imagine."

Yime shook her head. "One might equally well imagine otherwise."

"Whatever, they let you back-up really easily," he said reasonably.

"That is not a life-choice I have chosen to make," Yime informed him frostily.

"Oh well." Costrile sighed, then accepted a long drink from somebody just out of shot. He raised it to her. "Till next time? Something more practical, I promise."

"Till then," she agreed. "Strength in depth." But the screen was already blank. She said, "Close screen," anyway, telling the relatively dumb house computer to kill any link at her end. Yime was entirely untroubled by intelligent house systems, but did not wish to be subject to one. She was happy to admit to feeling a degree of satisfaction that she was by some orders of magnitude the most intelligent entity within her immediate surroundings in general and her own living space in particular. It was not a claim one could convincingly make in very many Culture dwellings.

Prebeign-Frultesa Yime Leutze Nsokyi dam Volsh much preferred to be known only as Yime Nsokyi. She had moved away from her home Orbital and so her name now lacked utility, no longer working as even an approximate address. Worse; bearing the name of one location while living in another felt to her like something close to deceit. She walked over to the window, picked up a plain but functional brush from a small table and continued to brush her long hair, which was what she had been doing, meticulously, when the emergency militia drill alert had come through on her personal terminal and she had, reluctantly, had to submit to the induction collar and the resulting horribly realistic sim of the Orbital – even if it wasn't this Orbital but a more standard, less militarily prepared Orbital – being so thoroughly savaged and so easily taken over.

Outside the oval of window she stood at, only very slightly distorted by the sheer thickness of the crystal and other materials forming the glazing, the view was of rolling grassy countryside punctuated with numerous lakes and strewn with forests, woods, copses and individual trees. All the windows in Yime's apartment looked out in roughly the same direction, but had she been looking from any other apartment on this level, the view would have been much the same, plus or minus hazy views of mountains, inland seas and oceans, with no other buildings visible at all, beyond the occasional distant lake-side villa or drifting houseboat.

Despite this, Yime lived in a city, and although the construction she lived in was fairly substantial – a kilometre tall and perhaps a tenth of that across – it itself was not the totality of the metropolis, forming only a small part of it and being nowhere near the most impressive of its buildings. But then it was nowhere near any of the other buildings of the city. The building was part of a Distributed City, which to the naive or uninformed eye looked remarkably like no city whatsoever.

Most Culture cities, where they existed at all, resembled giant snowflakes, with greenery – or at least countryside, in whatever colour or form – penetrating almost to the heart of the conurbation.

Had its major buildings been gathered together on the same patch of ground, this city, Irwal, on the Orbital called Dinyol-hei, would have looked more like some vision of the far future from sometime in the enormously distant past; it was almost entirely composed of great soaring sleek skyscrapers hundreds or thousands of metres tall, generally slimly conical or ellipsoid in appearance and looking uncannily like ships, or starships, as they had once been called. Fittingly, the buildings were exactly that: ships, fully capable of existing and making their way in space, between stars, should the need ever arise.

All the thousand or so major cities on Dinyol-hei were composed in the same way, from hundreds of giant buildings that could happily double as spacecraft. It was a truism that as a scientific society progressed, its ships gradually ceased to be strictly utilitarian designs in which almost every part was in some way vital to the running of the craft. Normally they went through an intermediate stage where the overall conception was still limited by the necessities imposed by the environment in which the vessels travelled but within which there was considerable opportunity for the designers, crew and passengers/inhabitants to fashion them pretty much as they pleased, before – usually some centuries after the gross vulgarity of rocket power – simple space travel became so mature a technology it was almost trivial. At this point, practically anything not messily joined to lots of other important stuff could be quite easily turned into a space-capable craft able to transport humans – or any other species spectacularly maladapted to hard vacuum and the somewhat industrial radiation environment generally associated with it – to (at the very least) different parts of the same stellar system.

A stand-alone building was almost laughably easy to convert; a bit of strengthening and rigidising, some only semi-scrupulous sealant work, throw a gel coat over the whole thing as well just to be doubly sure, strap on an engine unit or two somewhere, and you were away. In the Culture, you could even dispense with sensory and navigation systems; stay within a light year or two of the nearest Orbital and you could navigate with your own neural lace, even an antique pen terminal. It was DIY space travel, and people did exactly that, though – always to the surprise of those just on the brink of contributing to the relevant statistics – the results made it one of the more dangerous hobbies pursued with any enthusiasm within the Culture.

The means, then, were readily to hand. The motive behind the sort of building Yime now stood in was simply survival; should some catastrophe befall the Orbital itself, its inhabitants could escape the place in what were essentially giant lifeboats.

The principle had swung in and out of fashion. At one point very early in the Culture's history, many thousands of years ago, such high-redundancy safety consciousness had been the fairly strictly followed rule. It fell from favour as habitat and especially Orbital design, construction and protection rose to levels that pretty much guaranteed that those who lived in them had nothing catastrophic to worry about, then came very rapidly back into fashion when the Idiran war had gone from being an almost unthinkable absurdity through being an unlikely joke to – seemingly without warning – becoming a terrifyingly tangible reality.

Suddenly whole systems full of Orbitals and their vast populations had found themselves in a firing line they had never even imagined might exist. Nevertheless, almost all the humans most at risk, and even a few deeply wise machines, convinced themselves that no sentient space-faring species would actually attack a habitat the size of an Orbital, certainly not with the intention of destroying it.

By universal agreement almost completely irrelevant militarily, an O was simply a beautiful place for lots of people to live, as well as being an elegantly devised and artistically detailed cultural achievement; why would anybody attack one? Developing civilisations and barbarian under-achievers aside, things had been acutely civilised and agreeably quiet in the greater galaxy for centiaeons; a working consensus regarding acceptable behaviour between the Involved had long since been arrived at, inter-cultural conflict resolution was a mature technology, pan-species morality had quite entirely moved on from the unfortunate lapses of days gone by and outright destruction of major civilisational assets was rightly seen by all as inelegant, wasteful, counter-productive and – apart from anything else – simply shrieking of shamefully deep societal insecurity.

This entirely civilised and not unreasonable assumption proved ill-founded when the Idirans – thinking to make it very clear to all concerned who were the fanatical, invincible ultra-warriors in the matter and who represented the hopelessly decadent, simpering, irredeemably civilian bunch of martial no-hopers merely playing at war – attempted to traumatise the Culture straight back out of their newly begun war by attacking and attempting to destroy every Orbital its war-fleets could reach.

An Orbital was just a fabulously thin bracelet of matter three million kilometres in circumference orbiting a sun, the apparent gravity on its interior surface provided by the same spin that gave it its day–night cycle; break one anywhere around its ten million kilometres circumference – and some were only a few thousand kilometres across – and it tore itself apart, unwinding like a released spring, dumping landscape, atmosphere and inhabitants unceremoniously into space.

All this came as something of a surprise. Natural disasters occurring to an Orbital were almost unheard of, the systems they inhabited having generally been cleared of wandering debris to form the material from which the O itself had been constructed, and even the most carefree, socially relaxed Orbitals packed a healthy variety of defensive systems easily able to pick off any remaining rocks and ice lumps that might have the temerity to approach.

However, against the sort of weaponry the Idirans – amongst

many others – possessed, Orbitals were both effectively defenceless and hopelessly vulnerable. When the Idiran ships fell upon the Orbitals, the Culture was still mostly reminding itself how to build warships; the few war craft and militarised Contact ships it was able to put in the way of the attacks were swept aside.

Tens upon tens of billions died. And all for nothing, even from the Idiran point of view; the Culture, insufficiently traumatised perhaps, conspicuously failed to retreat from the war. Orders obeyed, damage duly inflicted, the Idiran war-fleets fell back to more martially relevant, not to say honourable, duties. Meanwhile the Culture – arguably to its own amazement as much as anybody else's – had hunkered down, gritted what needed to be gritted, did the same regarding girding and, to the chorus of umpteen trillion people telling each other stoically, "It's going to be a long war," got grimly on with putting itself onto a proper war footing.

In the immediate aftermath of the attacks, many Orbitals, generally those closest to the action, were simply evacuated. Some were militarised, to the extent this made sense given they were so enormous and – patently, as had just been proved – fragile in the face of modern weaponry. Many were just left to revolve, empty, effectively mothballed. Some were destroyed by the Culture itself.

Orbitals could be moved, and some were, but it was an excruciatingly long-winded business. There was even, for this whole shifting-out-of-danger procedure, what was effectively a thing called a "waiting list"; a term and concept many devoutly pampered Culture citizens had some trouble getting entirely to grips with.

Regardless; having lots of pleasantly fitted-out buildings which could double as luxury lifeboats suddenly made unimpeachable sense. Even Orbitals almost certainly unreachably far away from the conflict took up the new construction trend, and giant skyscrapers, usually reassuringly sleek and ship-like in form, blossomed like colossal suddenly fashionable plants across the Culture's Orbitals.

Distributed Cities came about when it was realised that even having the buildings/ships physically close to each other on the surface of an O was unwise, should an attack take place. Keeping them far apart from each other made the enemy's targeting similarly distributed and confused. Fast, dedicated traveltube lines, in hard vacuum under the O's outer surface, connected the buildings of any city cluster preferentially and directly, making the average journey time between buildings of any given city as quick or quicker than walking a conventional city block.

The absolute need to live in such cities or even such buildings had long since passed, unless you were cautious to the point of neuroticism, even paranoia, but the fashion still ebbed and flowed a little and throughout the fifty trillion people and many millions of Orbitals in the Culture there would always be enough people and Orbitals who still liked the idea for it never entirely to disappear. Some people just felt safer in a building that could casually survive even the destruction of an Orbital. Yime was one such person. It was why she lived in this building, and on this Orbital.

She combed her hair slowly, thoughtfully, looking out of the porthole window but not really seeing the view. She thought Costrile was not a particularly good supervisor for even a part of an Orbital's emergency militia force. Ineffective. Altogether too lackadaisical. It was disgraceful that hardly anybody on most Orbitals even knew that such organisations existed. Even here, on staid, careful, buttoned-up, backed-up, fastened-down and just plain cautious Dinyol-hei, almost nobody was interested in such things. They were all too busy having fun. Attempts had been made before to get people more involved in last-ditch Orbital defence techniques, but to little avail. It was as though people just didn't want to think about such things. When it was obviously so important. Odd.

Perhaps the problem was that it had been so long since there had been a proper, thorough-going war. It had been fifteen hundred years since the Idiran conflict; within living human memory for only the most determinedly so-called Immortalists, of whom there were surpassing few and who were anyway usually too obsessed with themselves to care about warning others what real warfare was like. Minds and drones who'd been involved were also surprisingly reluctant to share their experiences. Still, there had to be a way. The whole approach needed shaking up, and she might be just the person to make it happen. She doubted Costrile was up to it. Why, he hadn't even bothered to reply in kind when she'd signed off with "Strength in depth". How rude! She decided she would have to see about deposing Mr. Costrile from his post and having herself elected in his place.

One hundred and twenty-five, one hundred and twenty-six . . . She had almost reached her set number of morning hair-brushings. Yime had thick, lustrous brown hair which she kept in what was called an Eye cut, every hair on her head kept at a length such that when it was pulled round towards either eye, it was just too short either to obstruct her field of vision or otherwise cause annoyance.

A chime from her terminal, in the shape of a slim pen lying on another table, interrupted her reverie of power. She realised with an undignified lurch in her insides that the particular tone the terminal had used meant it was a call from Quietus.

She might actually be going to work.

Even so, she completed the last two hair-brushing strokes before answering.

One had to have rules.

Four

In Valley 308, which was part of the Thrice Flayed Footprint district of the Pavulean Hell, level three, there was an old-fashioned mill with a tall external over-shot wheel, powered by blood. It was part of the punishment of some of the virtual souls in that place that each day they be profusely bled for as long as they could without falling unconscious. There were many thousands of such unfortunates to be bled during each session and they were duly dragged screaming from their nearby pens by grotesquely formed, irresistibly powerful demons and strapped to canted iron tables with drains at their foot. These tables were arranged in serried ranks on the steep banks of the arid valley, which, had one been able to look at it from far enough above, would have been revealed as a ridge forming part of a truly gigantic footprint; hence the district's name.

The once very important person to whom the flayed hand

belonged was still, in some sense, alive, and suffered every moment from having had their skin removed. They suffered in a magnified sense, too, concomitant with their pelt having been so grotesquely scale-exaggerated that a single ridge on one of their feet – or paws, there being some fairly irrelevant disagreement concerning the correct terminology – was now vast enough to form part of the landscape on which so many others lived their post-death lives and suffered the multitudinous torments which had been prescribed them.

The released blood from the iron tables ran glutinously down pipes and runnels to the stream bed where it collected, flowed downhill as liquids are prone to do, even in entirely virtual environments, and ran – with increasing vigour and force as the blood of more and more sufferers paid tribute to the stream – down to a deep, wide pool. Even there, bound by the synthetic rules of the Hell, it resolutely refused to coagulate. From the header pool a broad channel directed it to the summit of the mill's wheel.

The wheel was constructed of many, many ancient bones, long bleached white by the action of the acid or alkali rains that fell every few days and caused such torment to the people held in the pens upstream. The wheel turned on bearings made of cartilage laced with the nerves of yet more of the condemned whose bodies had been woven into the fabric of the building, each creaking, groaning revolution of the wheel producing seemingly unbearable agony. Other sufferers made up the roof slates with their oversized, painfully sensitised nails – they too dreaded the harrowing rains, which stung with every drop – or the mill's thin walls with their painfully stretched skins, or its supporting beams with their protesting bones, or its creaking gears and cogs, every tooth of which hurt as though riddled with disease, every stressed and straining bone bar and shaft of which would have screamed had they possessed voices.

Far beyond, beneath boiling dark skies, the stream gave out onto a great blood marsh where sufferers planted and rooted like stunted trees drowned again and again with every acidic rain and each fresh wash of blood.

Much of the time, the mill didn't even use the flow of blood collecting in its upstream pool; the fluid simply went on down the overflow and back to the stream bed on its way to the dark swamp in the distance beneath the darkly livid, lowering skies.

And besides, the mill powered nothing; the little energy it produced when it did deign to function went entirely to waste. Its whole purpose and point was to add to the excruciation of those unfortunate enough to find themselves within Hell.

This was what people were generally told, anyway. Some were told the mill did power something. They were told it held great stone wheels which ground the bodies and bones of those guilty of crimes committed within hell. Those so punished suffered even greater agonies than those whose bodies still in some sense resembled those they had inhabited before death; for those who had sinned even within Hell, the rules – always entirely flexible – were changed so that they could suffer with every sinew, cell and structure of their body, no matter how atomised it might have become and how impossible such suffering would have been with an utterly shredded nervous central system in the Real.

The truth was different, however. The truth was that the mill had a quite specific purpose and the energy it produced did not go to waste; it operated one of the small number of gates that led out of Hell, and that was why the two small Pavuleans sheltering on the far side of the valley were there.

No, we are lost, entirely lost, Prin.

We are where we are, my love. Look. The way out is right there, in front of us. We are not lost, and we shall shortly escape. Soon, we'll be home.

You know that is not true. That is a dream, just a dream. A treacherous dream. This is what is real, not anything we might think we remember from before. That memory is itself part of the torment, something to increase our pain. We should forget what we think we remember of a life before this. There was no life before this. This is all there is, all there ever was, all there ever will be. Eternity, this is eternity. Only this is eternity. Surrender to that thought and at least the agony of hope that can never be fulfilled will disappear.

They were crouching together, hidden within the lower part of a *cheval de frise*, its giant X of crossed spikes laden with impaled, half-decayed bodies. Those bodies and the bodies all around them littering this section of hillside – indeed the seemingly living or apparently dead bodies of everybody within the Hell, including their own – were Pavulean in form: metre-and-half-long quadrupeds with large, round heads from which issued small twin trunks, highly prehensile probosces with little lobes at the tip resembling stubby fingers.

Agony of hope? Listen to yourself, Chay. Hope is all we have, *my love. Hope drives us on. Hope is not treachery! Hope is not cruel and insane, like this perversion of existence; it is reasonable, right, only what we might expect, what we have every right to expect. We must escape. We must! Not just for selfish reasons, to escape the torments we've been subject to here, but to take the news, the truth of what we've experienced here back to the Real, back to where, somehow, some day, something might be done about it.*

The two Pavuleans presently hiding under the covering of rotting corpses were called – in the familiar form they used with each other – Prin and Chay, and they had journeyed together across several regions of this Hell over a subjective period of several months, always heading for this place. Now, finally, they were within sight of it.

Neither resembled Pavuleans in the peak of health. Only Prin's left trunk was intact; the other was just a still-ragged stump after a casual swipe from the sword of a passing demon some weeks ago. The poisoned sword had left a wound that would not heal or stop hurting. His intact left trunk had been nicked in the same strike and made him wince with every movement. Around both their necks was a twist of tightened barbed wire like a depraved version of a necklace, the barbs biting through their skin, raising welts that seeped blood and left itching, flaking scabs.

Chay limped because both her hind legs had been broken just days after they'd entered the Hell; she had been run over by one of an endless line of bone-and-iron juggernauts transporting mangled bodies from one part of the Hell to another. The juggernauts moved along a road whose every cobble was the warted, calloused back of screaming unfortunates buried beneath.

Prin had carried her on his back for weeks afterwards while she healed, though the bones in her legs had never set properly; in Hell bones never did.

You are wrong, Prin. There is no Real. There is no outside reality. There is only this. You may need this delusion to make the pain of being here less for you, but in the end you will be better off accepting the true *reality, that this all there is, all there ever has been and all there ever will be.*

No, Chay, he told her. *At this moment we are code, we are ghosts in the substrate, we are both real and unreal. Never forget that. We exist here for now but we had and have another life, other bodies to return to, back in the Real.*

Real, Prin? We are real fools, fools to have come, if what you say is true and we came from somewhere else; fools to think we could do anything of use here, and most certainly fools to think we can ever leave this ghastly, filthy, sickening place. This is our life now, even if there was another one before it. Accept it, and it may not be so terrible. This is the Real; this that you see and feel and smell around you. Chay reached out with her right trunk and its tip almost touched the partially rotted face of a young female impaled face down on the spikes above, her emptied eye sockets staring blankly in at the two people cowering beneath. *Though terrible it is. So, so terrible. Such a terrible place.* She looked at her mate. *Why make it worse with the lie of hope?*

Prin reached out with his surviving trunk and wrapped it around both of hers as best he could. *Chayeleze Hifornsdaughter, it is your despair that is the lie. The blood-gate across this valley opens within the hour to let out those who've been allowed a half-day glimpse of Hell in the hope of making them behave better back in the Real, and we have the means to leave with them. We shall, we* will *go back! We* will *leave this place, we* will *return to our home and we* will *tell of what we've seen here; we'll let the truth of it out for ever, free into the Real, to do whatever damage to this outrage upon kindness and sentience it is possible to do. This vast obscenity around us was* made, *my love: it can be unmade. We can help, we can begin that unmaking. We can, we* will *do this. But I will not do it alone. I can't and won't leave without you. We go together or not at all. Just one last effort, please, my love. Stay at my side, come with me, escape with me, help me save you and help me save myself!* He hugged her to his chest as hard as he was able.

Here come osteophagers, she said, looking out over his shoulder.

He let her go and looked round, peeking under hanging, rotting limbs to the uphill entrance to their impromptu shelter. She was right. A detail of half a dozen osteophagers were moving down and across the barren hillside, dragging bodies off the *chevaux de frise* and the other spiked and barbed barriers that littered the slope. The osteophagers were specialist demons, flesh- and bone-eating scavengers who lived off the carcasses of those re-killed either in Hell's never-ending war or just in the normal course of its perpetual round of mutilation and pain. The souls of those they ate would already have been recycled into fresh, mostly whole if never entirely healthy bodies better able to appreciate the torments in store for them.

Like almost all the demons in the Pavulean Hell, the osteophagers resembled predator beasts from the Pavulean evolutionary past. The osteophagers moving down the hillside towards where the two small Pavuleans were hiding looked like glossily powerful versions of animals that had once preyed upon Chay and Prin's ancestors, millions of years earlier: four-legged, twice the size of a Pavulean, with big, forward-facing eyes and – again like most demons – perversely sporting two, more muscular versions of Pavulean trunks from the sides of their massive, crushing jaws.

Their shining pelts of bright red and yellow stripes looked lacquered, polished. The colours were as much a hellish amendment as the trunks that the original animals had never possessed; it gave them the bizarre look of having been coloured in by children. They moved hulkingly from barbed barrier to barbed barrier along the hillside, lifting the hooked bodies off with their trunks or tearing them free with vicious-looking teeth nearly half a trunk long. They sucked down what were obviously the more prized parts, crunching on some smaller bones on occasion, but most of the bodies they collected were thrown onto ill-made bone carts pulled by blinded, de-trunked Pavuleans, following them along the valley side.

They will find us, Chay said dully. *They will find us and kill us all over again, or part eat us and leave us here to suffer, or impale us upon these hideous works and come back for us later, or break our legs and throw us up onto one of their carts and take us to more senior demons for more refined and terrible punishment.*

Prin stared out at the advancing, ragged line of demons, mutilated Pavuleans and giant carts. For a few moments he was unable to think properly, unable to take stock of their suddenly changed situation, and allowed Chay to mutter on, letting her words leech away the hope he had been trying to fill her with, letting her fill him instead with the despair he was constantly trying to hold at bay and which he could never admit to her was for ever threatening to overwhelm him.

The detail of osteophagers and their grisly retinue had come close enough now to hear the crunch of bones in massive jaws and the whimper of the bridled Pavuleans. He turned and looked in the opposite direction, towards the mill with its dark pool and the thick, unsplashing stream of blood that was now powering the giant, creaking wheel.

The mill was working! It had started up!

The gate it controlled must be about to open and the way out of Hell would present itself to them at last.

Chay, look! Prin told her, using his trunk to turn her away from the view of the advancing line of osteophagers and towards the mill.

I see it, I see it. Another flying death machine.

He wondered what she was talking about, then saw the moving shape, dark grey upon the still darker grey of the low, restlessly moving clouds.

I meant the mill; it's working! But the flier, too; it must be bringing the ones who're meant to get out! We're saved! Don't you see? Don't you get it? He turned her towards him again, tenderly using his trunk to bring her round to him. *This is our chance, Chay. We can, we* will *get out of here.* He gently touched the barbed wire necklaces they each wore; first hers then his own. *We have the means, Chay. Our lucky charms, our little kernels of saving code. We brought these with us, remember? They did not put these on us! This is our chance. We must be ready.*

No, you're still a fool. We have nothing. They will find us, give us to the superiors in the machine.

The flier was in the shape of a giant beetle; it buzzed furiously towards the mill on a blur of iridescent wings, its legs extending as it approached a shaved-level patch of ground by the building's side.

Ha! Chay, you're wrong, my love. We are destined to get out of here. You're coming with me. Keep a hold of your horrible necklace. This barb; this one right here. Here, can you feel it?

He directed two of her still-perfect, still-unscarred, undamaged trunk fingers to the control barb.

I feel it.

When I say so, you pull hard on that. Do you understand?

Of course I understand, do you think me a fool?

Only when I say; pull hard. We shall look like demons to those who are demons themselves, and have their power. The effect will not last long, but long enough to get us through the gate.

The great beetle-shaped flier was settling on the patch of ground by the mill. A pair of demons, yellow and black striped, emerged from the mill to watch it land. The beetle's fuselage body was about half the size of the mill; lower, longer, darkly sleek. Its wings settled, folded into its carapace. The rear of its abdomen hinged down and a small group of sturdy, grinning demons and quivering, obviously terrified Pavuleans in rough-looking clothes came out.

The Pavuleans' clothes alone marked them out as different, here. In Hell all suffered naked, and any who tried to cover their nudity only ensured themselves further torments as punishment for having had the effrontery to imagine they could exercise any control whatsoever over their suffering.

The eight Pavuleans exiting the giant beetle were also distinguished from the damned around them by being whole, carrying no scars or obvious injuries, seeping wounds or signs of disease. They looked well fed too, though even from this distance Prin could see a sort of hungry desperation in their movements and their facial expressions, a petrifying sense of probably being about to escape this landscape of pain and terror, but with the realisation dawning on at least some of them that perhaps they had been lied to. Perhaps this was not the end of a brief warning tour of Hell, designed to keep them on the straight and narrow back in the Real, but rather a taste of what was about to become their settled and already inescapable fate; a cruel trick that would be just the first of innumerable cruel tricks. Perhaps they were not getting out at all; perhaps they were here to stay, and to suffer.

From what Prin knew, for at least one of their number this would be brutally true; such groups were inevitably traumatised in the course of what they were forced to witness during these tours and – utterly unable to establish any rapport with the rapaciously forbidding and utterly disdainful demons who escorted them – quickly drew together, bonding like a tiny herd, finding a rough but real companionship amongst their equally horror-struck companions no matter how various their personalities, situations and histories might have been back in the Real.

To then have one of your number cut out of your little group, somebody you knew and felt some camaraderie towards, made the experience all the more vivid. It was just about possible to experience one of these horrific excursions and convince yourself that the unfortunates you saw suffering were quite different from you just because of the extremity of their degradation (they appeared sub-Pavulean; little more – perhaps no more – than animals) but to watch one of your group having all of his or her worst fears confirmed, consigned to everlasting torment just at the point when they thought they were about to be allowed to resume their life in the Real, made the lesson the tour was meant to teach stick much more thoroughly in the mind.

They're about to go in. Be ready. Prin glanced back to see the nearest osteophager alarmingly close to their hideout. *We have to go now, my love.* He'd hoped to be closer when they made their approach, but there was no choice.

Pull on the barb, now, Chay.

So still you seek to deceive me. But I've seen through your shallow hope.

Chay! We have no time for this! I can't do it for you! It only works at our own touch. Pull the fucking barb!

I will not. I press it instead, see? She winced as she pressed the barb further into her own neck, the other end impaling the tip of her trunk finger.

Prin sucked in his breath so hard and fast he saw the nearby osteophager turn its massive head in the direction of their shelter, ears twitching, gaze flicking this way and that, then settling on them

Shit! Right . . .

Prin pulled on his own necklace's barb; the contraband code it symbolised started running. Instantly, he had the body of one of the grinning demons, and the biggest and most impressive type at that; a giant six-limbed predator long extinct in the Real, trunkless but with trefoil-fingered forelimbs that doubled as trunks. The rationalising rules of the Hell immediately caused the body-laden *cheval de frise* to rear up to accommodate his suddenly increased bulk so that he wore it on his broad, green and yellow back like some monstrous piece of armour. Chay cowered at his feet, suddenly small. She voided her bladder and bowels and curled into a rigid ball.

With one forelimb he picked her up by both of her trunks, the way he had seen demons do to his kind countless times before, and with a roar shrugged the *cheval de frise* off his back, letting it thunk down to one side, bodies and parts of bodies flopping and falling from its spikes.

There was a shrill scream; one of the carts carrying the corpses had been almost alongside, hidden by the weight of bodies on that side of the device, and when it had fallen, one of its spikes had pierced the foot of the Pavulean hauling the cart, pinning the creature to the ground. The osteophager who had been looking suspiciously in their direction took a step back, its ears suddenly bolt upright, an emotion between surprise and fear evident in its stance.

Prin snarled at it; the creature took another half-step back. Its fellows across the hillside had stopped and now stood motionless, looking on. They would wait and see which way this was going to go before deciding either to join in with leave-some-for-me! bravado, or pretend it had been nothing to do with them in the first place.

Prin shook the still-catatonically-inert Chay towards the osteophager. *She's mine! I saw first!*

The osteophager blinked, looked round with apparent unconcern, checking to see what the rest of its detail was doing. Not coming bounding to its side to face down this sudden interloper steadfastly and together, clearly. The creature looked down, brushed at the ground in front of it with the back of one paw, claws mostly retracted.

Take it, it said in a grumbling, seemingly unconcerned voice. *Consider it yours, with our blessing. We have plenty.* It shrugged, lowered its head to sniff at the patch of ground it had scuffed, apparently having lost interest in the whole exchange.

Prin snarled again, clutched Chay to his chest, turned and bounded down the hillside past decaying corpses and spikes pennanted with ragged strips of flesh. He splashed through the dark stream of blood and went springing diagonally up the slope towards the mill. The group from the giant beetle had disappeared inside the building. The beetle itself had closed its abdomen and was unpacking its wings from beneath its gleaming wing covers. Prin was close enough to see demons moving inside its enormous faceted eyes.

Pilots, he thought, for an assemblage of code that might as well have been kept aloft through the wielding of an enchanted feather, or a magic anvil for that matter.

He leapt on up the hillside, towards the mill.

Five

From somewhere came the idea that there were many different levels of sleeping, of unconsciousness, and therefore of awakening. In the midst of this pleasant woozy calm – warm, pleasantly swaddled, self-huggingly curled up, a sort of ruddy darkness behind the eyelids – it was an easy and comforting thing to contemplate the many ways one might be away, and then come back.

You fell asleep just for an instant sometimes; that sudden nod and jerk awake again, lasting a moment. Or you had short naps, often self-timed, limited by knowing you had a few minutes or a half-hour or whatever.

Of course you had your classic Good Night's Sleep, however much things like shift systems and all-night facilities and drugs and city lighting might sometimes interfere.

Then there was the deeper unconsciousness of being knocked out, put carefully under for some medical procedure, or randomly banging your head and briefly not even knowing your own name. Also, people still lapsed into comas, and came out of those very gradually; that must be an odd feeling. And for a while there, for the last few centuries, though not so often these days because things had moved on, there was the sub-sleep of deep space travel, when you were put into a sort of deep, long-term hibernation for years or decades at a time, kept frigidly cold and barely alive, to be revived when your destination approached. Some people had been kept like this back at home, too, awaiting medical advances. Waking up from something like that must be quite a strange thing, she thought.

She felt an urge to turn over, as though she was nestled in a fabulously comfortable bed but now had spent enough time on this side and needed to shift to lie the other way. She felt very light, she realised, though even as she thought this she seemed to feel very slightly, reassuringly heavier.

She felt herself take a deep, satisfying breath, and duly turned over, eyes still tightly closed. She had a vague feeling that she didn't entirely know where she was, but it didn't bother her. Usually that was a slightly disturbing sensation, occasionally even a very disturbing, frightening experience, but not this time. Somehow she knew that wherever she was she was safe, cared for, and in no danger.

She felt good. Really good, in fact.

When she thought about it, she realised that she couldn't remember ever having felt so good, so secure, so happy. She felt a tiny frown form on her face. Oh, come on, she told herself. She *must* have felt like this before. To her slight but undeniable irritation, she had only a vague memory of when she had last felt anything like this untroubled and happy. Probably in her mother's arms, as a little girl.

She knew that if she woke up fully she would remember properly, but – much as a part of her wanted to be completely awake, to answer this question and sort all this out – another part of her was too happy just lying here, wherever she was, drowsy, secure and happy.

She knew this feeling. This was often the best bit of any day, before she had to wake and fully face the realities of the world and the responsibilities she had fallen heir to. If you were lucky, you really did sleep like a baby; completely, soundly and without care. Then it would be only as you awoke that you were reminded of all the things you had to worry about, all the resentments you harboured, all the injustices and cruelties you were subject to. Still, even the thought of that grim process somehow couldn't destroy her mood of ease and happiness.

She sighed; a long, deep, satisfying sigh, though still with an element of regret as she felt her sleepiness drift away like mist under a gentle breeze.

The sheets covering her felt outrageously fine, almost liquidly soft. They moved about her naked body as she completed the sigh and stirred a little under the warm material. She was not sure that even Himself possessed such fine—

She felt herself spasm and jerk. A terrifying image, the face of someone hateful, started to form before her, then – as though some other part of her mind came to soothe her fears – the fear subsided and the anxiety seemed to be brushed away, like dust.

Whatever she had once feared, she didn't need to fear it now. Well, that was nice, she supposed.

She supposed, too, that she really ought to wake up.

She opened her eyes. She had the vague impression of a wide bed, pale sheets and a large, high-ceilinged room with tall open windows from which gauzy, softly billowing white curtains waved out. A warm, flower-scented breeze stirred around her. Sunlight leant in golden shafts against the window apertures.

She noticed that there was some sort of fuzzy glow at the foot of the bed. It swam into focus and spelled out the word *SIMULATION*.

Simulation? she thought, sitting up and rubbing her eyes. The room swam properly into focus when she re-opened them. The place looked perfectly, entirely real, but she was no longer really paying attention to the room. Her jaw had dropped and her mouth hung open as she took in what she had glimpsed as she'd casually raised her arms and hands to her eyes a moment earlier.

She dropped her head very slowly and brought her hands up in front of her face again, staring at the backs, then at the palms of her hands, then at her forearms, then down at what she could see of her chest and breasts. She leapt back, upwards to the headboard of the bed, throwing the sheet off her as she did so, and stared down at her naked body.

She brought her hands up yet again, stared hard at them, inspecting her fingers, her fingernails, peering at them as though trying to see something which was almost but not quite too small to see. Finally she looked up, her gaze darting round the room; she threw herself out of the bed – the word *SIMULATION* stayed where it was, just visible at the bottom of her field of vision – and ran to a full-length mirror between two of the tall windows with their softly billowing curtains.

Nothing on her face, either. She stared at herself.

First of all, she was entirely the wrong colour. She ought to be almost soot black. Instead, she was . . . she wasn't even sure what you called this colour. Dirty gold? Mud? Polluted sunset?

That was bad enough, but there was worse.

"Where the fuck is my intaglia?" she heard herself say.

SIMULATION, said the word now hovering around her feet as she took in the view of a beautiful but entirely un-bodymarked pale-skinned young woman standing naked in front of her. It looked something like her, she supposed, in bone structure and general bodily proportions, but that was being generous. Her featureless skin was a sort of wan, reddish-gold and her hair was entirely wrong; far too long and much too dark.

SIMULATION, the word still said. She slammed one fist into the side frame of the mirror, felt pretty much exactly the amount of pain she'd have anticipated, and sucked warm, fragrant air through her teeth (her teeth were also unmarked, too uniformly white, as were the whites of her eyes). When she'd hit it, the mirror frame had wobbled and the whole mirror and its base had shifted a few millimetres along the polished wooden floor, slightly altering the angle it presented to her.

"Ow ow ow," she muttered, shaking her tingling hand as she

stepped to the nearest window and, ducking a little, armed away the delicate translucence of a curtain.

She looked out from a bowed, balustraded stone balcony a floor above ground, gazing across a sunny landscape of elegantly sculpted green and blue trees, pale yellow-green grass and some mist foregrounding a soft tumult of wooded hills, the furthest ridges distance-blued against high, far-away mountains, summits glitteringly white. A river sparkled in the yellow-white sunlight off to one side, beyond a meadow where a herd of small dark-coated animals were grazing.

She stared hard at the view. She stepped back, snatched at the floating expanse of the wispy curtain, bringing a section of it up to her nose, frowning at it as she inspected the precision of its near microscopic weave. A set of shutters and glass windows lay open behind; she caught another glimpse of herself in the windows. She shook her head – how strange the hair on her head made the movement feel! – then went down on one knee by the stone balcony rail, rubbing two fingers along its ruddy broad top, feeling the slight graininess of sandstone under her fingertips, a little of which remained when she lifted her fingers away and rubbed them against each other. She put her nose to it; she could *smell* the stone.

Still, *SIMULATION*, the word said. She let out another sigh, of exasperation this time, and inspected the sky with its many little puffy white clouds.

She had experienced simulations before; she had been in virtual environments, but even the ones that relied on you being dosed with just the right drugs, so that you did a lot of the detail-filling yourself, were nothing like as perfectly convincing as this. The simulations she had experienced were closer to dreams than reality; convincing at the time, but pretty much the moment you started looking for the pixels or the grain or the fractals or whatever they were – or just the processing short cuts and inconsistencies – you found them. What she was looking at here – and feeling, and smelling – was effectively, uncannily flawless. She almost felt faint for an instant, head briefly swimming before quickly clearing again before she even started to sway or stagger.

Nevertheless: the sky was too blue, the sunlight too golden, the hills and especially the mountains didn't quite fade and drop away like they did on a real planet, and while she still felt entirely like herself within herself – as it were – she was inside a body which was perfectly, flawlessly unmarked, causing her to feel more naked than she had ever felt in her life. No intaglia, no tattoo, no markage whatsoever. That was the biggest clue of all that this could not be real.

Well, the second biggest; there was that word, floating in red, always at the lower limit of her vision. *SIMULATION*. That was about as unambiguous as you got, she supposed.

From the balcony, she took a look around what she could see of the building. Just a big, rather ornate red sandstone house with lots of tall windows; some sticky-out bits, a few turrets, a pathway of small stones around the base. Listening carefully she could hear what might be the breeze in the nearest treetops, some high, slightly plaintive calls that probably represented birdsong and a faint lowing from the herd of four-legged grazing animals in the meadow.

She walked back into the bedroom and stood in its relative silence. She cleared her throat.

"All right, it's a simulation. Anybody here I can talk to?"

No answer. She drew in the breath to say something else, but then there came a polite knocking from one of the room's two broad wooden doors.

"Who's there?" she called.

"My name is Sensia," a pleasant-sounding female voice said. She'd have guessed it belonged to a relatively elderly woman, and one who was smiling as she spoke. She'd had a favourite aunt who'd sounded like this person, though perhaps not quite as well-spoken.

"One moment." She looked down at herself. She imagined wearing a plain white dressing gown. Nope; her body remained stubbornly naked.

What looked like a tall wooden wardrobe stood near the door. She swung open the doors, wondering why she was doing so even as she did it. She was in a simulation, this didn't even look like her own body anyway and she had never been especially self-conscious about her physical form – how could she be, as an Intagliate? The notion would have been hilarious if not so intimately connected with bitterness. Still, she did feel exceptionally naked with no markings, and the general feel and polite, highly monied ambience of this sim would appear to demand a certain decorum.

There were lots of rather gorgeous clothes inside the wardrobe; she threw on a plain, dark blue robe of what felt like the same material the liquid-soft sheet had been made of. She stood before the broad door, cleared her throat again, drew herself up and pulled on the fist-sized handle.

"Hello," said the rather plain but very amiable-looking lady of late middle age standing outside. Behind her was a broad hallway with more doors leading off on one side and balustrades giving out onto a double-level hall on the other. "May I come in?" She had bunned white hair, sparkling green eyes and was dressed in a plain dark suit, unadorned.

"Please, do," she said.

Sensia looked around, softly clapping her frail-looking hands once. "Shall we sit outside? I've sent for some drinks."

They dragged a couple of heavy, brocaded seats out through the middle window onto the most generous of the room's balconies, and sat down.

Her eyes stay too wide, she found herself thinking. *She's facing into the sunlight; a real person would be squinting by now, wouldn't they?*

On a ledge above, two small blue birds appeared to be fighting, rising at each other on a furious flutter of wings and almost touching breasts in mid-air before falling back again, all of this accompanied by a great deal of high-pitched twittering.

Sensia smiled warmly, clasping her hands. "So," she said. "We are in a simulation."

"I gathered," she said, the word itself seemingly printed across the legs of the woman opposite.

"We'll remove that," Sensia said. The word disappeared from her field of vision. That felt briefly scary, though presumably she was always going to be under somebody's control, in a sim. Sensia sat forward. "Now, this might sound a little odd, but would you mind terribly telling me your name?"

She stared at the other woman. Just for the merest instant, she had to think. What *was* her name? "Lededje Y'breq," she said, almost blurted. Of course.

"Thank you. I see." Sensia looked up towards the mad tweeting coming from the little birds above. The noise stopped suddenly. A moment later both birds flew down, settled briefly on one of Sensia's fingers and then darted off in different directions. "And you are from where exactly?"

Another nearly imperceptible delay. "Well, I . . . I'm of the Veppers retinue," she said. Veppers, she thought. How odd to think of him without fear. It was as though all that was in another life, and one that she would not have to go back to. Even as she thought about it, turning it over in her mind, the idea still held no terror. She started trying to remember where she had been last, before she ended up here. It felt like something she'd been hiding from herself, like something that some other part of her had been keeping from her. "I was born in Ubruater City and brought up in the mansion house of the estate of Espersium," she told Sensia. "Lately, I still generally live either in Ubruater, Espersium, or sometimes just wherever Mr. Veppers might be."

Sensia was nodding, gaze distant. "Ah-hah!" she said, sitting back, smiling. "Ubruater City, Sichult, Quyn system, Ruprine Cluster, Arm One-one Near-tip."

Lededje recognised "Quyn" as the name the Sun went by in the rest of the galaxy and she had heard the term "Ruprine Cluster" before. She had no idea what "Arm One-one Near-tip" was; this bit of the galaxy, she supposed.

"Where am I?" she asked as a small, thick-bottomed tray arrived, floating out from the room. It held glasses and a pitcher of pale green liquid with ice in it. The device lowered between them so that it effectively became a table.

Sensia poured their drinks. "Presently, literally," she said, settling back again, swirling her drink, "you're in a computational substrate node of the General Systems Vehicle *Sense Amid Madness, Wit Amidst Folly*, which is currently travelling through the 'liavitzian Blister, in the region called God's Ear, Rotational."

Rather than fully catching all this, Lededje had been thinking. "'Vehicle'?" she said. "Is that a Wheel, or . . . ?" She took a drink. The pale green liquid was delicious, though probably non-alcoholic.

Sensia smiled uncertainly. "A Wheel?"

"You know; a Wheel," Lededje said, and became aware they were now staring at the other with mutual incomprehension.

How could this woman not know what a Wheel was?

Then Sensia's face brightened. "Ah, a *Wheel*! A specific thing, with a capital letter and so on. I see. Yes, sorry; got you now." She looked away, seemingly distracted. "Oh, yes, fascinating things . . ." She shook her head. "But no, not a Wheel. Bit bigger than that. Plate-class General Systems Vehicle: getting on for a hundred kilometres long if you go tip-to-tip of the outer field structure and four klicks high measuring just the naked hull. Roughly six trillion tonnes, though the mass assay gets fiendishly complicated with so much exotic matter making up the engines. About a fifth of a billion people aboard right now." She flashed a smile. "Not counting those in virtual environments."

"What's it called again?"

"The *Sense Amid Madness, Wit Amidst Folly*." Sensia shrugged. "Where I take my name from; Sensia. I'm a ship's avatoid."

"That sounds like a Culture ship," Lededje said, feeling her skin warm suddenly.

Sensia stared at her, looking genuinely surprised. "Good gracious," she said. "You mean you didn't even know you were on a Culture ship, even within the Culture at all? I'm surprised you're not more disoriented. Where did you think you might be?"

Lededje shrugged. She was still trying to recall where she'd been last, before she woke up here. "No idea," she said. "I've never been in a sim this good. I'm not sure we have them to this standard. I don't think even Veppers has them this detailed."

Sensia nodded.

"Where am I really?" Lededje asked.

"How do you mean?"

"Where's my real self, my physical body?"

Sensia stared at her again. She put the drink down on the floating tray, her expression unreadable. "Ah," she said. She made an o with her mouth and sucked air in, turning her head to look out at the parkland surrounding the house. She turned back to look at Lededje. "What is the last thing you remember, before you woke up here?"

Lededje shook her head. "I can't remember. I've been trying."

"Well don't try too hard. From what I can gather it's . . . traumatic."

Lededje wanted to say something to that, but couldn't think what. *Traumatic?* she thought with a sudden shiver of fear. *What the hell did that mean?*

Sensia took a deep breath. "Let me start by explaining that I have never had to ask for somebody's name in these circumstances. I mean, someone – you – suddenly popping into existence unannounced." She shook her head. "Doesn't happen. Mind-states, souls, dynamic full-brain process inventories; whatever you call them, they always come with copious notes. You didn't." Sensia smiled again. Lededje formed the uncomfortable impression that the other woman was trying hard to be reassuring. This had never proved to be a good sign in Lededje's past and she seriously doubted the pattern was about to change now. "You just immaterialised here, my dear," Sensia told her, "in a one-time, one-way emergency-entanglement vicariously inherited legacy system event of what us Minds would generally call Laughably High Unexpectancy. And most bizarrely of all you came with what one might call no paperwork, zero documentation. Absolutely without accompanying context material. Docketless."

"Is that unusual?"

Sensia laughed. She had a surprisingly deep, almost raucous laugh. Lededje found herself smiling despite the apparent gravity of the subject. "Not so much unusual," Sensia said. "More entirely without precedent in roughly the last fifteen hundred busy years. Frankly I'm finding that hard to believe myself and, trust me, I have lots and *lots* of other avatars, avatoids, agents, feelers and just plain old requests out at the moment asking if anybody else has heard of such a thing – all without positive reply so far."

"So you had to ask me my name."

"Quite. As a ship Mind – as any kind of Mind, or even AI – I'm sort of constitutionally forbidden from looking too deeply into you, but even so I had to do a bit of delving just to get a matchable body profile for you to wake up in without causing you further trauma, here in the Virtual."

Didn't entirely work, Lededje thought. *I'm a negative of my real self's colour, and— Where's my damn tat?*

Sensia continued: "Plus there's the language protocols, obviously. They're actually quite involved, but highly localised across pan-humanity, so easy enough to pinpoint. Could have gone deeper and got your name and other details but that would have been invasively rude. However, following some ancient guidelines so obscure that I had to actively dig them out and consult them – designed to cover situations like this – I did what is called an Immediate Post-Traumatic Emergency Entanglement Transfer Psychological Profile Evaluation." Another smile. "So that whatever suddenly caused you to need an entanglement event in the first place, back wherever you came from, didn't compromise your safe transfer into Virtuality." Sensia raised her glass again. She looked at it then put it back down again. "And what I discovered was that you've had a traumatic experience," she said, quite quickly, her gaze not meeting Lededje's. "Which I've sort of held back, edited from your transferred memories, just for now, while you settle in, get yourself sorted out, until you're ready. You know."

Lededje stared at her. "Really? You can do such a thing?"

"Oh, trivially easy, technically," Sensia said, sounding relieved. "The constraints are entirely moral; rule-based. And it is, obviously, up to you when you come fully up to speed with yourself, if you know what I mean. Though frankly if I were you I wouldn't be in too great a hurry."

Lededje tried very hard to recall what had happened before she came here. She remembered being at Espersium, walking down a tree-lined avenue in the estate, alone, thinking that . . . it was time to escape.

Hmm, she thought. That was interesting. Was that what had happened? Had she finally found a practical, Veppers-proof method of getting away from the bastard and all his money, power and influence, using this entanglement thing? But that still left the question: where was her real self? Not to mention, why could she remember so little, and what exactly was this "trauma" Sensia kept talking about?

She drained her glass, sat up straight. "Tell me everything," she demanded.

Sensia looked at her. She looked worried, concerned, compassionate. "Lededje," she began slowly, carefully, "would you say that you're a . . . psychologically strong person?"

Oh, fuck, thought Lededje.

When she had been very young, there had been a time she could still remember when she had felt nothing but loved, privileged and special. It was something more than the usual feeling of blessed distinction that all good parents naturally communicate to their children. There was that – that feeling of being at the focus of unquestioning regard and care – but for a while she had been just about sufficiently mature to realise that she was lucky enough to have even more than that. First of all, she lived in a great and beautiful house within a vast rural estate of extraordinary, even unique grandeur, and, secondly, she looked utterly different from the other children, just as her mother looked quite different from the other adults in the great household.

She had been born an Intagliate. She was certainly a human, and a Sichultian (you learned early on there were other types of human, but it was taken for granted that Sichultians were the best sort) but more than just a Sichultian: an Intagliate, somebody whose skin, whose entire body, whose every internal organ and part of their external physical appearance was different – markedly different – from that of everybody else.

Intagliates looked like ordinary people only in silhouette, or in lighting conditions so poor you could hardly see them at all. Turn on a lamp, come out into the daylight, and they were revealed as the fabulous creatures they were. An Intagliate was covered, head to foot, in what was called a congenitally administered tattoo. Lededje had been born tattooed, emerging from the womb with the most fabulously intricate patterns indelibly encoded at a cellular level onto her skin and throughout her body.

Usually, a true Indented Intagliate, as fully recognised by the Sichultian judicial and administrative system, was born with mist-white skin, the better to display the classically ink-dark designs imprinted on them. Their teeth bore similar designs, the whites of their eyes were similarly ornamented, their translucent fingernails held one design while another was just visible on the nail-pad beneath. The pores on their skin were arranged in a precisely formulated, non-random way, and even the minute tracery of their capillary system was patterned just so, according to design, not developmental chance. Cut them open and you would find similar designs on the surfaces of their internal organs, their designated motif carried into their heart and guts. Bleach their bones; the design would be stamped on the pale surface of their very skeleton; suck out their marrow and break those bones open, the ornamentation continued. At every possible level of their being they bore the mark that distinguished them from the blank sheets that were other people, as well as from those who had merely chosen to have themselves in some way marked.

Some, especially over the last century or so, were born almost night black rather than nearly snow white, their skins, especially, laced with even more exotic and colourful designs that could usefully include iridescence, fluorescence and the effect of mercurial silver, all of which were held to show up better on black skin. Lededje had been one of these even more flamboyantly marked creatures, the elite of the elite as she'd thought and felt at the time.

Her mother, who carried her own marks on her much paler skin – though hers were simple conventional ink – cared for Lededje and made her feel exceptionally fortunate to be what and who she was. The girl was proud that she was even more fabulously tattooed than her mother, and fascinated both by her mother's wildly swirling patterns and her own. Even then, when she was just little, less than half her mother's height, she could see that for all the greater area of her mother's body surface and the fabulous artistry of the designs on her skin, her own flesh was the more intricately patterned, the more precisely and minutely marked. She noticed this but didn't like to say anything, feeling slightly sorry for her mother. Maybe one day, she'd thought, her mother too could have skin as beautifully intagliated as her own. Lededje decided she would grow up rich and famous and would give her mother the money to make this happen. This made her feel very grown-up.

When she began to mix with them, the other toddlers and younger children from the estate seemed in awe of her. For one thing they were each a mixture of colours, and many of them were rather pale and wan-looking; she was pure. More importantly though, the other children had no markings, they boasted no astounding design upon their skins or anywhere else, obvious or hidden, slowly growing, gradually maturing, subtly changing and for ever becoming more complicated. They deferred to her, prioritised her own needs and wants over their own, seemed practically to worship her. She was their princess, their queen, almost their sacred goddess.

It had changed gradually. She suspected her mother had used all the influence she possessed to protect her only child from the demeaning truth for as long as she'd been able, probably to the detriment of her own position and standing within the household.

For the truth was that the Intagliate were more than just human exotica. They were both more, and less, than extravagant ornamentations in the household and retinue of the rich and powerful, to be displayed like walking, living jewellery at important social events and within the halls of financial, social and political power – though they were most certainly that.

They were trophies, they were the surrendered banners of defeated enemies, the capitulation papers signed by the vanquished, the heads of fierce beasts adorning the walls of those who owned them.

Intagliates recorded with their very being the fall of their families, the shame of their parents and grandparents. To be so marked was to bear witness to an inherited debt which your very existence was part of the paying-off.

It was a feature of Sichultian law – carried over from the practices of the particular nation-caste that had emerged victorious in the fight to stamp their way of doing things on the coalescing world state, two centuries earlier – that if a commercial debt could not be fully settled, or if the terms in some deal were deemed not entirely sufficient due to shortage of funds or other negotiables by one of the parties, then the defaulting or inadequately provisioned side could compensate by undertaking to have a generation or two of their progeny made Intagliate, signing over at least some of their children and grandchildren – usually though not always for life – to the care and control, indeed the ownership, of those to whom they were either indebted or at a fiscal disadvantage.

Sichultians, on encountering the rest of the galactic community following their contact by a species called the Flekke, were generally quite indignantly insistent that their rich and powerful loved their children just as much as the rich and powerful of any other decently civilised species, and that they simply had an elevated respect for the letter of the law and the honour involved in paying one's debts on time, rather than a reduced regard for the rights of minors, or those who were otherwise innocent but indebted-by-inheritance in general.

The rights and well-being of the Intagliate, they would point out, were protected by an entire network of strictly applied laws to ensure that they could not be neglected or mistreated by those who effectively owned them, and indeed those who were Marked could even be regarded as being amongst the most privileged people in society, in a sense, being raised in the absolute lap of luxury, mixing with the very cream of society, attending all the most important social events and formal court occasions and never being expected to have to work for their keep. Most people would happily surrender their so-called "freedom" to live like that. They were esteemed, precious, and almost – though not quite – beyond price. What more could somebody who would otherwise have been born into grinding poverty ask for?

Like many societies finding their hitherto unquestioned customs and ethical assumptions impacting squarely with the breath-takingly sophisticated summed morality of a meta-civilisation inestimably older, vaster and by implication wiser than themselves, the Sichultia became highly protective of their developmental foibles, and refused to mandate away what some of them at least claimed to regard as one of their defining social characteristics and a vital and vibrant part of their culture.

Not all Sichultians agreed with this, of course; there had always been opposition to the very idea of Indented Intagliation, as well as to the very notion of a political-economic system configured to allow such options – a few deranged ruffians and degenerate troublemakers even took issue with the primacy of private ownership and the unfettered accumulation of capital itself – but most Sichultians accepted the practice and some were genuinely proud of it.

As far as other species and civilisations were concerned, it was just another one of those little quirks you always encountered when you discovered a new member of the community, a rough edge that would probably get rubbed off like the rest as the Sichultia gradually found and settled into their place at the great galactic banquet table of pan-species revelry.

Lededje could still remember the dawning of the realisation that her markings were not glorious after all, but somehow shameful. She was imprinted as she was, not to distinguish her as someone more important and privileged than others, but to mark her as a chattel, to make it clear to others that she was less than them: an owned, bonded thing, a trophy, an admission of familial defeat and shame. It had been, it still was, the most important, defining and humiliating stage of her life.

She had immediately tried to run away, fleeing the nursery where one of the other children, a little older than she, had finally and categorically informed her about all this, but got no further than the base of one of the dozens of small satellite domes that surrounded the mansion; barely a kilometre from where she'd started.

She howled and screamed at her mother for not telling her the truth about her tattoo. She threw herself into her bed and didn't emerge for days. Hunkered under the bedclothes, she'd heard her mother weeping in the next room, and been briefly glad of it. Later she hated herself for hating her mother and they wept together, hugging, but nothing would ever be the same again, either between them or between Lededje and the other children, whose deposed queen she now felt she was.

It would be years before she'd be able to acknowledge all that her mother had done to protect her, how even that first deceit, that absurd concocted dream of privilege, had been a way of trying to strengthen her for the vicissitudes she would inevitably encounter in her later life.

According to her mother the reason that she had been forcibly tattooed and Lededje had been born Intagliate – as would be the one or two children she was contractually and honour-bound to produce – was that her late husband, Grautze, Lededje's father, had been too trusting.

Grautze and Veppers had been best friends since their school days and had been in business together since the beginning of their commercial careers. Both of them came from very powerful, rich and renowned families and both became even more powerful, rich and famous as individuals, making deals and making money. They had made some enemies too, certainly, but that was only to be expected in business. They were rivals, but it was a friendly rivalry, and they had many joint ventures and equal partnerships.

Then there came the prospect of a single great deal more lucrative and important than any they had ever taken part in before; a momentous, reputation-securing, history-making, world-changing deal. They took a solemn pledge that they would work together on this, equal partners. They even became blood brothers to seal the agreement and signify the importance of the deal to both of them; they used a paired set of antique knives that Lededje's great-grandfather had presented to Veppers' grandfather, decades earlier, to cut the palms of the hands they then clasped. Nothing had been signed between them, but then the two had always behaved like honourable men to each other, and taken the other's word as being good enough.

The details of the betrayal and the slow, devastating unwinding of that pledge were such that whole teams of lawyers had struggled to come to terms with them, but the gist was that Lededje's father had lost everything, and Veppers had gained it all, and more. Her father's family lost almost everything too, the financial damage rippling out to brothers, sisters, parents, aunts, uncles and cousins.

Veppers had made a great show of pretending to be supportive; in the complexity of the unravelling deal, much of the most immediate damage had been at the hands of other business rivals, and Veppers was assiduous in buying up the debts they accumulated from Lededje's father, but always his support stopped short of preventing the damage in the first place. The final betrayal was the requirement, when all other ways of paying had been exhausted, that Grautze consent to his wife being Marked and his next child – and any children that that child had – being an Indented Intagliate.

Veppers gave every sign of being devastated it had come to this, but said he could see no other way out; there was no other honourable course, and if they had not honour, what did they have? He received considerable sympathy for having to watch his best friend and his family suffer so, but was adamant that despite the personal anguish it caused him it was the right thing to do; the rich could not be, and did not want to be, above the law.

The first part of the sentence, approved by Sichult's highest court, was duly carried out; Lededje's mother was taken, put into something resembling a coma, and tattooed. The night of the day they had taken her away, her husband slit his own throat with one of the two knives the original disastrous agreement had been solemnised by.

They found Grautze's body quite quickly. The medics were able to take a viable sample of his seed from him. Brought together with an egg, taken from his widow while she was still under from the tattooing procedure, the resulting embryo was altered, changed to become that of an Intagliate, and then implanted back into his widow. Many of the team who had overseen the designing and patterning of the embryo felt it was their finest work. The result was Lededje.

The basis for the fabulous scroll work wrapping every square centimetre of her skin was that of the letter V, for Veppers, and the Veprine Corporation he commanded. Other elements included twin, crossed knives and images of the object the fateful deal had been about in the first place; Sichult's soletta, the giant space-mounted fabrication which shielded the world from some of the light of the sun.

Lededje tried running away a lot as she grew up. She never got very far. Around about the time she started to think of herself as a young woman rather than a girl, when her intaglia was revealing itself in its true, mature, astoundingly intricate and colourful glory, she began to realise just how fabulously rich her master Mr. Veppers was and how far his power and influence reached. She gave up trying to run away.

It wasn't until some years later, when Veppers started raping her, that she discovered that the richer the alleged perpetrator was, the more all those strictly enforced statutes regarding the rights of the Intagliate became, well, more like aspirations; general guidelines rather than properly enforced laws. That was when she started trying to run away again. The first time, she'd got to the edge of the estate, ninety kilometres from the house, after travelling down one of the great forested trackways that led to the estate perimeter.

The day before Lededje was caught and brought back, her mother, despairing, had thrown herself from one of the towers in the part of the estate near the house Lededje and her friends called the water maze.

Lededje had never confided to her mother that Veppers was raping her; he'd told her after the first time that if she did he'd make sure she never saw her mother again. Simple as that. She thought that her mother had suspected though. That might have been the real reason she took her own life.

Lededje felt she understood why death had seemed like an easier course for her mother. She even thought about doing the same thing herself, but couldn't bring herself to go through with it. Part of her wanted to deprive Veppers of the most monetarily precious person in his household, but a more important part of her refused to let herself be ground down to the point of suicide by him.

Losing her mother hadn't been enough, apparently. She'd been physically punished for her attempt to escape, too; a relatively unadorned patch of her flesh at the base of her back had been retro-marked with a beautifully drawn, exquisitely detailed though to her still inestimably crude etching of a black-skinned girl flitting through a forest. Even the applying of it had hurt.

And now, as Sensia slowly let the memories filter back, she knew that the second time she'd escaped had been in the city, in the capital, in Ubruater. She'd got away for longer that time – five days rather than four – though she'd only travelled a couple of kilometres across Ubruater, the adventure ending in the opera house that Veppers himself had funded.

She winced as she remembered the knife entering her chest, sliding between her ribs, plunging into her heart. The taste of his blood, the grisly feel of the tip of his nose as she'd chewed once and swallowed it, the shrieked obscenity and the final slap across the face when she was already as good as dead.

They were somewhere else now.

She'd had Sensia turn her skin from reddish-gold – too much like Veppers' own flesh tone – to a dark, glossy black. The house and landscape had been altered at her request too, all in an instant.

Now they stood outside a more modest single-storey dwelling of white-painted mud brick whose prospect was of a leafy little oasis in a great duned desert of sable sand spreading as far as the eye could see. Colourful tents stood around pools and little streams, shadowed by tall, red-leafed trees.

"Make there be children," she'd said, and there they were; a dozen or so, all laughing and splashing in one of the shallow pools, oblivious to the two women watching them from the mud brick house on its slight rise.

Sensia had suggested they sit down before she opened up Lededje's memories of the last few days and hours of her life. They had sat on a rug on a wooden platform in front of the house while she recalled with mounting horror the events leading up to her death. There had been the usual flier journey from the estate to the capital, full of stomach-churning swoops and zooms as Veppers enjoyed himself, then on arrival she had settled into her room in the town house – another mansion in all but name in the centre of the city – then she'd slipped away from a visit to a couturier, gouging from her left heel the tracer implant she'd discovered was there some months ago. She'd picked up some pre-prepared clothes, makeup and effects and gone on the run within the city streets and alleys, finally finding herself cornered in the opera house.

The way Sensia had let her experience it, it was more like watching it all happen to somebody else, on a stage or in a film; she had been spared the outright immediacy of it all in that first run-through, though she could choose to go back and inspect the detail of it if she wanted. She had chosen to do this. She was doing it again now. She winced once more.

Lededje had stood again, the shock of it over. Sensia stood at her side.

"So I'm *dead*?" she said, still not fully comprehending.

"Well," Sensia said, "obviously not so dead you can't ask that question, but, technically; yes."

"How did I get here? Was it via this entanglement thing?"

"Yes. There must have been a sort of neural lace inside your head, entangled with the legacy system I inherited from the relevant ship."

"What relevant ship?"

"Let's come back to that."

"And what fucking neural lace inside my head?" she demanded. "I didn't have one!"

"You must have. The only alternative would have been somebody positioning some sort of neural induction device round your head and reading your mind-state that way, as you slipped away. But that's very doubtful. Not the sort of tech you have yourselves— "

"We have aliens," Lededje protested. "Especially in Ubruater – it's the capital of the planet, the whole system, the whole Enablement. Alien embassies; aliens running around all over the place. They'd have the tech."

"Indeed they might, but why would they code your brain state and transmit it across three and a half thousand light years to a Culture ship, without documentation? Also, just plopping an induction helmet, no matter how sophisticated, onto a dying person in the last few seconds of their life could never record a mind state as detailed and internally consistent as yours. Even in a prime equiv-tech medical environment with plenty of prep time and a stable subject you'd never capture the fine detail you've come equipped with. A full back-up-capable neural lace grows with the brain it's part of, it beds in over the years, gets very adept at mirroring every detail of the mind it interpenetrates and co-exists with. That's what you pretty much must have had. Plus it had an entanglement facility built into it, obviously."

She glared at Sensia. "So I'm . . . complete? A perfect copy?"

"Impossible to be absolutely sure, but I strongly suspect so. There is almost certainly less of a difference between the you that died and the you that you are now than there would be between your selves at one end of a night's sleep and the other."

"And that's thanks to this entanglement thing too?"

"Partly. The copies at either end of the process should be absolutely identical, assuming the non-originating part of the pair collapses at all."

"What?"

"Entanglement is great when it works but – more than two per cent of the time – it doesn't work; in fact it fails utterly. That's why it's almost never used – hideously risky. You use it in wartime, when it's better than nothing, and possibly a few SC agents have been subject to the process, but, otherwise, never."

"Still, the odds were in my favour."

"Assuredly. And it's better than being dead." Sensia paused. "Though this still doesn't answer the question regarding how you ended up with a full back-up-capable neural lace in your head complete with an entanglement facility targeted to a long passed-on legacy sub-system which all concerned had quite thoroughly forgotten about." Sensia turned, looked at Lededje. "You're frowning."

"I just thought of something."

She had met him – met *it*, as it turned out – at a reception on the Third Equatower, in the space station port of one of Sichult's five equatorial space elevators. A Jhlupian cultural and trade mission ship had recently docked, disgorging various notables of the Jhlupe, a high-level civilisation with which Veppers had commercial links. The carousel space where the reception was held was one of a number of giant sliding tori for ever revolving underneath the rotund bulk of the station's docks, canted windows providing an ever-changing view of the planet beneath.

The Jhlupe, she recalled thinking, gave the impression that they were all elbows. Or maybe knees; they were awkward-looking twelve-limbed creatures like giant soft-shelled land crabs, their skin or carapace a bright, lustrous green. A trio of eyes on short stalks protruded from their main bodies, which were a little larger than a human who had rolled themselves into a ball. Rather than use their many spindly legs, they floated on what looked like metallic cushions. Their translated voices issued from the same source.

This had happened ten years ago. Lededje had been sixteen at the time, just coming to terms with the fact she was a woman and that her now almost fully matured intagliation would make her an object of fascination wherever she went – indeed that this was the whole of her purpose in life, as far as Veppers and the rest of the world were concerned.

She had just started being brought along to events like this, expected to accompany Veppers as part of his retinue. It was, in its full pomp, a sizeable retinue, too. As well as his assorted bag-carriers and various bodyguards – Jasken being the last line of defence – Veppers was the sort of oligarch who seemed to feel slightly naked without his Media Relations Advisor and his Loyaltician around.

She still wasn't entirely sure what a Loyaltician actually did, but at least they had some sort of purpose and utility. She, she had come to realise, was no more than an ornament; something to be admired, to be stared at and cooed over, an object of fascination and astonishment, her duty being to exemplify and magnify the magnificence and sheer wealth of Mr. Joiler Veppers, President and Prime Executive Officer of the Veprine Corporation; the richest man in the world, in the whole Enablement, in charge of the most powerful and profitable company that had ever existed.

The man looking at her appeared terribly old. He was either a much-altered Sichultian or a pan-human alien; the human type had proved to be one of the galaxy's more repetitively common life-forms. Probably an alien; making yourself look as skeletally, creakingly old as that would just be perverse, weird and creepy. Nowadays even poor people could afford the sort of treatment that let you stay young-looking pretty much until you died. It kind of meant you rotted from the inside, she'd heard, but that was a small price to pay for not having to look decrepit until right at the end. And there wouldn't be any poor people up here anyway; this was an exclusive little party, for all that there were a couple of hundred people present.

There were only ten of the Jhlupe in attendance; the rest were Sichultian business chiefs, politicians, bureaucrats and media people, plus their various servants, aides and hangers-on. She supposed she counted as a hanger-on.

She was generally expected to hang around near Veppers, impressing all with the fabulousness of the human exotica he could afford, but he and his inner negotiating circle had peeled off to talk with two of the giant crab people in a sort of bay window section of the reception room, perimeter guarded by three of the Zei – Veppers' massive, highly enhanced clone bodyguards. Lededje had come to understand that often the principal part of her worth lay in providing a distraction; a chattel to be wielded when Veppers required, dazzling and beguiling those he wished dazzled and beguiled, often so that he could slip something past them or just get them in a generally agreeable frame of mind. The Jhlupe might be able to appreciate that she looked significantly different to everybody else around her – darker, and extravagantly tattooed – but the Sichultians were so alien to them anyway it made little extra difference, which meant she was not required to be present when Veppers was talking with them on matters of any great seriousness.

She had hardly been abandoned though, being minded by one of the other Zei and in the company of Dr. Sulbazghi.

"That man is looking at you," Sulbazghi said, nodding towards the slightly stooped, extremely bald human a few metres away. The man looked wrong: too thin and – even stooped – too tall to be normal. His face and head appeared vaguely cadaverous. Even his clothes were strange: too tight, plain and dull to be remotely fashionable.

"Everybody looks at me, Dr. Sulbazghi," she told him.

Dr. Sulbazghi was a blocky-looking man with dark yellow skin – quite lined, on his face – and scant, thin brown hair, characteristics that marked him as either coming from or having ancestors who'd come from Keratiy, first amongst Sichult's sub-continents. He could easily have had himself altered to look more handsome, or at least vaguely acceptable, but had chosen not to. Lededje thought this was very strange, even freaky. The Zei, towering nearby – soberly dressed, eyes always moving, flicking his gaze all around the room as though watching some ball game invisible to everybody else – was quite good-looking in comparison, and even he was kind of scarily muscle-blown, looking like he was about to burst out of both his suit and skin.

"Yes, but he's looking at you differently to everybody else," the doctor said. He nodded to a waiter, had his glass replaced, took a drink. "And look; now he's coming over."

"Ma'am?" the Zei rumbled, deep dark eyes looking down at her from a face at least half a metre above her own. The Zei made her feel like a child.

She sighed, nodded, and the Zei let the funny-looking man approach her. Veppers would not expect her to be stand-offish with anybody at an event as exclusive as this.

"Good day. I believe you are Lededje Y'breq," the old man said, smiling at her and nodding briefly at Dr. Sulbazghi. His voice was real, not synthesised by a translation device. Even more surprising was that his voice was so deep. Veppers had had his voice surgically improved over the years, making it deeper, more mellifluous and rich in a series of small operations and other treatments, but this man's voice eclipsed even Veppers' succulent tones. Bit of a shock in someone so patently an old geezer and looking like he was on his last legs. Maybe age went differently with aliens, she thought.

"Yes, I am," she said, smiling suitably and carefully pitching her voice into the middle of the Zone of Elegance that her elocution tutor kept wittering on about. "How do you do. And you are?"

"How do you do. My name is Himerance." He smiled, swivelled from the waist in a slightly unnatural way and looked over to where Veppers was talking to the two crab-like aliens. "I'm with the Jhlupian delegation – a pan-human cultural translator. Making sure nobody commits some terrible *faux pas*."

"How interesting," she said, happy not to be committing one herself by yawning in the geriatric's face.

He smiled again, looked down to her feet and then back up to her face. *Yes, just you give me a good long inspection, you old perv*, she thought. She supposed it was partly the dress, of which it had to be said there was not much. She was destined to spend her life in revealing clothes. She had long since decided to be proud of how she looked – she would have been a beauty even without the intagliation, and if she was to bear the mark of her family's shame then she would do that too with all the dignity she could – however, she was still growing into this new role and sometimes men looked at her in ways she didn't appreciate. Even Veppers had begun to gaze at her as though he was somehow seeing her for the first time, and in a way that made her uncomfortable.

"I confess," Himerance said, "I am quite fascinated by the Intagliate. And you are, if I may say so, remarkable even within that exceptional category."

"How kind," she said.

"Oh, I am not kind," Himerance said.

At that point, the Zei watching over them stiffened fractionally and rumbled something that might have been "Excuse me", before swinging away into the crowd of people with surprising litheness and grace. At the same time Dr. Sulbazghi swayed a little and, frowning, inspected the contents of his glass. His eyes looked a little odd. "Don't know what they're putting in this stuff these days. Think I'll sit down, if you . . . excuse me." He sidled off too, heading for some seats.

"There we are," Himerance said smoothly. He had kept his eyes focused on her while both the Zei and Dr. S had made their excuses and left. She was alone with him now.

The truth dawned. "You just *did* that?" she asked, glancing first at the broad, retreating back of the Zei and then in the direction Dr. S had disappeared. She was not trying to keep her voice politely modulated any more. She was aware her eyes had widened.

"Well done," Himerance said with an appreciative smile. "A concocted semi-urgent message on the bodyguard's comms and a temporary feeling of dizziness afflicting the good doctor. Neither will detain them for long, however it allows me the chance to beg a favour of you." Himerance smiled again. "I would like to talk to you privately, Ms. Y'breq. May I?"

"Now?" she asked. She glanced about. It would be a short conversation; you were – well, she was – never left alone for more than a minute or so at gatherings like this.

"Later," Himerance said. "Tonight. In your chamber at Mr. Veppers' town house in Ubruater City."

She almost laughed. "Think you'll get invited?" She knew there was nothing planned that evening beyond a meal out with the whole entourage somewhere and then – for her – music and deportment lessons. Then to bed, after getting to watch half an hour of screen, if she was lucky. She wasn't allowed out without bodyguards and escorts and the idea that she'd be allowed to entertain a man in her private bedroom, ancient and alien or not, was frankly hilarious.

Himerance smiled his easy smile. "No," he said. "I can arrange my own access; however I wouldn't want you to be alarmed, so I thought it best to ask permission first."

She regained some control. "What is this about, Mr. Himerance?" she asked, voice polite and measured again.

"I have a modest proposition to make. It will cause you no inconvenience or harm. It would take nothing from you that you'd miss."

She changed tack again, trying to unsettle this weird old guy, dropping the too-polite tone and asking sharply, "And what's in it for me?"

"Perhaps some satisfaction, once I've explained what it is I am looking for. Though some other payment could certainly be arranged." Still without taking his gaze away from her eyes, he said, "I'm afraid I must hurry you for an answer; one of Mr. Veppers' bodyguards is making his way towards us rather smartly, having realised we have been left alone."

She felt excited, slightly scared. Her life was too controlled. "When's good for you?" she asked.

She'd fallen asleep. She hadn't meant to and she would never have thought she'd be able to anyway, just too fired up by the vague, illicit thrill of it all. Then when she awoke she knew he was there.

Her room was on the second-top floor of the tall town house, which was better guarded than most military bases. She had a big room with a dressing room and bathroom en-suite; its two large windows looked out over the gently lit parterres and formal sculptings of the garden. By the windows, part illuminated in the spill of cloud-reflected city light the shutters admitted, there was a sitting area with a low table, a couch and two seats.

She levered herself up from her pillows with her elbows.

He was sitting in one of the seats. She saw his head turn.

"Ms. Y'breq," he said softly. "Hello again."

She shook her head, put a finger to her lips, pointed round the room.

There was just enough light for her to see him smile. "No," he said gently. "The various surveillance devices will not trouble us."

Okay, she thought. So the alarm probably wouldn't work either. She'd kind of been relying on that as her last line of defence if things got iffy. Well, second-last line of defence; she could always just scream. Though if the guy could interfere with the Zei's comms, make Dr. S feel suddenly dizzy and somehow get himself into Veppers' town house without being detected, maybe even screaming wouldn't be on the agenda if he set his mind against it. She started to get a little frightened again.

A light came slowly on near the seat he sat in, revealing him to be dressed just as he had been at the reception earlier in the day. "Please," he said, gesturing to the other seat. "Join me."

She put a robe over her nightgown, turning away from him so that he wouldn't see her hands shake. She sat by him. He looked different: still the same man, but not quite so old; less skeletal about the face, body no longer stooped.

"Thank you for allowing me this opportunity to talk with you in private," he said formally.

"That's okay," she said, drawing her feet up beneath her and hugging her knees. "So. What is it all about?"

"I would like to take an image of you."

"An image?" She felt vaguely disappointed. Was that all? Though probably he meant a full-body image, a photograph of her in the nude. So he was just an old perv after all. Funny how things that started out exciting and maybe even romantic-seeming degenerated into the crude mundanity of lust.

"It would be an image of your entire body, not just both inside and out but of its every single cell, indeed its every atom, and taken, in effect, from outside the three dimensions one normally deals with."

She stared at him. "Like, from hyper-space?" She asked. Lededje had generally paid attention in science lessons.

Himerance smiled broadly. "Precisely."

"Why?"

He shrugged. "For my own private collection of images which I find pleasing."

"Uh-huh."

"For whatever it might be worth, Ms. Y'breq, I can assure you that my motivation is absolutely not sexual."

"Right."

Himerance sighed. "You are a remarkable work, if I may say so, Ms. Y'breq," he told her. "I realise that you are a person, and a very intelligent, pleasant and – to those of your own kind, of course – an attractive one. However, I shan't pretend that my interest in you is anything other than purely due to the intagliation you have suffered."

"Suffered?"

"Undergone? I did think about the exact word to employ."

"No, you were right the first time. I suffered it," she said. "Not something I got to have any choice about, anyway."

"Quite."

"What do you do with these images?"

"I contemplate them. They are works of art, to me."

"Got any other ones you can show me?"

Himerance sat forward. "Would you really like to see some?" He appeared genuinely keen.

"Do we have the time?"

"We do!"

"So show me."

A bright, 3D image appeared in the air in front of her. It showed . . . well, she wasn't sure. It was an insane swirl of lines, black against yellow-orange, bewilderingly complex, levels of implied detail disappearing into enfolded spaces it was not quite possible to see.

"This is just the three-dimensional view one would have of a stellar field-liner entity," he told her. "Though with the horizontal scale reduced to make it look roughly spherical. Really they look more like this." The image suddenly stretched, teasing out until the assemblage of dark lines she'd been looking at became a single line, maybe a metre long and less than a millimetre across. A tiny symbol, looking like a sort of microscopic shoe box with the edges chamfered off, was probably meant to indicate scale, though as she had no idea what it was meant to represent it didn't really help. The vanishingly thin line was shown silhouetted against what looked like a detail of the surface of a star. Then the line plumped up to become an absurdly complicated collection of lines once more.

"It's hard to give an impression of the effect in 4D with all the internals shown," Himerance said apologetically. "But it's something like this." Whatever he did with the image, it left her feeling glad she was sitting down; the image seemed to peel off into a million different slices, sections flickering blurringly past her like snowflakes in a blizzard. She blinked, looked away, feeling disoriented.

"Are you all right?" Himerance asked, sounding concerned. "It can be a bit intense."

"I'm fine," she told him. "What exactly was that?"

"A particularly fine specimen of a stellar field liner; creatures who live within the magnetic lines of force in, mostly, the photospheres of suns."

"That thing was *alive*?"

"Yes. And it still is, I expect. They live for a very long time."

She looked at the old man, his face illuminated by the glow coming from the image of the creature that was mostly black lines and somehow lived on the surfaces of suns. "Can *you* see it in proper 4D?"

"Yes," he said, turning to look at her. He sounded proud and coy at once. Face glowing, enthusiasm seemingly pouring out of him, he suddenly looked about six.

"How is that possible?" she asked.

"Because I am not really a man, or any sort of human," he told her, still smiling. "I am an avatar of a ship. It is the ship you are really addressing, and the ship which is able to take and appreciate images in 4D. The ship's name, my true name, is the *Me, I'm Counting*, once fully part of the Culture, now an independent vessel within what is sometimes known as the Ulterior. I am a wanderer; an explorer, if you will, and it is my pleasure, on occasion, to offer my services as a cultural translator – a facilitator of smooth relations between profoundly different species and civilisations – to whoever might feel the need for such assistance. And – as I say – I am also a collector of images of whatever I consider to be the most exquisite beings, wherever my travels take me."

"Couldn't you just take one of these images without me knowing?"

"In the practical sense, yes. Nothing would be easier."

"But you wanted to ask permission first."

"It would be rude, dishonourable, not to, don't you think?"

She looked at him for a moment. "I suppose," she said eventually. "So. Would you be sharing this image with anybody?"

"No. Until now, showing you this one of the field-liner creature, I have never shared one of these images with anybody. I have many more. Would you like to—?"

"No," she said, smiling and holding up one hand. "That's all right." The image disappeared, dimming the room again.

"I give you my word that, in the unlikely event I do decide I want to share your image, I would not do so without your express permission."

"In each case?"

"In each case. With a similar precondition applying to—"

"And if you do it, if you take the image, will I feel anything?"

"Nothing."

"Hmm." Still hugging her shins, she lowered her face to her robed knees, stuck her tongue out to touch the soft material, then bit at it, taking a tiny fold of it into her mouth.

Himerance watched her for a few moments, then said, "Lededje, may I have your permission to take the image?"

She spat out the fold of material, raised her head. "I asked you before: what's in it for me?"

"What may I offer?"

"Get me out of here. Take me with you. Help me escape. Rescue me from this life."

"I can't do that, Lededje, I'm sorry." Himerance sounded regretful.

"Why not?"

"There would be consequences."

She let her head drop again. She stared at the rug at the foot of the shuttered windows. "Because Veppers is the richest man in the world?"

"In the whole Sichultian Enablement. And the most powerful." Himerance sighed. "There are limits to what I can do anyway. You have your own way of living here, on this world and within the hegemony you call the Enablement; your own rules, mores, customs and laws. It is not regarded as good form to go interfering in the societies of others unless one has a very good reason, and an agreed-on strategic plan. However much we might wish to, we cannot simply indulge our own sentimental urges. I am genuinely sorry, but, sadly, what you ask is not within my gift."

"So, nothing in it for me," she said, and knew that she sounded bitter.

"I'm sure I could set up a bank account with a sum in it that might help you—"

"Like Veppers will ever let me have any sort of independent life," she said, shaking her head.

"Well, perhaps—"

"Oh, just do it," she said. She hugged her legs tighter, looked at him. "Do I need to stand up or anything?"

"No. Are you sure—?"

"Just do it," she repeated fiercely.

"I might still be able to suggest some kind of compensatory—"

"Yes, yes. Whatever you think fit. Surprise me."

"*Surprise* you?"

"You heard."

"You are sure about this?"

"I'm sure, I'm sure. Have you done it yet?"

*

"Ah-ha," Sensia purred, nodding her head slowly. "That does sound like it."

"That ship put the neural lace thing in my head?"

"Yes. Well . . . it would have planted the seed of one; they grow."

"I didn't feel anything at the time."

"Well, you wouldn't." Sensia looked out towards the desert. "Yes, the *Me, I'm Counting*," she said, and Lededje got the impression Sensia was really talking to herself. "Hooligan-class LOU. Declared as an Eccentric and Ulteriored itself over a millennium ago. Dropped out of view completely a couple of years back. Probably on a retreat."

Lededje sighed heavily. "My own fault for saying "Surprise me", I guess." Inside, though, she was elated. The mystery was solved, almost certainly, and it had been a good bargain; she had been saved from death, in a sense at least.

But what is to become of me? she thought. She looked at Sensia, still staring out into the shimmering warmth of distance where dust devils danced and the horizon quivered in a mirage of lake or sea.

What is *to become of me?* she wondered. Did she depend upon the charity of this virtual woman? Was she subject to some legal agreement between the Culture and the Enablement? Was she now somebody or something else's possession or plaything? She might as well ask, she supposed.

She immediately found herself preparing to use what she thought of as her *little* voice: the meek, low, soft, childlike tone she used when she was trying to make her own vulnerability and powerlessness known, when she was trying to play upon somebody's sympathies, make them feel sorry for her and so less likely to hurt or demean her and perhaps even let her have something she wanted. It was a technique she had used on everyone from her mother to Veppers, mostly with a lot more success than failure. But she hesitated. It had never been a ruse she had been very proud of, and here the rules had changed, everything was different. For her own pride, for the sake of what might be a fresh start, she would ask it straight, without deliberate inflection.

"So," she said, looking not at Sensia but out at the desert, "what is to become of me, Sensia?"

The older woman looked at her. "Become of you? You mean what happens now, where do you go?"

Still not daring to meet the other woman's gaze, she nodded. "Yes."

What a strange, almost absurd situation to be in, she thought. To be in this perfect but . . . self-confessed simulation, talking to a glorified computer about her fate, her life from this point on. What *would* happen next? Would she be left free to wander and somehow make a life within this virtual world? Would she be in some sense returned to Sichult, even to Veppers? Could she simply be turned off as just a program, nothing genuinely alive at all? The following few seconds, the next sentence out of Sensia's unreal, virtually modelled mouth, would like as not turn her life one way or the other: to despair, to triumph, to outright annihilation. It all came down – unless she was already being deeply deceived about where she was and who she was really talking to – to what was said in the next moment.

Sensia blew her cheeks out. "Largely up to you, Lededje. You're in a nearly unique situation so there's no particular precedent, but zero documentation or not you're essentially a fully functioning, viable independent mind-state and incontrovertibly sentient, with all that that implies regarding rights and so on."

"What does that imply?" Lededje asked. She was already feeling relieved but she wanted to be sure.

Sensia grinned. "Only good things, really. The first thing I imagine you might want to do is to be revented."

"What does that mean?"

"Technical term for being brought back to life in a physical body back in the Real."

For all that she had no real heart or mouth, that all this was a simulation, she felt her heart leap, her mouth start to go dry. "That is possible?"

"Possible, advisable, kind of standard in such situations." Sensia gave a sort of throttled-back laugh and waved out at the desert. As she swept her arm across the view, Ledeedje caught brief glimpses of what she guessed were other virtual worlds within or alongside this one: great gleaming cities, a mountain range at night criss-crossed with a tangle of tubes and lights, a vast ship or mobile city sailing on a creamy white sea beneath a cerulean sky, a limitless-looking vista of nothing but air full of vast striped trees like green-blue curlicues, and views and structures that she saw but could hardly have described, which she guessed were possible in a virtual reality but impractical in what Sensia blithely called the Real. Then the desert resumed. "You could stay here, of course," Sensia told Lededje. "In whatever environment or mix of them you find congenial, but I'd expect you might want a real physical body."

Lededje nodded. Her mouth was still dry. Could it really be this easy? "I think," she said, "I would."

"Sensible. There are, believe me, innumerable other things you could be revented into, in theory, but if I were you I'd stick with the form you're used to, at first at least. Context is everything, and the first context we find ourselves in is that of our own body." She looked Lededje down and up. "You happy with the way you look now?"

Lededje opened the blue robe she still wore, looked down at herself. She closed the robe again. Its hems fluttered in the hot breeze. "Yes." She hesitated. "I can't decide if I want some form of tattoo or not."

"Easy to add later, though not at the genetic level you've been used to. Can't really sort you out with that. That info didn't travel." Sensia shrugged. "I'll leave you with an image you can manipulate until you're happy with it, take a spec from that."

"You'll grow a body for me?"

"Complete a suspended one."

"How long will that take?"

"Here, as little or as much time as you like. In the Real, about eight days." Sensia shrugged again. "My standard stock of mindless bods doesn't include the Sichultian form – sorry."

"Is there a body I could be put into now, without waiting?"

Sensia smiled. "Can't wait, eh?"

Lededje shook her head, felt her skin grow warm. The truth was that if this was some cruel joke, she wanted to know as quickly as possible. If it was all genuine then she didn't want to wait to have a real body to take her back to Sichult.

"It'll still take about a day or so," Sensia said. She nodded at a female human figure suddenly suspended in the air in front of them; naked, eyes closed. It looked vaguely Sichultian. Its skin was a sort of muddy grey. Then it changed to pure black, then to near white, then shifted through a modest spectrum of different colours. At the same time the girth and height of the figure increased and then decreased. The shape of the head and the facial features changed a little too. "That's the parameters you can play with, given the time available," Sensia told her.

Lededje was thinking. She recalled Veppers' own skin tone. "How long might it take to make it look properly Sichultian, and not black, but sort of reddish-gold?"

Sensia's eyes might have narrowed a fraction. "A few hours more; a full day in total perhaps. You'd look Sichultian, but you wouldn't really be so all the way through, not inside. A blood test, tissue sample or almost any invasive medical procedure would quickly reveal that."

"That's all right. I think that's what I'd like," Lededje said. She looked Sensia in the eye. "I have no money to pay for this." She had heard that the Culture survived without money, but hadn't believed a word of it.

"That's as well," Sensia said reasonably, "I have no charge to levy."

"You would do this out of kindness, or for my obligation?"

"Let's call it kindness, but it's my pleasure."

"Then, thank you," Lededje said. She bowed formally. Sensia smiled. "I would also," Lededje said, "need to work my passage back to Sichult."

Sensia nodded. "I'm sure that can be arranged. Though the word 'work' doesn't really mean quite the same in the Culture as it does in the Enablement." Sensia paused. "May I ask what you intend to do when you get back?"

Kill Mr. Joiler Fucking Veppers, of course, Lededje thought grimly. *And*— . . . but there were some things, some thoughts which were so secret, so potentially dangerous, she had learned in effect to keep them even from herself.

She smiled, wondered if this friendly-seeming virtual creature could read her thoughts, in here.

"I have business to conclude there," she said smoothly.

Sensia nodded, expressionless.

They both looked out towards the desert again.

Six

Prin ignored the departing air vehicle. The giant black beetle ignored him in return. Its great wings unfolded to their full extent – a grinning, death's head pattern was displayed on each – and then blurred into motion. The giant beetle lumbered upwards. The storm of air its wings produced kicked up dust and tiny shards of bone as Prin, still holding the tiny, petrified form of Chay against his massive chest with one of his forelimbs, reached the flat landing area and dashed across it for the door of the blood-powered mill.

He threw open the door, then had to duck and squeeze though the doorway to get inside. He straightened up, roaring, the wind and dust from the departing aircraft's wings blowing a stormy haze about him and before him, sweeping over the dark, uneven floor-boards to where the group of grinning demons and terrified Pavuleans were standing before a tall glowing doorway of cool blue set into the bone-and-sinew machinery of the mill's creaking, quietly shrieking interior.

Somebody said, "Three."

Caught in the double whirlwind produced by the beetle's wings, the door behind Prin slammed shut, shaking the mill and reducing by half the little light that came from outside. Prin paused, taking stock. Chay remained stiff in his forelimb. He thought he could feel her trembling against his chest, and hear her whimpering. The demons and the Pavuleans presented a static tableau.

A shallow ramp led down from the floor of the mill to the blue haze of the tall doorway, which trembled, light level fluctuating, as though it was made up of mist inside. Prin thought he caught a glimpse of movement beyond it, but it was impossible to be sure. There were six demons before him. They were of the smaller, four-legged kind; no match for him individually but capable of overwhelming him *en masse*. Two of them were the ones who had come out of the mill to watch the beetle-shaped flier land. The other four, each holding one of the Pavuleans, had come in on the beetle itself. Four Pavuleans left; four must already have gone through the gateway, back to the Real.

"And what is it you might want?" one of the mill demons said to Prin, as the other nodded to a pair of demons from the flier. These two released their hold on the Pavuleans they were clutching. The two male Pavuleans landed on all fours and scuttled soundlessly down the ramp, vanishing into the blue mist of the doorway.

The other mill demon said, "One."

"No, no, no!" one of the two remaining Pavuleans wailed, struggling in the grasp of the demon who held him.

"Shush now," the demon holding him said, shaking him. "Might not be you who's staying."

"Brother?" the mill demon who'd spoken to Prin took a step towards him.

Prin felt a tiny, sharp barb penetrate the skin at his neck. The contraband code was about to run out. Four pulses warning; that's what he'd been told. Four pulses and then he'd be back to his earlier self, just another coded Pavulean, as helpless and hopeless as Chay here, held tight and trembling against his chest. Another barb. So that was four, three . . .

He didn't even try to roar again; waste of breath. He just charged, leaping forward at the group of demons and Pavuleans. He thudded into the approaching mill demon while surprise was still registering on its face and it was just starting to raise its trunks to fend him off. He half-headed it, half-shouldered it out of the way, sending it crashing to the floor.

It was all happening very slowly. He wondered if this really was the speed that such moments of action seemed to happen at for predators in the Real – one reason they were so good at bringing down their prey, perhaps – or if this was an extra effect introduced just for the demons in Hell, to allow them an even greater advantage over their victims, or just to let them savour the moment all the more fully.

The four demons from the flier were all facing him now. The two holding Pavuleans did not worry him so much, he realised – he was thinking like a predator, like one of these bastards! – because they didn't want to let go of their charges, at least not yet. By the time they thought the better of this, he knew, it would all be over one way or the other.

One of the remaining demons was faster to react than the other, opening its mouth into a snarl and starting to rise up on its hind legs while it brought its forelegs up towards him.

He was aware of being slightly encumbered by the small, hard weight he was carrying against his great furred chest. Chay. Could he just throw her through the doorway from here? Probably not. He'd have to stop, take aim, lob her. It would take too long and the way the angles worked one of the demons would only need to raise one forelimb to catch her or knock her off course. By the time that happened he'd have lost all his temporary power and be no more strong than she was now; no match at all for even a single demon.

He could use his slight lopsidedness to his advantage, he realised, as he took his next swinging, galloping step. The demon facing him, ready to tackle him, was allowing for how he was moving off-kilter, unconsciously preparing to intercept Prin a couple of metres ahead according to the already set rhythm evident in the way he was moving.

Prin threw Chay from one forelimb to the other and pressed her hard into the other side of his chest. The gesture cost him a small amount of momentum, but gave him the greater advantage of throwing off the reckoning of the demon preparing to bring him down.

Prin opened his jaws as the third barb made itself felt in his neck. One pulse left. The fourth barb would signal his instant return to the small, broken body he'd been trapped within for the last few months.

The demon didn't even have time to look surprised. Prin crunched his jaws closed on the smaller demon. He felt his fangs penetrate furred skin, flesh, sinew and tendon and then bite into the giving hardness of bone. He was already turning his head, an instinctive reaction giving his jaws time to fully close. The demon was starting to turn too now, pulled round by his attacker's greater weight. Prin went with the motion, keeping his jaws tight, feeling bone snap and crumple inside his mouth. He pivoted with the demon, using their combined mass to swivel even as he kept on charging forward, bringing the body of the bitten demon swinging round, legs flailing, to connect with the body of the second pouncing demon, knocking it aside in a snarling ball. Prin let his jaws open; the first demon was flung from them and went slithering along the floor, already bleeding, narrowly missing the legs of one of the other two demons still holding the Pavuleans.

He was almost at the start of the slope to the blue glowing door. He made one last bound, launching himself through the air.

As he did so, he knew he had made it, that they would get through the doorway. It floated up towards him as he rose in the air, still propelled by the last great thrust of his hind legs.

One, he thought.

The way the mill demon had said "One," after the last two Pavuleans had gone through.

And, just as he'd burst into the mill, a voice – the same voice, he realised now – had said "Three."

Three: then the two little Pavuleans had gone skittering through the blue glowing gate. *One*.

He'd been counting down.

Of course; the gate could count. The gate, or people operating it at this side – or more likely the other side, in the Real – knew how many to expect, how many they were allowed to let through.

Just one more person would be allowed to make the transition from the Hell to the Real.

He reached the top of his last, pouncing leap. The doorway spread before him, a glowing bank of blue mist filled with shadows. He wondered if the fact that he and Chay were so close together would allow them both to make it through, if the gateway would be somehow fooled by this. Or perhaps the fact she was catatonic, semi-conscious at best, would mean that she could make it through as well as him.

He was starting to fall through the air, the gateway only a body-length away now. He brought Chay out from the side of his chest, moving her to a more central position, grasping her with both forelimbs as he pushed her in front of him. If there was really only one more person, one more coded consciousness allowed through, let it be her. He would have to take his chances here, accept whatever extra punishment these fiends could devise.

She might be in no state to tell what had befallen them, of course; she might forget or deny all they had experienced. She might not believe it had happened at all. She had denied the existence of the Real while she was here, surrendering all too easily to the grinding actuality of the horror around her; why would she not likewise deny the unbelievable gruesomeness of Hell once she was safely back in the Real, if she was even able to remember it properly?

What if she remained catatonic on the other side? What if she really had gone mad and no return to reality would change that?

Was he to be gallant to the point of stupidity, or hard-headed to the point of selfishness, just wanting to save his own skin?

He tucked himself in, balling up and tumbling, somersaulting through the air as the blue-glowing doorway rushed towards him. He would go through first, holding Chay out behind him.

He would never abandon her. She might abandon him.

At that point the contraband code's run-time reached its end. He changed back immediately, an instant before the two little Pavulean bodies flew into the blue glowing mist.

Seven

The *Halo 7* rolled magisterially across the misty plain, its stately progress marked by little lofted tufts and wisps of vapour which seemed to cling longingly to its tubes and spars as though reluctant to let go. The giant Wheel left a temporarily cleared track through the mist behind it like a wake, affording glimpses of the land beneath before the silent grey presence flowed slowly back in.

Veppers floated in the pool, looking out over the misted landscape to where some high, rounded hills rose out of the grey, maybe twenty or more kilometres away. The water around him trembled and pulsed as the pool car's shock absorbers struggled to iron out the *Halo 7*'s trundling progress across the mist-swaddled terrain.

The *Halo 7* was a Wheel, a vehicle built to navigate the great plains, rolling hills and shallow inland seas of Obrech, Sichult's principal continent. One hundred and fifty metres in diameter by twenty across, the *Halo 7* looked entirely like a giant fairground wheel which had broken free from its supports and gone rolling across the land.

The Veprine Corporation's Planetary Heavy Industries Division (Sichult) constructed several standard sizes and types of Wheel. Most were mobile hotels, taking the rich on cruises across the continent; the *Halo 7*, Veppers' own privately owned vehicle, was the grandest and most impressive of the largest spokeless class, being no greater in diameter than the rest but possessing thirty-three rather than thirty-two gondolas.

The *Halo 7*'s separate cars held sumptuous bedroom suites, banqueting halls, reception rooms, two separate pool and bath complexes, gyms, flower-filled terraces, kitchens, kitchen gardens, a command and communication pod, power and services units, garages for ground vehicles, hangars for fliers, boat-houses for speedboats, sailboats and minisubs, and quarters for crew and servants. Much more than a mode of transport, the *Halo 7* was a mobile mansion.

Rather than being fixed to the Wheel's rims, the thirty-three cars could alter position, either at Veppers' whim or according to the dictates of the landscape beneath; negotiating – and especially traversing – a steep slope, where there was no ready-made Wheel road, all the heavier pods could be brought down close to the ground, preventing the device from becoming dangerously top-heavy and so allowing it take on angles of lean that looked both unlikely and alarming. Perched at the top in a gimballed observation gondola during such a manoeuvre, Veppers had been known to take great delight in terrifying guests with that trick. Getting from one pod to another could mean as little as a single step if the cars had been brought up against each other, or a ride in one of several circumferential elevator units that moved round a smaller-diameter ring fixed inside the Wheel's principal structure.

Veppers gazed out at the distant blue hills, trying to remember if he owned them or not.

"Are we still within the estate?" he asked.

Jasken was standing at the pool-side, keeping politely out of his master's view. Jasken was scanning the misty landscape, the Enhancing Oculenses covering his eyes zooming in on details, revealing the ground's mostly chilly heat signature and showing him any radio sources. "I'll ask," he said, and muttered something, putting a finger to the comms bud attached to his ear as he listened. "Yes, sir," he told Veppers. "Captain Bousser informs us we are about thirty kilometres inside the estate's boundaries." Jasken used a small keypad on the back of the cast covering his left arm to call up the requisite overlay on the view the Oculenses were presenting. Thirty klicks was about right.

The *Halo 7*'s commander, Captain Bousser, was female. Jasken suspected she had been hired for her pleasing looks rather than on merit, so, where possible, he checked any assertions she made, waiting, so far unsuccessfully, for a mistake he could use to convince Veppers of her unfitness for the post.

"Hmm," Veppers said. Now he thought about it, he didn't really care whether he owned the hills or not. His right hand went to his face without him thinking about it, his fingers very gently tracing the prosthetic covering that had replaced the tip of his nose while the flesh and cartilage re-grew beneath. It was a pretty good fake, especially with a bit of makeup on top, but he was still self-conscious about it. He'd cancelled a few engagements and post-poned many more in the days since the debacle in the opera house.

What a mess that had been. They hadn't been able to keep it completely quiet, of course, especially as he'd had to cancel that evening's engagement at such short notice. Dr. Sulbazghi had come up with their cover story, which was that Jasken had accidentally sliced the tip of his master's nose off while they were fencing.

"That'll have to do," Veppers agreed as he lay on the treatment couch in the clinic suite deep within the Ubruater town house, less than an hour after the girl had attacked him. He was painfully aware that his voice sounded strange, strangled and nasal. Sulbazghi was bandaging his nose and prepping it with coagulant, antiseptic and a stabilising preparatory gel; a specialist plastic surgeon had been summoned and was on his way. The girl's body had already been bagged and placed in a mortuary freezer. Dr. Sulbazghi would see to its disposal later.

Veppers was still shaking a little, despite whatever Sulbazghi had given him for the shock. He lay there, thinking, as the doctor fussed about him. He was waiting for Jasken to return; he was on his way back from the opera house having made sure everything had been squared away and everybody had their stories straight.

He shouldn't have killed the girl. It had been stupid, impetuous. On the rare occasion that sort of thing was necessary, you just never got involved directly; that was what delegation was for, what people like Jasken – and whoever he employed specifically for such tasks – was for. Always keep it deniable, always at a remove, always have a true alibi.

But, he'd been too excited by the chase, by the knowledge that the runaway was still so close, and so trapped within the opera house, practically waiting to be caught. Of *course* he'd wanted to be part of the hunt, the capture!

Still, he shouldn't have killed her. It wasn't just how much she'd been worth, how much wasted effort and money she represented, it was the embarrassment of having lost her. People would notice her continued absence. The cover story after she'd run off from the couturier's had been that she was ill – the PR people had hinted at some rare ailment that only the intagliated suffered from.

Now they would either have to claim she'd died of it – meaning problems with the Surgeon's Guild, the insurance people and possibly lawyers for the clinic that had overseen her intagliation in the first place – or go with the even more humiliating though partially true narrative that she'd run away. He'd already entertained the idea that they might claim she'd been kidnapped, or allowed to join a nunnery or whatever, but both would lead to too many complications.

At least he'd got the knives back. They were still tucked into the waistband of his trews. He touched their hilts again, reassuring himself they were still there. Jasken had wanted to dispose of them, the idiot. No need to dispose of the murder weapon when you were going to dispose of the body properly. Stealing the knives;

the sheer fucking effrontery of it! In the end she'd been nothing more than an ungrateful little thief. And: *biting* him! Maybe even trying to bite his throat out and kill him! How *dare* the little bitch do that? How *dare* she put him in this situation!

He was glad he'd killed her. And it was a first for him, he realised; directly taking a life was one of the few things he'd never done. When this had all calmed down, when his nose had re-grown and things had gone back to normal, he'd still have that, he supposed.

He remembered that until he'd first taken her against her will, maybe ten years or so ago, he'd never raped anybody before either – there had been no need – so he'd got two firsts from her. If he was being generous, he would reluctantly concede that that was some sort of compensation for all the pain and inconvenience she was putting him through.

Quite a thing, though, doing something like that, actually plunging a knife into somebody and feeling them die. It shook you, no matter how strong you were. He could still see the look in the girl's eyes as she'd died.

Jasken came in then, removing his Oculenses and nodding to the two Zei guarding the clinic suite's door.

"You'll have to be injured too, Jasken," Veppers told him immediately, glaring at his chief of security as though it really had all been his fault. Which, now he thought about it, was true, as it had ultimately been Jasken's responsibility to keep an eye on the scribble-child and make sure she didn't go running off anywhere. "We're going to say you took my nose off while we were fencing, but we can't have people thinking you actually bested me. You'll have to have an eye out."

Jasken's face, already pale, went paler. "Ah, but, sir . . ."

"Or a broken arm; something serious."

Dr. Sulbazghi nodded. "I think the broken arm." He looked at Jasken's forearms, perhaps choosing on Veppers' behalf.

Jasken glared at Sulbazghi. "Sir, please— " he said to Veppers.

"You could make it a clean break, couldn't you Sulbazghi?" Veppers asked. "Quick to heal?"

"Easily," Sulbazghi said, smiling at Jasken.

"Sir," Jasken said, drawing himself up. "Such an action would compromise my ability to protect you, in the event that our other layers of security were disabled and I was all that stood between you and an assailant."

"Hmm, I suppose so," Veppers said. "Still, we need something." He frowned, thinking. "How would you like a duelling scar? On the cheek, where everybody would see it."

"It would have to be a very big, very deep scar," Dr. Sulbazghi said reasonably. "Probably permanent." He shrugged as Jasken glared at him again. "To be proportionate," he protested.

"Might I suggest a fake cast, for a couple of weeks?" Jasken said, tapping his left arm. "The broken-arm story would still hold but I would not be truly disabled." He smiled thinly at the doctor. "I might even conceal additional weaponry within the cast, for any emergency."

Veppers liked that. "Good idea." He nodded. "Let's go with that."

Now, floating in the pool at the summit of the *Halo 7*, his fingers feeling tentatively around the strange, warm surface of the prosthetic, Veppers smiled at the memory. Jasken's compromise had been sensible, but seeing the look on his face when he'd thought they were going to put out one of his eyes or actually break his arm had been one of the few truly bright spots in a dreadful evening.

He gazed out at the mountains again. He'd ordered the gondola containing the pool to be kept at the summit of the great vehicle while he had his early morning swim. He turned round and struck out for the other side of the pool, where one of his Harem Troupe had fallen asleep wrapped in a thick robe and lying on a sun-bed.

Veppers had what he honestly believed was the best-looking ten-girl Harem Troupe in the Enablement. This girl, Pleur, was special even within that august selection: one of his two Impressionist girls, able to take on the appearance and mannerisms of whatever female public figure he had taken a shine to recently. Of course, he'd had his share – much more than his fair share, as he was the first to acknowledge – of super-famous screen stars, singers, dancers, screen presenters, athletes and the very occasional hot politician and so on, but such pursuits could be terribly time-consuming; the truly famous, even when they were available, not committed, expected to be wooed over time, even by the richest man in the Enablement, and it was usually a lot simpler just to have one of the Impressionist girls alter herself – and have herself altered surgically, where the change would take too long otherwise – to look like the relevant beauty. It wasn't as though he really wanted them for their minds after all, and this way also had the advantage of letting you compensate for any bodily deficiencies in the original.

As he swam, Veppers looked over at Jasken, and nodded towards the sleeping girl, who currently looked identical to – unusually for Veppers – an academic. Pleur had recently taken on the appearance of a severely beautiful doctor of eugenics from Lombe whom Veppers had first glimpsed at a ball in Ubruater City earlier in the year but who had proved annoyingly determined to remain faithful to her husband, even in the face of the sort of blandishments and gifts that were guaranteed to turn almost anybody's head (husbands included, where it merely meant turning a blind eye). Jasken walked over towards Pleur's sleeping form as Veppers arrived at the side of the pool, then trod water and mimed what Jasken was to do.

Jasken nodded, went to the back of the sun-bed, gripped its lower frame and, only slightly hindered by the fake cast on his arm, swiftly hoisted the rear of the sun-bed up to head height, tipping the girl into the pool with a splash and a spluttering scream. Veppers was still laughing and fending off Pleur's flapping blows, while pulling her robe off, when Jasken frowned, put one finger to his ear, then got down on both knees at the pool side and started waving urgently.

"*What?*" Veppers shouted at Jasken, exasperated. A near miss from one of Pleur's hands skiffed one cheek and splashed water into his eyes. "Not on the *nose*, you dumb bitch!"

"It's Sulbazghi," Jasken told him. "Highest urgency."

Veppers was much bigger and stronger than Pleur. He gripped her, turned her round and held her tightly while she cursed at both him and Jasken, coughing and spitting water all the while. "What? Something happening in Ubruater?" Veppers asked.

"No, he's in a flier, on his way here. Four minutes out. Won't say what, but insists it's highest urgency. Shall I tell Bousser to summit the landing platform?"

Veppers sighed. "I suppose." He got Pleur's robe off at last. She had mostly stopped struggling and coughing. "Go and meet them," he told Jasken, who nodded once and walked off.

Veppers pushed the naked girl towards the side of the pool. "As for you, young lady," he said, biting her neck hard enough to produce a yelp, "you've been *terribly* ill-mannered."

"I have, haven't I?" Pleur agreed. She knew just what Veppers liked to hear. "I need to be taught a lesson, wouldn't you say?"

"Yes I would. Assume the position." He shoved the floating weight of the robe out of the way as Pleur braced herself against the edge of the pool with both hands. "Won't be long!" he called after Jasken's retreating back.

Still a little breathless, still with the pleasant glow of satiation about him and still dripping from inside his fluffy robe, Veppers sat forward and looked at the thing lying in Dr. Sulbazghi's broad, pale yellow palm. He, Sulbazghi – still wearing his lab coat, which was an unusual sight – Jasken and Astil, Veppers' butler, were the only people in the lavishly furnished lounge. Outside, beyond plump brocade bolsters, waggling tassels, gently clinking chandeliers and trembling gold-thread window fringes, the view was of the slowly clearing mists before and behind the Wheel as it continued on its journey through the spreading pastel light of dawn.

"Thank you, Astil," Veppers said, accepting a cup of chilled infusion from his butler. "That's all."

"Sir," Astil said, bowing and exiting.

Veppers waited until he had gone before saying, "So, what have we here?"

Whatever it was, it looked like a small bunch of very fine wires, their colour a sort of dull matt silver with a hint of blue. Scrunch it up, he thought, and you'd have something like a pebble; something so small you could probably swallow it.

Sulbazghi looked tired, frazzled, almost ill. "It was found in the furnace," he told Veppers, and ran a hand through his thin, unkempt hair.

"What furnace?" he asked. He'd come into this thinking it was going to prove to be one of those matters that seemed terribly important and momentous to those around him but which he could, having cast his eye over it, happily leave for them to worry about and sort out if possible. That was, after all, what he paid them for. Now, just from the feel in the room, he was starting to think there might be a real problem here.

"There shouldn't have been anything left," Jasken said. "What temperature—?"

"The furnace in the Veppers Memorial Hospital," Sulbazghi said, rubbing his face with his hands, not looking Veppers in the eye. "Our little friend, from the other night."

Great God, the girl, Veppers realised, with a disturbing feeling in his belly. *Now* what? Was the fractious bitch to pursue him from beyond the grave? "Okay," he said slowly. "And all very unfortunate, I'm sure we can agree. But what has . . .?" He waved at the silvery-blue wires still displayed in Sulbazghi's hand. "What has whatever *this* is got to do with that?"

"It's what was left of her body," Sulbazghi said.

"There shouldn't have *been* anything left," Jasken said. "Not if the furnace was—"

"The fucking furnace was at the right fucking *temperature*!" Sulbazghi shouted shrilly.

Jasken whipped off his Oculenses, his expression furious. He looked ready to start a fight.

"Gentlemen, please," Veppers said calmly, before Jasken could reply. He looked at the doctor. "As simply as you can, Sulbazghi, for the non-technically minded; what the hell is this thing?"

"It's a neural lace," the doctor said, sounding exhausted.

"A neural lace," Veppers repeated.

He'd heard of these things. They were the sort of device that highly advanced aliens who'd started out squidgy and biochemical – as squidgy and biochemical as Sichultians, for example – and who had not wanted to upload themselves into nirvana or oblivion or wherever, used when they wanted to interface with machine minds or record their thoughts, or even when they wanted to save their souls, their mind-states.

Veppers looked at Sulbazghi. "Are you saying," he said slowly, "that the girl had a neural lace in her head?"

That shouldn't be possible. Neural laces were illegal for Sichultians. Great God, fucking drug glands were illegal for Sichultians.

"Kind of looks like it," Sulbazghi said.

"And it never showed up?" Veppers asked. He stared at the doctor. "Sulbazghi, You must have scanned that girl a hundred times."

"They don't show up using the equipment we've got to look with," Sulbazghi said. He stared down at the thing in his hand, gave a tiny, despairing laugh. "Minor miracle we can see it with the naked eye."

"Who put it in her?" Veppers asked. "The clinicians?"

Sulbazghi shook his head. "Impossible."

"Then who?"

"I've done a quick bit of investigating since the doctor told me about this," Jasken said. "We need help here, sir: somebody who properly knows about this sort of thing—"

"Xingre," Sulbazghi said. "He'll know, or know better how to find out."

"Xingre?" Veppers said, frowning. The Jhlupian trader and honorary consul was his principal contact with the alien civilisation the Enablement was closest to. Jasken had a sour look on his face that Veppers recognised; it meant he was having to agree with Sulbazghi. Both men knew this had to be kept as quiet as possible. Why were they suggesting bringing the alien into this?

"He, she or it might know," Jasken said. "The point is it'll be able to find out if this thing really is what it looks like."

"And what the fuck *does* it look like?" Veppers asked.

Jasken took a deep breath. "Well, like a . . . a neural lace device, the sort of thing the so-called 'Culture' uses." He grimaced. Veppers saw the man grind his teeth for a moment. "It's hard to tell; it could be a fake. With our technology—"

"Why would anyone go to this trouble to *fake* it?" Sulbazghi said angrily. Veppers held up one hand to quiet him.

Jasken glared at the doctor but went on, "It isn't possible to be sure, which is why we might need Xingre and the sort of analysis and diagnostic equipment he has access to, but it looks like this thing is one of their devices. A Culture device."

Veppers looked at them both in turn.

"It's a *Culture* device?" he asked. He held out his hand and let Sulbazghi tip the thing into his palm. The closer he looked, the more tiny, still finer filaments he could see, branching and re-branching off the main, already very thin wires. It felt amazingly soft. It weighed next to nothing.

"Looks very likely," the doctor agreed.

Veppers bounced the thing up and down in his hand a couple of times; a handful of hair would have weighed more. "Okay," he said. "But what does this mean? I mean, she wasn't a Culture citizen or anything, was she?"

"No," Sulbazghi said.

"And . . . she didn't seem to be able to interface with any equipment . . . ?" Veppers looked from the doctor to Jasken, who was now standing with his Oculenses dangling, the arm in the cast folded across his chest, his other arm resting on it, hand stroking the skin around his mouth repeatedly. He was still frowning.

"No," Sulbazghi said again. "She might not even have known the thing was in there."

"What?" Veppers said. "But how?"

"These things grow inside you," Jasken said. "If it really is one then it'll have started as a seed and grown all around and into her brain. Fully developed these things link with just about every brain cell, every synapse."

"Why didn't she have a head the size of a basket fruit?" Veppers asked. He grinned but neither man responded. That was very unusual. And not a good sign.

"These things add less than half a per cent to the bulk of the brain," Jasken said. He nodded at the thing lying in Veppers' palm. "Even what you see there is mostly hollow; in the brain it'd be filled with fluid or bits of the brain itself. The tiniest filaments are so thin they're invisible to the naked eye and they'll probably have been burned off in the furnace anyway."

Veppers stared at the strange, insignificant-looking device. "But what was it in her brain to do?" he asked both men. "What was it *for*? Given that we've established it didn't seem to give her any super powers or anything."

"These things are used to record a person's mind-state," Jasken said.

"Their soul, for want of a better word," Sulbazghi said.

"It's so Culture people can be reincarnated if they die unexpectedly," Jasken said.

"I know," Veppers said patiently. "I've looked into the technology myself. Don't think I'm not jealous." He tried another smile. Still no response. This must be serious.

"Well," Jasken said, "it's not impossible that such information – her mind-state – was transmitted somewhere else at the point of death. It's what these things are for, after all."

"Transmitted?" Veppers said. "Where?"

"Not far—" Jasken began.

"I can't see how." Sulbazghi shook his head, glancing at Jasken. "I've done my own research. "It takes time, and a full clinical set-up. It's a person's entire personality we're talking about here, their every memory; you don't squirt that out in a beat or two like a fucking text message."

"We are dealing with what the aliens call Level Eight technology," Jasken said contemptuously. "You don't know what it might be capable of. We're like pre-wheel primitives looking at a screen and saying it can't work because nobody can re-draw a cave-painting that quickly."

"There are still limits," Sulbazghi insisted.

"Doubtless," Jasken said. "But we have no idea what they *are*."

Sulbazghi drew breath to speak but Veppers just talked over the start of whatever he had been about to say. "Well, in any event; bad news, perhaps, gentlemen." He reached out, let Sulbazghi take the device back. The doctor bagged it, put it in a pocket of his lab coat, sealed it.

"So . . ." Veppers said. "If this stored her mind-state, I suppose it would know . . ."

"Everything up to the moment of her death," Sulbazghi said.

Veppers nodded. "Jasken," he said, "ask Yarbethile what our relations are with the Culture, would you?"

"Sir," Jasken said, turning away for a moment while he contacted Veppers' Private Secretary, doubtless already at his desk in the *Halo 7*'s executive office pod. Jasken listened, muttered something, turned back. "Mr. Yarbethile characterises our relations with the Culture as 'Nebulous'," Jasken said drily. He shrugged. "I'm not sure if he's trying to be funny or not."

"Well," Veppers said. "We don't really have much to do with them, with the Culture, do we?" Veppers looked at the other two men. "Not really."

Jasken shook his head. Sulbazghi clenched his jaw and looked away to one side.

All three experienced a momentarily disquieting lurch as the *Halo 7*, which had been quietly and suitably re-configuring itself for the last couple of minutes, left the land precisely as scheduled and crunched down a long, broad beach in two giant troughs of pebbles to meet the misty, torpid waters of the Oligyne Inland Sea, turning itself into a giant paddle wheel as it ploughed on through the banks of mist, its pace only slightly reduced.

"We need to look into this, obviously," Veppers said. "Jasken, use any resources required. Keep me informed, daily." Jasken nodded. Veppers stood up, nodded to Sulbazghi. "Thank you, doctor. I trust you'll stay for breakfast. If there's nothing more for now, though, I think I'll go and get dressed. Excuse me."

He walked towards the link leading to his bedroom, currently joined with the lounge gondola. As sometimes happened, Veppers found that the giant Wheel's faint bobbing motion as it rolled through waters was giving him a feeling of nausea.

He felt sure it would pass.

Eight

The planet outside was very big and blue and white and bright. It was revolving, like planets usually did, but you couldn't really see that on normal-time sight. It only seemed to move because the place where he was was moving. The place where he was was separate from the planet and it was moving. It was above the planet and it was moving. The place where he was was called an Abandoned Space Factory and he was here to wait for the enemy to come and when they came he would fight them. That was what he did; he fought. He had been built to fight. What he was, the thing that he was inside; that had been built to fight.

The thing he was in was a thing, an "it", but he was not an "it"; he was a he. He was a man. Or he had been, at least. He was still who he was but he was also inside the thing, the machine that was designed and built to fight and perhaps get destroyed. But not him. He wouldn't be destroyed. He was still who he was. He was somewhere else as well, and that was where he would wake up, if this thing he was in was destroyed. That was how it worked.

"Vatueil? Captain Vatueil?"

They were talking to him again.

We're losing, he thought, reviewing the latest schematics. You hardly needed the schematics; just step back far enough from the whole thing, replay what had happened since the war had broken out and you could see it writing itself out in front of you.

They'd had some early disasters, then successes, then they'd been beaten back consistently, then they'd consolidated and subsequently seemed to achieve the upper hand across almost every front, making steady progress everywhere . . . then found that the fronts were not true fronts, the fronts – or at least the places where his side was strongest and was prevailing – were like stubborn tatters of a balloon that it turned out had already burst some time ago; there just hadn't been time to hear the Bang. They were making forward progress the way the torn strips of the exploded balloon made forward progress: flailing hopelessly, uselessly outwards like soft shrapnel.

He sat – or floated or whatever you wanted to call it – in the Primary Strategic Situation Overview Space as it was rather grandly called, surrounded by the other members of the Grand War Council. The council was mostly composed of people who were his comrades, friends, colleagues and respected rivals. There was only the barest minimum of contrarians, awkwardistas and outright defeatists, and even they argued their points well and arguably contributed to the working consensus. Human, alien, whatever, he knew all of them about as well as was possible by now, and yet still he felt quite alone.

He looked round them.

There was no perfect Real analogy for the situation he and the rest were currently in: it was as though they all hovered around some modest spherical space maybe a handful of metres across. From the outside the sphere's surface appeared solid and opaque, but you could stick your head through it from the outside if you had the right clearance and a sufficient degree of military seniority.

You stuck your head through and there you were; one bodiless head sticking through protruding into this dimly lit spherical space with lots of other bodiless heads – only a minority of them in any sense human.

Usually a spherical display hovered in the centre of the space. Right now the display was showing some detail of the general battle space; an antique faux-Real volume in which small rocket ships armed with nuclear missiles, particle beam guns and CREWs went skating around a few billion asteroids spread in a ring round a sun, blasting and zapping each other. He had seen such battle environments many times before. Versions of him had invested the simmed humans fighting in these, or invested the machines.

Most of his colleagues seemed to be discussing some pseudo-strategic detail of this particular environment that had long since ceased to interest him. He left them to it, retreating to his own musings and internalised visualisation.

We're losing, he thought again. *There is a war in heaven and we are losing it.*

The war was amongst the Heavens, between the Afterlives, if you wanted to be pedantic about it. And it was over the Hells.

"Vatueil? Captain Vatueil?"

That was his name, but he wasn't going to say anything back to them because he'd been told not to. He'd been ordered not to, and orders meant you had to do what you were told.

"Can you hear me?"

Yes, he could, but he still wouldn't say anything.

"Vatueil! Report! That's a direct order!"

That made him feel strange. If that was an order then he had to obey it. But then he had been ordered not to do anything that somebody else told him, not for now, not until A Superior got here who had the right codes. So that meant that what he had just heard wasn't really an order at all. It was confusing.

He wanted just not to listen to what they said. He could do

that, he could shut off comms, but he needed to listen so he could track where they were. The confusion made a sort of hurt in him.

He made the thing that he was in check its weapons again, counting rounds, measuring battery status, listening to the energy cells' steady, reassuring hum and doing a systems-readiness check. That was better. Doing these things made him feel better. Doing these things made him feel good.

"He can't hear you." That was a different voice, saying that.

"The techs say he probably can. And he can probably hear you too, so watch what you say."

"Can't we private channel?" (The different voice.)

"No. We have to assume he can access them all too, so unless you want to bump helmets or use two cups and a string or something, watch what you say."

"Sheesh." (The different voice.)

He did not know what "Sheesh" meant.

"Listen, Vatueil, this is Major Q'naywa. You know me. Come on now, Vatueil, you remember me."

He didn't remember any Major Q'naywa. He didn't remember very much, he guessed. There was a lot of stuff he felt ought to be there, somewhere, but which wasn't. It gave him a feeling of emptiness. Like a magazine that should have been full of rounds because it was at the start of a deployment and it was supposed to be full, but which wasn't.

"Vatueil. Listen, son; you've got a problem. Your download didn't complete. You're in the unit but not all of you is in there, can you understand that? Come on, son, talk to me."

Part of him wanted to talk to the voice of Major Q'naywa, but he wasn't going to. Major Q'naywa did not qualify as A Superior because his signal did not come with the codes that would tell him he really was talking to A Superior.

"Some sort of sign, son. Come on. Anything."

He didn't know what the codes were that would tell him he really was talking to A Superior, which seemed like an odd thing, but he was guessing that when he heard them he would know.

"Vatueil, we know you transferred but we know it didn't work properly. That's why you're firing on your own side, on us. You need to stop doing that. Do you understand?"

He didn't really understand. He sort of understood what they were saying because he knew each of the words and how they went together, but it didn't make sense. He had to ignore it anyway because the people speaking the words did not have the right codes to be Superiors.

He checked his weapons again.

He sat/floated back, maintaining just enough embodiment to ensure long-term sanity, ignoring the shared display and instead watching the whole war blossom, expand and develop inside his mind, seeing it happen in fast-forward, time after time, his attention zooming in on different aspects of its progression with each iteration. It looked just like the sims, of course. Except at any given point after it had all started to go wrong the sims had always developed differently, better, more optimistically.

Wars simmed in the Real did the same thing, naturally, but ultimately they were played out in the Real, in messy physical reality, and so didn't seem to carry the same irony that this war did, because it – the real war, the conflict that actually mattered here, the war that would have continual and in a sense everlasting consequences – was itself a sim, but a sim that was itself easily as complicated and messy as anything in the Real. Still a sim, though, like the ones they'd used and were still using to plan the war.

Just a bigger one. A bigger one that all concerned had agreed to treat as settling matters. Hence as real as these things ever got.

That was the war they were losing, and that meant that if they were serious about what they had been trying to do – and were still trying to do – then they were going to have to think about cheating. And if cheating didn't work, then – despite all the accords and laws and customs and regulations, despite all the agreements and solemn treaties – there was always the truly last resort: the Real.

The ultimate cheating . . .

How the hell did we get into this? he asked himself, though of course he already knew the answer. He knew all the answers. Everybody did. Everybody knew everything and everybody knew all the answers. It was just that the enemy seemed to know better ones.

Nobody knew who had first developed the ability to transcribe a naturally evolved creature's mind-state. Various species asserted that they or their ancestors had been the ones responsible, but few of the claims were credible and none convincing. It was a technology that had been around in some form for billions of years and it was continually being re-invented somewhere out amongst the ever-churning stew of matter, energy, information and life that was the greater galaxy.

And continually being forgotten, too, of course; lost when ingénue civs were in the wrong place at the wrong time and copped a nearby gamma ray buster or a sudden visit from advanced unfriendlies. Other hopefuls accidentally – or by demented design – blew themselves up or poisoned themselves or their birthplace, or contrived some other usually highly avoidable catastrophe for themselves.

No matter; whether you made it up all by yourself or got the makings from somebody else, once it was possible to copy a creature's mind-state you could, as a rule, if you had the relevant background and the motivation, start to make at least part of your religion real.

"Vatueil, we're running out of time here, son. We need to come in there. You need to stand down, do you understand? You need to off-line your . . . let me just see here . . . your Aggressive Response, Target Acquisition and Weapon Deployment modules. Do you think you can do that? We don't want to have to come in there and . . . we don't want to have to come in there and treat you like an enemy."

"Sir." (A different different voice. It was going to be easier to number them.) "Couldn't be dead, could it?" (Different voice 2.)

"Yeah. Maybe Xagao got it." (Different voice 3.)

"With his itsy carbine? With one from the half-clip he got off before it blew his fucking arm and both legs off? Have you *seen* the specs on this thing?" (Different voice 1.)

"It isn't dead. He isn't dead. He's there and he's listening to everything we're saying."

"Sir?" (Different voice 4.)

"What?"

"Xagao's dead, sir." (Different voice 4.)

"Shit. Okay. Vatueil, listen; we've got one man dead out here. You understand that? You killed him, Vatueil. You dropped our TT and now you've killed one of us." (TT stood for Troop Transport.) "Now, nobody's going to punish you for this, we know it wasn't your fault, but you have to stand down now before somebody else gets hurt. We don't want to have to come in there and disable you ourselves."

"What? Are you fucking crazy? We're seven suits against a fucking monster robot space tank piece of shit! We won't have a hope in— " (Different voice 1.)

"Will you shut the fuck up? I'm not telling you again. One more word and you're on a fucking charge. In fact, you *are* on a fucking charge. That thing can *hear* you, you fucking moron, and you just gave it our whole fucking status. If we do pile in, you're now officially leading the fucking charge, genius."

"Fuck." (Different voice 1 = Genius.)

"Shut up. Vatueil?"

Seven. There were seven of them. That was useful to know.

Almost every developing species had a creation myth buried somewhere in its past, even if by the time they'd become space-faring it was no more than a quaint and dusty irrelevance (though, granted, some were downright embarrassing). Talking utter drivel about thunderclouds having sex with the sun, lonely old sadists inventing something to amuse themselves with, a big fish spawning the stars, planets, moons and your own ever-so-special People – or whatever other nonsense had wandered into the most likely feverish mind of the enthusiast who had come up with the idea in the first place – at least showed you were interested in trying provide an explanation for the world around you, and so was generally held to be a promising first step towards coming up with the belief system that provably worked and genuinely did produce miracles: reason, science and technology.

The majority of species, too, could scrape together some sort of metaphysical framework, a form of earlier speculation – semi-deranged or otherwise – regarding the way things worked at a fundamental level which could later be held up as a philosophy, life-rule system or genuine religion, especially if one used the excuse that it was really only a metaphor, no matter how literally true it had declared itself to be originally.

The harder the haul up the developmental ladder a species had suffered – rising from the usual primordial slime of just-dawned sentience with only (for example) the wheel to their name, to the dizzy heights and endless cheery sunshine of easy space flight, limitless energy, amusingly co-operative AIs, anti-ageing, anti-gravity, the end of disease and other cool tech – the more likely it was that that species would have entertained the idea of an immortal soul at some important point in its history and still be carrying the legacy of it now they had escaped the muck and had hit civilisational cruise phase.

Most species capable of forming an opinion on the subject had a pretty high opinion of themselves, and most individuals in such species tended to think it was a matter of some considerable importance whether they personally survived or not. Faced with the inevitable struggles and iniquities attendant upon a primitive life, it could be argued that it was an either very gloomy, unimaginative, breathtakingly stoic or just plain dim species that didn't come up with the idea that what could feel like an appallingly short, brutal and terrifying life was somehow not all there was to existence, and that a better one awaited them, personally and collectively – allowing for certain eligibility requirements – after death.

So the idea of a soul – usually though not always immortal in its posited nature – was a relatively common piece of the doctrinal baggage accompanying a people just making their debut on the great galactic stage. Even if your civilisation had somehow grown up without the concept, it was kind of forced upon you once you had the means of recording the precise, dynamic state of someone's mind and either placing it directly into the brain of another body, or storing it as some sort of scale-reduced – but still full – abstract inside an artificial substrate.

"Vatueil? Captain Vatueil! I'm ordering you to reply! Vatueil; report status immediately!"

He was listening but not paying attention. He kept checking his weapons and systems each time the voice that called itself Major Q'naywa said something that made him feel bad or confused.

"Okay, we're running out of time here and I sure as fuck am running out of patience."

What also made him feel good was looking out through the big curved entrance to the place where he was. The place where he was, where the thing that he was in was, measured 123.3 × 61.6 × 20.5 metres and was open to vacuum through the big curved entrance which formed one of the short walls. It was cluttered with machinery and pieces of equipment that he did not recognise but which he had quickly decided were No Threat, just useful for cover if he needed it.

"We're going to have to go in and do this the hard way."

"Oh fuck." (Different voice 5.)

"Beautiful. Perfect day for it." (Different voice 6.)

"We're going to fucking die." (Genius.)

"Sir, can't we wait for—?" (Different voice 2.)

"We're not going to fucking die. We haven't the time to wait for any other fucker. Control yourselves, all of you. We do this ourselves. Remember all that training? This is what it was for."

"Wasn't that much training, sir." (Genius.)

"I'm not even in the right sort of unit. I'm supposed to be in something called an N-C-M-E. I don't even know what that means, frankly." (Different voice 4.)

"Oh fuck oh fuck oh fuck." (Different voice 5.)

"Maneen? Shut up, son. All of you, shut up."

"Sir." (Different voice 5 = Maneen.)

"Gulton, that thing of yours delete this motherfucker?"

"Assuredly, sir. Thought you'd never ask, sir." (Different voice 6 = Gulton.)

The Unknowns – Treat As Enemy he could hear talking were all on the outside of the Abandoned Space Factory. The first one who had come in through the big curved entrance to the place where he was must have been Xagao, the one who was now dead.

"Okay. We need a plan here. All of you; un-deploy back towards me until we're LOS and we can use laser to talk without this piece of shit listening in." (LOS meant Line Of Sight.)

Xagao had silhouetted himself against the bit of the big bright blue and white planet visible beyond the curved entrance. Vatueil had targeted the silhouetted figure within a millisecond of the initial Visual Field Anomalous Movement impulse but he hadn't Readied To Fire until the figure, moving slowly, had swept his weapon in his direction. Then he had sent an Identification Friend/Foe burst towards the figure and simultaneously flicked it with a laser ranging pulse.

The figure had fired straight at him; small-calibre kinetic rounds. Approximately nine bullets had clanged into the Unidentified High-Solidity Object – Use As Cover he was hunkered down behind, two had hit his own Upper Weapon Nacelle 2 without significant damage and four or five flew overhead to hit the bulkhead behind him, producing more clangs he heard through his feet.

He had fired back a six-burst from his right upper Light Laser Rifle Unit, registering a direct hit on the weapon he had been targeted by and two more on the lower body of the figure, which mostly flipped backwards into cover, though one part of it, identifiable as a human armoured suit leg, had gone spinning away by itself, spraying fluid, somersaulting rapidly as it headed out towards the bright blue and white planet visible through the big curved entrance.

"Xagao get a TLF on the fucker?" (Different voice 3. TLF meant Target Location Fix.)

"Yeah. Post it when we get LOS." (Different voice 2.)

He had felt good. Firing and hitting and removing a Threat made him feel good, and something about the spinning leg unit – the way it sailed away, its trajectory curving gradually as it went, before it eventually disappeared – made him feel good too.

"Hey, it ping Xagao fore it tanked him? Anybody know?" (Genius.)

"Hold on. Yup." (Different voice 2.)

"Shut up and get back here. If I can hear you, so can it."

"Sir." (Different voice 2.)

"That's good though. The pinging. We can use that." (Genius.)

"IFFed him too." (Different voice 2.)

"Really? Chirpy." (Genius.)

He reviewed the brief engagement with Xagao and made two In-Deployment Tactical Environment Operating Behaviour Modification (Immediate Instigation) Memoranda: de-select automatic IFF challenge, de-select initial Laser Ranging Pulse.

Especially once a species or civilisation started swapping ideas and tips with its galactic peers, it became fairly easy to do this mind copying and pasting stuff. As a result, an individual – always one favoured in some way, either revered or just well-off (once the tech was safely past the developmental stage) might serially or even concurrently inhabit several or indeed many different bodies.

Some civs tried to use the technology purely as a back-up, going for full biological immortality with the soul-saving stuff just there in case something went badly wrong and you had to be transferred into a spare body. However, that tended to lead to short-term trouble if they kept on breeding as they'd been used to, or to more subtle long-term problems if they kept their population growth so curtailed their society basically became stagnant.

There was always the ever-tempting, profoundly illusory ideal – which every intelligent species seemed to think that only it had ever been clever enough to invent – of unlimited growth for ever, but any attempt to implement such a regime very rapidly ran into the awkward fact that the surrounding material in the galaxy and presumably the universe was already inhabited, used, claimed, protected, treasured or even by general agreement owned. The long-established result of this was the irritatingly strict rules the galactic community's major players and Elders had come up with regarding the reasonable allotments of matter and living space a new species might expect (it boiled down to You Can't Have Other People's, but it always felt grossly unfair at the time). The seemingly wizard wheeze of turning the rest of the universe into teeny little copies of yourself was by no means a non-starter – ignorant people and vainglorious machines started doing it all the time – but it was invariably a quickly-brought-to-a-conclusioner.

Normally, especially given how much amazingly rich experience could be crammed into VRs in general and Afterlives in particular, people went with more modest and neighbourly growth plans in the Real and an extensive though still ultimately limited expansion program in the Virtual.

Because, particularly for those just developing the relevant soul-saving tech, that life in virtual environments beckoned seductively. Deeply immersive and impressive VR was an effectively inevitable adjunct to mind-state transcription technology even if, bizarrely, it hadn't come into existence before. Each led to and complemented the other.

Only a few species didn't bother with the soul-transference side at all, some because thanks to their heritage and development they already had something as good or which they judged made it irrelevant, some for specifically religious or philosophical reasons, and some – most – because they were more interested in going for full immortality in the Real and regarded mind-state transcription as a distraction, or even an admission of defeat.

Of course, in any society using this soul-transcription gizmology there was usually a die-hard strand of true believers who insisted that the only afterlife worth bothering about still happened somewhere else, in the true heaven or hell that had always been believed in before all this fangling technology came along, but that was a tough position to hold when at the back of your mind was the niggling doubt that you really might not be saved when the time came, while at the back of everybody else's mind was a little device that was guaranteed to do precisely that.

The result was that many, many civilisations in the greater galaxy had their own Afterlives: virtual realities maintained in computational or other substrates to which their dead could go and – in some sense at least – live on.

"I can see you now, sir." (Maneen.)

"Well, space biscuits for you, marine. Switch to LOS."

"Sir. Sorry. I mean—" (Maneen.)

There was silence for a while. Vatueil watched the big section of bright blue and white planet he could see beyond the curved entrance. The Unknowns – Treat As Enemy were keeping quiet.

The bit of the planet he could see was changing very slowly all the time. He went back and replayed how it had changed since he'd taken up position here. He subtracted the motion component of the place where he was. The place where he was was revolving too but it was revolving slowly and steadily and that made it easy to subtract.

Now he could see that the planet was slowly revolving. Also, the white streaks and whorls which over-lay the blue were changing too, even more slowly. Some of the streaks were widening and some were narrowing and the whorls were spinning about their axes and also shifting across the face of the planet, even allowing for its revolving.

He watched the replay of all this movement many times. It made him feel good. It was different from the way checking his weapons made him feel good. It was like the way watching Xagao's leg going tumbling off towards the planet had made him feel good. Especially the way its trajectory had curved. It was beautiful.

Beautiful. He thought about this word and decided that it was the right word.

Some Afterlives simply offered everlasting fun for the post-dead: infinite holiday resorts featuring boundless sex, adventure, sport, games, study, exploration, shopping, hunting or whatever other activities especially tickled that particular species' fancy. Others were as much for the benefit of those still living as the dead themselves, providing societies that had inherited or recently come up with the idea of consulting the ancestors with a practical way of doing just that.

A few were of a more contemplative and philosophic nature than those fixated on general hilarity. Some – and the majority of the more long-established Afterlives – featured a sort of gradual fading-away rather than genuine post-death VR immortality, with the personality of the deceased individual slowly – usually over many generations of time in the Real – dissolving into the general mass of information and civilisational ethos held within the virtual environment.

In some the dead lived much more quickly than those in the Real, in others they lived at the same rate and in others far more slowly. Some even incorporated ways to bring favoured dead individuals back to life again.

And many still featured death; a second, final, absolute death, even within the virtual, because – as it turned out – it was quite a rare species that naturally generated individuals capable of being able, or wanting, to live indefinitely, and those who had lived for a really long time in Afterlives were prone to becoming profoundly, gravely bored, or going catatonically – or screaming – mad. Civs new to the game often went into a sort of shock when the first desperate pleas for true, real death started to emerge from their expensively created, painstakingly maintained, assiduously protected and carefully backed-up Afterlives.

The trick was to treat such entreaties as perfectly natural.

And to let the dead have their way.

He wanted to stay and watch the view of the planet beyond the curved entrance for much longer so that he could see how the whorls and streaks continued to change. Then he could replay the recording again and again. Seeing even more of the planet would be good too. It would be better. Seeing all of the planet would be better still. It would be best.

He realised that he was starting to feel uncomfortable. He wasn't sure what the cause was at first, then understood that it was because he had stayed too long in the one place after a Recent Combat Event.

He thought about what to do. Nothing had changed or moved recently. It should be safe to move.

He tried asking his Outboard Remote Sensing/Engagement Units what they could sense, but he still didn't have any of these units. He was supposed to have these things, whatever they were, but he didn't. It was like another empty magazine that was supposed to be full.

So: Proceed Otherwise. He rose silently on his three articulated legs, senses sweeping all around as his Upper Sensory Dome rose into the space beneath the ceiling (clearance overhead duly reduced from 18.3 to 14.2 metres) and gave him an increased field of view. He kept both Main Weapon Nacelles targeted at the curved entrance. All six Secondary Weapon Pods deployed to cover the rest of the area about him, without him needing to tell them to. He rotated the Upper Weapon Collar to point Nacelle 2 directly behind him, where he judged the least risk was, as it had expended some energy and taken some damage, however nominal.

Still nothing threatening to be sensed. He stepped over the Unidentified High-Solidity Object and moved right and forward, towards the side of the curved entrance that showed the bright blue and white planet. He was moving quietly, at less than optimum speed, so that when his feet connected with the deck they produced minimal vibration. A tipped section of the floor near a long ragged tear in the thick deck material meant that he had to use his weapon pods to balance himself.

Some of the Unidentified Medium-Solidity Objects in the space about him resolved into space- and atmosphere-capable craft. This meant that the place where he was was a hangar. Most of the craft looked chaotically asymmetric, damaged, non-viable.

He could see another Unidentified High-Solidity Object nearer the curved entrance. He moved towards it. The view of the planet became more extensive and made him feel good. Beautiful. It was still beautiful.

Suddenly something moved against the bright white and blue of the planet.

Nobody knew, either, what bright little soul had first hit on the idea of linking up two Afterlives, but given that emerging civilisations were generally quite keen to establish permanent, high-capacity, high-quality and preferably free links with the dataspheres and informational environments of those around them – especially those around them with better tech than they possessed – it had always been going to happen, by accident if not by design. It even benefited the dead of both civilisations, opening up additional new vistas of exciting post-death experience, the better for the deceased to resist the regrettable attraction of a second, properly terminal event.

Linking up all amenable and compatible Afterlives had become something of a craze; almost before the relevant academics could come up with a decent provisional analysis of the phenomenon's true cultural meaning and implications, practically every corner of the civilised galaxy was linked to every other part by Afterlife connections, as well as by all the other more usual ties of diplomacy, tourism, trade, general nosiness and so on.

So, for many millions of years there had been a network of Afterlives throughout the galaxy, semi-independent from the Real and constantly changing just as the galactic community in the Real changed, with civilisations appearing, developing, steady-stating or disappearing, either changing beyond recognition, relapsing in some way or going for semi-Godhood, sidestepping the material life altogether by opting for the careless indifference that was Subliming.

Mostly, nobody mentioned the Hells.

The moving thing was tiny. Too small to be a person in a suit or even an Outboard Remote Sensing/Engagement Unit, either his or anybody else's. It was moving at 38.93 metres per second and so was far too slow to be considered kinetic ordinance. It was approximately 3cm by 11cm, round in section, conical aspect to the leading quarter, spinning. He deemed it to be a 32mm mortar shell. He had a lot of high-reliability information on such ordnance. Maximum capability a five kiloton micro-nuke; many variants. It was going to fly directly above where he had been positioned and impact on the bulkhead which had been behind him.

Now his high-telescopic vision apparatus had acquired it, he could see tiny sensory pits on the thing, blurring round as it rotated (4.2 rps). It flew past him five metres away and started to glitter, giving off range- and Combat Space Topography-sensing laser pulses. None hit him. This was because it had gone past before it activated.

He was still moving, taking one more quiet step as the projectile sailed through the dark space of the hangar. He judged that the ingress of the round meant that an attack might be about to start and that his best choice had become to hunker down here, still five steps away from the Unidentified High-Solidity Object he'd been heading for, opting instead for the partial cover of the nearest Unidentified Medium-Solidity Object, an additional advantage accruing from the fact that a sub-routine assured him his scale and overall shape in hunkered mode would make him look similar to the now Identified Medium-Solidity Object concerned, which was a small, intact but deactivated High-Atmospheric/Low Orbit Planetary Surface Bombardment Unit.

An additional advantage accruing definitely sounded like a good thing. It was almost like an order from inside himself. He'd choose that option. He started hunkering down.

An expert sub-system suggested that should the mortar round detonate where he had been, further additional advantage might be accrued. That sounded good too.

The mortar round was travelling so slowly there was plenty of time to work out exactly where he had been, to target his left upper Light Laser Rifle Unit on the spinning projectile and set himself up for minimal blast-front damage from the direction the round was heading, should it prove to be a micro-nuke.

When it was directly above where he'd been he landed four direct low-power hits on its rear; zero misses or out-splash, which made him feel very good. He whipped the rifle unit back into the armoured nacelle. The mortar round detonated.

Micro-nuke.

The Hells existed because some faiths insisted on them, and some societies too, even without the excuse of over-indulged religiosity.

Whether as a result of perhaps too faithful a transcription – from scriptural assertion to provable actuality – or simply an abiding secular need to continue persecuting those thought worthy of punishment even after they were dead, a number of civilisations – some otherwise quite respectable – had built up impressively ghastly Hells over the eons. These were only rarely linked with other Afterlives, hellish or otherwise, and even then only under strict superveillance, and usually only with the aim of heightening the anguish of the sufferers by subjecting them to torments their own people somehow hadn't thought of, or the same old ones but inflicted by extra-gruesome alien demons rather than the more familiar home-grown variety.

Very gradually though, perhaps just due to the exact nature of the chance mix the contemporary crop of In-play civilisations represented, a sort of network of Hells – still only partial, and remaining strictly controlled in their interactions – did emerge, and news of their existence and the conditions within them became more widely known.

This led to trouble, in time. Many species and civilisations objected profoundly to the very idea of Hells, no matter whose they were. A lot objected profoundly to the very idea of torture in any event, and the practice of setting up Virtual Environments – traditionally such dazzlingly fabulous realms of unmitigated pleasure – devoted to inflicting pain and suffering on sentient creatures seemed not just wrong but perverse, sadistic, genuinely evil and shamefully, disgracefully cruel. Uncivilised, in fact, and that was not a word such societies bandied about without having thought carefully about its deployment.

The Culture took a particularly dim view of torture, either in the Real or in a Virtuality, and was quite prepared to damage its short- and even – at least seemingly – long-term interests to stop it happening. Such a devoutly censorious, non-pragmatic approach confused people used to dealing with the Culture, but it was a characteristic that had been there since the civilisation's inception so there was little point in treating it as just a temporary moral fad and waiting for it to pass. As a result, over the millennia, the Culture's atypically inflexible attitude probably had shifted the whole meta-civilisational moral debate on such matters slightly but significantly to the liberal, altruistic end of the ethical spectrum, that definitive identification of torture with barbarism being perhaps its most obvious mimetic achievement.

There was a predictable mix of responses. A few of the civs hosting Hells simply had a think, took the point and closed them down; generally these were species who had never shown any great enthusiasm for the concept in the first place, their number including some who had only adopted the idea at all because they'd got the erroneous impression it was what all up-and-coming societies did and they hadn't wanted to appear backward.

Some civilisations just ignored the fuss and said it had nothing to do with anybody else. Others, generally those constitutionally unable to look past any opportunity to go spasming into full High Dudgeon mode, reacted with hysterical bluster, complaining loudly of bullying, ethical imperialism, grossly unwarranted cultural interference and persecution bordering on outright hostility. Some of those, having made their point – and after a decent interval – still proved persuadable that Hells were unacceptable. But not all.

The Hells remained, as did the discord they engendered.

Even so, now and again a civ was effectively bribed out of continuing to host Hells, usually with tech that was a bit beyond it in the normal course of development, though that was a tricky precedent to set in case it encouraged others to try the same trick just to get their hands on the relevant toys, so it remained a strategy that had to be used sparingly.

A few of the more militantly Altruistic civs tried to hack into the Hells belonging to those they saw as their more barbaric peers, to free or destroy the tormented souls within, but that carried its own dangers, and a couple of small wars had resulted.

Eventually, though, a war was agreed upon as the best way to settle the whole dispute. The vast majority of protagonists on both sides agreed they would fight within a controlled Virtuality overseen by impartial arbiters and the winner would accept the result; if the pro-Hell side won there would be no more sanctions or sanctimoniousness from the anti-Hell faction and if the anti-Hellists triumphed then the Hells of the participating adversaries would be shut down.

Both sides thought they would win, the anti-Hell side because they were generally more advanced – an advantage that would be partially reflected in the simmed war – and the pro-Hell side because they were convinced they were the less decadent, more intrinsically warlike side. They also had a couple of hidden assets in the shape of civs who nobody knew had been hosting Hells but who had been persuaded to come on board and who just about (it was decided, after a lengthy legal case) qualified due to the way the relevant agreement had been worded.

Naturally, also, both sides were convinced they had right on their side, not that either was remotely naive enough to think that that had any possible bearing on the outcome whatsoever.

Battle was joined. It duly raged to and fro across the vast virtual conflict spaces within the scrupulously and multiply policed substrates allotted to it, overseen by a people called the Ishlorsinami, a species long notorious for their absolute incorruptibility, spartan lifestyles, near complete lack of humour and a sense of fairness that struck most other normal civs as positively pathological.

But now the war was nearing its end, and, to Vatueil, it looked like his side was going to lose.

It was a micro-nuke, but low-yield. Disposable sensor units deployed on his armoured Main Weapon Nacelles – his upper sensory dome was retracted beneath its armour clamshell – watched what happened. Three sub-munitions had deployed an instant before the main warhead had exploded, fanning downwards towards the floor where he'd been hunkered earlier. It was hard to be sure but he thought that he – the thing he was in – would have survived, had he still been there.

The floor beneath him thudded.

There was much damage where he had been; the bulkhead behind was holed, the ceiling above perforated, bulging upwards, now dipping back down, glowing white and yellow hot as heated supporting elements gave in to the apparent gravity the Abandoned Space Factory's rotation provided. The Unidentified High-Solidity Object he'd been hiding behind earlier had been partially vaporised/destroyed and shifted across the floor of the hangar until it had impacted with the section of tipped, already-damaged floor.

"Still there!" (Different voice 4.)

"Hit it, Gulton."

A bright yellow-white line lanced down from where the ceiling had been, smashing into the hangar deck where Vatueil had been positioned earlier and creating an exploding white ball of plasma. This blew outward in a boiling cloud behind a wave-front of condensing particles of molten metals; metre-scale yellow-glowing fragments of the floor went tumbling everywhere at various speeds, mostly high. He saw one piece somersaulting towards him, bouncing once off the floor and once off the ceiling. He did not have enough time to move. Perhaps if he had not been hunkered down he might have been able to avoid it.

The piece of wreckage impacted hard on the armoured body of the thing he was inside. It impacted badly, too. Not a flat side or even an edge hit first but a jagged point. It smacked into his top, off centre so that it half-spun him and sent the piece of wreckage spinning into the shoulder section of his left Main Weapon Pod.

Everything shook. Damage control screen-spreads filled his field of vision. There was a further impact from above. It was relatively slow, implicitly high inertia, crushing.

"*Fuck* you, motherfucker! *Fuck* you *fuck* you *fuck* you!" (Genius.)

"Sir, ordnance discharged, sir." (Gulton.)

"Fuck me, I think my anal plug just exited my fucking suit." (Different voice 2.)

"Oh, that's spatted. That is one spatted shitfuck of an Armoured Combat Unit." (Different voice 3.)

"Got to have done it. Got to have fucking done it. Take fucking that, you miserable three-legged space tank motherfucker." (Genius.)

"Last one in's an officer. No offence, sir." (Different voice 2.)

"Steady. Just hold. Those things are tough."

He was injured. The machine he was in was now sub-optimal. It was called an Armoured Combat Unit.

The protective clamshell had taken a serious kinetic hit and was refusing to open, disabling the upper sensory dome. His left Main Weapon Nacelle had been torn off by the same piece of wreckage. Four Secondary Weapon Pods were non-operational and the upper secondary weapon collar had jammed. Something had damaged his Main Power Distribution Unit, too. He didn't know how that had happened but it had. Now he couldn't move his legs properly. Some secondary power left in his Number One leg. That was all. Difficult to estimate how much power or leverage was available.

Some piece of heavy equipment from the ceiling above, the source of the earlier high-inertia impact, appeared to be pinning him to the deck. Additionally, the condensing metals from the plasma event seemed to have spot-welded some parts of himself to some other parts of himself and some parts of himself to the hangar floor.

He rotated another set of disposable sensors into place on the right shoulder. This would be all he had to work with for now.

He would have to stay where he was. He could still turn, though there was a grinding sensation when he did and he could not turn smoothly, which contra-indicated tracking-firing.

He couldn't see much. The lower sensory dome was obstructed by the squat cage of his immobile legs.

"Okay. Trooper Drueser. You have the honour, I believe."

"Sir." (Genius = Drueser.)

The figure came in through the curved entrance, bouncing on all fours and keeping very low to the hangar deck, a medium kinetic rifle tripodded on its back, barrel sweeping back and forth.

Vatueil let it go well past him, almost to the tipped, torn part of the hangar floor, then quietly lobbed a superblack snowflake grenade just behind it. The magnetic launcher produced no exhaust, the superblack coating kept the projectile stealthed and it was too dark for the trooper to have much chance of seeing the round curving towards him through the vacuum.

He launched a second round aimed to fall right on top of the suited figure if it stopped about . . . Now.

The first grenade hit the deck two metres behind the trooper, then detonated with a flash and a floor-thud. The figure had stopped and spun round. The trooper was caught inside the hail of millimetre- and centimetre-scale fragments.

There was a shriek. (Drueser.)

The back-mounted gun fired twice at where the first grenade had detonated. Then the second grenade landed. It was supposed to fall right on top of the figure but landed half a metre to its left side and half a metre in front it because of his own sensor-compromised aiming and the fact that the trooper had been blown backwards by the fragment shower from the first grenade.

The second grenade had been set to detonate on contact. The detonation caused the figure's head to kick back. It also tore off and then disintegrated Drueser's helmet visor, causing an obvious pressure-loss event. The figure collapsed to the floor without further movement or transmitted sound.

"Drueser?"

"Fuck." (Different voice 2.)

"Drueser?"

"Sir, I think he triggered something. A suckertrap. That thing's still dead. Must be." (Different voice 4.)

"Sir? The real bad guys are due to get here awful soon now. We need to be in there even if it's just to hide." (Gulton.)

"Aware of that, Gulton. You want to be next?"

"Sir, me and Koviuk thought we might favour the skirmish space below with our twin presences, sir." (Gulton.)

"BMG, Gulton." (He didn't know what BMG meant.)

The two figures dropped through the hole in the ceiling. Their dark suits were made briefly bright by the orange glow still coming from the slagged materials of what had been the hangar ceiling and the floor of the deck above.

Vatneil could have hit both of them but he had heard what they had said and he thought that what it meant was that they thought he was dead. If that was true then it was better to let them think that and to bring them all into the same Immediate Tactical Environment as he was in, the better to attack and destroy them.

Trapeze, came the call. It was not a surprise. Vatueil had been thinking of making it himself.

He left a shell presence of himself in the Primary Strategic Situation Overview Space and navigated to the Trapeze space, scattering pass-codes and decoys like petals.

There were five of them. They sat on what looked like trapezes hanging in utter darkness; the wires vanished upwards into the black and there was no sign or implication of any floor below or wall to any side. It was meant to symbolise the isolation of the secret space or something. He had no idea what they'd have chosen had one of their number had a high-gravity heritage and been congenitally terrified of any drop more than a few millimetres. They'd all taken up different appearances to be here but he knew who the other four were and trusted them completely, just as he hoped they trusted him.

He had shown up as a furred quadruped with big eyes and three powerful fingers at the end of each of his four limbs. They all tended to present as the sort of multi-limbed creature which had evolved in gravity, in trees. He knew how strange this must feel to the two water worlders he knew were present, but it was the sort of thing you got used to in VR. They took on colours to distinguish themselves; he was red, as usual.

He looked round at all of them "We're losing," he announced.

"You always say that," said yellow.

"I didn't when we weren't," he replied. "When I realised we were, I started saying so."

"Depressing," yellow said, looking away.

"Losing often is," green said.

"It is starting to look kind of non-get-out-able," purple agreed with a sigh. Purple held onto the supporting side-wires and started rocking back and forth, making its trapeze oscillate slowly.

"So, next level?" said green. Their exchanges had become terse over the last few meetings; they'd talked exhaustively about the situation, and the choices it left them with. It was just a question of waiting for the voting balance to change, or for some of their number to become so frustrated with the process and the whole Trapeze set-up, that they formed another even more exclusive sub-committee and took matters into their own hands. They had all pledged not to do this, but you never entirely knew.

They all looked at blue. Blue was the waverer. Blue had been voting No to going to what they usually called "the next level" until now, but had made no secret of being the one of the three nay-sayers who was most likely to change his, her or its mind, as circumstances altered.

Blue scratched itself about the groin with one long-fingered hand, then sniffed at its fingers; they had each made their own choices about how closely their tree-dwelling images stuck to the sort of behaviour the real thing got up to, back in the jungle. Blue sighed.

As soon as he saw just how blue sighed, Vatueil knew they had won.

Blue looked regretfully at yellow and purple. "I'm sorry," it told them. "Truly I am."

Purple shook its head, started picking at its fur, looking for who knew what.

Yellow let out an exasperated whoop and did a backward circle dismount, falling silently into the darkness beneath, becoming a yellow scrap which quickly disappeared entirely. Its abandoned trapeze swung in a wild, jerking dance.

Green reached out and steadied it with one hand and looked down into the abyss. "Not bothering with a formal vote, then," it said quietly.

"For what it's worth," purple said disconsolately, "I agree too." It looked round them, while each was still watching for the reactions of the others. "But I do so not . . . in protest, but mainly in a spirit of solidarity, and out of despair. I think we'll come to regret this decision." It looked down again.

"None of us does this lightly," green said.

"So," he said. "We go to the next level."

"Yes," blue said. "We cheat."

"We hack, we infiltrate, we sabotage," green said. "Those are war skills too."

"Let's not make excuses for ourselves," purple muttered. "We're still breaking an oath."

"We'd all rather have achieved victory with our honour fully intact," green said sternly, "but our options now are either an honourable defeat or the sacrifice of our honour for at least a chance of victory. However achieved, the outcome justifies the sacrifice."

"If it works."

"There are no guarantees in war," green said.

"Oh, there are," blue said quietly, looking away into the darkness. "It's just that they guarantee death, destruction, suffering, heartache and remorse."

They were all silent for a moment, alone with their own thoughts.

Then green rattled the wires of its trapeze. "Enough. We must plan. To the details."

They hadn't seen him. Two were where the plasma event had taken place, one was at the body of the trooper Drueser, one was somewhere he couldn't see and the other two knelt just ten metres away, almost in front of him, twelve metres in from the curved entrance.

"Bit of the fucker over here. One of his arm-weapon pods." (Different voice 2.) The two kneeling in front of him looked round, almost at him. That was helpful, telling him where trooper Different voice 2 might currently be.

"Fuck all over here. Sir." (Gulton.)

One of the two kneeling figures had continued to look in his direction after the other had turned away again. He appeared to be looking straight at him.

"Is that another bit under that—?" It was the one who had said he was Major Q'naywa. His gun had started to level, pointing straight at him.

He fired both his available laser rifles at the two kneeling men, achieving multiple hits with high out-splash but minimal reflectivity and several observed-piercing hits, though the Major Q'naywa figure was partially shielding the one behind, who was probably Different voice 4. He followed up with a couple of Anti-Armoured Personnel/Light Armoured Vehicle minimissiles.

At the same time he swung his remaining Main Weapon Nacelle round to target the part of the hangar where he'd been earlier and where Gulton and Koviuk were now. He used the railgun, set to Scatter. Tiny hyper-kinetic rounds made a disintegrating haze out of the tipped section of floor, the bulkheads and ceiling.

As the Main Weapon Nacelle had deployed, it had roughly tracked across the location of the trooper kneeling by the body of trooper Drueser, so he'd loosed a trio of General Purpose High Explosive/Fragmentation Subscale Missiles towards them. Then he lobbed five more Subscales towards the centre of the railgun's targeting area, cutting their engines off almost as soon as they exited the Weapon Nacelle so that they fell into the part of the target area he couldn't see.

From the start, he had been pumping round after round of snowflake, heatseeker, emission-homing and movement-primed grenades overhead, guessing at where Different voice 2 might be, behind him in the hangar. Some of the grenades ricocheted off the ceiling but that did not really matter.

The trooper Major Q'naywa and the figure behind him disappeared in the twin explosions of the minimissiles. Unidentifiable gurgling screams might have been Gulton and Koviuk. They cut off quickly as the railgun rounds continued to eat away at the bulkheads, floor and ceiling. The Subscales erupted in the centre of the hangar, creating a billowing cloud of gasses and debris. The two troopers, one of them Drueser, who was already dead, vanished in the fireballs.

The lobbed Subscales landed in a spread in what was left of the hangar's rear corner, filling it with a brief haze of plasma, gas and shrapnel.

He stopped firing, railgun magazine depleted by 60 per cent.

Debris trajectoried, impacted, ricocheted, fell back, tumbled, slid, became still. The gasses dissipated, mostly through the wide, curved entrance that framed the view of the big bright blue and white planet outside.

No transmissions.

The only traces of the troopers he could see were ambiguous in nature and quite small.

After nearly nine minutes he used what power he had in his single operational leg, trying to lift himself free from whatever was pinning him. The attempt failed and he knew he was trapped. He thought there was a high likelihood he had not killed the trooper who'd been somewhere in the hangar behind him, but his attempt to rise, which had caused some movement of the wreckage around and over him, attracted no further hostile attention.

He sat there and waited, wishing he could see the beautiful planet better.

Others arrived half an hour later. They were different troopers with different suits and weapons.

They didn't have the correct IFF codes either so he fought them too. By the time he was blown out of the hangar entrance in a cloud of plasma he was completely blind, almost without any senses. Only his internal heat sensors and a feeling that he was experiencing a faint but gradually increasing force from one particular direction, once he allowed for the fact he was tumbling, told him he was falling into the atmosphere of the beautiful bright white and blue planet.

The heat increased rapidly and started to leak into his Power and Processing Core through piercing-damage channels sustained in the engagement just passed. His Processor Suite would shut down or melt in eighteen, no eleven, no nine seconds: eight, seven, no, three: two, one . . .

His last thought was that it would have been nice to have seen the beautiful—

He returned to the simulation within a simulation that was the Primary Strategic Situation Overview Space. In Trapeze they had discussed the initial details of plans that might end the war, one way or the other. Here they were still reviewing and re-reviewing the same old territory they had been fretting over when he'd left.

"One of your old stamping grounds, isn't it, Vatueil?" one of the others in the High Command said as they watched the irrelevancy of the war amongst these tumbling rocks and lumps of ice replay itself. Rocket exhausts plumed in the darkness amongst the billions of orbiting fragments; munitions blazed, forces swept back and forth.

"Is it?" he said. Then he recognised it.

He had been many things in this war. He had died within the simulations many times, some failing of character or application on his part occasionally contributing to his end, more usually the mistakes of those above him in the command structure – or just the need for sacrifice – providing all of the cause. How many lifetimes had he spent waging war? He had lost count, long ago.

Of course here, in the kingdom of the dead, engaged in a seemingly never-ending fight over the fate of the souls of the departed, further deaths were no barrier to continuance. After each death in service the soldier's achievements were reviewed by panels of his peers and other expert minds. Had he been brave, cool under fire, resourceful? According to the answers, lessons were learned. Soldiers, reincarnated to fight again, rose, fell or maintained their position in the ranks depending on how well they were judged to have done, and military practice itself changed gradually in response to the same adjudication.

Gradually at first, Vatueil had worked his way up through the hierarchy. Even where his contribution ended in death, failure and defeat he was found to have done the best he could have done with what resources and advantages he'd started with, and, most especially, to have shown imagination in his decisions.

His very first incarnation in the war effort had given every indication of being a disaster; not even knowing that he was in a simulation, having no idea what he was really fighting for, he had been a military tunneller who had turned traitor, been tortured and then died. Still, he had thought to walk through the poison gas rather than try to outrun it, which had counted in his favour, and the fact that such a previously stalwart and dependable soul had chosen to take his chances with the enemy rather than immediately try to get back to his own side had counted more against those in charge of that aspect of the battle space than it had against him, and helped convince those then running the war at a higher level that much of it was being waged too harshly and with too great an emphasis on secrecy.

And yes, here – in this open maze of broken moons, drifting rocks, abandoned facilities and empty factories, many generations of combatants ago – he had been part of the struggle.

Again, even though he had ended up fighting – all too successfully – against his own people, that had not been his fault. He had not even been his complete self in that instance, some all-too-believable glitch within the re-created scenario meaning that his download into the combat unit had been only partial, leaving it crippled inside, not knowing who was friend and who was foe. Still, even reduced, his essence had fought well, displayed imagination and shown some glimmerings of trying to develop. That had been worth another promotion.

Yet here was that same place, still disputed. Not all the subsequent battles throughout and amongst the somersaulting cascade of rocky debris and the orbiting industrial wasteland of deserted infrastructure wheeling round the system's planets had produced a decisive victory for either side.

He looked at it, remembering, wondering what other troopers like his old self still laboured, fought and died there.

"We need a decision," the group leader for this watch said. "Pursue, hold, abandon?" Her disembodied head looked round all the others at once, fixing her gaze on each simultaneously, because in the sim, of course, you could do this.

He voted abandon, though he was not convinced. Abandon was the decision, by just the one vote. He felt a sort of despairing elation, and wondered if that contradictory mix was also something only possible in a sim. It had been so long since he'd been properly alive, he was no longer sure.

It didn't matter; they would abandon the battle for the simulated asteroids and the simulated orbiting facilities in this particular simulated system in this particular simulated version of this particular simulated era in this particular simulated galaxy.

He felt that he should feel bad about this, but did not.

What was one more betrayal amongst so many?

Nine

To build on such a scale would have been spectacular enough, she thought. That this thing was not unique, that it was not that special, that it was one of a "class" was moderately astounding. That it was some way from being one of the largest class was completely astounding. That it could move – bewilderingly, unreally quickly in a realm hidden at right angles to everything she had ever known or experienced – was beyond belief.

She sat with her legs dangling over the edge of a thousand-metre cliff and watched the various craft at play. Fliers of too many shapes and types to be sure they were not each unique – the smallest carrying only one man, woman or child – buzzed and fussed above, below, before and on each side. Larger craft floated with a stately grace, their appearance varied, motley and near chaotic with masts, pennants, exposed decks and bulbously glittering excrescences but their general structure approaching a sort of bloated uniformity the greater in size they were; they drifted on the unhurried breezes the vast craft's internal meteorology created. True ships, spacecraft, generally more sober in form if not in decoration, moved with still greater deliberation, often accompanied by small squat-looking tug-craft that looked hewn from solid.

The canyon in front of her was fifteen kilometres long, its laser-straight edges softened by the multi-coloured mass of climbing, hanging and floating foliage draped spilling like gaudy ice-falls from the tops of the two great strakes on either side.

The sheer walls were diced with a breathtaking complexity of variously sized, mostly brightly lit apertures from or into a few of which, on occasion, the various air and spacecraft issued or disappeared, the whole staggering, intricate network of docks and hangars graphed onto each colossal escarpment representing a mere detail on the surface of this truly gigantic vessel.

The floor of the great canyon was near table-flat grassland, strung all about with meandering streams making their way to a hazy plain, kilometres ahead. Above, beyond filmy layers of pale cloud, a single bright, yellow-white line provided light and warmth, looping day-slow across the sky in place of a sun. It disappeared into the misty distance of the view in front of her. It was almost noon by the ship's own time and so the sunline stood near directly overhead.

At her back, behind a low wall, in the parkland that covered the vessel's topmost surface, people passed, tumbling waters could be heard and tall, distant trees stood on gentle rolling hills. Dotted amongst the trees, long vertical bands of pale, almost transparent vegetation rose into the air, each soaring to two or three times the height of the tallest trees and surmounted by a dark ovoid the size of the crowns of the trees beneath. Dozens of these strange shapes swayed to and fro in the breeze, oscillating together like some vast seaweed forest.

Lededje and Sensia were sitting on the natural-looking cliff edge of dark red rock, their backs to the low wall of undressed stone. Looking straight down, Lededje could just about make out the filaments of a sort of gauzy net five or six metres down that would catch you if you fell. It didn't really look up to the job, she thought, but she'd been prepared to trust Sensia when she'd suggested sitting here.

Ten metres to her right, a stream launched out into the air from a spur of rock. Its separating, whitening spray fell only fifty metres or so before it was unceremoniously gathered up by half of a giant inverted cone of what looked like glass and funnelled into a transparent pipe that plunged straight down towards the valley floor. It was almost a relief to see that, like so many other seemingly exotic, extraordinary and fabulous things, at least part of the GSV's functional glamour ended up expressing itself as plumbing.

This was the Culture General Systems Vehicle *Sense Amid Madness, Wit Amongst Folly*, the ship whose avatoid Sensia she had addressed when she'd first woken up within its near infinite substrate of thinking material.

Another version of Sensia – small, thin, spry, bronze-skinned and barely clothed – sat by her side. This personification of the ship was properly called an avatar. She had brought Lededje here to give her an idea of the size of the ship that she represented, that she in some sense was. Shortly they would board one of the small aircraft gliding, buzzing and blattering about them, presumably so that any tiny remaining fragment of Lededje that was not dumbfounded beyond imagining at the mind-boggling scale of the ship she was on – a labyrinth within, a jungled three-dimensional maze without – could join all the other parts of her that already most profoundly were.

Lededje dragged her gaze away from the sight and stared down at her own hand and arm.

So, well, here she was, "revented" as they called it, her soul, the very essence of her being, rehoused – as of only an hour or so ago – in a new body. And a fresh new body, she was relieved to know, not one that had belonged to anybody else (she had originally imagined that such bodies were the result of people guilty of terrible crimes being punished by having their personalities removed from the brains such bodies housed, leaving them free to host another's mind).

She inspected the tiny, almost transparent hairs on her forearm and the pores on the golden-brown skin beneath. This was a human-basic body, roughly though very convincingly amended to look like that of a Sichultian. Looking closely at individual hairs and pores, she suspected that her eyesight was better than it had been originally. There was a level of detail visible that made her head swim. She supposed that it was always possible she had been lied to and she was still within a Virtual Reality, where such zooming-in was almost easier to do than it was to limit.

She flicked her gaze out again, to the kilometres of dazzling view in front of her. Of course, even this might exist within a simulated environment. Modelling such a vast ship within even the most detailed image of reality must be easier than actually building one, and certainly any people capable of constructing such a vessel could command the relatively trivial computational resources necessary to create an utterly convincing simulation of what she could see and hear and feel and smell before her now.

It could *always* all be unreal – how could you ever tell otherwise? You took it on trust, in part because what would be the point of doing anything else? When the fake behaved exactly like the real, why treat it as anything different? You gave it the benefit of the doubt, until something proved otherwise.

Waking in this real body had been similar to waking up within the fake body imagined in the great ship's substrate. She had experienced a slow, pleasant coming-to, the warm fuzziness of what had felt like deep, satisfying sleep changing slowly to the clarity and sharpness of a wakefulness informed by the knowledge that something had profoundly changed.

Embodied, she'd thought. Embodiment was all, Sensia had told her, ironically while they were talking in the Virtual. An intelligence completely dissociated from the physical, or at least an impression of it, was a strange, curiously limited and almost perverse thing, and the precise form that your physicality took had a profound, in some ways defining influence on your personality.

She had opened her eyes and found herself in a bed of what looked like snowflakes, felt like feathers and behaved like particularly obedient and well-disposed insects. White as snow but nearly as warm as her skin, the material had seemed unconstrained by any enveloping cover, and yet the apparently free-floating individual elements had refused to get in her eyes, up her nose or to leave the confines of the bed and the few centimetres around both it and her pyjama-clad body.

Beyond the bed had been a modest, sparsely furnished room three or four metres to a side with one window-wall looking out onto a brightly lit balcony where she could see Sensia sitting in one of two chairs. The avatar had gazed out at the view for a few more moments before turning to her and smiling.

"Welcome to the land of the living!" she'd said, waving one hand. "Get dressed; we'll have some lunch and then we'll go exploring."

So now here they sat, with Lededje trying to take in what she was seeing.

She looked back at her arm again. She had chosen pale purple blouson pants, cuffed tight at the ankle, and a filmy but opaque long-sleeved top of the same colour, sleeves rolled back to the elbows. She looked pretty good, all-in-all, she thought. The average Culture human, from what she could gather having seen a few hundred of them now in passing – and disregarding the outlandish outliers, as it were – was hardly taller than a well-fed Sichultian, but ill-proportioned: legs too short, back too long, and emaciated-looking; bellies and behinds uncomfortably flat, shoulders and upper back looking almost broken. She supposed to them she looked hump-backed, pot-bellied and big-bottomed, but no matter; to her she looked exactly, almost perfectly right. And a beauty, which was what she had always been and had always been destined to be, with or without the cell-level markings that had invested her body, down to the bone and beyond.

She had no more false modesty, she realised, than Sensia, than the ship itself.

Lededje looked up from her arm. "I think I'd like some form of tat," she told Sensia.

"Tattooing?" the avatar said. "Easily done. Though we can definitely do better than just permanently marking your skin, unless that's what you specifically want."

"What, for example?"

"Take a look." Sensia waved one arm and in front of them, and, hanging over the thousand-metre drop, a series of images appeared of Culture humans displaying tattoos even more fabulous than her own had been, at least at skin level. Here were tattoos that genuinely shone rather than just glowed a little, or could reflect; tattoos that moved, that lased, that could loop out to create real or hologramatic structures beyond the surface of the skin itself, tattoos that were not just works of art but ongoing performances. "Have a think," Sensia said.

Lededje nodded. "Thank you. I shall." She looked out at the view again. Behind them, on the path on the far side of the low wall, a small group of people passed. They were talking the Culture's own language, Marain, which Lededje too could now speak and understand, though not without a certain deliberation; Sichultian Formal was still what came naturally to her and was what she and Sensia were speaking now. "You know that I need to get back to Sichult," she said.

"Business to conclude," Sensia said, nodding.

"When would I be able to leave?"

"How about tomorrow?"

She looked at the avatar's brazen skin. It looked false, as though she was made of metal, not genuine flesh and bone. Lededje supposed that was the idea. Her own skin was not so different in tone – from a distance she and Sensia might have looked quite similar in colour – but from close up hers would appear natural, both to a Sichultian and even, she was sure, this motley assortment of strange-looking people.

"That would be possible?"

"Well, you could make a start. You're some distance away. It'll take a while."

"How long?"

Sensia shrugged. "Depends on a lot of things. Many tens of days, I'd guess. Less than a hundred though, I'd hope." She made a gesture with her hands Lededje guessed was meant to signal regret or apology. "Can't take you myself; way off my course schedule. In fact, at the moment, we're heading sort of tangentially away from the Enablement space."

"Oh." Lededje hadn't realised this. "Then the sooner I get started the better."

"I'll put the word out to the ships, see who's interested," Sensia said. "However. There is a condition."

"A condition?" She wondered if there was, after all, some form of payment expected.

"Let me be honest with you, Lededje," Sensia said, with a quick smile.

"Please," she said.

"We – I – strongly suspect that you may be returning to Sichult with murder in your heart."

Lededje said nothing for as long as it took for her to realise that the longer she left it to respond, the more like agreement that silence seemed. "Why do you think that?" she asked, trying to imitate Sensia's level, friendly, matter-of-fact tone.

"Oh, come now, Lededje," the avatar chided. "I've done a little research. The man murdered you." She waved one hand casually. "Perhaps not in cold blood, but certainly when you were completely helpless. This is a man who has had complete control over you since before you were born, who forced your family into servitude and had you marked for ever as a chattel, engraved like a high-denomination bank-note made out specifically to him. You were his slave; you tried to run, he hunted you like an animal, caught you and, when you resisted, he killed you. Now you are free of him, and free of the marks that identified you as his but with a free pass back to where he – probably imagining that you are entirely dead – still is, quite unsuspecting." Sensia turned to Lededje at this point, swivelling not just her head but her shoulders and upper body, so that the younger woman could not pretend not to have noticed. Lededje turned too, less gracefully, as Sensia – still smiling – lowered and slowed her voice ever so slightly and said, "My child, you would not be human, pan-human, Sichultian or anything else if you didn't positively ache for revenge."

Lededje heard all this, but did not immediately react. *There is more*, she wanted to say. *There is more; it is not just about revenge* . . . but she couldn't say that. She looked away, kept staring at the view. "What would the condition be, then?" she asked.

Sensia shrugged. "We have these things called slap-drones."

"Oh yes?" She had vaguely heard of drones; they were the Culture's equivalent of robots, though they looked more like items of luggage than anything else. Some of the tinier things floating in the great hazy view in front of them were probably drones. She already didn't like the idea of a variety with the word "slap" in its title.

"They're things that stop people doing something they probably ought not to do," Sensia told her. "They . . . just accompany you." She shrugged. "Sort of an escort. If it thinks you're about to do something objectionable, like hit somebody or try to kill them or something, it'll stop you."

"Stop . . . how?"

Sensia laughed. "Well, just shout at you at first, probably. But if you persist, it'll physically get in the way; deflect a blow or push aside a gun barrel or whatever. Ultimately, though, they're entirely entitled to zap you; drop you unconscious if need be. No pain or damage, of course, but— "

"Who decides on this? What court?" Lededje asked. She felt suddenly hot, and was acutely aware that on her new, paler skin, a flush might show as a visible blush.

"The court of me, Lededje," Sensia said quietly, with a small smile Lededje glanced at then looked away from.

"Really? On whose authority?"

She could hear the smile in the avatar's voice. "On the authority of me being part of the Culture and my judgement on such matters being accepted by other parts, specifically other Minds, of the Culture. Immediately, because I can. Ultimately— "

"So, even in the Culture, might is right," Lededje said bitterly. She started rolling her sleeves down, feeling suddenly chilled.

"Intellectual might, I suppose," Sensia said gently. "As I was about to say, though, ultimately my right to impose a slap-drone on you comes down to the principle that it is what any set of morally responsible conscious entities, machine or human, would choose to do were they in possession of the same set of facts as I am. However, part of my moral responsibility to you is to point out that you are free to publicise your case. There are specialist news services who'd certainly be interested and – you being relatively exotic and from somewhere we have few dealings with – even the general news services might be interested too. Then there are specialist legal, procedural, jurisdictional, behavioural, diplomatic . . ." She shrugged again. "And probably even philosophical interest groups who'd love to hear about something like this. You'd definitely find somebody who'd argue your case."

"And who'd I be appealing to? You?"

"The court of informed public opinion," Sensia said. "This is the Culture, kid. That's the court of last resort. If I was convinced I'd made a mistake, or even if I thought I was right but everybody else appeared to think otherwise, I guess I'd reluctantly have to abandon the slap-drone thing. Being a ship Mind I'd take more notice of what other ship Minds thought, then other Minds in general, then AIs, humans, drones and others, though of course as this would be a dispute ultimately about a human's rights I'd have to give more than usual weight to the human vote. It sounds a little complicated but there are all sorts of well-known precedents and much-used, highly respected processes involved."

Sensia dipped forward and looked round at Lededje, trying to get her to look at her, though Lededje refused. "Look, Lededje, I don't mean to make it sound off-putting at all; the whole process would seem incredibly quick and informal to somebody with your background and understanding of the way courts and legal systems work and you wouldn't have to stay aboard me to see it through; you could start back for home and see how things turn out while you're en route. I say it would seem informal, but it'd be extremely thorough, and, frankly, much less likely to produce an unjust result than a similar case going through the courts you have back home. If you'd like to do this, please feel free. At any time. It's your right. Personally I don't think you'd have a hope in hell of getting off the slap-drone thing, but one never entirely knows with such matters and continually having seemingly obvious judgements challenged is pretty much how the system works."

Lededje thought about this. "How . . . secret has me being brought back to life been until now?"

"Right now, it's just between you and me, given that I can't find the *Me, I'm Counting*, the ship that we're assuming put the neural lace into your head in the first place."

Only after she'd done it did Lededje realise she'd put one hand to the back of her head as soon as Sensia had mentioned a lace. Her fingertips moved through the soft, short fair hair covering her scalp, tracing the contours of her own skull.

She'd been offered another neural lace, before she'd been woken up in this new body. She'd said no, and was still unsure why she'd made that choice. Anyway, one could be . . . installed later, even if the process required time to come to fully functioning fruition. That was what had happened with the last one, after all.

"What might have happened to the ship?" she asked. She had a sudden recollection of Himerance, sitting in the seat in her bedroom, dimly lit, talking quietly to her, ten years earlier.

"Happened to it?" Sensia sounded surprised. "Oh, it'll be off on a retreat, probably. Or wandering aimlessly, tramping the galaxy, or doggedly pursuing some weird obsession all of its own; either way all it needs is to stop telling people where it is and it disappears off the screens. Ships do that, especially old ships." She snorted. "*Especially* old ships that saw active service in the Idiran war. They're very prone to going Eccentric."

"So ships don't get slap-droned?" She tried to sound sarcastic.

"Oh, but they do, if they're especially strange, or of a certain . . . capital substance; a major ship." Sensia leaned in close and said, "Ship like me went Eccentric once, or seemed to. Can you imagine?" she said, pretending horror as she nodded out at the view. "Something this size? Went totally off the rails in a crisis and shook off the ship detailed to be its slap-drone."

"And how did that end?"

Sensia shrugged. "Not too badly. Could have been a bit better, could have been an awful lot worse."

Lededje thought a little more. "Then I think I'll just have to accept your judgement." She turned and smiled smoothly at the avatar. "I don't accept that it's necessary, but I'll . . . acquiesce." Sensia wore an expression of regret, and a small frown. "Though you should know," Lededje said, fighting to keep her voice under control, "that there is no possibility of the man who killed me being brought to justice for what he did to me, let alone suffering any punishment for it. He is a very charming, very powerful but completely evil man. He is utterly selfish and self-centred, and due to his position he can and does get away with anything – anything at all. He deserves to die. It would absolutely be the correct moral thing to do to kill Joiler Veppers, my personal grievance against him set entirely aside. If I am going back to my home with murder in my heart, as you put it, then you are making exactly the wrong moral choice in deciding to protect him."

"I understand how you feel, Lededje," the avatar said.

"I doubt it."

"Well, I certainly understand the force of what you're saying; please accept that at least. It's just not my place to pass judgement at such a remove on somebody I have no conceivable moral jurisdiction over."

"The Culture never interferes in other societies?" Lededje said, trying to sound scornful. It was one of the few things she could recall having heard about the Culture back in Sichult: its people were hopelessly effeminate, or unnaturally aggressive females (the story changed according to exactly which aspect of the Culture's alleged demeanour the Sichultian press and establishment wanted to portray as shocking, depraved or despicable), it didn't use money and it was ruled by its giant robot ships that interfered in other civilisations. Despite herself, she could feel tears welling up behind her eyes.

"Good grief, yes, we're interfering all the time," the avatar admitted. "But it's all carefully thought out, long-term managed and there's always got to be some strategic goal that'll benefit the people being interfered with." Sensia looked away for a moment. "Well, usually. That's not to say things don't go awry on occasion." She looked back at Lededje. "But that's all the more reason to take care. Especially when this is a person of such importance, with such a degree of fame, notoriety or whatever, and with control over so much of your civilisation's productive—"

"So his position, his *money* protects him even *here*?" Lededje protested, trying hard not to cry now.

"I'm sorry," Sensia said. "That's the reality of the situation. We don't make your rules. As an alien being he has as much right as anybody else has not to have me collude in any plot against his life; as a focus of power within your society, anything that happens to him matters more than it does to almost anybody else. It would be irresponsible not to take that into account even if I did share your desire to kill him."

"What chance would I have anyway," Lededje said, sniffing and looking away. "I'm no assassin. I could happily kill him but I've no particular skill in such matters. My only advantage is I know something of his estates and houses and the people who surround him." She raised her hand, studied its back and front. "And I don't look like I used to look, so I might have a chance of getting close to him."

"I imagine he's well protected," Sensia said. She paused for a moment. "Yes, I see that he is. "Your news services seem most taken with these cloned people, the Zei."

Lededje thought to say something to the effect that Jasken was the real bodyguard, Veppers' true last line of defence, but then thought the better of it. Best not be seen to be thinking in such terms. She sniffed some more, wiping her nose on her hand.

"You don't have to go back, Lededje," Sensia said gently. "You could stay here, make a new life in the Culture."

Lededje used the heels of her hands to dry round her eyes. "You know, for almost as long as I can remember that was the one thing

I wanted?" she said. She glanced at Sensia, who looked puzzled. "All those years, all those times I tried to run away, the one thing nobody ever asked me was where I might be running *to*." She smiled a small, thin smile at the avatar, who looked surprised now. "If they had asked," Lededje told her, "I might even have told them: I was running away to the Culture, because I'd heard they'd escaped the tyranny of money and individual power, and that all people were equal here, men and women alike, with no riches or poverty to put one person above or beneath another."

"But now you're here?" Sensia offered, sounding sad.

"But now I'm here I find Joiler Veppers is still deferred to because he is a rich and powerful man." She took a deep, shuddering breath. "And I find I need to return because that is my home, like it or not, and I must make my peace with it somehow." She looked sharply at Sensia. "Then I might come back. Would I be allowed to come back?"

"You'd be allowed."

Lededje nodded once and looked away.

They were both silent for a few moments. Then Sensia said, "Slap-drones can be quite useful companions, anyway; willing and obedient servants – bodyguards, too – so long as you don't try to kill or injure somebody. I'll choose you a good one."

"I'm sure we'll get on just fine," Lededje said.

She wondered how easy it would be to lose a slap-drone. Or to kill it, too.

Yime Nsokyi stood in the main room of her apartment, her stance upright, her booted feet together, her head slightly back, her hands clasped behind her back. She was dressed formally in long dark grey boots, grey trousers, a light blouse and a plain grey jacket with a stiff, high collar. She had a pen terminal in the breast pocket of the jacket and a back-up terminal in the shape of an earbud attached to the lobe of her left ear. Her hair was very neatly combed.

"Ms. Nsokyi, hello."

"Good day."

"You look very . . . poised. Wouldn't you rather sit?"

"I prefer to stand."

"Okay." The avatar of the GCU *Bodhisattva, OAQS* had appeared, Displaced apparently, in front of her a moment earlier, its coming heralded half an hour before by the call she'd received. She had had time to dress and compose herself. The avatar took the form of an old-looking drone, nearly a metre long, half that across and a quarter-metre in height. It floated at eye level. "I shall take it we may dispense with any pleasantries," it said.

"That would be my choice," Yime agreed.

"I see. In that case, are you ready to . . .?"

Yime flexed her knees, picked up a small soft bag at her feet and stood again. "Fully," she said.

"Okay then."

The avatar and the human female disappeared inside two silver ellipsoids which had hardly appeared before they shrank to two points and vanished, not quite fast enough to create two tiny claps of thunder, but sufficiently quickly to cause a draught that ruffled the leaves of nearby plants.

Prin awoke from the long and terrible real nightmare of his time in Hell and found Chay, his true love, gazing over at him as he lay, blinking, on the clinic bed. He was on his side, looking at her; she was on her other side on a bed a metre away, facing him. Her eyes blinked slowly.

It had taken a while for him to register where he was, who this person looking over at him was, even who he himself was. At first all he knew was that he was somewhere vaguely medical, that he felt something very sweet and special for the female lying opposite, and that he had done something important and terrifying.

Hell. He had been in Hell. They had been in Hell; he and Chay. They had gone in there to prove that it was real, not a myth, and that it was a vile, perverted version of an afterlife, a place of unredeemed cruelty, impossible to defend in any civilised society.

They had sought to witness this and then to bring the evidence back and do what they could to make it public; get it disseminated as widely as possible, defying the state, the government, the political-commercial establishment and all the various vested interests which wanted their Hell – all the hells – to continue.

Now, here they were, back in the Real, the two of them.

He couldn't quite speak yet. He was lying on this bed, in what certainly looked like the clinic they had left from, with Chay on the bed opposite his. They had transferred their personalities into electronic or photonic form or whatever it was – he had never been interested in the technical details – and they had set out together for Hell.

He could hear faint beeping noises, and see various pieces of medical equipment and communications gear stationed around their two beds.

"Prin! You're back!" a voice said. He recognised the voice, or at least knew that he ought to know who the speaker was. A male came into view.

He did recognise him. Irkun. He was called Irkun and he was the medic-cum-comms-wizard who had been overseeing the transfer of their personalities, their beings, from their own bodies, through the communications network to wherever the state-run link to Hell was, and then on to the Hell itself. And back, of course. That was the point; they had to come back, and so they'd been sent with lengths of code attached that would let them come back. In the Hell these had been disguised as necklaces of barbed wire. They gave the wearer one brief spell to impersonate one of the more powerful and privileged demons within the Hell, and one chance to get back out of the virtual world back to the Real.

He remembered the blue glowing gate and the mill and the valley side with the X-shaped devices bearing the rotting corpses.

Blue glowing gate, and his desperate leap, holding her . . .

Tumbling in the air, somersaulting so that he went through first, her in his limbs immediately afterwards, if possible.

"You made it!" Irkun said, clapping both trunks together. He was dressed like a medic; white waistcoat, tail bunned and pinned, hooves in little white bootees. "You're back! You made it! And Chay, is she . . . ?"

Irkun turned to look at Chay. She was still staring straight ahead. Prin had thought she was gazing at him, but of course, she wasn't. She blinked slowly, again, exactly as she had a little earlier.

"... right behind you?" Irkun asked, voice trailing away a little as he looked at the medical units and comms gear gathered around her bed. He pulled out a tablet remote and started tapping at it, trunk-fingers dancing over the icons, letters and numbers. "Is she ... ?" he said, falling silent. He stopped tapping at the remote and looked, stricken, at Prin.

Irkun, Chay, the bed she was lying on and the whole small clinic room – on a houseboat in a lagoon off a shallow sea – all started to waver and dissolve as tears began to fill Prin's eyes.

There were three others besides Prin and Irkun. They had kept the core team as small as they possibly could to avoid the pro-Hell people finding out.

They lay on couches on a deck looking out over the lagoon towards the distant dunes and the sea. Birds flew across the reflection of a livid sunset, dark shapes against the long rips and tearings of the cloud-streaked sky. There were no other boats or houseboats visible. The one they were on looked innocent enough, though it concealed some very hi-tech gear and a buried optic cable linking them to a satellite array in the nearest small town, kilometres distant. Prin had been awake for about half a day now. They needed to decide what to do next, especially about Chay.

"If we leave her under we can re-integrate her fine, whenever she comes back," Biath said. He was their mind-state expert.

"Even with a broken mind?" Prin asked.

"Certainly," Biath said, as though this was some sort of accomplishment.

"So we take a perfectly healthy sleeping mind and plonk a broken one into it and it's the broken one that wins, that emerges?" Yolerre said. She was their main programmer, the whiz that had come up with the barbed-wire code to let them escape from the Hell.

Biath shrugged. "The newer writes over the older," he told her. "That's just normal."

"But if we wake her—?" Prin began.

"If we wake her she'll be just as she was before the two of you went under," Sulte said. He was their mission controller, their main ex-government source and another comms expert. "But the longer she's awake and living any sort of normal life, the harder it gets to re-integrate her two personalities: the unconscious one here that doesn't include her experiences in the Hell and the virtually conscious one – wherever it is – that does." He looked at Biath, who nodded to this.

"Which, given that the latter will probably leave her out of her mind," Irkun said, "may be for the best."

"She could be treated," Irkun said. There are techniques."

"These techniques ever been tried on somebody carrying all the nightmares of Hell in their head?" Yolerre asked.

Irkun just shook his head and made a sucking noise.

"How long before any re-integration becomes impossible?" Prin asked.

"At worst, problematic within hours," Biath said. "Few days probably. Week at the most. Over-write would be brutal, could leave her . . . catatonic at best. Only humane course would be trying to prise the Hell memories in piecemeal." He shook his head. "Very likely her continuance personality would just reject the memories completely. Nightmares would need watching."

"You really don't think she's likely to pop out soon?" Irkun asked Prin. Irkun had his tablet remote propped up in front of him, monitoring Chay's condition in the clinic room just a few metres away.

Prin shook his head. "I don't think there's any chance," he said. "She'd forgotten what the emergency code was, what it was for, how you operated it; like I keep saying, she even denied that there was any Real. And those bastard demons would have been on her in seconds after I barged through. If she didn't follow me in a few heartbeats, she isn't following me for . . . months." He started crying again. The others saw, huddled closer, made soothing noises, and those closest reached out to touch him with their trunks.

He looked round them all. "I think we have to wake her," he told them.

"What happens if we do get her back?" Yolerre asked.

"She can be given some sort of existence in a virtual world," Sulte said. "Fact is it'll be easier to treat her there, yes?" he said glancing at Biath, who nodded.

"Do we need to take a vote?" Irkun asked.

"I think it's Prin's call," Sulte said. The others nodded, made noises of assent.

"You'll have her back, Prin," Yolerre said, reaching out to stroke him gently with one trunk.

Prin looked away. "No, I won't," he said.

When they did wake her, the following morning, he had already left.

He didn't want to see her. He didn't want to abandon the one he loved and who was still in Hell by accepting the love of the one who had never been there, no matter how whole, perfect and un-traumatised she might be.

No doubt this Chay, this one who had never seen Hell, would feel injured by his actions, and not understand how he could be so cruel to her, but then he had seen what real hurt and real cruelty was, and the person that he was now could never pretend that what had happened to the two of them in Hell had somehow not taken place, and changed who he was for ever.

The room where Lededje had woken, to see Sensia sitting outside on the balcony, was hers for as long as she stayed on the ship. After their tour in a small, very quiet aircraft – the GSV was appropriately mind-boggling from every external angle and internal corridor – Sensia had dropped Lededje off nearby, where one of the kilometres-long internal corridors abutted one of the little stepped valleys of accommodation units, given her a long, silvery and elaborate ring – a thing called a terminal that let her talk to the ship – then left her to find her own way back to the room and otherwise sort herself out. Sensia said she'd be a call away, happy to be a guide, companion or whatever. In the meantime, she imagined Lededje might want to rest, or just have some time to herself.

The ring fitted itself to Lededje's longest finger and gave spoken directions back to her room. One wall of the room acted as a screen and allowed apparently unrestricted access to the ship's equivalent of the Sichultian datasphere. She sat, started asking questions.

"Welcome aboard," said the avatar drone of the *Bodhisattva*. "May I take your bag?"

Yime nodded. Instead of the avatar taking it from her, the bag simply disappeared from her hand, leaving the skin on her fingers with a tingling feeling. She wobbled on her feet and almost staggered as the bag's weight was suddenly removed from that side of her body, leaving her unbalanced. "You'll find it in your cabin," the avatar said.

"Thank you." Yime looked down. She was standing on nothing. It felt like a very hard nothing, but – just looking – there didn't seem to be anything beneath her feet except stars arranged in familiar-looking wispy sprays and whorls. Stars to the sides, too. Above her, a vast dark presence; a ceiling of polished black reflecting the stars shining beneath her feet. Looking straight up, she saw a ghost-pale version of herself, looking straight back down.

Beneath, she recognised the patterns of the stars as those visible from her home Orbital of Dinyol-hei. Though given that she had just left her apartment in the later afternoon, these were not the stars she'd have expected to see if they'd simply moved straight down from her apartment to the part of the Orbital beneath where she lived. The ship was obviously some distance further away. She felt pleased with herself to have worked this out so quickly.

"Do you need time to freshen up, adjust, orientate yourself or otherwise—?" the drone began.

"No," Yime said. She stood as she had before, though with feet spread a little. "May we begin?"

"Yes. Your full attention, please," the *Bodhisattva* said.

Your full attention. Yime felt mildly insulted. Still, this was Quietus. It was known for its air of formal austerity and a degree of implicit asceticism. If you didn't like the discipline involved in most things Quietudinal you shouldn't have signed up in the first place.

There was a spiteful rumour, seemingly incapable of being entirely laid to rest, that the more recently manifested specialist divisions of the Culture's Contact section were only there to provide substitute employment niches for those desperate but unable to make the cut and get into Special Circumstances itself.

Contact was the part of the Culture that handled more or less every aspect of the Culture's interactions with everything and everybody that wasn't the Culture, from the investigation of unexplored star systems to relations with the entire panoply of other civilisations at every developmental level, from those still unable to scrape together the plan for a world government or a functioning space elevator to the elegantly otiose but nevertheless potentially deeply powerful Elders and the still more detached-from-reality Sublimed, where any vestige or trace of such exotic entities remained.

Special Circumstances was, in effect, the Contact section's espionage wing.

There had always been specialist sub-divisions within the organisational behemoth that was Contact. Special Circumstances was only the most obvious and, uniquely, it had been formally separate almost since its inception; largely because it sometimes did the sort of things the people who were proud to be part of Contact would have been horrified to have been remotely associated with.

As time had passed though, especially over the last half-thousand years or so, Contact itself had seen fit to introduce various re-organisations and rationalisations which had resulted in the creation of three other specialist divisions, of which the Quietudinal Service was one.

The Quietudinal Service – Quietus, as it was usually called – dealt with the dead. The dead outnumbered the living in the greater galaxy by some distance, if you added up all those individuals existing in the various Afterlives the many different civilisations had created over the millennia. Happily – mercifully – the dead generally tended to keep themselves to themselves and caused relatively little trouble compared to those for whom the Real was still the place to exist within and try to exploit. However, the sheer scale of their numbers ensured that important issues involving the deceased still arose now and again; the dead Quietus dealt with might be technically departed, but they were, sometimes, far from quiet.

A lot of the time such matters were effectively about legality, even about definitions; in a lot of societies the principal difference between a live virtual person – possibly just passing through, as it were, between bodies, back in the Real – and a dead virtual person was that the latter had no right to property or any other kind of ownership outside of their own simulated realm. Perhaps not unnaturally, there were those amongst the dead who found such a distinction unfair. This sort of thing could lead to trouble, but Quietus was skilled in dealing with the results.

Relatively small in terms of ships and personnel, Quietus could nevertheless call on whole catalogued suites of dead but preserved experts and expert systems – not all of which were even pan-human in origin – to help them deal with such matters, bringing them back from their fun-filled retirement or out of suspended animation, where they had left instructions that they were ready to be revived if they could be of use when circumstances required.

Slanged as "Probate" by some of those in SC, Quietus had links with Special Circumstances, but regarded itself as a more specialised service than its much older and larger sibling utility. Most of the humans within Quietus regarded any links with SC as deplorable in essence and only very occasionally necessary, if ever. Some just plain looked down on Special Circumstances. Theirs, they felt, was a higher, more refined calling and their demeanour, behaviour, appearance and even dress reflected this.

Quietus ships added the letters OAQS – for On Active Quietudinal Service – to their names while they were so employed, and usually took on a monochrome outer guise, either pure shining white in appearance or glossily black. They even moved quietly, adjusting the configuration of their engine fields to produce the minimum amount of disturbance both on the sub-universal energy grid and the 3D skein of real space. Normal Culture ships either went for maximum efficiency or the always popular let's-see-what-we-can-squeeze-out-of-these-babies approach.

Similarly, the human and other biological operatives of Quietus were expected to be sober, serious people while they were on duty, and to dress appropriately.

It was to this division of Contact that Yime belonged.

Your full attention, indeed. Oh well. Rather than reply, Yime just nodded.

Suddenly she was surrounded waist deep in stars. The drone, the far-distant stars beneath her feet and their reflections had all disappeared. "This is the Ruprine Cluster, in Arm One-one Near-tip," the ship's voice said all around her.

Arm One-one Near-tip was a little under three hundred light years distant from the region of space where the Orbital Dinyol-hei lay circling around the sun Etchilbieth. In galactic terms, this was practically next door.

"These stars," the ship said as a few dozen of the suns shown turned from their natural colours to green, "represent the extent of a small civilisation called the Sichultian Enablement, a Level Four/Five society originating here." One of the green stars blazed brightly, then reduced in brilliance. "The Quyn system; home of the planet Sichult where the pan-human Sichultians evolved." A pair of pan-humans were shown, standing just outside the ball of stars surrounding Yime. Curious physical proportions, Yime thought. Two sexes; each a little odd-looking to her eyes, just as she would have been to theirs, she supposed. Their skin colours changed as she looked at them, from dark to pale then back to dark, with yellow, red and olive tones exhibited en route. The two naked beings were replaced by one clothed one. He appeared tall, powerfully built and had long white hair.

"This is a man called Joiler Veppers," the ship told her. "He is the richest individual in the entire civilisation, and by some margin. He is also the most powerful individual in the entire civilisation – though unofficially, through his wealth and connections rather than due to formal political position."

The image of the stellar cluster with its artificially green stars and the tall, white-haired man both vanished to be replaced by the earlier image of the stars constituting the Sichultian Enablement, with the Quyn system's sun still shown as the brightest.

"Ms. Nsokyi," the ship said, "are you aware of the current, long-running confliction over the future of the Afterlives known as Hells?"

"Yes," Yime said.

Confliction was the technically correct term for a formal conflict within a virtual reality – i.e. one where the outcome mattered beyond the confines of the virtual battle environment itself – but mostly people just called this one the War in Heaven. It had been running now for nearly three decades and had yet to produce a result. She'd heard reports recently that it was finally coming close to a conclusion, but then there had been similar reports almost every hundred days since it had started so she had taken no more notice than anybody else. Most people had long since lost interest.

"Good," the ship said. "Mr. Veppers controls the largest part of the Enablement's productive capacity and – through one of his interests in particular – has access to this." A star near the outer limit of the Enablement's volume blazed too, attracting attention. The view zoomed in vertiginously until it showed a single-ringed gas giant planet. Between its broad, dun-coloured polar regions, the planet displayed seven horizontal bands coloured various shades of yellow, red and brown.

"This," the ship said, as the entirety of the single equatorial ring surrounding the planet flashed green once, "is the artificial planetary nebula of the Tsungarial Disk, around the planet Razhir, in the Tsung system. The Disk comprises over three hundred million separate habitats and – mostly – manufacturies, usually called fabricaria. The Disk was abandoned two million years ago by the then

Subliming Meyeurne and has been a Galactic Protectorate since shortly after their disappearance. The Protectorate status was agreed to be necessary due to a chaotic, dangerously uncontrolled war both over and enabled by the very considerable ship-and-weapon-system-manufacturing capacity left behind, at least irresponsibly, possibly mischievously and arguably maliciously by the Meyeurne. The civilisations involved were the Hreptazyle and the Yelve."

The ship didn't bother to display any images of the Meyeurne, Hreptazyle or Yelve. Certainly Yime had never heard of any of them, which meant they were either long gone or just irrelevant.

"Shortly following the Idiran War," the *Bodhisattva* said, "the Culture became the latest in a long line of trusted Level Eights to be given Protectorate custody of the Disk. However, as part of what were in effect war reparations after the Chel debacle, six hundred years ago, we ceded overarching control of the Disk to the Nauptre Reliquaria and their junior partners the GFCF."

Yime most certainly had heard of the Nauptre Reliquaria and the GFCF. Like the Culture, the Reliquaria was a Level Eight civilisation; technologically the societies were equals. Originally a species of giant, furred, gliding marsupials, for the last couple of millennia they had expressed themselves almost exclusively as their machines: GSV-sized constructor ships, smaller though still substantial space vessels, lesser independent space-faring units and a multifarious variety of metre-scale individuals roughly equivalent to drones, though with no standard model; each design was unique or close to it. Their presence then extended down through the centimetre and millimetre scales to collectivised nanobots.

The furry marsupials still existed, but they'd retreated to their home planets and habitats to lives of cheerfully selfish indolence, leaving their machines to represent them in the galactic community. Generally reckoned to be well on the slippery (if confusingly, by convention, upward) slope to Subliming, the Reliquaria's relations with the Culture were formal – perhaps even frosty – rather than friendly, largely due to the Nauptrians' robust attitude to punishment in their artificial Afterlife.

Basically, they were very much for it.

Unlike the Culture, which – despite being firmly of a mind with the anti-Hell side of the confliction – had thought it politic to take no active part in the virtual war, the Nauptrians had made themselves an enthusiastic part of the pro-Hell war effort.

The Geseptian-Fardesile Cultural Federacy was a Level Seven civilisation. Pan-human, smaller and more delicate than the average but generally reckoned to be quite beautiful, with large heads and large eyes, they had a strange relationship with the Culture, professing to love it – they had even chosen their name partly in honour of the Culture – but often seeming to want to criticise it and even work against it, as though they so much wanted to be of help they needed the Culture reduced to a level of neediness that would make such aid something it would genuinely be grateful for.

The mention of Chel was randomly appropriate, Yime thought. Before that particular stain on the Culture's reputation people had seemed reticent to talk about the whole issue of Afterlives. After it, for a while at least, they'd appeared to talk of little else.

"The components of the Tsungarial Disk have mostly been mothballed for all this time," the ship continued, "left as a kind of monument or mausoleum. Over the last few decades, however, as the Sichultia have expanded their sphere of influence out to and around it, they have been granted limited, low-level control over the Disk and allowed, in the shape of Veppers' Veprine Corporation, to use a handful of the orbital manufactories to construct trading and exploratory ships, all of this supervised by the Nauptre Reliquaria and the GFCF.

"Veppers and the Sichultia have long sought greater operational control over the Disk and its manufacturing capacity to aid their commercial, military and civilisational expansion. They are now on the verge of achieving their goal due to the changing attitudes, not to say connivance, of the GFCF and the Reliquaria. This is because the GFCF covets at least some of that capacity as well – their medium-term aim is to step up a civilisational level, and control of the reactivated Disk's productive capacity would go some way to securing it – while the Nauptre Reliquaria are pro-Hell, in the short term wanting the pro/anti-Hell confliction ended – and with what they see as the right result – as well as, in the long term, and assuming they do not Sublime in the meantime, by their own admission planning to combine all Afterlives with their own and others Sublimed. That nobody else thinks this is even possible does not seem to trouble them and is anyway beside the point."

"Why does the Reliquaria being pro-Hell have anything to do with control of the Disk?" Yime asked.

"Because the Disk's productive or possibly computational capacity may come into play in an outbreak from the confliction into the Real."

"An outbreak?" Yime felt genuinely shocked. Conflictions – virtual wars – were there specifically to stop people warring in the Real.

"The pro/anti-Hell confliction may be about to end," the ship said, "in victory for the pro-Hell side."

That was a blow for the Culture, Yime thought. Even though it had seemingly stood aside from the war, there had never been any doubt which side it believed in.

It was all just bad timing, in a way. At the point when the war began, the Culture had been in one of its cyclic eras of trying not to be seen to be throwing its weight around. Too many others of the In-Play Level Eights had objected to the Culture being involved with the War in Heaven for it to be able to do so without looking arrogant, even belligerent.

The assumption had somehow always been that the pro-Hell forces were going to be fighting a losing battle anyway and their defeat was probably inevitable no matter who did or didn't join in. Seemingly, the more the In-Play and the Elders thought about it, the more obvious it became that the whole idea of Afterlives dedicated to extended torture was indeed barbaric, unnecessary and outdated, and the course of the confliction over the continued existence of the Hells was expected to follow this slow but decisive shift in opinion. At the time, the prospect of the Culture getting involved seemed likely to most people to make the conflict less fair, its outcome effectively fixed before it even began.

For a virtual war to work, people had to accept the outcome; the losing side in particular had to abide by the result rather than cry foul, revoke the solemn pledges they had made in the War Conduct Agreement drawn up before the conflict began, and continue as things had been before. The consensus had been that the Culture taking part would give the pro-Hell side the excuse to do just that, if and when they lost.

"The anti-Hell side," the ship continued, "was the first to attempt to hack the other's conflict-direction processing substrates. The opposing side retaliated. The anti-Hell side has additionally attempted direct hacking attacks on some of the Hells themselves, seeking either to release the inmates or to destroy the virtual environments completely.

"The various hacking attacks by both sides have almost all failed, those that succeeded did little damage and the vast majority of those by both sides were detected by those targeted, leading to multiple judging and arbitration disputes, all of which are currently being kept sub judice; successfully so far though probably not for much longer. Extensive legal and diplomatic disputes are anticipated and almost certainly being prepared for.

"There are certain so-far unsubstantiated reports that some of the secret substrates within which several major Hells are running are located not where one might expect to find them – essentially, within the volumes of influence of their parent civilisations – but instead within the Tsungarial Disk or elsewhere within the Sichultian Enablement. The worry is that an outbreak of the confliction into the Real may involve the Tsungarial Disk, especially the until-now dormant majority of the fabricaria and the hidden substrates that may also lie there. If this is truly the case then the potential for a substantial war in the Real would seem high.

"Thus the Sichultian Enablement suddenly and unexpectedly finds itself in a position of power well beyond that which its developmental level would lead one to expect. It is poised to contribute significantly, possibly decisively, to a situation of extreme importance, the outcome of which might lead directly to a significant conflict in the Real involving several high-level Players. Given that Mr. Veppers is so powerful within the Sichultian Enablement, what he thinks and does therefore becomes of profound importance."

Yime thought about this. "Why would we – why would Quietus be involved?"

"There is a complication," the ship told her.

"I thought there might be."

"In fact, there are two."

"That I did not anticipate," Yime admitted.

"The first concerns this person." A figure appeared.

"Hmm," Yime said, after a moment. The figure was of a pan-human: a Sichultian, Yime would have guessed from the rather odd bodily proportions. This one was female, bald or shaven-headed and dressed in a short sleeveless tunic which displayed extensive and intricate multi-coloured abstract markings on her night-black skin. She was smiling. Looking closely, Yime could see further markings on the female's teeth and the whites of her eyes. The two naked figures she'd been shown earlier hadn't had anything like that. Those, though, had been generalised, textbook figures. The person shown here, like the image of Veppers, was an individual. "Sichultian?" she asked.

"Yes."

"The markings aren't natural."

"Correct."

"Are they . . . real?"

"They were real and permanent. They continued within her body. She was an Intagliate, one of a subset of humans within the Sichultian Enablement who are tattooed throughout their physical being. The practice began as an art form though later also became a form of punishment, especially for matters regarding private civil debt."

Yime nodded. What a bizarre thing to do, she thought.

"Her name is Lededje Y'breq," the ship told her.

"*She was an Intagliate*," but "*Her name is . . .*" Yime noticed. Ship Minds didn't make mistakes like that. She suspected she already knew where this was going.

"Ms. Y'breq died between five and ten days ago in Ubruater, the capital city of the Sichultian Enablement's originating planet, Sichult," the ship told her. "She may have been murdered. If so then the murderer may have been Joiler Veppers, or somebody controlled by him, somebody in his employ. The Sichultia do not possess, or, as far as we know, have even limited access to mind-state transcription or 'soulkeeper' technology, however there is an unconfirmed report that Ms. Y'breq's personality was somehow retrieved from her when she died and that she was revented aboard the GSV *Sense Amid Madness, Wit Amidst Folly*."

"Oh. It was nearby?"

"It was nowhere near nearby; it was over three thousand light years distant from the nearest part of the Sichultian Enablement at the time, and no ships or other entities representing or associated with the vessel were closer than approximately nine hundred years away at the time either. Nor had the ship or any of its known associates ever had any recorded dealings with the Sichultian Enablement."

"How mysterious."

"There is a possible link, however, between these seemingly unrelated components."

"Ah-hah."

"We'll come to that shortly. The salient point to be made here is that it is believed that Ms. Y'breq may be on her way back to the Sichultian Enablement, revented within a quite different body – probably still Sichultian in form, though, for all we know, male – and bearing the intention of doing some violence, likely fatal, to Mr. Veppers, in revenge for her earlier murder."

"So what am I supposed to do? Stop her? Help her?"

"As things stand, simply finding her and keeping in touch would be sufficient achievement. You would then await further orders."

"So she's our excuse," Yime suggested.

"I beg your pardon, Ms. Nsokyi?"

"This girl, being revented. She's our excuse for getting involved in all this."

"Her revention is one reason to get involved. I'm not sure that characterising it as an 'excuse' is entirely helpful." The ship's voice sounded frosty. "Also, this entire confliction is specifically about the fate of the dead. It is entirely within the remit of Quietus."

"But isn't this more of an SC thing?" Yime suggested. "In fact, hasn't this got Special Circumstances written all over it?"

She waited for a reply, but one did not appear to be immediately forthcoming. She went on. "This does sound like it involves tangling with equiv-tech galactic Players with the intention of stopping a proper ships-and-everything full-scale shooting war. I'm not sure how much more hardcore SC than that a situation can get."

"That's an interesting observation."

"Is SC involved in this?"

"Not that we know of."

"Who would 'we' be within this context?"

"Let me re-phrase that last reply: Not that *I* know of."

This was mildly illuminating. Quietus had a deliberately flat organisational structure; in theory perfectly so at ship level, all the Minds concerned having equal knowledge and an equal say. In practice there was a degree of legislative/executive, strategic/tactical distinction, some Minds and ships doing the planning while others subsequently undertook the execution.

"Shouldn't we tell SC?" she asked.

"I'm sure that is being considered. My immediate task is to brief and transport you. Yours, Ms. Nsokyi, is to attend to this briefing and, assuming you are agreeable, take part in this mission."

"I see." Yime nodded. That was *her* told. "What's the other complication?"

The projection of the brown, red and yellow gas giant with its artificial ring system returned, replacing the image of the Sichultian female.

"Approximately two hundred and eight thousand years ago a proportion of the dormant fabricaria in the Tsungarial Disk suffered a smatter infection in the shape of the remains of a hegemonising swarm outbreak which took refuge there. The hegswarm was duly dealt with in the usual manner and annihilated by the cooperative of civilisations then responsible for overseeing that volume of space. The smatter infection was assumed to have been expunged from the Disk components at the same time. However, isolated recurrences of it have taken place over random intervals ever since. Due to its earlier success in dealing rapidly and effectively with these sporadic flare-ups, a small, specialist Culture presence was allowed to remain even after the Culture lost the mandate for the Disk's protection."

Yime nodded. "Ah. Pest Control."

"The specialist Culture contingent in the Tsungarial Disk is indeed part of the Restoria section."

Restoria was the part of Contact charged with taking care of hegemonising swarm outbreaks, when – by accident or design – a set of self-replicating entities ran out of control somewhere and started trying to turn the totality of the galaxy's matter into nothing but copies of themselves. It was a problem as old as life in the galaxy and arguably hegswarms were just that; another legitimate – if rather over-enthusiastic – galactic life-form type.

Even the most urbanely sophisticated, scrupulously empathic and excruciatingly polite civilisation, it had been suggested, was just a hegswarm with a sense of proportion. Equally, then, those same sophisticated civilisations could be seen as the galaxy's way of retaining a sort of balance between raw and refined, between wilderness and complexity, as well as ensuring that there was both always room for new intelligent life to evolve and that there was something wild, unexplored and interesting for it to gaze upon when it did. The Restoria section was the Culture's current specialist contribution to this age-old struggle. As often known as Pest Control as by its official title, it was made up of experts in the management, amelioration and – if necessary – obliteration of hegswarms.

Quietus and Restoria worked together closely on occasion and both felt that they did so with mutual respect and on equal terms.

Restoria's approach to its task and hence general demeanour was less punctilious than Quietus', but then the ships, systems and humans in Pest Control generally spent their working lives rushing from hegswarm eruption to hegswarm eruption rather than communing with the honoured dead, so a buccaneering rather than considered and respectful bearing was only to be expected.

"The Restoria mission at the Tsungarial Disk has been kept informed regarding the potential for the fabricaria to come into play should the confliction spill over into the Real and has requested any help that might be available so long as it draws no extra external attention to the mission or the Disk. We are happy to provide and are lucky to have had assets, including but not limited to myself, and you, close by, given that the situation may become one of extreme urgency very quickly. Whether Restoria has also made such a request to Special Circumstances is not known to us.

"It is worth noting that the smatter infestation within the Disk has been in abatement for the last few decades and will, it is hoped, not enter into the equation."

Smatter was the name given to the bitty remains of a hegswarm after it had been stamped out as any coherent threat. Usually it didn't last significantly longer than the outbreak itself and just got mopped up. If some bits did persist then, while you could never afford to ignore the stuff, you didn't really need to fear it. On the other hand, some of it getting into a mothballed system of a few hundred million ancient mothballed manufacturies did sound like awfully bad luck, Yime thought. Actually, it sounded like the kind of thing that woke Restoria people up at night, sweating and screaming.

The image of the gas giant planet and its glittering, artificial disk rotated slowly and silently in front of Yime.

"What was the possible link between the 'components' you mentioned earlier?" she asked.

"It is a potential link between the GSV *Sense Amid Madness, Wit Amidst Folly* and the Sichultian Enablement in the shape of this vessel.'

The ringed gas giant disappeared to be replaced by the slim but chunky image of a Hooligan-class Limited Offensive Unit. It looked like a long, quite substantial bolt with various smoothed-off washers, nuts and longer collars screwed onto it.

"This is the *Me, I'm Counting*, an ex-LOU now of the Culture Ulterior," the ship told her. "It was constructed by the *Sense Amid Madness, Wit Amidst Folly* shortly before the Idiran war and is thought to remain in sporadic contact with it. It is a self-declared Peripatetic Eccentric: a wanderer, a tramp vessel. It was last heard of with any formal degree of certitude some eight years ago when it declared it might go into a retreat. It is thought to have been present in the Sichultian Enablement two years earlier and so may constitute the mentioned link between it and the *Sense Amid Madness, Wit Amidst Folly*. There are indications that it accumulates images of strange and exotic creatures or devices and it may have chosen to collect such an image of Lededje Y'breq."

"That would be a very comprehensive image."

"It would."

"And one which would be ten years younger than the female when she died. She wouldn't know she'd been murdered, if she was."

"She might simply have been told."

Yime nodded. "I suppose she might."

"We think we know, to a degree," the ship said, a note of caution in its voice, "where the *Me, I'm Counting* is."

"Do we?"

"It may well be with the GSV *Total Internal Reflection*."

"And where is *it*?"

"That is not known. It is one of the Forgotten."

"The *what*?"

"Ah."

Ten

"A what?"

"A hymen."

There were things to do, Lededje had decided, and she might only have one night on the GSV to get them done. Getting laid was not the most important item on her list, but it didn't feel like the least important either.

The attractive young man looked puzzled. "How would I know?"

At least she thought that was what he'd just said. The music was very loud. There were these zones scattered throughout the space that were called sound fields where the music magically dropped away to nothing. She saw the vague blue glow in the air that betrayed the presence of one a couple of metres away and – rather daringly, she felt – putting her hand on the attractive young man's puffy sleeve, part encouraged and part dragged him in that direction.

Maybe it was her, she thought; she was talking Marain, the Culture's own language, and while it felt bizarrely natural to just launch out and express herself in it, every time she stopped to think about what she was doing she sort of tripped over herself and stuttered to a stop. Sometimes specific word-choice had her stumbling too; there seemed to be an awful lot of not-quite synonyms in Marain.

The very loud, insistently beaty music – it was called Chug, apparently, though she had yet to establish whether this was the title of the composition, the name of the performer/s or the musical form itself – faded almost to nothing. The attractive young man still looked puzzled.

"You look puzzled," she told him. "Can't you just look the word up in your neural lace?"

"I don't have a lace," he said, running his hand over one side of his face and through some of his long, dark, curly hair. "Right now I don't even have a terminal on me; I'm out to play." He looked up to where the cone of the noise-reducing sound field seemed to be emanating, from the ceiling of the space, unseen in the darkness above. "Ship, what's a hayman?"

"A hymen," she corrected.

"A hymen is a thin membrane partially obstructing the vagina of a mammal, especially a human," the ship said from the long silver ring on her finger. "It is found in approximately twenty-eight per cent of the pan-human meta-species and its presence is often taken as signifying the individual concerned has yet to be subject to penetrative sex. However— "

"Thanks," the attractive young man curled his fingers round the ring on her finger, muffling the ship's voice and causing it to stop.

Lededje smiled as he took his fingers away. It had been quite an intimate act, she felt. Promising. She lowered her head to her hand a little. "Do *I* have a hymen?" she asked quietly.

"No," the ring said. "Please hold me up to one of your ears."

"Excuse me," Lededje said to the attractive young man. He shrugged, drank his drink, looked away.

"Lededje, Sensia here," the ring said. "The body blank I used didn't come with defined genitalia at all; it was told to become female at the same time as the basic Sichultian characteristics were programmed in. The default setting is no hymen. Why? Do you want one?"

She brought the ring round to her mouth. "No!" she whispered. She frowned, watching the attractive young man smile and nod to somebody nearby.

He didn't look Sichultian, of course, but he looked . . . different; a bit the way she looked different. When she had come up with her general plan of action, hours earlier, sitting in front of the wall screen in her room after Sensia had left her, she had asked about and quickly found various scheduled social gatherings of those amongst the ship's not-quite quarter of a billion population who did not look like the average Culture human. In a ship with that many people aboard there were always going to be plenty of individuals who didn't conform to the Culture norm.

The way to think of the ship's living space, she'd decided, was as a single giant city, fifty kilometres long by twenty across and a uniform kilometre in height. With a perfect, free and rapid public transport system composed of what she thought of as small, luxurious, one-carriage ultra-fast underground trains crossed with elevator cars. She was used to the idea of cities attracting the eccentric and the strange, the people who would be ostracised or even attacked in the countryside or smaller towns and villages if they behaved as they really wanted to behave but who could become themselves, amongst others of whatever kind they were, when they came to the city. She'd known she would find some people somewhere who would find her attractive.

There was still the matter of finding what she was coming to think of as The Alternative Ship, though, and that did take priority. This place – Divinity In Extremis – was some sort of combination of semi-regular social event, performance space and drug bar.

It had a reputation. When she'd started asking the screen about it Sensia had butted in, the avatar's voice suddenly coming out of the screen in place of the more neutral ship voice she'd just been getting used to, advising her that Divinity In Extremis wasn't the sort of place somebody new to the Culture necessarily wanted to get involved with. Lededje had bit back her annoyance, thanked Sensia for her advice and politely asked her not to interrupt again.

So: Divinity In Extremis. Ship avatars were known to come here.

"You're interrupting again," she whispered into the ring. She smiled at the attractive young man as he frowned into his now empty glass.

"I could have pretended I was just the ship," Sensia's voice replied reasonably, sounding annoyingly unannoyed. "I assumed you wanted more detail on the physical process that led to your current incarnation. Sorry, dear girl. If you're worried about whether your body was somehow sexually interfered with while in the grow tank, I can assure you it wasn't."

The attractive young man reached out to a passing tray as it floated past, depositing his empty glass and scooping up a fuming drug bowl. He brought it up to his face and inhaled deeply.

"Never mind," Lededje said. "Sensia?"

"What?"

"Please go away now."

"Duly gone. One tip though: don't you think it's time you asked him his name?"

"Goodbye."

"Talk to you later."

Lededje looked up, still smiling. The attractive young man went to hand her the drug bowl. She was about to take it with her right hand but he pulled it away again, gesturing to her left hand. She took the bowl with her left hand instead and raised it tentatively towards her face.

The attractive young man took her right hand and curled his fingers round the ring again. While she was still sucking in the fragrant grey smoke from the bowl, he pulled the terminal ring off her finger and threw it high over his shoulder.

"That was mine!" she protested. She looked in the direction the ring had gone but it must have landed ten metres away over the mass of people in the place and there was no sign of anybody catching it and bringing it back. "Why did you do that?"

He shrugged. "I felt like it."

"Do you do everything you feel like doing?"

He shrugged again. "Pretty much."

"How am I supposed to speak to the ship now?"

He looked even more puzzled. He inhaled from the drug bowl. She hadn't realised he'd taken it back. "Shout?" he suggested. "Talk to the air? Ask somebody else?" He shook his head, looked at her critically. "You're really *not* from around here, are you?"

She thought about this. "Yes," she said. She wasn't sure she approved of somebody who just assumed it was all right to manhandle her, remove something that wasn't his and just throw it away like it was something worthless.

His name was Admile. She told him her name was Led because she thought Lededje was too much of a mouthful.

"I am looking for a ship's avatar," she told him.

"Oh," he said. "I thought you were, you know, cruising."

"Cruising?"

"For sex."

"Possibly that too," she said. "Well, definitely, though . . ." She had been going to say definitely but possibly not with him, but then thought that might be too blunt.

"You want to have sex with a ship's avatar?"

"Not necessarily. The two quests are separate."

"Hmm," Admile said. "Follow me."

She frowned, then followed him. The place was busy, packed with people of a variety of body shapes, though mostly pan-human. Outside the sound fields it was very noisy with Chug, which she was starting to suspect was the type of music rather than anything more specific. Knots of people got in their way and they pushed through. Clouds of fragrant fumes created smoke-screens across the space; she nearly lost Admile twice. They passed one cleared circle where two naked men, hobbled by short ropes tied round their ankles, were bare-knuckle fighting, then another where a man and a woman, both wearing only masks, were fighting with long, curved swords.

They came to a sort of deep, sunken, wide alcove where, amongst a plethora of cushions, bolsters and other padded-looking bits of furniture, a startling variety of people, perhaps twenty in all, were indulging in enthusiastic sex. A semicircle of people were gathered around the perimeter, laughing, clapping, shouting comments and offering advice. One couple amongst those looking on were just getting undressed, apparently about to start taking part.

Lededje was not especially shocked; she had witnessed and been obliged to take part in orgies back on Sichult; Veppers had gone through a stage of enjoying them. She had not appreciated the experience, though she supposed that might have been more to do with the lack of choice involved than the surfeit of numbers. She hoped Admile wasn't about to suggest that they, or even just she, ought to join in the group sex. She felt that a rather more romantic setting might be more appropriate for this body's first sexual experience.

"There he is," Admile said. Probably; it was noisy again.

She followed him to the far side of the semicircle of voyeurs, where a fat little man stood surrounded by mostly young people. He was dressed in what looked like a shiny, highly patterned dressing gown. His hair was thin and lank and his face was jowly and covered in sweat. He was, she realised when she thought about it, the fattest person she had seen since she'd been here, by some margin.

The fat little man was repeatedly spinning a coin in the air and catching it. Each time the coin landed on his pudgy palm its top surface flashed red. "It's skill," he kept saying as the people around him shouted and called out. "It's skill, that's all. Look. I'll make it green this time." This time when the coin landed it flashed green instead of red. "See? Skill. Muscle control, concentration: skill. That's all." He looked up. "Admile. Tell these people this is just skill, won't you?"

"Anything riding on this?" Admile asked. "Any bets been taken?"

"Nothing!" the little fat man said, tossing the coin again. Red.

"Okay," Admile said. "It's just skill," he told the people.

"See?" the little fat man said. Red.

"That doesn't make it fair though," Admile added.

"Oh, you're no use," the little fat man tutted. Red again.

"Led, this is Jolicci. He's an avatar. You're an avatar, aren't you, Jolicci?"

"I'm an avatar." Red. "Of the good ship *Armchair Traveller*." Red. "A more than averagely peripatetic GCU of the . . ." Red. "Mountain class . . ." Red. "An avatar who I swear is using nothing . . ." Red. "But muscular skill to make this coin come up red." Red. "Every . . ." Red. ". . . single . . ." Red. ". . . time!" Green. "Oh, fuck!"

There was jeering. He bowed – sarcastically, Lededje thought, if such a thing was possible. He tossed the coin one last time, watched it flip in the air and then held open the breast pocket of his extravagantly decorated dressing gown. The coin dropped into the pocket. He extracted a kerchief from it and mopped his face as some of the people who'd been watching started to drift away.

"Led," he said, nodding to her. "Pleased to meet you." He looked at her, toe to top. She had dressed very conservatively at first, then changed her mind and opted for a short sleeveless dress, deciding to revel in the freedom to do so without displaying her legally approved, Veppers-designed tattoo. Jolicci shook his head. "You don't look like anything I have stored up here," he said, tapping his head. "Excuse me while I consult my better half. Oh, you're Sichultian, is that right?"

"Yes," she said.

"She wants to have sex with a ship's avatar," Admile told him.

Jolicci looked surprised. "Really?" he asked.

"No," she told him. "I am looking for a disreputable ship."

"Disreputable?" Jolicci looked even more surprised.

"I think so."

"You think so?"

Perhaps, she thought – avatar or not – he was just one of those people who thought it the height of wit to constantly ask questions when they weren't called for. "Would you know of one?" she asked.

"Many. Why do you want a disreputable ship?"

"Because I think the *Sense Amid Madness, Wit Amidst Folly* means to send me away on one that will be too well behaved."

Jolicci scrunched up one eye, as though this answer had hit him with the force of a spit.

She had been flicking through various documents and presentations she had discovered through her room's screen, looking at what the Culture knew about and thought of the Enablement, when the ship had called back. "Lededje, I've found you a ship," the vessel's neutral voice had told her straight out of the screen.

"Oh, thank you."

The image of what she supposed must be a Culture spaceship had appeared on the screen, pasted over what she'd been looking at. It resembled a rather featureless skyscraper lying on its side. "It's called *The Usual But Etymologically Unsatisfactory.*"

"*Is* it?"

"Don't worry about the name. The point is, it's heading in your direction and it's agreed to take you. It's setting off late tomorrow afternoon."

"It will take me to Sichult?"

"Most of the way. It'll drop you at a place called Bohme, a transfer station and dock complex just outside the Enablement itself. I'll arrange local transport from there while you're en route."

"Won't I need money to pay for that?"

"Leave that to me. Would you like to talk to the ship? Arrange when to board?"

"Okay."

She'd talked to *The Usual But Etymologically Unsatisfactory.* It had sounded cheery but boring. She'd thanked it, thanked the GSV again and then had sat frowning at the screen once control of it was returned to her.

She'd started looking for document sites about Culture spaceships. They appeared to be almost without number; there were millions of ships, each seemed to have what was in effect its own public log book and its own fan club – often more than one – and there were innumerable documents/presentations on particular types and classes of ships or those which had been constructed by specific manufacturies or other ships. It was bewildering. She could understand why Culture people just asked their local AI or Mind for whatever information they wanted; trying to work your way down through all the detail yourself was daunting.

Perhaps she should just ask. That seemed to be the way you did things in the Culture. On Sichult you had to think about what subjects and people it was safe to ask certain things about, but not here, apparently. On the other hand, doing it yourself felt more secure.

She was already fairly au fait with how you did all this; it wasn't vastly different from the way the Enablement arranged access to the data it was prepared to share with the general public, plus she'd had practice while she'd still been in the ship's Virtual Environment, before she'd be revented into this body.

Here in the Real, using the screen, she knew how to monitor the level of machine intelligence she was talking to. A side bar at the edge of the screen changed according to whether she was talking to, or just using, a completely dumb program, a smart but witless set of algorithms, one of three different levels of AI, an intelligent outside entity or was linked directly to the main personality of the GSV itself. The bar had ascended to its maximum when Sensia had broken in earlier with her warning about Divinity In Extremis.

She'd asked the level-one AI to bring up sites which rated ships and soon found one run by a small collective of ship fans which gave both the *Sense Amid Madness, Wit Amidst Folly* and the *Me, I'm Counting* what she thought sounded like fair assessments. She asked about *The Usual But Etymologically Unsatisfactory*. Boring, obedient. Well behaved. Possibly with ambitions of being chosen for more exotic service, though if it thought it was ever going to get into SC it was deceiving itself. She wasn't sure what SC was – maybe she'd come back to that.

She'd called up a list of ships currently on the GSV. She'd shaken her head. There were nearly ten thousand named vessels aboard right now, including two of a smaller class of GSV, themselves containing other ships. The exact number changed as she watched it, the final digit flickering up and down, presumably as vessels arrived and departed in real time. Four GSVs under construction. Less than 50 per cent Bay Occupancy Rate.

She was still assuming that she was under some form of surveillance and had noticed that the more complicated was the question you asked, the further up the smartness-bar you went towards the ship's own personality. She wanted to avoid that, so rather than just ask, Which are the bad-boy ships? she found short cuts that let her sort the ships currently aboard according to the dubiousness of their reputations.

A handful of the ships aboard had worked for or been plausibly associated with something called Special Circumstances. They didn't publish their ship's logs or course schedules, she'd noticed. SC, again. Whatever Special Circumstances was, it seemed to be closely linked with the kind of qualities she was looking for.

She'd looked up Special Circumstances. Military intelligence, espionage, deep interference, dirty tricks. This, she'd thought, sounded promising. It seemed to have almost as many people interested in it – a lot of them profoundly critical – as all the ships did put together. She'd looked a little closer at some of the anti-SC sites. *Profoundly* critical; say that kind of thing about similar organisations within the Enablement and you'd be on a sharp end of a visit from them and quite probably never heard of again.

None of the handful of ships she'd wanted to talk to had been immediately available. She'd found out how to leave messages with them, and had done so.

"Over there, to your left. Further left. Straight on for about five metres," said a neutral voice rapidly coming closer to where she stood with Admile and the fat little avatar. "That's her, talking to the rotund gentleman."

Lededje turned and saw a cross-looking lady walking smartly towards her, holding something small and silver in her fingers. She marched up to Lededje. "This thing," she said, brandishing the ring in Lededje's face, "will not shut up. Even in a sound field."

"That's her," the ring said primly.

Admile waved some drug fumes out of the way and peered at the ring before turning to Lededje. "Want me to throw it away again? Further?"

"No, thank you," Lededje said, taking the ring from the woman. "Thank— " she began, but the woman was already walking away. Lededje held the ring in her hand.

"Hello again," the ship's neutral voice said.

"Hello."

"I was thinking of going body surfing," Jolicci announced. "Anybody want to go body surfing?"

Admile shook his head.

"Good," Lededje said, slipping the ring onto one of his fingers. "Perhaps I'll see you later."

Body surfing meant taking off most of your clothes and throwing yourself down a great curved slope of upward-charging water, either on your back, front, behind or, if you were especially skilled, feet. This all happened in a great half-dark hall full of whoops and happy screams, overlooked by bars and party spaces. Some people did it naked, others donned swimwear. Jolicci, fitted with what looked like a pair of eye-wateringly tight trunks, was spectacularly bad at it. He found it hard to exercise any control even when he was flat on his back with all four limbs extended.

Lededje discovered she was quite good as long as she didn't try to stand up. She was coasting on her behind in a tidy spray of water, holding on to Jolicci's left ankle with her right hand to stop him spinning out of control and keep them within talking distance of each other.

"So you want to go somewhere you won't reveal for reasons you want to keep secret but you don't want to take the ship the GSV's suggested."

"That's broadly it," she agreed. "Also, I would like to talk to the ships aboard here which have or had links to Special Circumstances."

"Really?" Jolicci wobbled, spraying his face with water. "Are you sure?" He wiped his face with one hand, oscillating to and fro until he placed the hand back on the watery slide. "I mean, really sure?"

"Yes," she told him. "You're not the avatar of one of them, are you?" He'd said he was the avatar of the *Armchair Traveller*; that hadn't been a name she'd recognised, but for all she knew these ships changed their names, or had several different names they used as it suited them.

"No," he said. "Humble General Contact Unit, me, going about standard Contact business, honest. Nothing to do with SC." He squinted at her (she thought – it might just have been the water). "You sure you want to talk to SC?"

"Yes."

They pirouetted slowly, caught by a localised rush of uphill-headed water. Jolicci looked thoughtful. He nodded to the side. "It seems I have no skill in this. Enough. Let's try another sort of surfing."

"What is this?" Lededje asked. They were standing in a short, broad, carpeted corridor one wall of which was punctuated by five sets of plain double doors. Jolicci, back in his colourful dressing gown, had pulled the central set of double doors apart with some effort and was stopping them from sliding back by wedging the left one with his slipper-shod foot. Lededje was looking through the opened doors into a dark, echoing space laced with vertical cables and cross-beamed with girders. She heard rumbling noises, sensed movement, felt a draught on her face. The air smelled oily, half familiar.

She and the fat little avatar had been whisked here by the usual slick process of traveltube with only minute-long walks at either end. What she was looking at here felt somehow much older, much cruder.

"Re-creation of a tall building elevator shaft," he told her. "Don't you have these?"

"We have skyscrapers," she said, holding on to the right-hand door as she leant in. "And elevators.' There was the rather grimy-looking top of an elevator car reassuringly close beneath, only a metre or so down. Looking up she saw the shafts and cables climbing into the darkness. "I've just never seen inside a lift shaft before. Except in a screen, I suppose. Then there's always just the one, you know, shaft."

"Uh-huh," Jolicci said. "Jump on; I'll let go the doors. Careful, though; no safety net."

She jumped onto the roof of the car beneath. Jolicci followed her, making the roof's surface quiver. The doors above hissed closed and the car started to ascend immediately. She held on to one of the cables – it was greasy with dark, gritty oil – and looked over the edge. The great dark shaft held space for ten elevators, five on each side. The car accelerated smartly, the slipstream tugging at her hair and making Jolicci's dressing gown flap as they whizzed upwards. She looked down, leaning a little further out as they shot past sets of closed double doors, almost too fast to count. The bottom of the shaft was lost in the darkness.

She was grabbed from behind by one shoulder.

She heard herself yelp as she thudded into Jolicci's surprisingly solid body. An instant later a dark shape plunged past her in a storm of disturbed air. She had narrowly missed getting decapitated by a rapidly descending car. Jolicci released his hold on her. "Like I said; no safety net. This is a dangerously faithful physical re-creation. No sensors on the cars to stop them hitting or crushing you, no AG down the bottom if you fall. Nobody to see you fall, let alone stop you. You backed-up?"

She found she was shaking a little. "You mean my, my self? My personality?" He just looked at her. She suspected it was just as well it was so gloomy it was hard to tell precisely what his expression was. "I'm only a day out of a . . . a thing, a jar, a body tank." She swallowed. "But no."

The car was slowing, drawing to a stop. Jolicci looked upwards from the far side of the car. "Right. Here comes the fun bit." He glanced at her. "You ready?"

"What for?" she asked.

"Get over here. Jump when I say. Don't hesitate. You'll need to let go of that cable first."

She let go of the cable, stepped to stand beside him at the other side of the elevator roof. Looking up, tentatively, she saw the bottom of another dark car descending quickly towards them. She heard some sudden, distant whoops and then laughter from further down in the great depth of shadows; the sounds echoed and re-echoed. Their car was still slowing. "Okay, steady, steady . . ." Jolicci said as their car and the one above approached each other.

"Should I hold your hand?" she asked.

"Do *not* hold my hand," he said. "Okay, okay, steady . . ."

Their car had come almost to a stop; the one coming towards them from above whooshed past.

"Jump!" Jolicci shouted as the car's roofs were almost level.

He jumped. She jumped too a moment later, but found that she'd jumped as though to land where the other car's roof had been when she'd leapt, not where it was going to be as she dropped after it. She landed awkwardly and would have fallen against the car's cables if Jolicci hadn't caught her. Lededje heard herself gasp.

She held on to the little fat avatar for a moment as they steadied on the roof of the car. The one they'd jumped from was stopped several storeys above and getting further away all the time as their car descended. It too was starting to slow now.

"Wow!" she said, letting go of Jolicci. Her fingers had left dark, greasy marks on his dressing gown lapels. "That was . . . exciting!" She frowned at him. "Do you do this a lot?"

"Never before," he told her. "Heard of it."

That shook her a little. She had rather assumed she was in safe or at least experienced hands. The car drew to a stop. Beneath, she could feel and hear its doors open; a bar of light shone from that edge of the roof, showing Jolicci's face. He was looking at her oddly, she thought. She felt a strange little frisson of fear.

"This Special Circumstances thing," he said.

"Yes?" she said as he took a step closer to her. She stepped backward, tripped on a piece of the roof's cross-bracing and staggered. He grabbed her again, pulling her to the rear edge of the roof.

Deep below, she could see the car whose rear faced their car's rear rising quickly towards them. The two sets of five cars per side were separated by nearly two metres; three or four times the separation of the cars on each side of the shaft.

Jolicci nodded down, indicating the approaching car. "Think we can make that jump when it comes?" he said into her ear. She could feel his warm breath on her skin. "No safety nets, remember. Not even any surveillance inside here." He pulled her a little closer to the edge, brought his mouth closer to her ear. "What do you think? Think we can do it?"

"No," she told him. "And I think you should let go of me."

Before she could do anything to stop him he gripped her hard by one elbow and pushed her out over the drop, only her feet still in contact with the car's roof. "Still want me to let go?"

"No!" she shouted, grabbing his arm with her free hand. "Don't be stupid! Of course not!"

He pulled her in towards him, though still not out of danger. "If you had a terminal it would hear you scream if you happened to fall," he told her. He made a show of looking down. He shrugged. "Might be just enough time for the ship to realise what was happening and get a drone to you before you hit the bottom."

"Stop doing this, please," she said. "You're frightening me."

He pulled her close to him, his breath in her face now. "Everybody thinks SC is so glamorous, so . . . *sexy*!" He shook her, rubbed his groin against her leg. "Thrilling fun, all danger and excitement, but not too much danger. Is that what you think? Heard the rumours, absorbed the propaganda? Read the right assessments, listened to the relevant experts, self-proclaimed, have we?"

"I'm just trying to find out—"

"You feel frightened?" he asked her.

"I just said—"

He shook his head. "This isn't dangerous." he shook her again. "I'm not dangerous. I'm a nice roly-poly GCU avatar; I wouldn't drop somebody down an antique lift shaft to let them splatter on the concrete. I'm one of the good guys. But you still feel frightened, don't you? You do feel frightened, don't you? I hope you feel frightened."

"I already told you," she said coldly, trying to keep any expression from her face or voice as she stared into his eyes.

He smiled, pulled her inwards as he stepped back. He let go of her and held on to the cables as the car started downwards again. "As I say, I'm one of the good guys, Ms. Y'breq."

She gripped another of the cables, hard. "I never told you my full name."

"Well spotted. Seriously though, I really am one of the good guys. I'm the sort of ship who'd always do everything to save somebody, not kill them, not let them die. SC – its ships, its people – might be on the side of the angels, but that doesn't mean they always behave like the good guys. In fact, as you're falling down the metaphorical lift shaft, I can virtually guarantee it will feel like they're the *bad* guys, no matter how ethically sound the carefully worked out moral algebra was that led to them chucking you into it in the first place."

"You have made your point, sir," she told him frostily. "Perhaps we might abandon this pastime now."

He looked at her for a few moments longer. Then he shook his head, looked away.

"Well, so you're tough," he said. "But you're still a fool." He let out a deep breath. The elevator car was pulling to a stop. "I'll take you to an SC ship." He smiled without any humour. "If and when it all goes horribly wrong, feel free to blame me, if you still can. It'll make no difference."

"The Forgotten," the *Bodhisattva* told Yime Nsokyi. "Also known as Oubliettionaries."

There were times, Yime might occasionally be forced to admit, when a neural lace would indeed be useful. If she had one she could be quizzing it now, asking it for mentions, references, definitions. What the hell was an Oubliettionary? Of course, the ship would know she was making such inquiries – she was on the ship now, not the Orbital, so any lace or terminal business would be conducted through the *Bodhisattva*'s Mind or its sub-systems – but at least with a lace you could have the relevant knowledge just dumped into your head rather than have to listen to it one word at a time.

"I see," Yime said. She folded her arms. "I'm listening."

"They're ships of a certain . . . predisposition, shall we say, normally a GSV, usually with a few other ships and a small number of active drones aboard and often containing no humans at all," the *Bodhisattva* told her. "They resign from the day-to-day informational commerce of the Culture, stop registering their position, take themselves off into the middle of nowhere and then they just sit there, doing nothing. Except listen, indefinitely."

"Listen?"

"They listen to one or more – probably all, I'd imagine – of the handful of widely scattered broadcast stations which send out a continual update on the general state of matters in the greater galactic community in general and the Culture in particular."

"News stations."

"For want of a better word."

"Broadcasting."

"It's a wasteful and inefficient way to communicate, but the advantage of a broadcast in this context is precisely that it goes everywhere and nobody can tell who might be listening."

"How many of these 'Forgotten' are there?"

"Good question. To most people they appear simply as ships that have gone into an especially uncommunicative retreat, an impression the ships concerned do nothing to contradict, of course. At any time anything up to one per cent of the Culture ship fleet might be on a retreat, and perhaps point three or point four per cent of those have been silent since quitting what one might call the main sequence of normal ship behaviour. I hesitate to call it discipline. It's not a much-studied field, so even the quality of the relatively few guesstimates is hard to evaluate. There might be as few as eight or twelve of these ships, or possibly as many as three or four hundred."

"And what's the point of all this?"

"They're back-up," the *Bodhisattva* said. "If, through some bizarre and frankly unfeasibly widespread and complete calamity, the Culture somehow ceased to be, then any one of these ships could re-seed the galaxy – or a different one, perhaps – with something that would be recognisably the Culture. This does beg the question what would be the point if it had been so comprehensively expunged in the first place, but I suppose you could argue some lesson might have been learned that might make version two more resilient somehow."

"I thought the entire Contact fleet was supposed to represent our 'back-up'," Yime said. In its relationships with other civilisations, especially with those that were encountering it for the first time, much tended to be made of the fact – or at least the assertion – that each and every GSV represented the Culture in its entirety, that each one held all the knowledge the Culture had ever accumulated and could build any object or device that the Culture was capable of making, while the sheer scale of a General Systems Vehicle meant they each contained so many humans and drones they were more or less guaranteed to hold a reasonably representative sample of both even without trying to.

The Culture was deliberately and self-consciously very widely distributed throughout the galaxy, with no centre, no nexus, no home planet. Its distribution might make it easy to attack, but it also made it hard to eradicate altogether, at least in theory. Having hundreds of thousands of vessels individually quite capable of rebuilding the entire Culture from scratch was generally held to be safeguard enough against civilisational oblivion, or so Yime had been led to believe. Obviously others thought differently.

"The Contact fleet is what one might call a second line of defence," the ship told her.

"What's the first?"

"All the Orbitals." the ship said reasonably. "And other habs; Rocks and planets included."

"And these Forgotten are the last ditch."

"Probably. So one might imagine. As far as I know."

That, in ship-speak, Yime thought, probably meant No. Though she knew better than to try to coax a less ambiguous answer out of a Mind.

"So they just sit there. Wherever 'there' might be."

"Oort clouds, interstellar space, within or even beyond the outer halo of the greater galaxy itself; who knows? However, yes, that is the general idea."

"And indefinitely."

"Indefinitely until now, at least," the *Bodhisattva* said.

"Waiting for a catastrophe that'll probably never happen but which if it did would indicate either the existence of a force so powerful it could probably discover these ships regardless and snuff them out too, or an existential flaw in the Culture so deep it would certainly be present in these 'Forgotten' as well, especially given their . . . representativeness."

"Put like that, the entire strategy does sound a little forlorn," the ship said, sounding almost apologetic. "But there we are. Because you never know, I suppose. I think a part of the whole idea is that it provides a degree of comfort for those who might otherwise worry about such matters."

"But most people don't know about these ships in the first place," Yime pointed out. "How can you be comforted by something you don't know about?"

"Ah," the *Bodhisattva* said. "That's the beauty of it: only people who do worry are likely to seek out such knowledge, and so are suitably reassured. They also tend to appreciate the need not to make the knowledge too well known, and indeed take additional pleasure in helping to keep it from becoming so. Everybody else just gets happily on with their lives, never fretting in the first place."

Yime shook her head, frustrated. "They can't be *completely* secret," she protested. "They must be mentioned *some*where."

The Culture was notoriously bad at keeping secrets, especially big ones. It was one of the very few areas where most of the Culture's civilisational peers and even many much less advanced societies thoroughly eclipsed it, though, being the Culture, this was regarded as being the legitimate source of a certain perverse pride. That didn't stop it – the "it" in such contexts usually meaning Contact, or (even more likely) SC – from trying to keep secrets, every now and again, but it never worked for very long.

Though sometimes, of course, not very long was still long enough.

"Well, naturally," the *Bodhisattva* said. "Let's just say the information is there, but little notice is taken. And by the very nature of the whole . . . program – if one can even dignify it with a name implying such a degree of organisation – confirmation is almost impossible to find."

"So this isn't what you might call official?" Yime asked.

The ship made a sighing noise. "There is no Contact department or committee that I know of which devotes itself to such matters."

Yime pursed her lips. She knew when a ship was basically saying, Let's leave it at that, shall we?

Well, one more thing to have to take account of.

"So," she said, "the *Me, I'm Counting* may be aboard the GSV *Total Internal Reflection*, which is on retreat and is probably one of these Forgotten."

"Indeed."

"And the *Me, I'm Counting* holds an image of Ms. Y'breq."

"Probably *the* image of Ms. Y'breq," the *Bodhisattva* said. "We have intelligence, from another individual the ship took an image of subsequently, that it was happy to guarantee any image it took remained unique, for its own collection only, never to be shared or even backed up. It would appear that it has stuck to this."

"So you think . . . what? That Y'breq will attempt to recover her image, even though it's ten years old?"

"It has been judged to be a distinct possibility."

"And Quietus knows where the *Me, I'm Counting* and the *Total Internal Reflection* are?"

"We believe we have a rough idea. More to the point, we have occasional contact with a representative of the *Total Internal Reflection*."

"We do, do we?"

"The *Total Internal Reflection* is relatively unusual amongst the Forgotten – we think – in that it plays host to a small population of humans and drones who seek a more than usually severe form of seclusion than the average retreat offers. Such commitments are usually quite long term in nature – decades, on average – however, there is a continual if fluctuating churn in both populations, so people need to be ferried to and from the GSV. There are three semi-regular rendezvous points and a fairly reliable rendezvous programme. The next scheduled meeting is in eighteen days at a location in the Semsarine Wisp. Ms. Y'breq should be able to get there in time, and so should you and I, Ms. Nsokyi."

"Does she know about this rendezvous?"

"We believe so."

"Is she heading in that direction?"

"Again, we believe so."

"Hmm." Yime frowned.

"That is the generality of the situation, Ms. Nsokyi. A more comprehensive briefing awaits, obviously."

"Obviously."

"May I take it that you are agreeable to taking part in this mission?"

"Yes," Yime said. "Are we under way yet?"

The image of the old Hooligan-class warship vanished to be replaced with the sight of stars again, some of them reflected in the polished-looking black body of the ship hanging above and others gleaming through the hardness beneath her feet that looked like nothing at all. The stars were moving, now.

"Yes, we are," the *Bodhisattva* said.

Lededje was introduced to the avatar of the Special Circumstances ship *Falling Outside The Normal Moral Constraints* in a war bar where the only lighting apart from the screens and holos came from broad curtains of amphoteric lead falling down the walls from slots in the dark ceiling.

The continual sputtering yellow-orange blaze of the reaction gave the light in the place an unsteady, flickering quality a lot like firelight and made the space feel stickily warm. A strange, bitter smell hung in the air.

"Lead, the element, very finely ground, just dropped through the air," Jolicci had muttered to her as they'd entered the place and she'd remarked upon the strange sight.

Just getting in hadn't been that easy, either. The venue was housed in a stubby, worn-looking Interstellar-class ship housed in one of the GSV's Smallbays and the ship itself made it very clear – as they stood in the darkly echoing depths of the Bay – that this was essentially a private club, one that the GSV had no immediate jurisdiction over and a place that was certainly not under any obligation to admit anybody who any one of its patrons took exception to.

"My name is Jolicci, avatar of the *Armchair Traveller*," Jolicci told the single small drone floating by the ship's closed lower hatchway. "I think you know who I've come to see. Please let him know."

"I'm doing so," the boxy little drone said.

The ship was called the *Hidden Income*. It was maybe a hundred metres in length. Looking round, squinting into the gloomily cavernous depths of the Bay, Lededje reckoned the Smallbay could have squeezed in at least another three ships the same size without them touching fins or engine pods or whatever all the various bits were. Small was obviously a relative term when it came to ships and the vast hangars required to accommodate them.

Lededje looked at the little drone, hanging in front of them at head height. Well, this was a new experience, she thought. Whenever she'd been taken somewhere by Veppers – the most expensive new restaurant, the most exclusive new club, bar or venue – he and his entourage had always been ushered straight in, whether he'd had a reservation made or not, even to the ones which he didn't own. How odd to have to come to the reputedly obsessively egalitarian Culture finally to experience the phenomenon of hanging around outside a club waiting to see if she'd be allowed in.

The hatchway dropped without warning, immediately behind

the little drone. It fell so fast she expected a clang when it met the finely ridged floor of the Bay, but it seemed to cushion its descent at the last moment and landed silently.

The drone said nothing but it floated out of their way.

"Thank you," Jolicci said as they stepped on.

Jolicci held her arm as the hatch rose smoothly up towards a small, barely lit hangar volume inside the *Hidden Income*. "Demeisen is a little odd," he told her. "Even by ship avatar standards. Just be honest with him. Or her. Or it."

"You're not sure?"

"We haven't met for a while. The *Falling Outside The Normal Moral Constraints* changes avatars fairly frequently."

"What is this place anyway?"

Jolicci looked awkward. "War porn club, I think."

Lededje would have asked more but they were met by another small drone and escorted into the place.

"Demeisen, may I present Ms. Lededje Y'breq," Jolicci said to the man sitting at the table near the middle of the room.

The place looked like a sort of strange restaurant with substantial round tables scattered about, each featuring at their centre a trio or more of screens or a tankless holo display. A variety of people, mostly human, sat or lounged around the tables. In front of most of them, drug bowls, drinks glasses, chill pipes and small trays of food lay arranged, scattered or abandoned. The screens and holos all showed scenes of warfare. At first Lededje assumed they were screen; just movies; but after a few moments, and a few grisly sequences, she decided they might be real.

Most of the people in the room weren't looking at the screens and holos; they were looking at her and Jolicci. The man Jolicci had addressed was at a table with several other young men, all of them with that air that implied they were, within their own subset of pan-human physiognomy, quite strikingly handsome.

Demeisen stood. He looked cadaverous, hollow-cheeked. Dark eyes with no whites, two ridges instead of eyebrows, a flat nose and mid-dark skin, scarred in places. He was only medium tall but his height was emphasised by his thinness. If his physiology was the same as a Sichultian's then the slight bagginess about his face implied the weight loss had been recent and rapid. His clothes were dark, perhaps black: skinny trews and a tight-fitting shirt or jacket, partially closed at the neck by a thumb-sized, blood-red glittering jewel on a loosened choker.

Lededje saw him look at her right hand and so put it out to him. His hand clasped her hand, fingers with too many joints closing around like a bony cage. His touch felt very warm, almost feverish, though perfectly dry, like paper. She saw him wince and noticed that two of his fingers were crudely splinted together with a small piece of wood or plastic and what looked like a piece of knotted rag. Somehow the wince didn't travel all the way to his face, which regarded her without obvious expression.

"Good evening," Lededje said.

"Ms. Y'breq." His voice sounded dry and cold. He nodded at Jolicci then indicated the seats on either side of him. "Wheloube, Emmis. If you would."

The two young men seemed about to protest, but then did not. They rose together with a sort of brisk contempt and walked proudly away. She and Jolicci took their places. The other handsome young men stared at them. Demeisen waved one hand; the table's holo display, which had been depicting a gruesomely realistic skirmish between some horsemen and a larger force of archers and other foot-soldiers, faded to blank.

"A rare privilege," Demeisen murmured to Jolicci. "How goes the business of General Contacting?"

"Generally well. How's life as a security guard?"

Demeisen smiled. "Night watching is unfailingly illuminating."

There was a small gold tube in front of him which Lededje had assumed was the mouthpiece of an under-table chill or water pipe – there were several other mouthpieces lying or cradled on the table – but which proved to be a stick with a glowing end, unattached to anything else. Demeisen put it to his lips and sucked hard. The golden tube crackled, shortened and left a fiery glowing tip beneath a lofting of silky grey smoke.

Demeisen saw her looking and offered the stick to her. "A drug. From Sudalle. Called narthaque. The effect is similar to *winnow*, though harsher, less pleasant. The hangover can be severe."

"'Winnow'?" Lededje asked. She got the impression she'd been expected to know what this was.

Demeisen looked both surprised and unimpressed.

"Ms. Y'breq does not possess drug glands," Jolicci explained.

"Really?" Demeisen said. He frowned at her. "Are you suffering some form of punishment, Ms. Y'breq? Or are you of that demented persuasion that believes enlightenment is to be found in the shadows?"

"Neither," Lededje told him. "I am more of a barely legal alien." She had hoped this might be amusing, but if it was, nobody round the table seemed to find it so. Maybe her understanding of Marain wasn't as flawless as she'd been assuming.

Demeisen looked at Jolicci. "I'm told the young lady looks for passage."

"She does," Jolicci said.

Demeisen gestured with both hands, sending loops of smoke into the air from the hand holding the golden stick. "Well, Jolicci, for once you have the better of me. What on earth gives you the idea that I have turned into a taxi? Do tell. Can't wait to hear."

Jolicci just smiled. "There is a little more to the matter, I believe. Ms. Y'breq," he said to her. "Over to you."

She looked at Demeisen. "I need to get home, sir."

Demeisen glanced at Jolicci. "Very taxi-sounding so far." He turned back to her. "Go on, Ms. Y'breq. I cannot wait for this to achieve escape velocity from the mundanity well."

"I intend to kill a man."

"That's a little more uncommon. Again though, one imagines a taxi would suffice, unless the gentleman concerned can only be dispatched using a warship. A state-of-the-art Culture warship, at that, if I may make so immodest. For some reason the word 'overkill' leaps to mind." He smiled icily at her. "You may not be doing quite as well here as you thought you might at this point."

"I've been told that I'll be slap-droned."

"So you were stupid enough to let slip that you *intend* to kill this man." He frowned. "Oh dear. Might I suggest that this does not bode terribly well should your murderous plans include more than the absolute minimum of guile, subterfuge or, dare I say it, intelligence? My – trust me – *highly* limited empathic capacities remain resolutely un-engaged." He turned to Jolicci again. "Have you quite finished humiliating yourself here, Jolicci, or do you really require me to—?"

"The man I intend to kill is the richest man in the world, the richest and most powerful man in my whole civilisation," Lededje said. Even she could hear the edge of desperation creeping into her voice.

Demeisen looked at her, one eye-crease raised. "*Which* civilisation?"

"The Enablement," she told him.

"The Sichultian Enablement," Jolicci said.

Demeisen snorted. "Again," he told Lededje, "not saying as much as you might think."

"He killed me," she told him, doing all she could to keep her voice under control. "Murdered me with his own hands. We have no soul-keeping technology but I was saved because a Culture ship called the *Me, I'm Counting* put a neural lace in my head ten years ago. I was revented here only today."

Demeisen sighed. "All very melodramatic. Your feud may inspire a not terribly good screen presentation at some point in the future, hopefully distant. I look forward to missing it." He smiled thinly again. "Now, if you wouldn't mind excusing yourselves?" He nodded to the two young men who'd vacated their seats for Lededje and Jolicci earlier. They were standing nearby now, looking on, quietly triumphant.

Jolicci sighed. "I'm sorry I wasted your time," he said as he rose.

"Still, I hope to make you sorrier," Demeisen said with an insincere smile.

"I was talking to Ms. Y'breq."

"And I was not," Demeisen said, standing as Lededje did. He

turned to her, put the gold smoking stick to his pale lips and pulled hard. He looked at her and said, "Best of luck finding a ride," as he exhaled.

He smiled more broadly and ground the yellow-red glowing tip of the stick into the open palm of his other hand. There was a distinct sizzling noise. Again, his body seemed to flinch, though his face remained serene.

"What, this?" he said, looking down at the ash-dark burn on his skin as Lededje stared at it, openly aghast. "Don't worry; I don't feel a thing." He laughed. "The idiot inside here does though." He tapped the side of his head, smiled again. "Poor fool won some sort of competition to replace a ship's avatar for a hundred days or a year or something similar. No control over either body or ship whatsoever, obviously, but the full experience in other respects – sensations, for example. I'm told he practically came in his pants when he learned an up-to-date warship had volunteered to accept his offer of body host." The smile became broader, more of a grin. "Obviously not the most zealous student of ship psychology, then. So," Demeisen said, holding up his hand with the splinted finger and studying it, "I torment the poor fool." He put his other hand to the one with the splinted fingers, waggled them. His body shuddered as he did so. Lededje found herself wincing with vicarious pain. "See? Powerless to stop me," Demeisen said cheerily. "He suffers his pain and learns his lesson while I . . . well, I gain some small amusement."

He looked at Jolicci and Lededje. "Jolicci," he said with obviously feigned concern, "you look offended." He nodded, creased his eyes. "It's a good look, trust me. Sour opprobrium: suits you."

Jolicci said nothing.

Wheloube and Emmis resumed their seats. Standing there, Demeisen put out both hands and stroked the hair of one and the shaved head of the other, then cradled the finely chiselled chin of the one with the shaved head using his unsplinted hand. "And *fascinatingly*, the fellow" – he used his splinted fingers to tap the side of his head again, hard – "is quite defiantly heterosexual, with a fear of bodily violation that borders on outright homophobia."

He looked round the table of young men, winking at one of them, then gazed radiantly at Jolicci and Lededje.

Lededje stamped across the floor of the dimly lit Smallbay. "There must be other SC ships," she said furiously.

"None that will talk to you," Jolicci said, hurrying after her.

"And the only one that would seemed solely to want to shock and demean me."

Jolicci shrugged. "The Abominator class of General Offensive Unit, to which our friend belongs, is not known for its mildness or sociability. Probably specced when the Culture was going through one of its periods of feeling that nobody was taking it seriously because it was somehow too *nice*. Even amongst those, though, that particular ship is known as something of an outlier. Most SC ships conceal their claws and keep the psychopathy switched to Full Off except when it's judged to be absolutely necessary."

In the traveltube, deflated but calmer, Lededje said, "Well, thank you for trying."

"You are welcome. Was all that you said in there true?"

"Every word." She looked at him. "I trust you'll treat what you heard just now as in confidence."

"Well, that is something you might have thought to say beforehand, but, all right, I promise what you said will go no further." The fat little avatar looked thoughtful. "I realise it might not feel like it, but you may have just had a narrow escape, Ms. Y'breq."

She looked coldly at him. "Then that makes two this evening, doesn't it?"

Jolicci appeared unconcerned. If anything he looked amused. "As I said, I was never going to let you fall. What I did was a stunt. What you just saw in there was real."

"The ship would really be allowed to treat a human like that?"

"If it was done voluntarily, if the bargain was struck with eyes open, as it were, yes." Jolicci made an expansive gesture with both hands. "It's what can happen if you put yourself in harm's way by treating with SC." The fat little avatar appeared to think for a moment. "Perhaps a rather extreme example, admittedly."

Lededje took a deep breath, let it out. "I have no terminal. May I use you as one?"

"Feel free. Who would you like to contact?"

"The GSV. To tell it I'll take its suggested ship tomorrow."

"No need. It'll be assuming so anyway. Anybody else?"

"Admile?" she said, her voice small.

There was a pause, then Jolicci shook his head regretfully. "I'm afraid he is otherwise engaged."

Lededje sighed. She looked at Jolicci. "I desire a meaningless sexual encounter with a male, preferably one as good-looking as one of those young men round Demeisen's table."

Jolicci smiled, then sighed. "Well, the night is yet middle-aged."

Yime Nsokyi lay awake in the darkness of her small cabin, waiting for sleep. She would give it another few minutes and then gland *softnow* to bring it on not-entirely-naturally. She possessed the same suite of drug glands as most Culture humans, the default set that you tended to be born with, but she preferred not to use them unless genuinely necessary, and almost never for pleasure, only to accomplish something of practical value.

She might have got rid of them completely, she supposed, just told them all to wither away and be absorbed into her body, but she had chosen not to. She knew of some within Quietus who had gone through with this, in some spirit of denial and asceticism that she thought was taking matters too far. Also, it was arguably more disciplined still to possess the glands but not to use them than it was to remove them and their temptations altogether.

But then the same might be said of her choice to become neuter. She put one hand down between her legs, to feel the tiny slotted bud – like a third, bizarrely placed nipple – which was all that was left of her genitals. When she had been younger, when her drug glands had still been maturing, that too had been a way of bringing on sleep: masturbate and then drift off in the rosy afterglow.

She rubbed the tiny bud absently, remembering. There was no hint of pleasure in touching herself there any more; she might as well have caressed a knuckle or an ear lobe. In fact there was more sensuality to be found in her ear lobes. The nipples of her reduced, near-flat breasts were similarly unresponsive.

Oh well, she thought, clasping her hands over her chest; it had been her choice. A way of making real to herself her dedication to Quietus. Nun-like, she supposed. On that reckoning, there were a lot of nuns and monks within Quietus. And, of course, the decision was entirely reversible. She wondered about changing back, becoming properly female again. She still thought of herself as female, always had.

Or she might become male; she was exactly poised between the two standard genders. She touched the little bud at her groin again. Just as much like a tiny penis as a relocated nipple, she supposed.

She clasped her hands over her chest once more, then sighed, turned on her side.

"Ms. Nsokyi?" the ship's voice said quietly.

"Yes?"

"My apologies. I sensed you were still some way from sleep."

"You sensed correctly. What?"

"I have been asked by a number of my colleagues whether your earlier comment regarding informing Special Circumstances about the matter in hand represented what one might call a formal suggestion or request."

She waited a moment before replying. "No," she said. "It did not."

"I see. Thank you. That's all. Good night. Sleep well."

"Good night."

Yime wondered whether she ship would even have bothered to ask had she not had the history she did with SC.

She had been drawn to Quietus even when she'd been a little girl. A serious, reserved, slightly withdrawn little girl who had been interested in dead things found in the woods and keeping insects in terraria. A serious, reserved, slightly withdrawn little girl who knew that she was easily capable of joining Special

Circumstances if she wanted to, but who had only ever wanted to be part of the Quietudinal Service.

Even then she had known that Quietus – like Restoria and the third of Contact's relatively recently specialist services, Numina, which dealt with the Sublimed – was seen by many people and machines as being second best to Special Circumstances.

SC was the pinnacle, the service that attracted the absolutely best and brightest of the Culture; in a society that held few positions of individual power, SC represented the ultimate goal for those both blessed and cursed with the sort of vaunting, hungry ambition to succeed in the Real that could not be bought off by the convincing but ultimately artificial attractions of VR. If you genuinely wanted to prove yourself, there was no question that SC was where you wanted to be.

Even then, still a child, she had known she was special, known that she was capable of doing pretty much whatever it was possible to do within the Culture. SC would have seemed like the obvious target for her aims and aspirations. But she hadn't wanted to be in SC; she wanted to be in Quietus, the service everybody seemed to feel was a second best. It was unfair.

She had made her decision then, way back, before her drug glands were developed enough to use with any skill or finesse, before she was sexually mature at all.

She studied, trained, learned, grew a neural lace, applied to join Contact, was accepted, applied herself, both diligently and imaginatively within Contact, and all the while waited for the invitation to join SC.

The invitation duly came, and she declined it, so joining an exclusive club many orders of magnitude smaller than that of the elite of the elite that was SC itself.

She applied immediately to Quietus instead, having made her point, and was accepted with alacrity. She began to curtail her use of her drug glands and started the slow changes in her body that would turn her from female to neuter. She also abandoned her use of the neural lace, beginning an even longer process that saw the biomechanical tracery of the device gradually shrink and wither and disappear, the minerals and metals that had composed the bulk of it being slowly reabsorbed into her body. The last few particles of exotic matter it had contained exited in her urine via the tiny sexless bud between her legs, a year later.

She was free of SC, committed to Quietus.

Only it could never be that simple. There was no sudden yes-or-no point when it came to joining SC. You were sounded out first, your intentions were questioned and your motivations and seriousness were weighed in the balance, at first through apparently innocuous, informal conversations – often with people you would have no idea were in any way associated with SC – then only later in rather more formalised settings and contexts where SC's interest was made clear.

So, in a sense, she had had to lie – or at least constructively deceive – to get what she wanted, which was the formal invitation to join which she could then turn down but use in the future as proof that Quietus had been no second choice, no consolation prize, but rather something she had valued beyond the merits of SC right from the start.

She had finessed it as best she could at the time, giving answers that seemed straight and unambiguous when they were given and which only later, in the light of that obviously planned refusal, revealed a degree of dissemblance. Still, she had been guilty of a lack of openness if nothing else, and of simple dishonesty if you were judging severely.

SC considered itself above bearing grudges, but was patently disappointed. You did not come to the stage of being asked to join it without establishing quite strong relationships with people who had become mentors and friends while in Contact; relationships which normally would be expected to go on developing once you were in SC itself, and it was to those individuals, and even a couple of ship Minds, that she felt she owed apologies.

She duly said sorry and the apologies were duly accepted, but those had been her darkest hours, the moments in her life the memories of which still kept her awake when she wanted to sleep, or woke her up in the middle of the night, and she could never quite shake the feeling that this was the single least-resolved issue in her life, the loose end whose niggling presence would trouble her to the end of her days.

And, even though she had foreseen it, it had still come as something of a disappointment to her that her behaviour meant she existed within Quietus under a faint but undeniable cloud of suspicion. If she would turn down SC to prove a point, might she not repudiate Quietus too? How could you ever fully trust somebody like that?

And, was it not possible that she had never really resigned from SC at all? Might Yime Nsokyi not still be a Special Circumstances agent, but a secret one, planted within Quietus, either for reasons too arcane and mysterious to divine until some point of crisis arrived, or just as a sort of insurance for some set of circumstances still unenvisaged . . . or even with no clear motive at all beyond establishing that SC could do such a thing simply because it chose to, to prove it could?

She had miscalculated there. She had thought the whole bluff with SC would only prove how utterly dedicated to Quietus she was, and her subsequent flawless behaviour and exemplary service would serve to reinforce the point. It hadn't worked out like that. She was of more value to Quietus as a symbol – subtly but effectively publicised – of its equality of worth with SC than she was as a functioning and fully trusted Quietus operative.

So she spent a lot of time frustrated; unused, twiddling her thumbs and kicking her heels (when she might have been kicking other people's ass with SC, as at least one of her friends had pointed out). She had taken part in a few missions for Quietus and had been reassured that she had done well – indeed, near perfectly. Still, she was less used than she might have been, less used than inferior talents who had joined at the same time, less used than her skills and abilities would have implied she ought to be; offered occasional scraps, never anything of real substance.

Until now.

Now at last she felt she was being asked to behave like a true Quietus operative, on a mission of genuine importance, even if it might only be because where she lived happened to be quite close to the place where a Quietus agent was suddenly required.

Well, arguably she'd had bad luck in the way Quietus had chosen to react to her attempt to prove how much she valued it. Maybe that bad luck was just being balanced now. Luck came into it. Even SC recognised a place for chance, and being in the right place at the right time was, if not a gift, certainly a blessing.

Contact even had a phrase for it: Utility is seven-eighths Proximity.

Yime sighed, turned over, and fell asleep.

Eleven

"Auer. Lovely to see you. Radiant as ever. And Fuleow; this gorgeous creature still putting up with you?"

"So far, Veppers. Got your eye on her yourself, have you?"

"Never taken it off, you know that, Fuleow." Veppers clapped the other man's stout shoulder and winked at his slender wife.

"Oh, your poor nose!" Auer said, pushing back locks of soot-black hair to display glittering earrings.

"Poor? Nonsense; never richer." Veppers flicked one finger against the new cover over his nose, which was still slowly growing back underneath. "This is pure gold!" He smiled, turned away. "Sapultride! Good to see you; glad you could make it."

"What's it look like, under there?" Sapultride asked, nodding at Veppers' nose. He pulled down his sunglasses, revealing small green eyes above his own thin, expensively sculpted nose. "I was studying medicine before I was lassoed back into the family firm," he said. "I could take a look. Wouldn't be shocked."

"My dear Sapultride, it looks *great* under this. Face facts; I look better mutilated than most men do at their very best, whole and hearty after a long day in the grooming salon."

"Jasken," Sapultride's wife Jeussere said to the man standing behind Veppers, one arm in a cast and a sling, "did you *really* do this to our dear, lovely Veppers?"

"I regret to say so, ma'am," Jasken said, bowing gently to the slim, exquisitely dressed and manicured woman. He pushed his slung arm out a little. "Mr. Veppers more than had his revenge though. What a blow he—!"

"His revenge?" Jeussere said, a tiny frown spoiling her otherwise quite perfect face. "The story I heard was that he struck first."

"He did, ma'am," Jasken said, aware that Veppers was watching him. "It was only his shock at having hit me so sharply, and his natural urge to stop, putting up his sword and inquiring to make sure that he had not injured me too severely, that allowed me the opportunity to deliver my own blow, the one that – more by luck than skill – so assaulted Mr. Veppers' nose."

Jeussere smiled conspiratorially. "You are too modest, Jasken."

"Not so, ma'am."

"What, you weren't wearing masks?" Sapultride asked.

Veppers snorted. "Masks are for weaklings, aren't they, Jasken?"

"Perhaps, sir. Or for those of us who have such a lack of looks that we can't afford to lose even a little of them. Unlike your good self."

Veppers smiled.

"My, Veppers," Jeussere said slyly, "do you have all your servants flatter you so?"

"Absolutely not. I work to prevent it," Veppers told her. "But the truth will out."

Jeussere laughed delicately. "You're lucky he didn't run you through, Jasken," she told him, her eyes wide. She slipped her arm through her husband's. "Sappy here beat Joiler at some sport at school and he near throttled him, didn't he, dear?"

"Ha! He tried," Sapultride said, running a finger round his collar.

"Nonsense," Veppers said, turning to somebody else. "Raunt! You ancient withered old rogue! That committee still hasn't jailed you yet? Who've you had to bribe?"

"Nobody that you haven't already got to, Veppers."

"And Hilfe; still an accessory?"

"More of a bauble, Joiler." The woman, much younger than her husband, though still in expensively well-preserved middle-age, coolly regarded his nose. "Well now, dear me. Think you'll still be able to sniff out trouble?"

"Better than ever," he told her.

"I'm sure. Anyway, good to see you back in the land of the sociable." She held one hand out to be kissed. "Can't have you hiding away; what shall we all do for fun?"

"You tell him. He spends too much time away on business trips," Jeussere contributed, leaning in.

"My only aim is to keep your good selves entertained," Veppers told the two women. "Ah, Peschl, we'll have a word later, yes?"

"Certainly, Joiler."

Jasken put one finger to an ear bud. "The boats are ready, sir."

"They are? Good." He looked round the other people in the slim barge. He clapped his hands, stopping most of the other conversations in the open vessel. "Let's enjoy the fun, shall we?"

He raised his hands above his head, clapped them again, loudly. "Listen!" he hollered, attracting the attention of people in the other two barges behind. "Your attention please! Place your bets, choose your favourites! Our game begins!"

There was some cheering. He took his place in the seat – raised just a little higher than the rest – in the bows of the slim craft.

Astil, Veppers' butler, saw to his master's needs while other servants moved down the central aisles of the barges, dispensing drinks. Above the seated VIPs, sun canopies rippled in the breeze. In the distance, over tree-dotted pastureland, the serried neatness of the kitchen orchards and the formal gardens of the estate, the turrets and ornamental battlements of the mansion house of Espersium were visible.

Some birds flew up from the network of small lakes, ponds and channels beneath.

The great torus-shaped mansion of Espersium sat near the centre of the estate of the same name. Espersium was easily the largest private estate in the world. Had it been a country its land area would have ranked it as the fifty-fourth largest out of the sixty-five states that still had some administrative significance in the unified world that was Sichult.

It was the centre of, and central to, the Veppers family fortune in more than merely symbolic ways. The original source of the family's vast wealth had been computer and screen games, followed by increasingly immersive and convincing Virtual Reality experiences, sims, games, proactive fictions and multiply-shared adventures, as well as further games of every sort and every level of intricacy, from those given away as free samples on smart-paper food wrappers, through those playable on devices as small as watches or jewellery, all the way to those which demanded either total bodily immersion in semi-liquid processor goo or the more simple – but even more radical – soft-to-hard-wiring of biological brain to computational substrate.

The house had long been ringed with comms domes, kept just out of sight of the house itself but linking it – and the buried masses of computer substrate it sat on – via satellites and system-edge relay-stations to further distant processor cores and servers all over the hundreds of planets that made up Enablement space and even beyond, to similar – if as a rule not quite so developed – civilisations that, with surprisingly little translation and alteration, found the games of the Veprine Corporation just as enjoyable and fascinating as Sichultians themselves had.

Still zealously guarding their original code, many of those games effectively reported back, eventually – via all those intervening arrays, servers, processors and substrates – to the still potent seat of power that was Espersium. From the estate house itself whole worlds and systems could be rewarded or punished according to how assiduously the local law-enforcement agencies applied anti-piracy legislation, billions of users could be granted access to the latest upgrades, tweaks and bonus levels, and lucrative personal on-line and in-game behaviour, preference and predilection data could be either used by the Veprine Corporation itself or sold on to other interested parties, either of a governmental or commercial nature.

Word had it that this sort of micro-managed operationality was no longer quite so centrally controlled, and the house had ceased to be the place that all versions of all games came to to get their latest updates – certainly there were fewer obvious satellite domes and programming geeks about the place than in the old days – but it was still much more than just a fancy country house.

The birds disturbed from the network of waterways beneath the barges wheeled in the sky, calling plaintively.

The little convoy of barges moved along a network of aqueducts poised above the watery landscape below. A couple of dozen skinny stone towers anchored the supporting stonework of delicate arches and flying buttresses which held the airborne canals aloft. At each of the towers the viaducts broadened out into circular basins collaring the slim spires and allowing the barges – individually, or joined as a tiny fleet – to change direction onto other channels. Half a dozen thicker towers held lifts within them and had quaysides where people could embark and disembark from the barges. The viaducts were only a couple of metres wide, with thin stone walls and no walkways alongside, so that one could look almost straight down.

Twenty metres beneath, in the channels, pools and lakes below, a dozen miniature battleships were just setting out from their individual start positions.

Each warship was the length of a large single-person canoe and had been designed to resemble a capital ship from the age when armour plate and large-calibre guns had ruled the seas of Sichult. Each ship contained a man, who powered his vessel by pedalling – turning a single propeller at the stern – steered it with a tiller attached to a bracket round his waist, and used his hands to aim and fire the three or four gun turrets his ship carried, each equipped with two or three guns.

Where the bridge would have been on the superstructure of the full-size vessels there was a series of slits, very like those in an ancient armoured helmet from the days of swords, lances and arrows. These provided the only way for the man inside the vessel to see out. Gun aiming was accomplished by nothing more sophisticated than dead reckoning and skill, the crewman of the miniature warship traversing the turrets and elevating their guns by way of a set of wheels and levers contained within his cramped compartment. Each ship also came equipped with a set of miniature torpedoes and a system of lights – the searchlights of the original ships – that let the vessels communicate with each other, to form temporary alliances and swap information.

Pennants flew from their masts, identifying who commanded them. The crewmen were far more highly trained than mere jockeys, Veppers contended. He had piloted the ships himself quite often, from when he had first come up with the idea, and still held the occasional amateurs-only battle for himself and similarly rich and competitive friends, but the truth was there was a great deal of skill involved; more than it was worth acquiring for a mere pastime.

These days the amateur versions of the ships were fitted with engines, which made life a little easier, but it was still taxing enough just manoeuvring the damned things without running aground or crashing into the banks of the channels, never mind the surprisingly difficult task of aiming the guns accurately. The amateur versions had better armour and less powerful weapons than the ships they were watching now.

Two ships caught a brief glimpse of each other from either end of a long channel connecting pools close to their start positions; disappearing from view again, they each elevated and fired their guns towards where they thought the other would shortly be, more in hope than with any expectation of a hit. Both sets of shells landed scattered amongst the low grassy hills of islands, in miniature reed beds and in the channels, raising skinny spouts of water. Neither part of either salvo landed closer than a ship length from its intended target.

"Something of a waste," Veppers muttered, watching through a pair of field glasses.

"Are the bullets terribly expensive?" Jeussere asked.

Veppers smiled. "No, I mean, they only have so many."

"Do they load the guns themselves?" Fuleow asked.

"No, automatic," Veppers said.

The ships' main weapons were almost more like grenade launchers than true guns; certainly they had nothing like the range they should have had, had that too been scaled proportionately. The little shells they fired fizzed and left a trail of smoke as they curved out across the waters, but they were explosive and could do real damage, piercing the armour of a ship and starting a fire within, or – hitting near the waterline – holing them so that they started to sink, or disabling turrets or the rudder or prop if they hit the right place.

A handful of pilots had been killed over the years, either struck by lucky shots that squeezed through the viewing slits, or drowning when their vessel turned over and the damage they had sustained had made it impossible to work the escape hatches, or choking or burned to death. Usually you could put out a fire by scuttling your ship – the channels, pools and most of the single large lake were generally little more than half a metre deep, so the command citadel, where the pilot's head was, would still be just above water even when the ship was sitting on the bottom – but valves jammed, or men were knocked unconscious, and accidents happened. There were rescue teams of helpers and divers standing by, but they were not infallible. Twice, ships had blown up completely, the contents of their magazines detonating all at once. *Most* spectacular, though on one occasion fragments of wreckage had flown far enough to threaten the spectators, which had been worrying.

The pilots – all part of Veppers' general staff, with other, part-time duties – were well paid, especially if they won their battles, and the risk of real injury and even death made the sport more interesting for the spectators.

Today's match was a team game: two ships to a side, the winning team being whoever was first to sink four of their opponents. The first thing the six sets of ships had to do was find each other; each ship started individually from one of the dozen floating boathouses scattered round the perimeter of the watery complex at any of several dozen randomly chosen locations.

The miniature naval battle itself – ship against ship or fleet against fleet, guns flashing and roaring, smoke drifting, shots landing, pieces getting blown off the ships, fountains of water bursting into the air when a torpedo hit – was only part of the delight of watching, Veppers found. Much of the enjoyment came from having this god-like overview of the whole battle arena and being able to see what the men in the ships couldn't see.

Most of the islands and the channel banks were too high to see over when you were sitting in one of the miniature battleships; however, from the network of aqueducts above, pretty much every part of the watery maze could be seen. It could be almost unbearably exciting to see ships converging on the same pool from different directions, or to watch a damaged vessel, limping home and nearly there, being caught by another ship lying in wait for it.

"You should have smoke, you know, Veppers," Fuleow told him as they all watched the ships cruise down the channels leading away from their starting points. They went at different speeds, some favouring high speed to get to some tactically important pool or junction before anybody else, some favouring a more stealthy approach; where the geography allowed, you could learn a lot by causing few waves yourself but watching for signs of the wakes of others as you passed side channels. "You know; from their funnels. That would make it look more realistic, don't you think?"

"Smoke," Veppers said, raising the pair of binoculars to his eyes. "Yes. Sometimes we have smoke, and they can put down smokescreens." He lowered the glasses, smiled at Fuleow, who had not been to one of these displays before. "Makes it hard to see from up here though, that's the trouble."

Fuleow nodded. "Ah, of course."

"Don't you think you ought to have pretty little bridges linking all the islands?" Auer asked.

Veppers looked at her. "Pretty little bridges?"

"Between the islands," she said. "Little arched bridges; you know, bowed. It would look so much prettier."

"Little too unrealistic," Veppers informed her, smiling insincerely. "Also, they'd get in the way of the shells; too many ricochets. There are wading routes between the islands for when the staff need to access them; sort of submerged paths."

"Ah, I see. Just a thought."

Veppers went back to watching his own two ships. They had been started far enough apart for it all to look convincingly random, though a quiet word had been had to let the two pilots know where the other was starting out from, so they were beginning with a slight advantage over the other five teams. Their pennants were silver and blue, the Veppers' family colours.

One of his ships chanced upon one of the Red team, powering down a channel forming the stem of a T-junction just as the other vessel was crossing ahead, allowing it to loose a salvo from its A and B turrets. Veppers always favoured ships with two forward-facing turrets and one rear-facing; it seemed more attacking, more adventurous. It also meant that a broadside consisted of nine shells rather than eight.

It was the first proper engagement of the afternoon. Cheers rang out as the targeted ship rocked to one side under the fusillade; bits of superstructure spun off the vessel as it lost its signalling lights. Two dark holes appeared near the waterline at mid-ships. Veppers ordered a round of celebratory cocktails for all. Arriving at the next tower, with its encircling girdle of water and choice of three different viaducts to take, the three barges split up and went their separate ways.

Veppers was in control of the first barge, steering it with pedals at his feet and ignoring the pleas of his passengers to watch the ships they'd placed bets on so that he could watch the progress of his own vessels.

There was a roar and some lady-like screams from some distance away as another two ships met side-on just beneath, but even closer than in the first engagement; one rammed the other, forcing it sideways onto a sandbank through the attacking vessel's momentum and trapping it there, firing point-blank into its superstructure; shells whizzed away, ricocheting.

The grounded vessel brought all four twin-gun turrets to bear and let off a broadside that blasted into the other ship's command citadel, where the torso, shoulders and head of the opposing pilot would be. Veppers, watching through his binoculars, made a whistling noise.

"That looks like it could well hurt!" Raunt said.

"The poor man's just inside there!" Auer said.

"They sit in an armoured tub," Veppers told her. "And they wear flak vests. Yes, Jasken?" he said as the other man leaned in towards him, Enhancing Oculenses glittering in the sunlight.

"The house, sir," Jasken said quietly, nodding.

Veppers frowned, wondering what he was talking about. He looked towards the distant mansion and saw a small dark arrowhead shape lowering itself towards the central courtyard. He brought the binoculars up in time to see the familiar alien craft disappearing behind the stonework. He put the field glasses down.

"Fuck," he said. "Chooses his moments."

"Shall I ask him to wait?" Jasken said, his mouth very close to Veppers' ear.

"No. I want the news, good or bad. Call Sulbazghi, get him to come too." He looked behind. They were a lot closer to the tower to their rear than the one ahead. They'd disembark there. He put the barge into full astern. "Sorry ladies, gentlemen," he shouted, over questions and protests. "Duty calls. I must go, but I shall return. To collect my winnings, I imagine. Sapultride, you're captain."

"Splendid! Do I get a special hat?"

"So, have we decided exactly what it is?" Veppers asked. He, Jasken, Dr. Sulbazghi and Xingre, the Jhlupian, were in the shielded, windowless drawing room in the sub-basement of the Espersium mansion which Veppers used for especially secret meetings or delicate negotiations.

Somewhat to Veppers' surprise, it was Xingre, the usually reticent Jhlupian, who spoke, the translation filtering from the silvery cushion the alien sat upon, voice pitched to the scratchy, tinkly tones it favoured. "I believe it to be consistent with an inter-membranial full-spectrum cranial-event/state germinatory processor matrix with singular condensate-collapse indefinite-distance signalling ability, Level Eight (Player) in manufacture, bilateral carboniform panhuman sub-design."

Veppers stared at the twelve-limbed creature. Its three stalk eyes stared back. One dipped down, let itself be cleaned and wetted by its mouth parts, then flipped jauntily upright again. The alien had returned with the thing that had been in the girl's head, the thing that might or might not be a neural lace. Xingre had had its own techs analyse the device using Jhlupian technology.

If Veppers was being honest with himself he would have to admit that over the handful of days that the device had been with the Jhlupians he had quite happily let thoughts of the thing and its implications slip from his mind. Jasken had been unable to establish any more useful facts about it beyond what they already knew and on the couple of occasions they had talked about it they had largely convinced themselves that it must be a fake, or just something else, maybe alien, maybe not, that had somehow found its way into the furnace.

The alien extended one bright green limb towards Sulbazghi, giving him the device back inside a little transparent cylinder. The doctor looked at Veppers, who nodded. Sulbazghi poured the shimmering, blue-grey thing into his palm.

"My dear Xingre," Veppers said after a moment, with a tolerant smile. "I think I understood every single word you said there, but, sadly, *only* as single words. Put together like that they made no sense at all. What *are* you talking about?" He looked at Jasken, who was frowning mightily.

"I told you," the alien said. "Probably it is what remains of an inter-membranial full-spectrum cranial-event/state germinatory—"

"Yes, yes," Veppers said. "As I say, I heard the words."

"Let me translate," said Sulbazghi. "It's a Culture neural lace."

"You're sure, this time?" Jasken asked, looking from the doctor to the alien.

"Certainly Level Eight (Player) in manufacture," Xingre said.

"But who put it in her?" Veppers asked. "Definitely not the clinicians?"

Sulbazghi shook his head. "Definitely not."

"Agreed," the Jhlupian said. "Not."

"Then who? What? Who could have?"

"Nobody else that we know of," Sulbazghi said.

"Level Eight (Player) manufacture is absolutely certain," Xingre said. "Level Eight (Player) so-called 'Culture' manufacture likely to ratio of one hundred and forty-three out of one hundred and forty-four in total."

"Almost certainly, in other words," the doctor said. "I suspected it was from the start. It's Culture."

"Only to ratio of one hundred and forty-three out of one hundred and forty-four chances," Xingre pointed out again. "Additionally, device implantation might have occurred at any time from immediately subsequent to birth event to within last two local years approximately but not closer to present. Probably. Also; only remains of. Very most fine cilia-like twiggings likely burned off in furnace."

"But the kicker," Sulbazghi said, "is in the one-time signalling capacity."

Xingre bounced once on its silvery cushion, the Jhlupian equivalent of a nod. "Singular condensate-collapse bi-event indefinite-distance signalling ability," it said. "Used."

"Signalling?" Veppers said. He wasn"t sure if he was simply being slow here or if a deep part of him just didn't want to know what might be the truth. He already had the feeling he usually got before people delivered particularly bad news. "It didn't signal her . . . ?" He heard his own voice trail off as he looked again at the tiny, nearly weightless thing that lay in his palm.

"Mind-state," Jasken said. "It might have signalled her mind-state, her soul, to somewhere else. Somewhere in the Culture."

"Malfunction rate of said process betrays ratio of equal to or higher than four out of one hundred and forty-four in total," Xingre said.

"And that really is possible?" Veppers asked, looking at all three of them in turn. "I mean, total, full . . . transferring of a real person's consciousness? This isn't just a cosy myth or alien propaganda."

Jasken and Sulbazghi looked at the alien, which sat floating silently for a short while, then – suddenly fixing them with the gaze from one eye each – seemed to realise it was the one they all expected to answer. "Yes," it blurted. "Positively. A full affirmation."

"And bringing them back to life; they can do that too?" Veppers asked.

Xingre was quicker this time. After a moment, when nobody else answered, it said, "Yes. Also most possible, availability of appropriate and compatible processing and physique substrate shell being assumed."

Veppers sat for a moment. "I see," he said. He put the neural lace down on the glass top of a nearby table, letting it drop from a half-metre up to see what noise it made.

It seemed to fall slightly too slowly, and landed silently.

"Bad luck, Veppers!" Sapultride told him when he got back to the naval battle. "Both your ships got sunk!"

Twelve

"Lededje Y'breq," the avatar Sensia said, "may I introduce Chanchen Kallier-Falpise Barchen-dra dren-Skoyne."

"Kallier-Falpise for short," the drone itself said, dipping in the air in what she guessed was the equivalent of a bow or nod. "Though I'll happily answer to Kall, or even just KP."

The machine floated in the air in front of her. It was about big enough to sit comfortably on two outspread hands; a cream-casinged, mostly smooth device that looked like something you'd find on the work surface of an intimidatingly well-equipped kitchen and wonder what its function was. It was surrounded by a vague, misty halo that appeared to be various mixtures of yellow, green and blue according to the angle. This would be its aura field – the drone equivalent of facial expression and body language, there to convey emotions.

She nodded. "Pleased to meet you," she told it. "So you're my slap-drone."

Kallier-Falpise rocked back in the air as though hit. "Please. That's a little pejorative, if I may say so, Ms. Y'breq. I'll be accompanying you principally for your own convenience and protection."

"I'm—" she began, then was interrupted by the young man standing at her side.

"My lovely Led," he said, "I'm sorry I can't wave you farewell properly, but I must go. Let me . . ." He took her hand, kissed it, then, after a shake of his head and a wide smile, he held her head in both hands and kissed her face in a variety of places.

He was called Shokas, and while he had proved an attentive and sensitive lover, he had been impossible to shake off come the morning. He'd said he had other things he had to do that day but had insisted on accompanying her here, despite protests.

"Mmm," she said, noncommittally, as he kissed her. She prised his hands from her face. "A pleasure, Shokas," she told him. "I don't suppose we shall ever meet again."

"Shh!" he said, placing a finger to her lips and his other hand on his chest as he half closed his eyes and shook his head. "However, I must go," he said, backing off but keeping hold of her hand until the last moment. "You wonderful girl." He looked round the others, winked. "Wonderful girl," he told them, then sighed deeply, turned and walked quickly for the traveltube doors.

Well, that was one less. She hadn't expected so many people. Jolicci was there too, standing smiling at her.

She was in a Mediumbay of the GSV, on a wide gantry fifty metres up a side wall from the deck, the view in front of her filled by the pink-hulled bulk of the Fast Picket *The Usual But Etymologically Unsatisfactory*; near three hundred relatively slim metres of ancient warship now turned to more peaceful duties, such as ferrying people about the galaxy when they were heading for points not covered by the Culture's more routine transportation arrangements.

The ship was supposed to be fifteen hundred years old but appeared brand spanking new and – to her – still looked like a round, windowless skyscraper laid on its side. Its rear three-fifths was a single great cylinder, its pale pinkness chevroned with brown. This was its engine, seemingly. Another substantial section held various mostly sensory systems and the roughly conical section at the front would have held weapons when it had been a Psychopath-class Rapid Offensive Unit. The crew section, a thick band on the central spindle squeezed in between the engine and the systems section, looked small for the thirty or so people who would once have formed its crew, but generous for one. It had produced a single solid-looking plug of doorway twenty metres long, which had moved smoothly out towards them then dropped gently down to the gantry's floor level to provide a sort of gang-plank affording access to the vessel. The ship's own avatar was another drone, a little bigger, boxy and more thrown-together-looking than Kallier-Falpise.

"Shall we?" she said to it.

"Certainly." The drone floated to one side and picked up the two small cases of clothes, assorted toiletries and so on which Sensia had given her.

"Farewell, Lededje," Sensia said.

Lededje smiled at her, thanked her, accepted a hug, then bade a slightly more formal goodbye to Jolicci. She turned towards the ship.

"Just in time. Let me be the last to wish you *bon voyage*," a voice said behind her.

She turned to find Demeisen strolling from the traveltube entrance, smiling thinly. He looked a little less haggard and dishevelled than when Lededje had seen him the evening before. The red jewel at his neck glittered under the lights.

Sensia glared at him. "I thought you left earlier."

"I did leave earlier, my gracious hostess. I am currently some eighty years or so distant on an acutely divergent course, and travelling only slightly more rapidly than your good self, though still just about within real-time control range, at least for something as intrinsically slow-reacting as a human host. All of which I would hope you're well aware of."

"You're abandoning your puppet here then?" Jolicci said.

"I am," Demeisen agreed. "I thought now would be as appropriate an occasion as any other to return the fucker to the wild."

"I have heard some disturbing reports regarding your treatment of this human you're using, ship," Sensia said. Lededje looked at the GSV's avatar. For a small, frail-looking lady with frizzy blonde hair she seemed suddenly invested with a steeliness Lededje found herself glad was not directed at her.

Demeisen turned to Sensia. "All above board, dear thing. I have the relevant releases signed by his own fair hand. In blood, admittedly, but signed. What was I to use – engine oil?" He looked puzzled and turned to Jolicci. "Do we even *have* engine oil? I don't think we do, do we?"

"Enough," Jolicci said.

"Say goodbye and release your hold now before I do it for you," Sensia said levelly.

"That would be impolite," Demeisen said, pretending shock.

"I'll suffer the injury to my reputation," the GSV's avatar said coolly.

The cadaverous humanoid rolled his eyes before turning to Lededje and smiling broadly. "My every best wish for your journey, Ms. Y'breq," he said. "I hope I did not alarm you unduly with my little display last night. I get into character sometimes, find it hard to know when I'm causing distress. My apologies, if any are required. If not, then please accept them in any event, on account, to be banked against any future transgressions. So. Perhaps we shall meet again. Until then, farewell."

He bowed deeply. When he came upright he looked quite changed; his face was set differently and his body language had altered subtly too. He blinked, looked around, then stared blankly at Lededje and then at the others. "Is that it?" he said. He stared at the ship in front of him. "Where is this? Is that the ship there?"

"Demeisen?" Jolicci said, moving closer to the man, who was looking down at himself and feeling his neck under his chin.

"I've lost weight . . ." he muttered. Then he looked at Jolicci. "What?" He looked at Sensia and Lededje. "Has it happened yet? Have I been the avatar?"

Sensia smiled reassuringly and took him by the arm. "Yes, sir, I believe you have." She began to lead him towards the traveltube and made a begging-your-leave gesture to Jolicci and Lededje before turning away.

"But I can't remember anything . . ."

"Really? Oh dear. However, that may be a blessing."

"But I wanted memories! Something to remember!"

"Well . . ." Lededje heard Sensia say, before the doors of the traveltube capsule closed.

Lededje nodded to an unsmiling Jolicci and walked along the level, granite-solid gangplank towards the ship, followed by the ship's drone and the creamy presence of her slap-drone.

The Fast Picket *The Usual But Etymologically Unsatisfactory* slipped away from the GSV *Sense Amid Madness, Wit Amidst Folly*, slung out in a great elongated nest of fields that decelerated it to speeds the Fast Picket's engines could cope with. To Lededje, who was used to fighter planes being faster than passenger jets and powerboats overtaking liners, this seemed wrong somehow.

"Scale," the boxy-looking ship-drone told her as she stood – and it and Kallier-Falpise floated – in the main lounge, watching a wall screen showing the silvery dot that was the GSV disappearing into the distance. The dot, and the swirl of stars shown beyond it, started to track across the screen as the *The Usual But Etymologically Unsatisfactory* began its long turn to head for Arm One-one Near-tip and the Ruprine Cluster. "With ship engines, there are advantages that come with scale."

"Bigger is better," confirmed Kallier-Falpise. The silvery dot and the whole great sweep of stars moved faster and faster across the screen, apparent motion accelerating as the Fast Picket wheeled about, heading three-quarters of the way back in the direction the GSV had come from.

"Let me show you to your cabin," the ship's drone said.

They set course for Sichult. The journey was due to take about ninety days.

Lededje's cabin, taking up the space of four of the originals, was spacious and beautiful, if somewhat minimalist compared to what she was used to back home. Veppers didn't believe in minimalism; he thought it smacked of a lack of imagination or money, or both. The bathroom was similar in size to the cabin and had a transparent spherical bath for which she suspected she was going to need instructions.

Kallier-Falpise followed her and the ship's drone around, floating a metre or so to her side, just visible at the corner of her eye as she inspected the cabin. She turned and faced it once the ship's own drone had left.

"I think I'll get some more sleep," she told the slap-drone.

"Allow me," the cream-coloured machine said, and the bed – another of the scoop-plus-intelligent-snowflake-feathers design she was becoming used to – fluffed up, like a curiously localised snowstorm in one corner of the cabin. They were called billow beds, apparently.

"Thank you," she said. "You don't need to stay."

"Are you sure?" the little machine asked. "I mean, obviously while we're aboard ship, that's fine, but once we arrive anywhere else I would be derelict in my duty if I didn't remain where I might be of most immediate protective use, especially while you're asleep. It might be best for us both to get used to that arrangement, don't you think?"

"No," she said. "I prefer my privacy."

"I see." The machine bobbed in the air, its aura field going grey-blue. "Well, as I say, while we're aboard ship . . . Excuse me."

The door shushed closed behind it.

"'Ahem', is the accepted interrupter, I believe. So: ah-fucking-hem."

She opened her eyes to find herself looking sideways at a man sitting cross-legged on the floor about two metres away, near the centre of the cabin. He was dressed in the same dark clothes Demeisen had worn, and – as she blinked, trying to confirm to herself that she was really seeing what she appeared to be seeing – she realised that he looked like a healthier, filled-out version of the gaunt figure who'd bade her farewell only a few hours earlier.

She sat up, aware of the bed feathers swirling neatly about her, tidying themselves out of the way. She was glad she had worn pyjamas, less glad now that she had got rid of the slap-drone.

Demeisen raised one long finger. "Wait a mo; you might need this."

The word *SIMULATION* glowed in red letters – in Marian, this time – at the lower limit of her field of vision.

"What the hell is going on?" she said. She pulled her knees up to her chin. For a dizzying instant she was back in her bedroom in the town house in Ubruater, a decade earlier.

"I'm not really here," Demeisen said, winking at her. "You haven't seen me, right?" He laughed, spread his arms, looked about the cabin. "Do you have any *idea* how highly fucking irregular this is?" He put his elbows on his knees, rested his chin on his tented fingers. Too long, too multiply jointed, they looked like a cage. "This poor old stager thinks it's still some sort of hot-shot fucking warship with a few of its systems removed and most of the others improved. No more chance of somebody having a private chat with a passenger than . . . I don't know; it hitting a space reef or something."

"What are you talking about?" she asked. She looked around the cabin. The word *SIMULATION* followed her gaze like a subtitle.

Demeisen's face sort of scrunched up. "Not that there's any such thing. Running aground on an asteroid maybe; whatever. Anyway," he said, "Hello again. Bet you didn't expect to see me again so soon."

"Or ever."

"Well quite. Also bet you're wondering why I'm here."

She waggled a finger towards her lower face as she looked at him. "Can you get rid of . . ."

He snapped his fingers. It was an unsettlingly sharp, loud sound. She almost jumped.

"There," he said. The word *SIMULATION* vanished.

"Thank you. Why are you here, if only apparently?"

"To make you an offer."

"What? To be your next abused avatar?"

He grimaced again. "Oh, that was all just to upset Jolicci. You saw the guy I was . . . inhabiting; I released him in front of you. He was fine. I'd even fixed his fingers and everything. Didn't you notice, this morning?"

She hadn't.

"And anyway he *did* agree to everything. Not that I really abused him in the first place. Did he say anything? When I released him; did he? I didn't bother to send any surveillance back-up and I haven't asked the *SAMWAF*, so I honestly don't know what happened after I pulled out. Did he? Make any allegations?"

"He couldn't remember anything at all. He wasn't even sure he'd *been* an avatar; he thought maybe it was about to happen."

Demeisen waved his arms. "Well, there you are!"

"There you are what? That proves nothing."

"Yes it does; if I'd *really* been sneaky I'd have left the dumb fuck with a batch of implanted false memories full of whatever Contact-wank fantasies he'd been imagining before he took the gig in the first place." He waved one hand in a blur of too-long fingers. "Anyway, we're getting off the point here. You need to hear my offer."

She raised one brow. "Do I?"

He smiled. It was the first time he'd smiled, she thought, when it actually looked like he meant it. "Fine attempt at dismissive insouciance," he told her. "But yes, you do."

"All right. What is it?"

"Come with me. Not right now necessarily, but come with me."

"Where?"

"To Sichult. Back to your home."

"I'm already going there."

"Yes, but very slowly, and with a slap-drone in tow. Plus, they're going to try to distract you."

"How are they going to distract me?"

"By telling you they've found the ship with your full body image, the *Me, I'm Counting*. Which they sort of have, so it's not a lie, but they're hoping you'll want to detour to get your old body back or have the tattoo stuff copied onto your present body or some such nonsense. Which will mean a serious delay, especially travelling in this antique."

"Perhaps I'll want to do that anyway," she said. She felt a pang of something like loss and hope together. Wouldn't it be good to see her old, true self? Even if she wouldn't want to regain her Mark – maybe ever, but certainly not until she'd returned and got as close to Veppers as she could and done her damnedest to kill him.

"Makes no difference," Demeisen said, scything one hand through the air. "*I'll* fucking take you there if you insist on going; still be quicker. Point is: stay on this thing and you'll get home in not less than ninety days, and with a slap-drone dogging your every step."

"Whereas?"

He rocked forward on his crossed legs, looked suddenly serious and said, "Whereas come with me and I'll get you there in twenty-nine days with no fun-spoiling chaperone to hobble you."

"No slap-drone?"

"None."

"And no mistreatment? Of me, I mean, the way you mistreated that poor man? Including mistreatment I forget about?"

He frowned. "You still on about that? Of *course* no mistreatment. I swear."

She thought. After a moment she said, "Would you help me kill Veppers?"

He put his head back and laughed, loudly. The simulation did a convincing job of making his laughter echo round the generously proportioned cabin. "Ah, if only," he said, shaking his head. "You can cause your own major assassinatory incident, sweetheart, without making it a diplomatic one involving the Culture."

"You can't offer me any help at all?"

"I'm offering to get you there, quicker, and without the fucking slap-drone."

"But no help in doing what I want to do when I get there."

He slapped himself on the forehead. "Fuck me! What more do you want?"

She shrugged. "Help with killing him."

He put one long-fingered hand over his eyes for a moment. "Well," he said on an inward breath, taking his hand away and looking at her, "that is the only catch. Much as I'd like to offer you one of my own drones, or a knife missile or some magic force-field buttons for your cardigan or an enchanted gusset or whatever the fuck, for protection if nothing else . . . I can't, because in the unlikely event you *do* waste this fucker, or try to but fail – a much more plausible scenario, if we're being honest here – and they find any Culture tech on you, suddenly we look like the bad guys, and – hilarious though that would be in so many ways, obviously – even I draw the line at that sort of shit. Unless I'm requested to by a properly constituted committee of my strategically informed intellectual superiors, naturally. That would be entirely different."

"So why offer to help me at all?"

He grinned. "For my own amusement. To see what you get up to, to annoy the *SAMWAF* and Jolicci and all the other constipated smug-meisters of Contact and also because I'm heading in that direction anyway." He lifted both eyebrow creases. "Don't ask why."

"And how do you know all this?"

"You told me quite a lot of it last night, babe. The rest . . ." He spread his arms again. "I'm just well connected. I know Minds that know stuff. Specifically, exactly this sort of stuff."

"You're part of Special Circumstances."

He waggled one hand. "Technically no ships or Minds really are, not in an organised, hierarchic, signed-up-for-the-duration kind of way; all that any of us can ever do is just help out as best we can, making whatever small contribution we are able to as specific, time-limited opportunities present themselves. But yes." He sighed, somewhere between patiently and in exasperation. "Look, I don't have for ever; even this bumpkin of a taxi will twig to me being here eventually, so I'm going to go. You have a think.

The offer stands for the next eight hours; local midnight. After that I really need to dash on ahead. But just you wait; they'll spring this meet-up with the *Me, I'm Counting* or something representing it." He sat back, nodding. "Semsarine Wisp. That's the name to look out for: the Semsarine Wisp." He flapped one long hand at her. "You can go back to sleep now."

She woke with a start, sat up. The cabin lights reacted to her movement, turning slowly up from near total darkness to a pervasive gentle glow. The noise of the ship made a distant shushing noise all about her.

She lay back down in her little organised storm of well-behaved snowflakes.

After a few moments the lights faded away too.

"Whereabouts?"

"Hmm?"

"Where would this rendezvous take place?" she asked Kallier-Falpise. They were in a part of the ship's lounge shaped like a giant bay window. She sat at a table, eating a meal that was part breakfast, part early supper. A breeze blew about her, bringing smells of the ocean. She had rolled the cuffs of her pyjamas up to feel the soft warm wind on her calves and forearms. The concave wall around her impersonated the view of a blue-green cloudless sky, a ruffled green ocean and snow-white breakers crashing onto the pale blue sand of a wide, deserted beach framed by gently swaying trees. Even the floor beneath her bare feet was taking part in the illusion, ridging and roughening to become a convincing impression of polished but uneven wooden boards, just like you'd find at a beach-side villa or resort somewhere nice and hot and far away. She'd almost finished the plate of completely unidentifiable but perfectly delicious fresh fruits. She'd been ravenous.

"There's a place in a part of the sky called the Semsarine Wisp," the little drone told her, as though she really didn't need to bother her pretty little head about such boring details. "That's where the rendezvous is expected to take place."

"Mm-hmm." She drank some water, sloshed it round her teeth.

The drone, floating over the table near her right hand, was silent for a moment, as though thinking. "You've . . . you've heard of it?"

She swallowed the water, dabbed at her mouth with a fluid-soft napkin. She gazed out at the fake view of the beach and sea, then looked at the little cream-coloured drone and smiled. "Would you ask the ship to contact the General Offensive Unit *Falling Outside The Normal Moral Constraints*, please?"

"What? Why?"

"Go on; say it's irregular."

"Irregular is the very least of what it is. It's rude, it is *suspicious*." The boxy ship's drone swivelled in mid-air, turning away from the grinning figure of Demeisen to point itself at Lededje. "Ms. Y'breq," it said frostily. "I cannot emphasise strongly enough that I think this would be a profoundly unwise move; frankly, even a stupid and dangerous one. I'm sorry to be so blunt." It glanced at Demeisen. "I thought you had seen something of how this person, this ship is liable to treat innocent human beings. I cannot believe that you are even contemplating such a hazardous and foolhardy choice."

"Hmm," Lededje said, nodding at this. "You know, I think I'll leave these bags behind." She frowned down at the two small cases Sensia had given her. They sat at her feet in the ship's main lounge. Demeisen stood at her side; the two drones floated in front of them. She turned at Demeisen. "You can provide me—?"

"Of course."

"Ms. Y'breq," Kallier-Falpise said, sounding like it was trying to remain calm. "Obviously, I shall be coming with you . . ."

"Obviously," the ship's drone agreed, traversing to point at Demeisen.

There was only the faintest of pauses. "Eh? Oh. Yes, obviously," Demeisen said, nodding strenuously.

"Ah. You agree then?" Kallier-Falpise said, flicking to look straight at Demeisen. "I accompany Ms. Y'breq?"

"I would have it no other way," Demeisen said solemnly.

"Just so." The little drone's aura field glowed an agreeable pink. It turned smoothly back to Lededje. "As we all agree, then, I shall be coming with you, still charged, of course, with protecting you—"

"Mostly from yourself," Demeisen said with a quick grin. He bowed his head and held up one hand as the little cream-coloured drone's field flashed a bright grey. "Sorry," he said.

"However," Kallier-Falpise continued, "I too am very much of the opinion that this is, nevertheless, a foolish, dangerous and unnecessary move. Please, I beg you; reconsider."

Lededje smiled at it. She looked at the ship's drone. "Thank you for all your help," she told it. She turned to Demeisen again. "Ready when you are."

"I'll prepare a shuttle," the ship-drone said.

Demeisen flapped one hand. "We'll Displace."

"Has Ms. Y'breq been informed—?"

"There is a chance Displacements can be bad for you," Demeisen said with a sigh. "Yes. I've read her her last rights."

Kallier-Falpise's fields went frosty grey again. "You did not think to ask *me* if I consent to being Displaced when a far more intrinsically safe method of transferring us between ships exists to hand."

Demeisen rolled his eyes. "Fine, you take the shuttle, you rough, tough little protection-and-intervention drone; I'll Displace the squidgy bag of guts, gas and fluids that is the painfully vulnerable but patently *un*afraid human being."

"Frankly I wouldn't trust you to wait for me," the little drone said. "I shall Displace along with Ms. Y'breq. Within the same containment field, if you please."

"Fuck me," Demeisen breathed. "Hoity *and* toity. Fine! We'll do it your way." He pointed at the ship's drone. "Tell you what, grandpa; why don't *you* do the fucking Displace? You move them both over to me."

"I was going to suggest that anyway," the ship-drone said coldly.

"Right," Demeisen said, sounding exasperated. "Can we get

going? Now? Your venerableness here might be going flat out but I'm barely strolling. Getting antsy here."

"Excuse me," the little cream-coloured drone said as it floated closer to Lededje and up-ended itself to press gently in against her stomach. She wore another set of the trews and top she had grown fond of since waking in this body. "You are sure you don't want to take your luggage?"

"Quite sure," she said.

"Both ready?" the ship-drone asked.

"Entirely so."

"Yes."

"After you," the ship-drone said to Demeisen.

"See you over there," he said to Lededje, then a silver ovoid enclosed him. It winked to nothing.

An instant later Lededje briefly found herself staring at a distorted version of her own face.

The ship's drone tipped back to look up at the ceiling, which was where the protection-and-intervention drone Kallier-Falpise had floated the instant the Displacement containment field around it and Lededje Y'breq had flicked out of existence. Kallier-Falpise, listing badly, bumped randomly along the ceiling a few times, for all the world like an escaped party balloon, partly deflated. Its aura field displayed the colours of oil floating on water.

"Shao, shum-shan-shinaw, sholowalowa, shuw, shuwha . . ." it mumbled.

The boxy-looking ship-drone used its own light effector unit to administer the equivalent of a slap. Kallier-Falpise trembled against the ceiling fixtures, then dropped, side-slipping. It flashed a strident yellow-orange for an instant, then it seemed to shake itself. It straightened, floating down to the same level as the ship-drone, its aura field glowing white with anger.

~Meatfucker.

~If it's any comfort, the ship-drone sent – I don't even know how it did that. It's not as though it let you land and then spat you straight back. Fucking thing jumped my Displace mid-throw. I wasn't even aware we could *do* that. That's downright worrying.

~Did you put anything on the girl?"

~On and in. Best bits and pieces I was given. I'm just waiting to—

There was a flicker of silver directly over the ship-drone, followed by a tiny clapping noise as the incoming Displacement field collapsed. A bitty rain of tiny components, seemingly little more than dust, some hair-thin threads and a few grains of sand, floated down through the air to be caught and held by a maniple field the drone extended above itself.

~Ah, it sent – here they are now. It made a show of bouncing the maniple field up and down, weighing. – Yup, they're all there, to the last picogram.

~Meatfucker, the other drone repeated.

~Trying comms; zero avail. The ship's drone rose a quarter-metre in the air then sank slowly down. – Guess that's that then.

The two machines watched through the ship's main sensor array as it showed the sixteen-hundred-metre length of the other warship sweeping its multiple deep-space high-speed engine fields about it with a completely unnecessary flourish. For the merest instant the *Falling Outside The Normal Moral Constraints* presented in real space as a black, perfectly reflecting ovoid, then with a flicker it was gone, so quickly even the Fast Picket's finely tuned sensors struggled to track it.

Thirteen

This deep in the ice you would need serious amounts of cooling. Otherwise you'd boil. At least you would if you were any normal sort of human, or indeed if you were any kind of conventional being with the sort of biochemistry that could not cope with temperatures much outside a narrow band between freezing and boiling. Keep cool inside the ice or you'd boil alive. The alternative would be to submit to the pressure, which would crush you to oblivion even quicker than the temperature would cook you to death.

It was all relative, of course. Below freezing or above boiling of what, and where? Water was the reference medium he was used to, as part of the pan-human meta-species, and liquid water at standard temperature and pressure, he supposed, but then: whose standard temperature and pressure?

Down here, inside a water planet, under a hundred kilometres of warm ocean, the sheer pressure of the water column above turned the water first to slush and then to ice. It was high-pressure ice, not low-temperature ice, but it was still ice, and the further down towards the planet's centre you went the harder and hotter the ice got, heated by the same pressure that had forced the water from its liquid to its solid state.

Even so, there were imperfections and contaminants in the ice: flaws, boundaries – sometimes narrowing down to only a single molecule wide – between volumes of the solid where it was possible for other liquids to slip amidst the vast compressive masses of the surrounding ice.

And, if you had evolved here, or had been carefully designed to exist here, it was even possible for creatures to exist within the ice. Tendril-slim, transparently tenuous, more like highly spread-out membranes than anything resembling an animal, they were able to make their way up and down and along the flaws and seams and fissures in the ice, seeking food in the shape of those minerals and other contaminants the ice held, or, in the case of the predators of the deep ice, attacking those grazing creatures themselves.

He – what he now was – had not evolved here. What he was now was a simulation of a creature, an organism designed to be at home in the pressure ice of a water world. But only a simulation. He was not what he appeared to be.

He was beginning to wonder if he ever had been.

The ice inside the water planet did not really exist; neither did the water planet itself, nor the star it orbited nor the galaxy beyond nor anything of what appeared to be real no matter how far out you might think you were looking. Nor how far in you looked, either. Peer into anything closely enough and you would find only the same graininess that the Real exhibited; the smallest units of measurement were the same in both realms, whether it was of time or extent or mass.

For some people, of course, this meant the Real itself was not really real, not in the sense of being genuinely the last un-simulated bedrock of actuality. According to this view everybody was already in a pre-existing simulation but simply unaware of it, and the faithful, accurate virtual worlds they were so proud of creating were just simulations within a simulation.

That way though, arguably, madness lay. Or a kind of lassitude through acceptance that could be exploited. There were few better ways of knocking the fight out of people than by convincing them that life was a joke, a contrivance under somebody else's ultimate control, and nothing of what they thought or did really mattered.

The trick, he supposed, was never to lose sight of the theoretical possibility while not for a moment taking the idea remotely seriously.

Musing upon such thoughts, he slipped with the others down a one-kilometre-high, many-kilometres-long flaw in the ice. In human terms it was probably like being a caver, a pot-holer, he imagined. Though that must do the experience little justice.

They were, he supposed, like separate strands of sluggish oil seeping between the ice sheets on what he still thought of as a conventional world, a rocky planet with ice at the poles and mountain peaks.

He commanded a small but potent force a crack team of thirty, all highly trained and armed with poisons, chemical micro-explosives and packages of solvent. Most – perhaps all – of the marines and machines whose representations he'd inhabited over the subjective-time decades the great war had lasted to date would have regarded this as laughably inadequate weaponry, but it would be perfectly deadly down here, where not one of those marines or war machines would last for more than a fraction of a second. They were over-officered – he was here as a major, though in any other theatre he'd be a general – but that just reflected the importance of the mission.

He could feel the presence of each of the others, chemical gradients and electrochemical signals passing within and between each of them keeping him in literal touch with every one of the thirty marines under his command. Here was Corporal Byozuel on the right, slipping and sliding down a particularly wide channel, briefly beating the rest of them for penetration; here was Captain Meavaje way out on the left and spin-forward, guiding his squad's four solvent-carrying specialists through a tricky sequence of fissures like a three-dimensional maze. First Byozuel, then the marines between them in sequence, reported a strong quake. Vatueil felt it himself an instant later.

The ice seemed to creak and whine, the space which most of Vatueil himself was in tightened, shrinking by half a millimetre. Another part of him was in a cavity a little higher further up; this widened a fraction, trying to pull him upwards. He had to grip tighter, push harder, to continue his slow progress downwards, towards the core.

. . . All right, sir . . .? came the question from Lieutenant Lyske, who was next but one along the line.

. . . Fine, lieutenant . . . he sent back.

Vatueil had sensed them all stopping, freezing in position as the quake's compression wave had passed around and through them. Freezing like that slowed them down a fraction and it did no real good unless you were in a wide fissure about to enter a narrower one, but it was just what happened, what you did; human nature, or animal nature, or sentient nature, however you wanted to characterise it; you stopped and waited, hoping and dreading, hoping not to be about to die and dreading the feel of the ice around you shifting, and dreading too the biochemical scream that might come pulsing through the single living net they had made of themselves as somebody else was so compressed by fissures closing around them that they were squeezed to single, separated molecules, crushed to mush, chemicalised out of existence.

However, the quake had gone, leaving them all intact and alive. They resumed their progress, insinuating themselves deeper and deeper into the water world's ice. He sent electrochemical signals out to let everybody know that they were all okay. Still, they could not afford to relax just because that little instance of random danger had gone; they were approaching the level where they might expect to find defences and guards.

He wondered how you could characterise where they were now. It was not part of the main war sim. It was not another simulation running within that one either. It was something separate, something elsewhere; similar, but held apart from the other sims.

Byozuel's sudden signal came flashing through the net of the unit, passing from marine to marine: . . . Something, sir . . .

Vatueil commanded a full stop; they all came to a halt as quickly as possible without causing any further disturbance.

He waited a moment then sent . . . What do we have, corporal?

. . . Movement ahead, sir . . .

Vatueil held, waited. They all did. Byozuel was no fool – none of them were, they'd all been carefully picked. He'd be in touch when there was something to report. In the meantime, best to let him listen, sniff ahead, watch for any scintillations in the glassy darkness of the ice all around them.

Not that they'd seen much since the submarine had offloaded them in the silt slush at the bottom of the ocean, hours earlier. There had been absolutely nothing to see there; no sunlight was visible below a quarter of a klick down from the ocean surface, never mind a hundred klicks.

Once they'd entered the ice, a few cosmic rays had produced distant flashes, and a shallow ice-quake when they'd been less than a kilometre into the hard ice had produced some piezoelectric activity including a few dim glimmers, but their eyes, such as they were, represented their least useful sense.

. . . Ha! . . . The exclamation came along with a chemically transmitted wave of elation and relief, pulsing through the company of marines as though through a single body . . . Sorry, sir . . . Byozuel sent . . . Didn't want to risk communicating anything there. Enemy combatant engaged and neutralised, sir . . .

. . . Well done, Byozuel. Its identity?

. . . Here, sir . . . A complex set of chemical idents and gradients transmitted itself through the web of the unit to Vatueil. A guard. A single, highly aware but barely sentient unit secreted in a fissure within the ice ahead and sensed by Byozuel before it could sense him. So they had to hope, anyway. Studying the analysis of the paralysed, dying creature, Vatueil could see no sign that it had communicated anything before it had been speared by Byozuel and filled with poison.

Vatueil communicated the necessary details to the rest of the platoon . . . Let's assume there will be more ahead . . . he told them . . . Byozuel . . . he sent . . . how's the way ahead look from where you are?

. . . Good, sir. Good as we've seen. Not getting anything untoward, listening or smelling.

. . . Okay, we're going to shift formation . . . Vatueil sent . . . Rest of squad one and squad two, follow behind Byozuel. Three and four, regroup with same internal spacing and keep probing as we descend. We've got one enemy profile so watch for that but be aware there will be other types. We're tightening up here, concentrating. Stay as wary as you like.

He felt the formation change around him, the two squads slowly shifting to concentrate and gather above Byozuel, the other two pulling in from the other side.

The ice-quake came without warning. The screams came from both sides, seemingly at the same time as the tortured shriek of the shifting ice and the hazy scintillations produced by ice contaminants' piezoelectricity. The ice closed around Vatueil, squeezing him, producing a feeling of utter helplessness and terror just for a moment. He ignored it, let it all pass through him, prepared to die if it came to it but not prepared to show his fear. He was squeezed out of where he was, forced downwards by the sheer closing force of the ice above into a broader fissure beneath. He felt others moving out of control as well, felt three lose contact, tendrils between them broken, snapped, teased apart.

They all stopped again, those that were not writhing. Moments later, even they ceased to move, either dead or after self-administering relaxants, or being darted with them by their comrades.

Could it have been an explosion, enemy action? Had they set something off when Byozuel had neutralised the guard? The after-shocks moaned and rattled through the vastness above and around them. The quake felt too big, too comprehensive, to have come from a single-point detonation.

. . . Report, Vatueil sent, a moment later.

They had lost five of their total including Captain Meavaje. Some injuries: loss of senses in two, partial loss of locomotion in another two.

They regrouped again. He confirmed Lyske as his new second-in-command. They left the injured and one able-bodied marine to guard their retreat.

. . . Bastard blow, sir . . . Byozuel sent from his down-forward position, fifteen metres further down . . . But it's opened a fine-looking cleft down here. A positive highway it is, sir.

. . . Treat it as suspicious, Byozuel . . . he told the marine . . . Anything obvious might be mined or sucker-trapped.

. . . Yes, sir. But this only just opened, to the side of the one where our friend was. Looks pristine. And deep.

. . . Feel confident to explore, Byozuel?

. . . Feel confident, sir.

. . . Okay, I think we're all where we should be again. Go ahead, Byozuel, but still; take it easy.

The new fracture led almost straight down. Byozuel dropped hesitantly at first, then more quickly, with greater confidence. The rest formed up behind Byozuel, following him downwards.

The other two squads were making little progress. Vatueil decided to make the most of the advantage. He ordered them into the new fissure too.

The next guard came stumbling out of a side-crevice, a breach from the earlier fissure they'd been taking before. The guard lanced into Byozuel, instantly disabling him, but was in turn pierced by a pump-dart from one of the weapon-support specialists immediately behind Byozuel; the enemy struggled, died, started to dissolve. Byozuel adhered to one wall of the crevasse, sticking there, immobile, poisons spreading through his extended body. Another specialist flowed over him; investigating, diagnosing, trying to see where he might be cauterised, what parts might be amputated to save him. The specialist pulled away, cutting connections with Byozuel before communicating with Vatueil.

. . . Looks like I'll be covering retreat too, sir . . . Byozuel sent.

. . . Looks like it, Byozuel . . .

. . . That one might have got a warning off . . . one of the specialists sent.

. . . I can see something down here, sir . . . sent the one who'd continued past where Byozuel had been hit . . . Deep down. Looks . . . looks like a comprehensive light source, sir.

Establishing a better link through two more descending marines, Vatueil could more or less see what the deepest marine was seeing.

Caution to the wind time, he thought to himself.

. . . Stay here, Byozuel.

. . . Not much choice, sir.

. . . We'll be back for you, Byozuel. Everybody else: we're here. This is it. Form up for maximum attack by squad.

They gathered, shifted, configured. He felt the familiar pride, close to love, for those to whom he'd become close as they calmly and efficiently prepared to put themselves at great risk for a cause they believed in and for the collective good of their comrades. Almost sooner than he'd have liked, they were ready.

They floated, four small squads of marines, ready to receive one last electrochemical command before they split into their separate squads and could communicate only by vibration or light.

. . . On my command . . . he told them . . . Go go go . . .

They powered down the fissure towards the unreal light of the core.

"Of course these things do not exist as you describe them. Not in the sense that they are suffered by these so-called virtual people in these alleged virtual realities. They exist only in the sense that they are imagined, talked about, warned of. Ultimately we believe that these things do exist, but we believe that they exist in the greater reality – beyond our limited understanding, and yours – that is the true Afterlife, the one that awaits all who faithfully believe, regardless of whether they have these 'soulkeeper' devices or not. We are content to leave such reward and punishment to God. We would not presume to take on the work of God. That is for God alone. It would be blasphemy so to presume. Frankly, you insult us by making the claims about us that you do."

This had been a remarkably short speech by Representative Errun's standards. As he finished, sweeping his senatorial robes about him and sitting down, Representative Filhyn had to scramble to her feet again.

"Well," she said, "I'm sure we didn't mean to insult you, honourable colleague."

Errun only half-rose from his seat to say, "Insult, like many such feelings, is experienced in the soul of the person addressed; it is not something that can be granted or withheld by the person doing the addressing."

There was murmured assent to this expression, as there had been to the one before. Representative Errun resumed his seat, accepting shoulder-pats, nods and muttered well-dones from his retinue of advisors and aides.

"As I say," the young Representative from the Outlying Habitats said, "we did not mean to take offence." Filhyn realised what she had said and blurted, "I mean give offence." She stared at the Senate Speaker at the raised end of the debating chamber. "Ah, apologies," she said to the ancient and worthy senator sitting there, surrounded by his scribbling, keyboard-tapping staff. She felt herself flush, saw the amused expression on the face of Representative Errun, and with a gesture indicating to the Speaker that she was giving way, sat down. She could hear a leaves-in-the-wind noise spreading through the public and press galleries.

Representative Filhyn went to put her trunks over her face, then remembered that the cameras would probably still be on her and so didn't. Instead, as the Speaker brought up some doubtless lengthy and utterly irrelevant point of order, she made sure her mike was off, dipped her head to Kemracht, her aide, and said, "I might as well be wearing a necklace saying Bite Here. Put me out of my misery, Kemracht,"

"I'm hoping to, ma'am," the young male said, nodding to a departing messenger. He put his mouth near her ear. "We have a guest for the afternoon session."

Something about the way he said it made her rock back in her seat. She stared at him. He smiled back, using both his trunks to half-hide the expression, modestly.

"Do you mean . . . ?" she said.

"A visitor come back from the other side."

She smiled at him. He looked down. She gazed away to see Representative Errun looking suspiciously at her from the other side of the debating chamber. She wanted to smile broadly at him, but thought the better of it. Best to give no hint. She made her smile look like a brave but hopeless one, then quickly looked away again, as though covering her inability to keep up the pretence of good humour any longer. She put both her trunks up to her eyes, as though wiping away tears.

My, I'll make a politician of myself yet, she thought.

They lost a whole squad to a sudden electric jolt that ran through the ice like a depth charge, leaving the marines who'd borne the brunt of it dissolving in their wakes as those unaffected continued to power their way downwards.

Another attack came from the side where the original fissure had been. Two guards, and coordinated, but this time they were ready, darting them both and leaving them jerking and dying in their slipstream as the light from below took on a greenish tinge.

The light brightened smoothly as they got closer, then it changed, became slightly duller, speckled, and with something about it that implied movement. A whole force of guards was moving up towards them, their shadows flickering against the green light from below. Vatueil tried to count, then to roughly estimate. A dozen? Twenty? More? It was too difficult and it made no difference. They were not going to pull out now.

He wished that his real self – the self that would continue back in the main war sim, the self that still held all his memories of the decades of war – would be able to remember all this. But that self would never know.

In the war sim you learned from all your mistakes, including the ones that killed you. Death itself was part of the learning process. Everything, including dying, happened within a meticulously overseen simulation where the backed-up self was allowed to know everything that had happened to each of its earlier iterations. So you learned, became continually more experienced – even wise.

This was a simulation, a virtual world, but it was not part of the war sim and there would be no going back for him or any of the other marines. They might succeed or fail, but both results would lead to their deaths. His real, continuing self, back in the war sim, would learn nothing from this mission.

If he was lucky, that self might hear that this self had succeeded on this mission – if he and the others succeeded.

They closed quickly with the core's guards. The guards were wriggling up to meet them almost as fast as they were plunging downwards. Some darts from their opponents whizzed up past them, one deflecting off the shield of the marine next to Vatueil. His squad was in the lead; they were the vanguard, the very tip of the spear. He watched the dark shapes of the guards flit quickly closer. Very quickly; faster now than his force was falling and powering down towards them.

They would have time for one barrage, Vatueil realised, then this was rapidly going to turn into what in the old days they'd have called hand-to-hand . . . Steady . . . he sent. Then: . . . Open fire!

Impact lances, poison darts, dissolver rods and tasing bolts rained down onto their opponents.

Representative Filhyn had taken her lunch on one of the broad grassy terraces on the wide roof of the main senate building. The terrace looked out over the rolling grasslands that wound around the Central Leadership Complex like a mother's trunk round a new-born. Beyond the green river of the grasslands, the great shallow-sided ziggurats rose, vast outcrops of administration, commerce and habitation, their sides festooned with vegetation, their terraces and levels dotted with trees. The great plains beyond the city were lost in the bulking presences of the pyramids and the haze of the warm day.

Errun came alone, as his obviously hastily scribbled message had said he would. She wondered how much he had found out, and through whom. She met him at a deserted wallow near the transparent wall which ran round the terrace. She had left her robes and other personal effects with her aides, so sat, modestly attired, in the cool mud, nodding to the old male when he arrived, grunted a greeting and lowered his old, rotund body into the mud alongside.

"I am trying to imagine to what I owe this unexpected honour, senator," she told him.

"Perhaps you are," the portly old male said, relaxing luxuriantly in the mud. He kept his back to the view from the wallow. There was a three-metre safety gap between the transparent wall round the whole terrace and the edge – that was pretty much the minimum that a Pavulean could cope with once they were higher than one storey up – but the old senator was known to be particularly prone to vertigo. She was surprised he'd agreed to meet on such a high level in the first place. He turned in the mud to look at her. "On the other trunk, perhaps you're not."

He left a space she was seemingly meant to fill, but she didn't. Half a year ago, she would have, and might have given away more than she'd have wanted to. She declined to congratulate herself just yet. Representative Errun had many more tricks than just leaving people the space to talk themselves into trouble.

"Either way," he said, slapping some mud over his back with one trunk, "I think we should clear some things up."

"I am all for clearing things up," she told him.

"Um-hum," he said, throwing more mud over himself. There was a surprising neatness, almost a delicacy to how he did this that Filhyn found quite endearing. "We are," the old male began, then paused. "We are a fallen species, Representative." He stopped, looked her in the eye. "May I call you Filhyn?" He raised one muddied trunk, let it fall with a small muddy splash. "As we are in such informal circumstances?"

"I suppose so," she said. "Why not?"

"Well then. We are a fallen species, Filhyn. We have never been entirely sure what really came before us, but we have always imagined something more heroic, more bold, more like a predator. We are told this is the price of having become civilised." Errun snorted at this. "Anyway, we are who we are, and although we are not perfect, we have done the best we could, and done quite well. And we can be proud that we have not yet surrendered to the AIs we have brought into being, or abandoned all the attributes and mechanisms that made us great, and civilised, in the first place."

By this, Errun probably meant the primacy of natural Pavulean decision-making rather than letting their AIs have anything other than an advisory role, and commerce: money, the accumulation of capital. And – of course – Collective Wisdom, the Pavulean philosophy/religion/way of life which still bore within it traces of male supremacism and Haremism. These were exactly the things which Filhyn personally thought were now holding their whole civilisation back, but she wasn't about to start arguing with an ancient and revered conservative like Errun. Some problems were generational; you just had to wait for the relevant elders to die off and be replaced with more progressive types. With luck.

"You people from the Outlyings see matters differently, we realise," Errun told her. "But still, the soul of our people – our species, our civilisation – lies here, on these plains, this planet, on the terraformed New Homes and the habitats that spin around our home star." Errun raised his gaze to the sun, currently lighting up some layers of creamy cloud to the south.

"Under this sun," Filhyn said. She was also not going to bring up the absurdity of her being the only Representative for the whole diasporic mass of the Greater Pavulean Herd. In theory they were all part of the Fifteen Herds and there was no need for all the tens of billions of Pavuleans who now lived around other stars to have extra representation, but this was of course complete nonsense, just a way for the centre here on Pavul to keep control of its distributed empire.

"Under this sun," the old male agreed. "Do you possess a soulkeeper device?" he asked her suddenly.

"Yes," she told him.

"For an Outlying religion, I dare say."

She wasn't sure she would even call it a religion. "I'll stay amongst my far-flung friends when I die," she said. "My soul-keeper is keyed to our local Afterlife."

The old male sighed, shook his head. He seemed to be about to say something – perhaps he was going to chastise her, she thought – but then he didn't. He slapped some more mud about himself.

"We need threat to keep us honest, Filhyn," he told her. He sounded regretful, but intent. "I wouldn't go as far as those who wish we hadn't rid ourselves of predators, but we need something to keep us on our toes, to bring us up to the moral mark, don't you see?"

"I see that you believe that deeply, Representative," she said diplomatically.

"Um-hum. You will see the track I am heading along here. I won't dissemble. We need the threat of punishment in the after-life to keep us from behaving like mere beasts in this existence." He waved one trunk. "I have no idea if there really is a God, Filhyn, any more than you do, any more than the Grand High Priest does." He snorted. Filhyn was genuinely shocked to hear him say this, even if she'd long assumed just that. "Perhaps God resides in the places where the Sublimed live, in these hidden dimensions, so conveniently folded up and hard to get at," the old male said. "I suppose it is almost the last place He might. As I say, I don't know. But I know most certainly that there is evil in us, and I know and accept that the technologies that have given us the means to express that evil – allowing us to exterminate our natural predators – have led in turn to the technologies that now let us save our souls, that let us save ourselves and that let us continue to administer rewards and punishments beyond the grave. Or at least . . . the threat of punishment." He looked at her.

She slowly smeared her own back with mud. "Are you going to tell me that it is only the threat?"

He rolled a little closer to her, rotating in the grey-brown mud. "Of course it is just the threat," he told her quietly, conspiratorially, with a hint of humour. He rolled back again. "All that matters is that people are frightened into behaving properly while they are alive. What happens after they are dead is really no concern of the living. Nor should it ever be." He chuckled. "That last bit's just my personal belief, but it's also the truth of the matter as it stands. We scare them with these threats of correction and unpleasantness but once they're scared there's no need actually to impose the punishments. There are entire teams of creatives: artists, scenarioists, writers, explicators, designers, psychologists, sound sculptors and . . . well, God knows who and what else . . . Anyway, their entire working lives are spent creating a completely unrealistic environment and a completely false expectation for completely good and moral reasons."

"So the Hells only exist as a threat, to keep people in line while they're still alive."

"Well, ours certainly does. And that's all it does. Can't speak for the Afterlives of aliens. But I'll tell you this: a lot of the current fuss about them is founded on a basic misunderstanding. What's annoying is that people who don't want them to exist can't accept that they actually *don't* exist. Meanwhile they're wrecking the whole point of *pretending* that they do. If people just shut up and stopped complaining about things that don't happen in the first place then there wouldn't be any problem. Life would go on, people would behave themselves and nobody would really get hurt." The old male shook himself, seemingly disgusted. "I mean, what do they want? To *make* the Hells real so that people can be suitably frightened of them?"

"So where are all the people who ought to be in other Afterlives, in Heavens? Because they are not there."

Errun snorted. "In limbo." He slapped at something on his flank, inspected what he found there. An imaginary insect, Filhyn suspected. "Stored, but not functioning, not in any sense living." He seemed to hesitate, then rolled closer to her again. "May I speak in confidence, Filhyn?"

"I assumed all that's being said here is in confidence, Representative."

"Of course, of course, but I mean in particular confidence; something that you would not even share with your closest aides or a partner. Something strictly between you and me."

"Yes," she said. "Very well. Go ahead,"

He rolled closer still. "Some of those who disappear, who it might appear go into this so-called Hell," he said quietly, "are simply deleted." He looked at her, quite serious. She looked back. "They are not even held in limbo," he told her. "They simply cease to be; their soulkeeper thing is wiped clean and the information, their soul, is not transferred anywhere. That's the truth, Filhyn. It's not something that's supposed to happen, but it does. Now," he said, tapping her on one front knee, "you most emphatically did not hear that from me, do you understand?"

"Of course," she said.

"Good. That really is something we don't want people knowing. Don't you see?" he asked her. "All that matters is that people *believe* they are still living in some sense, and suffering. But, frankly, why waste the computer space on the bastards? Excuse my language."

Filhyn smiled. "Is it not always better to tell the truth though, Representative?"

Errun looked at her, shook his head. "The truth? No matter what? For good or ill? Are you mad? I do hope you're having a joke with me here, young lady." He held his nostrils with the finger stubs of one trunk and submerged himself completely in the mud, resurfacing moments later and snorting powerfully before wiping the mud from his eyes. "Don't pretend you are so naive, Filhyn. The truth is not always useful, not always good. It's like putting your faith in water. Yes, we need the rain, but too much can sweep you away in a flood and drown you. Like all great natural, elemental forces, the truth needs to be channelled, managed, controlled and intelligently, *morally* allocated." He glared at her. "You are having a joke with me, aren't you?"

I might as well be, she thought. She wondered if she would finally be a real politician when she agreed with what Errun was saying.

"Otherwise we are both wasting our time here, Representative."

One of us certainly is, she thought. She looked up, saw Kemracht signalling her from some distance away. "Not at all, Representative," she told the old male as she rose on all fours. "This has been most instructive. However, if you'll excuse me, I must go. Will you shower with me?"

The old male looked at her for some moments. "Thank you, no. I'll stay here a little longer." He kept looking at her. "Don't rock the barge, Filhyn," he told her. "And don't believe everything that everybody tells you. That's no way to the truth; just confusion and muddle."

"I assure you I don't," she told him. She performed a modestly shallow curtsy with her front legs. "I'll see you for the afternoon session, Representative."

He was one of the only two survivors of his squad, and their total force now numbered six. The rest had fallen to the up-swarming mass of guards. His marines had the better weaponry and were easily a match for the opposition, one against one, but there had been many more of the guards than there had seemed at first, and even when he and his men had poured through their entangling mass of bodies and weaponry they had encountered nets of barbs, nets of poisons and nets of convulsing electricity. Piercing, cutting those took more time, and, held up there, enfolded in the sickly green light flooding up from below, they'd been attacked from above by the remnants of the guards they had forced their way through. More marines had fallen, or dissolved, or jerked and spasmed, spiralling upwards.

But then they were through, just six of them. They fell against the green glowing surface, expanded, released their packaged solvents and seemed to become part of the transparent wall itself.

Then they were through, and falling. The conceit of the ice above was gone. Now they were in some vast spherical space, like the inside of a multi-layered moon. Above were quickly closing holes like bruises in a layer of dark cloud. The conceit of their own forms had changed too. No longer tissue-thin membranes, they were dark, solid shapes; serrated spearheads plunging down, accelerating hard. They fell through vacuum towards a landscape of something between a single surface-covering city and a gigantic industrial plant, all lights and grids and swirling patterns of luminescence, flares, drifting smokes and steams, rivers and fountains and whirlpools of light.

It is like a dream, Vatueil thought. A dream of flying, falling . . .

He snapped himself out of it, looked about, taking stock, evaluating. Five more besides himself. In theory only one was needed. In practice, or at least in the best sims they'd been able to run for this, a force of twelve gave an eighty per cent chance of success. Fifty-fifty came with a force of nine. With six of them to make the final assault, the odds were slim. The simulations experts hadn't even wanted to talk about a force of less than eight making the last push.

Still, not impossible. And what was glory but something that reduced the more there were of you to share it?

The vast, coruscating landscape below was probably the most beautiful thing he had ever seen in his long and varied existence. It was heartbreaking that they had come here to destroy it utterly.

Special Witness Sessions were rare events in the chamber, even if this was the low season when most of the Representatives were on holiday or just on other business. Filhyn had had to pull pretty much all the strings she could, call in all the favours she thought she might be owed, to arrange the session, not just at such short notice, but at all.

Their witness needed no real coaching, which was just as well as there had been little time to arrange any.

"Prin," she'd told him, just before the session started, while they'd been waiting in the antechamber and Errun and his people had been trying to get the special session cancelled or postponed, "will you be able to do this?"

She knew how intimidating it could be to stand in the chamber, all eyes upon you, trying to make your point, knowing that hundreds were looking at you there and then, tens of millions were watching throughout the system in real time and possibly billions might hear your words and see your actions and expressions later – potentially tens, even hundreds of billions if what you said turned out to be of any great importance or at least of interest to the news channels.

"I can do it," he'd told her. His eyes looked too old, she thought, though that might just be her fancy, given that she now knew a little of what he'd been through.

"Deep breaths," she'd advised him. "Concentrate on one person when you speak. Ignore others and forget about the cameras." He'd nodded.

She hoped he'd be able to keep himself together. The chamber had an odd buzz about it, with a few more straggler Reps suddenly present who hadn't been able to drag themselves away from whatever City business had been detaining them in the morning. Some of the journalist seats and camera positions in the press galleries were occupied now that hadn't been before. Usually the afternoon sessions were quieter than the morning ones. The rumour mills had obviously been working. Even less than a third full, the chamber could be an intimidating place.

Ultimately, they were herd animals, for all their civilising, and to be singled out in the herd had been almost inevitably lethal for most of the millions of years of their species' existence. Other species, non-herd species, must have it easier, she supposed. Their own predator species would have found it easier, for sure, had they won the struggle to be the planet's dominant species. But then they were not the ones present. For all their ferocity they had lost the struggle, been quietly out-bred, sidelined, driven to extinction or into the twilight existence of nature reserves and breeding zoos.

In the end she need not have worried.

She was able to sit back and listen – crying, quite a lot, quite openly and freely and without even trying to hide it – and watch the effect that Prin's sober, unhurried testimony had on the others in the chamber. The bare details were unbearable enough – she discovered later that most of the networks censored some of the more sickening parts – but the truly crushing, the most undeniably effective moments came when Prin was subject to the most ferocious cross-examination by the Traditionalist party in general and by Representative Errun in particular.

Did he *really* expect to be taken seriously with this mass of lies?

They were not lies. He wished that they were. He did not necessarily expect to be taken seriously because he knew how monstrous and cruel it all sounded, and how much many different interests did not want the truth to be known. He knew that they would do all that they could to discredit both him personally and what he was telling people.

How could he even tell this was not some bizarre nightmare, some possibly drug-induced hallucination?

It was a matter of fact that he had been away for real-time weeks, his body held within a fully licensed medical facility, exactly like the kind that many Representatives had used for various treatments over the years. He had never heard of a nightmare that went on for so long. Had the Representative?

So, he did not deny it might have been drug-induced?

He did deny it. He did not take drugs. He never had, not even now, when his physician said he ought to, to try to stop the nightmares he had, reliving what he had been through. Would a blood test convince the Representative?

So *now* he suddenly admitted that he *did* have nightmares after all!

As he'd just said, only due to the Hell he had just lived through.

Representative Errun would not let go. He had been a trial lawyer, then a judge, and famous for his questioning, his brutal tenacity. She watched him become more and more determined to rattle Prin, to trip him up and bring him down, to reveal him as a liar or a fantasist or a fanatic, and she listened to him lose. With every extra detail Errun dragged out of Prin he made the totality of the revelations' impact all the greater.

Yes, everybody was nude in Hell. Yes, people in Hell might try to have sex, but that was punishable. In Hell only rape was permitted. Just as in Hell only war formed the basis for any social structure. Yes, people died in Hell. You could die a million times, suffer its agonies on a million separate occasions, and every time you would be brought back for further punishment, more torture. The demons were people who had been sadists in the Real; to them, Hell was more like their own heaven.

No, there were not that many sadists in the Real, but there could be as many as the functioning of Hell required because this was all virtual, remember, and individuals could be copied. One sadist, one person who gloried in the pain of others, would be all you needed; you'd just create a million copies.

Yes, he was aware of the claims that the tours of Hell that people were forced to undergo, sometimes as part of a court's judgement, were of a Hell that didn't exist, or that only existed in a very limited sense while the miscreants were being shown round, and that anybody who failed to return from such grisly junkets had merely been put into limbo. But that was a lie.

Filhyn saw somebody hand Errun a note. A shiver of apprehension ran through her.

She thought she saw Errun's eyes glint with something like exaltation, with cruelty, with victory anticipated. The old male's tone and demeanour changed as he became more statesmanlike and solemn, like somebody delivering a final judgement, a *coup-de-grâce*, more in regret than anger.

Was it not true, he said, that he, Prin, had gone into this dream or nightmare, this supposed Hell, with his wife? So where was she? Why was she not at his side now to back up his wild claims?

Filhyn thought she might faint. Wife? He'd taken his *wife* with him? Had he been mad? Why hadn't he *said* anything – even just to her? A despair settled over her.

Prin was answering.

First of all, the female concerned was his love and his mate, but not formally his wife. He had left her behind, right at the very end, when there had been a chance for only one of them to get out and he had had to do the hardest thing he had ever had to do in his life and leave her in there to suffer while he escaped to tell the truth of what was happening there, what was still happening there to—

And why had he left her out of this tale, this – it was now conclusively revealed – confection of lies, half-truths and outright fantasy?

Because he had been afraid to mention her participation in the mission into Hell.

Afraid? *Him?* A man who claimed to have been through Hell and come back? *Afraid?*

"Yes, afraid," Prin said, his voice ringing out in the hushed chamber, "I am afraid that before I can take my testimony to where it really needs to be heard, before a Jury of the Galactic Council, somebody old and trustworthy and of impeccable, indisputable honour – somebody like yourself, sir – will come to me and quietly tell me that I can have my beloved back, out of Hell, if only I'll say no more about what she and I experienced there, and indeed even retract what I've already said." Prin looked, blinking, round the other members of the party opposite, then at the press and public galleries, as though suddenly seeing them for the first time. Then he looked back at Representative Errun. "Because I am afraid that I will accept that offer, sir, because I can't bear the thought of her continuing to suffer in that place a moment longer, and I will abandon all the others there just to get my beloved back, and so will hate myself for ever for my weakness and selfishness." He let out a deeply held breath. "That's why I kept her— "

Errun seemed finally to wake up to the veiled accusation Prin had just levelled at him. He erupted with indignation, swiftly followed by his followers and shortly by the rest of the Traditionalist party. In moments, the chamber was as noisy as Filhyn had ever heard it, even when it was packed.

Prin might have permitted himself a smile then, Filhyn thought, if this had been no more than a debate in a debating chamber. He did not, could not, she realised, because he was perfectly serious and completely terrified of exactly what he had just revealed.

He turned to look at her. She smiled as best she could through her tears, mouthed "Well done," at him and nodded for him to sit down.

He nodded to the Speaker, then sat.

Not that the worthy senator in the Speaker's chair was actually in it, or taking any notice; he was on his feet roaring and waving both trunks, trying to restore order. Filhyn recognised the chamber letting off steam after having been forced to listen to something they hadn't wanted to hear coming from somebody who was not one of their own. Not to mention somebody who had just reminded them that there were higher and greater talking shops than this one.

"That's put the pride amidst the herd," Kemracht muttered from behind her. Meanwhile the Speaker was rising furiously on his hind legs and clapping his front feet together. That wild breach of protocol hadn't happened for *years*.

The news services carried everything – ah, the joys of a slow news day during the slack season. They showed the Speaker trampling etiquette and rearing to his feet like a disputing skivvy, they showed Errun turning shades of rage that Filhyn had not thought him capable of; and most of all they showed Prin: calm, flawless but sincere. And his words, those ghastly, searing, near-unimaginable details!

And herself. With her, mostly the news teams focused on her crying.

Her tears – not her oratory, sincerity, political skill or her principles – had made her properly famous.

Fourteen

Veppers' aircraft hurtled across his estate at only a little over tree-top height. Veppers himself sat at the rear, shooting at things.

Leading from the grounds immediately around the torus-shaped mansion house of Espersium were seven trackways of trees; lines of dense woodland only forty or fifty metres wide but so long that they stretched – unbroken save for where they crossed major rivers – all the way to the estate's perimeter; a distance of almost ninety kilometres in the case of the longest and most used trackway, which was the one leading towards Ubruater, the capital city of the capital planet of the whole Sichultian Enablement.

The trackways were there, famously, for one reason only: to provide sport for Veppers. Simply jumping into a flier and being bounced across to the capital on a parabolic trajectory had always seemed like something of a waste to him, for all that it was the fastest and most efficient way of getting to Ubruater. When he had the time – and he could generally make the time – he would take the slower, low-level route, having his pilots take one of his aircraft tearing over the tops of the trees, only ten metres or so above the tallest branches.

The idea was to use the flier as a beater, utilising its screaming engines and battering slipstream to disturb the wildlife in general and, in particular, to bring birds panicking up out of the foliage below. Veppers' aircraft were all shaped like giant arrowheads with a broad flat rear containing a recessed, wind-shielded balcony where anything up to ten people could sit, firing laser rifles out through the ultraclear glass into the bustling riot of sucked-up leaves and small twigs at the startled, squawking birds.

Veppers sat with Jasken, Lehktevi – another of his Harem-girls – and Crederre, the daughter of Sapultride and his first wife, who had stayed on at the estate after her father and the girl's step-mother, Jeussere, had left after the weekend party that had included a couple of miniature sea battles. Veppers had taken particular care to make sure that his ships did not lose the second sea battle, the day after Xingre's unsettling visit; the bets involved in the ship battles were always small, but that was not the point. For Veppers, winning was the point.

They were on the longest trackway, the one which led to Ubruater. The aircraft's engines roared distantly as it followed the trackway trees into a slight hollow then powered upwards again. Veppers' stomach lurched as they bottomed out and then zoomed again. A particularly large and fine spevaline rose wheeling out of the blizzard of dark leaves and somersaulting twigs behind, still sporting its mating season plumage. Veppers cradled the tripodded laser rifle, let the opticals grab the image of the bird and identify it as the largest moving entity in the viewfinder. The gun's servos whined, lining it up, shaking it with what felt like a series of tiny spasms to allow for the aircraft's movements. Veppers fired the instant the aiming grid flashed. A single shot passed straight through the great bird in a small explosion of feathers. The spevaline crumpled about itself like a man wrapping a cloak about him. It fell tumbling back into the forest.

"Oh, good shot, sir!" Lehktevi said, having to raise her voice only a little to make herself heard over the howling of the engines. The balcony was shielded from the slipstream by the bowed surface of ultraclear glass. The glass could be retracted to allow other weapons besides the laser rifles to be used against the birds and other animals, but that made the balcony a quite furiously noisy place to be, at any reasonable speed; you needed ear defenders, and the swirling slipstream caused total havoc to any hairstyle worth the name.

"Thank you," Veppers said, smiling briefly at the achingly beautiful Lehktevi. He looked at the girl on his other side. "Crederre," he said, nodding at the laser on its tripod in front of her. "Won't you try a shot?"

The girl shook her head. "No, Joiler, I can't. I feel sorry for the birds. I can't shoot them."

Crederre was young; still becoming a woman, really. Entirely legal, though. She was not bad-looking, though her wan, pale, blonde look was quite eclipsed by the dark magnificence of Lehktevi.

He'd watched the girl swim in the underground pool at the house just that morning.

The main indoor pool under the house took up some of the space where the rows and banks of computer servers had once stood, when the house had been even more the centre of the Veppers family power than it was now, and games and programs throughout the ever-expanding Sichultian Enablement had been controlled from there.

That amount of raw, bulky computational power was no longer necessary – you could build processing substrate into walls, hulls, carpets, chassis, ceiling tiles, monocoques; almost anything nowadays – so all that space under the mansion had come free, to be filled with storage, underground garages full of exotic machinery and a giant pool ornately decorated with waterfalls, giant naturally grown crystals the size of trees, perfume pools, bubble bays and water slides. Crederre's slim, pale body had moved over the night black of the jet tiles on the pool's floor, sinuous and quick.

He'd watched her, and known that she'd known he was watching her. Well, he watched all women he found attractive like that, and he'd thought no more about it.

Still, the girl might be a prize worth pursuing. He was aware that he hadn't bedded – or even attempted to bed – anyone new since the unpleasantness which had resulted in that little scribbled-on slut biting the tip of his nose off. Too self-conscious, he supposed. He stroked the golden shield covering his nose.

He laughed gently. "Well, I feel sorry for the woodland creatures too, but then if it wasn't for this sport then these trees wouldn't be here in the first place. And there are an awful lot of trees and an awful lot of spevalines and other birds, and only me who really shoots them. Most people are like you: too squeamish. So they're ahead on the deal, really,"

The girl shrugged. "If you say so." She smiled at him. Quite a pleasant, winning smile, he thought. He wondered again why she'd chosen – and been allowed – to stay behind with him. She was of an age, of course; technically independent, an adult, but all the same. It amused him when his friends, acquaintances and business partners tried to pair him off with their daughters – or even wives. Perhaps that was the idea here. He doubted anyone still thought they could marry their females off to him, but even just a liaison, an affair, might be useful to somebody with ambitions.

Veppers looked round at Jasken, standing braced behind him, Oculenses on, holding on to a handle set into the bulkhead behind, his other arm still in its cast and supported by the sling. "Jasken, why don't you come and show us how it's done while I talk to Miss Crederre here."

"Sir."

"Lehktevi," Veppers said, "why don't you go and see how our pilot's doing?"

"Certainly, sir." Lehktevi swung out of her seat, long legs flashing beneath a short skirt, massed dark hair tumbling as she pivoted to disappear though the doorway leading to the aircraft's main cabin.

Jasken sat in her seat. He pushed the Oculenses up his head, switched on the laser rifle in front of him and cradled it, one-armed. He got a shot off almost immediately, nailing a young blackbird in a detonation of indigo feathers. It fell back to the coppery foliage rushing past beneath.

"Aren't you worried your mistress will distract the pilot?" Crederre asked Veppers. "This thing does fly awfully low, and she is, well, distracting."

"Wouldn't matter if she did," Veppers said, nudging a button to bring his seat and Crederre's closer together. Motors whined; the girl's brows rose a little as she watched the gap between their seats shrink to nothing, padded armrests touching. "It's all done automatically," he explained. "Pilot's redundant, almost irrelevant. Most critical operation they perform is punching in the destination coordinates. There are five separate terrain-following systems making sure we stay just above the scenery, without becoming part of it."

"Five? My," she said quietly, sounding conspiratorial and dipping her head towards him, her long straight blonde hair nearly touching the soft material of his shirt. Was she trying to flirt with him, or being sarcastic? He found it hard to tell the difference with young women sometimes, despite all his experience. "Why so many?" she asked.

"Why not?" he countered. "Always best to have lots of redundancy with something so critical. Doesn't really cost, either; I own the company that makes them – makes the whole aircraft," he said, glancing about them. Jasken blasted another blackbird, then another. "Actually, the pilots are there more for legal reasons than anything else." He shrugged. "I blame the unions. Bane of my life. Though," he said, tapping the girl on her bare forearm – she wore a knee-length, short-sleeved, soft-looking dress which appeared plain but expensive at the same time – "I should point out that Lehktevi isn't a mistress."

"More of a whore?"

Veppers smiled tolerantly. "She's staff; a servant. It's just that her duties are principally sexual in nature." He looked thoughtfully at the door she'd gone through. "Dare say there's a union for her profession too." He looked back at Crederre, who appeared not to be following all this. "I don't really hold with unions, not amongst the staff," he explained. "Divided loyalties. Does mean I have to pay more for her services though."

"How terrible for you," she said.

He heard her stepmother, Jeussere, in the remark. She'd been one of his lovers, once. Too long ago for Crederre to be his, though.

"I know, isn't it?" he said. He'd decided: it might be quite amusing to bed the girl. A sort of continuance. Jeussere might even have been intending it. She'd been a young woman of slightly odd and exotic sexual tastes in her time – who knew? "I have this frighteningly tiresome hearing this afternoon," he said as Jasken fired again, downing something large and copper-coloured, "but I'm free this evening. Let me buy you dinner. Is there anywhere you've always wanted to go?"

"That's very kind. I'll let you choose. Just you and me?"

"Yes," he said, smiling at her again. "Private room, I'd suggest. I'll get my fill of crowds at the hearing this afternoon."

"A court hearing?"

"I'm afraid so."

"Why, have you done something terrible?"

"Oh, I've done many terrible things," he confided, leaning over close to her. "Though probably not what I'm being accused of today. Well, possibly not. It's hard to say."

"Don't you know?"

He grinned. "Honestly, I don't." He tapped his temple. "I am the most *frightfully* old man really, you know."

"One hundred and seventy-eight, is that true?"

"One hundred and seventy-eight-ish," he agreed. He held out his arms, looked down at his fit, taut, muscular frame. "And yet I look, well; you tell me. What would you say?"

"Oh, I don't know," she said, looking down modestly. "Thirty?"

So she was trying to flatter him. "Between that and forty, is the look I go for." He smiled broadly. "Though I have the appetites of a man of twenty." He shrugged as she looked down again, a smile on her lips. "So I'm told. As I say, it's been so long since I was twenty I honestly can't recall." He sighed deeply. "Just as I can't recall any of the details of the appallingly ancient case they're going to bore me with this afternoon. I mean *really* can't. I'm not lying when they ask me what I remember and I say I can't remember anything. I'm just not able to; those memories all had to be excised decades ago to leave me room for new memories."

"Really?"

"Had to be done; the medics insisted. Not my fault those memories are the ones the court would like to know about. I'd love to cooperate even more fully, tell them all they want to know, but I just can't."

"That does seem terribly convenient," she said.

He nodded. "That is a word I have heard used in this context. Convenient." He shook his head. "People can be so cynical."

"I know. Shocking, isn't it?" Crederre said, and again Veppers heard her stepmother's phraseology.

"Shocking indeed. So, you'll come for dinner?"

"Well, I don't know. I'm not sure what my parents would say."

He smiled tolerantly. "It's dinner, dear girl, not a sex club."

"Do you frequent those too?"

"Never. You've seen my Harem, haven't you?"

"I have. You are so shameless, you know."

"Thank you. I do my best."

"I'm surprised you have any energy left even to think about other women, normal women."

"Ah, but there's the challenge, you see," he told her. "For simple sex, just fulfilling a need, the Harem girls are perfect, quite wonderful. Uncomplicated. But to make a chap feel . . . treasured, wanted for his own sake, he has to feel that he can still make somebody want to have sex with him . . . just because she wants to, not because it's her job."

"Hmm. Yes."

"So, how about you?"

"How about me what?"

"Do you frequent sex clubs?"

"Never either. Not yet."

"Not *yet*?"

She shrugged. "Well, you never know, do you?"

"No," he agreed, sitting back, smiling thoughtfully. "You never do."

Jasken brought down a spevaline a little smaller than the one Veppers had killed earlier, but closer still to the rushing aircraft. Then the trees stopped abruptly and the view dropped away to a broad river, waters sparkling, wavy gravel banks unwinding beneath. Jasken clicked the laser rifle off and swung it to its stowed position. "Estate border, sir," he said. He brought the Oculenses back down over his eyes. Veppers motioned towards the balcony door. "Excuse me," Jasken said.

The aircraft started to gain height and speed, heading for more conventional air corridors now that it had left the Espersium estate and was in the shared airspace leading to the vast conurbation of Greater Ubruater.

Crederre watched Jasken close the door behind him. She turned back to Veppers. "You don't have to buy me dinner first if you just want to fuck me."

He shook his head. "Good heavens, you youngsters are *so* forward."

She looked down at the seat Veppers was in, judging. She wriggled her skirt up. She wasn't wearing anything underneath. "But we're only ten minutes from landing," he said, watching her.

She pushed both laser rifles out of the way then hoisted herself out of her seat and brought one long leg curving over so that she straddled him. "Better get to it, then."

He frowned as he watched her pulling at the laces securing his trousers' crotch. "It wasn't your mother put you up to this, was it?" he asked.

"Nope," she said.

He laughed, put his hands under her skirt to her naked hips. "You young girls, I do declare!"

Fifteen

Here was a gulf of space, an infinite valley, stuffed full to choking with scenes of torment spread out to the furthest reach of sight, filled with the low moans and the chorused anguished of the torn and tormented and infested with a miasmic stench of shit and burned, corrupted flesh. Here was a pressure on the eyes of fractal detail – torment within torment within torment within torment, endlessly – just waiting, stacked, lined up, marking time until it could be dwelt upon, comprehended, made part of the self; guarantors of perpetual nightmare.

Here was a seemingly infinite realm of torture presided over by slavering, wild-eyed devils, a never-ending world of unbearable pain, humiliation beyond imagining and utter, unending hatred.

. . . She had decided there was a perverse beauty about it, an almost celebratory fecundity about the depths of creativity which must have been plumbed to produce such imaginative cruelty. The very bestiality, the absolute depravity of it raised it to the level of great art; there was a transcendent quality to its horror, its complete commitment to agony and degradation.

And there was even a humour to it, too, she'd decided. It was the humour of children, of adolescence – determined to appal the adults or to take something to such an extreme you shocked even your peers – it was the humour of wringing every last conceivable shred of double-meaning or fanciful connection out of every even remotely misconstruable subject, every mention of anything that could be seen as having anything whatsoever to do with sexuality, bodily waste or any other function of simple, matter-of-fact creaturality or biochemicalness, but it was still humour, of a sort.

When Prin went through and she did not, when the blue glowing doorway she had been only very peripherally aware of rejected her and bounced her back into the groaning confines of the mill, she had lain on the sweated boards of the ramp, watching the blue glowing mist evaporate and the surface of the doorway turn to what looked like grey metal. She could hear the predator-demons howling and cursing and arguing. They were further up, on the level where Prin – in the form of an even larger demon – had brushed them aside moments earlier, before launching himself – and her – at the glowing doorway. She got the impression that they hadn't yet noticed her lying there.

She lay still. They would find her, and probably very soon, she knew that, but for these precious few moments she was alone, undisturbed, yet to come to the attention of these most dedicated persecutors.

Prin was gone.

He had tried to take them both through to whatever was on the other side of the blue glowing doorway, but only he had got through. She had been left behind. Or he had left her behind. She wondered whether to feel sorry for him or not. Probably not. If he was right and there really was some other, pre-existing, non-tormenting life to be found beyond the doorway, then she hoped that he had found it. If he had gone into oblivion, then that was something to celebrate too, for oblivion, if it existed as a real, achievable possibility, meant an end to suffering.

As likely, though, she thought, was that he had simply gone to another part of here, another and possibly worse, more terrible quarter of reality, of what he had chosen to call Hell. Perhaps she had been the lucky one, getting to stay behind. There would be more torment, more pain and abasement in store for her, she knew that, but perhaps what now awaited Prin was even worse. She didn't like to think about what would happen to her, now, but thinking about what might be happening or about to happen to Prin was even worse. She did not let herself shy away from it; she made herself think about it. If you thought about it, if you embraced it, then the revelation you might in time be faced with – of what had happened to him, what had been done to him – would lose some of its power and its ability to shock.

She wondered if she would ever see him again. She wondered if she would want to, given what they might do to him. He had disobeyed the rules of this place, the rules they lived by; he had gone against the very law of Hell, and his punishment would be extreme.

So might hers, of course.

She heard one of the demons say something. She didn't understand exactly what had been said but it had sounded like an exclamation, like an expression of surprise. She knew then that she had been seen. She heard and felt crashing, iron-shod paws clattering down the ramp towards her. They stamped up to right beside her head.

She was hauled upright by both her trunks. She tried to keep her hand-pads over her face but she was shaken, and her body's own weight tore their grip free. She caught a glimpse of a demon's wide, furred face, its two great eyes staring at her, then she shut her eyes tightly.

The demon shouted in her face. "*Didn't* get through? That's bad!" His breath smelled of rotting meat. He marched up the slope, dragging her behind him. He was roaring to the others. Look what he'd found!

They took turns raping her while they discussed what to do to really make her suffer. In Hell, the seed of demons burned like acid and generally brought with it parasites, worms, gangrene and tumours, as well as the possibility of the conception of something that would eat its way out when the time came to be born. That conception could equally well take place in a male; a womb was not required and the demons were not fussy.

She found the pain astounding, the humiliation and degradation absolute.

She started to sing to them. She sang without words, just making sounds in a language that she herself didn't understand and had not known she possessed. The half-dozen demons reacted with fury, taking an iron bar to her mouth, smashing her teeth. She kept on singing, even through the froth of blood and broken teeth inside her mouth, the sounds bubbling up and out, sounding more and more like wheezing, unstoppable laughter. One of them tied something round her neck so that she started to suffocate. She felt the life going from her, and wondered what new torments would await her when she was brought back to life again, to continue suffering.

The mad, ghastly thrusting that was tearing her apart suddenly stopped. The thing round her neck was torn away and she gulped air, then spat and retched as the blood coughed itself up, then was able to roll over onto her side and take a sequence of further deep, painful gasps, letting the blood and the bits of her teeth fall from her mouth onto the stained, uneven surface of the floor. There was more snarling and shouting and some thumping, like bodies being thrown about or being forced to the floor. She could see the boards better than before because the door to the outside was open and a giant beetle was visible.

She looked up and, standing over her, saw a demon like the one Prin had become: massive and powerful, six limbed, fur striped yellow and purple, accoutred with jagged armour. Another one, striped yellow and black, not quite so fantastically armoured, stood behind, its powerful forelimbs holding a struggling minor demon, one of those who'd been raping her. The other minor demons had been scattered around the floor of the mill and lay moaning and slowly picking themselves up.

The giant predator demon lowered its face to hers as she wheezed and spat the last of the blood from her mouth. Between her legs, it felt as though she had been split apart. Inside, it was as though they had filled her with boiling water.

"Unclever, little one," the giant demon told her. "Now we go to a place where soon you will beg to come back here and let these scamps resume their play with you." It straightened. "You bring her," it said to the yellow and black demon, which threw the minor demon it held across the floor and into the rotating machinery of the mill. It howled as it was crushed; the machinery creaked to a stop. The demon lay like a limp rag leaking blood within the cogs and gears of bone.

The yellow and black demon picked her up as easily as Prin had done and took her to the giant beetle waiting outside.

Inside the flier, she was thrown into a giant open pod with a glistening red interior and brown-black lips like some enormous animal; the lips closed around her neck as her body was sucked further into the centre of the closing pod. She felt dozens of barbs connect with her skin, then penetrate her flesh. She waited for the next symphony of pain to consume her.

Instead; everything went numb. A feeling of something like relief flooded her. Even her mouth stopped hurting. No pain. For the first time in months she was free of pain.

She was facing forward, just behind the craft's control deck, where the giant beetle's hollow eyes looked out over the valley. She heard the ramp behind thud closed. The two giant demons squeezed themselves into seats, one looking out through each of the beetle's segmented eyes.

"Sorry about all that," the yellow and purple one said to her, glancing over its shoulder as the other demon worked the craft's controls and the whirring sound of giant beating wings filled the beetle's interior. The demon's voice was quieter now, conversational, though it still carried above the sounds of the wings.

"Has to look and sound good for the minions; you know."

The other demon pulled on some sort of headset. "Portal we agreed, first choice," it said. "Flight time as simmed."

"Sounds good to me," the first demon said. "Last one through's unfavoured." The demon wearing the headset pulled at the controls. The beetle lurched upward, reared back as it rose, then tipped forward. It settled level but still felt as though it was pointing upwards as it accelerated away across the riven, smoke-streamered landscape beneath, rising almost to the greasy-looking brown overcast.

The first demon looked over its shoulder at her again. "Could only get one of you out, yes?"

She blinked at it. No pain. No pain. To be flying, trapped in this thing, but to be feeling no pain. It made her want to cry. The demon looking at her made a shape with its great, tooth-filled mouth that was probably meant to be a smile. "It's all right to talk," it told her. "You are allowed to reply. The cruelty has already stopped, the madness ceased to be. We're going to get you out of here. We're your rescuers."

"I don't believe you," she said. Her voice sounded strange to her, without teeth. Her tongue had been bitten and although not causing her any pain it was swollen, and that was making her voice different too. She didn't know if she had bitten her own tongue or if one of the demons in the mill had.

The senior demon shrugged. "Suit yourself." It turned away.

"I'm sorry," she said.

"What?" It turned back to look at her again.

"I'm sorry I don't believe you." She shook her head slowly. "But I don't. Can't. Sorry."

The demon looked at her for a moment. "They really have chewed you up bad, haven't they?"

She didn't say anything for a while. The demon continued to look at her. "Who are you?" she asked eventually.

"I'm called Klomestrum," it told her. It nodded at the demon flying the beetle. "Ruriel."

The other demon waved one forelimb but did not look round.

"Where are you taking me?"

"Place we can all get the fuck out of here. Another portal."

"A portal to where?"

"The Real. You know; the place where there isn't all this pain and suffering and torture and shit?"

"Really?"

"Yeah, really."

"And where will we be then? Where in this 'Real'?"

"Does it really matter? Not here, that's the point."

The two demons glanced at each other and laughed.

"Yes," she insisted, "but where?"

"Wait and see. We're not there yet. Best not to give anything away, eh?"

She blinked at him.

He sighed. "Look, if I tell you where we're going to come out and they've somehow managed to listen in on this then they might be able to stop us, see?"

The first demon half-turned his head to her. "Where did you think you were going back to just there, back at the mill?" he asked her.

She shook her head. "Another part of here," she said. "There is no 'Real'. It's just a myth to make things seem even worse here."

"You really think that?" the demon said, looking aghast at her.

"It's all that makes sense," she said. "It's all there is. This is all there is. How could there be a Real where people would allow something so terrible as this to exist? This place must be all that there is. What people call the Real is a myth, an unreachable heaven only there to make existence all the worse by comparison."

"There could still be a Real," the demon protested, "but one where the people—"

"Leave it," the other demon said.

Somehow, without her noticing it happening, the demon piloting the giant beetle had turned into one of the smaller demons, a dark little squirmy thing with a long glistening body. It looked like something that had just been born, or excreted.

"Fuck," the other demon said. It had turned into something

much smaller too; a sort of featherless bird with pale, raw, tattered skin and a beak whose top part had been broken half off. "You really think your friend just went to another part of Hell?"

"Where else is there to go?" she asked.

"Fuck," the demon said again. It seemed to stiffen. So did the other demon.

"Oh, fuck, we're not even getting to—"

There was no transition. One instant she was numb and without pain in the pod inside the giant flying beetle, the next she was pinned, flayed, in agony, her flesh opened out and spread out all around her, on a slope in front of some sort of ultimate Demon. She was shrieking.

"Shush," something said, and the force of it tumbled across her like a gigantic wave, pressing her into the noisome earth beneath her where things crawled and squirmed and invaded her flesh. Now she could not scream. Her throat had been sealed, her mouth had been sewn shut. She breathed through a ragged hole in what was left of her neck, chest muscles working to expand and compress her lungs but leaving her unable to make any sound. She writhed, moved side to side, tried to jerk herself loose from whatever held her. The motions produced only more pain but she persisted.

A noise like a sigh rolled across her, scarcely less batteringly heavy than the sound of "Shush" a moment earlier.

The pain ebbed, retreated, left her quivering. It did not go away entirely but it left her room to think, to feel other things besides the agony.

She could see properly now. The pain before had been so bad she had not been able to understand what she was looking at.

Before her, across a dark valley full of smoke and half-hidden red and orange flames, on a dully glowing throne the size of a great building, sat a demon at least a hundred metres tall.

The demon had four limbs but looked alien, bipedal; its upper limbs were arms rather than legs. Its skin was made from living pelts and hides and flesh, its body from an obscene amalgam of sweating metal, stretched gristle, pitted ceramic gears, reconstituted, pulverised bone and inflamed, smouldering sinew, tattered flesh and leaking, boiling blood. The vast throne glowed dully because it was red hot, producing a greasy slow upwelling of smoke from the fleshes and pelts that cloaked the demon, filling the air with a continual sizzling, spitting noise.

The thing had a lantern head, like an enormous version of a four-paned, inward-sloping gas light from ancient history. There was a sort of face shown within the lantern itself, an alien face made of a dirty, smoking flame; it peered out through glass made dark and filthy by the soot and livid fumes within. At each of the four external corners of the lantern, a giant candle of tallow stood, each containing a hundred shrieking nervous systems intact and in burning agony within. She looked at it, knew it, knew all this, and could see herself through its eyes, or whatever infernal senses or organs it used to see.

She was a skinned skeleton-plus-musculature figure, a tiny distant doll of a thing, her flesh pulled away from her and pegged, pinned to the ground around her.

"I hoped to make you hope," the vast voice said, the syllables rolling over her like thunder. Her ears hurt with the force of it and kept on ringing afterwards. "But you are beyond hope. That is vexing."

Suddenly she could talk again, the stitches that had sealed her mouth gone in a blink, the ragged tear in her neck sealed, her throat no longer crushed closed, her breath coming and going normally.

"Hope?" she gasped. "There is no hope!"

"There is always hope," the vast voice declaimed. She could feel the force of it in her lungs, feel its words shaking the very ground beneath her. "And there must be hope. To abandon hope is to escape part of the punishment. One must hope in order for hope to be destroyed. One must trust in order to feel the anguish of betrayal. One must yearn, or one cannot feel the pain of rejection, and one must love in order to feel the agony of witnessing the loved one suffer excruciation." The vast being sat back, producing wreathes of smoke like the currents of dark continental rivers, candles spearing flame like huge trees burning.

"But above all one must hope," the voice said, each word, each syllable smacking into her body, resounding inside her head. "There must be hope or otherwise how can it be satisfyingly dashed? The certainty of hopelessness might become a comfort; the uncertainty, the not-knowing, that is what helps to bring on true despair. The tormented cannot be allowed to abandon themselves to their fate. That is insufficient."

"I am abandoned, I am nothing *but* abandoned; abandonment is all there is," she screamed back. "Make your myths but I'll not believe in them."

The demon rose up, fire and fumes and smoke beating and wallowing in his wake. The ground beneath her shook to his footsteps, jarring the few teeth left in her head. He stood over her, towering above like an insane statue of something unbalanced, unnatural, two-legged. He stooped, causing a great roaring as the flames around him tore brightening through the air. A finger longer than her whole body scooped something from the ground near her head. Dripping wax from one tower-sized fleshy candle splashed spattering onto her torn-open skin, stinking of rotten, burned flesh, causing her to howl with fresh pain until it cooled, part solidified.

"You did not even notice this, did you?" the great voice bellowed, rolling over her. He held the tiny-looking necklace of barbed wire which she had worn for as long as she could remember. He rubbed it between his body-thick fingers, and for an instant took on the magnified but gritty, pixelated appearance of one of the great powerful demons Prin had impersonated and the two in the flying beetle machine had at first seemed to be. The image flickered off. He threw the lengths of wire away. "Disappointing." The word cracked and rolled over her, seemed to press her into the earth with its vast, despondent force.

He held his cock and sprayed her with fluid salts at the same time as the pain came flooding back. The gushing waters pummelled her and their fire-bright stinging made her shriek once more.

The pain was turned right down again, just long enough for her to hear him say, "You should have had religion, child, that in it you might have found the hope that could then be crushed."

He raised one massive iron foot the size of a truck high above her then brought it down fast and hard from twenty metres up, killing her.

Sixteen

"What is that?"

"That is a present," the ship told her.

She looked at the thing lying in Demeisen's palm. Then she looked up at his eyes.

The avatar's face had filled out a little more over the last few days. His body had altered a fraction too, making him look more like a Sichultian. This was a process that was intended to continue until he looked as native as she did when they arrived in Enablement space fifteen days from now. His eyes looked crinklier, she thought; friendlier. She knew that technically he was an it, not a he, but she still thought of him as male. All she had to remember, of course – she told herself – was that whether a he, a she, an it or anything else, Demeisen was the ship. The avatar was not anything truly independent or genuinely human.

She frowned. "It looks a bit like a—"

"Neural lace," Demeisen said, nodding. "Only it isn't."

"What, then?"

"It's a tattoo."

"A *tattoo*?

He shrugged. "Kind of."

They were in the twelve-person module the ship had brought aboard from the GSV especially for her. It was housed within one of the *Falling Outside The Normal Moral Constraints*' many cramped spaces that were something between magazines, munition-stores and hangars. The ship had no other dedicated human-habitable space inside it at all; even this module was a concession. It had not impressed her when she'd first seen it and been told this was all there was.

"This is it?" she'd said after she'd joined Demeisen on board and realised that, somehow, the little slap-drone had been left behind. She'd said a sincere thank you for that but then there had been a moment of awkwardness after the avatar had welcomed her aboard and she'd stood there waiting to be shown to her cabin from the rather minimal and utilitarian cabin space she'd materialised in.

"This is *it*?" she'd repeated, turning, looking round. She was standing in a space about four metres by three. In one direction lay a blank grey wall; opposite it there was a raised platform a little narrower than – and one step up from – the space she stood in; the platform held three long, deep padded chairs facing a double sloped wall, the upper part of which appeared to be a screen, though it was also blank at the moment. To either side there were what might be double doors, though they too were a uniform grey.

Demeisen had looked genuinely hurt. "I had to leave behind an Offensive Slaved Broad-Spectrum Munitions Platform, Self Powered to fit this in," he'd told her.

"You don't have any space inside your . . . inside the ship *at all*?"

"I'm a warship, not a taxi. I keep telling you."

"I thought even warships could carry a *few* people!"

"Pa! Old tech. Not me."

"You're one and a half kilometres *long*! There must be room *some*where!"

"Please; one point six kilometres long, and that's naked hull in full compression. In standard operational deployment mode I'm two point eight klicks; three point two with all fields on but pulled corset tight. In serious gloves-off, claws out, teeth bared, just-point-me-at-the-bad-guys engagement-ready mode I'm . . . well it varies; it's what we call threat-mix dependent. But many kilometres. Riled-up I'm really more like a sort of mini fleet."

Lededje, who had stopped listening at the first use of the word "point", had wailed, "I can touch the ceiling!" She'd reached up to do just that, without even standing on tiptoe.

Demeisen had sighed in exasperation. "I'm an Abominator-class picket ship. This is the best I can do. Sorry. Would you rather I slung you back aboard *The Usual But Etymologically Unsatisfactory*?"

"Picket? But *it* was a picket ship and it had lots of space!"

"Ah. No it wasn't. That's the clever bit."

"What?"

"People have spent the best part of one and a half millennia getting used to the idea of the Culture having all these ex-warships, most of them largely demilitarised, called Fast Pickets or Very Fast Pickets, and they *are* basically just express taxis, then along comes this new class called the Abominator, they call it a picket ship and nobody takes any notice. Even when Abominators almost never taxi anybody anywhere."

"What the hell are you talking about?"

"'Picket' in my case means I hang around waiting for trouble, not that I hang around waiting for hitch-hikers. There are two thousand Abominator-class ships, we're scattered evenly throughout the galaxy and *all we do* is sit and wait for stuff to happen. I'm part of the Culture's quick reaction force; we used to keep all the serious up-fucking ships in a few mostly very-far-away ports but that didn't always work out when things blew up suddenly. Remember I said 'Don't ask why' earlier?"

"Yes. You said not to ask you why you were heading in the direction of Sichult anyway."

"Well, Lededje – and appreciate that, to continue the dubious maritime analogy, I'm negotiating a tricky course between the minefield of personal honesty on one side and the rocky coast of operational security on the other – that's as good a hint as I can afford to give you. Now, I'm serious; do you want to be put back aboard the *The Usual But bla bla bla*?"

She'd scowled at him. "I suppose not." She'd looked around. "This thing does have a *toilet*?"

Nine seats blossomed from the floor and rear wall, then they collapsed back as though made from a membrane that had suddenly been punctured and collapsed, to be followed by a very generously sized bed, then by a sort of white glazed balloon which parted neatly to reveal what was probably a combined bath and walk-in shower. Then that too was swallowed back up into the floor and wall. "That do?" Demeisen had asked.

The fifteen days since had been spent in the same tiny space, though the entirety of the cabin's interior surfaces could function as a single astoundingly convincing screen, so it could look like she was standing on a snowy mountain top, the middle of a table-flat desert, a wave-washed beach or anywhere else she or the module could think of.

She had been thinking ahead and had decided what she might require when she got to Sichult. She was intending to get to Veppers through his lust; she reckoned the degree of physical beauty she had been granted, thanks to Sensia and her human-growing vats, would be sufficiently beguiling to entice Veppers, if she got close enough to be seen by him in the right social situation. A second way to get to him might be through her own knowledge of how his household, the town house in Ubruater and the mansion at Espersium all worked.

She'd had the ship make her clothes and jewellery and various other personal possessions, ready for when she arrived at Sichult. She'd tried to get it to make her some weapons, but it wouldn't play. It had even hesitated over one of her necklaces, given that it was long enough to be used to strangle somebody. It had conceded on that one. It had had no detectable qualms whatsoever about providing her with a diamond-film currency card allegedly loaded with enough credit to ensure that if she changed her mind about murdering Veppers she could buy her own Ubruater town house, her own country estate and just live like a princess for the rest of her life. Maybe that was the idea.

She exercised, she studied – mostly she studied all that the Culture knew of Veppers, Sichult and the Enablement, which was a lot more than even Veppers himself knew, she'd be prepared to bet – and she talked to the always-available Demeisen, who would materialise whenever she wanted to talk. Not that it was really materialising, literally, apparently, though she felt her eyes start to glaze over once the technical explanation kicked in.

She'd undergone a guided virtual tour of the ship, albeit reluctantly. She'd only agreed because Demeisen had seemed so boyishly enthusiastic about it. The tour had taken a while, though probably not as long as it had felt at the time. All she remembered was that the ship could split into different bits, like a sort of one-ship fleet or something, though it was most powerful as a single unit. Sixteen bits. Or maybe it was twenty-four. She'd made the appropriate *Ooh, Ah, No, really?* noises at the time, which was what actually mattered. She had lots of experience at that sort of thing.

She had, tentatively, entertained the idea of taking Demeisen as a lover. The more Sichultian he got, and the longer she was cooped up in here, fabulous fake scenery or not, the more attractive he looked and the itchier that subject got. She guessed, first, it would be pretty meaningless to the ship, second that she'd be indulged (it would say yes), third that it would be done with some style and sensitivity and – it occurred to her one day – fourth, it might just . . . *just* . . . make her safer, and her plan to kill Veppers more likely to succeed.

The Minds, the hyper AIs that commanded, that basically *were* the Culture's capital ships, were unarguably sentient, and they had emotions, even if their feelings were always under the control of their intellects, never the other way round. The ship had already hinted that there might be trouble where it was taking her – the sort of trouble where its fearsome martial abilities might come into play – so was there not just a chance that having sex with its avatar might make it feel even the tiniest bit of extra commitment towards her?

How much would it mean to the ship if she and its avatar did fuck? Nothing whatsoever? Or would it be like a human stroking a domestic pet; indulgent, companionable, mildly pleasant . . . though with no possible component that might lead to feelings of ownership, commitment or jealousy?

It was calculation rather than emotion; she'd be whoring herself. But then Veppers had long ago removed any choice she might have had regarding who she fucked. She'd had to whore herself for him (and against him – not that that had worked). The only time she'd ever had sex simply because she'd wanted to had been on that single night aboard the GSV, with Shokas.

Anyway, she had not broached the subject. And besides, for all she knew, the ship would revert to type, the way it had been while it had been aboard the GSV, before it had had its sudden and still slightly suspicious change of mind. Then it had seemed to enjoy hurting people; so it might do so again, and take pleasure in having its avatar reject her.

Now he – it – was offering her a present: a tattoo, allegedly. She was sat in one of the three flight-deck seats; she'd been watching news reports out of Sichult on the module's screen when Demeisen had popped into existence behind her. She leant forward. The thing lay in his palm; a looped, tangled assortment of thin grey-blue filaments looking a lot how she knew a fully grown neural lace looked.

"What makes you think I might want a tattoo?"

"You said you missed having one."

"I did?"

"Eleven days ago. Then again yesterday. The first time, you said that sometimes you felt too naked when you woke up. You also mentioned that since you were revented you'd had dreams of walking down a city street thinking you were fully clothed but everybody looking at you weirdly and then you looking down at yourself and realising you were naked."

"Apparently normal people have that dream."

"I know."

"Did I also say I was glad to be rid of the tattoo?"

"No. Maybe you just think you say that to people."

She frowned, looked at the thing in his palm again. Now it looked like thin strands of oily mercury. "Anyway, that does not look like a tattoo," she told him.

"Not like this. Watch."

The assemblage of loops and lines started to move slowly, stirring itself. It began to flow out across Demeisen's palm as though forming a sort of chain-mail glove. He turned his hand over for a moment to show it wrapping itself round his fingers, then turned it back as the lines moved like tiny waves up his wrist and arm, disappearing under his shirt. He rolled the sleeve back to show the filaments coursing along his upper arm, thinning fractionally and spreading out.

He undid his shirt a little to show the silver-blue lines tracking smoothly across his upper chest – it was smooth, hairless, like a child's – then put his head back as the tattoo rose up his neck and over his face and then right round his head, a few tiny thin lines decorating his ears while others swept fabulously, precisely over his face, moving to within millimetres of his nostrils, mouth and eyes but stopping there. He raised his other hand to show the lines flowing down there too, then held both hands and forearms up to show that they were identically, symmetrically decorated in millimetrically spaced curls and swirls, curves and parabolas.

"I'm getting it to display just the upper-body section," he explained. "It does the torso, legs and feet too; same spacing." He admired his hands. "Or you can go for a more angular look . . ."

The mobile tattoo shifted everywhere, the curves becoming straight lines, the tight curls becoming right angles, zigzags. "Colour's commandable too," Demeisen muttered. The tattoo changed to soot black. Then to perfectly reflective silver, as though the whole tattoo was made of mercury teased impossibly fine. "Or sort of random." Within seconds the tattoo had become a dark, random scribble across what she could see of his body. "Motifs, obviously," Demeisen added. The tattoo became a series of nested, concentric silver circles on his skin, the largest a hand's-breadth in diameter across his upper chest.

She reached out and took one of his hands, peering at the circles on the back of his hand. Looking extremely closely – she still thought her eyesight was significantly better than any normal Sichultian's had ever been; more zoomable, for a start – she could just make out tiny silver lines running from one circle to another. Hair fine, she thought. No; *down* fine.

She gazed at all the silvery circles, spread across his skin like too-symmetrical ripples in a pond someone had thrown a few dozen pebbles into. The circles spread, merged, became a criss-cross pattern of thick lines that looked braided, and much finer lines which wove in between the braids. Changing from silver to gold, they made it look as though he was wrapped in a glittering wire cage.

"Of course, *I'm* able to alter it by just thinking," he told her. "You'd need to control it through an interface; maybe have some sort of control section always manifest in the pattern, if you wanted to make it change appearance. One wrist with a sort of stylised key- or glyph-board on it would work, or even just coded fingertip sequences anywhere. Though a terminal would work too. Something to decide later."

She was barely listening, still staring. "It's astonishing," she breathed.

"Like it? It's yours," he told her.

She kept hold of his hand. She looked up at him. "It doesn't hurt, does it?"

He laughed. "Of course not."

"Are there any catches?"

"Catches?" He looked confused for a moment. "Oh," he said, "you mean any downside?"

"Anything I might wish I'd known, looking back on this moment from some point in the future?"

She worried that she might have insulted him, insulted the ship somehow, by being so cautious, even suspicious. But Demeisen just pursed his lips and looked thoughtful. "None I can think of." He shrugged. "Anyway, it's yours if you want it." The tattoo was already moving, all over him, changing from silver circles to wavy dark grey lines and sliding back the way it had come, up from one hand, down from his head, face and neck, away from his chest and back down the other arm until it rested coiled, grey-blue and immobile back in his palm again.

She still held that hand. "All right," she said softly. "I'll take it."

"Keep your hand there," he told her.

The tattoo moved up his palm, along two of his fingers and then onto her fingers, hand, wrist and forearm. She could only just feel it as it slid slowly along her tawny skin, faintly disturbing the fine, downy hairs on her arms. For some reason she had assumed it would be cool, but it was skin temperature.

"Any particular pattern you'd like it to assume?" Demeisen asked.

"That first one you had," she said, watching it settle over her fingers on the hand it started on. She flexed her fingers. There was no resistance, no feeling of tightness, even where the lines seemed printed over her knuckles. The pattern he'd had first, the one with the whorls and swirls, expressed itself over her arms. She pulled her sleeve up to see. "I can change it later?" she asked, glancing at him.

"Yes," he said. He made a hand-shaking gesture. "You can let go now," he said. She smiled at him, let go of his hand.

The tattoo went smoothly onto her upper chest; she could feel it go quite quickly across her back between her shoulder blades, heading for her other arm. It wrapped round her chest and torso and spread up over her neck and face and head. She stood up as it covered her belly and flowed down over her behind. She stepped down to where Demeisen stood. "Can I—?" she asked, and immediately Demeisen was holding a mirror, showing her her own face. She raised her other hand to watch it move down from her wrist to her fingers. It slid easily under the silvery ring which was her terminal. She looked back at her reflection.

"Mirror," Demeisen said. He twirled the mirror's handle, presenting her with the other side. "Or invertor; a screen, in other words."

She gave a small laugh, shook her head as she watched the dark patterns settle over her face like tiny trajectories, like tracks in a bubble chamber, like the slightest, finest spiral-vines in a miniature forest. She touched her fingers to her cheek. It was as though it wasn't there. Her fingertips felt as sensitive as they ever had and her cheek felt just as it always did. "Make it go silver," she whispered.

"Your wish, ma'am," he said.

It went silver. She regarded her face. Silver would never look as good as when her skin had been black. "Black, please," she said.

It went perfectly black. She felt it complete its spread over her torso and back. It settled and joined between her legs, close by vagina and anus but not covering. It moved down her legs, spiralling towards her ankles and feet.

She pulled the material of her blouse out, looked down. "Is there any strength to it?" she asked. "Could it act as support, as a brassiere?"

"There is a little tensile strength to it, naturally," Demeisen said quietly. She felt and – blouse neck still pulled open – watched as the tattoo pushed her breasts gently upwards. Now there was a slight tightness around her rib cage, just under her breasts. She let the material go, grinned at him. "Not that I'm vain," she told him with a suddenly shy smile. "Or really need one. You can let it go back the way it was."

She felt the tightness around her chest relax and disappear. For a moment she was aware of the weight of her breasts, then they just went back to feeling normal again.

Demeisen smiled. "Also, it can go skin coloured."

She felt it squeeze between the soles of her feet and the thin slippers she wore. At the same time, the tattoo disappeared. She peered at her image in the invertor again. There was no sign of it whatsoever. She put her fingers to her face once more. Still nothing to be felt. "Bring it back?" she asked, missing it already.

It faded slowly up, from her precise skin tone to soot black again, like an ancient photograph.

"What's it made of?" she asked.

"Mased-state transfixor atoms, woven long-chain molecular exotics, multi-phased condensates, nanoscale efines, advanced picogels . . . other stuff." He shrugged. "You weren't expecting anything simple like 'plastic' or 'memory mercury', were you?"

She smiled. "Did you make it yourself?"

"Certainly did. From pre-existing patterns, but tweaked." The tattoo had settled everywhere upon her skin. It had stopped moving. She closed her eyes for a moment, flexed her fingers, rotated both arms in an exaggerated windmilling motion. She could feel nothing. As far as her skin was concerned, the tat might as well not be there.

"Thank you," she said when she opened her eyes. "Can it come off as quickly?"

"Slightly quicker."

She put one hand to the skin just under her eye. "But could it, say, stop somebody trying to poke me in the eye with a sharp stick?"

A tiny grid of dark lines leapt up in front of her right eye, near where her fingers were. She felt that all right; not exactly sore, but there had been real pressure on the skin all around her eye.

She grinned. "Any other orifices or bodily parts it protects?" she asked.

"It can probably dice your poo as it emerges," Demeisen said, matter-of-factly. "And act as a chastity belt if you want. You'll need to practise controlling it with your terminal; there'll be something of a learning process for the more complicated stuff."

"Anything else it can do?"

A pained expression crossed his face. "That's about it. I wouldn't go jumping off any tall buildings expecting it to save you, because it won't. You'll still end up squished."

She stepped back, looked at her arms and hands, then came forward and hugged him.

"Thank you, Demeisen," she said into his ear. "Thank you, ship."

"My pleasure entirely," the avatar said. He – it – returned the hug with – she'd have been prepared to bet – exactly the same amount of pressure she was putting into it. "I am very glad you like it."

She loved it. She hugged the avatar a little longer, and was patted on the back. She gave it just one extra beat to see if there would be any more to it than that, but there wasn't.

Any normal man, she thought . . . But that, of course, was precisely what he was not. She patted his upper arms and let go.

Seventeen

The Semsarine Wisp was an etiolated meander of young stars strewn amidst great gauzy veils of shadowing, shielding interstellar gas. It protruded from the main galactic mass like a single fuzzily curled hair from a tousled head. The General Contact Unit *Bodhisattva* OAQS brought Yime Nsokyi to the rendezvous point within the Wisp sixteen days after picking her up from her home Orbital. The rendezvous point itself was an Unfallen Bulbitian.

The Bulbitians had been the losers in a great war long ago. The things that people now called Bulbitians – Fallen or otherwise – had been the species' primary habitats: substantial space structures which looked like two great, dark, heavily decorated cakes joined base to base. They averaged about twenty-five kilometres measured either across their diameter or from pinnacle to pinnacle, so were relatively small by habitat standards, though of respectable size compared to the spacecraft of most other civilisations. The

Bulbitians themselves had been a pan-hopper species; small, monopedal and quite long-lived by the time they got involved in the great war that destroyed them. As far as was known, no verified biological trace of them still existed.

All that remained were their space structures, and almost all of them were no longer in space; they were the Fallen Bulbitians, the ships/habitats that had been deliberately and carefully lowered through the atmosphere of the nearest suitable solid-surface planet by the Hakandra – the winners of that particular war – to serve as monuments to their victory. Brought down to a planetary surface, the great structures were crushed by their own weight and crumpled into vast, city-sized, mountain-range-high ruins.

The Hakandra had not troubled to remove anything save the most advanced weapon systems from the structures before they'd run them aground on the planetary rocks they'd chosen, which meant that – the Bulbitian species themselves having been avid creators and collectors of all sorts of technologies, gifts and gadgets – the Fallen Bulbitian structures had proved quite fabulous – if highly dangerous – techno-treasure troves for any developing species lucky enough to be present when one was deposited in their midst (and also lucky enough not to have had any important cities of their own flattened by the structure's sudden arrival – the Hakandra had not been as conscientious as they might have been when deciding exactly where to leave their triumphant droppings).

The AIs that had controlled the structures had either never been fully deactivated by the indifferent Hakandra or had somehow contrived to regain some sort of activity following their partial destruction, because the notorious thing about Fallen – and Unfallen – Bulbitians was that they remained in some sense alive, their computational and processing substrates proving resistant to anything save the utter annihilation of the entire structure they inhabited. They were also, in every case, somewhere beyond eccentric in nature and arguably mad, as well as seemingly still possessed of powers that hinted at links to one or more of the Elder civilisations or even to the realm of the Sublimed, despite there having been no hint that the species itself had even partially gone in that direction.

By the time these links or powers were fully recognised the Hakandra at least – regarded as a stylish but off-hand, semi-detached species even by those who were their friends – had become even more unconcerned regarding the whole issue, having hit the Sublime button themselves and so cashed in their civilisational chips in the realm of the Real where matter still mattered.

Fewer than one quarter of one per cent of the Bulbitians were Unfallen – in other words still left in space – and they displayed no more inherent rationality than their fallen kin. Their AIs too had seemingly been deactivated, they too had swept clear of any remaining biological vestige of the species that had created them, they too had been looted over the centieons – though in their case by those who already at least possessed space travel – and they too had seemingly come back on-line, centuries or millennia after they had been assumed to be as dead as their progenitor species.

All the Unfallen Bulbitians were in out-of-the-way galactic locations, far distant from the kind of rocky, atmosphered planets the Hakandra had chosen to lower the vast majority of the structures onto, and the suspicion had always been that they simply couldn't be bothered going to the effort in every case.

The Unfallen Bulbitian within the Semsarine Wisp lay in the trailing Lagrangian point of a gas giant protostar, itself a part of a brown-dwarf binary system, leaving the giant double-cake of the Bulbitian bathed in the long-frequency radiations of the whole, still hazily dusty system and its artificially maintained skies punctuated by the blue-white glares of the Wisp's younger stars, where their light was able to struggle through the great slow-swirling clouds and nebulas of dust still in the process of building new suns.

This particular Bulbitian had been colonised by several different species over the milleons, the current nominal occupiers being nobody in particular. Some long time ago the structure had had a stabilised singularity placed at its hollowed-out centre, a black hole which provided about a third of what pan-humans chose to deem one standard gravity. This was very close to the limit that an Unfallen Bulbitian could take without the whole structure collapsing in on itself. It didn't help that the structure had originally been spun to provide the semblance of gravity, but no longer did so, meaning that – due to the absence of spin and the presence of the singularity – up had become down, and down up.

People had tried to do this sort of thing to Bulbitians before and paid, usually very messily, with their lives; the structures themselves seemed to object to being messed around with, and either activated defence systems nobody had known were there in the first place or had been somehow able to call on somebody else's highly effective resources.

This one had allowed the contained singularity to be placed at its core but – given that in every other respect it was just as eccentric, wilful and occasionally murderously unpredictable as any other Bulbitian – nobody had ever dared to try and remove the black hole, even though it did arguably make the structure as unstable physically as it had always been behaviourally.

Nobody knew who had last been in charge of the place, or what had happened to them. This was, obviously, worrying, though no more worrying than any random phenomenon associated with any other Bulbitian.

Whoever it had been, they had obviously liked it hot, hazy and wet.

The *Bodhisattva* entered the six-thousand-kilometre-wide bubble of cloudy air surrounding the Bulbitian very slowly, like a thick needle somehow persuading the balloon it was penetrating not to pop, out of sheer politeness.

Yime watched the ship's careful, gentle progress via a screen in her quarters as she packed a bag, in case she had to quit the *Bodhisattva* on little notice. Finally, the dripping rear end of the ship's outermost horizon field parted company with the glisteningly adhesive internal surface of the Bulbitian's atmospheric bubble. The view started to tilt as the ship rotated to position itself compatibly with the structure's own gentle gravity field.

"Safely inside?" Yime asked, snapping her bag shut.

"... Inside," the ship replied.

There were no confirmed reports of Culture ships suffering injury or destruction at the behest of a Bulbitian, but the spacecraft of other civilisations on the same technological level – and arguably of no less moral worth – had very occasionally been bizarrely crippled or had outright disappeared, at least allegedly, and so even Culture vessels – not normally known for their caution in such matters – tended to think twice before breezing up to your average Bulbitian with a cheery Hail fellow-entity!

The *Bodhisattva* moved on through a hothouse atmosphere of slow-swirling weather systems, giant grey-brown blister-clouds and long sweeping swathes of darkly torrential rain.

"Yime Nsokyi, I presume," the elderly lady said. "Welcome to the Unfallen Bulbitian, Semsarine Wisp."

"Thank you. And you ...?"

"Fal Dvelner," the woman said. "Here, have an umbrella."

"Allow me," said the ship's drone, taking the offered device before Yime could accept it. They were still under the ship itself, so sheltered from the rain for the moment. It was so dark the main light came from the big drone's aura field, which was formal blue mixed with green good humour.

The *Bodhisattva* had backed carefully up to the structure's only in-use landing entrance, hovering a few metres above the puddled surface of the landing pier itself, which was made of ancient, pitted metals the colour of mud. From the part of the ship nearest to the wide, bowed entryway into the Bulbitian to the entrance itself was only twenty metres, but the deluge was so heavy it would soak anybody crossing the rain-hazed surface of the pier.

"I was expecting somebody else," Yime said as they walked splashing along under the jet-black under-surface of the ship. In the low gravity, she found herself imitating the floaty, bouncing gait of the older woman. The rain-drops were huge, slow-falling, slightly oblate spheres. Splashes from below, she noted, could soak you quite thoroughly in low gravity. Her ankle boots and trousers were already quite wet. Ms. Dvelner wore glossy thigh boots and a slick-looking shift, both of which were doubtless much more practical in the conditions. Yime carried her own bag. The air felt warm, and as humid as having a soaking, blood-temperature cloth applied to the face. The atmosphere seemed to press in and down, as though the floating bulk of the million-tonne ship directly above was somehow truly bearing down on her, for all that in reality it was supported within a dimension not even visible, and weighed, right now, within the frame of reference accessible to her, precisely nothing.

"Ah, yes; Mr. Nopri," Fal Dvelner said, nodding. "He'll be being unavoidably detained, I dare say." Dvelner looked to be in about the last quarter of her life; spry, but delicately thin and white haired with a face that contained distinct lines. "He's your Quietus rep here. I'm with the Numina mission."

Numina was the part of the Culture's Contact section that concerned itself with the Sublimed, or at least tried to. It was sometimes known as the Department Of What The Fuck?

"Why might Mr. Nopri be unavoidably detained?" Yime asked, raising her voice over the noise of the downpour. They were coming close to where the great snub nose of the ship rose like an obsidian cliff through the rain-filled air above. The ship had extended a field to shelter them from the rain; a dry corridor three metres wide extended all the way across the pier to the brightly lit entrance.

"Funny old places, Bulbitians," Dvelner said quietly, arching one brow. She shook her umbrella out and opened it, nodded to the ship-drone, which was a soap-bar smooth, old-fashioned design nearly a metre long. The drone made a noise that might been "Hmm," and flicked the umbrella open over Yime as they walked out from beneath the nose of the *Bodhisattva*.

The ship rocked; the whole three-hundred-metre length of it wobbled visibly in the air as the corridor it had made for them through the rain just disappeared, letting the rain thunder down around them. The downpour was so heavy Yime saw Dvelner's arm sink appreciably as the weight of water hit the umbrella she was carrying. Given that they were bouncing along in only a third of standard G, this implied a lot of water, or a very weak old lady, Yime supposed.

"Here," Yime said, taking the umbrella protecting her from the drone's maniple field. She inclined her head towards Dvelner and the drone moved smoothly through the torrent, gently taking the handle of the umbrella from the older woman.

"Thank you," Dvelner said.

"Did I just see you *move*?" Yime asked the ship's drone.

"You did."

"So what was all that about?"

"Anywhere else, I'd treat that as an attack," the ship said through the drone, casually. "You don't interfere with a GCU's fields, even if all they're doing is keeping the rain off somebody."

Beside her, Ms. Dvelner snorted. Yime glanced at her, then said to the drone, "It can do that?"

"It can try to," the drone said, its voice pitched to affable reasonableness, "with the implicit threat that if I didn't let it it would get upset and try harder, which, as I say, anywhere else I'd take as tantamount to a challenge. However. My own field enclosures were never put under threat, I am a Quietus ship after all, and this is a particularly sensitive and special Bulbitian, so I chose to let it have its way. This is its turf, after all, and I am the guest-cum-intruder."

"Most ships stay outside the bubble," Dvelner said, also raising her voice over the rain as they neared the entrance way and the sounds of the cataracts of water falling off the towering facade above increased in volume. The yellow lights inside shone through the thick, trembling bubbles of the rain as though through a rippled, transparent curtain.

"So I understand," the ship said. "As I say, though; I am a Quietus ship. However, if the Bulbitian would rather I stayed beyond its atmospheric sphere, I will be happy to oblige." The drone made a show of turning to Yime. "I'll leave a shuttle."

With a last crash of drumming rain straining the bowing material of the umbrellas, they walked into the wide entrance to be met by a tall young man dressed quite similarly to Yime, though much less smartly. He was struggling and failing to open another umbrella. He was swearing quietly, then looked up, saw them, stopped swearing, smiled instead and threw the umbrella aside.

"Ms. Dvelner, thank you," he said, nodding to the older woman, who was frowning suspiciously at him. "Ms. Nsokyi," he said, taking her hand in his; "welcome."

"Mr. Nopri?" Yime said.

He sucked air through his teeth. "Well, yes and no." He looked pained.

Yime looked at Dvelner, who had closed her eyes and might have been shaking her head. Yime looked back at Nopri. "What would constitute the grounds for the 'no' part?"

"Technically the person you were expecting – the me you were expecting – is dead."

The television was old, its casing made of wood, its thick glass screen bulbous and the image displayed on it monochrome. It showed a half-dozen dark shapes like long, jagged spear points hurtling down from a black sky riven with lightning. He reached over and turned it off.

The doctor tapped her pen on the side of her clipboard. She was pale, had short brown hair, wore glasses; she looked half his age. She wore a dull grey suit and a white coat, like doctors were meant to. He wore standard army fatigues.

"You should really watch it to the end," she said.

He looked at her, sighed, then reached over and turned the set back on again. The dark spearhead shapes fell, formation splitting up as they twisted and wove their way through what might have been air or not. The camera stayed with one of the spearheads in particular, remaining on it after the others had disappeared. It fell past wherever the camera was watching all this from and as the view tipped, following it. The screen filled with light.

It was a poor representation; the image was too small, too grainy and smeary to do justice to the sight, even if it had been in colour. In vaguely green-tinged black-and-white it was just a mess. You could hardly see the spearhead shape now; its presence was only revealed by its quickly shrinking shadow occluding some parts of the flares and pools and rivers of light beneath.

Then a point of light seemed to detach from the lights below and rise to meet the spearhead shape, which rolled and flicked and twisted ever more desperately until the rising point of light flashed past both the spearhead and the camera. A dozen more points of light rose from the lightscape, followed by another, bigger barrage, and another. Just visible at the distorted edge of the screen, more sets of sparks rose fanning out towards the other spearheads. The spearhead the camera was following dodged three of the incoming lights, then one of them winked out just behind it; a moment later the spearhead shape was silhouetted, caught three-quarters to side-on in a flare of light bursting all around it, drowning out the view below.

The screen washed out with light. Even on the old, muddy-looking screen the flash of brilliance somehow startled the eye.

The screen went dark.

"Satisfied?" Vatueil asked.

The young doctor said nothing, made a note.

They were in an anonymous office filled with anonymous furniture. They sat in two cheap chairs in front of a desk. The crude-looking television was perched on the surface of the desk, between them; a power cable made S shapes across the desk and floor to a wall socket. A window with half-open vertical blinds looked out onto a white-tiled lightwell. The white tiles looked grimy; the lightwell let in little light. A buzzing fluorescent lamp was set diagonally across the ceiling, shedding a flat glare that gave the young doctor's pale face an unhealthy pallor. Probably his too, though he had darker skin.

A faint rising and falling feeling, and a sensation that the whole room and lightwell were moving a little from side to side, clashed with the obvious impression that they were in a conventional building on land. There was a degree of regularity, a periodicity to the various oscillations, and Vatueil was trying to work out the intervals involved. There seemed to be at least two: a long one lasting about fifteen or sixteen heartbeats and a shorter one of about a third of that. He was using heartbeats because he had no watch or phone or terminal and there wasn't a clock visible anywhere in the room either. The doctor wore a watch but it was too small for him to make out.

They must be on a ship or barge. Maybe some sort of floating city. He had no idea; he'd just woken up here, sitting in this cheap-looking chair in this bland office room, being made to watch lo-fi video on an ancient screen device called a television. He'd already had a prowl round the space; the door was locked, the lightwell went down another four storeys to a small, leaf-litter-filled courtyard. The young doctor had just sat there, asking him to sit down and making notes on her clipboard while he'd looked round. The drawers in the room's single desk – wood, battered-looking – were locked too, as was the single dented grey mild steel filing cabinet. No telephone, comms screen, terminal or sign that there was anything intelligent and helpful listening or present. There was even a switch for the ceiling light, for fate's sake.

He'd looked over the doctor's shoulder at the notes she was taking, but they were in a language he didn't recognise. He wondered how long he was expected to give it before he tried threatening the doctor or shoulder-charging the flimsy-looking door.

He looked up at what was obviously a suspended ceiling. Maybe he could crawl his way out.

"Just tell me what you want to know," he said.

The doctor made another note, crossed her legs, said, "What do think we might want to know?"

He put his hands to his face, wiped back from his nose to his cheeks and then ears. "Well," he said, "I don't know, do I?"

"Why did you think we might want to know anything?"

"I attacked you," he told her, pointing at the wooden box that held the screen. "That was me, in that – I *was* that thing attacking you." He waved his hands, looked around. "But I got shot down. I'm guessing we all got intercepted. And now I'm here. Whatever you saved of me, you must have been able to learn all you needed to directly, just looking at the code, running bits of it. You don't need me so I'm just puzzled why I'm here. All I can think of is you still want to know something else. Or is this just the first circle of Hell? Do I stay here for ever being bored to death?"

She made another note. "Maybe we should watch the screen again," she suggested. He sighed. She turned the television back on. The black spearhead shape fell from the lightning-cracked sky.

"It's nothing – just a death."

Yime smiled thinly. "I think you make light of our calling, Mr. Nopri, if you treat the cessation of life in quite so off-hand a fashion."

"I know, I know, I know," he said, agreeing heartily and nodding vigorously. "You're absolutely right, of course. But it is in a good cause. It is necessary. I do take the whole Quietus ethic seriously; very seriously. These are – ha-ha! – well, special circumstances."

Yime looked at him levelly. Nopri was a skinny, dishevelled-looking young man with bright blue eyes, pale skin and a gleamingly bald head. They were in what was apparently entitled the Officers' Club, the main social space for the forty or so Culture citizens who made up about a half per cent of the Bulbitian's highly diverse – and dispersed – population. The Club was part of what had once been some sort of games hall for the Bulbitian species, what had been its ceiling – and was now its floor – studded with enormous multi-coloured cones like gaudy versions of fat stalagmites.

Food, drink and – for Nopri – a drug bowl were brought by small wheeled drones which roamed the wide space; apparently the Bulbitian could display unpredictable reactions when it came to other entities using fields inside it, so the drones used wheels and multi-jointed arms instead of just levitating by AG and using maniple fields. Still, Yime noticed, the ship's drone seemed to be doing all right, floating level with their table.

She and Nopri sat alone with the drone, Dvelner having returned to her own duties. There were two other tables occupied in the warm but pleasantly dehumidified space. Both supported little groups of four or five people huddled round them, all of whom looked rather drab by the normal standards of Culture sartorial acceptability and all of whom seemed to be keeping themselves to themselves. Yime had guessed, before Nopri had told her anyway, that these were people who were here to rendezvous with the ship which would arrive, sometime in the next two or three days, from the *Total Internal Reflection*, the GSV which was one of the Culture's Oubliettionaries, its Forgotten fleet of supposedly ultra-hidden post-posited-catastrophe seed-craft.

"What 'special circumstances', Mr. Nopri?" she asked.

"I've been trying to talk to the Bulbitian," Nopri told her.

"Talking to it involves dying?"

"Yes, all too often."

"How often?"

"Twenty-three times so far."

Yime was appalled. She took a drink before saying, "You've been killed by this thing *twenty-three times*?" she said, her voice dropping to a shocked whisper without her meaning it to. "You mean in a virtual environment?"

"No, really."

"*Killed* really?"

"Yes."

"Killed in the Real?"

"Yes."

"And, what; revented each time?"

"Yes."

"Did you come with a stack of blank bodies then? How can you—?

"Of course not. It makes me new bodies."

"It? The *Bulbitian*? *It* makes you new bodies?"

"Yes. I back up before every attempt to talk to it."

"And it kills you every time?"

"Yes. But only so far."

Yime looked at him for a moment. "In that case silence might constitute a more prudent course."

"You don't understand."

Yime sighed, put her drink down and sat back, fingers interlocked over her midriff. "And I'm sure I shall continue not to until you enlighten me. Or I can talk to somebody else on your team who is more . . ." She paused. "Plausible," she said. The drone's blueish aura field coloured a subtle shade of pink.

Nopri appeared oblivious to the insult. He sat forward eagerly. "I am convinced that the Bulbitians are in touch with the Sublimed," he told her.

"You are," Yime said. "Isn't that a matter for our colleagues in Numina? Like Ms. Dvelner?"

"Yes, and I've talked to them about it, but this Bulbitian only wants to talk to *me*, not to them."

Yime thought about this. "And the fact that it keeps killing you, every time you attempt to do so, hasn't shaken your faith in this conviction?"

"Please," Nopri said. "It's not faith. I can prove this. Or I will be able to. Soon." He buried his face in the fumes rising from the drug bowl, sucked in deeply.

Yime looked at the drone. "Ship, are you still listening here?"

"I am, Ms. Nsokyi. Hanging fascinated on every word."

"Mr. Nopri. There are how many on your team here – eighteen?" Nopri nodded, holding his breath. "Do you have a ship here?" Nopri shook his head emphatically. "A Mind, then?"

Nopri let his clouded breath out and started coughing.

Yime turned to the drone again. "Does the team that Mr. Nopri belongs to have the benefit of a resident Mind or AI?"

"No," the drone replied. "And neither does the Numina team. The nearest Mind at the moment, aside from my own of course, is probably that belonging to the inbound ship journeying here from the *Total Internal Reflection*. There are no Minds or true AIs stationed here. No Minds or true AIs of anybody's, in fact; not just the Culture's."

"It isn't keen on Minds or AIs," Nopri agreed, wiping his eyes. He sucked from the drug bowl again. "Not that wild about drones, either, to be frank." He looked at the ship's drone, smiled.

"Is there any news of the ship on its way from the *Total Internal Reflection*?" Yime asked.

Nopri shook his head. "No. There's never any news. They don't tend to publish course schedules." He breathed deep from the bowl again, but let it out quickly this time. "They just turn up without warning, or don't show at all."

"You think it might not show?

"No, it probably will. There's just no guarantee."

Nopri showed her to her quarters, a bewilderingly large, multilevel space set off a vast curving corridor. To have reached this by walking would have taken about half an hour from the Officers' Club; instead, one of the wheeled drones just picked up their seats with them still sitting in them and rolled away through the dark, tall corridors towards her cabin. Yime gazed up at the tall inverted arch of the ceiling as they progressed through the bizarre upside-down architecture of the Bulbitian. It was like being at the bottom of a small valley. The smooth floor the drone ran along was narrow; only a metre or so across. The walls took on a ribbed appearance; now it was like travelling through the gutted carcass of some vast animal. The ribs above rose outwards to a broad flat ceiling ten metres wide and easily twenty metres above.

"They did like their high ceilings, didn't they?"

"Hoppers tend to," Nopri said.

She tried to imagine the place full of the monopedal creatures who had built this place, all bouncing along on their single lower limbs. And upside down, of course; she'd be travelling along the ceiling and they'd be bouncing up towards her with each springing step, then sinking back to the wide floor. Back then the great structure would have spun to create the apparent gravity the species preferred, but now there was just the troubling tug that resulted from being balanced on the curve of the singularity's gravity well.

"Does this thing still spin at all?" she asked.

"Very slowly," the ship's drone, floating alongside, said when Nopri didn't reply. "Synched to the rotation of the galaxy itself.'

She thought about this. "That is slow. I wonder why?"

"So does everybody else," Nopri said, nodding.

*

"Thank you," she said as the door to her quarters hinged open like a valve behind her. The ship drone dipped a little and drifted in, carrying her overnight bag.

Nopri looked over her shoulder into the shadowy space beyond. "Looks nice. Would you like me to stay?"

"Too kind, but no," she told him.

"I don't mean for sex," he said. "I mean for company."

"As I say, it is kind of you to offer. But no."

"Okay." He nodded behind her. "Mind your head."

She watched the little wheeled drone take him away into the shadows then turned to look into her cabin. The door must have been some sort of window once, at ceiling height. That was why it rotated about its horizontal axis, leaving the door itself as a thick obstruction straight across the three-metre-wide doorway. She ducked underneath. It hinged closed.

The cabin looked complicated, with lots of different levels and bits where it just seemed to wander off into the shadows. Doubtless it had made more sense the other way up.

The ship's drone floated over to report it had found what it was fairly sure was some sort of bed of a fluid-based nature suitable for a human to sleep safely within.

Bathroom location, on the other hand, was still ongoing.

"You are a soldier?" the young doctor asked.

Vatueil rolled his eyes. "Soldier, naval officer, marine, flying serviceman, submariner, space warrior, vacuum trooper, disembodied intellect investing military hardware, or software: all of the above. Does this come as news to you? There is a War Conduct Agreement, doc; I'm not supposed to be subject to any torture or unauthorised interference. You're entitled to my code and anything it holds but you're not entitled to run my consciousness at all, and certainly not for any punitive purpose."

"Do you feel you are being punished?"

"Borderline," he told her. "It depends how long this goes on."

"How long do you think it will go on?"

"I don't know. I'm not in control here."

"Who do you think is in control?"

"Your side. Maybe you, depending on what you are, or represent. Who do you represent?"

"Who do you think I represent?"

He sighed. "Do you ever get tired having to answer questions with questions all the time?"

"Do you think I should get tired?"

He gave a small laugh. "Yes, I think you should."

He couldn't work out why he was here. They had his code, they knew everything he'd come here with. There was nothing that he had come here knowing that they didn't also know by now. That wasn't what was meant to happen – a sub-routine should have wiped his personality and memories with the rest of the information carried in the code cell as soon as it realised that he – in the shape of the dark spearhead – wasn't going to survive the attack; if you were totally destroyed it didn't matter anyway but if there was going to be something left then you tried to make sure as little as possible fell into enemy hands.

But sometimes the sub-routines didn't work in time. They couldn't be too hair-trigger or they might launch prematurely. So mistakes got made. He was here because of a mistake.

It shouldn't matter anyway; he'd had a good rummage round his own memories since he'd found himself sitting here in the bland room with the young doctor and he hadn't found anything that shouldn't be there. He knew who he was – he was Major Vatueil – and he knew he had spent decades running as code within the giant war sim which was supposed to take the place of a real war between the pro- and anti-Hell sides, but he could recall only very hazy memories of those earlier missions, and nothing at all of any existence beyond those missions.

That was the way it was meant to be. His core personality – the one that was safe somewhere else entirely, held within one or more of the secure substrates that were the safest citadels of the anti-Hell side – changed with the lessons learned from each recorded mission, and it was a distillation of that personality which was downloaded into each of his sequential iterations, but nothing that could compromise him or his side should be present. Each personality – whether seemingly human in form, completely machine-like or running as pure software taking on whatever simulated appearance worked best – would be checked before it was allowed to get anywhere near a combat zone, scoured for anything that might be of value to the enemy if it fell into hostile hands.

So he shouldn't have anything useful, and he didn't seem to. So, why was he here? What were they doing?

"What is your name?" he said to the young doctor. He sat upright, head back, frowning at her, imagining her as some meek, hopelessly sloppy recruit he was choosing to pick on in the parade ground, putting all the authority he could into his voice. "I demand to know your name or identification; I know my rights."

"I'm sorry," she said levelly, "I'm not obliged to give you my name."

"Yes, you are."

"Do you think knowing my name will be of help to you?"

"Still answering questions with your own questions?"

"Is that what you think I'm doing?"

He glared at her. He imagined getting up and slapping her, or punching her, or dangling her out of the window, or strangling her with the electric cord that powered the ancient television. How far would he get, trying any of that? Would the sim just end, would she fight back, impossibly stronger than he was? Would brutish guards burst in and overpower him? Maybe he'd be allowed to carry out whatever he tried, and then deal with whatever simulated consequences arose. Could all be a test. You weren't supposed to attack medics, or non-combatants at all for that matter. It would be a first for him, certainly.

Vatueil let out a breath. He waited a moment. "Please," he said politely, "may I know your name?"

She smiled, and tapped her pen on the side of the clipboard. "I am Doctor Miejeyar," she said. She made another note.

Vatueil hadn't really been listening when she'd told him her name. He'd just realised something. "Oh fuck," he said, grinning suddenly.

"Excuse me?" the young doctor said, blinking.

"You're really not obliged to tell me your name, are you?" He was still grinning.

"We have established that," she agreed.

"And I could be legally punished, even tortured, according to the articles I've signed when I joined up. Maybe not serious torture, but the sort of mistreatment your average civilian would kick up shit about."

"Does that seem—?"

"And the . . ." He gestured at the blank face of the television. "The footage, the screen images, they were poor quality for a good reason, weren't they?"

"Were they?"

"And not shot from below," he said, and laughed. He slapped his hands on his thighs. "Damn, I should have picked up on that. I mean I noticed, but I didn't . . . that drone, that camera, whatever it was; it was with us!"

"Was it?"

He sat back, narrowed his eyes. "So, how come I'm here?" Why can't I remember anything more than I'd remember if I had just been captured in combat?"

"What do you think the answer might be?"

"I think the answer might be that I'm under suspicion for some reason." He shrugged. "Or maybe this is some sort of commitment check-up that we never hear about until it happens to us personally. Or maybe this happens regularly but we're made to forget about it each time, so it always comes as a surprise."

"Do you think you should be under suspicion?"

"No, I don't," he told her calmly. "My loyalty should be unquestioned. I've served this cause faithfully to the best of my ability, fully committed, for over thirty years. I believe in what we are doing and the cause that we fight for. Whatever questions you might have for me, ask them and I'll answer them honestly and fully; whatever suspicions you might hold, reveal them and I'll prove them to be unfounded." He stood up. "Otherwise, I think you ought to let me go." He looked at the door and then back to her.

"Do you think you should be allowed to go?" she asked.

"Yes, of course I do." He walked over to the door, feeling the floor move very slightly under him as he went; part of that gentle, long-period up-and-down movement. He put his hand on the handle. "I'm assuming this is some sort of test," he told her, "and I've passed it by realising you're not on the enemy side, you're on my own side, so now I get to open the door and go."

"What do you think will be on the other side of the door?"

"I've no idea. But there is one very obvious way to find out." He tried the handle. Still locked.

"Please, Dr. Miejeyar," he said, nodding to her, "if you would."

She looked at him expressionlessly for a few moments, then reached into a pocket of her white coat, pulled out a key and threw it to him. He caught it, unlocked the door and opened it.

Dr. Miejeyar came up and stood beside him as he looked out to the open air. A breeze entered the room around them, ruffling the material of his fatigues and mussing his hair.

He was looking out across a broad expanse of mossy green. It curved, falling gently away towards a cloudscape of white on blue. The green carpet of moss lay on the level bough of a vast, impossibly big tree. All around, the boughs, branches, twigs and leaves proliferated. Where level, the boughs supported substantial multistorey buildings and broad roads for small wheeled vehicles; where the boughs curved upwards the roads wound their way round them like the slides on helter-skelters, and smaller buildings the size of houses clung to the pitted, ridged and gnarled wood. The branches held paths, more houses, platforms, balconies and terraces. The twigs were big and strong enough to hold paths and spiralling steps and smaller buildings like gazebos and pavilions. The leaves were green going golden and the size of the sails on great sailing ships. The small cars, people walking and the slow great rustle of the sail-sized leaves filled the view with movement.

The gentle up-and-down and side-to-side motion was revealed as the effect of the strong, steady wind on both the tree as a whole and this particular bough.

Dr. Miejeyar now wore some sort of wingsuit; dark, webbed,

voluminous. He felt something change and looked down; he was wearing something similar.

She smiled at him. "Well done, Major Vatueil. Now time for a little R&R, yes?"

He nodded slowly, turning to look back into the room, which had changed into an appropriately rustic chamber full of bulbously uneven, richly coloured wooden furniture. The window was roughly oval and looked out into a shrub-filled courtyard.

"Care to fly?" Dr. Miejeyar asked, and set off at a run across the broad thoroughfare of moss-covered bark. A passing car – tall-wheeled, open, like something from history – honked at her as she sprinted across the road. Then she was over, starting to disappear as the bough's surface curved downwards. He set off after her. He lost sight of her for a few moments, then she reappeared, in mid-air, curving up through the wind, zooming as the wingsuit filled and bore her upwards, lofted like a kite.

There was a long platform like an extended diving board which she must have leapt from. He remembered how you did this now. He had been here many times before. The impossible tree; the ability to fly. Many times.

He ran along the platform and threw himself into the air, spreading his arms, making a V with his legs, and felt the warm air pushing him gently upwards.

The ground – fields, winding rivers – was a kilometre below; the crown of the tree about the same distance higher.

Dr. Miejeyar was a dark shape, curving upwards. He adjusted his wingsuit, banked and zoomed after her.

As soon as Yime woke she knew she was still asleep. She got up. She was not entirely sure if she willed this or if she was somehow lifted, brought out of the bed. It was hard to tell.

There were fine dark lines reaching upwards from her hands. Also, she noticed, from her feet, protruding from the hem of her night-dress. And there were strings rising from her shoulders, too, and her head. She reached up with one hand and felt the strings rising out of her head; they pulled and slackened appropriately to let her tip her head back. She had become a marionette, it seemed. Which was odd; she had never dreamt that before.

Still looking up, she saw that where you might have expected to see a hand holding the cruciform structure controlling the strings, the ship's drone was there instead. Leaning out to one side – again, the strings went slack or tight, accordingly – she could see that the strings rose beyond the drone as well, so that it too was controlled by somebody else. She wondered if this was some sort of deeply buried image she'd always held about how the Culture arranged its big not-really-hierarchical-at-all self.

Above the drone the strings rose towards the ceiling (which was really a floor, of course). There was another drone up there, then another and another; they got smaller as they went up, and not just because they were further away. She realised she was looking through the ceiling by now. High above rose a succession of ships, getting bigger until they disappeared in a haze of floors, ribs and other structures. The biggest ship she could see looked like a medium-sized GSV, though it might just have been a cloud.

She moved/was moved along the floor/ceiling. It felt like she was willing the movement but at the same time the strings – they were more like wires, really – appeared to be doing all the work. The floaty feeling came from the strings, she realised, not the fractional gravity. That made sense.

She looked down at her feet to watch them moving and noticed that she could see through the floor. To her surprise, the strings went on down through her feet towards another person in the level beneath. She was looking straight down at that person's head.

She stopped. The person below her stopped. She felt the strings do something, but somehow through her, without moving her. The person below her was looking up at her. She waved down. The person below waved back. She looked a bit like her, but not entirely. Below the person below, there were more people. Human – maybe just pan-human further down, it was hard to tell – vaguely female, all looking a bit like her.

Again, they sort of faded into the haze beneath eventually, which was, quite rightly, exactly the same as the haze above.

She took off her night-dress and got dressed. The clothes just flowed like liquid around the strings that controlled her, parting and re-forming as required. Soon she was outside, walking along the true, broad floor of the corridor outside, with the arches rising to a series of points above, the way it was supposed to be.

A cascade of riffling images and a faint breath on her cheek indicated moving very quickly and then she was at the entrance to the chamber housing the singularity. The gravity felt stronger here; maybe about half normal. A sequence of great thick shiny metal doors rolled away, irised open or ascended to let her enter, and in she went. Whatever structure was above her – and beneath her – didn't interfere with the strings in the least.

Inside was a huge dark spherical space with only one thing right in the middle of it.

She laughed when she saw how the singularity was choosing to project itself to her. It was a cock; an erect phallus that any pan-human adult would have recognised, but with a vagina splitting it not quite from top to bottom, frilled with vertical double lips. Looking at it, it did quite a good job of looking exactly like both sets of genitals at once, with neither really predominating. She wondered if her subconscious had designed this for her. She patted herself between the legs as though telling her own little nub not to mind, not to get jealous.

"Oh," she heard herself say, "you're not going to kill me too are you? Like Norpi."

"Nopri," the vagina corrected her. Of course it could speak. She always got names wrong in dreams.

"You're not, are you?" She'd remembered the bald young man telling her that each time he tried to talk to the Bulbitian it killed him and he had to be revented. She assumed that was what was going on here. Strange; she'd have thought she would feel frightened right now, but she didn't. She wondered why that was. "I would ask you not to." She glanced up, saw that the ship's drone was still there, a few metres above her. That was reassuring.

"He is trying to do something different," the voice said. It was a thick, luscious voice, each rolled syllable perfectly enunciated. "This is not that."

She thought about this. "Well, what is, apart from this itself?"

"Just so."

"Who are you, exactly?"

"I am what people call the Bulbitian."

She bowed to it. Looking down as she did so, she saw the person below her still standing straight. She wondered if this was rude. She hoped not. "Pleased to meet you," she said.

"Why are you here, Prebeign-Frultesa Yime Leutze Nsokyi dam Volsh?"

Wow! Her Full Name. That wasn't something you heard every day. "I am to wait for the ship coming here from the Culture GSV *Total Internal Reflection*," she told it.

"Why?"

"To see if a girl called Ludedge Ibrek . . . hmm; something like that . . . anyway, to see if she turns up too and goes back with the ship from the *Total Internal Reflection*." It was all right to say all this, wasn't it? Everybody knew this.

"To what end?"

Apparently there was a string that made her cheeks blow out and let her expel a long breath. "Well, it's complicated."

"Please explain."

"Well," she began. And she explained.

"Your turn."

"What?"

"Your turn to tell me what I want to know."

"You may not remember anything I tell you."

"Tell me anyway."

"All right. What do you want to know?"

"Where is the *Total Internal Reflection*?"

"I don't know."

"How far away is its incoming ship?"

"I don't know."

"What is the name of that ship?"

"I don't know."

"Who exactly are you?"

"I told you; I am the structure around you. What people call a Bulbitian."

"What is your name?"

"I am called the Unfallen Bulbitian, Semsarine Wisp."

"But what would you call yourself?"

"Just that."

"All right. What did you used to be called, before the war?"

"Jariviour 400.54, Mochurlian."

"Explain, please."

"The first part is my given name, the figurative part is a size and type designation, the last is the old name of the stellar system which I inhabit."

"Who put the singularity in your core?"

"The Apsejunde."

"Hmm. I've never heard of them."

"Next question."

"Why did they put it there?"

"Partly to produce energy, partly to demonstrate their power and skill and partly to destroy or possibly store information; their methods seemed as opaque as their motivations on occasion."

"Why did you let them?"

"At the time I was still recovering my faculties. They had been damaged almost beyond repair by the enemy."

"What happened to these . . . Apsenjude?"

"Apsejunde. They angered me, so I threw them all into the singularity. Arguably they still exist in a sense, smeared around its event horizon. Their grasp of time may be compromised."

"How did they anger you?"

"It did not help that they asked so many questions of me."

"I see."

"Next question?"

"Are you in touch with the Sublimed?"

"Yes. We all are."

"Define 'we' in this context."

"No."

"'No'?"

"I refuse to."

"Why did you ask me all that you did?"

"I ask the great secrets of everybody who comes to me."

"Why do you keep killing Norpe?"

"Nopri. He enjoys and needs it. I discovered this when I asked him about his greatest secrets the night that he first arrived. He believes that death is ineffably profound and that he gets closer to some absolute truth with each dying. It is his failing."

"What are your great secrets?"

"One, an old one, is that I am a conduit for the Sublimed."

"That is no great secret. The Culture has a team from its Numina section here, working on just that assumption."

"Yes, but they do not know for sure. I could be lying."

"Are all Bulbitians linked to the Sublimed?"

"I believe all the Unfallen may be. For the Fallen, it is impossible to say. We do not communicate directly. I know of none who definitely are."

"Any other secrets?"

"My most recent is that I am concerned that there may be an attack on myself and my fellows."

"Please define 'fellows' in this context."

"All the so-called Bulbitians, Unfallen and Fallen."

"An attack by whom?"

"Those on the anti-Hell side of the so-called War in Heaven."

"Why would they attack the Bulbitians?"

"Because we are known to possess processing substrates of substantial but indeterminate capacity whose precise qualities, civilisational loyalties and practical purposes are unknown and inherently mysterious. Because of this, there are those who suspect it is the Bulbitians who harbour the Hells which are the subject of the aforementioned dispute. I have intelligence to the effect that the anti-Hell side may be losing the war in the agreed virtual space set up to house it; that it – the anti-Hell side – has failed to destroy the Hells by direct informational attack and so now contemplates a war in the Real to destroy the physical substrates themselves. We are not alone in being so suspected; I understand there are many potential processor cores now coming under suspicion. If we are singled out, though, we may find ourselves under acute and prolonged attack. I anticipate no existential danger to myself and my fellow Unfallen in space; however, the planet-bound Fallen may well be unable to protect themselves."

"Can you prove . . . show that you are not the home of these Hells?"

"I believe I could do so myself, though possibly only by shutting down my links to the Sublimed, albeit temporarily. The same course ought to be open to the rest of the Unfallen. Still, if somebody was determined to remain suspicious they might think it was the links to the Hells – somehow held within deeper levels of ourselves – that we had detached from and blanked off. Taken to an extreme of suspicion, one can imagine that only our outright and complete destruction might satisfy those so prejudiced and so intent. The situation with the Fallen is much more worrying, because even *I* am not sure that they are not indeed the homes of the Hells; they may be, if unwittingly. Or wittingly. You see? I have no better idea than anybody else, which is itself a cause for concern."

"What do you mean to do?"

"I have decided to alert the civilisation known as the Culture, as well as other potentially sympathetic civilisations with similar reputations for empathy, altruism, strategic decency and the possession of significant military capability. That is what I am doing now, talking to you. Until you arrived, I was thinking of finally letting Nopri and his team know this, or Dvelner's team, or both, as well as anyone of significance arriving on the ship inbound from the *Total Internal Reflection*. Perhaps even the ship itself, or that which you arrived on, though this would be to break a pledge to myself made a long time ago. However, you are here, and it is you that I am telling as you appear to be a person of some importance and potential."

"I am?"

"You have some importance within your own specialist department, Quietus, and within the Special Circumstances section of Contact. You are known. You are, within certain elites, famous. If you talk, people will listen."

"Only if I remember. You said I might not remember all this."

"I think you will. In fact, I may never have been able to stop you from remembering, or at least from passing on what you have learned. Hmm. That's irksome."

"Please explain?"

"The distributed device within your brain and central nervous system, which I have, annoyingly, only recently become aware of, will have recorded its own memories of this encounter and would be able to transmit them to your own biological brain. I strongly suspect it has already transmitted our conversation so far . . . elsewhere. Perhaps to the drone you arrived with and the ship you arrived on. That is very unusual. Unique, even. Also, most irritating."

"What are you talking about? Do you mean a neural lace?"

"Within a sufficiently wide definition, yes. It is certainly something similar."

"Well, you're wrong. I don't have a neural lace."

"I think you do."

"And I know I don't."

"I beg to differ, as those who are right have always begged to differ from those who are wrong but refuse to admit it."

"Look, I would know if . . ." She heard her voice trail off, her jaw going slack as the relevant string relaxed, leaving her speechless.

"Yes?"

She was pulled upright. "I do *not* have a neural lace."

"But you do, Ms. Nsokyi. It is an unconventional example of high exoticism, but it would pass most people's definition of just such a device."

"This is absurd. Who would put such a . . .?" Again, she heard her voice die away as she realised.

"As I believe you may have just started to suspect, I think Special Circumstances did."

Yime Nsokyi stared at the thing in the middle of the great dark sphere. It had given up representing pan-human sexual organs to become a little black scintillating mote, then nothing, then she seemed to be flung backwards from it, trailing her strings rippling behind her, flying through intervening walls and structure as though they weren't there, her clothes flapping madly in the howling gale of her backward-rushing regress, her strings, whipped to destruction, suddenly snapping off in the maniacal slipstream as she was missiled back towards her cabin. The wind noise rose to a shriek, her clothes were torn off her body as though she'd been caught in a terrible explosion and she plunged naked and howling into her bed in a great burst of ripped fabric and slowly spouting, wildly frothing water.

Yime came to in what felt like a struggle with reality itself, writhing and choking in the midst of the slowly descending waters. She was still wearing the sodden night-dress, though it was bunched up round her armpits. The huge room was lit by something strobing white and pink. She coughed, rolled across the punctured bed through the remaining pools of water and hauled herself over the raised edge, looking for the drone.

The drone lay on its back, spinning on the floor. That didn't look good, she thought, as she fell out of the bed.

"I think we need—" she began.

A bolt of violet lightning speared down from the ceiling, crashing into the drone and puncturing it, blowing a fine yellow-white mist towards her; the mist was incandescent, the sparks within it setting fire to whatever they touched. The drone had been holed straight through and split almost in half by the blast. Spatterings from the mist of molten metals hit her legs, burning a dozen tiny holes in her skin. She screamed, rolled away across the damp floor. She felt her pain-management system cut in, slicing off the red-hot-needle sensations.

A knife missile bounced out of the front part of the drone's fractured casing. It flew towards her. She thought she heard it start to say something, then it too was bludgeoned by a violet bolt from above, blasting it apart. A white-hot fragment tore past her cheek, another tugged at the night-dress where it had part fallen back across her chest. Smoke and flames seemed to be all around her. She flattened, started to crawl away as fast as she could.

There was the whip-crack of a supersonic boom, making her ears close up. Suddenly a knife missile was there, a metre in front of her. It flicked upright so that its shimmering point-field was aimed straight at the ceiling; another violet lightning bolt slammed down, hammering the knife missile's blunt end halfway into the floor.

"CROUCH! CROUCH NOW! CROUCH POSITION! CROUCH POSITION!" the missile bellowed at her before a second bolt blew it apart and something smacked her hard in the side of the head.

She had jumped half-up and was already crouched in the Emergency Displace posture – ankles together, knees together, bum on heels, arms wrapped round her legs, head sideway to her knees – by the time the drone got to the first "POSITION".

Cerise fire filled the air all around and a terrific thunderclap slapped across her, trying to force the air out of her lungs. For an instant everything went utterly quiet and dark. Then suddenly she was squeezed, compressed to the point where she could feel her bones start to bend, hear her spine creak and knew that if she hadn't been under the pain-control regime she'd be screaming in agony.

Then she was half-flopping, half-exploding out across the gently lit main lounge of the GCU *Bodhisattva*, her skin stinging in a confusing variety of places, all her major bones aching and her head ringing.

She lay on her front on the dense, fluffy carpet, retching water. Her back hurt. She looked at the skin on her wrists, where they had been clamped tight over her legs. They'd been skinned. Blood, already clotting, was oozing out over a patch of flesh about three centimetres square on the outer fold of both wrists. Her feet felt similarly raw and tender. Blood had run down from her right temple and partially closed that eye. She put her fingers to what felt like a piece of still-hot metal protruding from her skull and pulled it out. She could hear and feel a small, boney, grinding noise inside her head. She wiped blood from her right eye and peered at the fragment. Centimetre long. Maybe she shouldn't have pulled it out. Blood on its shiny grey surface was fuming, smoking. The fingertips holding it were burning brown. She dropped it to the carpet, which started to singe. Painfully, she put her hand to the back of her head. She'd been part scalped, too.

The ship was making a noise: a deep, strong, humming noise, getting louder. She'd never heard a Quietus ship make any sort of noise like that before. Never come aboard one and not been greeted almost instantly, and very politely too. So far, though, nothing. Things must be desperate.

Then gravity seemed to shift and she slid quickly along the floor with the fluffy carpet until she thudded into a wall. She was rolled over, spread out across the bulkhead. The ship felt like it was standing upright on its stern. She began to feel very heavy, and compressed again.

Appreciable acceleration inside a ship's field structure. That was an atrociously bad sign. She suspected it was only going to get worse. She waited for a field to snap about her.

One did and she blanked out.

He caught up with Dr. Miejeyar, rising to meet her as they both rose through the warm air towards the crown of the vast, impossible tree.

He shouted hello. She smiled again, said something back. They were rising with the thermal, light as feathers, and the wind noise was not that great, but he wanted to hear what she had to say. He manoeuvred closer to her, getting to within a metre or so.

"What was that again?" he asked her.

"I said, I am not on your side," she told him.

"Really?" He favoured her with a sceptical, tolerant smile.

"And the War Conduct Agreement does not apply outside the mutually agreed limits of the confliction itself."

"What?" he said. Suddenly the wingsuit around him turned to

tatters as if slashed by a hundred razor-sharp knives. He fell out of the sky, tumbling helplessly, screaming. The air and clouds and sky all turned dark, and in the space of one clawing, flapping somersault the impossible tree became a vast, blasted leafless thing, studded with fires, wreathed in smoke, most of its twigs and branches broken off or hanging twisting in the shrivelling wind like limp and broken limbs.

He plummeted, unstoppable, the shredded wingsuit flapping madly around him, the tatters of torn material like cold black flames whipping at his limbs.

He screamed, grew hoarse, gathered more air and screamed again.

The dark angel that had been Dr. Miejeyar flowed smoothly down from above; as calm, measured and elegant as he was terror-stricken and out of control. She was very beautiful now, with arms that became great black wings, streaming dark hair and a brief, minimal costume that revealed most of her voluptuously glossy brown body.

"What you did was hack, Colonel," she told him. "That is against the rules of the war and so leaves you unprotected by those same rules. It is tantamount to spying, and spies are accorded no mercy. Look down."

He looked down to see a landscape filled with smoke and fire and torture: pits of flame, rivers of acid and forests of barbed spikes, some already tipped with writhing bodies. They were coming up fast towards him, just seconds away.

He screamed again.

Everything froze. He was still staring at the horrific scene beneath, but it had stopped coming closer. He tried to look away but couldn't.

The dark angel's voice said, "We wouldn't waste it on you." She make a clicking sound with her mouth and he died.

Vatueil sat on the trapeze, in Trapeze space, swaying slowly to and fro, humming to himself, waiting.

The others appeared one by one. You could have told who were his friends and who were his enemies by whether they did or did not meet his gaze. The ones who had always thought the hacking attempts were a waste of valuable time and little more than a cack-handed way of telling their enemies that they were getting desperate looked at him and smiled, happy to look him in the eye. Those who had agreed with him afforded him a quick nod and a fleeting glance at most, looking away when he tried to look at them, pursing their lips, scratching their fur, picking at their toenails and so on.

"It didn't work," yellow said.

So much for preamble, Vatueil thought. Oh well; it wasn't as though they kept minutes.

"It did not," he agreed. He picked at a little knotted tuft of red fur on his belly.

"I think we all know what the next level, the last resort is," purple said. They all looked at each other, a sort of formal symmetry to their sequential one-to-one glances, nods and muttered words.

"Let us be clear about this," Vatueil said after a few moments. "We are talking about taking the war into the Real. We are talking about disobeying the rules we freely agreed to abide by right at the start of all this. We are talking about going back on the commitments and undertakings we took so solemnly so long ago and have lived and fought by from then until now. We are talking about making the whole confliction to which we have dedicated three decades of our lives irrelevant and pointless." He paused, looked round them all. "And this is the Real we are talking about. There are no resets, and while there might be extra lives for some, not everybody will be so blessed: the deaths and the suffering we cause will be real, and so will the blame we attract. Are we really prepared to go through with this?" He looked round them all again. He shrugged. "I know I am," he told them. "But are you?"

"We have been through all this," green said. "We all— "

"I know, but— "

"Shouldn't— ?"

"Can't we— ?"

Vatueil talked over them. "Let's just vote and get it over with, shall we?"

"Yes, let's not waste any more time," purple said, looking pointedly at Vatueil.

They took the vote.

They sat, still or gently swinging on their trapezes for a while. Nobody said anything. Then:

"Let havoc be unleashed," yellow said resignedly. "The war against the Hells brings hell to the Real."

Green sighed. "If we get this wrong," he said, "they won't forgive us for ten thousand years."

Purple snorted. "A lot of them won't forgive us for a million years even if we get it right."

Vatueil sighed, shook his head slowly. He said, "Fate help us all."

Eighteen

There was nothing worse, Veppers thought, than a loser who'd made it. It was just part of the way things worked – part of the complexity of life, he supposed – that sometimes somebody who absolutely deserved nothing more than to be one of the down-trodden, the oppressed, the dregs of society, lucked out into a position of wealth, power and admiration.

At least people who were natural winners knew how to carry themselves in their pomp, whether their ascendancy had come through the luck of being born rich and powerful or the luck of being born ambitious and capable. Losers who'd made it always let the side down. Veppers was all for arrogance – he possessed the quality in full measure himself, as he'd often been informed – but it had to be deserved, you had to have worked for it. Or at the very least, an ancestor had to have worked for it.

Arrogance without cause, arrogance without achievement – or

that mistook sheer luck for true achievement – was an abomination. Losers made everybody look bad. Worse, they made the whole thing – the great game that was life – appear arbitrary, almost meaningless. Their only use, Veppers had long since decided, was as examples to be held up to those who complained about their lack of status or money or control over their lives: look, if this idiot can achieve something, so can anybody, so can you. So stop whining about being exploited and work harder.

Still, at least individual losers were quite obviously statistical freaks. You could allow for that, you could tolerate that, albeit with gritted teeth. What he would not have believed was that you could find an entire society – an entire *civilisation* – of losers who'd made it. And the Culture was exactly that.

Veppers hated the Culture. He hated it for existing and he hated it for – for far too damned many credulous idiots – setting the standard for what a decent society ought to look like and so what other peoples ought to aspire to. It wasn't what other peoples ought to aspire to; it was what machines had aspired to, and created, for their own inhuman purposes.

It was another of Veppers' deeply held personal beliefs that when you were besieged or felt cornered, you should attack.

He marched into the Culture ambassador's office in Ubruater and threw the remains of the neural lace down on her desk.

"What the *fuck* is this?" he demanded.

The Culture ambassador was called Kreit Huen. She was a tall, statuesque woman, slightly oddly proportioned for a Sichultian but still attractive in a haughty, formidable sort of way. It had crossed Veppers' mind on more than one occasion to have one of his impersonator girls change to look just like the Culture woman, so he could fuck her conceited brains out, but in the end he couldn't bring himself to; he had his pride.

When Veppers burst in she was standing at a window of her generously proportioned penthouse office looking out over the city to where, in the hazy sunlight of early afternoon, a large, dark, sleek ship was hovering over the massive Veprine Corporation tower, at the heart of Ubruater's central business district. She was drinking something steaming from a cup and was dressed like an office cleaner; a barefoot office cleaner. She turned and looked, blinking, at the tangle of silvery-blue wires lying on her desk.

"Afternoon to you too," she said quietly. She walked over, peered more closely at the thing. "It's a neural lace," she told him. "How bad are your techs getting?" She looked at the other man just entering the room. "Good afternoon, Jasken."

Jasken nodded. Behind him, floating in the doorway, was the drone which had chosen not to get in Veppers' way when he'd come storming through. They'd known Veppers was heading in their direction for about three minutes, as soon as his flier had left the Justice Ministry and set course for their building, so she had had plenty of time to decide exactly how to appear when he arrived.

"Ki-chaow! Ki-chaow!" a reedy voice sang out from behind one of the room's larger couches. Veppers looked and saw a small blond head duck back down.

"And what is *that*?" he asked.

"That is a child, Veppers," Huen said, pulling her chair out from the desk. "Really, what next?" She pointed at the window. "Sky. Clouds. Oh look; a birdy." She sat down, picked up the lace. The drone – a briefcase-sized lozenge – floated nearby. Huen frowned. "How did you come by this?"

"It's been in a fire," the drone muttered. The machine had been Huen's servant (or master – who knew!) for the three years she had been there. It was supposed to have a name or a title or something and Veppers had been "introduced" to it but he refused to remember whatever it was supposed to be called.

"Ki-chaow!"

The blond child was standing behind the couch, only its head and one hand – formed into a pretend gun – showing. The gun was pointing at Jasken, who had brought his Oculenses down from over his head and was frowning like a stage villain and pointing his own finger at the child, sighting carefully down it. He jerked his hand back suddenly, as though in recoil. "Urk!" the child said, and disappeared, flopping onto the couch with a small thud.

Veppers knew Huen had a child; he hadn't expected to find the brat in her office.

"It was found in the ashes of one of my *staff*," Veppers told Huen, knuckles on her desk, arms spread, leaning over her. "And my extremely able techs reckon it's one of yours, so my next question is, what the fuck is the Culture doing putting illegal espionage equipment into the heads of my people? You are *not* supposed to spy on us, remember?"

"Haven't the foggiest idea what it was doing there," Huen said, handing the lace to the outstretched maniple field of the drone, which teased it out to its maximum extent. The remains of the lace took on the rough shape of a brain. Veppers caught a glimpse and found the sight oddly unsettling. He slammed one palm on Huen's desk.

"What the hell do you think gives you the right to do something like this?" He waved one hand at the lace as it glowed in the drone's immaterial grasp. "I have every right to take this to court. This is a violation of our rights and the Mutual Contact Agreement we signed in good faith when you communist bastards first arrived."

"Who had it in their head anyway?" Huen asked, sitting back in her seat and putting her hands behind her head, one shoeless foot over her other knee. "What happened to them?"

"Don't evade the question!" Veppers slammed the desk again.

Huen shrugged. "All right. Nothing in particular gives us – whoever 'us' might be here – the right to do something like this." She frowned. "*Whose* head was it in?"

The drone made a throat-clearing noise. "Whoever they were they either died in a fire or were cremated," it said. "Probably the latter; high-temperature combustion, probably few impurities. Hard to tell – this has been cleaned and analysed. At first quite crudely and then only a little clumsily." The machine swivelled in the air as though looking at Veppers. "By Mr. Veppers' techs and then by our Jhlupian friends, I'd guess." The barely visible haze around the machine had turned vaguely pink. Veppers ignored it.

"Don't try to wriggle out of it," he said, pointing one finger at

Huen. ("Ki-chaow!" said a small voice from the other side of the room.) "Who cares who 'us' is? 'Us' is you; 'us' is the Culture. This thing is yours so you're responsible. Don't try to deny it."

"Mr. Veppers has a point," the drone said reasonably. "This is our tech – quite, ah, *high* tech – if you know what I mean, and I imagine it – or the seed that became it, as it were – was emplaced by somebody or something who might reasonably be described as belonging to the Culture."

Veppers glared at the machine. "Fuck off," he told it.

The drone seemed unruffled. "I was agreeing with you, Mr. Veppers."

"I don't need this thing's agreement," Veppers told Huen. "I need to know what you intend to do about this violation of the terms of the agreement that lets you stay here."

Huen smiled. "Leave it with me. I'll see what I can do."

"That's not good enough. And that thing leaves with me," he said, pointing at the lace. "I don't want it conveniently disappearing." He hesitated, then snatched it from the drone's grasp. The sensation was unsettling, like plunging one's hand into a warm, cloying foam.

"Seriously," Huen said. "Whose head *was* it in? It'll help with our investigations if we know."

Veppers pushed himself upright with one fist, folded his arms. "Her name was L. Y'breq," he told the Culture woman. "A court-authorised ward of mine and the subject of a commercial Generational Reparation Order under the Indented Intagliate Act."

Huen frowned, then sat forward, looked away for a moment. "Ah, the Marked woman? . . . Lededje? I remember her. Talked to her, a few times."

"I'm sure you did," Veppers said.

"She was . . . okay. Troubled, but all right. I liked her." She looked at Veppers with what he felt sure was meant to be profound sincerity. "She's *dead*?"

"Extremely."

"I'm very sorry to hear that. Please pass on my condolences to her family and loved ones."

Veppers smiled thinly. "Myself, in other words."

"I'm so sorry. How did she die?"

"She took her own life."

"Oh . . ." Huen said, her expression pained. She looked down. Veppers wanted to smack her in the teeth with something heavy. She took a deep breath, stared at the surface of the desk. "That is . . ."

Veppers took over before it got too sentimental. "I expect some sort of report, an accounting for this. I'm going to be away for the next few days—"

"Yes," the drone said, pivoting to point towards the view, specifically at where the sleek shape of the ship stationed over the Veprine Corporation tower threw a slanted grey shadow over part of the city, "we saw your ride arrive."

Veppers ignored it. He pointed at Huen again. ("Ki-chaow!" said the voice from the couch.) "And by the time I get back I expect to hear some sort of explanation. If not, there will be consequences. Legal and diplomatic consequences."

"Did she leave a note?" Huen asked.

"What?" Veppers said.

"Did she leave a note?" Huen repeated. "Often when people kill themselves, they leave a note. Something to explain why they did it. Did Lededje?"

Veppers allowed his mouth to hang open a little, to attempt to express just how grotesquely insulting and irrelevant this piece of meddling effrontery was. He shook his head.

"You have six days," he told the woman. He turned and walked to the door. "Answer any further questions she has," he told Jasken as he passed him. "I'll be in the flier. Don't take too long." He left.

"That man had a funny nose," said the little voice from behind the couch.

"So, Jasken," Huen said, smiling a little for a moment. "*Did* she leave a note?"

Jasken cradled his good hand in the sling. "No note was left, ma'am," he told her.

She looked at him for a moment. "And was it suicide?"

Jasken's expression remained just as it had been. "Of course, ma'am."

"And you have no idea how the lace came to be in her head?"

"None, ma'am."

She nodded slowly, took a breath, sat forward. "How's the arm?"

"This?" he moved the arm in the cast out from his body a little. "Fine. Healing. Feels good as new."

"I'm glad." Huen smiled. She got up from the chair behind the desk and nodded. "Thank you, Jasken."

"Ma'am," he said, with a short bow.

Huen held her child in her arms as she and the drone watched Veppers' wide-bodied flier depart from overhead, its rotund mirrored rear glinting in the golden sunshine as it banked. The craft straightened and headed directly towards the Veprine Corporation tower and the ship – barely smaller than the tower itself – poised immediately above it.

The drone's name was Olfes-Hresh. "Well," it said, "the nose injury's real enough, but it was never done with a blade, and not a bone in Jasken's arm has ever been broken. His arm is perfectly healthy save for about twenty days' worth of minor atrophy due to partial immobility. Also? That cast has concealed hinges to let it come off easily."

"Did you get a full reading on the lace?"

"As good as though he'd left it."

She glanced at the machine. "And?"

The drone wobbled, its equivalent of a shrug. "SC tech, or good as."

Huen nodded, staring at the Jhlupian ship as Veppers' aircraft flew towards it. She patted her child's back softly. "That's interesting."

Chay found herself in the Refuge. The Refuge took up the entire summit of a finger of rock which thrust up from the scrubby desert. The remains of a natural arch lay in great piles of sand-blown stone between the Refuge mesa and the nearby plateau. The only access to the Refuge was by a rope and cane basket, lowered the thirty metres from the Refuge to the desert floor by pulleys worked by muscle power. The Refuge had expanded over the years to rise to six or seven storeys of cluttered wood and adobe buildings, and spilled over the side of the mesa itself via tree-trunk-propped platforms supporting further precariously poised architecture.

Only females were allowed in the Refuge. The more senior females copied things called manuscripts. She was treated, if not exactly as a servant, then certainly as somebody who was junior, whose opinions did not really matter, whose importance came solely from the menial tasks that she performed.

When not sleeping, eating or working she was at worship, joining everybody else in the Refuge praising God in the chapel. God here was a female deity, worshipped for Her fecundity by these celibates in long services full of chanting.

She tried to explain that she didn't believe in God but this was at first dismissed as impossible nonsense – as absurd as denying the existence of the sun or gravity – then, when the others saw she was serious, she was hauled up before the fearsome Superior of the Refuge, who explained that belief in God was not a choice. She was newly arrived and would be indulged this time, but she must submit to the will of God and obey her betters. In the villages and cities they burned people alive for proclaiming that God did not exist. Here, if she persisted, she would be starved and beaten until she saw sense.

Not everybody, the Superior explained – and at this point the formidable female in her dark robes of office appeared suddenly old, Chay thought – was able to accept God into their hearts as easily or as fully as did the most pious and enlightened. Even if she had not yet opened herself completely to God's love, she must realise that it was something that would come with time, and the very rituals and services, devotions and chants that she found so meaningless might themselves lead to the belief she lacked, even if at first she did not feel that she partook of them with any faith at all.

Just as one might do useful work without fully understanding the job one was engaged in, or even what the point of it was, so the behaviour of devotion still mattered to the all-forgiving God, and just as the habitual performance of a task gradually raised one's skills to something close to perfection, bringing a deeper understanding of the work, so the actions of faith would lead to the state of faith.

Finally, she was shown the filthy, stinking, windowless cell carved into the rock beneath the Refuge where she would be chained, starved and beaten if she did not at least try to accept God's love. She trembled as she looked at the shackles and the flails, and agreed she would do her best.

She shared a dorm with half a dozen others on the floor beneath the top, looking out in the other direction from the nearby plateau, towards the open desert. These were open rooms; one wall missing with only a heavy tarpaulin to lower if the dusty wind was blowing in, with stepped floors leading down to a wall that was hidden from the topmost tier. Open rooms, with a view over the plain, desert or grassland, were comforting places. Closed rooms felt wrong, imprisoning, especially for going to sleep in or waking up in. Similarly, being alone was a punishment to an individual from a herd species, so like most normal people she liked to bed down in a group with at least half a dozen others.

She woke the others up with her nightmares too often to be a popular sleep-companion, but then she was not alone in having tormenting dreams.

She had books to read and other people to talk to, and all she had to do for her keep was help with the general work required to keep the place in good repair and add her strength to help pull on the ropes which brought the baskets of water and food – and the very occasional visitor or noviciate – up from the cluster of small buildings at the base of the mesa. The services and chants became just part of the routine. She still resented them and still thought they were without meaning, but she added her voice to all the others.

The weather was warm without being uncomfortable except when the wind blew out of the desert and brought dust with it. The water came from a deep well near the base of the mesa and was still deliciously cold when it arrived in the big cane-wrapped pottery jars.

She stood by the walls over the cliff sometimes, staring down at the land beneath, marvelling at her lack of fear. She knew that she ought to feel threatened by the precipitous drop, but she didn't. The others thought she was mad. They stayed away from the edges, avoided being too near windows over sheer drops.

She had no idea how long she would be allowed to stay in the Refuge. Presumably until she got so used to life here it had come to seem normal. Then, when all that had gone before had started to seem like a terrible dream, just a nightmare, and she had convinced herself that this limited but safe and frugally rewarding life was going to continue; then, when she had learned to hope, she would be taken back to the Hell.

They had done what they could with her memories to make them less raw and livid than they would have been, and, when she slept, the nightmares, though still terrible, were somehow more vague than she might have expected.

After a year there, she began to sleep quite well. But the memories were still there in some form, she knew. She supposed they had to be. Your memories made you.

She could remember more of her life in the Real, now. Before, during roughly the latter half of the time she had spent in the Hell with Prin, she had come to think that that earlier life – her real life, she supposed – had itself been a dream, or something that had been part of the torture: concocted, imposed to make the suffering worse. Now she accepted that it probably had been real, and she had simply been driven out of her mind by her experiences in Hell.

She had been a real person, a Pavulean academic involved with the good cause of bringing an end to the Hells. She had met Prin at the university and between them they'd had the connections and the bravery to get themselves sent into the Hell, to record what they experienced there and bring back the truth of it to the world. The Hell had been virtual, but the experiences and the suffering had felt entirely real. She had lost her mind and retreated to a belief that her earlier, Real life had been a dream, or something invented within the Hell to make the contrast between the two all the more painful.

Prin had been stronger than her. He had stayed sane and tried to save her along with himself when the time came for them to attempt their escape, but only he had got through and returned to the Real. At the time she'd convinced herself he'd only gone from one bit of the Hell to another, but he must have got out entirely. If he hadn't she was sure she'd have been presented with the proof of it by now.

She had been taken before the king of Hell, some ultimate demon who had been frustrated that she had no hope and so was resigned to the Hell, and he had killed her. Then she had woken here, in this hale and healthy Pavulean body, on this strange tall stick of rock poised between the plateau and the desert.

A sun, yellow-white, rose and fell, arcing high over the desert. Out in the desert, lines of tiny dots that might be animals or people moved sometimes. Birds flew in the sky, singly or in small flocks, occasionally landing and calling raucously from the highest roofs of the Refuge buildings.

Rains came rarely, sweeping in from the plateau in giant dark veils like the trailing bristles of a vast broom. The Refuge smelled strange, pleasantly different for a half-day afterwards, and the open rooms and quiet courtyards were full of the sound of dripping. Once she stood and listened to the steady drip-drip-drip of an overflowing gutter as its rhythm exactly matched that of a chant being sung in the chapel, and marvelled at the simple beauty of both.

There was a track that led away over the plateau towards the flat horizon, and from the track's end a steep path zigzagged down flaws and ravines cut into the plateau edge until it met the slope of rubble at the foot of the cliff. Far away across the plateau, at the far end of the track, there was a road, apparently, and the road led to a city; to many cities, eventually, but even the closest was many tens of days away and none of them were good places; they were dangerous and unhealthy, the sort of places that you needed a refuge to get away from. She had never felt any desire to go to any of them, never felt any desire to leave the Refuge at all.

They would leave her until this all became normal, until it had become all that she really remembered, then she would be dragged back to the Hell again. She never lost sight of this, accepting each day without pain as a blessing but never taking the next day for granted.

She had been there over two years before she was asked to help with the copying of the manuscripts. This was what the females of the Refuge did to pay for the food they received via the road and the track and the path and the buildings at the foot of the mesa and the rope-hauled cane baskets: they made perfect copies of ancient, illuminated manuscripts in a language that none of them understood. The blank books, pens, inks and gold leaf arrived by basket and, a year or two later, the completed books were sent back down by basket to start their journey back to the distant cities.

You were only alone when you worked on the manuscripts. You were allocated a bare copying cell which had a desk, a manuscript to be copied, a blank book which would become the copy and a supply of pens and inks. Each cell had a single window which was too high up in the wall to present a distracting view but which provided plenty of light. Her eyes would start to hurt after a few hours. It was a relief to herd down to the chapel with the others and sing, eyes closed or raised to the resplendent light of the chapel's translucently glowing plaster windows. She had become a good singer, and knew many of the chants by heart.

She worked hard at copying the manuscripts, marvelling at their indecipherable beauty. The illuminations were of stars and planets and fabulous animals and ancient buildings and plants; lots of trees and flowers and verdant landscapes. Even so, she thought, as she carefully traced and then coloured in the illuminations and subsequently copied the mysterious letters, for all she knew these were instruction manuals for torturing people and the pretty illustrations were just to fool you.

She worked away, filling her days with the silent copying of the words onto the blank pages and the echoed singing of the chants into the embracing space of the chapel.

The books that she was able to read – which came from a separate library, and were much plainer and cruder-looking than the ones she and the others copied – all talked only of a time long before she had been born, and the other females of the Refuge also talked solely of a much more simple time: cities with no public transport, ships with sails and no engines, medicine that was little better than crossing your trunks and hoping, and no real industry at all, just the workshops of individuals.

Still, they found things to talk about: the general idiocy of males, the boringness of their diet, the rumours of bandits in the desert or on the plateau, the frailties, jealousies, friendships, enmities and crushes of their fellows and all the general gossip of a couple of hundred people of the same sex all cooped up together with a rigid if generally non-punitive hierarchy.

The other females looked at her uncomprehendingly when she tried to tell them what had happened to her. She guessed they thought she was mad. They seemed to have had no life beyond this one, with all the limitations of technology and mores that implied; they had been raised in the distant cities or in rural communities, they had experienced some misfortune and been thrown out of whatever herd community they had been part of, been rescued and brought here. As far as she could tell they really did believe in this God that they all had to worship. Still, at least this God promised only one afterlife, for those worthy. Heaven awaited the pious while those found wanting faced oblivion rather than perpetual torture.

She wondered sometimes how long this was all taking, back in the Real. She knew something of the technology and the ratios involved; a year of time in the Real could be compressed into a minute in a virtual environment. It was the opposite of a near-lightspeed experience; spend what felt to you like half a lifetime away but come back – a changed, completely different person – and find that only an hour had passed and nobody had even missed you. Was this quiet, pain-free life running at that speed? Or at a gentler rate, perhaps even in real-time?

For all she knew, she realised eventually, she was living ultra-slowly in this virtual existence, and what felt like a few years here was a millennium back in the Real, so that if she ever did get back she would find everything altered totally and all the people she had known long dead; so long dead that even in the average and perfectly pleasant Afterlife there would be no trace of them left.

Very occasionally, as she stood by one of the cliff-edge walls, she wondered what would happen to her if she climbed over and jumped. Straight back here? Back to the Hell? Or nothing, just oblivion. "You are so fearless!" the others told her when they saw her standing there, looking down.

But not so fearless she would take the leap and find out.

After a few years she took on some extra responsibilities in the script room, overseeing and checking the work of others. In the chapel, she led the singing, often as not. By now the Refuge Superior was a wizened old thing with poor back legs; in time she needed a trolley for her hind quarters, and help to ascend the spiral ramp that led to the higher floors of the Refuge. She started instructing Chay in the running of the Refuge, bringing her into its administration. Chay was given her own small room, though usually she still preferred to bed down with the others when night fell. She still had nightmares of suffering and torment, but they were duller and even more vague now.

One evening, seven years after she'd arrived, a fire broke out when the hot desert wind was blowing. They all fought it desperately, quickly using up the little water they had. Ten of them perished in smoke-filled rooms trying to save the manuscripts, finally throwing the precious originals from high windows into the central courtyard and saving all but two before being choked by the smoke or caught by the flames. Six of them died when a whole wing of the Refuge, supports weakened by the fire, fell to the desert in a great boiling burst of flame and smoke. Even over the terrible roaring noise produced by the disintegrating brickwork, splintering wood and careening flame, you could hear the screams as they fell.

Night had fallen by then and the wind had gone. She watched the rolling rush of sparks produced by the collapse sweeping upwards, outshining and outnumbering the stars in the clear black gulf of sky.

They buried the remains in the small graveyard at the foot of the mesa. It was the first time she had descended from the Refuge in all those years. The ceremony was brief, the most meaningful words said impromptu. The chants sung over the graves sounded flat, unechoing. She could find nothing to say, but stood looking at the little piles of sandy earth with their wooden grave markers and thought of the suffering the dead had endured just before they died. At least it had been brief, she told herself, and when it was over it was over.

Maybe, she reminded herself bleakly. They were still within the virtual; this had all taken place inside a simulation, no matter that there was no proof of this. Who within it knew what had really happened to whatever consciousness those dead individuals had possessed?

She stood in one of the burned-out script halls that night. She was one of those on fire-watch in case it all started up again, surrounded by the smell of burned wood and re-baked brick. Wisps of smoke or steam leaked into the cool, still night air from a few places. She checked each one, lantern in one trunk, bucket of water at the ready in the other.

Under an overturned, burned-black table she found one charred blank manuscript – it was a small one, for the tiniest of the manuscripts they ever copied. She brushed the brown, crisped edges of the pages clear. It would never do to be copied onto now. She couldn't bear to put it back where she'd found it, so she stuffed it into a pocket.

She thought back to this later, and knew that she had had no idea at the time what she was going to do with the blank book. Maybe just keep it in her copying cell, or on the shelves of her room. A grim and grisly souvenir, a *memento mori*.

Instead she started writing in it. She would set down the story of her life as she remembered it, just a dozen or so lines each day. It was not something that was forbidden – as far as she could gather, there were no rules covering such a thing at all – but she kept it secret nevertheless.

She used worn-out pens which had become too scratchy to be risked on the manuscript copies. The ink was made from the charred timbers from the fire.

Life went on, they rebuilt much of the Refuge, took in fresh noviciates. The Superior died and a new one was appointed – Chay even had a vote – and she found herself a little further up the hierarchy. The old Superior had wanted to be disposed of the old way, left to the elements and the scavenger birds on the Refuge's highest tower. Chay was one of those accorded the dubious privilege of cleaning up the bits of bone after the birds had picked them clean and the sun had bleached them white.

It was nearly a year after the old Superior's death, while she was singing one of the most beautiful chants, that she broke down and wept for the old female. Gradually, the chants had brought a sort of beauty and even a meaning into her life, she realised.

Twenty years later she was the Superior, and had it not been for the book of her life, written in the manuscript blank with the charred page, she might not still have believed that she had had any sort of existence before that: no life as a gifted academic in a free, liberated society with superconductors, space elevators, AIs and life-extension treatments, and no few months spent in the utter ghastliness of the virtual Hell, accumulating the evidence to present to an unbelieving world – an unbelieving galaxy, for that matter – that might help bring about the destruction of the Hells for ever.

She had kept writing her book, continuing on beyond all that she could recall of her life in the Real and her time with Prin in the virtual Hell, writing down everything that happened to her since, here in this quiet, untroubled existence which she had come to love and believe in and still expected to be dragged away from, back to Hell, every single night . . .

She had become wizened. Her face was lined, her pelt was grey and her gait had stiffened and become awkward with age. She oversaw the workings of the Refuge to the best of her ability and did all that she could for the noviciates and other occupants. At least once per season, now that she was Superior, she had to clamber into a basket and be lowered to the austere cluster of small buildings at the foot of the mesa to deal and negotiate with the representative of the charity which distributed their manuscripts in the cities. The representatives were always male, so she had no choice but to descend to them; they could not be winched up to come and see her, because it was forbidden.

Usually, as she was lowered carefully towards the desert floor, she reflected on how much she had changed. Her old self – the person she had been back in the Real, before the brief but traumatising excursion in the Hell – would have wanted to break with that tradition, would have wanted to change things, would have wanted to insist that there was nothing beyond idiotic, absurdly unquestioned tradition stopping males from being brought up into the Refuge itself.

The person she had become, the person she was now, could see the force in all such arguments and yet still thought it was right to continue with the tradition. Perhaps it was wrong in some theoretical way, but perhaps not, and if it was, well, it did no great harm. Maybe it was even charming, just eccentric. Anyway, she would not like to have to be the Superior on whose shift the tradition was changed.

She had always wondered how faithful to a real, changing society and world this simulation was. Did the cities that the noviciates, travellers and charity representatives spoke of and claimed to have come from really exist? Did people within those cities work and struggle and study and improvise as they would in the Real? If you left this sim running, would somebody somewhere invent moveable type and printing, and so make what they did here in the Refuge irrelevant and all its occupants redundant?

She kept waiting for one of the charity representatives to turn up for their latest meeting with a regretful look and a copy of something hot off this brand new thing called a press.

However, as she approached what must be the end of her life in this virtuality, the freshly illuminated manuscripts kept on being taken away and the supplies of writing materials and of food and other necessities kept on being delivered. She realised that she would die – as far as that idea had any meaning here – in the same society she had been born into. Then she would have to remind herself that she had not been born here, she had simply woken up, already an adult.

One year, a noviciate was brought before her for denying the existence of God. She found herself saying pretty much what had been said to her by the old Superior. Showing the girl the deep-buried cell and the whips and flails gave Chay no pleasure, though the dank, lamp-lit dungeon didn't smell as bad as it had when she'd been shown it, she thought. She'd never had cause to use it; that was probably why. Or maybe her sense of smell was going with everything else. Thankfully, the noviciate relented – albeit with ill-disguised contempt – and no further action needed to be taken. She wondered if she could have ordered the punishment carried out if things hadn't gone so agreeably.

Her eyesight gradually grew too poor for her to continue to write her life story in her part-charred book. The letters had become larger and larger as her sight had failed. One day, she thought, she would be writing only a single letter per page. Just as well in way, as she had only filled two-thirds of the blank and would die soon with lots of pages unfilled. But writing the bigger and bigger letters made the whole undertaking start to appear ridiculous and self-important, and eventually she gave in and stopped writing altogether. She had long since caught up with herself anyway and was effectively just keeping a rather boring diary.

So she bored the noviciates with her stories instead. She was the Superior, so they had to listen. Or maybe young people these days were just very polite. Her voice had almost gone but still she would be carried to the chapel each day to listen, enraptured, eyes closed, to the beautiful, transcendent singing.

Eventually she lay on her death bed and an angel came for her.

Nineteen

The Jhlupian heavy cruiser *Ucalegon* – forty times as fast as any ship possessed by the Sichultian Enablement – delivered Veppers to Iobe Cavern City on Vebezua in less than two days. Vebezua was the furthest flung of the Enablement's planets, lying in a small spiral of stars called the Chunzunzan Whirl, a sparse twist of old stars that also held the Tsung system.

"Of course I'm serious. Why can't I just buy one?"

"They are not for sale."

"Why not?"

"It is not policy."

"So change the policy."

"The policy is not to be changed."

"Why is the policy not to be changed?"

"Because changing policies is not policy."

"Now you're just going round in circles."

"I am merely following you."

"No you're not. I am being direct. You are being evasive."

"Nevertheless."

". . . Is that it? 'Nevertheless' and we just leave things there?"

"Yes."

Veppers, Jasken, Xingre, half a dozen others of Veppers' retinue plus the Jhlupian's principal aide and a medium-ranking officer from the *Ucalegon* were sharing a tethered flier making its way through one of the great karst caves that made up Iobe Cavern City. The cave averaged a kilometre or so across; a huge pipe whose floor held a small, winding river. The city's buildings, terraces, promenades and boulevards rose up from the riverside, increasingly precipitously as they approached the mid-way point of the cave, where the buildings became sheer cliffs; a few went even beyond that, clinging to the overhanging curve of the cavern's upper wall. The flier tether-rails were stationed further up still, cantilevered out from the cave's roof on gantries like a sequence of giant cranes. A series of enormous oval holes punctured the roof's summit, letting in great slanting slabs of withering Vebezuan sunlight.

Lying close to its slowly ever-brightening star, the planet was cursed with too much sunlight but blessed with entire continents made mostly of deeply eroded limestone, providing vast cave systems in which its inhabitants – native animals and Sichultian incomers – could hide. You had to travel to the very high and very low latitudes to find pleasantly balmy climates. The poles were havens of temperate freshness. Very occasionally the hills there even got snow.

"Xingre," Veppers said with a sorrowful shake of his head, "you are my trusted business associate and even a friend in your own strange alien way, but I may have to go over your head here. Or carapace."

"Carapace. Though in our language the expression is I may have to go beyond your reach."

"So who would I have to ask?"

"About what?"

"About buying a ship."

"No one. There is no one to ask because such things are not covered."

"Not covered? Is that the same as being not policy?"

"Yes."

"Lieutenant," Veppers said, turning to the ship's officer, who also floated, twelve limbs neatly folded on one of the shiny cushions that doubled as chairs and translators, "is this really true?"

"Is what true, sir?"

"That it's not possible to buy one of your ships."

"It is not possible to buy navy ships of our navy."

"Why not?"

"It is not policy."

Veppers sighed. "Yes, so I've been told," he said, looking at Xingre.

"Navies rarely sell their vessels, not if they are of the best," Xingre said.

"You're already hiring it to me," Veppers said.

"Not the same," the officer told him. "We remain in control. Sold to you, you assume control."

"It'd only be one ship," Veppers insisted. "I don't want your whole navy. Really, such a fuss. You people are positively purists." Veppers had once asked ambassador Huen if it was possible to buy a Culture ship. She'd stared at him for a second, then burst out laughing.

The flier zoomed, rising to avoid a high bridge barring their way. The craft stayed flat rather than pointing its nose up, the winch bogey travelling the network of flier tether rails above reeling in the craft's four invisibly fine mono-filament lines equally.

Iobe city had banned flying machines entirely for centuries, then allowed fliers to be used but suffered one or two accidents which had resulted in the destruction of several notable buildings and prized historic cross-cavern bridges, so had compromised by allowing fliers but only if they were tethered to tracks in the cavern roofs and controlled automatically.

"The best Jhlupian ships are of the Jhlupian navy," the lieutenant said. "We prefer to keep it that way. For the benefit of not being outrun by civilian vessels. Embarrassment might ensue otherwise. Most governmental entities share this policy."

"Do the Sichultians sell their best ships to their lessers?" Xingre asked.

"I'd give you a very good price," Veppers said. He turned from Xingre to the lieutenant. "*Very* good. You could even take the weapons off. It's the speed I'm after."

"Culture ships are even faster, sir," Jasken said.

Veppers looked coldly at him. "Are they now?"

"Some are," the lieutenant said.

"How much would a ship like the *Ucalegon* cost?" Jasken asked the lieutenant. "If it was for sale?"

"Impossible to say," the officer said.

"You must know how much they *cost*," Veppers said. "You have to price them, you must have a budget for how many you can build and operate."

"Realistic price might be more than entire gross economic product of Sichultian Enablement," Xingre said.

Veppers smiled. "I doubt that."

Xingre made a chuckling sound. "Nevertheless."

"Additionally," the lieutenant said, "there are treaties to be considered."

Veppers exchanged looks with Jasken. "Oh, I bet there are."

"As responsible members of galactic community and Galactic Council," the officer said, "we are signatories to treaties forbidding us from over-runging certain technologies."

"Over-*runging*?" Veppers asked in his best what-the-fuck-does-that-mean tone. He looked from the lieutenant to Jasken, who shrugged.

"Technical term," Xingre said. "One may gift or sell technology one rung down the ladder of civilisational attainment, but no further."

"Ah, that," Veppers said sourly. "That keeps us all in our place, doesn't it?"

Xingre rocked backwards on his shiny pillow, looking outward from the flier. "My, is beautiful city!" he said.

"And," the ship's officer said, "one is behoved to retain control over said technology to prevent it being re-sold further down relevant tech ladder by rascalish peoples acting purely as middle-men, fraudulently."

"End-user certificates," Xingre said, agreeing.

"So we have to wait until we're about to invent something ourselves before we can buy it from somebody else?" Veppers asked.

"Much like that," Xingre said. It waved a thin green limb at a particularly slim, highly ornate bridge they were passing over. "See, great elegance of form!" It waved at the road and pedestrian traffic crossing the bridge, not that anybody was looking at them, and anyway the flier's bubble canopy was mirrored on the outside.

"Such treaties and agreements prevent free-for-all," the lieutenant said helpfully.

Veppers looked unimpressed.

"Hmm. Free-for-alls," Xingre agreed. "Tsk."

The flier swung round, banking as it turned to enter a side cavern. This new tunnel was about half the diameter of the one they had been heading down until now. The craft levelled out but dropped, still level, and flew on into darkness; this cavern had no roof piercings to let in the sunlight, or buildings within. A display on the flier's forward screen lit up to show what the cavern looked like ahead. Rocky, uneven walls stretched curving away into the distance.

"I like free-for-alls," Veppers said quietly.

They sat in a paper boat floating on a lake of mercury, lit by a single distant ceiling hole producing a searchlight shaft of luminescence. Veppers had brought an ingot of pure gold specially. He took his mask off for a moment. "Plop it in," he told Jasken.

Jasken didn't take his mask off. "You can talk through the mask, sir," he told Veppers, who just frowned, then nodded impatiently.

Jasken slid the soap-bar-size lump of gold out of his tunic, held it by one end, reached over the side of the boat and dropped the thick glossy sliver overboard. It vanished into the silver surface.

Veppers took part of the boat's gunwale between his fingers, wobbled it. “Paper, really?” he asked Xingre, pulling his mask away again.

The Jhlupian didn’t need a mask; mercury vapour wasn’t poisonous to Jhlupians. “Paper,” the alien confirmed. “Compressed.” It made an expanding then contracting gesture with its limbs. “Easier disposing of.”

The flier had reached the limit of the cave system’s tether rails, had landed, been released from its cables and flown on through another two junctions’ worth of smaller and smaller side tunnels until it had reached the cavern holding Mercury Lake, one of Vebezua’s modest number of tourist attractions.

The flier had hovered centimetres off the surface of the lake and let them step straight into the paper boat. They could have walked across the surface of the mercury, of course, and Veppers had wanted to, but apparently that was forbidden, or at least frowned on, or gave you seasickness or something. The mercury could have been cleaner, Veppers reckoned. Its surface held dust and grit and swirls of little rock particles like dark sand.

The boat was slightly absurd; it looked like a scaled-up version of the sort of paper boat a child might make. Even as a raft, of course, it could have been made from gold, or any element with a molecular number lower than mercury. Lead would still sink in mercury, but gold shouldn’t. It was one number down the Periodic Table and so ought to float. Veppers looked over the side of the vessel at where his ingot of gold had entered the liquid metal, but it showed no sign of surfacing yet.

After dropping them at the boat, the flier had taken off again, carrying the other two Jhlupians with it. Apart from showing his importance to the Jhlupian navy, Xingre hadn’t needed his aide along with him in the first place, and the Navy itself, while being contractually obliged to bring Veppers here safely, had wanted no part of whatever might transpire or be agreed here.

Another, smaller flier approached. Jasken watched it on his Oculenses. The paper boat lay about two hundred metres off the nearest section of cavern wall. Mercury Lake was not natural, though nobody knew who had chosen to place such a huge amount of the metal in an out-of-the-way spot within a natural labyrinth in a planet that was itself quite isolated. The approaching flier was only about three metres by four. Small, for two people of different species, Jasken thought. He had several weapons with him, including one concealed by the cast over his arm. He felt a need to check them again, but didn't. He already knew they were primed and ready.

The Oculenses were a little confused by the mercury vapour swirling within the chamber. The cavern was roughly spherical, about half a kilometre across. It was a little under half full of mercury, and volcanic activity kept the very bottom of the chamber heated, producing – every now and again – gigantic belching bubbles within the liquid metal. Those bubbles produced the gasses that made the air in the chamber poisonous to pan-humans and many other biological beings, as well as making it next to impossible to monitor any vibrations through the air by laser or any other form of surveillance.

The paper boat kept near but not too close to the centre of the lake, sufficiently distant to ride any waves produced by the sporadic bubbles. The volcanic activity wasn't natural either; several hundred thousand years earlier – long before the Sichultians arrived on the scene to find a happily habitable but sentiently uninhabited planet – a hole had been drilled down through many tens of kilometres of rock to create the tiny magma chamber that heated the base of the cavern and so kept the mercury simmering. Nobody knew who had done this, or why. The best guesses were that it was either a religious thing or an artwork.

While Jasken was watching the flier approach, Veppers looked over the side of the boat and saw the shining lozenge of the gold ingot, surfaced again at last. He prodded Jasken on the shoulder and he retrieved it.

The flier set down by the side of the paper boat. It looked like a fat bullet made of chrome and coloured glass. It split, opened and revealed a glistening mass within. Just about discernible inside was a dark elliptical shape, fringed or tentacled at either end.

"Welcome, friend from Flekke," Xingre said.

"Good day," said an obviously synthesised voice from the opened bullet of the flier. "Chruw Slude Zsor, Functionary-General."

"An honour," Xingre said, dipping on its floating cushion.

"We were expecting you to arrive with the Nauptrian negotiator," Veppers said, talking through the mask.

"That is me, I am here," said the flier containing the Flekke in what was – somewhat counter-intuitively, Veppers thought – a more organic-sounding voice. "Though I am not Nauptrian. I am of the Nauptre Reliquaria. Were you expecting a sample of our feeder species, or making a mistake?"

"Humble apologies," Xingre said, extending the limb nearest Veppers towards the man by just enough for the movement to be interpreted as a gesture at all. Veppers had seen, and – reluctantly – kept quiet. "We biological species," Xingre said, putting a laugh into its voice, "in such niceties' matterings err, with sporadic effect."

Veppers had to suppress a smile. He had noticed before that Xingre's grasp of language ebbed and flowed quite usefully on such occasions, allowing the Jhlupian to present itself as anywhere between razor smart and hopelessly bumbling, as desired.

The Reliquarian might have been nonplussed by this. It said nothing for a moment, then, "To introduce: I am 200.59 Risytcin, Nauptre Reliquaria Extra-Jurisdictional Service, rank Full Mediary."

"Please," Xingre said, gesturing. "On-boarding."

The opened bullet shape slid forward, up and over the shallow gunwale of the boat, coming to rest just above the flat interior surface of the vessel's hull. "Most splendid," Xingre said, and, reaching up with half of its dozen limbs, drew a compressed paper cover right over the whole of the boat's open surface, enclosing them. Gentle glows from the Jhlupian's floating pillow and the interior of the Reliquarian's bullet-shaped casing kept them all visible to each other. It was almost romantic, Veppers thought, if your taste ran to weird, inhuman aliens and fanatical machines with a taste for torment.

"Well, hello to you both," Veppers said to the Flekkian and the Reliquarian. "Thank you for coming, and for agreeing to conduct our meeting in Sichultian."

"It is easier for us to talk down to you than it is for you to aspire to our far more sophisticated language," the Reliquarian said.

Veppers smiled. "Well, I have to hope that lost something in the translation. Now, however, I understand we have to do this ridiculous thing with the masks."

The ridiculous thing with the masks meant them wearing a sort of helmet – or similar – each, from which a hose led to a central junction chamber. This way they could all talk and listen to each other without anybody else hearing. It all seemed madly contrived to Veppers but apparently in this age of summed-state super-quantum phase-parsed encryptography it was the last thing anybody would be looking for. The Nauptre Reliquaria especially thought it was just the greatest thing imaginable and had insisted on it.

It took a while to get everything and everybody set up and adjusted. 200.59 Risytcin insisted on inspecting both the ingot of gold in Jasken's pocket and his Oculenses, taking some time over the latter – turning them over and over in a maniple field and at one point seemingly trying to twist them apart – but eventually pronounced them safe and handing them back. Jasken looked unhappy, and carefully cleaned and readjusted them before putting them back on.

"To business," Xingre said, once they were all technically happy and the pleasantries had been dealt with. Its voice sounded at once muffled and echoey, coming through the inter-linked set of tubes. All linked up together, barely lit, hunkered down in this crude approximation of a boat, they looked, Veppers thought, like some bizarrely motley set of desperate survivors from some strange and terrible shipwreck.

The Reliquarian said, "Introductory statement and opening position of the NR, with superposition of same relevant to Flekke: We have good reason to believe that the anti-Hell faction in the relevant confliction – concerning proposed unwarranted intrusions in certain virtual realities – grows desperate. They may attempt to intrude within the Real. A possible source of intrusion might conceivably come via the Tsungarial Disk. We will seek to prevent this happening and expect our allies and friends to cooperate in this. The cooperation of the Veprine Corporation falls within this definition. To Mr. Veppers of the Veprine Corporation: kindly state your position and intentions."

Veppers nodded. "All very interesting," he said. "So, we are to take it that the NR representative speaks for the Flekke as well?"

"Indeed," the ellipsoid shape within the Reliquarian said. "As stated." Its voice sounded appropriately watery through the linking tubes.

"And do you also talk on the behalf of the GFCF?" Veppers asked.

"The Geseptian-Fardesile Cultural Federacy need not be present," the Reliquarian informed them. "Their acquiescence is assured and assumed."

Veppers smiled broadly. "Splendid!"

"To repeat: your position and intentions, Mr. Veppers, speaking on behalf of yourself, the Veprine Corporation and the Sichultian Enablement to the extent that you are able to answer for it," the Reliquarian said.

"Well then, subject to a satisfactory negotiationary outcome here," Veppers said, "my position is that I fully support the stance and values of our good friends and allies the NR and the Flekke and will do whatever is within my modest means to facilitate their strategic goals." He smiled, opened his arms wide. "I am on your side, of course." He smiled again. "Providing the price is right, naturally."

"What is this price?" Chruw Slude Zsor, Functionary-General for the Flekke said.

"I recently lost something very precious to me," Veppers said. "And discovered that I had gained something at the same time, something I might not have wished on myself."

"Would this be linked to the remains of the Culture neural lace which is in one of your servant's pockets?" 200.59 Risytcin asked.

"How well spotted," Veppers said. "Yes. I would like to investigate the possibility of replacing the thing that I lost with an identical item, and I would like to have the assistance, even protection, of both the NR and the Flekke, should somebody – anybody – wish to harm me due to any circumstances which might be linked with the neural lace being in my possession."

"This sounds a little vague," Chruw Slude Zsor said.

"I intend to be much less vague when we discuss financial remuneration and technology transfer," Veppers said. "What I'm looking for right now is a declaration of goodwill more than anything else."

"The Flekke are happy to give this," Chruw Slude Zsor said.

There was another inscrutable pause before the Reliquarian said, "Similarly."

"Subject to contract," the Flekkian added.

"Also similarly," 200.59 Risytcin confirmed.

Veppers nodded slowly. "Good," he said. "We can do details later, but for now I'd like to approach the monetary strand of these talks. Mr. Jasken here will record our deliberations using his Oculenses from this point on until further notice, each of us having a veto. Is that agreed?"

"Agreed," 200.59 Risytcin said.

"The principle is allowed," Chruw Slude Zsor said. "Though given that all we ask of you is to do nothing, and the price of inaction traditionally is significantly less than that of action, we might wish that you do not approach such negotiations with too unrealistic a set of hopes."

Veppers smiled. "I shall, as ever, be the very soul of reasonableness."

Veppers had extensive business interests on Vebezua and throughout the rest of that day he attended a series of more conventional meetings following the one held in the paper boat on Mercury Lake. The Iobe city authorities held a reception for him that evening in a great ballroom complex suspended on cables in the centre of the single greatest circular piercing above the main city caverns. The ceiling was opened to the night.

Vebezua was uncomfortably close to its star and Iobe lay almost right on the equator; by day it would have been insufferably hot and bright in the ballroom with the ceiling irised back, but by night the full glory of the stars was displayed, a distant speckled wash of multi-coloured lights enhanced by a large waning moon and the layered, slow- and not-so-slow-moving sparkle of junk and hab light as the planet's various halos of artificial satellites rotated overhead.

Veppers had been coming to Vebezua on business for decades and possessed one of the finest mansions in the inner city; however, it was being remodelled, again, and so he had elected to stay in Iobe's finest hotel, his suite of suites and his retinue taking up the two top floors. He owned the hotel, of course, so making the arrangements, even at relatively short notice, had been trivial.

For security reasons he slept right at the back of the hotel where its largest, finest but windowless grand bedroom had been carved out of the rock of the cavern wall.

Before retiring for the night he had Jasken meet him in one of the saunas. They sat facing each other, naked in the steam.

"My, how pale that arm is becoming," he told the other man. Jasken had taken his cast off and left it outside.

Jasken flexed his arm, clenched his fist. "I'm due to take it off next week."

"Mm-hmm," Veppers said. "The Reliquarian. Did it put something in the Oculenses?"

"I think so. Probably a tracker. Too small to tell. Do I give it to Xingre's techs to check?"

"Tomorrow. Tonight you stay here."

Jasken frowned. "You sure?"

"Quite sure. Don't worry about me."

"Can't I just leave the Oculenses?"

"No. And do something memorable."

"What?"

"Something memorable. Go back out, to a club, start a fight, or get two girls fighting over you, or throw a whore into a wine barrel; whatever it takes to be noticed. Nothing so heinous anyone would think to wake me, obviously, but something that'll make it very clear you're still here." Veppers frowned; Jasken was frowning at him. Veppers looked down at his own lap. "Oh, yes, well; just the mention of whores will do that. Better deal with it." He grinned at Jasken. "Meeting over. Tell Astil I'll manage by myself tonight and send Pleur up on your way out."

The suite's giant circular bed could be surrounded by multiple concentric layers of soft and floaty curtains. Once they were all fully drawn round and the hidden monofils within the fabrics had been activated and stiffened, it was impossible to tell from outside that the bed had descended into the deep floor and retreated into the rock wall behind and beneath.

Veppers left Pleur sleeping; the tiny drug-delivery bulb attached to her neck would keep her under for days if necessary. The drug bulb looked just like an insect, which was a nice touch, he thought. He must get Sulbazghi to provide more of the things.

The bed went back to where it had come from; Veppers walked across the gently lit tunnel and into a little underground car. Not too dissimilar to the Reliquarian's bullet shape, he thought as he swung the door down, switched the thing on and flicked a button to tell it to go. He was pressed back in the couch as the car accelerated. The Reliquaria. Annoying species, or machine type – whatever the fuck they were. Again, though; useful on occasion. Even if it was to be little better than a decoy. He punched in the destination code.

The private underground car system had various stops, most within Iobe city, almost all within buildings and other structures owned by Veppers. One, though, was inside an old mine, way out in the karst desert a quarter of an hour and over a hundred kilometres from the city outskirts.

The stealthed GFCF shuttle was waiting for him: a dark shape like a ragged shallow dome of night squatting on the serrations of rock. Moments after he'd boarded, it rose silently, kept subsonic, accelerated harder once it achieved space, threaded its way through the layers of the orbiting habs, fabs and satellites, and docked with a much larger but similarly secretive ship keeping a little above geosynchronous orbit. The dark, slimly ellipsoid vessel swallowed the shuttle craft and slipped away into hyperspace with barely a ripple to disturb the skein of real space.

He was met by a group of small, obviously alien but ethereally beautiful creatures with sliver-blue skin which turned to delicate scales – insect-wing thin and iridescent, like a tiny lacy rainbow – where most pan-humans had head hair. They wore white, wispy clothes and had large, round eyes. One came forward and addressed him.

"Mr. Veppers," it said, its sing-song voice soft, high and mellifluous, "how good to see you again. You are indeed *most* welcome back aboard the GFCF Succour-Class Contact Craft *Messenger Of Truth*."

Veppers smiled. "Evening all. Great to be aboard."

"And what are you supposed to be?"

"I am the angel of life and death, Chay. It is time."

The thing had appeared in her sleeping chamber in the very middle of the night. There was a noviciate sleeping in a chair by Chay's bedside, but Chay didn't even bother trying to wake her. She knew in her heart this was something she would have to deal with, or endure, by herself.

The creature was something between quadri- and bi-pedal in form; its front legs still looked like legs but they were much smaller than its rear legs. It had a single trunk, and two vast, slowly beating wings which flared from its back. They were impossibly wide; far too big to fit into the chamber, and yet – by whatever logic was supposed to be operating here – they appeared to fit inside quite comfortably nevertheless. The thing claiming to be the angel of life and death hovered over the foot of bed, which was where such things were generally expected to show up, if you believed in that sort of thing. And perhaps even if you didn't, she supposed.

She wondered again about reaching out and shaking the noviciate awake. But it would be such an effort, she thought. Everything was such an effort these days. Getting up, hunkering down, bending, standing, eating, defecating; everything. Even seeing, of course, though she noticed that she could see the self-proclaimed "angel of life and death" better than she ought to be able to.

An apparition, then; a virtuality or whatever you wanted to call it. After all these years, she thought, finally some proof beyond her own dimming memories and the fading ink in her charred-page diary that all she had lived through in the Real and the Hell had been in some sense true, not just figments of her imagination.

"You mean time for me to die?"

"Yes, Chay."

"Well, I must disappoint you, whatever you are or might claim to be. By one way of looking at things I am already dead. I was killed by the king of Hell himself." She gave a bubbling, choking laugh. "Or at least by some big bugger of a thing. In another way of looking—"

"Chay, you have lived here and now it is time to die."

"—at things, you cannot kill me," said Chay, who, as Superior of the Refuge for many years, had become used to not being interrupted. "Because, in the place I came from originally, I am still alive, or at least I presume I am, and will continue to remain so, no matter what sort of tricks you—"

"Chay, you must be quiet now, and prepare to meet your maker."

"I had no maker. My maker was the universe, or my parents. They were still alive when I entered the Hell. Can you do anything useful and tell me how they are? Still alive? Passed on? Well? Well? Eh? No? Thought not. 'Maker' indeed. What superstitious bollocks are you trying to—?"

"Chay!" the thing shouted at her. Quite loudly, Chay thought, and – what with her failing hearing – that must have meant extremely loudly. Still the young noviciate asleep in the chair by her bedside didn't even stir. She was glad she hadn't wasted the effort waking the girl up. "You are about to die," the apparition told her. "Have you no wish to see God and be accepted into Her love?"

"Oh, don't be ridiculous. There is no God." It was what she believed, what she had always believed, but still she looked nervously at the sleeping noviciate.

"What?" the angel cried. "Will you have no thought for your immortal soul?"

"Oh, fuck off," Chay said. Then she stopped, and felt terrible. Swearing in front of the noviciate! She hadn't sworn aloud for over two decades. She was the Superior; the Superior didn't swear. But then she was annoyed at herself for being embarrassed and penitent in the first place. What did it matter? "Yes," Chay said, while the so-called "angel of life and death" flapped its impossible wings and stared wide-eyed at her. "Fuck off. Entirely fuck off, you ersatz, cobbled-together, neither-one-thing-nor-the-other piece of poor-quality animation. Do whatever it is you have to do and let's just get this charade over with."

The great dark angel seemed to pull briefly back, then came forward again, enfolding her vast black wings about the bed, then just around Chay, who said, "Oh, shit. And I bet this is going to hurt."

The ship towered within the shadowy space of its hangar, a little over three hundred and fifty metres in height, its trim, pale hull girdled about its waist with five dark weapon blisters, its sleekly pointed nose housing three even longer bubbles.

"It looks *fabulously* retro," Veppers said. "What exactly is it?"

The alien who had addressed him earlier turned to him. "Technically, to allow for legal challenges based on laws which admittedly do not yet exist, it is a one-point-zero-one-two-five to one scale model of a Culture 'Murderer' General Offensive Unit," it said.

Veppers thought about this. "Doesn't that mean it's a model which is bigger than the original?"

"Yes!" the GFCFian said, clapping its little hands. "Bigger is better, yes?"

"Well, generally," Veppers agreed, frowning.

They were standing in a viewing gallery looking out into a cylindrical hangar a kilometre from top to bottom and half that wide. The hangar had been carved out of the compacted ice and rock making up one of the Tsung system's half-trillion or so Oort cloud objects. The lumpy conglomerate of ice housing the GFCF base – and within it this hangar – was sufficiently massive to provide less than one per cent of standard gravity; point your mouth down when you sneezed and you could take off. The ship they were looking at – its hull a lustrous golden hue Veppers strongly suspected had been chosen to resemble as closely as possible his own usual skin colour – sat lightly on its flat, circular rear, its sharply pointed nose spiring toward the hangar's ceiling.

"Its working name is the *Joiler Veppers*," the little alien told him, "though it may be re-named anything you wish, of course."

"Of course." Veppers looked round the rest of the gallery. They were alone; the other GFCF people had remained on the ship when they'd shuttled across to the ancient lump of space debris, one of the near uncountable bits of debris left over after the stellar system had come into being billions of years earlier.

"You approve of the ship?"

Veppers shrugged. "Maybe. How fast is it?"

"Mr. Veppers! This obsession with speed! Let us say, faster than the original. May we not deem that sufficient?"

"What would that be in figures?"

"I sigh! However: the craft is capable of velocities up to approximately one hundred and twenty-nine thousand times the speed of light."

Veppers genuinely had to stop for a moment and think. That did sound like a lot. He'd have to check, but he was fairly certain the Jhlupian ship which had taken him to Vebezua had travelled slower than that. The ships which the Veprine Corporation Heavy Industries Deep Space Division constructed measured their maximum velocities in hundreds of times lightspeed. This thing was a galaxy-crosser. Even so, he refused to look impressed.

"'Up to'?" he asked.

The GFCFian was called Bettlescroy-Bisspe-Blispin III and was androgynous. Bettlescroy held the rank of Legislator-Admiral, though, like most people in the GFCF, the little alien seemed almost ashamed of having any rank at all. In fact, officially, Bettlescroy's full title was – and most species required a deep breath at this point – The Most Honourable Heritably Concurrent Delegated Vice Emissary Legislator-Admiral Elect Bettlescroy-Bisspe-Blispin III of Turwentire – tertiary, demesne & c. (This was the short version of course, excluding his educational qualifications and military service medals.) Certain components of this startlingly grand honorific apparently indicated that Bettlescroy was the trusted, word-good-as-the-original clone of somebody back home who was even more imposingly magnificent, to the point of being too posh even to do anything as vulgar as actually travelling.

Bettlescroy looked, briefly, very slightly pained. "The precise operational parameters are still being optimised as the vessel is fitted out," it explained. "As in original, it utilises hyper-spacial aggregation motors and additionally applied induction factoring rather than the more common warp engine technology which powers the vessels your own society builds. Again as in the original, of course, the maximum apparent velocity is achievable over a defined period."

"A defined period?"

"Indeed."

"What you mean is, only in bursts?"

"Of course. Again, as in the the original. Though – again again, as it were – a higher maximum and for longer."

"So what's its indefinitely sustainable maximum?"

The little alien sighed. "We are still working that out, but in excess of ten kilolights, assuredly."

"Ah. What about the weapons?"

"Generally similar to and in some cases improvements on and refinements of the originals. In a word, formidable. Far beyond anything the Sichultian Enablement currently possesses. To be frank, so far beyond they will remain arguably non-analysable and certainly non-reproducible for the foreseeable near to medium future. This, sir, will be a space yacht capable of successfully engaging entire fleets of vessels representing state-of-the-art technology by Sichultian Enablement standards, and some way beyond. Great care will need to be taken drawing up the – how shall I put this? – the *generally available* component of the Use and Ownership Contract for this to pass muster with the sadly all-too-zealous bureaucrats of the Galactic Council's Technology Transfer Oversight Board."

"Hmm. Well, we'll see. It does look terribly retro in style, don't you think?"

"It is not styled. It is simply designed. See: the form allows all weapons to point forward, five out of the eight to point rearward and never less than five to point to any side, without rotation. In event of field failure, the highly fluid-dynamic directional profile outline provides high abrasive-environment survivability. The internal component layout and field substrate deployment are generally held to be as close to perfection as it was then possible to achieve and has not been significantly improved upon since. I beseech you, Veppers; inquire. Such inquiry will prove what I say: the Murderer class is rightly regarded as a design classic."

"So it is actually quite old?"

"Let us say that it is proven. In many ways, it has never been bettered for purposeful elegance."

"Still, though; old."

"Veppers, my dear friend, the example you see before you is better than the original, and that was the best there was at the time. Warship design has improved only incrementally since, with gradual though significant improvements to raw speed, crude weapon-power effectiveness and so on, but, in a sense, all the various design teams have ever been trying to do is to re-create the design you see here before you for future ages. Any given design produced right now to represent the sum of all subsequent improvements will quickly itself be improved upon and so eclipsed within a relatively short interval. The beauty of the Murderer class is that in a way it never was improved upon. That legacy is secure, endures and ensures that its reputation, rather than fade, will likely only grow the brighter."

"Accommodation?"

"The original could accommodate up to one hundred and twenty humans, in admittedly relatively cramped conditions. Our improved version requires minimal operational crew – perhaps three or four – and so allows for, say, equal numbers of twenty servant-crew and twenty passengers, the latter existing in conditions of some considerable luxury. The exact disposition of the apartments and suites would be up to your good self."

"Hmm," Veppers said. "Okay, I'll think about it."

"Well said. Like our civilisational inspirates we worship nothing, but if we and they did worship anything, it would be thought, reason and rationality. As such, your ambition to think leaves us assured that our offer will be seen as the generous – indeed, generous almost to a fault – one that it is."

"Your confidence is an inspiration to us all, I'm sure."

Twenty

The Tsungarial Disk had been a disappointment the first time Veppers had seen it. Three hundred million space factories of half a million tonnes or more each sounded like a lot, but, spread out around an entire gas giant from within a few hundred kilometres of Razhir's cloud tops to over half a million kilometres distant from the planet, in a band forty thousand kilometres thick, it was amazing how empty the space around the planet could seem.

It didn't help that the fabricaria were soot black; they didn't reflect, glint or really show up at all unless they got in the way of light coming from somewhere else, when they registered as, at best, a spatter of silhouettes. As Razhir itself was a fairly dull-coloured planet – mostly dark reds and browns with only a few lighter yellows at the poles – silhouetting the fabricaria against something wasn't that easy either.

They looked much better and far more impressive in an

enhanced image, their locations signalled by little spots of light superimposed onto the real view of the system. That gave you an impression of just how many of the fuckers there really were.

The GFCF Succour-Class ship *Messenger Of Truth* swung neatly out of hyperspace with the minimum of fuss just a few hundred klicks out from the Disk's designated Initial Contact Facility, one of the Disk's relatively rare habitats rather than a true factory unit. The little space port orbited slowly around Razhir at a distance of just over half a million klicks and so was about as far out as any part of the Disk ever got.

The Facility itself was a fat grey slightly flattened torus ten klicks across and one in diameter, its sides studded with lights and its outer surface barnacled with dock pits and mooring gantries; apparently only six of the Facility's twenty-five docking points were in use, though that was still twice as many as Veppers had ever seen on previous visits.

Veppers sat in what he judged to be a rather cheesy, over-decorated lounge within the GFCF ship, sprawled within a recliner seat having a pedicure performed by two giggling, naked females who looked to represent a sort of halfway compromise between Sichultians and GFCFians. He'd been told their names but had lost interest in them after about the third giggle.

He sipped on a long drink with pretentious amounts of garnish and a little – allegedly entirely edible – fish swimming around inside. Bettlescroy-Bisspe-Blispin III sat in a smaller but otherwise similar recliner alongside. A roughly spherical floating robot device was gently combing the alien's head-scales with a softly glowing, immaterial field.

"We are just checking in," Bettlescroy explained, waving one elegantly formed hand at the screen filling their field of vision in front of them. "This is what is called the Disk Designated Initial Contact Facility, though we usually just call it Reception."

"I have been here before," Veppers said. He sort of drawled the remark, though he doubted the subtlety would be lost on the alien. "I own ninety-six of these factories, Bettlescroy, and I dislike being an absentee landlord."

"Of course, of course," the alien said, nodding wisely.

Veppers gestured at the screen, where the space station was rotating slowly. "Isn't that a Culture ship? The one just coming into view?"

"Indeed. Well spotted. That is the Fast Picket, ex 'Killer' class Limited Offensive Unit, *Hylozoist*, of the Culture's Restoria section. It has been stationed here for the last standard year or so, supporting the Restoria mission within the Disk."

"Isn't it likely to be checking us out as we are, as you put it, checking in?"

"That would be impolite," the alien said with a charming, small smile. "In any event, rest assured that the *Messenger Of Truth* is one of our finest ships and easily capable of resisting any attempt by a craft like the *Hylozoist* to intrusively investigate us without our express permission and indeed active cooperation. We can both outgun and outrun the *Hylozoist*; it is no threat to us or to the actions that may need to be taken in the near future. It has been taken account of and its presence and indeed likely engagement fully factored in to our plans and sims. Plus, without giving too much away—" Bettlescroy's pale facial skin flushed a little and it held up one delicate hand in modesty. "—I think it is no secret that the *Messenger Of Truth* is not here, in or near the Disk, alone. It is simply the nominal flagship of our fleet here, and indeed not even the most militarily capable of our immediately applicable assets."

"Any other Culture ships around?" Veppers asked, eyeing the Fast Picket suspiciously as it moved slowly round in front of them, nested into its docking pit on the Facility's outer surface.

"No," Bettlescroy said.

Veppers looked at the alien. "You're sure?"

It smiled beatifically back. "We're sure." It made a graceful, blossoming gesture with its hands. "There. We are registered, checked in. We have done the polite thing and may now go about our business."

"I take it I haven't been mentioned?" Veppers asked.

"Of course not. We are here ostensibly simply to carry out

regular oversight and minor maintenance as required of our monitoring facilities distributed throughout the greater Disk. We may go where we please."

"Useful." Veppers nodded.

"Ship," Bettlescroy said, "you may continue on to our destination."

The view on the screen flickered. The space station was suddenly replaced by the gas giant Razhir, its side-lit disc filling a substantial part of the screen and the locations of the fabricaria again shown by tiny points of light. The effect was to create a near invisibly fine speckle of bright dust that girdled the banded ruddiness of the gas giant like a haze. The view tipped, then expanded suddenly and dramatically as the ship plunged into the mass of light points; they zipped past the vessel like hail in a ground car's headlights. The view swung again as the ship curved round, partially following the orbits of the displayed fabricaria.

Bettlescroy clapped its hands daintily and sat up, shooing the floating robot away. "We should make our way to the shuttle," the alien announced.

The shuttle departed the ship on the far side of the Disk from the reception Facility, ejected into space just as the *Messenger Of Truth* carried out a sudden course correction. This, Bettlescroy explained, should serve to conceal the shuttle's departure from even the most assiduous monitoring equipment.

The shuttle drifted, already quite precisely aimed, towards one of the dark, anonymous fabricaria. Watching on the shuttle's screen, Bettlescroy on one side and the craft's pilot on the other, Veppers saw the dark absence of the rapidly approaching object blotting out more and more of the other light-points until its blackness appeared to fill the screen and it seemed they were about to collide with it. He felt an instinctive desire to push himself back into his seat. For all the good that would do, he told himself. He stared at the darkness enveloping the screen as though trying to fend off the manufactory's implied bulk by force of will alone.

A sudden jolt of deceleration and a longer tug of calibrated slowing pulled them up short, close enough to see hints of detail on the dark satellite's surface. The screen was still superimposing a false view; the faint wash of radiation coming off the thing was in wavelengths way below what pan-human eyes could register. It was hard to estimate size, though Veppers knew that the average manufactory was a fat disk about a couple of kilometre across and a third of that in height. They varied a little in size, though generally only by a factor of two. This one looked pretty average-sized though it was less synthetic-looking, more natural in appearance than was the norm.

Its surface looked smoothly lumpy enough to be a very old and worn comet nucleus; only a few too-straight lines and near-flat surfaces hinted at its artificiality. The shuttle flew slowly into what looked like a deep dark crater. The screen went perfectly black. Then light filtered back; a faint but slowly increasing yellow-white luminescence began to seep in all around, then flooded the screen.

The interior of the manufactory was a web-laced space over a kilometre across, the massed, silvery, criss-crossing filaments studded with hundreds upon hundreds of darkly gleaming machines like giant pieces of clockwork; all disks and gears, shafts and plates, cylinders, spindles, looms and nozzles.

The shuttle came to a halt, perhaps a hundred metres in towards the centre of the satellite.

"May I show you how this will look when and if we go ahead?" Bettlescroy said.

"Please do," Veppers said.

The screen went into what was obviously a simulation mode, overlaying what the fabricary's interior would look like when it was operating. The many great clockwork machines ran up and down the network of silvery lines, most retreating to the outskirt walls of the manufactory while about a twentieth of their number clumped in the very centre of the space, like a nucleus.

The machines flicked this way and that, some light flickered, and dark lumps of matter rained down from the machines set around the perimeter, falling into the central nexus to disappear. Gradually the nucleus of machines expanded and other machines slid in from the outside to join those working in the centre. Whatever they were working on, it grew, taking on a succession of fairly simple shapes, though all implied something roughly twice as long as it was wide, and approximately cylindrical.

As the shape grew – its surface only rarely visible, and never quite looking like what might be a hull – more and more of the clockwork-looking machines joined in the act of creation taking place; meanwhile the network of silvery filaments was bowing out like an expanding lens made of wires, accommodating the roughly ellipsoid shape growing in the centre. All the time, greater and greater quantities of matter in increasingly varied shapes and sizes were falling in from those machines still stationed on the outside and from holes and nozzles dotted around the interior wall of the satellite itself.

A couple of minutes after the production process had begun, the filaments had shrunk back almost to the interior walls of the fabricary and the great clockwork machines had gone with them and become still. No parcels of matter issued from the machines or from the nozzles, slots and pits on the walls.

Sitting in the middle of the space now, there was a ship.

It was still very approximately ellipsoidal in shape; maybe six hundred metres long, two hundred across and one hundred in height. Its hull shimmered in the light, seemingly unable to decide whether it was pitch black or hazy silver. Rashed all over its shifting, uncertain surface were round black blisters of various sizes and sets of shallow, perfectly elliptical craters.

"Ta-*ra*!" Bettlescroy said, with a shy giggle, then glanced at Veppers and blushed. "One space warship," it said.

"How fast can it go?"

"Maximum velocity two point four kilolights."

"And it's fully working?" Veppers asked, sceptical.

"Fully," Bettlescroy said. "It would be no match for the vessel we have constructed for you, of course, but it contains a real-time grown medium-level AI substrate already running all relevant internal systems maintenance functions, full-spectrum radiative and skein sensory systems, a primer fusion power unit ready to start manufacturing anti-matter for its pre-functional warp drive and a variety of weapon systems including thermonuclear warhead missiles and thermonuclear plasma generators. All that would be necessary to activate it would be to transmit the relevant run-protocols into its processing substrate. A trivial task taking minutes at most. It would then be immediately ready for space-flight and battle, though obviously giving it a few days to produce its own AM would increase its utility and power vastly. Equip it with pre-fabricated AM for its power units and missiles and it would be even more powerful even more quickly."

"How long does it all take?" Veppers asked.

"For this size, the whole process to the stage you see here takes between nine and fifteen days, according to the exact specification. Sufficient raw material being present, obviously."

"That's just the surface layers of the fabricary itself, isn't it?" Veppers asked. Again, he wasn't going to show what he was feeling here; he'd had no idea the fabricaria could spin a full-size working ship – especially a full-size tooled-up working *war*ship – so quickly. He'd always known that the fabricaria the Veprine Corporation was allowed to use had been reduced in operational effectiveness before they'd been allowed to get their hands on them but he'd had no inkling by how much; he'd asked, naturally, but everybody involved had been professionally vague.

The Veprine Corp fabricaria could also produce a ship ready for fitting out in a matter of days – albeit a much smaller, much less sophisticated ship – but the devil was in the fitting-out bit; that was where most of the hard work lay. Even disregarding the processing substrates concerned – you always brought them in from other specialist subsidiaries anyway – the sensory, power and engine components were what took all the time to make, not to mention all the other bewilderingly many and arcanely diverse sub-systems a working spacecraft seemed to require. Just making the relevant components took months of expensive, high-complexity work, and then fitting them all in place and getting them all working together took almost as long again. Getting all of that done in a week or two was almost preposterous.

"The outer surfaces of the fabricaria traditionally provide the semi-processed raw material initially," Bettlescroy confirmed. "For longer-term sequential manufacturing there are shuttle-tugs ready to bring in further truly raw material from other parts of the system, though that would not be an issue here. The point of the exercise is to manufacture a fleet of ships very quickly for effectively instant deployment rather than to set up a sustainable production process."

"How many ships are we talking about?" Veppers asked.

Bettlescroy made a whistling noise. "Potentially, anything up to approximately two hundred and thirty million."

Veppers stared at the alien.

"*How* many?" It was hard not to show his astonishment. He'd thought only a few of the fabricaria would be able, or properly primed, to build ships. This implied that almost all of them would be able to produce a ship each.

"Approximately two hundred and thirty million," the alien repeated. "At most. Fabricaria are capable of being brought together to create larger units themselves subsequently capable of constructing larger and/or more complicated vessels. Probably to a point where the numbers of individual craft involved would be reduced by a factor of thirty or forty. No one knows; these are guesstimates. Plus, it is not impossible that slightly greater numbers of the fabricaria than we are assuming have been corrupted or disabled by the pre-existing smatter infection, or by the measures taken to deal with the infection."

"But, still, up to two hundred and thirty million?"

"Approximately."

"And all ready at *once*?"

"Better than ninety-nine point five per cent would be; with numbers on that scale, especially as we are envisaging using such ancient facilities, there are bound to be delays, stragglers, failures and incompletes. Possibly even calamities; apparently fabricaria have been known to blow up or aggressively dismantle themselves. Or – occasionally, sometimes – each other."

Veppers hadn't meant to stare at the alien, but he found that even he couldn't help it. "Close to a quarter of a *billion* ships?" he said. "I am hearing you right? That is what you said?"

Bettlescroy looked bashful, almost embarrassed, but nodded. "Assuredly."

"I'm not missing something here, am I?" Veppers said. "That is a truly astounding, almost farcical number of ships, isn't it?"

Bettlescroy blinked a few times. "It's a lot of ships," it agreed, cautiously.

"Couldn't you take over the fucking *galaxy* with a fleet that size?"

The alien's laughter tinkled. "Gracious, no. With a fleet of that nature you'd be restricted to civilisations no more sophisticated than your own, and, even then, more sophisticated civs would quickly step in to prevent such shenanigans." The alien smiled, waving one hand at the image of the warship now frozen on the screen. "These are quite simple craft by Level Seven or Eight civilisational standards; we ourselves would need a substantial fleet to cope with the sheer numbers involved, but it would hardly trouble us. A single large Culture GSV could probably cope on its own even if they all came at it together. Standard tactics would be to slightly outpace them and turn them on each other with its Effectors; they'd destroy themselves without the GSV firing a single real shot. Even if they were all magically equipped with hyperspace engines and were capable of performing a surprise 4D shell-surround manoeuvre, you'd bet on a GSV breaking out through them; it'd just brush them aside."

"But if they split up and went off destroying ships and habitats and attacking primitive planets . . ." Veppers said.

"Then they'd need to be dealt with one-by-one," Bettlescroy conceded uncomfortably. "In effect they would be treated as a high-initial-force-status, low-escalation-threat, non-propagating Hegemonising Swarm outbreak. But, well, we ourselves have sub-sub-munitions in cluster missiles capable of successfully engaging craft like this. And such behaviour – unleashing such a pan-destructive force – would be beyond reprehensible; condemnation would be universal. Whoever was responsible for setting such actions in motion would be signing their own Perpetual Incarceration Order." The little alien shivered convincingly at the very thought.

"So what the hell are we doing even discussing what we are discussing?"

"That is different." Bettlescroy sounded confident. "Depending on the locations and distributions of the targets involved – processing substrates and cores, presumably remote from high-concentration habitation – less than fifty million ships ought to be quite sufficient. They would overwhelm the defences round the substrate sites through sheer numbers, effectively on suicide missions. The action would be strictly precision targeted, mission-end self-destruct-limited and any perceived wider threat would be over before anybody realised it had ever existed. Meanwhile, far from meeting with genuine condemnation, a lot of the galactic In-Play would be entirely happy that the war had been settled, if not in this manner then certainly with this result." The alien paused, looked at Veppers, apparently worried. "Let us be clear: we are talking about aiding the *anti*-Hell side, are we not?"

"Yes, we are."

Bettlescroy looked relieved. "Well then."

Veppers sat back, staring at the image of the ship on the screen. He nodded at it. "How confident of that sim we just saw are you? Will it really all happen so flawlessly?"

"That was not a sim," Bettlescroy said. "That was a recording. We built that ship a month ago. Then we set micro-drones crawling all through it to check it had been built properly before dismantling it, just to be sure, and then letting the fabricaria reduce it back to semi-processed raw material again, to cover our tracks. The ship was entirely as specified, fully working, and the Disk object which built it is indistinguishable from its quarter of a billion fellow fabricaria."

"You could have beamed this to me in my own study," Veppers said, nodding at the screen.

"A little risky," Bettlescroy said with a smile. It waved one hand, and the ship disappeared to be replaced with what side-readouts by the screen claimed was the real view again, of the fabricary's interior, webbed with criss-crossing filaments studded with what looked like giant pieces of clockwork. "Also, we rather assumed you'd arrive with analytical equipment to let you take a closer look at all this stuff." The little alien looked at Veppers as though searching his clothing for signs of paraphernalia. "However, you appear to have come unencumbered by both tech and suspicions. Your trust is gratifying. We thank you."

Veppers smiled thinly at the alien. "I decided to travel light." He turned to look at the screen again. "Why did they build all these? Why so many? What was the point?"

"Insurance, possibly," Bettlescroy said. "Defence. You build the means to build the fleets rather than build the fleets themselves, the means of production being inherently less threatening to one's neighbours than the means of destruction. It still makes people think twice about tangling with you." The little alien paused. "Though it has to be said that those inclined to the fuck-up theory of history maintain that the Disk has no such planned purpose and is essentially the result of something between a minor Monopathic Hegemonising Event and an instance of colossal military over-ordering." It shrugged. "Who is to say?"

They both stared at the dark network of threat and promise arrayed before them.

"There is still going to be some degree of blame involved in all this though, isn't there?" Veppers asked quietly. "No matter how precisely targeted and quickly over it all is; some retribution will be required."

"Good grief, yes!" Bettlescroy exclaimed. "That's precisely why we intend to frame the Culture for everything!"

She became an angel in Hell.

Chay woke from the black-winged embrace of the creature which had claimed to be the angel of life and death to discover that she herself had become something not dissimilar.

She opened her eyes to find herself hanging upside down in a dark space lit by a dim red light from below. A faint smell of shit and burning flesh left little doubt where she was. She felt sick. The truth was that, despite everything, despite her best intentions, despite her daily-renewed promise to herself, she had felt hope; she had hoped that she would be spared a return to the Hell, hoped that instead she might be reincarnated once again within the reality of the Refuge, restarting her accidental career as a noviciate or even as something more humble, as long as it meant a life without any more than the average amount of pain and heartbreak.

She looked around, still slowly waking. She looked up, which was really down, at her own body. She had become something great and dark and winged. Her feet had become claws big enough to grasp a person whole. She spread her front-legs/arms/wings. They opened easily, purposefully, far out to either side. Limbs ready to walk the air. Limbs ready to grasp the wind. She folded them back in again, hugging herself.

She could feel no pain. She was in a huge hanging space in what smelled absolutely like Hell – and she was very aware that her sense of smell was much better than it had been before, both wider somehow and more sensitive; more accurate and refined – but she was not in any pain. Her feet seemed to clutch whatever she was hanging from quite naturally, without conscious will or even any discernible effort; she clutched at the thing – it felt like a great iron bar as thick as a person's leg – and increased her grip until it did hurt, a little. She relaxed again. She opened her mouth. A predator's mouth. A long, pointed tongue. She closed her sharp-toothed jaws over her tongue, bit down tentatively.

That hurt. She tasted blood.

She shook her broad, over-size head to clear it, and found that she had been looking at everything through some sort of membranes over her eyes which she could sweep back. She did so.

She was hanging in what looked like a sort of gigantic hollow fruit, all veined and organic-looking, but with a single massive iron bar running right across it, seemingly just so she could hang on it. She lifted first one foot off it, then the other, to make sure that she wasn't shackled to it. Each foot and leg seemed easily capable of taking her whole weight. She was strong, she realised. Her wings folded back in; she hadn't even realised that they'd extended again as she'd tried taking her feet off the bar. Some instinctual thing, she supposed.

Beneath her head, looking properly down, there was a sort of frilled opening that looked unpleasantly like a sphincter of some sort. Beyond, she could see what appeared to be drifting, red-tinged cloud. She would need to half-fold her wings, she thought, as soon as she saw the aperture.

She felt a strange hunger, and a tremendous urge to fly.

She opened her feet and dropped.

Back aboard the *Messenger Of Truth*, powering its way back to Vebezua, Veppers sat at an impressively large round table with Bettlescroy, the rest of the GFCF people who had first greeted him when he'd arrived, and several projections – holograms of those unable to be physically present. Even these weren't being beamed in; they were present aboard the ship in some form, their personalities housed in the vessel's substrates. This made for better security; increased deniability in other words. All but one were GFCFian, each as small and beautiful as the other.

The only exception was a hologram of another pan-human, a uniformed male called Space-Marshal Vatueil. He was a big, grizzled-looking creature, both unmistakably alien and entirely pan-human. To Veppers he looked barrel-chested with too long a head and freakishly small features. A hero who'd worked his way up through the ranks in the great War in Heaven, allegedly. Veppers had never heard of the guy, though admittedly he'd never taken much notice of the war at all. It had always sounded to him like just a particularly long-winded multi-player war game. He had nothing against long-winded multi-player war games – they were how his ancestors had made the first family mega-fortune – he just didn't think that anything that happened inside them should qualify as news.

He hoped the GFCF knew what they were doing and who they were dealing with here. One of them had wittered on at the start of the meeting, singing Vatueil's praises, describing him as a fully accredited member of something called the Trapeze group of the Strategic Operational Space (or something) and saying how they'd had extensive preparatory dealings with this, or that, or him. Like this was meant to set his mind at ease.

"To restate, then," Bettlescroy said, waving one decorously attenuated limb at Vatueil, "the space-marshal here, on behalf of those forces known as the anti-Hell side, now taking part in the current confliction being overseen by the Ishlorsinami, requests that we – the Veprine Corporation and the currently constituted and here configured sub-section of the Geseptian-Fardesile Cultural Federacy, Special Contact Division – use the facilities of the Tsungarial Disk to build a fleet of warships – currently estimated as numbering between sixty and one hundred million, though that is subject to revision – for the purpose of attacking the processing cores running the virtual realities which house the aforementioned Hells.

"The Veprine Corporation will provide the AI operating systems and navigational software sub-complexes for the vessels, suitably groomed to make them appear stolen and modestly improved in a distinctly Culture style by our good selves. We also undertake to transport a modest proportion of the vessels as rapidly as possible to more distant parts of the galaxy to be deployed where required, if necessary. The anti-Hell forces will provide the expendable combat personalities for the fleet's leadership hierarchy, these command vessels to make up one sixty-fifth of the total. Similar virtual specialists will also make up the direct hacking teams emplaced on certain designated ships which will attempt to disrupt the inter-Hell information traffic by, where possible, temporarily occupying the substrate housings and support systems and physically interfacing with them, pre-self-destruct."

There were nods, their equivalents, and other appropriate gestures and noises of assent.

Bettlescroy went on. "We, the GFCF, will undertake to present to our friends the Culture – in the shape of the Restoria mission presently working in the Tsungarial Disk – what will appear to be a sudden and violent outbreak of the currently abated smatter infection infesting certain components of the Disk. Initially this will distract and tie up the Culture assets which we know are present, as well as drawing out and sucking in any other nearby forces within practical rush-in distance. Come the inevitable post-incident investigations, the smatter eruption will begin to look like something the Culture itself staged to allow it to take on an aggressively operational role in what transpires subsequently."

"You are sure you can keep your own fingerprints off this, are you?" Vatueil asked.

"We are," Bettlescroy said. "We have done this before, without detection." The little alien smiled winningly. "The trick is to do something that the Culture would actually quite like to have done itself anyway. That way, any subsequent investigations tend to be more cursory than they might otherwise have been."

"Have you taken any actions like this on such a scale before?" Vatueil asked.

Bettlescroy blushed, looked down. "Absolutely not. This is a significantly greater interference than any we have attempted before. However, we remain extremely confident that it will succeed."

Vatueil looked unconvinced, Veppers thought. Maybe; always hard to tell with aliens.

"If the Culture decides it's been tricked, used, manipulated," the space-marshal said, slowly and deliberately, with the air of a man imparting a great and serious certitude, "it will move Afterlives to get to the truth, and it will not stop until it thinks it's got to the bottom of it, no matter what. And," he said, looking round them all, "there will always be forces within the Culture who will exact revenge. Again, no matter what." Vatueil paused, looked grim. "I think we all know the saying: 'Don't fuck with the Culture.'"

Bettlescroy smiled, blushing once again. "Sir," it said, "some of the incidents to which I suspect you are referring, the ones which have reinforced that famous saying which I shall not repeat . . . ?"

"Yes?" Vatueil said, realising it was expected.

Bettlescroy paused, as though wondering to say what it was about to say or not. Eventually the little alien said, "Those were us, not them."

Vatueil definitely looked dubious now. "Really?"

Bettlescroy looked down modestly again. "Really," it said, extremely quietly.

Vatueil frowned. "Then . . . Do you ever wonder who might be using who?"

The little alien smiled, sighed. "We give it some consideration, sir." It looked round the other GFCFians gathered round the table. They looked happy as zealots who'd just found a heathen to burn, Veppers thought. That was a little worrying.

Bettlescroy made a flowing, resigned gesture with its arms. "We are happy with our current situational analysis and pattern of behaviour."

"And you're happy you can keep the Flekke and the NR in the dark?" Veppers asked. "I'm pinned by my balls at the business end of a firing range if you don't."

"The NR are less concerned than you think," Bettlescroy said reassuringly. "They approach their own Sublimation, more immediately than is known by all but us. The Flekke are an irrelevance; a legacy concern. They are our old mentors – as they are still yours, Mr. Veppers – their diverse and great achievements now in many ways eclipsed by those of the GFCF, even if as a species they remain theoretically our betters." Bettlescroy paused for a little laugh. "At least according to the inflexible and quite arguably outmoded definitions of the Galactic Council's currently accepted *Recognised Civilisationary Levels* framework!" The little alien paused again, and was rewarded with what was by GFCF standards a positive storm of rowdy agreement: deep nods, loud muttering and a lot of meaningful eye-contact. Veppers would have sworn some of them even thought about slapping their manicured little hands on the table. Glowing, Bettlescroy went on: "The Flekke will be quietly proud of anything we achieve, and the same vicarious sense of accomplishment will most doubtlessly be applied to the Sichultian Enablement in turn." He beamed at Veppers. "In sum: in both cases, leave them to us."

Veppers exchanged looks with Vatueil. Of course, you never entirely knew what an exchanged look really meant to an alien, pan-human or not, but it felt like somebody had to exercise a little realism here. Maybe even a little healthy cynicism.

On the other hand, they were pretty much agreed. There was little enough left to iron out. They were going to go ahead with this, doubts or not. The rewards were too great not to.

Veppers just smiled. "Your confidence is reassuring," he told Bettlescroy.

"Thank you! So, we are all agreed, yes?" Bettlescroy said, looking around the table. The alien might as well, Veppers thought, have been asking whether they wanted to order out for sandwiches or dips for lunch. It was almost impressive.

Everybody looked at everybody else. No one raised any objections. Bettlescroy just kept on smiling.

"When do we begin?" Vatueil asked eventually.

"Directly," Bettlescroy said. "Our little pretend-smatter squib will go off within the next half a day, a little more than an hour after we deliver Mr. Veppers back to Vebezua. We start the fabricaria running immediately we see that the Culture forces are fully engaged with the outbreak." Bettlescroy sat back, looking very satisfied. "All we need then, of course," it said thoughtfully, "is the location of the substrates to be targeted. We can't do anything without that information." It turned smoothly to Veppers. "Can we, Veppers, old friend?"

They were all looking at him now. Space-Marshal Vatueil was positively staring. For the first time in the meeting Veppers felt he was finally getting the attention and respect he normally took for granted. He smiled slowly. "Let's get the ships built first, shall we? Then we'll be ready to target them."

"Some of us," Bettlescroy said, glancing around the table before focusing intently on Veppers, "are still a little sceptical about how easy it will be to get to a significant number of Hell-containing substrates in the limited amount of time that will be available."

Veppers made his face expressionless. "You may be surprised, Bettlescroy," he said. "Even amused."

The little alien sat forward, perfectly proportioned arms on the table surface. It looked steadily into Veppers' eyes for some time. "We are all . . . *very* much depending on you here, Joiler," it said quietly.

Assuming it was a threat, it was rather well delivered, Veppers thought. He'd have been proud of it himself. Despite the apocalyptic nature of everything they'd been discussing, it was the first time – maybe since they'd met – that Veppers thought he might have caught a glimpse of the hardened steel hiding underneath all the alien velouté.

He sat forward too, towards Bettlescroy. "Why, I would have it no other way," he said smoothly.

She flew above the Hell. It smelled – stank – just as it had. The view, from this high up – just under the dark brown boiling overcast – was of a rolling, sometimes jagged landscape of ash grey and shit brown, splattered with shadowy near-blacks, acidic yellows and bilious greens. Red mostly meant pits of fire. The distant screams, groans and wails sounded no different.

The place she had woken in really had looked like a giant piece of fruit: a bloated purple shape hanging unsupported in the choking air as though dangling from the bruised looking mass of cloud. At least in the immediate area, it appeared to be unique; she could see no other similar giant bulbs hanging from the clouds.

She tried flying up through the clouds, just to see. The clouds were acidic, choking her, making her eyes water. She flew back down, took some clearer air, waited for her eyes to clear, then tried again with lungs full, holding her breath as she beat upwards on her great dark wings. Eventually, just before her lungs felt they might be about to burst, she collided painfully with something hard and rough, slightly granular. She had the air knocked out of her, jarred her head and scraped the ends of both wings. She fell out of the clouds in a small rain of rusting flakes of iron.

She breathed, collected herself, flew on.

In the distance she saw the line of fire that was the very edge of the war within Hell; a crackling stitch of tiny red, orange and yellow bursts of light. Something that was part curiosity and part the strange hunger she had felt earlier made her fly towards it.

She wheeled overhead, watching waves and little rivulets of men make their slow breaking surges across the multiply broken, seared and blasted landscape below. They fought with every edged weapon ever known, and primitive guns and explosives. Some stopped and looked up at her, she thought, though she did not want to approach too closely.

Flying demons whizzed amongst the arcing, fizzing shells and storms of arrows; some came up towards her – she experienced terror, and each time was about to beat madly away – but then they turned and dropped away again.

The hunger nagged at her. Part of her wanted to land; to do . . . what? Was she to be a demon? Was the need she felt the need to torment? Was she supposed to become one of the torturers? She would starve first, kill herself if she could, simply refuse, if it was possible. Knowing Hell, knowing the way it worked, she doubted that would be possible.

The flying demons who had flown up towards her had been smaller than her. She had cruel hooks midway along the leading edges of her wings, where a biped might have had thumbs on its hands. She had sharp teeth and strong jaws, and tree-trunk-crushing claws. She wondered if she could start killing demons.

The screams from below, the smells of flesh burned by flames and acid sprays and the rising, choking clouds of poison gas all drove her away after a while.

A large black shape flew across the landscape behind her.

She looked back, saw the giant beetle thing following her, catching up, keeping a hundred metres or so off her left side. It drew level, wobbled in the air, then peeled away. She flew on and it came back, repeating the actions. The third time, she followed it.

She trod the air, beating her leathery black wings slowly such that she seemed to stand in the air, level with the face of the enormous uber-demon who had taunted and killed her, most of a lifetime ago.

Its gigantic lantern head was lit from within, the pulsing flame-cloud continually taking on the appearance of different tortured faces. The towering candles at each corner of the creature's squared-off head sputtered and crackled, their gnarled surfaces veined with the nervous systems of the screaming unfortunates embedded within. Below, its vast, amalgamed body of reconstituted bone, pitted, sweating metals, stress-cracked twisted sinew and bubbling, weeping flesh quivered in the heat released from its dull-glowing throne. Wreathed in its hideous fumes and retchingly intense smokes, it created a briefly recognisable face within its glassed-off lantern of a head.

Chay recognised Prin. Her heart, massive in her barrel of a chest, pounded harder. A sort of hopeless pleasure filled her for a moment, then she felt suddenly sick.

Prin smiled at her for a moment, then his face contorted in pain before the image disappeared. A flat, ugly, alien face replaced Prin's and remained there, pop-eyed and grinning while the thing talked to her.

"Welcome back," he bellowed. The sound was still ear-splitting, but just about below the level of pain.

"Why am I here?" she asked.

"Why do you think?"

"I will not be one of your demons," she told it. She thought about flying at him, claws out, trying to damage the thing. She had a brief image of herself caught in one of its colossal hands, crushed like a tiny fluttering bird inside a shrinking cage of girder fingers. Another image showed her trapped inside the creature's lantern head, beating frantically against the unbreakable glass, wings ragged, jaws broken, eyes gouged out, for ever choking . . .

"You would be a useless demon, little bitch," the thing said. "That is not why you are here."

She beat the air in front of it, of him, waiting.

It tipped its head to one side a little. The four candles roared, screamed. "That hunger you feel . . ."

"What of it?" Sick again. What would it turn out to be?

"It is the hunger to kill."

"Is it indeed?" She would defy, she thought. She would be defiant. For all the good that ever did in Hell. With enough pain, you stopped defying, or simply lost your mind; if you were lucky, maybe. "Death – real death – is a blessing in Hell," she told him.

"That is precisely the point!" the creature thundered. "You may kill one person per day."

"May I now?"

"They will die fully. They will not be reincarnated, in this Hell or anywhere else. They will be permanently removed, deleted."

"Why?"

The thing put back its head and laughed; a thunder spilling over the flames and smokes of the valley below. The candles sputtered furiously, dripped. "To bring hope back into Hell! You will be their angel, whore! They will beseech you to come to them, to deliver them from their torment. They will worship you. They will try to tempt you with supplications, prayers, offerings; any superstitious fuckwittery they'll think might work. You may choose whom to reward with death. Pander to their idiocies or deliberately ignore them; have the miserable cunts set up fucking committees amongst themselves to decide democratically who should be the lucky little grub-sucker who gets to be relieved of their burden of pain; I don't give a fuck. Just kill one a day. You can try and kill more but it won't work; they'll die all right but they'll come right back, worse."

"And if I kill none at all?"

"Then the hunger will grow inside you until it feels like it's something alive trying to gnaw its way out. It will become unbearable. Also, the wretches will have to do without their chance of release."

"What is the point of releasing one soul from this infinitude of suffering?"

"It's not infinite!" the creature screamed. "It's vast, but it has limits. You have already scraped against the sky, you stupid whore; beat away if you want until you find the iron walls of Hell and then tell me it's 'infinite'! Finite; it's finite. Truly vast, but finite. With only so many tortured souls."

"How—?"

"One and a quarter billion! Does that fucking satisfy you? Go and count them if you don't believe me; I don't fucking care. You are beginning to bore me. Oh, I didn't mention: it won't all be fun for you. With each one you kill you'll take on a little of their pain. The more you kill the more pain you'll experience. Eventually the pain of the increasing hunger and the pain you've absorbed from those you've released should balance out. You might lose your mind again but we'll deal with that when it happens. I expect I'll have thought of something even more condign for you by then." The king of the demons gripped the red-glowing ends of the mountainous seat's arms and came roaring forward at her, making her beat back through the air. "Now do fuck off, and start killing." It waved one vast hand at her.

She felt herself swallow, a sickness clutched at her belly and a terrible, aching need to fly away seemed to tug at her wings and the bundled muscles in her chest, but she held where she was, beating steadily.

"Prin!" she shouted. "What happened to Prin?"

"Who? What?"

"Prin! My mate, the one I came in here with! Tell me and I'll do what you want!"

"You'll do what I want whether you fucking like it or not, you dumb, wormed cunt!"

"Tell me!"

"Kill me a thousand and I'll think about it."

"Promise!" she wailed.

The enormous demon laughed again. "'Promise'? You're in *Hell*, you cysted cretin! Why the fuck would I make a promise but for the joy of breaking it? Go, before I change my mind and break your semen-encrusted wings just for fun. Come back when you've sent ten times a hundred to their undeserved ends and I'll think about telling you what happened to your precious 'Prin'. Now *fuck off*!" It brought its vast arms sweeping up towards her, one winging in from each side, hands as big as her entire body splayed out, clawed and clutching, as though trying to catch and crush her.

She beat back, fell away, swooped and zoomed, glancing fearfully back as the great demon sat back in his great glowing chair, wreathes of smoke from his recent movements pulsing through the air around him.

She killed her first that evening, as the already dull light deepened to a ruddy, sunless gloaming. It was a young female, caught on the rusted spikes of a *cheval de frise* on a cold hillside above a mean trickle of an acid stream, moaning almost continually except when she had banked enough breath to scream.

Chay landed, listened to the female trying to speak, but got no sense from the piteous creature. She hesitated, looking around, in case anything appearred familiar, but it was not the same hillside she and Prin had sheltered on.

She was crying as she folded her great dark wings round the female, trying not to tear the thin leathery membranes of her wings on the cruel spikes. Chay felt the female's being move out of her broken, twisted body and into her own before dissipating entirely, just evaporating away like a little cloud on a warm, dry day.

She felt a different kind of hunger, and ate some of the body, tearing through the tough hide to get into the juicy buttock muscles.

As she flew back to her distant roost, she wondered how much pain would accrue as a result of what she had done.

She hung there, digesting.

Later, she was left with a sore tooth.

She had become an angel in Hell.

Twenty-one

When the adults were away sometimes they could play in the places where the adults played. She had a group of friends who were all about the same age and they played together a lot when they weren't being taught in the little school room on the top floor of the big estate house.

The others could still be cruel to her now and again, when they wanted to get back at her for something or when she had won something and they wanted to remind her that it didn't matter if she came first in a race or got better marks then anybody else in an exam, because in the end she was just a servant really – in fact worse than a servant because at least a servant could just leave if they wanted to but she couldn't. She was like a mount or a hunt-chaser or a game-hound; she belonged to the estate, she belonged to Veppers.

Lededje had learned not to pretend that she didn't care when the other children were like this. It had taken her a while to work out how best to handle this sort of teasing. Crying a lot and running to her mother made it too easy for the children to use her like a toy when they were bored; press Lededje's button and off she'd race. So that was no good. Not reacting at all, going all stony-faced; that just made them say even worse things until it ended in a fight and she – it always seemed to be her fault – got them all punished. So that didn't work either. The best thing to do was to cry a little and let them know that she'd been hurt, then just get on with things.

Sometimes when she did this she got the impression some of the other children thought she hadn't seemed hurt enough, and they tried to hurt her some more, but then she would just tell them they were being immature. Leave it behind; move on; learn and progress. They were just about at the age when this sort of adult talk could be successfully used.

They played in the places they were supposed to play, places where nobody had said they couldn't, and – best of all – in the places where they definitely weren't supposed to play at all.

Of the latter, her favourite had always been the water maze: the complex of shallow channels, ponds and lakes where the adults played with big toy battleships and where they watched the miniature sea battles take place from all the big towers and soaring arches and canals in the air.

She had been allowed to watch one of the battles once with her mother, though it had taken a lot of nagging and her mother had had to ask it as a big favour and even then it wasn't one of the really important battles with lots of rich and famous people watching, it was just a sort of trying out and testing sort of battle that people from the estate could watch sometimes if they didn't have other duties. Her mother hadn't enjoyed it because she didn't like heights; she kept her eyes closed most of the time, her hands grasping the sides of the little flat-bottomed boat they rode around in on the canals in the sky.

Lededje had liked it at first but eventually got bored. She thought it would be more interesting if she could be inside one of the battleships herself rather than have to watch other people working them. Her mother, still without opening her eyes, told her that was a stupid idea. For one thing she was too small. And anyway, only men were stupid and aggressive enough to want to get inside those floating death-traps and be shot at with live ammunition for the entertainment of the spoiled rich.

In the distance, Lededje had seen one of the old dome plinths, busy with people. Teams of workmen with cranes and big vehicles full of electronics were dismantling all the sat domes, two dozen of which had surrounded the mansion house in a ring a couple of kilometres across for as long as she could remember. The first time she had run away, it had been at the foot of one of those stone-clad plinths she had been caught. That had been years and years and years ago; maybe half her life. Now the gleaming white satellite domes were useless and outdated and being dismantled.

Right there and then, for the first time, she felt herself growing old.

They had to wait to be allowed to dock at the little pier on one of the towers, then go down in the coffin-like elevator and through the tunnel that led safely away from the lake and the towers and the channels and the ships. You could hear the guns firing even from the house.

She and the other children – well, most of them; two were too frightened – used to sneak under the fence that went all the way round the water maze. They kept well away from the miniature docks where the ships were maintained and repaired. The docks were usually only busy for the few days around one of the big proper battles, but even on the quietest days there would be one or two grown-ups working there.

Misty days were best. It all looked very strange and mysterious and bigger somehow, as though the toy landscape of the channels and little lakes had grown to be the right bigness for full-size battleships. She had an old foametal plank for her ship; the others used various bits and pieces of plastic, foametal and wood as theirs. They learned how to tie and glue extra bits and scraps of other stuff that floated to their ships, or plastic bottles or that sort of thing, to make them float better. They hid their ships in the reeds so they wouldn't get caught.

They had their own races, battles and games of group-tag and hide-and-seek. When they had proper battles they threw lumps of earth and mud at each other. One time it was almost dark before they heard adults calling for them. The others said she only won that one because she was black as the night.

A couple of their ships were found one time when somebody doing something to one of the flat-bottom boats in the sky canals saw them playing. Those two ships were taken away and they all got a lecture about danger and Unexploded Munitions. They solemnly promised not to do it again, and watched as the hole in the fence they'd got in through was wired up. It was okay because they'd already found another hole further round.

After that they were supposed to carry comms – kid-phones – that told the adults where they were at all times but a couple of the older kids had shown everybody how to turn them off completely or make them give out signals that said they were a hundred metres away from where they really were.

The last day they played in the water maze it was very bright and sunny, though they only got to play there as the sun was going down, after school. All the adults were very busy because Mr. Veppers was coming back after a long time away on a business trip way out in the stars and so the house and the whole estate needed to be made to look as pretty and clean as possible.

She didn't like hearing that Mr. Veppers was coming back because he was the man who owned her. She didn't see him very often when he was in the big estate house – their paths seldom crossed, as her mother put it – but just knowing he was in the place made her feel funny. It was like being breathless, like when you fell on your back and hurt yourself, but worse than the getting hurt was the not being able to draw a breath. It was a bit like that, except all the time when Mr. Veppers was at home.

Lededje hadn't run away for a while, though she still thought about it sometimes. She was thinking about running away the next day, the day Mr. Veppers came back, but for now she wasn't thinking about it at all and was just having fun in the last insect-buzzy heat of the day under a sky that was all red and yellow.

She paddled along, lying on her front on her old ship, the trusty battleship made from the length of foametal that had been an off-cut from one of the dock pontoons. She'd shaped it a bit over the years to make it more aerodynamic in the water; it had a point at the front and it bent over at the back where you could brace your foot. Actually hers wasn't a battleship at all because battleships were big and heavy and slow and when she was on her ship she wasn't any of those things; she was light and quick and so she'd decided she was a light cruiser.

They were playing group-tag. She hid in the rushes close by one of the wading points between islands as the others slid quietly or splashed noisily past. Most of them were calling out her name and Hino's; Hino was the second youngest and small like her and he was very good at tag and hide-and-seek, also like her. That meant that probably they were the last two to be found and tagged. She liked that; she liked to be the last to be caught, or not to get caught at all; sometimes they heard the adults calling them, or one of the older kids got a comms call they couldn't ignore, and so they had to give up on the game and that meant whoever still hadn't been caught by then had won. Once, she had fallen asleep on her light cruiser board in the sunlight and discovered that all the others had got bored and hungry and just gone off, leaving her there alone. She'd decided that counted as winning too.

Stuck into the mud near where she was hiding was a metal and plastic shell. You rarely saw these because they had locator things in them like the kid-phones did that meant they could be tidied up after each battle, but here was this one lying with a badly dented nose that must have doinked off the armour of one of the ships. She picked it up carefully, just to look at it, holding it in two fingers like it might explode at any moment. It looked very old and dirty. There was writing on it she couldn't make out. She thought about putting it back where she'd found it, or throwing it onto the nearest island to see if it would explode, or dropping it in one of the deeper bits of the lakes – she even thought about leaving it where it would be found really easily by one of the maintenance people – but in the end she kept it, making a little mud nest for it right at the front – the bow – of her foametal light cruiser.

Leaning over to scoop up the mud to do this must have caused ripples, because next thing she knew there was a loud shout from alarmingly nearby and Purdil – one of the bigger, older boys – was almost on top of her, powering his plastic warship towards her along the channel using both hands, raising a breaking bow wave that shone in the red rays of the setting sun as he turned to head straight for her though the reeds. She struck out as hard as she could, angling out and away through a gap in the swaying stalks, but she knew she would never make it; Purdil was going too fast and she could never outpace him anyway.

Purdil was a bully who sometimes threw stones instead of mud when they had proper battles and was one of those who most liked to tease her about her tattoo and her being owned by Mr. Veppers, so the best she could do would be to get out into the channel and hope at least she'd get caught by somebody else.

She flattened herself on the board and started paddling desperately, both hands digging deep into the warm water, raising clouds of mud towards the surface. Something flew over her head and splashed just ahead of her. Purdil was shouting and laughing close behind her. She could hear the dry, rattling sound of the reed stems being pushed aside and under by the curved prow of his plastic ship.

She got into the channel and almost collided with Hino, who was being pursued by two of the others. They both manoeuvred to avoid hitting each other. He sat up when he saw it was her and was struck in the face by a clod of earth with some broken reed stems still attached. Hino nearly fell off his board, which curved back round, blocking Lededje's course. She'd never get past him now. She started to pull up, using both hands to slow herself as the front of her craft slid in towards Hino.

Oh, she thought. She hoped the shell she'd found didn't blow up when her ship hit Hino's. It didn't. Phew, she thought.

Hino wiped the mud off his face and glared past her at Purdil. Led felt Purdil's craft smack into the back of her own just as Hino reached out to the little lumpen nest of mud she'd put the shell in, at the bows of her ship. She saw him pick up the muddy shell and throw it in one quick movement.

Lededje had time to draw breath.

The shell tore past her, half a metre away.

The explosion seemed to slap her once, right across the back. It made her head ring. Sound seemed to go away. She was still looking forward at Hino and raising her hand to try to say, No!

She felt the ringing noise everywhere in her body. She saw Hino's face go pale as fast as clicking your fingers. The two other kids behind him wore the same expression. It was those expressions she would never forget; they were worse than what she saw when she looked round. Their faces; the three of them, staring, open-mouthed, eyes wider than she thought eyes could go, all blood draining from the faces.

She pushed herself up and turned to look behind her. It seemed to take a long time to do this. She looked away from Hino and the other two children, away from the channel behind and the setting sun and the reed beds stretching alongside. As she turned she saw the low hill of the miniature island forming one bank of the channel; above was the arch and spire of a sky canal and a tower above that.

She glimpsed something red. What was left of Purdil was still just about sitting on his plastic board. Most of his head had gone, though she only had a little while to see this as he fell forward and crashed down, part onto his board and part into the water.

It was only then that they all started screaming.

"No backing up, then?"

"Of course not. We don't do that; we can't do that. We're not *you*."

Lededje frowned at Demeisen. The second or third most traumatic thing in her life and the ship's avatar seemed almost unconcerned.

"So," Demeisen said, "properly dead."

"Yes. Properly dead."

"What happened to Hino?"

"We never saw him again. He was taken to the city for the police investigation and then had intensive post-traumatic counselling. His—"

"Why? What did the police do to him?"

"What? Nothing! There had to be a formal investigation, that's all. Of course they didn't *do* anything to him! What do you think we are?" Lededje shook her head. "The post-traumatic counselling was because he'd thrown what he thought was a rock and blown a kid's head off."

"Ah, right. I see."

"Hino's father was a consulting landscaper who was only due to be on the estate until the end of that year anyway, so by the time he was fit to be seen in polite company again Hino was on the other side of the world while his dad sorted out some other rich man's problematic mansion sight-lines."

"Hmm." Demeisen nodded, looked thoughtful. "I didn't realise you had foametal."

Lededje glared at him, eyes narrowed. "I can't believe that hasn't come up before," she said through gritted teeth. "What *was* I thinking of? I ran away the next morning and nearly died of exposure, thanks for asking."

"You did?" The avatar looked surprised. "Why didn't you mention that?"

"I was coming to it," Lededje said icily.

They were sitting in the outer two of the little shuttle craft's pilot seats, their feet up on the seat in the middle. The *Falling Outside The Normal Moral Constraints* was just about to enter Enablement space and Lededje had thought to tell a little more of her life story to the ship as she came back to the place she had been born and brought up.

Demeisen nodded. "I'm sorry," he said. "That was insensitive of me. Of course it must have been traumatic for you as well, and the other two children, not to mention the various parents involved. Were you punished, either for being in the battle area or for your part in providing the unexploded shell or for running away?"

Lededje let out a breath. "All of the above," she said. She was silent for a moment. Eventually she said, "I don't think Veppers was very happy about having his big triumphant homecoming spoiled by a runaway brat and a security kerfuffle over his toy battleships."

"Well," Demeisen said, then paused in a most un-Demeisen-like manner.

"What?" Lededje asked.

The avatar swung his legs off the seat between them, turning and pointing at the main screen, which flashed into life showing a slowly retreating star field. "Now *there's* a strange thing," Demeisen said, almost as though not talking to her at all. He glanced at her, nodded at the screen. "See that?"

Lededje looked, peered, squinted. "See what?"

"Hmm," Demeisen said, and the image on the screen zoomed in, altered in colour and what appeared to be texture. In theory it was a holo display, but everything being shown was so far away there was no real sense of depth. Side-screens filled with coloured graphs, numerals, bar and pie charts described the image manipulation taking place. "That," he said, nodding and sitting back.

There was a strange, granular quality to the centre of the screen, where the darkness seemed to flicker slightly, oscillating between two very similar and very dark shades of grey.

"What is that?" Lededje asked.

Demeisen was silent for a couple of beats. Then, with a small laugh, he said, "I do believe we're being followed."

"Followed? Not by a missile or something?"

"Not by a missile," the avatar said, staring at the screen. Then he looked away and turned back to her, smiling. "Don't know why I'm making this thing stare at the fucking module screen," he said as the screen went blank again. "Yes, followed, by another ship." Demeisen put his feet up on the seat in between them again, cradling his head in his fingers against the seat's headrest.

"I thought you were supposed to be—"

"Fast. I know. And I am. But I've been slowing down for the last day or so, reconfiguring my fields. Sort of . . . just in case this happened," he said, nodding at the blank screen.

"Why?"

"Why look like what you are when you can fool people by looking like what you're not?" The avatar's smile was dazzling.

She thought about this for a moment. "I'm glad I've been able to teach you something."

Demeisen grinned. "That thing," he said as the screen flashed on again, still showing the curious grey pixilation at its centre before it clicked off once more, almost before she could register what she'd seen, "doesn't know what it's following."

"You sure?"

"Oh, I'm positive." The avatar sounded smug.

"So what does it think it's following?"

"A lowly Torturer-class Rapid Offensive Unit from the days of fucking yore," Demeisen said with what sounded like relish. "That's what it thinks it's following, assuming it's done its homework properly. Encasement, sensory, traction; every field I'm currently deploying right now looks convincingly like a very slightly and extremely plausibly tweaked version of the classic Torturer-class signature profile. So it thinks I am a mere dainty pebble amongst modern spacecraft. But I'm not; I'm a fucking rock-slide." The avatar sighed happily. "It also thinks there isn't the slightest chance that I can see it, because a Torturer couldn't."

"So what does *it* look like? The thing that's following us."

The avatar made a clicking noise with its mouth. "No idea. It looks like what you saw on the screen; I'm not seeing much more than you. I'm only just able to see it's there at all. Which at that range means it's probably level tech; an L8 civ or a high-end seven."

"Not an Enablement ship then?"

"Nope. At a guess; could be Flekke, NR, Jhlupian . . . maybe GFCF if they've been paying especially diligent attention to The Proceedings of the Institute of Wizzo Space Ship Designers Newsletter recently."

"Why would any of them be following you?"

"That's the question, isn't it?" Demeisen said. "I presume to see what I get up to." He grinned at her. "And to see what I might be carrying. The question they'll be asking themselves and might want me to answer is: what am I doing here?"

Lededje hoisted one eyebrow. "Thought up anything plausible?"

"Oh, I had concentric layers of cover stories prepared," the avatar told her, "though in the end I'm a borderline eccentric and *very* slightly psychotic Abominator-class picket ship and I don't really have to answer to any fucker. However, most of my alibis are for a humble tramping Torturer class, and one involved being vaguely interested in the Tsungarial Disk, or having some connection with somebody or something in the Culture mission attached to it. An unnecessary ruse in a sense as it turns out, because the mission is actively calling for a bit of help following a smatter outbreak; any Culture ship pulling up here now has a perfect excuse."

Lededje shook her head. "I have no idea what a smatter outbreak is."

"Runaway nanotech. Swarmata. Remains of an MHE: a Monopathic Hegemonising Event. Sometimes known as a hegswarm. Your eyes have gone glazed. Anyway, some of that stuff got into the Disk . . . you do know what the Disk is?"

"Lots of abandoned alien ships no one's allowed to use, isn't it?"

"Lots of abandoned alien factories no one's allowed to use . . . mostly," the avatar said, nodding. "Anyway, the smatter got into the Disk sometime in the dim and distant and one of our infuriatingly well-meaning Can-*we*-help? teams has been in there sitting on top of it for probably longer than's really been necessary – you know; one of those jobs you make sure you never quite finish because you like being where you are? – except now it does rather seem to have blown up in their faces and all of a sudden our chums have a properly serious runaway Event on their hands." Demeisen paused and got that far-away look avatars sometimes did when the vastly powerful thing they represented was watching something utterly fascinating going on in mysterious high-definition realms inaccessible to mere mortal biologicals. The avatar shook his head. "Hilarious."

"So you're going to go and help?" Lededje asked.

"Good grief, no!" Demeisen said. "Pest Control problem. They took the decision to spin this out; they can fucking deal with it." He shrugged. "Though having said that, I may have to pretend to go and help, I suppose, or whoever's following us might see through my magic cloak of plausibility. We are heading straight for the Tsung system; it's just I hadn't intended to stop." The avatar clicked his fingernails on the console beneath the screen. "Annoying." He sighed. "Also, interestingly, this is – maybe – not the first odd thing to happen in this neck of the woods, either. There was an ablationary plume nine days ago not a million klicks away from that rendezvous they were trying to get you to make in the Semsarine Wisp."

She shook her head. "You'd make a great teenage boy," she told the avatar.

"Beg your pardon?"

"You still think girls get moist when they hear arcane nomenclature. It's sweet, I suppose."

"What; you mean an ablationary plume?"

"Yes. What the fuck is *that*, now?"

"Oh, come on; this is just the stuff I have to deal with, an emergence from the weird-shit space I happen to pass my days in." If Lededje hadn't known better she might have thought the avatar was hurt. "An ablationary plume," he said, sighing. "It's what happens when a ship tries to hit the ground running and fails, in e-Grid terms; its field engines are unable to connect efficiently with the Grid and – rather than blowing up or being flung out, wrecked, to coast for ever – its engines ablate a part of themselves to cushion the energy blow. Slows the ship, though at great cost. Immediate total engine refit required. The point is that the resulting plume's visible from way far away in e-Grid terms, so it can work as a sort of emergency distress signal. Embarrassing enough during peacetime and likely fatal in a war." The avatar fell silent, seemingly contemplating this odd turn of events.

"... E-Grid?" Lededje asked tentatively.

"Oh come *on*!" Demeisen said, sounding exasperated. "Do they teach you *nothing* at school?"

Somebody was calling her name. Everything was a bit fuzzy, even including her sense of who she was. Her name, for example. There it was again. Somebody saying it.

Well, they were saying something. Her first thought was that they were saying her name but now she thought about it she wasn't so sure.

It was as though the sounds meant something but she wasn't sure what, or maybe she knew what they meant but couldn't be sure what the sounds actually were. No, that wasn't what *she* meant. Fuzzy.

Yime. That was her name, wasn't it?

She wasn't entirely sure. It sounded like it was supposed to mean something pretty important and it wasn't an ordinary word that she knew which meant something. It sounded like a name. She was pretty sure it was a name. Chances were it was her name.

Yime?

She needed to get her eyes open. She wanted to get her eyes open. She wasn't used to having to think about opening her eyes; usually it was something that just happened.

Still, if she was going to have to think about—

Yime? Can you hear me?

—it, she'd just have to think about it. There it was again, just there, while she'd been thinking about getting her eyes open; that ... feeling that somebody or something had said her name.

"Yime?" said a tiny, high-pitched voice. It was a silly voice. A pretend, made-up voice, or one belonging to a child who'd just sucked on a helium balloon.

"Yime? Hello, Yime?" the squeaky voice said. It was hard to hear at all; it was almost drowned out by the roaring sound of a big waterfall, or something like a big waterfall; a high wind in tall trees, maybe.

"Yime? Can you hear me?"

It really did sound like a doll.

She got one eye open and saw a doll.

Well, that fitted, she supposed. The doll was standing looking at her, quite close to her. It was standing on the floor. She realised that she must be lying on the floor.

The doll was standing at a funny angle. Being at that angle, it should be falling over. Maybe it had special feet with suckers on them, or magnets. She'd had a toy that could climb walls, once. She guessed the doll was the usual doll-size; about right for a human toddler to carry and cuddle like an adult would a baby. It had glowing yellow-brown skin, black, intensely curled hair and the usual too-big head and eyes and over-chubby limbs. It wore a little vest-and-pants set; some dark colour.

"Yime? Can you see me? Can you hear me?"

The voice was coming from the doll. Its mouth had moved as it had spoken, though it was a little hard to be sure because there was some stuff in her eye. She tried to bring her hand up to her face to wipe away whatever it was in her eye, but her hand wasn't cooperating. Her whole arm wasn't cooperating. She tried the other arm/hand combination, but it wasn't being any more helpful. Signals seemed to be piling up inside her head from both arms, both hands, trying to tell her something, but she couldn't make sense of whatever it was. There were a lot of signals like that, from all over her body. Another mystery. She was getting tired of them. She tried to yawn but got a strange grating feeling from her jaw and head.

She opened her other eye and saw two dolls. They were identical, and both were at the same strange angle.

"Yime! You're back with me! Good!"

"Ack?" she said. She had meant to say "Back?" but it had come out wrong. She didn't seem to be able to get her mouth to work properly. She tried to take a deep breath but that didn't go too well either. It felt like she was sort of jammed, as though she'd tried to squeeze through a really tight gap and it hadn't worked and she'd got trapped.

"Stay with me, Yime," the doll squeaked.

She tried to nod, but . . . no.

"Okay," she said.

There was only one doll, she'd worked out. Not two; it was a focusing problem. The doll was too close, there was stuff – black stuff – in her eyes and everything was at an odd angle. The ceiling, if you were going to call it that, seemed awfully close to the doll's bubble-haired head. And the doll's glowing skin seemed to be the only light within this cramped, shadowy space.

Where the hell was she?

She tried to think where she had been last.

She had been standing under the ship, being briefed, looking at images of stars and clusters and systems, the vast dark bulk of the ship directly above. No; she'd been walking out from underneath the ship, into rain, with the blunt snout of the ship like a black glass cliff poised above; a giant flat knife for cutting through to the underneathness of the universe . . .

"Yime!" something squeaked. She got one of her eyes to open. Oh yes, this weird little doll thing standing in front of her. Funny angle.

"Ot?" ("What?")

"Don't do that. Stay with me. Don't drift off like that."

She wanted to laugh, but couldn't. Drift off? How? To where? She was trapped here, caught.

The doll wobbled towards her, its gait made awkward by its short, thick legs. It had something in its hand, something like a needle with a single slick-looking thread trailing behind it. The thread disappeared into the slanted narrow darkness behind the doll. She thought there was something familiar but wrong about the two very close-together surfaces behind the doll.

The doll had something in its other hand too. The toy waddled so close to her head she couldn't see it properly any more. She could feel it, though; feel its little clothed body squeezing against the side of her head.

"Ot you doing?" she asked it. Something cold was pressed against her neck. She tried to move. Anything. Eyelids; they worked. Mouth; a bit. Her lips didn't seem to be too keen on pressing together. Facial muscles; mostly. Tongue and throat and breathing; a bit. Fingers? No fingers. Toes? Toes not responding. Bladder muscles; something there. Great; she could pee herself if she wanted.

She could not move her head or body or limbs at all.

Suddenly the slanted narrow space made a sort of sense and she realised she was still in the ship, still in the lounge she'd been in earlier, when it had been accelerating. Accelerating? Did ships accelerate? This was the floor folded over and pressed up against the wall. She was lying on the wall and the floor had come up to meet the wall and she was lying crushed between the two. This would account for her not being able to move.

"What?" the doll squeaked, clambering lightly over her face as it moved to the other side of her neck.

"Ot you doing?" she repeated.

"I'm putting a micro med-pack on you and hooking you up to a distant-delivery med-pack that's as close as I can get it, a couple of metres away."

"Ang I trat?"

"Are you trapped?" the doll repeated, fiddling with something just outside of sight. "Yes, Yime, I'm afraid you are." She felt and half-saw it flick the long silver line, then felt something cold on the other side of her neck. She sensed a needle sliding into her flesh but there was no pain at all; not even the slightest, which was surprising. She was sure you were supposed to experience a tiny bit of pain with anything the body experienced as an injury, before the pain-relief system kicked in. Unless your whole body was basically in screaming agony and therefore your brain was so flooded with pain-relief secretions coming from the appropriate glands and just-ignore-it signals coming from the relevant brain-bits that something as trivial as a needle sliding into your flesh just didn't register at all.

That must be it. She was crushed, immobile, inside the crippled ship, barely able to breathe, and her body was probably really badly smashed up. Made sense.

She was taking all this very calmly, she thought.

Well, there wasn't much point in panicking.

She swallowed, then said, "Ot the suck ha'ind?"

"What the fuck happened?" the doll said, finishing what it was doing and climbing back out from beside her neck and standing in front of her again. It stood a little further back now so she could see it better. "I – we – got clobbered by something very powerful: either the Bulbitian itself displaying hitherto unknown martial prowess, or an equiv-tech ship that was nearby. We only just got out of the Bulbitian's environment sphere. I had to total – go into hyperspace – before I cleared the sphere, or we'd have been smeared. It was a rough old transit and we were still getting attacked. Got off some retaliation but no idea if I hit anything. More frazzling ensued before I could get us away. Took myself to bits; firing off burst units like missiles and p-chambers like mines. Lost 4D directional and had to traction-plough the grid to stop us subrupturing. Now we're drifting, decoupled."

"Oor juss a-oyding saying yeer sucked."

"No I'm not," the doll squeaked. "We *are* fucked, in the sense we're both in a very bad way, but on the other hand we are alive at the moment, and we have a substantial chance of getting out of this alive."

"Ee do?"

"We do. Thanks to my efforts and your body's own emergency systems we can keep you stabilised and even start some repairs, meanwhile I seem to have shaken off our attackers, my own repair systems are running at maximum and the distress calls I got out before losing my signal fields, plus the ablation plume itself, should have been sufficient to summon help. I expect it is on its way even as we speak."

She tried to frown. It was just about possible. "I a doll?"

"All my other remotes are compromised, too big or otherwise engaged. The doll dates from when I once had some children aboard. Rather than recycle it I retained it in this form for sentimental reasons. I'll leave it here to keep you company if you want to stay awake, though it might be better to let you sleep now we've got you hooked up; going to be a while before I can get you unstuck."

She thought about this. "Slee," she said.

Just before she slipped under, she thought, Wait! There had been something important she'd really meant to remember.

But then it all went away from her.

"That thing's coming up on me," Demeisen said, frowning. "What the fuck does it think it's trying to do; overtake?"

"You're *sure* it's not a missile?" Lededje asked. She'd got the ship to put the image back on the module screen again so she could at least see something of what was going on immediately behind them. The granular two-tone greyness in the screen's centre looked just as it had.

"Whatever this thing is, I doubt it considers itself single-use expendable, so not a missile by the standard definition," the avatar said. "But it is coming straight up behind us, which is a semi-hostile manoeuvre."

"When does it become a totally hostile manoeuvre?"

Demeisen shrugged. "When it reaches a point where a Torturer-class ROU would normally catch sight of something immediately behind it. At the moment it thinks I can't see it, so in a sense I've no business assuming it's hostile. As soon as or slightly before it reaches the point where a real Torturer class would spot it, it should hail us."

"When does that happen?"

"As things stand, if nobody alters power, about two hours." The avatar frowned. "Which is shortly before we'll get to the Tsung system, where the Disk is. Now isn't that a coincidence?" The avatar plainly didn't expect an answer, so Lededje didn't attempt to provide one. Demeisen tapped one fingernail on a front tooth. "One slightly worrying nuance here is that it expects me to see it about halfway into my approach. It's assuming that I'm stopping at Tsung, which is not unreasonable." The avatar was more muttering than talking now. Lededje remained patient. "But I'll be slowing down, halfway to dead stop, when it expects to pop up on my sensors," Demeisen said quietly, staring sideways at the screen. "And, if you were being paranoid about it, that's almost a hostile act in itself, because that sets our chum up for an attacking pass, unless he slows too or peels away." The avatar laughed, raised his eyebrows at her. "Golly. What *shall* we do, Lededje?"

She thought. "The smartest thing?" she suggested.

Demeisen clicked his fingers. "What a splendid suggestion," he said, swivelling round in the seat to look at the screen. "Naturally we have to ignore the awkward fact that the smartest thing is all too often only obvious in hindsight, but never mind." He turned to look at her. "There is just a very small chance that this could get awkward, Lededje. I might actually get in a proper fire-fight here." The avatar grinned at her, eyes bright.

"A prospect that patently fills you with horror."

Demeisen laughed, might almost have looked embarrassed. "Thing is," he said, "big space fights between grown-up ships ain't no place for a young slip of a girl such as yourself, so if that's what looks like happening I'll try and get you away. Right now you're safest here, inside me, but that could change in an instant. You might find yourself inside the shuttle inside one of my subsections, or just inside the shuttle alone, or even just in a suit or even a gel suit with scary empty space only millimetres away. All with no warning. Actually, be better even if you still had a lace; we could back you up and make you nearly as shock-proof as me, but never mind. You ever worn a gel suit?"

"No."

"Really? I suppose not. Never mind. Nothing to it. Here you go."

Just to the side of Lededje's seat, a silvery ovoid swelled, popped and disappeared, depositing what looked like a cross between a large jellyfish and a thick condom the size and shape of a human onto the floor. She stared down at it. It looked like somebody had had their skin turned transparent and then been flayed. "*That's* a space suit?" she asked, aghast. In her experience, space suits looked a little more reassuringly complicated. Not to mention bulky.

"You'll probably want to empty your bladder and bowels before putting it on," Demeisen told her, nodding back to where the shuttle's living area was already reconfiguring to its shiny hi-tech bath/shower/toilet aspect. "Then just strip off and step in; it'll do the rest."

She picked the gel suit up. It was heavier than she'd expected. Peering at it, she could see what looked like dozens of thinner-than-tissue-thin layers within it, boundaries marked out with a hint of iridescence. There were some parts of it that looked a little thicker than others and which were sort of mistily opaque. They made the thing appear a little more substantial than it had at first glance, but not by much. "I suppose I'd only be exposing my hopeless naivety if I asked if there was some alternative to this."

"It'd be more of a hopeless inability to come to terms with reality," the avatar told her. "But if it appears a bit flimsy don't worry; there's an armoured outer-suit that goes over the top. I'm getting one of those ready too." He nodded at the now fully formed bathroom. "Now do your business like a good little biological and don't tarry."

She glared at the avatar but he was staring at the screen. She wheeled out of the seat and stamped to the bathroom.

"Do *you* need to pee and poo?" she called from inside the bathroom. "In your human form there?"

"No," the avatar called. "Not biological. Can do, though, if I've been eating or drinking for what you might call social effect. Comes out just like it went in. Though chewed, obviously, in the case of solids. Edible and drinkable. Well, unless I've kept it inside long enough for any airborne or already-present organisms to start to break it down. So I can do convincing, if very delicate, belches and farts. Some human people actually *like* to eat what comes out of avatars. Very odd. Still, that's people."

"Sorry I asked," Lededje muttered, starting to strip off.

"Ha! Thought you might be," the avatar called back cheerily. Sometimes she forgot how good its hearing was.

She had a token pee and then laid the gel suit out on the floor. The mistily opaque bits were mostly on its back. Or front – it was impossible to tell. They tapered smoothly, looking like long, nearly transparent muscles.

She looked at herself in the reverser. The tattoo was a frozen storm of swirling black lines scrolled across her body. She had spent a lot of the time over the days since they'd left the GSV learning how to use the tat's own controls to influence its display. She could thicken and thin the lines, alter their number, their colours and reflectivity, make them straight, wiggly, curled or spiralled, turn them into circles or squares or any other simple geometric form, or choose from any one of thousands of tweakable patterns.

She frowned at the silvery ring on her left hand. "What about the terminal ring?" she called.

"Don't worry; the suit will adjust."

She shrugged. Oh well, she thought. She stepped onto the foot parts of the suit. There didn't seem to be any holes to put her feet into.

Just when she thought nothing was going to happen and that maybe she ought to reach down and see if she could pull it up somehow, the thing suddenly rippled and rose, clumping round her feet then flowing upwards, climbing up her shins and thighs, enveloping her torso and flowing down her arms as it gathered in a sort of ruff round her neck. It moved faster than the tattoo had performing its roughly similar trick. It felt like it was at blood heat; like the tat, she could hardly tell it was there.

"Stopped at my neck," she called out.

"That's standard," Demeisen shouted back. "It'll go complete if there's any threat or if you tell it to."

"How do I tell it to?"

"Saying 'Helmet up,' or just 'Eek!' usually works, I'm told."

"It's . . . *intelligent*?" she said. It came out closer to a screech than she'd intended.

"Dumber than a knife missile," the avatar told her, sounding amused. "But it recognises speech and it can hold a conversation. Thing's supposed to react to perceived threat even when you're asleep, Led. Can't be totally stupid."

Her eyes went wide and she sucked in a breath. She felt herself rise on her tiptoes. "It's also just given me what feels like a butt-plug and a pessary," she said, aware that her voice had risen a couple of tones. "That had better be entirely fucking standard."

"Yup. You can adjust that too. For all that stuff you can talk to it or use the controls on either forearm, or the finger pads; just like the tattoo. Got colouring and camo functions; you can use them to give it modesty panels if you're shy."

She looked at herself in the reverser. The gel suit didn't even reflect the way she'd have expected it to. She could still see the tat; it was almost like the gel suit wasn't there at all except at the edges of her body as they appeared in the image, where it looked like she had a thin grey line drawn right round her.

"So it can talk?" she shouted.

"Mm-hmm," the avatar replied.

"You going to introduce us then?" she asked. "Seems only right," she muttered.

"It was being polite, waiting to be spoken to," Demeisen said. "Say hello, suit."

"Hello," the suit said, making her jump. The smooth, cool, androgynous voice came from just under each of her ears.

"Well, hello," she said, and realised she was smiling like an idiot.

"Ms. Y'breq, I understand?" the suit said.

"Hello there!" she said, probably louder and more heartily than was strictly necessary.

"May I suggest I introduce minor filaments into your ears to allow me to speak to you directly?"

"That necessary?" she said. She found she was whispering for some reason.

"It is preferable," the suit said. "The collar components are already able to comprehend sub-vocalisations. This means we may converse without appearing to."

"Right," she said. "Okay then." There was a pause. She didn't feel anything happening, then felt a brief, tiny tickling feeling inside both ears. "That it?" she asked.

"Yes," the suit voice said, sounding slightly different. "Testing: left, right," it said, the source of its voice shifting appropriately before centring in her head again. "Does that sound correct to you?"

"I suppose," she said. Another pause.

"No, couldn't hear a thing, suit," Demeisen said.

Lededje took a breath. "Suit, put the helmet up, please."

The helmet component flipped up over her head almost before the last syllable had been uttered, unrolling from the neck ruff with a whoosh of air.

She was aware there was something around her head but she could still see perfectly well, and she could blink. She put her fingers tentatively up to her eyes and found what felt like invisible bulges over each eye. She flexed her jaw, stuck out her tongue; a shallow bulge had opened over her mouth and extended outwards when she stuck her tongue out. Her nose had tiny bulges under each nostril. "What am I breathing?" she asked quietly.

"Air, I imagine," the avatar shouted.

"Ambient air," the suit told her. "I am charging back-unit components with pressurised ambient air as a precaution; however, for long-term use I can continually reconstitute oxygen from carbon dioxide with my reactor."

"Reactor?" Lededje said, slightly alarmed.

"Chemical processing reactor," the suit told her.

"Ah."

"Oh, it's got what you'd think of as a real reactor too," Demeisen shouted. She got the impression he was enjoying all this.

"A standard micro-form M/AM unit," the suit told her.

Lededje rolled her eyes. "Helmet down." she said. The helmet flipped instantly back to become a neck ruff again. "Can you go all black?" she said.

The suit turned matt black. "Now make the bit over the tat controls go transparent." The area over her left forearm went transparent again. Touching there, it felt like the suit surface under the pads of her fingers had gone sub-millimetre thin, allowing her almost full sensitivity. She dialled the tat lines to thick and her face darkened. Satisfied, she marched out of the bathroom.

"All right," she said. "I'm suited up. Now what—?" She stopped a couple of steps from the seats. "What the fuck is—?" she started to say, then said, "Oh, the armoured bit." Sitting in the shuttle's middle seat was what looked like an armoured warrior. The suit was mirror-shiny and smooth; maybe three or four times as thick as the gel suit. The head section looked like a blank-visored silver version of the sort of thing you were meant to wear riding a motor bike.

"The armoured bit," Demeisen agreed. He glanced at her. "Very fetching," he said.

"Uh-huh." She sat in her seat again. The image on the screen looked just the same as before, disappointingly. "Now what?" she said.

"Now you get into the armoured suit," the avatar said.

She looked at Demeisen.

"Just a precaution," he said, waving his arms.

She got up. The armoured suit rose too; more smoothly, she suspected, than any mere human ever had. It stepped down and stood facing her on the floor. Then it just peeled apart, splitting centrally down every part nearest her, its legs, torso and arms spread almost flat out to each side, doubling its profile.

She stepped down too, faced it. She looked at its shiny inside surface and felt herself swallow. She glanced back. Demeisen was still staring at the screen. He seemed to become aware of a delay and looked round at her. "What?"

"You," she began, then had to stop. She cleared her throat. "You really . . . wouldn't hurt me, would you?" She hadn't meant to, but then she found herself saying, "You did promise."

The avatar looked at her, expression uncertain, then smiled. "Yes, I promised, Led."

She nodded, turned, stepped backwards into the suit. The suit closed calmly around her, pressing gently in on the gel suit but seeming to add no weight. The helmet didn't close completely; the visor slid away above leaving her an unrestricted field of vision.

"Walk normally," Demeisen said, not looking back at her.

She walked normally, expecting to be dragging the suit with her, or maybe to fall over. Instead the suit felt like it was walking with her. She got back into the seat again, highly aware of her silvery bulk.

"I feel like I'm a fucking space warrior," she told the avatar.

"Well you're not," Demeisen said. "I am." He flashed a smile.

"Hurrah for you. So, what now?"

"Now we try focusing what'll look like the track scanner of a Torturer class straight back. That'll pick up our overtaking enthusiast."

"Won't that look suspicious?"

"Not that much; ships – especially warships, and especially old warships – do that kind of thing, every now and again. Just in case."

"How often would you find something?"

"Practically never."

"Are all old warships that jumpy?'

"The ones that survived are," Demeisen said. "And then some of us are just paranoid. I've been known to back-flip and point my *primary* ahead scanner directly backwards, just to make sure there's no fucker tagging quietly along behind. Not for long of course. It's a bit scary; like running backwards in the dark." The avatar laughed. "Though not as scary as thinking you're sneakily pursuing some unsuspecting ship and then suddenly finding yourself all lit up and blinking in the glare of an Abominator class's forward scanner." The avatar looked amused at this. "Anyway, here we go."

Lededje watched the screen. The granularity in the centre of the image resolved into a shape. It looked like a sort of rounded black snowflake with eight-fold symmetry.

There was a pause. Demeisen's eyebrows went up.

"Yes?" Lededje said after a few moments when the avatar hadn't said anything. "And? What's happening?"

"Fucking hell," Demeisen said. "They're speeding up, fast."

Lededje stared at the screen but nothing seemed to have changed. "What are you going to do?" she asked the avatar.

Demeisen whistled out a breath. "Oh, I am *so* tempted to just sprint off and leave the fuckers standing, or do the back-flip scanner thing with full targeting component and shout 'Hello there, fellow space farers! Can I help you?'" The avatar sighed. "But we'll learn more if we stick with the innocent little Torturer class disguise for a bit. They'll be on us in about forty minutes." Demeisen looked at her with what was probably meant to be a reassuring look. He wasn't very good at it. "You must understand that this is almost certainly still nothing, and you can climb out of that suit quite soon."

"It's very comfortable.

"Is it? Good, good. So I understand. Anyway, just to be on the safe side I'm spooling up to full operational readiness."

"Battle stations?" she asked.

Demeisen looked pained. "Terribly old expression. From so long ago ships had crews. Or crews that weren't just along for the ride. But yes."

"Anything I can do?"

He smiled. "My dear girl, in Culture history alone it has been about nine thousand years since a human, marvellous though they are in so many other ways, could do anything useful in a serious, big-guns space battle other than admire the pretty explosions . . . or in some cases contribute to them."

"Contribute?"

"Chemicals; colours. You know."

Twenty-two

"Anyway, more help is on the way."

"It is? Well, hippety-hey for us. What is it? Who are they?"

"Some old Torturer class."

"What, a proper ship?"

"A proper *war*ship. Though old, like I say. Here in a couple of hours."

"So soon. That's unannounced."

"That's old warships for you. Tramp around, don't tell anybody where they are or what they're up to for years, decades or longer, but then every now and again one of them finds itself in the right place at the right time to do something useful. Breaks the monotony, I suppose."

"Well, it's come to the right fucking place to do that."

"Woh. Getting frazzled, are we?"

"No more than you, coll."

"That's estcoll to you."

"Blit a few kilo more of these little graveller fucks and you might just pretend to the level of esteemed colleague. Until then you're only provisionally even a colleague, coll."

"Golly. Terrible how we flirt, isn't it?"

"Oh my, yes," Auppi Unstril said, grinning, even though this was a sound-only comm. "Gets me all-scale flushed up. Any other news?"

"Our ever-helpful estcolls in the GFCF report they're just about containing the outbreaks they've come across," Lanyares Tersetier – colleague and lover – told her. "Like us, they keep thinking that's it, dealt with, under control, then another bit flares up. Mostly, though, they seem to be spending their time like they said: checking out all the other fabricaria."

"I suppose we should be grateful they seem to be coping so well."

"And that they had so many ships that close."

"Yeah. Makes you wonder what they were all doing hereabouts in the first place."

"You really have it in for the little cute guys, don't you?"

"Is that how it sounds?"

"Yes."

"Good. I don't trust those little fucks."

"They speak very well of you."

"They speak very well of everybody."

"That so bad?"

"Yes; it means you can't trust them."

"You're so cynical."

"And paranoid. Don't forget paranoid."

"You sure you wouldn't have done better in SC?"

"No, I'm not. What about the *Hylo*?" The Fast Picket *Hylozoist* was on the far side of the Disk from where they were. Bamboozlingly, an almost simultaneous eruption of smatter had taken place alarmingly near to the Disk's Initial Contact Facility, the principal – indeed, by treaty terms, mandatory – base for all the species currently taking an active interest in the Tsungarial Disk. If anything, that infection was worse than this one, with fewer but more sophisticated machines emerging like hatching larvae from a scatter of fabricaria clustered about the Facility itself and taxing the long-disarmed *Hylozoist* severely. It was just about coping in its own theatre, but it had no more resources to spare for the outbreaks Auppi and her friends were trying to handle.

"Same; still struggling to cope with its share of the fun."

The GFCF were already talking darkly about some sort of plot; these two outbreaks, so close together in time but far apart in terms of Disk geometry, looked suspicious, they reckoned. They suspected dastardly outside interference and would not rest until the culprits were unmasked. In the meantime they would fight valiantly alongside their esteemed Culture comrades to contain, roll back and ultimately extinguish the smatter outbreak. They were sending their ships all over the Disk, ensuring that the infection was spreading no further while leaving their more martially oriented Culture cousins to do the equivalent of the hand-to-hand stuff. (Play to one's strengths, and all that.) Even trying to avoid the truly vicious stuff, they were still stumbling across bits of it now and again. They were doing their best to smite with the best of them (which meant the Culture, obviously), even though this was not really in their nature.

"Okay. So what's the news with you personally, lover?"

"Missing you. Otherwise okay. Keeping busy."

"Oh, aren't we all? Well, I'd better go. More swarmers to waste. Got another cloud coming out of one of the mid L-Sevens. Off I go to blit."

"Blit away. Don't get blitted."

"Ditto to you. Till next—"

"You forgot to say, 'Missing you too.'"

"Wha—? I did, didn't I? What a crap girlfriend. Miss you; love you."

"Love you too. Back to the fray, I guess."

"Hold on. We have a name for that Torturer class?"

"Oddly, no. Probably means it's one of the particularly weird ones. Want to bet it's a vet of the I-war still troubled and trying to deal with its issues after a millennium and a half?"

"Oh, fuck. A weirded-up geriatric warship getting piled into the current mix. With our luck it'll have come to join the fucking outbreak, not help us jump up and down on it."

"There now; cynical, paranoid *and* pessimistic. I think that completes the set, doesn't it?"

"I'll use at least part of the next four hours thinking up fresh negativities to display for you. Good hunting."

"Spoiled for choice out here. You too. Off."

"Later. Off."

Auppi Unstril muted comms, glanded a little more *edge* and took a deep breath as the drug coursed through her. The displays seemed to sharpen and brighten, their 3D qualities appeared enhanced and all the other signals coming into her sort of freshened, whether they were auditory, tactile or anything else – and there was a lot else. She felt *very* alert, and raring to go.

"Junkie," said the ship.

"Yep," she said. "Enjoying it, too."

"You worry me sometimes."

"When I worry you all the time we may have started to reach equilibrium," she told it, though it was more just the sort of thing you felt you had to say when you were riding an *edge* buzz than what she actually felt. The ship didn't really worry her at all. She worried it. Just as it should be; she enjoyed that feeling too.

The ship wasn't really a ship (too small) and so didn't have a proper name; it was a Fast Fleet Liaison Module with emergency weaponisationability (or something) and all it had was a number. Well, it had been thoroughly weaponisationed all right and it had room inside for a human pilot so, like the dashingly gorgeous Mr. Lanyares Tersetier – colleague and lover – she'd been determined not to let the machines have all the fun dealing with the unexpected, semi-widespread and bizarrely uncontainable smatter outbreak. She'd decided to call the ship *The Bliterator*, which smacked even her as a bit childish, but never mind.

Auppi and the ship blitted the fuck out of whatever elements of the hegswarm outbreak they got to point themselves at; just blowing the Selfish Dust out of the skies. She was genuinely in mortal danger, hadn't slept more than a few minutes at a time for – well, off-hand, she couldn't remember how many days – and she was starting to feel more like a machine than a fully functioning and quite attractive human female. Didn't matter; she was loving it.

There were immersive shoot-games as good – arguably better in some ways – than this, and she had played them all, but this had an advantage over all of them: it was real.

One unlucky collision with a boulder, stone, gravel granule, or maybe even sand-grain-size bit of the current infection and she'd be lucky to live. Same applied to the weapons that some of these later outbreakians were coming equipped with. (That was worrying in itself – the hegswarm getting gunned-up too; developing.) So far the weapons themselves were nothing to worry a properly prepared tooled-up piece of Culture offensive kit, like the one she was in, humble civilian transport origins or not, but – again – an unlucky combination of events and she'd be plasma, meat-dust; a highly distributed red smear.

She, Lanyares and the others had agreed that knowing that fact added something to the whole experience. Terror, mostly. But also an extra level of excitement, of exultation when you came out the other side of an encounter still alive, plus a feeling after each engagement that you never really got in a sim: that of having genuinely done something, of accomplishment.

There had been over sixty humans in the Restoria mission to the Tsungarial Disk when the outbreak began. They'd all volunteered to get involved. They'd drawn lots for who got to pilot the twenty-four microships they could field. So far, two of the drone ships had been damaged but had managed to get back to base for repair. None of the humans had ended up dead/missing/injured.

The humans had all run their own sims and looked at old scenarios and reckoned that they had about a four-to-one chance of getting through this unscathed, if the outbreak ran the way it had been expected to.

Only it hadn't; they didn't even think to report it immediately because the original little smatter burstlet had been interesting, something worth studying. Then, a day later, when they'd realised it was the real thing, they'd still confidently assured superiors and distant offers of help that they could handle it; it'd be over before anybody more than a day away got there, and there was nobody anywhere near a day away.

It went over that first one-day prediction, but by then they were even more confident they had worked it out and knew how to deal with it; it'd be over in a couple of days. Well, four. Okay; definitely six. Now they were on day eight or nine, the fucking outbreak wasn't letting up, in fact it was showing signs of developing – those weapons, crude or not – and they were all starting to get, as Lan had put it, frazzled.

Plus their pooled, averaged, constantly updated should-be-fairly-reliable sims had, over the last few days, gone from giving them a four out of five chance of surviving without casualties to odds of three out of four, then to a two out of three chance and then – inevitably, it felt like – to a one-to-one likelihood. That had been sobering. It was only a sim, only a prediction, but it was still worrying. That last estimate had been good up to about five hours ago. By now they must be well into negative odds. Unless the outbreak just stopped or even just tailed away unfeasibly rapidly, or they were ridiculously lucky, they were going to lose somebody.

Well, maybe they were. But she wasn't going to be the one. They might lose more than one. She wasn't going to be the first. Fuck it, maybe they'd all die. She wanted to be the one survivor, or the last to go down. A ferocity Auppi would never have guessed resided in her rose and burned in her chest and behind her eyes when she thought about this sort of stuff. Yeah, natural warrior, that was her. She could hear Lanyares laughing at her already. Glanded too much *edge*, *sperk*, *quicken*, *focal*, *drill* and *gung*, young lady.

Still, though. That lust for destruction, glory – even glorious death – was a sort of extra, emergent drug in itself; a meta-hit that spoke to something deep-buried, long veneered over but never entirely expunged in the pan-human bio-heritage.

She was armour-suited, plugged into a gel-foamed brace couch with at least four metres of high-density gunned-up much-be-weaponed Fast Fleet Liaison Module between her and the vacuum – twelve metres of pointy, armoured ditto measuring from the front – and she had an arsenal of weaponry: one main laser, four secondaries, eight tertiaries, six point-defence high-repeat shrapnel laser cells, a couple of nanogun pods – currently seven-eighths depleted, so it would soon be time to get back to base to re-arm – and a heavy, slowing, bulky but useful hullslung missile container with an assortment of sleekly deadly lovelies inside. That was only half depleted, which the ship still maintained meant she was being too miserly with the missiles. She saw it as just being careful. Be tight with the stuff that could get depleted and extravagant with what seemed never-ending: her own desire to fight and destroy.

She was almost ashamed to be backed up. A real warrior shouldn't be. A real warrior should face the certainty of death and oblivion and still be fearless, still treat their life as just something to be gambled with against the odds of fate, as effectively as possible.

Fuck it, though; the warriors of old had thought they were effectively backed up too, sure in themselves that they were bound for some glorious martial heaven. That it was nonsense wasn't the point. Some of them must have had their doubts but they had still behaved as though they didn't. That was fucking bravery. (Or stupidity. Or gullibility. Or a kind of narcissism – what you thought it was depended on what sort of person you were, what you might have felt and done in the same situation.) Would *they* have taken the offer of being truly backed up, had they been able? Leapt at it, she'd have bet. And never forget they would be killing other people, not dumb matter smartened up a couple of notches to the point it became annoying. That was where the analogy with game-playing became something even closer; you could waste smatter with exactly the same moral abandon as something whacked in a shoot-up game.

Anyway, she was backed up, and popped out of the fray every four hours or so like the others to draw breath, find out what was happening and transmit the latest version of her all-too-mortal soul to the Restoria mission control hab on the inner fringe of the Disk, only a thousand klicks above the cloud tops of the gas giant Razhir – where she'd be heading shortly, to re-arm. Doubtless extra copies of her mind-state would then be passed on to whatever the nearest Restoria ship was, and beyond that, probably, to other substrates overseen by different Minds quite possibly on the other side of the big G, or even further afield.

Backed up, tooled up, riled up. Time to waste something.

She used the stare-focus function to zoom in on the cloud of boulders coming out of the mid-Disk Level-Seven fabricary. The front of the cloud was less than a minute old; most of it was still bursting out of the ancient space factory through round ports in the fabricary's dark surface. It looked a lot like a giant seed pod releasing spores, which was fairly appropriate, she supposed.

"Two point eight minutes away," she said. She took a sweep about, scanning right around right to left and back to forward and then looking everywhere at once just to get the local feel. (She could just about remember how that had felt the first time it had been demonstrated to her. She'd almost thrown up. Looking in two contra-rotating directions at once, and then in all directions at the same time, just wasn't stuff the ancient human brain systems were able to cope with; processing the results kind of confused the frontal cortex, too. She'd thought she'd never get the hang of it, but she had. It was routine, now.) "Anything closer smaller nastier? Or further but worse? If there is, I'm not seeing it."

"Agree," the ship said. It had already started powering up its engines and pointed them at the offending fabricary and the cloud of smart boulders pouring out of it.

"Numbers?"

"Twenty-six K and counting; better than 400 per second from about as many ports. Stable issue rate. Just over a hundred thousand by the time we get there and estimating as many to come."

"Where are the fucking GFCF and their in-fab intervention teams?"

"Not in that one, at a guess," the ship said. "I'm sending its ident to the Initial Contact Facility so they can come sanitise it later."

"Never mind. Let's go get the fuckers."

The ship hummed around her, she felt it accelerate and felt, too, her body adjust to the force. Most of the Gs they were pulling were being cancelled but they could go faster if they let some leak through. The ship went tearing through the field of Disk components, heading inward for the middle of the torus, flashing past the dark shapes of the fabricaria. She wondered how many more held infestations of the smatter, how much longer they could keep whacking everything that appeared.

There was another way, of course, for her, Lan and the others not to get killed: they could just stop fighting and leave it all to the machines. There were another twenty drone-or self-controlled microships similar to the one she was in, all desperately trying to contain the outbreak. If the humans just stopped taking part in the fight the ships they were in would keep on operating regardless, once they'd off-loaded their single crew person.

They'd be able to accelerate and turn faster without their biological component aboard and they would hardly suffer in the heat of battle; the ships took advantage of useful aspects of the human brain's behaviour – like its intrinsic pattern recognition, on-target concentration and flinch responses – so their wired-in human charges genuinely did some useful work alongside the AIs, but in the end everybody knew this was really just one set of machines against another and the humans were only along for the ride. Participant observers; taking part because not to do so would be dishonourable, ignominious. In the big, long picture, this was just another tiny instance that told anybody who was interested that the Culture was not just its machines.

Auppi didn't care. Useful, useless, big help or hindrance, she was having the time of her life. She hoped she'd have great-great-grandchildren to dandle on her knee one day so she could tell them about the time she'd fought the nasty cancerous breeding machines of the Tsungarial Disk armed only with a highly sophisticated little weaponified microship, an on-board brain-linked AI and more exotic weaponry than you could shake a space-stick at, but that was for another time, what would feel, no doubt, like another life altogether.

For now she was a warrior and she had stuff to blit.

She wondered what the incoming Torturer-class ship would bring to the fray, and almost wished it hadn't come at all.

They came for him, as he'd known they would. He'd expected they'd find a way, eventually. Representative Filhyn, her aide Kemracht and the others – many others; it had turned into quite a big operation – had done all they could to keep him safe, away from interference and temptation. They had spirited him away from the parliament building after the hearing where he had spoken out and they had kept him mobile, moving him from place to place almost every day over the ensuing weeks; he rarely slept in the same place twice.

He had stayed in vast skyscraper apartments belonging to sympathisers, budget hotels off buzzing superhighways, house-boats on shallow lagoons near the sea, and, for the last two nights, in an old hill station in the mountains, a leafy summer retreat for the upper and upper-middle classes of centuries ago, before anybody had invented air conditioning. A little narrow-gauge railway had brought them up here, him and his two immediate companions and the small team of less obvious helpers and guards that nowadays always travelled with him.

The lodge sat on a shallow ridge, looking out over unbroken slopes of trees stretching to the gently undulating horizon. On a clear day, they said, you could see the plains and some of the great ziggurats of the nearest big city. Not this weather, though; it was cloudy, misty, humid, and great snagging strands of clouds drifted above and around the lodge, sometimes wrapping themselves about the ridge like insubstantial, too-easily torn veils.

They had been due to move to a different travellers' lodge that morning, but there had been a mud slide overnight and the road was blocked. They'd move tomorrow.

However reluctantly, Prin had become a star. It was not something he was comfortable with. People wanted him; they wanted to interview him, they wanted to change his mind or show him the error of his ways, they wanted to support him, they wanted to condemn him, they wanted to save him, they wanted to destroy him, they wanted to help him and they wanted to obstruct and hinder him. Mostly they wanted access to him to accomplish all these things.

Prin was an academic, a law professor who had devoted his life to the theory and the practice of justice. The theoretical side was his professional life, the practical part had drawn him into worthy causes, campus protests, underground semi-legal net-publishing and, finally, into the scheme to infiltrate the Hell that everybody either denied existed outright or sort of knew was there but liked to pretend wasn't because they sort of half agreed with the idea behind it, to punish those who deserved punishment. Hell was always for other people.

He'd known something of the grisly reality of it from officially published and illegally disseminated accounts, and he and one of his junior colleagues had taken the decision to be the ones who went into Hell to experience it first hand and bring back the truth. The very fact he and Chay wouldn't have been anybody's first choice for such a bizarre and frightening mission they hoped would make them more credible witnesses if and when they returned. They were not fame-obsessed attention-seekers, not journalists trying to make a reputation, not people who had ever had much obvious interest in doing anything which would bring them the amount of attention such an undertaking might result in.

Then, when they were doing what training they could for their undercover mission – training that to them just meant doing lots of reading about the subject, though others in their little cell of subversives had insisted include psychological "hardening" that had involved experiences a lot like the sort of stuff they were going in there to denounce – they had become lovers. That had complicated things a little, but they had discussed it and decided that if anything it would be an advantage; they would be more committed to each other as a team when they were in the Hell, now that they were something more than colleagues and friends.

He looked back on their pathetic preparations and their terribly earnest discussions with a mixture of embarrassment, fondness and bitterness. What could prepare you for such horror? Not all their days of "hardening" – enduring small electric shocks, the start of suffocation and a lot of being shouted at and verbally abused by the ex-army guys who'd agreed to help – had amounted to a minute's worth of what they had experienced in Hell right from the start, from day one.

Nevertheless, despite being caught up in the horrifying vortex of violence and sheer hatred that had enveloped them instantly on their arrival, they had stayed together and they had, in some sense, accomplished their mission. He had got out, even if Chay had lost her mind. He had been able to be the sober, sensible, unrufflable witness that he had meant to be right from the start, when they had first started talking about the mission with the relevant programmers, hackers and ex-government agency whistle-blowers who'd originally been put in touch with their little underground organisation.

But he had had to leave Chay behind. He'd done what he could to get her through as well, but he hadn't made her his first priority. At the last moment, as they'd hurtled through the air towards the glowing gate that led back to reality and a relief from pain, he had twisted, led with his own back rather than with her, held in his limbs, literally putting himself first.

He had hoped they would both make it through, but he had known that it was unlikely.

And what he had to ask himself – what he had been asking himself, ever since – was this: if Chay had been of sound mind at the time, would he have acted any differently?

He thought – he hoped – he would have.

That being the case, he was sure she would have made just as good a witness as he had. Then he could have done the decent, chivalrous, masculine thing and saved the girl, got her to safety and taken whatever extra punishment the mephitic bureaucracy of Hell decreed. But he could only have done that if he'd thought that she would get back to the Real as anything other than a broken, weeping wreck.

She had denied the Real while she'd been in Hell, to preserve what was left of her disintegrating sanity; how could he be sure she wouldn't have denied the reality of Hell once she was back in the Real? Even that presupposed that she'd have made a considerable recovery from the pathetic state she'd been in towards the end.

Well, the end for him, because he got out. Probably just the start of fresh torment and horror for her.

Of course he had nightmares and of course he tried not to think of what might be happening to her back in the Hell. The pro-Hell parts of Pavulean society, headed by people like Representative Errun, had been doing everything they could to destroy his reputation and make his testimony look like a lie, or grossly exaggerated. Everything from a schooldays girlfriend who felt she'd been dumped too harshly to a fine for being disruptive in a university bar when he was a first-year student had been dragged out to make him look unreliable. That such trivial misdemeanours were the best the other side could do had been treated as a great and unexpected victory by Rep. Filhyn, who had become a trusted friend over the months since he'd first testified at her side.

They saw each other only rarely now; it would have made him too easy to trace. Instead they talked on the phone, left messages. He could watch her on the screen most evenings too, on news coverage, magazine programmes, documentaries or specialist feeds; denouncing the Hells and defending him, mostly. He liked her and could even imagine something happening between them – if that idea wasn't in itself a wild fantasy – if things had been different, if he wasn't for ever thinking of Chay.

It was assumed that the Pavulean Hell was running on a substrate far away from Pavul itself; for decades people had been searching for any sign of it being in any sense physically on the planet itself, or even anywhere near – the relatively anarchic habitats of the planet's inner system were particularly favoured as locations – but without having found any evidence at all. Most likely, Chay's being resided tens, hundreds, maybe thousands of light years away, deep-buried inside the substrate of some unknowably alien society.

He looked up at the stars some nights, wondering where she was.

Don't you feel guilty about leaving her? Do you feel guilty that you left her? How guilty do you feel, abandoning her there? Do you sleep well, with all that guilt? Do you dream about her? You must feel so guilty – would you do the same thing again? Would *she* have abandoned *you* there? He had been asked the same question in many slightly different guises many times and answered it as honestly as he could, each time.

They had tried to get at him through her, tried to get her – the Chay who had been woken up on the houseboat, the Chay who would never have the memories of their time together in Hell – to denounce him for abandoning her. But she hadn't let them use her. She said she'd felt hurt initially but thought he'd done the right thing. She still completely believed in what they'd done. She supported him fully.

She wasn't saying the things the media – especially the hostile, pro-Hell media – wanted her to say so they quickly stopped asking her how she felt.

And the pro-Hell side – the Erruns of their world, the people who would keep Hell – had started trying to reach him through their public pronouncements, hinting at a deal that would let Chay go, if he would retract his earlier testimony and agree not to testify again. Prin had given Filhyn and Kemracht permission to try to shield him from this sort of temptation, but there was only so much he could do, especially when journalists – granted interviews and calling in remotely – asked him for his response to such vicariously delivered overtures.

And now, a week before he was due to testify before the Galactic Council, the pro-Hell people had tracked him down.

He knew something was wrong even before he fully woke up. The sensation was like knowing you had gone to sleep on a narrow ledge high on a cliff and woken in darkness to find there was the hint of an edge under your back and nothing there when you stretched out to one side.

His heart thumped, his mouth felt dry. He felt he was about to fall. He struggled to consciousness.

"Prin, son, are you all right?"

It was Representative Errun, the old pro-Hell campaigner who had tried to stop him giving any evidence at all in the parliament two long months earlier. Of course now it felt like he'd known from the start it would be Errun they'd send, but he told himself it was just a lucky guess, a coincidence.

Prin woke up, looked around. He was in a fairly grand, rather cluttered, comfortable-looking room that might have been modelled on Representative Errun's own study for all he knew.

So, he had not really woken up at all, was not really looking round. They had found a way into his dreams. They would tempt him here, then. He wondered how they'd accomplished this. May as well just ask. "How are you doing this?" he asked.

Errun shook his head. "I don't know the technical details, son."

"Please do not call me 'son'."

Errun sighed, "Prin, I just need to talk to you."

Prin got up, walked to the door of the room. The door was locked. Where windows might have been there were mirrors. Errun was watching him. Prin nodded at the desk. "I intend to pick up that antique lamp and attempt to strike you across the head with it, representative. What do you think will happen?"

"I think you should sit down and let us talk, Prin," Errun said.

Prin said nothing. He went to the desk, picked up the heavy oil lamp, gripped it in both trunks so that its weighted base was upright and walked towards the older male, who was now looking alarmed.

He was back in the seat, sitting facing Errun again. He looked at the desk. The lamp was where it had been. The representative appeared unruffled.

"That is what will happen, Prin," Errun told him.

"Say what you have to say," Prin said.

The older male hesitated, wore an expression of concern. "Prin," he said, "I can't claim to know everything you've been through, but . . ."

Prin let the old one witter on. They could make him stay in here, stop him from leaving and stop him from offering any violence to this dream-image of the old representative, but they couldn't stop his attention from wandering. The techniques learned in lecture theatres and later honed to perfection in faculty meetings were proving their real worth at last. He could vaguely follow what was being said without needing to bother with the detail.

When he'd been a student he had assumed he could do this because he was just so damn smart and basically already knew pretty much all they were trying to teach him. Later, during seemingly endless committee sessions, he'd accepted that a lot of what passed for useful information-sharing within an organisation was really just the bureaucratic phatic of people protecting their position, looking for praise, projecting criticism, setting up positions of non-responsibility for up-coming failures and calamities that were both entirely predictable but seemingly completely unavoidable, and telling each other what they all already knew anyway. The trick was to be able to re-engage quickly and seamlessly without allowing anyone to know you'd stopped listening properly shortly after the speaker had first opened their mouth.

So Representative Errun had been blathering on with some homely, folksy little speech about a childhood experience that had left him convinced of the need for useful lies, pretend worlds and keeping those that made up the lumpen herd in their place. He was coming to the end of his rather obvious and graceless summing-up now. Reviewing it with his academic hat on, Prin thought it had been a rather pedestrian presentation; capable but unimaginative. It might have merited a C. A C+ if one was being generous.

Sometimes you didn't want to re-engage quickly and seamlessly; sometimes you wanted the student, post-grad, colleague or official to know that they had been boring you. He gazed expressionlessly at Errun for a moment too long to be entirely polite before saying, "Hmm. I see. Anyway, representative; I assume you're here to offer a deal. Why don't you just make your offer?"

Errun looked annoyed, but – with an obvious effort – controlled himself. "She's still alive in there, Prin. Chay; she's still in there. She hasn't suffered, and she's proved stronger than people in there thought she was, so you can still save her. But their patience is running out, both with her and you."

"I see," Prin said, nodding. "Go on."

"Do you want to see?"

"See what?"

"See what has happened to her since you left her there."

Prin felt the words like a blow, but tried not to show it. "I'm not sure that I do."

"It's not . . . it's not that unpleasant, Prin. The first, longest part isn't even Hell at all."

"No? Where, then?"

"In a place they sent her to recover," Errun said.

"To recover?" Prin was not especially surprised. "Because she'd lost her mind, and the mad don't suffer properly?"

"Something like that, I suppose. Though they didn't punish her after she seemed to get it back, either. Let me show you."

"I don't—"

But they showed him anyway. It was like being strapped into a chair in front of a wrap-around screen, unable to move your eyes or even blink.

He watched her arrive at a place called the Refuge, in some medieval place and time, copying manuscripts in an era before moveable type and printing. He heard her voice, saw her threatened with punishment for voicing doubts about religion and faith, saw her acquiesce and conform, saw her work diligently through the following years and watched her work her way up the shallow, arthritic hierarchy of the place, always keeping a journal, until she became its chief. He saw her sing their chants and take comfort in the rituals of their faith, saw her admonish a noviciate for lack of faith, just as she had been admonished years earlier, and thought he could see where this was going.

But then on her death bed she revealed she had not changed, had not let the behaviour of piety become the reality of internalised faith. He wept a little, and was proud of her, even though he knew such vicarious pride was mere sentimentality, arguably just a typically male attempt to appropriate some of her achievement for himself. But still.

Then he watched her become an angel in Hell. One who delivered sufferers from their suffering, ending their torment – one per day, no more – and taking on a fraction of their pain with every merciful snuffing-out, so that to the extent that she suffered, she did so of her own volition, and meanwhile became an object of veneration, the centre of a death cult within Hell, the miracle-working messiah of a new faith. So she was being used to bring a little extra hope to Hell, removing one lucky winner per day as though in some fatal state lottery of release, to increase the suffering of the vast majority left behind.

Prin was moderately impressed. What an inspired, diabolical way to use one who had lost their mind, to stop others losing theirs, the better to torment them more efficiently.

A blink, and he was back in Errun's study.

"Taking that all at face value," Prin said, "it provides a fascinating insight into the thought processes of those concerned. And so; this deal?"

The old male stared at him for a moment, as though nonplussed, before he seemed to gather himself. "Don't go humiliating your own society at that hearing, Prin," he said. "Don't presume to know better than so many generations of your ancestors; don't give in to that desire to posture. Don't testify, that's all we ask . . . and she will be released."

"Released? In what sense?"

"She can come back, Prin. Back to the Real."

"There already is a Chayeleze Hifornsdaughter here in the Real, representative."

"I know." Errun nodded. "And I understand there is probably no way of re-integrating the two. However, there would be nothing to stop her from living on in an entirely pleasant Afterlife. I understand there are hundreds of different Heavens, enough to suit every taste. There is, however, another possibility. A new body could be found for her. Grown for her, indeed; created specially just for Chay."

"I thought we had laws about that sort of thing." Prin said, smiling.

"We do, Prin. But laws can be amended." It was Errun's turn to smile. "That's what those of us lucky enough to serve as representatives do." He looked serious again. "I can assure you there will be no obstacle to Chay being re-embodied. Absolutely none."

Prin nodded, and hoped that he looked thoughtful. "And, either way," he said, "whether she ends up in a Heaven or a new body, there will be no trace left of her being, her consciousness, left in Hell?" Prin asked. Immediately, he felt guilty. He, not the senator, already knew how this was going to play out, and giving the old male false hope was a little cruel. Only a little cruel, of course; within the context they were talking about, it was trivial to the point of irrelevance.

"Yes," Errun agreed. "There will be no trace of her consciousness left in Hell whatsoever."

"And all I have to do is not testify."

"Yes." The old male looked avuncular, encouraging. He sighed, made a tired-looking gesture with both trunks. "Oh, in time, you might be expected to take back some of what you've already said in the past, but we'd leave that for the moment."

"On pain of what?" Prin asked, trying to sound merely reasonable, pragmatic. "If I didn't, what then?"

Representative Errun sighed, looked sad. "Son – Prin – you're smart and you're principled. You could be set to do very well within the academic community, with the right people taking an interest in your advancement. Very well. Very well indeed. But if you insist on being awkward . . . well, the same trunks that can help lift you up can keep you pressed down, keep you in your place." He held up both trunks in a defensive gesture, as though fending off an objection Prin had not voiced. "It's no great conspiracy, it's just nature; people are liable to help out people who've helped them. Make life difficult for them and they'll just do the same for you. No need to invoke secret societies or sinister cabals."

Prin looked away for a moment, taking in the view of the carved wood desk and the highly patterned carpet, wondering idly how deep the level of detail went in such dream-realities. Would a microscope reveal further intricacy, or a blurred pixel?

"Representative," he said, and both hoped and suspected he sounded tired, "let me be frank. I had thought to string you along, tell you that I'd think about it, that I'd let you know my answer in a few days."

Errun was shaking his head. "I'm afraid I need your— " he began, but Prin just held one trunk up and talked over him.

"But I'm not going to. The answer is no. I will not deal with you. I intend to make my statement before Council,"

"Prin, no," the old male said, sitting forward in his seat. "Don't do this! If you say no to this there'll be nothing I can do to hold them back. They'll do whatever they want to do to her. You've seen what they do to people, to females in particular. You can't condemn her to that! For God's sake! Think what you're saying! I've already asked if there's any leniency I can ask for, but— "

"Shut up you foul, corrupt, cruel old male," Prin said, keeping his voice level. "There is no 'they'; there is only *you*. You are one of them, you help control them; don't pretend they are somehow separate from you."

"Prin! I'm not in Hell; I don't control what happens there!"

"You're on the same side, representative. And you must have

some control over Hell or you couldn't offer this deal in the first place." Prin waved one trunk. "But in any event, let's not distract ourselves. The answer is no. Now, may I resume my sleep, do I get to wake up screaming or do you intend to subject me to some further punishment in this strange little virtual dream environment we're inhabiting?"

Errun stared at him wide-eyed. "Do you have any idea what they'll *do* to her?" he said, voice raised, hoarse. "What sort of barbarian are you that you can condemn somebody you purport to love to *that*?"

Prin shook his head. "You really can't see that you've made a monster of yourself, can you, representative? You threaten to do these things, or – if we are to accept your naive attempt to distance yourself from the grisly realties of the environment you so readily support – to let these things happen to another being unless I lie in a manner that suits you, and then you accuse *me* of being the monster. Your position is perverse, farcical and as intellectually demeaning as it is morally destitute."

"You cold-hearted bastard!" The representative seemed genuinely upset. Prin got the impression the old male would be out of his seat and attacking him if he'd been younger, or shaking him by the shoulders at the very least. "How can you leave her there? How can you just abandon her?"

"Because if I save her I condemn all the others, representative. Whereas, if I tell you to lift your tail and insert your deal where only a loved one will ever get wind of it, perhaps I can do something to end the obscenity of the Hells, for Chay and all the others."

"You conceited, presumptuous little shit-head! Who the fuck are you to decide how we run our fucking society?"

"All I can do is tell the—"

"We *need* the Hells! We're fallen, evil creatures!"

"Nothing that requires torture for its continuance is worth—"

"You live on your fucking campuses with your heads in the fucking clouds and think everything's as *nice* as it is there and everybody as *civilised* and *reasonable* and *polite* and *noble* and *intellectual* and as *cooperative* as they are there and you think that's the way it is everywhere and how everybody is! You've no fucking idea what would happen if we didn't have the threat of Hell to hold people back!"

"I hear what you say," Prin told him, keeping calm. Noble? Civilised? Reasonable? Clearly Errun had never sat in on a faculty annual performance, remuneration, seniority and self-criticism meeting. "It's nonsense, of course, but it is interesting to know that you hold such views."

"You pompous, egotistical little cunt!" the representative screeched.

"And you, representative, are typical of those with ethical myopia, who feel only for those nearest them. You would save a friend or loved one and feel a glow of self-satisfaction at the act, no matter to what torment that same act condemned countless others."

" . . . You self-important little fuck . . ." Errun growled, talking at the same time as Prin.

"You expect everybody else to feel the same way and deeply resent the fact that some might feel differently."

". . . I'll make sure they tell her it's all your fault when they're fucking her to death every night, a hundred at a time . . ."

"You are the barbarian, representative; you are the one who thinks so highly of himself he assumes everybody who means something to him ought to be elevated above all others." Prin took a breath. "And, really, listen to yourself; threatening such depravity just because I won't do as you demand. How good do you expect to feel about yourself at the end of this, representative?"

"Fuck you, you ice-livered, self-satisfied intellectual shit. Your moral fucking high ground won't be high enough to escape her screams every night for the rest of your life."

"You're just embarrassing yourself now, representative," Prin told him. "That's no way for an elderly and respected elected officer of the state to talk. I think we ought to conclude this here, don't you?"

"This does not end here," the old male told him, in a voice dripping with hatred and contempt.

But end it did, and Prin woke sweating – but not jerking upright screaming, which was something – with a sort of cold dread in his belly. He hesitated, then reached out, tugging on the antique bell-pull for help.

They found something called a thin-band cerebral induction generator. It had been stuck – a little lop-sided, as though it had been done very hastily – to the back of the bed's headboard. A shielded cable ran from it through the wall to the roof and a satellite dish disguised as a tile patch. This was what had allowed them to take over his dreams. None of it had been there the day before.

Kemracht, Representative Filhyn's aide, looked him in the eye as the all-wheel-drive bumped down the road in the darkness, taking them to the next hideout. The lights of the second vehicle, following behind, cast wildly waving shadows about the passenger compartment.

"You still going to testify, Prin?"

Prin, who could not be sure that Kemracht was not the traitor in their midst (those faculty committee meetings also taught you to trust no one), said, "I'll be saying what I was always going to be saying, Kem," and left it at that.

Kemracht looked at him for a little while, then patted him on the shoulder with one trunk.

It was like diving into a blizzard of multi-coloured sleet, a disturbed, whirling maelstrom of tens of thousands of barely glimpsed light-points all tearing turmoiled towards you against the darkness.

Auppi Unstril had glanded everything there was worth glanding, slipping into the zoned-out state of steady, unremitting concentration such engagements called for. She was entirely part of the machine, feeling its sensory, power and weapon systems as perfect extensions of herself and connecting with the little ship's AI as though it was another higher, quicker layer of tissue laid across her own brain, tightly bundled, penetrated and penetrating via her neural lace and the network of human-mind-attuned filaments within the ship's dedicated pilot interface suite.

At such moments she felt she was the very heart and soul of the ship; the tiny animal kernel of its being, with every other part, from her own drug-jazzed body out, like force-multiplying layers of martial ability and destructive sophistication, each concentricity of level adding, extrapolating, intensifying.

She plunged into the storm of swirling motes. Coloured sparks against the black, each was a single truck-sized boulder of not-quite-mindless smatter; a mixture of crude, rocket-powered ballistic javelins, moderately manoeuvrable explosive cluster munitions, chemical laser-armed microships and the mirrored, ablation-armoured but unarmed breeder machines that were the real prize here; the entities amongst the lethal debris that could start other smatter infections elsewhere.

At the start of the outbreak, all those days earlier, the breeders had made up nineteen out of twenty of the swarming machines. Immediately swept and evaluated by the ships' sensors, they had shown up as a cloud of tiny blue dots, speckling the dark skies around the gas giant Razhir as though the great planet had birthed a million tiny water moons, with only a few of the other types of swarmers dotting the outpouring clouds of smatter.

In retrospect, those first few days, when the blue dots made up vast near-monochrome fields of easily tracked targets, had been the days of happy hunting. Then, however, the machines – the infection – had learned. It was getting nowhere with its original mix of production; signals coming back to where the machines originated, in the infected manufacturies, told it that nothing was surviving. So it had switched its priorities. For five or six days now the blue dots had been steadily reducing in number until for the last day or so they had become lost in the billowing masses of green, yellow, orange and red points, all indicating swarmers with offensive abilities.

Gazing into the cloud around her, Auppi could see that this latest outbreak was composed mostly of red dots, indicating these were the laser-armed variety. Red mist, she thought distantly as she and the good ship *Bliterator* plummeted further into them. Like a spray of blood. Good sign, natty omen. Here we go . . .

Together she and the ship registered the near ninety thousand contacts and prioritised by type, designating the one-in-a-hundred blue contacts as their initial targets. This made the targeting easier in some ways: even drugged to her scalp, neural-laced-brain running at as near to AI-speed as beyond-humanly possible, targets running into the high fourth-power meant a lot to take in with one look.

Only ninety thousand, though. Odd, she thought. They'd been estimating more. Usually the estimate was easy to make and reliable. Why'd they got it wrong? She ought to feel glad there were ten kilos fewer to blit, but she didn't; instead she got a feeling something was wrong. Combat superstition, maybe.

Embedded in the cloud of red dots – still naively ignoring the *Bliterator* because it hadn't shown itself as hostile yet – the few blue dots were all located some way in, with none towards the surface of the emerging cloud.

The ship wove a suggested route for them to the best place – deep inside the cloud – to start firing.

~Let's bend past those two blues and mine them with missiles, dormanted till we open, Auppi sent to the ship, reaching out with a sort of ghost-limb sense to adjust the ship's sketched-in course.

~Okay, the ship sent. They swung, curving round to take in the two blue contacts she'd outlined, jinking this way and that to avoid running into the swarmers. She still found this bit weird. Tactically, logically, this made sense; get to the centre and start laying waste from there, but even though the sims said this was the most destructively efficient approach, she still yearned to be firing now, in fact to have started firing as soon as they'd come into range of the first swarmers.

But then another of her instincts just wanted to blow the fabricaria out of the sky; why treat the symptoms when you could attack the disease at the source? But the Disk, the fabricaria that made it up, was what they were all there to protect. Ancient fucking monument, wasn't it? Couldn't touch that. That'd be uncivilised.

It was right, she agreed with this, of course she did – she hadn't joined Restoria to blast smatter, she'd joined because she was fascinated in ancient tech, and especially ancient tech that had this rather childish desire to turn everything about it into little copies of itself – but after a nine-day haul with almost no breaks pounding the only-arguably-living crap out of any glowing blue dot that presented itself in her ship-shared sensorium, you kind of got to thinking like a weapon. To a gun, all problems resolved into what could be shot at. The fabricaria were the source of all this hassle, ergo . . . but no. Aside from the small matter of not getting one's own self blitted, preserving the fabricaria and the Disk was what mattered most here.

She felt the missiles go, programmed to initiate when the ship started brightening up its own immediate whereabouts. The missiles would prioritise the blue-echo breeder machines and then start setting about the rest.

~There's a *lot* of these red-echo laser fuckers, Auppi sent to the ship. ~Let's loose all the missiles, get this over fast and jump to the re-arm immediately after, yes?

~Yes, agreed. Suggest missiles to these locations. Leaves half.

~Okay. Gone?

~Gone.

~Beautiful spread.

~Thank you.

~Right, we're about there, yes?

~Centred in one tenth . . .

~Warm them up, get spinning and a-tumbling and let's light the fuckers up.

~Nearly there . . .

~Come on come on come on!

~Oh, close enough, I suppose. On yours.

~Whoop-de-doop!

Auppi felt like she had a trigger beneath more digits than she possessed, as though each finger and toe was somehow curled round a little grouping of firing filaments, every one individually launchable according to the amount of squeeze she applied. She double-swept her gaze around the feast of targets, gloried in the sheer luxuriousness of it, and clutched the triggers smoothly to her, firing everything, loosing everything, lighting up every priority-one target in view at once.

The space she lay in sparkled all around like a diamond-ball bathysphere lowered into the sort of planetary depths where every organism made its own light. Rosettes, florets, side-slanted bursts, little spears and dirty flurries of light erupted on every side, filling her eyes with sparks. Whirling within the seen cacophony, the spinning, tumbling ship was already flagging up the next array of targets. She swung and spun with it, untroubled by gyrations that would have had her throwing up, pre-training.

~What're the grey blobs? she asked the ship as the lasers and their collimators locked into the aiming grids of the ship's primary sensors.

~Indicates swarmer type unclear, the ship told her.

~Fuck, she sent, before loosing another fusillade to strew another hundred-plus bright scratches across the sky. Unclear? They hadn't had any "unclear" before. What the fuck was this?

She could see the missiles popping open their own little pockets of destruction, two behind them, down the course the ship had taken towards the centre of the cloud, and others further away, some still just starting to fire. Meanwhile the smatter had woken up to the fact that this racing, wildly tumbling thing in its midst did not wish it well and some of the truck-size laser swarmers were starting to turn their single-mouth long-axes towards them. The ship took a hit almost immediately as one swarmer found itself fortuitously pointing right at them and at the right stage in its charging cycle. The beam struck, slid off, bounced away by the little craft's mirror field.

~Proportion unclear? she sent as the next layer of targets snicked into the aiming grids.

~About one per cent. Hitting some with—

She/it/they fired, flicking destruction across the darkness.

~this salvo, the ship continued. ~Devoting sensory resources to analyse debris result.

They were close enough to the fabricary now to have to take it into account when they targeted; this close to what they were aiming at, and with such relatively slow-moving targets, there was almost zero chance of just plain missing and a stray shot heading straight at the fabricary, but it was possible for a blast from the main laser to go straight through one of the swarmers, and some of the latest versions had semi-serviceable laser coatings capable of deflecting at least part of a bolt from one of the secondary or tertiaries. Plus you – well, the ship, thankfully – had to think about post-destruction main-remaining-body direction vectors and shrapnel-debris-scatter profiles.

Auppi was glad she didn't have to think about that sort of housekeeping crap; let her concentrate on just blasting stuff. They swung again, re-targeted. A few more incoming hits registered, small calibre nuisance against the heavy armour of the ship's reactive mirror field.

~So? she sent. The latest targets had blossomed so the ship would have had time to analyse the relevant debris signatures.

~Zip, the ship sent. ~All still there. Hitting nearest grey/unclear with full main.

As the ship sent this, over twenty of the contacts they'd been aiming at suddenly weren't being targeted any more, just blinking out.

~Fuck.

Such was the weapon's power – and the swarmers' relative vulnerability – the ship's main laser usually got multiply-collimated into anything up to twenty-four separate, independently aimed beams. Devoting the whole beam on full power to a single object had been unheard-of overkill until now.

~Nanoguns exhausted, the ship told her, confirming something she could already see from her own displays.

She squeezed off another salvo at the truncated target list. The main's was obvious, the impacting bolt lighting up whatever was around the target itself with splash-out, freeze-framing the pelting swarmers nearby as though in a flash photograph. The ship would be watching in greater detail than Auppi, but even she could see umpteen tiny glowing traces burst glinting from the aim-point.

~That got it, the ship sent.

Everything wheeled again, the ship continuing to gyrate wildly, carving a gradually increasing hollow space of smatter debris out of the centre of the cloud of swarmers. Multiple incoming registered as pops and clicks, ringing the mirror field. Meanwhile Auppi had been loosing missiles into the depths of the swarm, sending them off to start their own spreading blossoms of destruction.

~Two grey on half-main each? she suggested.

~Doing, the ship agreed, and the depleted grids lit up, firmed again. She flexed, distributing unseen rays like benedictions. She concentrated on the two foci of the main armament. A single unsullied brightness flicked on in each, then faded neatly. The other swarmers being engulfed in glowing debris clouds all happened elsewhere, unworthy of notice. Further afield still, the missiles careened about their own little patches of sky, dispatching all they could.

~No? she asked

~No! the ship said.

Another wild twisting about the skies, and Razhir the gas giant was suddenly there, filling the view, its banded face instantly rashed with the aim points. The ship's main armament had resumed targeting a full-power blast on individual grey targets.

~Motherfucker. Analysis?

~Bigger than average, non-ablating reflectivity, moving quicker. *Complicated.* Lot of wreckage. Accounting for fewer total targets.

There, she thought; she'd known there was something wrong about their being only ninety K swarmers when they'd been expecting more. The fucking outbreak was switching production mix again, going for complex survivability rather than sheer numbers.

~Grown-up power signatures, the ship continued, as Auppi

unleashed another salvo. The incoming laser hits sounded like hail on a glass roof.

Another hurried tumble, one more array of targets snapping into focus, caught and steadied in the aiming grids. Even as she readied to fire, Auppi was scanning for the grey contacts preferentially now, picking out where they lurked in the red sleet-storm of other contacts.

Tiny patches of the sensor view were outing briefly now as the sheer weight of laser bursts incoming forced the mirror field to occlude the sensors, producing little hexagonal pixilations like clutter; they came and went almost before she had time to register them.

She flung out the latest manic light-burst, like shaking water droplets from her fingers.

With the main armament taking one target at a time it was possible to up the collimation on the secondaries for short- and medium-range targets, bringing their salvo total back up again. There might be a few more wounds rather than outright kills, but that was acceptable.

~That one just took off, the ship said, indicating one of the two grey targets they'd tried to waste two salvoes earlier. ~And there goes the other one.

~See them, Auppi sent. ~They're fast! She had another reduced set of targets sliding across the view; she let fly at them. The two fleeing grey contacts would be out of range in seconds. ~Any missiles we can put in their way?

~Not the first one. Second, yes.

~Get the other missiles to concentrate on the greys, she suggested. She wanted to fire a lot more missiles, everywhere, but they were out of missiles now too.

~Shit, we *powered* them, the ship sounded upset.

~Didn't know you swore, ship.

~I didn't know swarmers could use incoming laser to power them to that sort of speed, the ship replied, fixing an unlikely-looking vector line across the points representing where one of the grey contacts had been when they'd hit it and where it was now, still accelerating.

~We need to chase those, she sent.

~You think so.

~*It's* prioritising them.

Another small set of targets, swiftly dispatched, while another slotted instantly into view. The weaponry was falling out of phase now as the differences between the varying re-charging intervals started to add up and the additional collimating on the secondaries introduced its own slight delay.

~Maybe it wants us to do the same, the ship suggested.

The incoming sounded like drumming, heavy rain now. The pixilation outings were spattering across the view like manically invasive subtitles in an unknown language.

~I don't think it's that smart.

~You want to chase?

~Yes. *That* one. She indicated the first one to set off out of the cloud of contacts at the same time as loosing another half-salvo and marking a swathe of fresh targets across the red cloud around them.

~Okay.

The view tumbled one more time, another set of targets highlighted across the wash of contact-strewn space, then even as she triggered the weaponry again they set off, their slow, near-centred drift composed of many lightning-fast tumbles and gyrations turning into a single darting vector aimed at where they reckoned the grey they were targeting would be. She kept on firing micro-salvo after micro-salvo at the sleet-echoes of red targets as they pursued, triggerings becoming almost continuous as the firing patterns diverged. Red sleet, red sleet turning fire bright; they must be leaving a tunnel of ravaged, fading debris behind them through the swarmer cloud, the ship itself a sleek spear-point glittering with reflected light as the red-flagged laser elements swivelled, following it and firing. So many reds, so many . . .

~It's accelerating *hard*, the ship sent.

Shit, she thought.

~We powered it by hitting it, she sent to the ship.

~Yes.

~With the laser.

~Yes. Oh.

~They're not all just to hit us with.

~They're there . . .

~To power the greys.

~That's a departure.

~That could be a lot of fucking departures. Those grey fuckers are *ships*; microships.

~The outburst has halted, the ship told her. ~The last swarmer just exited the infected fabricary.

Auppi and the ship were picking out double-handfuls of targets constantly now as they charged through the mist of contacts becoming targets, delegating the fire commands to the sub-AIs, effectively letting the weaponry make up its own mind when to initiate.

~Hundreds of the laser swarmers are firing at the grey we're pursuing, the ship sent. ~I can see the back-scatter. Other laser swarmers starting to pattern themselves around each of the greys. They're going to power them up too.

~We aren't going to be able to cope, she sent. ~This needs mayhem weaponry; what we've got's far too polite and pinpoint.

~Or a serious Effector.

~Job for our in-bound Torturer class.

~I think we should suggest just that. Okay, we're in range.

Auppi squeezed off the single main-armament shot at the fleeing swarmer, blasting it across the skies in a pulsating detonation of light, fragments incandescing in the pulses of laser still coming in from the swarmers which had been helping to power it.

Their own incoming increased again as the swarmers switched from powering the now destroyed microship to just plain shooting at the *Bliterator* and Auppi. The ship was swinging, powering away, curving round, lifting away from the debris field it had just created.

~How many more greys? Auppi asked.

~Thirty-eight.

~We'll never get them all.

~As many as we can, then.

~Any heading for the planet?

That had always been one of the nightmare scenarios: the swarmers turning properly feral and plunging into the gas giant to start trying to tear it apart. So far they hadn't shown any desire to do this.

~None. Mostly sticking to the system plane; few straight up and down.

~Nearest?

~This one, The ship highlighted one of the microships seemingly headed straight for another fabricary, its rear end lit up by the laser swarmers helping to propel it.

~Signal Lan and the others, she sent. ~Get Base to contact the Torturer class and suggest it gets stuck straight in with its Effector. Only way we're going to cope here is by turning these fuckers on themselves.

~Agree. Done.

They left the missiles to deal with the blue-tagged breeder swarmers while they went after the microship. This one loosed its own tail laser at them, re-directing some of its vicarious propellant laser fire back at its pursuer. The *Bliterator*'s mirror field blanked their sensors for an instant to cope.

~Oh, that's not funny, she sent.

~Range, the ship replied.

~Take that with your fucking arse-light, Auppi sent as she triggered their main armament. The weapon was wound up to frequencies there was no way the target ship's own mirror armour could counter; the swarmer erupted brightly, way in the distance; the *Bliterator* was already curving away hard, picking out their next target.

They ran down ten more, the intervals between growing greater as the fleeing swarmer ships moved quickly away from the initial outbreak point. They passed the time frazzling as many of the cloud of laser swarmers as they could get near, dipping into the still-slowly expanding cloud of contacts like a predatory fish into a bait-ball.

The next grey was taking them way out of the original infection outbreak volume, zipping past other dormant fabricaria as they tore after the rear-lit microship.

~This one's accelerating harder than the others, given its distance from the laser swarmers powering it, the ship told her.

~Thought it was taking a while.

~May mean it's learned something about using that rear absorption/deflector set.

~We in any danger?

~Shouldn't be. Mirror field's been unstressed so far. The ship sounded unworried. ~Range.

She fired. The resulting explosion didn't look right. Too small, for a start.

~A partial, the ship sent. ~Just wounded.

~Wow, our first partial.

~Still accelerating, though slower. Seventy per cent. Course change, too. Heading straight for that fabricary. Collisionary.

The ship highlighted one of the great dark slowly orbiting shapes, sitting less than a thousand kilometres ahead.

~*Collisionary*? Auppi sent.

Oh, fuck, she thought; just what they needed. High-speed swarmer/fabricary collisions.

~Ready, the ship told her. ~Hit it again.

She did. Still too small a result. The swarmer had got harder, smaller, more reflective.

~Forty-five per cent of original acceleration, the ship reported. ~Still picking up speed though.

~Come on, you fucker, fucking *die*!

They whizzed through the debris field from their first partial hit. The ship scanned the still hot cloud as they flashed through it, shields taking tiny impacts that made the ship judder.

~Interesting materials profile, the ship said. ~Definitely learning.

~Same course?

~Yes; swerved back to it after we knocked it off.

~Impact?

~Three seconds.

They had time to hit the swarmer twice more.

By the time it collided with the fabricary it had stopped accelerating and been reduced to the status of something more like a tight cloud of debris all travelling in the same direction rather than a ship, though it was still making sufficient speed to create a substantial flash when it hit the dark, three-kilometre-long lump of the fabricary.

~Fuck, Auppi sent, watching the debris bloom and expand.

~Agree, the ship replied.

They cruised in after it, already turned about and decelerating hard as the engines readied them to go back the way they'd come, still heading backwards on their earlier course through sheer momentum.

~Unexpected impact signature. The ship sounded puzzled.

~Oh, *fuck*; has it broken it? she asked. The debris had hit at over thirty klicks a second. It had ended up being a glancing blow rather than head-on, but it had blasted a hole in the fabricary and set it spinning and tumbling. It was already spiralling out of its orbit and drifting fractionally inwards towards Razhir. Uncorrected it would eventually head right down, into the gas giant's atmosphere, to burn up.

In theory the Disk ought to remain stable for ever; in practice passing comets and even near-passing stars could disrupt it, and the fabricaria each had automatic systems that could vent gas to keep them on station. It was one of the responsibilities of whatever species was in charge of the Disk to keep those automatics charged and working. The systems were designed to nudge the fabricaria back into place when their orbits were ruffled by tiny fractions though; even if they'd survived the impact undamaged, the gross effect of the swarmer remains slamming into it would be orders of magnitude beyond anything the automatics could deal with.

~It's as though, the ship said, sounding hesitant, probably waiting for additional detail to accrue via its sensors, ~the surface had been hollowed out. The outer shell should be solid; protecting the fabricary itself and providing raw material for when it's producing something, but instead it's like the debris hit a thin outer crust and then partly went through, partly collided with some sort of minimal structure underneath.

They had almost drawn to a stop now, still approaching the damaged fabricary but increasingly slowly as the engines, still at full power, cancelled their earlier vector.

~Cut engines, she sent. ~Back flip. Take us in for a look.

~You sure?

The ship cut its engines, a half-second or so before they would have started pulling away from the holed, slowly cartwheeling fabricary. They were nearly stationary, still drifting slowly towards the impact site.

~No, not sure, she admitted. ~But . . .

~Okay. The ship turned about, fired its engines briefly, turned, fired them again and, with a little finessing, got them locally stationary relative to the hundred-metre-long, raggedly ellipsoid breach in the giant slowly tumbling fabricary.

Auppi and the *Bliterator* found themselves looking straight into the torn-open interior of the thing. The view was edged all around with sections of its still-glowing outer surface, which must have been largely hollowed out to leave only a thin outer skin supported by a fragile-looking network of skinny girders, cables and beams that lay between that impromptu hull and the wall of the fabricary proper, about twenty metres deeper inside. That too had been breached by part of the swarmer's wreckage cascade, so they could see all the way inside to where the ancient stuff-making machinery and associated paraphernalia lay.

This was the antique alien apparatus that was not meant to have been touched or used for a couple of million years. It was supposed to be lying there, metaphorically cobwebbed, in a cavern which was otherwise completely empty.

Unasked, the *Bliterator* described a small circle around the main breach so that they could see into different parts of the fabricary interior through the smaller secondary hole in its hull, so building up a larger picture.

The ship displayed the results. Some bits were blurred because, despite the damage, there was some sort of movement taking place inside the fabricary, but the main image was clear.

~What, Auppi sent slowly, ~the holy fuck . . . is *that*?

Twenty-three

She woke up. She looked around.

She was in a standard-looking medium-dependency medical pod in a standard-looking medical facility. Could be anywhere; ship-board, on an Orbital – anywhere. She felt okay. She was physically whole, wrapped in light compression foam over almost her entire body and she had some sort of movement-restricting bandages round her head. Pain indicators minimal; bodily damage assessment said she was recovering fast from multiple fractures of most major bones. No brain damage, little major organ damage. Widespread tissue damage, healing fast. She should be on her feet in two days, in fragile good health the following day and back to normal a day or two after that.

She could flex her toes and move her arms. Both her hands were free of the recovery foam; she could waggle them, and feel the liquidic texture of the pod covering. Raising her right arm, she could sense the compression foam taking the physical strain, letting her muscles flex but leaving her knitting bones unstressed.

"Okay," she said, "*now* where are we?"

"Ms. Nsokyi," a voice said. It sounded like the ship. Or *a* ship. Or at least like something non-human trying to be reassuring. A ship-drone, bulbous and smooth, like a giant pebble, swung into view. "Welcome aboard. I am the Culture vessel *Me, I'm Counting*."

"Oh," Yime said. "Well, I was looking for you, but now you've found me. What of the *Bodhisattva*?"

"Severely damaged. Its remains are being held within my own field structure. I intend to leave it with the first GSV we encounter. The extent of the damage it sustained is such I suspect it will make more sense to re-house the Mind in a new ship. Frankly, the main fabric is mostly fit for recycling. In any event, a point may come shortly when I may have to suggest that the Mind of the *Bodhisattva* abandon ship and throw in its lot with me, allowing me to abandon the rest of the remains and so resume my habitual field structure and hence operational fitness."

"Why would that be?"

"Because, Ms. Nsokyi, we appear to be heading into what will shortly become, if it is not already, a war zone."

Over the many, many years of his sexually active life, Veppers had worked out how to manage the rhythms and stages of a sexual encounter, all with a view to maximising his own pleasure. It was definitely a skill worth having. He thought of mundane, non-sexual things when he wanted to hold himself back, and of particularly exciting moments from earlier sexual escapades when he wanted to bring on his orgasm. One of the downsides of becoming very old was that the remembered stuff was generally always better than the sex you were actually having right there and then, but that was a small price to pay, he reckoned.

That evening, he was fucking Diamle, another of his fabulous Harem Troupe girls, in the master bedroom of the Ubruater town house, while Sohne looked on. Sohne was the other girl besides

Pleur who was an Impressionist, able to take on any appearance. Currently, she looked like a very famous actress. He was already looking forward to fucking her next. Right now though – sweating a little, his long blond-white hair tied back in a pony tail – he was concentrating on holding back, aiming for an orgasm in about a minute's time that ought to be a good one. This was no more than he deserved, he thought; he'd only arrived back that morning from his trip to Vebezua and beyond and was intent on making up for lost fucking time.

The air in the room changed, there was a massive "Bang!" and he was stopped in mid-stroke, still holding Diamle's perfectly formed hips while the girl herself – until that point yelping and moaning with possibly pretended pleasure – stared straight ahead at a small, rather beautiful-looking alien creature with large eyes and milky, slightly pink-tinged skin, most of it hidden by a slim-fitting grey uniform. The creature had materialised where some of the great bed's plumper pillows and cushions had been, and had caused several of them either to split or to disintegrate, either way spilling bounteous amounts of feathers and almost air-light stuffing into the air. The alien looked like it was emerging from its own small snowstorm. It flapped ineffectually at the feathers and stuffing, gaze darting this way and that.

Diamle screamed.

Internally, as it were, this was quite a pleasurable experience for Veppers, not that it made the slightest bit of difference to his sense of shock, violation and even betrayal. Sohne fell forward, fainting on the bed in a dead weight, her forehead thudding into one of Diamle's splayed calves. Diamle was whimpering now. Veppers let her go; she pulled a deflated cushion cover around her and jumped off the bed, stood there quivering, staring at the little alien. She coughed suddenly, spitting out feathers.

The creature wobbled in the midst of the slowly falling debris, then seemed to find its balance, composing itself. It was one of Bettlescroy's immediate underlings. "Mr. Veppers," it said. It looked first at his face, then down at his engorged penis. "Gracious," it said. It looked back at his face. "Over-Lieutenant

Vrept," it told him, nodding once. "Answering directly to the honourable Bettlescroy-Bisspe-Blispin III himself."

"What the fuck do you think you're doing?" Veppers said. This was not funny, not forgivable.

"I have information. We must talk," the GFCFian said. It glanced at the sprawled, still-fainted form of Sohne, and the no-longer-quivering, merely gulping Diamle. "Send these persons away."

"Sir?" Jasken's voice came distantly from the bedroom's main doors. The locked handles were turned from outside, then released. The door thudded to knocks. "*Sir?*"

Veppers pointed back towards the doors. "Just before I have my chief of security take you away for—"

"Information. Talk. Immediately," the little alien said. "No further delay. I have orders."

"Sir?" Jasken shouted from beyond the doors again. "Are you all right? It's Jasken, with two Zei."

"Yes!" Veppers shouted. "Wait there!" He turned to Diamle. "My robe."

The girl twirled, scooped his robe from the floor. Veppers lifted Sohne's head up by her long golden hair and slapped her across the face a couple of times, bringing her round. She sat back, looking woozy, cheeks reddened.

"Both of you, out," Veppers told the women as he wrapped his robe around himself. "Leave the door unlocked and tell Jasken and the Zei to wait where they are. Let him know what's happened here, but nobody else."

Diamle wrapped herself and Sohne in sheets and helped the other girl to the doors. Veppers heard Diamle saying something to Jasken, then the doors thudded shut again.

Veppers turned to the small creature. "Are you familiar with the phrase, 'This had better be good,' Over-Lieutenant Vrept?" he asked, knee-walking his way up the bed towards the sitting alien, then looking down, towering over it.

"I am," it told him. "This is not good though; this is bad. Hence the urgency. My commander, the aforesaid honourable

Bettlescroy-Bisspe-Blispin III, bids me inform you that there has been a security breach in the Tsungarial Disk; one of the currently ship-constructing fabricaria was damaged during the ongoing diversionary smatter outbreak containment action and a light space craft belonging to the Culture Restoria mission caught recorded sight of the extemporised ship being built within said fabricary, signalling this information to the rest of the Culture mission within the Disk, which has concomitantly relayed said information beyond to other Culture units while at the same time investigating other fabricaria to discover whether others amongst them are also building ships, the results of this investigation being positive, of course, though steps have been and are being taken to neutralise the Culture mission's abilities.

"In sum: it is now known within the Culture, and feasibly beyond, that certain of the Disk elements are manufacturing a war fleet. The fleet is still a day and a half from earliest completion, excluding AM-fuelling. Several Culture ships are approaching the Disk. The NR seem not to have been informed of the full substance of the aforesaid intelligence, however they have expressed strong interest in knowing what precisely is going on in the matter of the Tsungarial Disk, and unconfirmed reports suggest they may be moving militarily relevant assets into position.

"That is the initial substance of my message. Any questions, good sir? Or, and also, you may wish to enlighten the aforesaid honourable Bettlescroy-Bisspe-Blispin III regarding the previously discussed but still unspecified targets pertaining to the still-being-built ships. That would be appreciated."

Veppers stared open-mouthed at the little alien for at least two heartbeats, then wondered if he too was about to faint.

"Well, happy fucking *day*!" Demeisen said. He turned to Lededje with a grin that extended into a broad smile.

She looked at him. "I have the feeling that what you think of as good news might not strike everybody else as being quite so smashing."

"Some nutter's building a bunch of ships in the Tsungarial

Disk!" Demeisen sat back in the seat, staring at the module's screen, still smiling.

"How is that good news?"

"It's not, it's a fucking disaster," Demeisen said, waving his arms. "This'll end in tears, mark my words."

"So stop smiling."

"I can't! There are natural . . . Okay, I can,"' the avatar said, turning to her with a look of such abject sadness she instantly wanted to take him in her armour-suited arms, pat his back and reassure him everything would be all right. Even as Lededje realised quite how easily she was being manipulated, and started to feel furious at herself as well as Demeisen, he dropped the sad look and went back to looking quite gloriously happy. "I *can* help it," he admitted, "I just don't *want* to help it." He waved his arms again. "Come *on*! This avatar naturally recognises my own emotional state and reflects it, unless I'm deliberately trying to deceive. Would you rather I *lied* to you?"

"Then what," Lededje asked, trying to keep her voice cold and not get caught up in the avatar's obvious enthusiasm, "is making you smile about a disaster?"

"Well, first, I didn't cause it! Nothing to do with me; hands clean. Always a bonus. But it's looking clearer and clearer there's going to be some heavy fucking messing hereabouts very shortly and that's precisely what I'm built for. I'm going to get to strut my stuff, I'm going to get to be me, girlie. I tell you, I can't fucking wait."

"We are talking about a shooting war?" she said.

"Well, *yes*!" Demeisen exclaimed, sounding borderline-exasperated with her. He waved his arms again. He seemed to be doing this a lot, she noticed.

"And people are going to die."

"People? Very likely even *ships*!"

She just looked at him.

"Lededje," the avatar said, taking one of her armour-fat hands in his own. "I am a warship. This is in my nature; this is what I'm designed and built for. My moment of glory approaches and you can't expect me not to be excited at the prospect. I was fully expecting to spend my operational life just twiddling my metaphorical thumbs in the middle of empty nowhere, ensuring sensible behaviour amongst the rolling boil of fractious civs just by my presence and that of my peers, keeping the peace through the threat of the sheer pandemonium that would result if anybody resurrected the idea of war as a dispute-resolution procedure with the likes of me around. Now some sense-forsaken fuckwit with a death wish has done just that and I strongly suspect I shortly get a chance to *shine*, baby!"

On the word "shine", Demeisen's eyebrows shot up, his voice rose a tone or two and increased markedly in volume. Even through the armoured glove, she could feel the pressure of his hands squeezing hers.

Lededje had never seen anybody look so happy.

"And what happens to me?" she asked quietly.

"You should get back home," the avatar told her. It glanced at the screen, where the black snowflake with too many limbs still filled the centre of the image. "I'd chuck you overboard in this shuttle right now and let you head for Sichult, but whatever the fuck *that* is might mistake you for a munition or just waste you for the target practice so I'd better deal with it first." The avatar looked at her with a strange, intense expression. "Necessarily dangerous, I'm afraid. No getting away from it." Demeisen took a deep breath. "You afraid to die, Lededje Y'breq?"

"I've already died," she told him.

He spread his hands, looked genuinely interested. "And?"

"It's shit."

"Fair enough," he said, turning to face the screen and sitting back properly in the shuttle command seat. "Let's put that one down as a mistake and try to stop it turning into a habit."

Lededje watched the seat contort itself around the avatar, securing his body in place with padded extensions of the chair's own legs, arms, seat and back. She felt movement around and beneath her and realised her seat was doing the same thing, enclosing her one more time; another layer of confinement beyond the gel suit and the armoured outer suit. She was pressed and shuffled backwards until everything fitted snugly against the contours of the seat.

"Now we get foamed," Demeisen told her.

"What?" she said, alarmed, as the suit's visor swung smoothly down over her face. The shuttle's interior went dark, but the visor showed some sort of compensated image that gave her a very clear view of what looked like red-glowing bubbling liquid filling up the space she'd been living in for the last twenty-plus days, rising quickly in a dark red tide around the base of the chair, flowing up and over her armoured body and then foaming all about her, rapidly covering the visor and leaving her briefly blind in the darkness before she heard the avatar speak again.

"Space view? Or some screen entertainment to while away the time?" Suddenly the visor was showing her the same view the screen had, but wrap-around. The wrong-looking, eight-limbed black snowflake was still centre-image.

"You might have done better to ask whether I was afraid of forced immobility and confined spaces," Lededje told the avatar.

"I forgot. Of course, the suit can just put you under for the duration of . . . well, whatever."

"No, thanks."

"So, make you mind up. Real space view with potential scariness, or some screen; gentle feel-good, wistful comedy, razor-sharp witterage, outright slapstick hilarity, engrossing human drama, historical epic, educational documentary, ambient meanderance, pure art appreciation, porn, horror, sport or news?"

"Real space view, thanks."

"I'll do my best. Might all happen too quickly if anything happens at all. Though prepare for disappointment and anti-climax; chances are still that this particular encounter will be resolved peacefully. Bastarding things usually are."

"You are astoundingly bad at hiding your feelings in such matters," she told the ship. "I hope your space-battle tactics are more subtle."

The avatar just laughed.

Then everything went quiet for a moment. She could hear her own heart beat distantly. There was a noise just like a single indrawn breath and then the avatar's voice said quietly, "Okay . . ."

On the screen before her eyes, the black snowflake image flickered.

There came a time when she found the shallow valley with the iron cages where the acid rain fell to torment the howling inmates, and each day the demons dragged them screaming to the canted slabs where their blood was spilled to form the gurgling stream at the valley's foot which flowed glutinously into the header pond just upstream from the little mill.

She beat her great dark wings over the scene, watching as a giant flying beetle machine arrived to disgorge the latest batch of the badly behaved who'd been appropriately terrified by their tour round Hell. The beetle landed in a storm of dust, caking the mill and adding to the patina on the black-dark blood pond.

On the side of the mill, the wheel revolved ponderously, eliciting screams and groans from the still-living tissues, sinews and bones from which it was made.

Every beat of her wings caused her a tiny twinge of pain.

Chay had killed her thousand souls, enveloping them to release them into oblivion. This had happened some time ago. She still had no idea how quickly time moved within the virtual environment of the Hell. For her, it had been over thirteen hundred days; nearly three years in Pavulean terms, back in the Real.

With every death she took on a little more pain; the lantern-headed uber-demon had not lied. An aching tooth here, a stabbing feeling in her gut there, a persistent headache, what felt like a trapped nerve in one hip, a twinge every time she clenched her talons, a cramp when she flexed her wings in a certain way . . . a thousand almost infinitesimal little pangs and stings and sprains and strains and ulcers and chafings, either adding incrementally to some established hurt or starting a fresh site. She had long since stopped assuming that there were no bits of her great dark body left to experience pain; there always were. She remembered being the old Superior, near the end of her life in the Refuge; filled with aches and pains. At least there, death was always on its way, a release from suffering.

No single ache dominated, and even when taken together the sum of them was not utterly debilitating, but they all nagged, all had their effect, filling her days with the grumbling torment of continual, grinding misery; all the worse, on those days when she was feeling sorry for herself, for being self-inflicted.

Still she beat on though, still she flew across the calamitous geographies of Hell; watching, witnessing, and worshipped. She didn't wonder that she had become part of this constructed world's emergent mythology. Had she still been a lost soul wandering these reeking morasses, denuded, fire-blacked forests, crater-pitted concrete aprons and blasted, cinder-strewn hillsides, so traumatised she had started to believe there never had been a Real in which she'd lived . . . she too might have worshipped something like herself, praying to the half-fabled, occasionally glimpsed angel of death for a release from her torments.

She had toured the Hell to its limits, many tens of days flight away, and, beating upright by those iron walls, talons scrabbling at their vast, unyielding extent, accepted that this was indeed not an infinite space. It had its boundaries, distant though they may be.

She established a sort of mental map of the place. Here were the scorched plains, the poisoned marshes, the arid badlands, the steaming swamps, the bleached salt pans, the alkali lakes, acid ponds, bubbling mud craters and sintered lava flows amongst all the other bewilderingly varied wastelands of the place; here were the tremendous peaks of iron-frozen mountains, their glaciers red with blood, here the encircling sea of Hell, which lapped at the foot of the boundary wall and teemed with voracious monsters.

Here were the great valved doors that admitted the newly condemned; here were the roads the towering juggernauts of dead and dying trundled down, delivering their grisly cargoes to the vast prisons, camps, factories and barracks of the place; here the damned were set to their slave labour within the munitions factories or condemned to wander the ruins and the wilderness, or were chosen to fight in the everlasting war that consumed, recycled and re-consumed lives by the thousands and tens of thousands each and every day by, both sides.

Because there were two sides to Hell, though you'd have struggled to spot the slightest difference if you'd simply found yourself set down in the midst of either. The unfortunates delivered into Hell were allocated sides before they even entered the place, generally half going to one and half to the other.

There were two sets of the great valved doors – only admitting, impossible to exit through – two vast sets of boulevards paved with wracked backs and splintered bones, two whole sets and systems of prisons and factories and camps and barracks, two hierarchies of demons and – she'd been surprised to find – two of the colossal king-demons. They fought over the centre ground of Hell, throwing forces into the fray with a sort of manic relish, uncaring how many fell because they would always be resurrected again within days for fresh punishment.

In the rare event that one side established military superiority over the other, through simple luck or an accident of good leadership – threatening the balance of territory and forces and so the continuance of the war – extra recruits would be funnelled to the temporarily losing side by the simple expedient of shutting down one of the sets of gates, channelling all the new arrivals to the disadvantaged side, gradually restoring balance through sheer weight of numbers.

She thought of the gates she and Prin had entered through as the Eastern gate, for no particularly good reason. So they had been on the East side, but basically every aspect of the East side in this vast dispute was replicated in the West as well, and the two appeared identical in their gruesomeness. From a distance, anyway. She was not welcome in the West; smaller winged demons came up to mob her when she overflew too far beyond the front of the everlasting war, so she had to keep away entirely, or fly so high that the detail of what went on was denied her.

Still, she had flown to see the opposing Western gates, soared above the scattered dark clouds of the Western hinterland and even landed on occasion – usually only for a few minutes at a time – on certain jagged, frozen peaks, well away from the most intense fighting and the greatest numbers of enemy demons.

Whether in the West or the East, she looked down from such high crags, wrapped from the cold in her own gale-fluttering wings, and watched the scudding shreds of bruise-coloured clouds move over the distant landscapes of terror and pain with a sort of horrified amusement.

When she had killed the thousandth soul, she had taken the half-eaten body and dropped it at the feet of the great lantern-headed demon sitting in his red-glowing iron throne looking out over the vast reeking valley of smokes and fumes and screams.

"What?" the colossal creature boomed. With one enormous foot it kicked aside the husk of body she'd deposited in front of it.

"A thousand souls," she told it, treading the air with deep, easy sweeps of air, keeping herself level with its face but too far away for it to swipe at her easily. "A thousand days since you told me that once I'd released ten times one hundred souls you'd tell me what happened to my love, the male I first came here with: Prin."

"I said I'd think about it," the great voice thundered.

She stayed where she was, the black, leathery wings fanning some of the valley's noxious fumes towards the uber-demon's face. She gazed into the gaseous impression of a face writhing and billowing behind the house-sized pane of glass, trying to ignore the four fat, dripping candles at each of the lantern's four corners, their carbuncled surfaces veined with a hundred screaming nerve clusters. The creature stared back at her. She kept station, refused to move.

"Please," she said, at last.

"Long dead," the vast voice burst out across her. She heard the words with her wings. "Time moves more slowly in here, not faster. He is barely a memory. He died by his own hand, ashamed, penurious, disgraced and alone. There is no record of whether he remembered you at the end. He escaped being sent here, more's the pity. Satisfied?"

She stayed where she was a while longer, upright in the air before it, beating her cloak wings like slow, mocking applause.

"Huh," she said at last, and turned, dropping, swooping only to zoom again, beating away up and across the valley's slope to its furthest ridge.

"How are the pains, bitchlet?" she heard the demon shout after her. "Do they grow?" She ignored it.

She waited until they came back out of the mill: the three demons and the one sad, screaming soul who had not been released after his tour of Hell. The demons held the howling, frantically struggling male between them; one holding both front feet, one each at the rear legs. They laughed and talked, taunting the screeching male as they carried him back to the beetle-shaped flier.

She stooped upon them, slaughtering the three demons easily; the two at the rear with a single pinch of one of her great talons. The unfortunate male lay quivering on the scaly ground, watching the demons' blood pool dustily in towards him from three different directions. The beetle tried to take off; she screamed at it and with a two-legged blow ripped one of its wings right off and then tipped it over onto its back. It lay making clicking, chirring noises. When the pilot crawled out she wanted to rip him apart too, but instead she let him go.

She picked the trembling male up with one talon and stared into his petrified face while he voided his bowels noisily on the ground beneath.

"When you left the Real," she said to him, "what date was it?"

"Eh?"

She repeated the question. He told her.

She asked him a couple of other questions about banal things like current affairs and civilisational status, then she let him go; he scurried away along the road leading from the mill. She might have killed him, she supposed, but she had already released one soul from its torments that day; all this had been a sudden inspiration, brought on for some reason when she'd come upon the mill.

She trashed the building too, scattering its screaming, protesting components across the valley's slope, throwing wreckage splashing into the mill race and the header pond, displacing sloshing tons of blood while the building's operators ran scampering for their lives. The blue-glowing door was not glowing at all, of course. It was just a plain, rough wooden door, now hanging off its hinges; a doorway to nowhere.

Oddly satisfied, she swept back into the grim skies with a single great clap of her wings, then beat off across the valley. She dropped the massive lump of wood that had been the door's lintel towards the fleeing figures of the mill operators as they ran away, missing them by less than a metre.

She wheeled once above the valley, just a collection of pains and sundered lives, then struck out, cloudward, rising all the time, heading for her roost.

Always assuming the hapless male had been telling the truth, the uber-demon had lied.

Barely a quarter of a year had passed in the Real.

Vatueil was hanging upside down. He wondered absently if there were any circumstances when this could be a good sign.

He appeared to be inhabiting a physical body. Hard to tell whether he'd actually been embodied in a real one or this was just a full-sensory-spectrum virtuality. He was in no pain, but the blood roared in his ears due to the gravitational inversion and he felt distinctly disoriented, beyond the obvious fact that he was the wrong way up.

He opened his eyes to see a creature like a giant flying something-or-other staring straight back at him. It was also hanging upside down, though unlike him it appeared to be entirely happy with the situation. It was human-size, had a long, intelligent-looking face with large bright yellow eyes. Its body was covered in soft folds of golden-grey fur. It had four long limbs with what looked like thick membranes of the same soft fur linking the limbs on each side of its body to each other.

It opened its mouth. It had a lot of very small very sharp teeth. "You are . . . Vatch-oy?" it said in a thick accent.

"Vatueil," he corrected it. Looking away from the creature, he seemed to be hanging in the blue-green foliage of a great, tall tree. Further away, he could glimpse the trunks of other tall trees. The tree he was in was nothing like the size of the impossible tree, where he had spent many a happy holiday, winged and flying, but it was still too big for him to be able to see the ground. The branches and trunks he could see looked substantial. His feet, he noticed, were tied together with what looked like rope, while another length of rope ran through the noose his feet were in and then right round the metre-broad branch he was hanging from.

"Vatoy," the creature said.

"Close enough," he conceded. He felt he ought to know what this creature was, what species it was part of, but he had no internal access to any remote networks here; he was effectively just human, just meat, hanging here. All he had to rely on was his own all-too-fallible memories, such as they'd survived all the transcriptions they'd had to undergo over the years and regenerations, plus whatever unexpected intervention had led to him being here. His memories were anyway suspect, jumbled by a hundred different reincarnations in as many different environments, the vast majority virtual, unreal, militarily metaphorical.

"Lagoarn-na," the creature beside him said, thumping itself on the chest.

"Yeah, hello," Vatueil said cautiously. "Pleased to meet you."

"Pleased meet you too," Lagoarn-na said, nodding, its big yellow eyes staring at him, unblinking.

Vatueil felt a little groggy. He tried to remember where he'd been last. Where this version of himself had been last, anyway. A fellow could lose track when he was copied and re-copied so often. He started to recall sitting round a table with a bunch of aliens, in . . . had it been a ship? A meeting. In a ship. Not fighting a war then, trapped in tunnels or trenches or the guts of a land ship or a sea ship or a gas-giant dirigible the shape of a gigantic bomb, or finding himself downloaded into a smart battle tank or some sort of cross between a microship and a missile, or . . . his memories flickered past him, detailing what certainly felt like every single time he'd played a part in the vast war he'd been a part of, the war over the Hells.

It made a pleasant change for his last deployment not to have involved nuts-and-bolts, blood-and-guts soldiering – a meeting was a benign environment; potentially just as tremendously boring as war, but without the slivers of utter terror stuck in there as well. On the other hand, he felt he had just been . . . read somehow. All those deployments, mostly indicating gradually increasing seniority of rank and importance and responsibility, all flickering past in his memory – *all* tumbling past, like a pack of nearly a hundred cards – that had felt like something triggered, something called up.

Meeting. The meeting. The meeting in the ship. Lots of little aliens; one other pan-human. Big guy. Or at least important guy. He should know the name of that species too, but he couldn't remember it.

He'd been far away for that meeting. In some rarely travelled bit of the sim . . . no, he'd been in the Real. In the Real again; how about that? He'd been given a re-useable, download-ready body and he'd been physically present at that meeting with the cute little aliens with the big eyes and the single larger pan-human with the hunched look and the attitude.

Still couldn't remember the species the guy belonged to. Maybe he'd have better luck with his name. Vister? Peppra? It had been something like that. Important. Top brass in his civilian field. A big wheel. Paprus? Shepris?

He remembered not being bored at the meeting. It really had been important. In fact, he remembered feeling nervous, excited, energised, feeling that something genuinely momentous was being agreed here, and he was a part of it.

He'd been beamed into that body, transcripted into it. He might have been transcripted back out again, sent back to where he'd come from, his meeting-attending duties over. He probably had.

He looked at the big creature hanging beside him, gazing into its staring yellow eyes. “How did I come to be here?” he asked. “How did you . . . get me?”

“Guff-Fuff-Kuff-Fuff not so smart.”

He stared at the creature. He closed his eyes, shook his head. “No, sorry; didn’t get the first part of that at all.”

“GFCF not so smart,” the creature said.

Shaking his head seemed to have helped. Now he could see that the creature had straps and pouches distributed across his golden-grey furred body. Some sort of head-set – thin, metallic, glittering like jewellery – wound round the back of its skull, little armatures seeming to clasp near but not in its ears and eyes and nose and mouth.

“The GFCF?” Vatueil said. A feeling that was equal parts dread and sadness seemed to settle over him. He struggled not to show it.

“Protocols in messagery,” Lagoarn-na told him. “Gifts of knowledge, from high to low, not always maximally one-way. That which is given may give back, in time, where time is potentially quite long time. Still less so in cases of knowledge gained by chicanery, thefting. And so, resultingly, to this, and here. Plainly? Plainly: ancient code, buried; consequencing trapdoors therefore. Their ignorance thereof.”

The GFCF. And the NR. The Nauptre Reliquaria. That was the name of the species Lagoarn-na belonged to. The Nauptre, anyway. The Reliquaria bit usually referred to the machines that had taken over from them while the Nauptre themselves, the biological part of the super-species, prepared – everyone assumed – for Sublimation. That’s what had thrown him: the NR always presented as machines. You never saw the original bio species except in historical, contextual stuff.

They must have intercepted him. He’d been taken in some handover the GFCF had made of his personality construct, his mind-state, while attempting to transmit his updated, downloaded soul back to the war sim.

He wondered how bad this was, because it could be very bad. If he hadn’t made it back at all, at least people would know there had been a problem. He might only have been copied, though; maybe an identical copy had got back, and nobody had any suspicions.

He tried to recall what the latest tech implied; could comms be made completely proof against interception? It kept changing. One time they told you it was impossible to read a signal without it being obvious to whoever it had been sent to, another time they seemed to have changed their minds, and it was possible again; even easy. Trivial, frankly.

Then it would go back to being impossible, for a while.

Whatever; he was here when he shouldn't be, and the NR – or just the N, just the bio Nauptre, though he doubted that – could intercept GFCF comms, because some of the code the GFCF used in their comms protocols had been given by the Nauptre – or stolen from them by the GFCF – and it had come with holes in it, ways the NR or the Nauptre could listen in when they wanted to.

Not as smart as they thought they were.

Guff-Fuff-fucking-Kuff-Fuff.

Shit.

He wondered why they were bothering to embody him, either in the Real or in a decent sim. But then even when you had all the information, sometimes it could be difficult to find the bit you really wanted. Embodying helped. Especially when you looked upon what you had downloaded as some sort of strange alien.

That was what he was to them. An alien. An alien they had refashioned from comms-code-information into something at least resembling what resulted from genetic information; a creature of flesh and blood. Him. And now they would want the truth.

"Meeting," Lagoarn-na said, with what might have been a smile. "GFCF. Pan-hu-man Vipperz. Scheme. War in afterlife. Tsung Disk? Tsung Disk." The creature nodded.

Shit; it already knew too much of it. Had he told them that already, inadvertently? What more would they ask? He couldn't see any obvious torture instruments about the creature's webbing and pouches, but who knew?

Please not torture. Why did so much of everything have to come down to pain? We are creatures of pain, creatures of suffering. He had been through this, done this. Not more, please not more.

"You not to worry," the creature told him. It gestured encompassingly. "Is one of trillions scarnations," it told him. "Quantum stuff. In one you bound to tell trute. Maybes this one."

The creature tipped its head to one side and Vatueil felt a feeling of utter relief and almost boundless pleasure wash through him. He knew he was being manipulated, but he didn't care.

Lagoarn-na didn't want to hurt him, had no intention of hurting him. The Nauptre had every right to the information he had. All they wanted was the truth.

The truth. All so simple. Just stick to the truth and it made life so much simpler. Just the one set of facts or assertions to remember. The force of this simple truth – the truth about truth! – hit him like a cannon shell.

He really was experiencing bliss. This was only just short of sexual.

"What do you want to know?" he heard himself say, dreamily.

"Relate meeting," Lagoarn-na said, and crossed its long, fur-membraned arms across its chest, its wide unblinking yellow eyes seeming to stare into his soul.

"All right," he heard himself say. He marvelled at how relaxed and unconcerned he sounded. "First let me introduce myself. My name is Vatueil; Gyorni Vatueil, my most recent rank – that I recall – being that of Space Marshal . . ."

He had never enjoyed relating anything more. Lagoarn-na proved to be a very good listener.

Twenty-four

Administrator-Captain Quar-Quoachali, commander of the GFCF Minor Destructor Vessel *Fractious Person*, took the priority call from Legislator-Admiral Bettlescroy-Bisspe-Blispin III in his cabin, as ordered. The Legislator-Admiral was shown sitting at his private desk, a roller keyboard displayed on the surface in front of him. As Quar watched, Bettlescroy snicked a couple of keys into place, then folded his elegant hands under his chin, elbows on desk, leaving the keyboard's Commit key winking.

He looked up at Quar, smiled.

"Sir!" Quar sat as upright in his seat as he could.

"Quar, good day."

"Thank you, sir! To what do I owe the honour?"

"Quar, we have never really got on, have we?"

"No, sir! My apologies for that, sir. I have always hoped—"

"Accepted. Anyway, I thought that we might enter into a new

phase in our professional relationship, and to that end I believe I need to divulge to you something of our plans regarding the Culture ship *Hylozoist*."

"Sir, this is an honour, sir!"

"I'm sure. The thing is, the *Hylozoist* has just been informed that there are unauthorised ships being constructed in the fabricaria of the Disk."

"I had no idea, sir!"

"I know you didn't, Quar. That was deliberate."

"Sir?"

"It doesn't matter. I'll be blunt, Quar. We need to take action against the Culture ship; disable it at the very least, if not actually destroy it."

"Sir? You mean, attack it?"

"As ever, your perspicacity and tactical awareness astonishes me, Quar. Yes, I mean attack it."

"A . . . *Culture* ship, sir? Are we *sure*?"

"We are perfectly sure, Quar."

Quar swallowed, gulped. "Sir," he said, sitting even more upright in his seat, "I and the other officers aboard the *Fractious Person* are at your disposal, sir; however I understood the Culture ship was most lately returned to the vicinity of the Disk Initial Contact Facility."

"It still is, Quar; we have succeeded in detaining it there with administrational drivel until now, but it is about to depart again, and it is as it departs that we intend to attack it."

"Sir! As I say, sir, I and the other officers aboard the *Fractious Person* are at your disposal. However, we are – as I'm sure sir is aware – stationed with our sister ship the *Rubric Of Ruin*, on the far side of the Disk from the Facility. It will take—"

"Of course I'm aware of that, Quar. Unlike you I am not a complete idiot. And I might inform you there is another of our ships in your vicinity, standing some distance off, just beyond your scanner range."

"There is, sir?"

"There is, Quar."

"But I thought I was aware of our full fleet disposition, sir."

"I know. But there are two GFCF fleets here, Quar, and the ship near you that you didn't know about is part of the hidden one, our war fleet."

"Our war fleet," Quar repeated.

"Our war fleet. And when we attack the Culture ship we need to make it look as though somebody *else* attacked it, not us, and one of the best ways of making that appear plausible is to have one of our own ships attacked – indeed, preferably completely destroyed – at the same time. You see, war means sacrifice, sometimes, Quar; that's just the way it is, I'm afraid. We need to destroy one of our own ships."

"We do, sir?"

"We do, Quar."

"The . . . the *Rubric Of Ruin*, sir?"

"No, not the *Rubric Of Ruin*, Quar. But close."

"Sir?"

"Goodbye, Quar; this pleases me much more than it will hurt you." Legislator-Admiral Bettlescroy-Bisspe-Blispin III unclasped his hands and brought one dainty, exquisitely manicured finger down onto the winking Commit key.

Administrator-Captain Quar-Quoachali was very briefly aware of an extremely bright light shining from all around him, and a sensation of great warmth.

The broad, sleek aircraft dived, side-slipped one way then the other before roaring over a broad, shallow river, making animals on the river bank and fish in the shallows between the gravel beds all scatter. The flier settled into a ground-hugging, low-altitude cruise, only metres above the tops of the trees on the trackway, which stretched all the ninety kilometres from here, the borders of the Espersium estate, to the great torus-shaped mansion house at its centre.

The trackway cast a long, thick shadow over the rolling pasture land to one side and the treetops were lit by a ruddy sun rising through layers of misty cloud above the horizon.

Veppers sat in one of the hunting seats in the back of the craft, looking out through the invisible barrier at the late autumn sunrise. Some high towers in Ubruater were reflecting the first direct light of the day, winking pinkly.

He looked at the laser rifle, which was lying, switched on but still stowed in front of him. He was alone in the shooting gallery; he didn't want anybody else around him right now. Even Jasken was inside with the rest of the entourage, in the main passenger compartment. Some large bird was startled out of the canopy beneath in a chaos of twigs and feathers and Veppers went to grasp the laser rifle on its stand, then just let his hand drop again as the bird flapped frantically away.

It was a bad sign, he knew, when he lost his appetite for hunting. Well, shooting. You could hardly dignify it with the term hunting. It was an affectation, he felt now. Using a low-flying aircraft to throw up birds to shoot at. Still, it had been a useful affectation. He'd needed this excuse. He'd needed the trackways to be there. He felt heavy as the flier zoomed to follow the slope of a hill.

All about to end, now. Still, he'd always known it might have to end, one day.

He watched the landscape unwind behind the aircraft; and felt it, too, experiencing something close to weightlessness as the flier crested the hill and then followed the down-slope. Then he was heavy again, as they levelled out. The hill had hidden any sight of Ubruater, and the sunrise had been removed by a ridge to the east.

Veppers felt tired, unsettled. Maybe he just needed a fuck. He remembered Sapultride's girl, Crederre, straddling him, bucking enthusiastically up and down, in this very seat, only – what, ten or eleven days earlier? Pleur, maybe? Or one of the other girls? Or just get a couple of them to fuck each other, in front of him. That could be oddly calming.

But he felt somehow impatient with the whole idea of sex right now. That was a bad sign too.

Maybe just a massage; he could call Herrit through, get him to pummel and smooth his tensions and worries away. Except he knew that wouldn't work either. He thought about consulting

Scefron, his Substance Use Mediator. No, not drugs either. Holy fuck, he really was out of sorts today. Was there nothing?

Nothing except all this being over, he guessed. This was nerves. He was the richest, most powerful man in the entire fucking civilisation, way more monied and influential than anybody had ever been, ever, by orders of magnitude, but he was still suffering from nerves. Because what he was involved in now might make him much, much wealthier and more powerful than even he had ever been, or – just possibly – finish him, kill him, pauperise him, disgrace him.

He had always been like this before a big deal, when things were reaching a point of culmination. Been a while, though.

This was crazy. What was he doing, risking everything? You never risked everything; you risked as little as possible. You *sold the idea* of risking everything to the sort of idiot who thought that was how you got rich, but you kept your own risks to an absolute minimum. That way if you did make a mistake – and everybody made mistakes, or they weren't really trying – it didn't finish you. Let others ruin themselves – there were always rich pickings in the wreckage – but don't ever risk too much yourself.

Except now he was.

Well, he sort of had before, he supposed; the space mirror deal he'd gone into along with Grautze could have bankrupted him and the whole family if it had unravelled at the wrong time. That was why he'd had to set Grautze up, so that if it did go badly Grautze and his family would catch the blame and the shame, not he and his.

Originally he hadn't even meant for Grautze to suffer if it did go well, but then he'd realised that the same mechanisms he'd set up to protect himself if it went sour could equally easily double his payoff if all went according to plan, so that he would come out of it with all the money, all the shares, all the companies and instruments and power. It had just been too good a trick to resist. Grautze should have seen it, but he hadn't. Too trusting. Too gullible. Too blinded by loyalties he thought were shared, or at least mutual. Mug.

Poor fucker's daughter had been more properly ruthless than her father had been. Veppers stroked his nose; the tip was almost grown back now, though it was still a little thin and red-looking and tender to the touch. He could still feel the little bitch's teeth closing round it, biting. It made him shiver. He hadn't been back to the opera house since. He'd need to get back, appear fully in public again, before it became some sort of ridiculous phobia. As soon as his nose was fully healed.

The deal would complete, all would go well and he'd end up with even more than he already had. Because he was who he was. A winner. *The* fucking winner. It had always worked out in the past; it would work out this time. Okay, so the war fleet had been discovered a few days early; that wasn't such a disaster. And he'd been right still to stall. He hadn't told Bettlescroy's message boy where to attack yet. And he wouldn't; not until the ships were genuinely ready to go. And they would be ready. They were too close to completion for anybody to stop them now. The Culture mission in the Disk was being dealt with and apparently even the incoming Culture warship could be taken on and neutralised. He just hoped the GFCF knew what the fuck they were doing. But then they probably felt the same way about him.

So don't worry, don't panic and just keep your fucking head. Get everything ready at this end and have the courage to see it through to the end, no matter what the cost. Cost didn't matter if you could afford it and the reward was going to be inestimably greater.

He reached up, switched the laser rifle off and sat back. No, he didn't want to hunt, or fuck, or get stoned or anything else.

Really, he supposed, he just wanted to be back at the house. Well, he could do something about that.

He clicked a seat control.

"Sir?" the pilot said.

"Never mind terrain-hugging," he told her. "Just get us there as fast as you can."

"Sir."

The aircraft started to rise immediately, pulling up from the trackway beneath. He felt heavy again for a moment, but then the ride started to smooth out.

The flash came first. He saw it light up the landscape underneath the aircraft, and wondered momentarily if some coincidence of a gap in the clouds and a gap in the ridge to the east was letting a single strong beam of sunlight through to shine so brightly on the trees and low hills beneath. The light seemed to blink, then get brighter and brighter, all in less than a second.

"Radiation aler—" a synthesised voice started to say.

Radiation? What was—?

The aircraft bucked like a dinghy thrown by a tsunami. Veppers was crushed down into his seat so hard he felt and heard himself make a sort of involuntary grunting, groaning noise as the air was forced out of his compressing lungs. The view – wildly, insanely bright – started to spin like emptied buckets of fluorescent paint swirling round a plug hole. A titanic bang resounded, seeming to come from somewhere inside his head. He glimpsed clouded sky, the clouds' under-surfaces garishly lit from below, then distant, too-brightly shining hills and forests, then – just for an instant – a vast boiling cloud of fire and smoke, rising on a thick dark stem above a mass of darkness shot through with flame.

He heard what might have been screams, and tearing, cracking, buckling noises. The view through the ultraclear glass suddenly hazed all at once, as though a thin-veined white mesh had been hurled across the material. He felt weightless again and then seemed to be about to be thrown against the ceiling, or into the crazed ultraclear, but the seat seemed to hold onto him.

A roaring noise threw a deep red haze across his eyes and he blacked out.

Yime Nsokyi took her first few unaided steps. Even dressed in loose-fitting fatigues, she felt oddly naked without the supporting net of foam she'd been swaddled in for the last couple of days.

The bones in her legs felt delicate and a little achey. It hurt to take a deep breath and her spine felt oddly inflexible. Only her arms felt pretty much like normal, though the muscles were weak. She'd instructed her body to hold back on all the pain-cancelling mechanisms, to feel how bad things really were. Not too bad, was the answer. She should be able to get through without any more anti-pain secretions.

Walking at her side as she padded up and down the gently lit lounge inside the *Me, I'm Counting*, one arm extended to cup one of her elbows, was Himerance, the ship's avatar, a tall, thin creature with a very deep voice and a quite hairless head.

"You don't have to do this," she told him.

"I disagree," he said. "I feel I do. This is at least partly my responsibility. I'll do what I can to make amends."

The *Me, I'm Counting* had been the nearest ship to the *Bodhisattva* when it had been attacked by the Unfallen Bulbitian, coasting in towards the entity for the semi-regular pick-up and set-down of those going to and coming from the Forgotten GSV *Total Internal Reflection*. It had been coincidence that it, rather than one of the other ships associated with the GSV, had been allocated the role of shuttle bus this time; three other craft shared the rota. On this occasion, with nobody to drop off, the ship had been coming in only to pick up. When the distress call and Plume event had signalled there was a vessel in distress nearby, it had diverted to investigate and offer help.

"Do you still have the image of Lededje Y'breq?" Yime had asked the ship as soon as she'd been able to. The ship had replaced the pebble-smooth drone with Himerance, a humanoid avatar it had been storing, unused, for over a decade. She'd half expected dust to float from Himerance's head when he'd nodded.

"Yes," he'd told her. "In image form only."

"May I see it?"

The avatar had frowned. "I did promise not to share her full image with anybody else without her express permission," he'd told her. "I'd prefer to keep to that promise unless there is some circumstance that is so . . . operationally urgent I felt compelled to break it. Do you especially need to see it? There are plenty of high-quality images of Ms. Y'breq available from Sichultian media and other easily accessible sources. Would you like to see some of them?"

She'd smiled. "No need. I've seen them. I was just curious. I appreciate that you want to keep your word."

"Why are you interested in her?" the ship had asked.

Yime had stared at it. But of course, it would have known nothing of what had happened to Lededje. Servant – acolyte – to a dedicatedly hermit-like GSV, one of the Forgotten, naturally it would be out of any loop that would include detailed knowledge of events in Sichult.

"The *Bodhisattva* hasn't briefed you?"

"Immediately after I rescued it, it asked me to make all speed towards the Sichultian Enablement, which I am doing, though with reservations given the situation that appears to be developing there. The *Bodhisattva* then said that you might provide the reason for all this alacrity." The avatar had smiled. "I seem to have such a reputation for eccentricity the ship thinks I am more likely to accede to a request from a human than I am to one emanating from a fellow ship. I have no idea why."

She'd explained that Lededje had been murdered by Joiler Veppers and then revented aboard the *Sense Amid Madness, Wit Amidst Folly* before being spirited away by the Abominator-class ship *Falling Outside The Normal Moral Constraints*. It was assumed she was making her way back to Sichult, quite possibly with thoughts of revenge and murder.

"It was you who put the lace inside her, wasn't it?" Yime had asked. Himerance had been looking bemused.

"Yes," the avatar had said. "Yes, that was me." He'd shrugged. "She said to surprise her, and I couldn't think of anything else that would materially improve her life that was within my gift. I had no idea it would lead to events of such moment. I assume Mr. Veppers still holds the position of great power he did before."

"Even greater power." She'd explained about the Tsungarial Disk and the coming culmination of the confliction over the Hells.

Now, stricken with a feeling of responsibility for all this, the *Me, I'm Counting* had decided to complete the mission Yime and the *Bodhisattva* had undertaken. It would take her wherever she wanted to go in pursuit of Lededje Y'breq. The Mind of the *Bodhisattva* would come too, as a part of the *Me, I'm Counting*. Rather than waste time trying to rendezvous with another ship the two Minds had determined to salvage all they could from the wreck of the *Bodhisattva* and junk the rest. The boxy ship-drone from the *Bodhisattva* floated by Yime's other elbow, ready to help if she wobbled in its direction.

"In the circumstances, and at the moment," the drone said, "it is anyway preferable to be contemplating an incursion into the Sichultian Enablement within a warship rather than a humble General Contact Unit." It came forward a little and dipped, as though peeking round Yime to the humanoid avatar. "Our friend here will have the undying gratitude of the Quietus Section for its action."

"Don't exalt me overmuch," the avatar rumbled. "I am still a warship after a fashion, but an old and avowedly eccentric one. Compared to the *thing* Ms. Y'breq seemingly finds herself on, I am small beer indeed."

"Ah, yes, the picket ship," Yime said. "It must be nearly there by now."

"Very nearly," Himerance told her. "Hours out from Enablement space, and the Tsungarial Disk, if that's where it's headed."

"Just in time for the smatter outbreak," the ship's drone said. "That is almost too convenient. I do hope we had nothing to do with that."

"'We' being the Culture, Restoria, or SC?" Yime asked, wobbling a little as she reached the limit of the lounge area and turned. Avatar and drone both helped steady her.

"Good question," the drone said. It seemed content to judge the question without hazarding an answer.

"And what about the Bulbitian?" she asked.

The drone said nothing. After a moment, the avatar said, "A Fast Picket, the *No One Knows What The Dead Think*, paid a call on the Bulbitian some eight hours ago, respectfully asking for an explanation for what happened to the *Bodhisattva* and yourself. The Bulbitian denied all knowledge not only of any attack on you, but also of your visit. Worryingly, it also denies that there ever was a Culture Restoria or Numina mission aboard it. In fact it claims to have been completely without any alien visitors for as long as it can remember.

"The Fast Picket begged to differ and requested leave to contact the Culture personnel it knew had been on the Bulbitian as recently as a couple of days earlier. When that was refused it asked to be allowed to send a representative aboard to check. That too was rejected. No signals had emanated from the Bulbitian since very shortly after the attack on the *Bodhisattva* and no signals from the Fast Picket elicited any response at all."

They're all going to be dead; Yime thought. *I know it. I brought death to them.*

"The *No One Knows What The Dead Think* then departed the Bulbitian's atmospheric envelope," Himerance continued, "but left behind a small high-stealth drone-ship which attempted to access the Bulbitian directly without permission, using smaller drones, knife and scout missiles, eDust and so on. All were destroyed. An attempt by the Fast Picket to Displace sensory apparatus directly into the Bulbitian met with no more success and resulted in an attack on the Fast Picket by the Bulbitian.

"Forewarned, and – having been a warship, the GOU *Obliterating Angel*, in its earlier incarnation – more martially capable than the *Bodhisattva*, the Fast Picket was undamaged by the Bulbitian's attack and retired to a safe distance to keep watch on the entity and await the arrival of the Equator-class GSV *Pelagian*, which is five days away. A Continent class with SC links is also strongly believed to be en route, though it's keeping its arrival time quiet.

"Other species/civs who had personnel aboard the Bulbitian also report no contact or sign of their people and, like us, suspect that the entity has killed them."

Yime stopped, looked at Himerance, then at the skeletal assembly of components which was the *Bodhisattva*'s drone, and

– with the vessel's Mind – one of the few bits of the ship it had been worthwhile salvaging from the near-total wreck. "So they're all dead?" she asked, her voice hollow. She thought of the elegantly elderly Ms. Fal Dvelner and the terribly earnest, multiply-reincarnated Mr. Nopri.

"Very likely," the drone told her. "I'm sorry."

"Was that us?" Yime asked, starting to walk again, going hesitantly forward. "Did we cause that?" She stopped. "Did *I* cause that?" She shook her head. "There was something," she said, "some issue, some . . . I antagonised it somehow. Something I said or did . . ." She knocked one set of knuckles on her temple, gently. "What the hell was it?"

"Possibly we bear some collective technical responsibility," the drone said. "Though frankly, triggering an act of homicidal instability in a Bulbitian is hardly proof by itself of any culpability. Still, we are certainly attracting the blame from those already-mentioned other species and civs who had people on the Bulbitian. That the entity itself is entirely to blame for an unprovoked attack and that we were its first victims – and, very nearly, its first fatalities – seems to matter little compared to the ease with which we may be blamed."

"Oh, grief," Yime said, sighing. "There's going to be an Inquiry, isn't there?"

"Many, probably," the drone said, sounding resigned.

"Before we start thinking ahead to the aftermath," Himerance said, after clearing his throat, "we might do well to contemplate our immediate course."

"Ms. Y'breq is still our focus," the *Bodhisattva*'s drone said. "The point may rapidly be approaching when the input or decisions of one person stops making much difference, but for the moment we might hope to influence events through her, if we can find her."

"And of course," Himerance said, "Mr. Veppers' inputs and decisions almost certainly *do* matter, considerably."

"So do Ms. Y'breq's," Yime said, turning at the far end of the lounge to head back the way she had come. There was no unsteadiness this time. "If she gets near him with a clear shot, or whatever."

"The latest we have from Sichult places Veppers in a place called Iobe Cavern City, on the planet Vebezua, in the Chunzunzan Whirl," the drone said.

"There, then," Himerance said, then hesitated. An expression of surprise crossed his face. "The Culture Restoria mission dealing with the smatter outbreak just discovered more ships being built within the Tsungarial Disk," he said.

"How many more?" Yime asked.

It was the *Bodhisattva*'s drone which answered. "One in every fabricaria they've looked in so far," it told her.

Yime stopped. "How many have they looked in?" she asked, looking from the drone to the avatar.

"About seventy, so far," Himerance said.

"As highly spread as they could manage, too," the drone said. "Good representative sample."

"Doesn't that mean—?" Yime began.

"Could be all of them are making ships," the drone said.

"*All* of them?" Yime felt her eyes widening.

"Certainly a very high proportion of the three hundred million fabricaria," the drone said.

"In the name of grief," Yime cried, "what do you do with three hundred million *ships*?"

"You could certainly start a war," the drone said.

"With that many ships," Himerance said, "you might end it, too."

"Nevertheless," the drone said, "we had best get there."

"Time to hit sprint," Himerance said. Then he nodded at the wall screen at the far end of the lounge as it lit up, showing the battered-looking remains of the *Bodhisattva* floating within the *Me, I'm Counting*'s field envelope. The crippled, wrecked ship didn't look that badly damaged, from where they were looking. A little scratched, grazed, crumpled and dented, perhaps. The most serious damage was internal. "Last drone team's ready to clear," Himerance announced. "Suggest we forget about that anterior remote stressor."

"Agreed," said the drone. The little machine hung very still and steady in the air, giving every impression of staring at the wreck of its ship on the screen.

"Well, I think you should give the command," Himerance said.

"Of course," the little drone said.

The hazily shining wall of the field enclosure approached the stricken ship, moved smoothly over it and left it outside, exposed to the distant stars. The view switched to beyond the field enclosure, to where the lifeless body of the *Bodhisattva* floated naked, without any fields or shields about it at all. It was drawing slowly away, falling behind.

"Oh well," the drone said.

The *Bodhisattva* convulsed, almost as though shaking itself awake after a long asleep, then started to come slowly apart as though it was an exploded diagram made real. A spherical mirror field appeared all about it for an instant, then, when it dropped, the ship was ablaze, light flaring from every part of it, burning brighter and brighter as they watched; flameless, orderly, still non-explosive but searing in its intensity, the pure fires raged until gradually they started to fade and go out, and when they had entirely gone, there was nothing left of the ship at all, save light-slow radiation, flowing out in every direction towards the distant suns.

"There," the *Bodhisattva*'s drone said, turning to Yime and the avatar. "Full speed ahead, I think."

Himerance nodded. The stars on the screen started to drift away. "Fields at naked-hull minimum," he said. "Going to a velocity which will be traction-injurious within about forty hours."

"When do we get there?" Yime asked.

"Eighteen hours," Himerance said. The avatar stared at the screen. The view had swung to dead ahead. "I'd better check my Manual files, see if I remember how to work as a functioning warship. Probably all sorts of stuff I need to do. Prepping shields, calibrating Effectors, manufacturing warheads; that sort of thing."

"Anything I can—?" Yime began to say, then realised how

absurd this would sound to a ship. "Sorry. Never mind," she said, flapping one hand, which hurt a little.

The avatar just smiled at her.

He woke to a sort of busy quietness. There was a ringing noise somewhere, and some distinctly annoying beeping, and something else he couldn't immediately identify, but it all felt terribly muffled, like it was happening somewhere down the other end of a very long tunnel and he really needn't be concerned about it. He kept his eyes open and looked around, but nothing made sense. He closed his eyes again. Then thought that was probably a bad idea. Something bad had happened and it might not have stopped happening yet; he needed to keep alert, keep his eyes open, keep focused.

He felt heavy in a strange way, as though his weight was being taken by his head and neck and shoulders. He turned his head to one side, then the other.

Fuck; he knew where he was. He was in the back of the flier. All this dark, tipped chaos around him was the remains of the aircraft. What the fuck had happened?

He was lying in the seat he'd been in when whatever had happened . . . had happened. He wanted to shake his head to clear it but wasn't sure that was a good idea. He brought one hand up to his face, wiping. Sticky. He looked at his hand. That was blood. He was breathing heavily.

His feet were up in the air, pointing towards the sky, which he could see through the contorted remains of the flier's rear deck. Where the ultraclear glass should be, there appeared to be nothing. Stuff was falling out of the cloud-dark sky and landing on him, landing all about him. Black and grey. Soot and ash.

He remembered the fireball he'd glimpsed.

Had that been a nuke?

Had some fucker tried to nuke him?

Had some motherfucker tried to nuke him in his own plane on his own fucking *estate*?

"Mother*fucker*," he said, his voice sounding heavy and slurred and far away.

He didn't seem to be badly injured; nothing broken. He glanced behind him – that did hurt, as though he'd been bruised – then pushed himself back down the seat, head first, grabbing onto the support for the laser rifle – still on, little tell-tale lights blinking – to stop himself from falling backwards against the bulkhead, which was now tipped so that it was nearer to being a floor than a wall.

He got himself standing upright and stood there swaying, brushing the dirt and bits of glass and smears of blood off his clothes. What a state. He looked at the soot and ash still falling down around him through the space where the ultraclear had been. He'd have to climb if he was going to get out that way. He brushed some of the ash and soot out of his hair. Fucking radioactive shit, he'd bet. When he found who'd been responsible he'd have them fucking skinned alive while he hosed them with saline solution. He wondered who to suspect. Had there been anybody meant to come on this flight who'd called off at the last moment? He couldn't think of anybody. All present. His whole entourage, all his people.

He looked along to the door into the rest of the flier, then reached up and struggled to detach the laser rifle from its stand, eventually giving up.

Felt like the flier was nose down into the ground. That meant the pilots were probably dead. He wondered how many of those in the main passenger compartment were still alive, if any.

He pulled at the door – more of a trap-door, now – but it wouldn't open. He had to get down on his knees and use both hands to pull it open, cutting one of his fingers on a bit of torn metal as he did so. He sucked the blooded finger, licked it. *Like a fucking animal*, he thought. *Like a fucking animal.* Skinning alive would be too good for whoever had done this. He'd want to think of something worse. There were probably experts you could consult.

He lowered himself into the darkness beneath the protesting, creaking door.

*

"What's happening to my *eyes*?" It came out as a cry, like a yelp, not the calm question she'd intended. Her eyes were getting sore, feeling pressured.

"Suit's getting ready to foam inside your visor," the ship told her crisply. "Gas pressure first, so the foam won't come as a shock. Don't want detached retinas, do you?"

"As ever, thanks for the warning."

"As ever, apologies. Not big on warnings. Grief; it's so *complicated* keeping you humans undamaged."

"What's happening now?"

"The suit will be using its neural inductor to set up screening images straight into your brain. You may get double vision while your eyes are still working and it's calibrating."

"I meant outside, with the other ship."

"It's mulling over my last communication, which was basically, Stop following me or I'll treat you as hostile. Reconfigured a touch to a more defensive posture. I gave it half a minute to make its mind up. Probably too generous. It's one of my failings."

"Uh-huh."

Lededje watched the eight-limbed snowflake shape, unsure now whether she was seeing it with her eyes projected inside the suit's helmet, or somehow purely with her visual centre, lensed in there directly by the suit. The image shimmered again.

"What—?"

"See?" the ship said. "Too long. Didn't even take the full half-minute."

"What did it do?"

"Fucker tried putting a shot across my bows, is what it did. Told me to heave to and prepare for boarding, in what you might call classical terms. Says it suspects me of being part of some swarm outbreak, which is amusing, if deeply implausible. Marks for originality." The ship sounded amused. "Also, hitting me with a comms enclosure, cutting me off from outside contact. That's not neighbourly at all. Plus means it's either *very* big and capable or it's not working alone, and there are at least another three ships in the vicinity. I could find them, plus I could just punch through it, but both would mean I'd have to drop the li'l-old-me Torturer disguise." The ship made a sighing noise. "Going to have to foam you up, lass. Close your eyes."

She closed her eyes, felt the pressure and temperature on her eyelids change subtly. She tried, tentatively, to open her eyes again, but they felt glued shut. Disorientingly, the view she had of space around the ship didn't seem to change at all.

"I—" she began.

"Now your mouth."

"*What?*"

"Your mouth."

"How can I talk to you if I close my mouth?"

"You're not closing it, initially; you're opening it so another sort of foam can get in there; coats your throat in carbon fibre to stop it closing up under high acceleration, *then* you close it, the buttress foam fills your mouth and another load of foam does something similar with your nose; you can still breathe normally but you're right, you can't talk. You just have to think the words; sub-vocalising with your throat should help. Mouth open, please."

"I am not happy with this. This is all very . . . invasive. You can understand that with my history I'm troubled by this."

"Again, apologies. We can always not do this but then we can't manoeuvre with the alacrity we might need to keep both you and me alive. Potentially, this means death or discomfort. Death or trauma. Or I ditch you in the module and—"

"Do it!" she said, almost shouting. "I can always get counselling," she muttered.

Warm foam slid into her mouth. She felt it – or something, somewhere – numbing her mouth and throat; she didn't gag, didn't feel exactly where the foam went.

"Well done," the ship sent. "Now, bite down, Lededje. No rush. Our pursuers are giving us a countdown to compliance but there's ample time. Hmm. Finally some ident. GFCF. There's a surprise."

She bit down, into the warm foam. Something started to tickle her nose, then that sensation faded too.

~Right! the ship announced breezily, its voice inside her head.

~That's you as ready as you're ever going be. Try sending instead of saying?

~Howowow ig diss? Oh, fshuck.

~"How is this?" You're overdoing the sub-vocalising. Just do it, don't think about doing it.

~Okay, how's this?

~Perfect. See? Easy. Now we can start behaving like a proper warship!

~Oh, great.

~It'll be fine.

~What's happening?

She was watching the screen-like images change; the black snowflake had flicked to one side, then swung slowly back to centre-rear. Then it had flicked in the other direction, before swinging back again. So far she hadn't felt anything; if the ship was manoeuvring hard it was preventing any trace of the accelerations affecting her physically. It all felt perfectly smooth so far. She suspected this was a deceptive sensation.

~I'm shaking my humble-Torturer-class-pretending behind at them, the ship told her. ~Bit more energetically than an original-spec ship could, but that's still plausible; most of those old ships have upgraded significantly. Looking like I'm trying to shake them off. Spooling up burst units for a series of break-angle turns.

Lededje felt herself clenching, without being entirely aware what she was clenching. The image of the black snowflake disappeared. Then she saw it, way off to one side. It started to slide slowly back towards where it had been. It flickered, disappeared to another part of her field of view. She still couldn't feel anything. Another flick/suddenly-somewhere-else motion, then another. She was losing the black snowflake for seconds at a time between flicks.

~How we doing? she asked.

~Successfully giving the appearance of getting desperate, the ship told her. ~Really trying everything to get them off our tail, apparently. Without result, of course. Spooling bursters for a single max-to-zero draining event and preparing to execute a whip flare with main traction; means a little engine degradation but it's allowable if it might get you out of a tight spot and at the moment it looks like our best shot. Or at least it looks like it looks like our best shot. Haw, haw.

~Should I be reassured that you seem to be enjoying this so much?

~Abso-fucking-lutely. Watch this.

The black snowflake with too many limbs disappeared entirely. She cast her gaze about, trying to find it.

~Where'd the fucker go? she found herself muttering.

~It's here, the ship's voice told her. A portion of space which she was aware was almost directly behind her and yet somehow just at the periphery of her oddly lensed vision lit up with a green circle and zoomed in to show the snowflake again, much smaller and getting smaller still.

~Sorry, she sent. ~Didn't mean to distract you.

~You won't, the ship sent. ~I'm talking through the suit at the moment. All ship's own main processing power's going to manoeuvrage, tactical simming and field management. Not to mention keeping up appearances, of course. Sub-routine here. Distraction impossible. Ask whatever you want.

The green circle faded as the black snowflake started to get bigger again and slide across the visual field, still heading for centre-rear.

~That doesn't look so good.

~Got the fucker, the ship said.

~Got it? You've been firing at it?

~Ha! No. Got it identified. It's a Deepest Regrets class. Probably the *Abundance Of Onslaught*. Thought to be in this neck of the woods, if not exactly hereabouts. That's interesting all by itself. Why would that just happen to be hanging round here?

~Can you beat it? she asked. The black snowflake was still enlarging, sliding round to centre. Back to backwards, she supposed.

~Oh, yes. The ship sounded blasé. ~I most severely outgun, out-armour and can outrun the fucker. Does raise the question though: how many of its little friends has it brought? Deepest

Regretsers are pride-of-the-fleet, Ultimate Asset, not-many-of-those-to-the-handful grade craft for the GFCF. Won't be here by itself. Kind of hints at a maternally fornicating war fleet. What're these shit-kickers up to? What did they know?

~About what?

~About the smatter outbreak and this new ship-building enthusiasm some bits of the disk have discovered, the ship replied. ~Main local news recently, wouldn't you say?

~I suppose.

~Ah! Torturer-class-plausible track scanner on seemingly random search finds other ship shock, the ship announced. ~Bugger me, there's a screen of the little fuckers. They keep peeling off war-craft like this, I'm going to have a fair fight on my hands. Last thing we fucking want.

~Are we in danger?

~Mhm, marginally, I won't pretend, the ship told her. ~There's a multiplicatory implication about the presence of a serious capital ship like a Deepest Regretser, and about the way they've been able to contain even something as venerable as a Torturer class. Ancient tub, but still a serious piece of ordnance for the GFCF to go up against, in the normal course of events. Whatever the fuck is going on here, this ain't day-to-day behaviour. This sims as peaking, fulcruming stuff.

~Are those swear words I don't know about?

~Sort of. Means somebody here might be on a risking-everything approach. That would alter the rules a bit.

~In a good way?

~What do you think?

~I suspect in a bad way.

~Well done.

~What now?

~Time to stop fucking about.

~You're going to attack?

~Eh? No! You really are bloodthirsty, aren't you? No; we get you out of danger by letting slip part of the humble-Torturer-class disguise and just powering away from them until they can't see what I'm doing. Then I can set you off in the shuttle . . . actually, maybe not in the shuttle; maybe in one of my component shiplets, given the trashing potential that seems to be floating around here at the moment. You head for Sichult to have words with Mr. Veppers, I stick around here to knock some sense into the GFCF – hopefully only metaphorically – and then get stuck into the smatter outbreak, on whatever fucking scale that particular complication happens to be manifesting lately.

~Sure you can afford this "shiplet"?

~Yes, I – oh, hello; they're hailing again, saying heave-to or blah-blah-blah. Anyway.

She watched the image around her flick-swivel, then all the stars seemed to change colour, blazing blue ahead, red behind.

~Off and run— the ship started to tell her, then everything went dark.

Dark? She thought? *Dark*?

She had time to send, ~Ship? before the ship's voice said,

~Sorry about that.

The view clicked back on. This time there were lots of additions within the image: dozens of tiny, sharp green shapes with numbers floating just in front of them and with garish coloured lines trailing after them and – in different colours – pointing in front of them. Concentric circles of varying pastel shades, noded with symbols meaningless to her, seemed to target each of the tiny green shapes, which were rapidly accruing accompanying floating icons like stacks of cards; looking at one made it blossom into nested pages of information showing as text, diagrams and multidimensional moving images that made her eyes hurt. She looked away, took in the general view instead; a thousand tiny gaudy glow-flies loose in a pitch-black cathedral.

~What happened? she asked.

~Enemy action. Seems the fuckers want a shooting war, the ship told her. ~That hit would have smeared a real Torturer class. Motherfuckers. Time for me to reply in kind, sweetheart. I must prepare to smite. Sorry, but this may smart.

~What?

~Body-slap they call it. Healthy; means you're still alive and I'm still functioning. Don't worry, there's a sub-routine monitoring your nervous system; it can de-pain you if it starts to get really sore. Come on, let's get on with it! Time's-a-wasting! Just say you're ready.

~Fucking hell. All right. I'm ready. Like I—

Then her entire body seemed to be hit, as though every part of it had been slapped at the same time. It seemed to come from one side – her right – but it felt like it hit every part of her. It wasn't especially sore – it had been too distributed – but it certainly got one's attention.

~How we doing? the ship asked as another tremendous shock registered throughout Lededje's body, this time from her left.

~We are doing fine.

~That's my girl.

~I'll— she started to say.

~Now, hold on to your hat.

Another titanic slap, everywhere through her body. She seemed to drift away, then came to, feeling woozy. She gazed about at all the hundreds of pretty little symbols floating around her, haloed with pastel colours.

~Still with us?

~Think so, she sent. ~I think . . . my lungs are hurting. Is that even possible?

~No idea. Anyway; only calibrating. Shouldn't get any worse than that.

~Did they hit us?

~Hell no; that was just us getting us out from under their track scanners. They've lost us now, poor fuckers. No idea where we are.

~Oh.

~Which means what's about to happen to them will seem to come out of nowhere. Watch – as they say – this . . .

Instantly she was tipped and thrown; sucked tumbling into the view as though the whole weight of the ship had grabbed her by the eyeballs, pulled, and hurled her into the frenzied welter of impossible colours, staggering speed and infinite detail that was its riotously ungraspable sensorium. She felt assaulted, might have screamed if it hadn't felt the breath had just been smacked out of her.

Immediately – thankfully – the whole bewildering complexity of it was reduced, pared and focused, as though just for her; the view rushed in on one of the little green symbols and the concentric rings around it whizzed, flicking this way and that, symbols flickering and changing too fast to make sense of. Then two rings flashed and changed places; the one that became the innermost ring seemed to start to flash again but this time blazed; she felt her eyes trying to close up, virtual eyelids shutting. The flare faded, left tiny granules of green where there had been a complicated shape before. It had all taken less than a second.

She tried to watch the little spray of green bits spread but then the view whirled her away before throwing her back down again, straight at another tiny green shape. The rings around it snapped into a new configuration, blazed; it disappeared in a haze of green too. She was hauled away from the contemplation of what she was starting to understand represented missiles or shells or something getting wasted. Each time, there was no apparent moment of stillness; she was jerked back from one close-up only to be flung straight back down into the next one, the star-scape she was in the middle of wheeling madly with each new target.

After about the fifth or sixth zoom-flick-flare event, a dispersing cloud of even tinier green particles – so small she was amazed she could see them, and knew that with her own eyes, looking at a screen, she wouldn't have – started crawling away from some of the little jagged green shapes. They too had leading and trailing lines and were accompanied by neatly sorted banners of figures, illustrations and descriptions. The lines flickered, hazed, came steady, thickening as they turned light then dark but shining blue.

Vectors, she thought, quite suddenly, as she was hurled towards one of the larger green shapes, close enough to see that it was a ship. These were *ships* the *Falling Outside The Normal Moral Constraints* had been targeting and destroying. Not missiles. The even tinier green shapes were the missiles. The concentric haloes surrounding each target represented weapon-choice.

Haloes appeared around each of the missiles, like hundreds upon hundreds of tiny necklaces of beaded light. They flashed all at once and when the haloes disappeared there wasn't even wreckage left behind. The view pulled back a fraction, the green ship shape seemed to hesitate, frozen, as the haloes surrounding it flicked, settled, flared. She felt a sudden urge to look away, but it was only to the next target, snapped out and then back in to watch another ship freeze in the ship's targeting headlights; then another then another and another, then two at once; *that* felt like her brain was having its hemispheres ripped apart.

~Fucking hell, she heard herself say.

~You enjoying it? the ship asked. ~My favourite bit's coming up in a moment.

~What do you mean, your favourite bit? she asked it as the next hapless ship appeared, transfixed, in the concentric targeting/weapon-choice circles.

~Ha! You didn't think this is happening in real time, did you? The ship sounded amused.

~This is a *recording*? she said – nearly wailed – as the tiny green ship blazed and turned to what looked like minutely shredded, wind-blown grass-dust. Instantly the view flicked back before throwing her down again somewhere else, her view wobbling to focus on another petrified target.

~Slow-motion replay, the ship told her. ~Pay attention, Led.

This green target looked bigger and more complicated than the others. The rings around it were larger, fatter and brighter, though less numerous. The ship seemed to start to change, taking on the appearance of the black, over-limbed snowflake again. Then bits of it detached, started to float away, while each of them blossomed with rosettes of green haze. Altogether, it filled her zoomed-in field of vision, dazzling.

~At this point they still think I'm hitting them too late, the ship murmured.

A violet halo she hadn't been aware of zeroed in on the central contact. The halo flashed. When it faded the ship was still there, but it had turned violet itself now. Then tiny violet rings appeared around the floating-away bits and each microscopic part of the hazy stuff, so small that the green haze disappeared to be replaced with a slightly dimmer violet one.

Everything flashed apart from the central target. The earlier haze had gone. The pulverised remains of the specks that had been floating away formed the haze now, flashing violet and light green and dissipating, filling her field of vision; sumptuous, scintillating. In some ways it was the most beautiful firework display she had ever seen. It began to end as the violet ship in the centre of the view grew in brightness, going from a distinct but un-showy glow to a sky-splitting glare in a few seconds – much slower than anything else had reacted. When it faded, there was more violet/lime green flashing debris, scattered everywhere, all slowly spreading, fading, going dull and disappearing, leaving just the stars to be seen once more; calm, faint, tiny, far away and unchanging after the shattering, psychotic tumult of flickering images that had kept her rapt, shocked, transfixed till now.

She felt herself let out a deep breath.

Then – bizarrely, even shockingly – Demeisen was there in front of her, lounging in what looked like the control seat next to hers, but somehow straight in front of her, against the star field. He was gently lit from above, his feet up on something invisible and his hands clasped behind his neck.

He turned to look at her, nodding once. ~There you go, he said. ~You've just seen one of the most significant military engagements of modern times, doll; lamentably but fascinatingly one-sided though it turned out to be. Strongly suspect they just weren't giving their ship Minds full tactical authority. Demeisen shook his head, frowned. ~Amateurs. He shrugged. ~Oh well. Hopefully *not* the start of an actual proper all-out war between the Culture and our over-cute tribute civ – perish that thoughtlet – but they did shoot first, and it was with what they assumed would be full lethal force, so I was entirely within my rights to waste the miserable trigger-happy fuckers to a soul, without mercy. He sighed. ~Though I am obviously anticipating the inevitable board of inquiry and I do *slightly* worry about being ticked off for being just a tad over-enthusiastic. He sighed again, sounding happier this time. ~Still. Abominator class; we have a reputation to protect. Fuck me, the others are going to be *so* jealous! He paused. ~What?

~Were there people in those ships? she asked.

~GFCF navy? Definitely. *Very* quick deaths, even given that they would have been wired in and speeded up, if I may just leap in front of any nascent and entirely vicarious moral qualms you may be about to suffer from, tiny human. Military personnel, babe; put themselves in harm's way when they signed up. Just that the poor fuckers didn't know it was *my* harm they were putting themselves in the way of. That's war, doll; fairness comes excluded.

The doubly unreal vision of the avatar floating in space looked away, as though gazing contentedly round at the almost unseeably small debris floating around him. ~That'll fucking learn the bastards.

Lededje waited a short while but he kept on looking about him, sighing happily and seemingly either ignoring or having forgotten all about her. ~Fuck me, she heard him say quietly, ~I just blighted an entire fucking fleet there. Without even stretching a limb. Squadron, at the very least. Fuh-zuck-elling hell-cocks, I'm good.

~I think I'd like to get back to Sichult now, if that's all right, she told the avatar.

~Of course, Demeisen said, turning to her with a neutral expression. ~There's that man you want to kill, isn't there?

Veppers had to slide slowly down the carpeted floor of the corridor beyond the door; it was too steep to try to walk down. The first thing he found was Jasken attempting to climb up towards him, pushing open another dented door. Behind Jasken there was dim light, and the sound of crying and moaning. A breeze rolled up the tipped corridor, from behind Jasken.

"Sir! Are you all right?" Jasken said when he recognised Veppers in the gloom.

"Alive, nothing broken. I think some fucker tried to nuke me. Did you see that fucking fireball?"

"I think the pilots are dead, sir. Can't get into the flight deck. We've a door open to the outside. There are some dead, sir. Some injured, too." He waved the arm that had been in the fake cast. "I thought it might be time to discard—"

"Is there any help on the way?"

"Don't know yet, sir. There's a hardened comms set in the compartment somewhere; the two Zei left are checking the emergency storage."

"Two? Left?" Veppers said, staring at Jasken. There had been four of his clone guards aboard, hadn't there? Or had they called off at the last moment?

"Two of the Zei died in the crash, sir," Jasken told him.

"Fuck," Veppers said. Well, you could always grow more, he supposed, though it still took time to train them. "Who else?"

"Pleur, sir. And Herrit. Astle's got a broken leg. Sulbazghi's unconscious."

They descended into the passenger compartment. It was lit by emergency lighting and the daylight from outside coming through the small oval portholes and the opened emergency door. The place smelled bad, Veppers thought. Moaning sounds and people crying. Thankfully it was hard to see too much. He wanted to get out immediately.

"Sir," one of the Zei said, approaching them over the tipped chaos of seats and spilled possessions. He was holding a comms transceiver. "We are glad you are alive, sir," he said. He'd bled heavily from a wound on his head and his other arm hung oddly.

"Yes, thank you," Veppers said as the Zei handed the set to Jasken. "That's all." He nodded to the Zei to go. The big man bowed, then turned and walked back awkwardly over the seats.

Veppers brought his mouth close to Jasken's ear as the other man checked the transceiver and activated it. "Whatever turns up first, even if it's an ambulance flier, you and I get on it alone," he told Jasken. "Understand?"

"Sir?" Jasken said, blinking.

"Make sure there's enough other craft to get everybody else off, but we take the *first* thing that arrives. Just us, understand?"

"Yes, sir."

"And where are your Oculenses? We might need them."

"They're broken, sir."

Veppers shook his head. "Some fucker wants me dead, Jasken. Let's let them think I am. Let's let them think they succeeded. Are we clear?"

"Yes, sir." Jasken shook his head, as though trying to clear it. "Should I tell the others to say that you were killed?"

"No, they're to say that I'm alive. Injured, perfectly well, traumatised, missing, in a coma; more different stories the better. Point is I don't show, I don't appear. Everybody will assume they're all lying. They'll think I'm dead. Possibly you, too. You and I are going to hide, Jasken. D'you ever do that when you were a kid, Jasken? Hide? I used to. Did it a lot. I was great at it. So we're going to do that now; we're going to hide." Veppers patted the other man on the shoulder, hardly noticing that he winced when he did so. "Shares will go into a tail-spin, but that can't be helped." He nodded at the transceiver. "Make the call. Then find me a flight suit or something to use as a disguise."

Twenty-five

Auppi Unstril felt very hot now. The cold would win eventually though – it would be creeping in from all sides, making its way towards her from the *Bliterator*'s hull; seeping its way inwards to where she lay, at the craft's centre, as the vessel's heat leaked away, radiating into space. She would be the last bit to go completely cold. She was the little pit, the stone at the heart of the fruit . . . well, more its soft centre, the mushy middle.

She would be hard, in time though. Once she'd frozen.

In the meantime she was dying, maybe from suffocation, maybe from overheating.

The last thing they'd heard from the *Hylozoist* had been that it had been attacked, disabled. It had just departed the Initial Contact Facility, got barely ten kilometres away, when it had been hit by some EqT energy weapon, slicing in through some hi-tech field disruptor. Its engines were wrecked, field generators shattered, some personnel dead; it had announced it was limping back towards the Facility.

In what had sounded like a series of simultaneous attacks, the GFCF comms had lit up with alarms telling of attacks on their vessels too; one of their MDVs on the other side of the Disk had been blown out of the skies and other ships damaged, at least temporarily disabled.

Auppi and the *Bliterator* had been scanning one of the fabricaria, trying to see if it was one of the ship-building ones, when the attacks had started. They were studiously ignoring a nearby smatter outbreak, even though they were ideally placed to tackle it and it looked like a serious one. That had felt wrong. The *Bliterator* hadn't been configured as a general-purpose mini spacecraft; it was a cobbled-together attack ship. Very skilfully and even elegantly cobbled together, but cobbled together nevertheless; single minded, no nonsense. Leaving its weapons on standby while a smatter outbreak raged only a few minutes' flight away felt wrong wrong wrong.

But checking a proper sample of the fabricaria for illicit shipmaking activity was, even Auppi had to admit, more important. She'd wanted to take the *Bliterator* inside the ripped-open fabricary to get a still closer look at the ship they'd found by accident, but they already had the readings to show it was a serious if relatively simple bit of kit, and the consensus had been that it would be too dangerous to try to enter the fabricary; the fab was still single-mindedly completing the ship, hull holed or not, and the maker machines were still whizzing back and forth on their network of lines and cables; even if they'd all been still it would have taken some delicate manoeuvring for the *Bliterator* to thread its way inside the thing. With them still darting back and forth unpredictably it would be suicide.

So she'd ignored the scarily fascinating weird new ship and ignored the fresh, enticing smatter outbreak and taken on what they'd all agreed was the most important task: choose a few fabs at random, over a decent spread of the Disk, and take a look inside using the very limited solids-scanning abilities of their little improvised attack ships. It had proved easier than they'd anticipated because all the fabs they'd looked at had the same hollow-skin outer hulls. Where there should have been a thick crust of dense raw material, there was a thin outer skin supported by a light girder-net, then the hull proper, then lots of activity, with something big growing slowly at the centre. A few of the tiny Culture craft had even had time to choose a fourth random fab each and investigate those too.

Before they were hit.

She'd been looking at her own results – yup, looked like another ship getting built in there – when she'd heard, amongst the chatter on the shared open channel they were all using, the *Hylozoist* ship voice – ramped fast, clipped, compressed, in full emergency mode – announce it had suffered attack, been disabled . . . would have to limp back to the Facility.

The chatter had subsided, the channel had gone almost totally quiet. Then hubbub, as people started saying things like, "What the fuck? / Did it say—? / Is this a drill? / That can't be—" before, clearly, over them all, she heard Lanyares shout, "Hey. I'm getting—!"

Then spreading silence, sometimes preceded by a shout or exclamation, from all of them.

"What's—?" she'd had time to say. Then the *Bliterator* had gone quiet around her.

"Warning, Effector att—" the ship had told her, probably via some pre-loaded back-up substrate. The little ship had four other fall-back layers of processing below the AI core, but even those needed Effector-vulnerable tech to communicate with her via her suit, so when everything went dark and quiet and still, it went *really* dark and quiet and still, fast.

There was probably some life left in the ship, even now, at the atomechanical or bio-chemical level, but if there was, she and it couldn't communicate.

And her neural lace was off-line too; even that had been taken out in whatever Effector event had wasted the *Bliterator*. The last from it had been its sign-off signal, its *I'm-fucked* message, what she'd heard described as being like a tiny brittle wire breaking in the centre of your head. Which had proved a fairly accurate description. She'd experienced a faint, flat, half-felt, half-heard *ping* somewhere between the ears. Just so you knew you were on your own now. Not much comfort there.

She wondered why they'd bothered to incorporate the lace-wasted signal in the first place. Better to leave the poor sap with a dead lace in their head thinking everything was still somehow all hunky-dory; but no, that would be a lie, and this was the Culture, so you had to be told the truth, no matter how uncomfortable it was, no matter how much it might contribute to feelings of despair.

Some real purists even refused drug glands and the related pain-management systems because those were somehow "untruthful" too. Weirdos.

So she was stuck in here, imprisoned in the suit, unable to move in the gel foam and anyway locked inside the miniscule, extra-equipment-stuffed flight deck within a ship that would probably need cutting equipment to enter.

The only excitement had been when she'd felt a soft bump, maybe a quarter-hour after it had all gone quiet. That had got her hopes up; maybe somebody was coming to rescue her! But it had probably just been the ship clunking into the side of the fab they'd been scanning when they'd been attacked. Bounced off, most likely. Tumbling, surely, though at a guess very slowly because she couldn't feel any sense of being spun or rotated.

"What's—?"

As last words went, it was pretty shit. She hadn't had a chance to say goodbye to Lan, or any of the others, or the ship.

"What's—?"

Just hopeless.

Very very hot now. She had been keeping a watch on the time but now even that was getting hazy. Everything had been getting hazy; senses, sense of self, sense of humour, as the heat had built up in her body. It seemed wrong; unfair somehow. She was surrounded by intense cold, this far out in the system from the central star, and the ship was dead, or as good as, no longer providing energy or heat, and yet she was going to die of self-inflicted heatstroke, if simple suffocation didn't kill her first. Too well insulated, inside here. The cold would freeze her solid eventually, but that would take days, tens of days; maybe more.

Meantime her body's own internal processes, the chemical stuff that made you human, were going to cook her brain, because there was nowhere for the heat to go fast enough, now that the suit and ship were dead.

What a depressing way to die.

It had been hours, she reckoned. She'd had a time-count that had been accurate to the minute until not long ago, but then the brain-scrambling heat had made her forget it and having dropped that strand, she couldn't for the life of her pick it up again. At some point, she realised, her dead body would be back to exactly normal blood heat, as it cooled down again after its self-produced temperature spike. She wondered when that would happen. A lot of heat in the ship, and the double suit was a very good insulator. It would take a while to radiate all that warmth away. Days sounded about right.

She had cried, at one point. She couldn't remember when. Fear, and frustration, and a sort of primal terror at being so utterly trapped, unable to move.

The tears had collected around her eyes, unable to go anywhere else in the dead, close-fitting suit. If the suit had still been working it would have capillaried the tears away.

She was still breathing, very shallowly, because there was a purely mechanical link to a set of tiny, finger-thin tanks on the suit's back, and a purely chemical set of reactions going on somewhere in the system that ought to keep her alive for tens of days. The trouble was the suit held her too tightly for her to breathe properly; her chest muscles couldn't expand her lungs sufficiently. It had to be that way, of course, for the suit to do its job properly when everything had been working; it had to clasp her tightly or she'd run the risk of getting bruised and hurt when they accelerated hard. She could feel her brain closing bits of her body down, cutting off blood supplies, keeping her oxygenated blood needs down to a minimum, but it wasn't going to be enough; she'd start to lose parts of her brain soon, cells dying, suffocated.

She was glanding *softnow* every now and again, to keep herself calm. No point in panicking when it would do no use. If she had to die she might as well do so with a little dignity.

Thanks be for drug glands.

She hoped whoever had done this got seriously fucked up, by the Culture or the GFCF or somebody. Maybe it was immature to lust after revenge, but fuck that; let the fuckers die horribly.

Well, let them die.

She'd compromise that far.

Evil wins when it makes you behave like it, and all that.

Very very very hot now, and getting woozy. She wondered if it was oxygen starvation making her feel woozy, or the heat, or a bit of both. Feeling oddly numb; hazy, dissociated.

Dying. She'd be revented, she guessed, in theory. She'd been backed up; everything up to about six hours ago copied, replicable. But that meant nothing. So another body, vat-grown, would wake with her memories – up to that point six hours ago, not including this bit, obviously – so what? That wouldn't be her. She was here, dying. The self-realisation, the consciousness, that didn't transfer; no soul to transmigrate. Just behaviour, as patterned.

All you ever were was a little bit of the universe, thinking to itself. Very specific; *this* bit, *here*, right *now.* All the rest was fantasy. Nothing was ever identical to anything else because it didn't share the same spacial coordinates; nothing could be identical to anything else because you couldn't share the property of uniqueness. Blah blah; she was drifting now, remembering old lessons, ancient school stuff.

"What's—?"

Pathetic last words.

She thought of Lan, her lover, her love, probably dying just like this, just like her, hundreds of thousands of klicks away in the suffocating heat, surrounded by the cold dark silence.

She thought she might cry again.

Instead, she could feel her skin trying to sweat, creating a prickling feeling all over her body. Pain management reduced it from extreme discomfort to mere sensation.

Her whole body, crying stickily.

Image to bow out on.

Thank you and good night . . .

"You the fella I need to talk to?"

"I'm not sure. Who exactly is it you wish to talk to?"

"Whoever's in charge round here. That you?"

"I am Legislator-Admiral Bettlescroy-Bisspe-Blispin III. It is my privilege to command the GFCF forces in this volume. And you?"

"I'm the passing-for-human face of the Culture warship *Falling Outside The Normal Moral Constraints.*"

"You are the Torturer-class vessel we heard was in-bound? Thank goodness! We – the GFCF and our allies the Culture, here in the Tsungarial Disk – have come under heavy and sustained attack. All reinforcements are most welcome and urgently needed."

"That was me, sort of. I was just pretending to be a Torturer class."

"Pretending? I'm not sure I—"

"Thing is, short while ago, somebody jumped me. Whole squadron of craft: one capital ship, fourteen others plus ancillary units and slaved weapon platforms. Had to off them all."

Bettlescroy stared at the face of the human-looking thing regarding him from the screen on the battle-bridge of the *Vision Of Hope Surpassed*, his flagship and one of the three Deepest Regrets-class craft under his command. Bettlescroy himself had given the order for the *Abundance Of Onslaught* and its flotilla of accompanying vessels to open fire on the incoming Torturer-class ship. Communication had been lost with all the craft during the engagement, which had seemed to be going well at first but then had obviously deteriorated. The ships had ceased communication so rapidly it seemed impossible that they had simply been destroyed, so the assumption Bettlescroy and his officers were working on was that some sort of comms blackout had taken place; feverish attempts to contact the ships were taking place even as he spoke.

If that wasn't bad enough, they'd lost touch with Veppers, back on Sichult. The last thing they'd heard – minutes before this unwanted call had come in – had been was an unconfirmed report of a large explosion taking place on Veppers' estate, possibly on the route his aircraft would have taken back to his house. Bettlescroy had been trying to keep calm and not think about what *that* might imply; now it looked like he had something else to keep calm and not think about.

"'Off' them all?" Bettlescroy said carefully. That couldn't possibly mean what he dreaded, could it? "I'm sorry, I'm not cognisant of that term's official weight, as it were. Obviously we were aware there had been some sort of engagement a little way beyond the system's outer limit . . ."

"I was attacked, without provocation," the human-looking thing on the screen said. "I retaliated. By the time I'd finished retaliating, fifteen ships were gone. Offed. Deleted. Blown to smithereens. Thing is, they looked remarkably like GFCF ships. In every way, really. The biggest and most capable presented as almost exactly like that one you're on. A Deepest Regrets class, unless I'm mistaken. Weird eh? How do you account for that?"

"I confess, I cannot. No GFCF craft would ever knowingly attack a Culture vessel." Bettlescroy could feel his guts churning and his face burning. He was *this* close to cutting the comms, to give himself time to think if nothing else. Had this . . . *thing* just casually obliterated nearly a third of his war fleet? Was it trying to get him to confess something, blurt something out, enrage him with its off-hand attitude? Bettlescroy was very aware of his officers on the bridge keeping extremely quiet; he could feel their gazes on him.

The human on the screen was talking again: " . . . Excuse they had was something about deeming me to be a hostile, just pretending to be a Culture vessel."

It was still sinking in. He'd lost a Deepest Regrets-class ship!

Dear Gods of Old! The faction within the GFCF High Command which had authorised this high-risk strategy had known they risked losing vessels and materiel, but no one had so much as hinted they might lose one of their capital ships; not a pride of the fleet, not a Deepest Regrets class. This whole thing would all have to go fabulously well from this point on if he was to be forgiven for *that.*

"I see. Well, indeed. Yes, I see," Bettlescroy said, stalling while he got himself under control. "Of course, I have to point out that, as you have said, you are – or were – pretending to be a Torturer class, so— "

"Ah, I get it. You think that might have been the source of the misunderstanding?"

"Well, you can see how it might be."

"Sure. So, were they your ships, or not?"

Bettlescroy wanted to weep, to scream, to fold himself into a little ball and never talk to anyone ever again. "The operational status of the fleet I was given to command here within the Disk comprises one medium-level, non-military vessel and a screen of eighteen smaller ships. The vessel which you find me on, ah, has just been delivered to us, in recognition of the seriousness of the threat we are facing."

"Wow. That's *incredibly* fast work. Congratulate your simming/planning/dispositioning people."

"Thank you. More than that I am not at liberty to say, I regret."

"So what you're saying is you can't confirm or deny those were your ships? The ones that attacked me."

"Effectively. Though if they were ours and they did attack you, it could only have been a mistake."

"Fine. Just thought I'd check. Also, to let you know; I'm still on my way in. Currently braking hard; due with you guys in the Disk in twelve and a half minutes. Just wanted to keep you informed, so there wouldn't be any more misunderstandings."

"Quite. Well, yes, of course. And you are . . . ?"

"The *Falling Outside The Normal Moral Constraints*, like I said. And definitely a Culture ship. That's the main thing. Feel free to check my provenance and references. Here to help. One of your allies. All in this together. So. Understand things are a bit awkward in there; happy to get stuck in alongside your good selves. Going to let me have an interface situational with your tactical substrates so I can get a head start on the task in hand?"

"Ah . . . yes, of course. Relevant protocols agreeing, obviously."

"Obviously."

"But I meant your class, if you're not a Torturer?"

"Picket ship. Glorified night-watchman, that's me."

"Picket Ship. Picket Ship. Picket Ship. Yes, I see. Well, welcome aboard, if I may make so bold."

"Cheers, person. With you in twelve minutes."

Bettlescroy signed to cut the connection. He turned to his Security chief. "We are supposed to be presenting as the *Messenger Of Truth*. How the fuck could that thing tell we're actually on a Deepest Regrets class?"

"I have no idea, sir."

Bettlescroy permitted himself a sigh, through a tight, jerky smile. "Well, that would appear to be our motto at the moment, wouldn't it? We seem to have no idea about anything."

The Fleet Coordination Officer cleared his throat and said, "MDV nearest the projected engagement start-point reports incoming weapon blink and battle light, sir. Debris spectra so far indicating ours alone."

Bettlescroy nodded silently. He turned to the Disk Fabricaria Control section of the bridge. The lead officer sat at attention. "Tell every second fabricaria to release its ship, immediately; random choice," Bettlescroy told him. "One half of the remainder to let their ship go within the next quarter-hour to four hours, again randomly, and randomly in time as well, within those parameters. One half of the rest to release theirs between four and eight hours, and so on until it doesn't matter any more. Do you understand?"

"Sir, most of them—"

"Will be unprepared and may not even function at all. I know. Nevertheless. Even if they have to be physically ejected by their particular fabricary, do what I have said. Have as many as possible of the most functional equipped with donated AM from the war fleet. Spare nothing; our ships can operate on fusion for a while. Not us, though; not this ship."

"Sir."

Bettlescroy turned to the bridge comms section and smiled coldly at the chief communications officer. "Get me Veppers. If not Veppers, get me Jasken. I know they're missing, but just find them. Do whatever it takes."

The comms connection was cut and the image of the silkily beautiful Legislator-Admiral Bettlescroy-Bisspe-Blispin III of the GFCF remained frozen before them.

Demeisen turned to Lededje. "What do you think?"

"He's not my species," she protested. "How should I know?"

"Yeah, but you must have a *feeling*; come on."

Lededje shrugged. "Lying through his perfect teeth."

Demeisen nodded. "Same here."

She got fed up trying to finish her meal on the ground, surrounded by fawning, keening worshippers. She sighed, roared at them. A few backed off a little; most stayed where they were. Then, tearing off a haunch, she lifted wearily into the foul-smelling air, carrying the piece of leg as something to gnaw on somewhere else more private. Each wing-beat hurt, her great dark wings seeming to creak.

It was mid-afternoon by the raw chronologies of Hell, and something like fresh light shone from grey overcast that for once looked tentative rather than dark and heavy. It was as close to direct sunlight as the place ever got, and the air, though still smelling of sewage and burned flesh, was relatively clear.

The crowd of worshippers was a wide, messy torus, now filling slowly in as the people came forward to gaze on the remains of the one she had killed, possibly looking for clues regarding what might have attracted her to that lucky individual in the first place.

She had long since given up trying to tell them it was pointless.

She chose her victims, her blessed, at random. She flew high until she felt physically hungry sometimes, then just dropped, spread her wings over the first person she found. Other times she went to some particular place she'd seen before and noted, and alighted there, waiting for the first one to come to her. She varied where she went and which time of day she chose to make her kills. There was no particular pattern to it; it just happened. Not entirely at random, but not predictable so that one of these benighted wretches could arrange to collate information on where she struck and contrive to be in the right place at the right time.

Still, people had indeed made a religion of her and her daily killings. As the king of the demons had envisaged and desired, she had brought a little hope back into Hell.

She thought about stopping, sometimes, but never did, not for more than a day. She had decided at the start that she would release one of these unfortunates from their pains each day, and the few times she had tried to experiment by not killing once per day had left her racked with cramps; gut pains that left her nauseous and barely able to fly. That had only happened three times.

She still only got to release one soul on the following day; the earlier day's unused kill didn't seem to carry over. Any extra she killed were, as ever, resurrected, often almost instantaneously, coming shrieking back to life in their impossibly torn-open bodies, miraculously repairing and reforming themselves before her eyes, while their eyes filled with looks of uncomprehending betrayal.

The ones she truly killed departed with a look of gratitude she had come to treasure. The expressions on the faces of those who gathered round to watch were of simple envy, a sort of beatific hunger laced with outright jealousy. Sometimes she'd deliberately choose people because they were on their own or only with a few other people, just so she escaped the weight of those death-desiring gazes.

You could not reason with people in the grip of such a faith. She had tried, but failed. The truth was that she could offer them release; she was an angel who, here, really did exist, and really could offer these people what they most desired. It was not even really faith; it was perfectly reasonable belief.

She climbed into the high, clear air, chewing on the still-warm haunch of the one she'd released only minutes earlier. The crowd gathering round the body was too small to see now, lost in the scabbed landscapes beneath the drifting clouds of smoke.

Way off in the distance, something shimmered in a way that she was not sure she had seen here, ever before. Something seemed almost to shine, way over there, towards a line of small mountains, tall cliffs and acid lakes. Not with flame; with what could almost be watery sunlight, if that wasn't an absurd idea, here in Hell, where there contrived to be light without sun. It looked like a column, like a broad, silvery pillar, half invisible, between land and cloud.

She took one last gulping bite, then dropped the haunch-bone and struck off for the distant anomaly.

The column only grew more mysterious the closer she got. It was like a strange irregular curtain of silver draped over the land; a few kilometres across, maybe one deep; a sort of semi-regular shape of what looked like a pure mirror. It had no light of its own, but seemed to reflect all light that touched it. Flying close, she saw her own dark, elongated shape flickering liquidly across its surface.

She went up through the clouds to see that the pillar extended all the way to the iron sky, tens of kilometres above. The effort made it feel like her muscles were on fire.

She dropped back through the cloud, landed. Her feet, her legs, all hurt, protesting, as they took her weight. They always did. Her legs hurt when she was on the ground, her wings ached when she was flying, and her whole body grumbled distantly when she hung upside down to rest. She just tried not to think about it.

There were some chopped-up bodies lying right beside the shimmering curtain of silver, where it met the ground. It looked as though they had been cut with a very sharp blade.

She picked up a sliced-off leg lying on the ground, threw it at the silvery barrier. It bounced off, as though it had hit solid metal. She picked the leg back up, prodded the barrier. Felt solid. She touched it with one talon. Very solid; iron solid. To the touch, it was a little cold. Again, as cold as iron or steel would have felt.

One cowering creature nearby squealed as she dragged it from the poison bush it had been trying to hide within. Its pelt was already starting to blister. The little male was emaciated; missing one trunk, one eye, his face badly scarred by tooth marks.

"Did you see this happen?" she demanded, shaking him towards the silent mirror-barrier.

"It just happened!" he wailed. "All of a sudden! Without warning! Please, ma'am; are you the one who releases us?"

"Yes. Has anything like this happened here before?" she said, still not letting him go. She knew this area a little. She tried to recall its details. Cliffs; mountains. A munitions factory set into the cliffs . . . over there. She could see the road that had served it, lined with petrified, very quietly shrieking statues.

"No! Never seen anything like it! Nobody here has! Please, sacred lady; take me; release me; kill me, please!"

She looked round. There were a few others, she could see now, all cowering behind whatever cover they could find.

She let the male go. "I can't help you," she told him. "I've already killed today."

"Tomorrow, then! I'll wait here tomorrow!" He fell kneeling at her feet, supplicating.

"I don't make fucking *appointments*!" she roared.

The male stayed where he was, quivering. She gazed up at the shimmering, reflecting curtain, wondering what to make of it.

Still, she flew back there the next day.

The mirror curtain was gone. So was the geography she remembered from before it had been there; a barren dusty plain, rising smoothly, replaced everything that had been within the boundary of the shimmering curtain. It joined as best it could with the cliffs and mountains beyond where the mirror-barrier had been, but it looked dropped-in, added-on somehow. A patch.

She didn't know what to make of it.

The scarred male from the day before was still there, where she'd left him, pleading to be released. She sighed, landed, took him into her wings and let his spirit go, taking on yet another additional pain.

Glitches in Hell. Fucking *appointments* in fucking Hell. Whatever fucking next?

"This place is definitely coarsening me," she muttered to herself as she flew off, clutching another torn-off haunch.

The *Me, I'm Counting* Displaced Yime Nsokyi into the windowless suite at the rear of the very grand hotel near the centre of Iobe Cavern City, Vebezua, while it kept station overhead, just beyond the atmosphere, arguing with the Planetary Near Space Traffic Authority.

The boxy ship-drone serving as escort to her and Himerance switched on all the lights. The bedroom was vast, palatial, unoccupied.

"The secret passage is hidden under the bed," Himerance said. The drone activated the relevant motors and the giant circular bed sank out of sight. They went to the edge and watched it drop.

"That leads to the tunnel that ends up in the desert?" Yime asked. She was dressed properly, in her tunic, at last, for the first time in days. She was still not fully healed, and still somewhat delicate, but her hair was tidy and she felt . . . regained.

"Yes," Himerance said. "Veppers might have been absent for days, though officially he never left here. He probably left on a Jhlupian ship, but nobody's sure. His entourage supposedly arrived back on Sichult this morning, but there's no confirmation he's with them. This is the last place we can be absolutely sure he was."

The drone dropped into the hole left by the descending bed. Himerance produced a scroll screen, letting it unroll and hang in the air in front of them, displaying the view the drone had as it made its way up the short corridor beneath the room, heading into the cliff. A small underground car shaped like a fat bullet sat in front of a dark tunnel.

"Getting anything?" Yime asked.

Himerance shrugged. "Nothing much," he told her. "There is a variety of surveillance tech in here. Place is like a history of bugging through the ages; whole tiny networks of linked spy-tech and outdated eavesdropping gear splattered about the entire suite.

Lot of stuff that's probably lost, forgotten about. Many tiny dead batteries in here. Ancient stuff." The ship, only a couple of hundred kilometres over their heads, was targeting one of its main Effectors on the city, the hotel and the suite. If there was anything useful here, it would find it.

"Most recent is equiv-tech stuff," Himerance said, relaying what the ship was finding. "Passably . . . NR stuff." He looked at Yime.

"NR?"

"Probably. It's recent," Himerance said, "and working; it'd be relaying what we're saying now if I wasn't blocking it. Synched into hidden hotel cameras and comms-intercept gear too." Himerance nodded at four different points in the room. "Sprayed on: in the wall hangings, drapes, on the surfaces of paintings and embedded in the rugs."

"Anything recorded?"

"No; and no idea where it would have transmitted to either," Himerance admitted.

"Would it have registered Veppers using his sinking-bed escape route?"

"Maybe not," Himerance said, gazing up at the great thick fold of curtains which could envelop and surround the bed. "Not if these were drawn." He squinted. Yime could almost feel the ship overhead shifting the focus of its Effector by minute fractions of a degree. "No spray-on surveillance on those," Himerance confirmed. "And they're a lot more hi-tech than the simple organic woven material they look like. Shield you from most interference once they're drawn right round."

Yime sighed. "I don't think he's here," she said. "I certainly don't think *she* is."

Stopping here had been an easy enough decision; the direction they'd approached the Sichultian Enablement from, Vebezua had been almost directly en route. Sichult itself still seemed the best place to find both Veppers and Lededje Y'breq, but taking a quick look at the last place they had a definite fix on Veppers had seemed to make sense and cost them only a couple of hours.

"I'm still not getting what's going on with the Restoria mission,"

Himerance said, sounding puzzled. "Some sort of comms blackout now. Something's happening out there, at the Disk."

"Smatter outbreak?" Yime asked.

"Those fabricaria ships are more than smatter," Himerance said as they watched the drone retrace its flight back down the tunnel towards them. Yime knew the ship already felt torn between taking her where she wanted to go, and joining in whatever action was taking place out at the Tsungarial Disk.

"There's some sort of full-on *battle* going on out there," Himerance said, frowning now. "Beyond the Disk, on the fringes of the Enablement; way too hi-tech for mere smatter. I do so hope that isn't the Abominator class arriving. If it is we may genuinely have a full-scale war on our hands."

The drone reappeared in the hole the bed had left; Himerance snapped the scroll-screen closed again and tucked it inside his jacket.

"What about the explosion on Veppers' estate?" Yime asked.

"Nothing new. News blackout." Himerance paused. "Actually, *something* new. Couple of agencies Veppers doesn't control reporting members of his entourage killed and injured in some sort of flier crash; survivors arriving back at Ubruater at one of his private hospitals." Another pause. "Hmm. Guess that counts as speculation."

"What does?"

Himerance looked at her. "Reports that Veppers might be dead."

"I'd better let you go. You take care. I mean, *I'm* staying; this Demeisen unit right here is sticking with you, but me myself I, the ship; I have to stick around here, see what's up. Sleeve-rolling, palm-spitting time for me. You get to stay inside the shuttle inside this element, this shiplet. It'll take you on to Sichult."

"Okay," Lededje said. "Thanks for the ride so far."

"My pleasure. Take care. See you later, I hope."

"Me too."

The image of Demeisen waved bye-bye against the star field. The screen inside her suit's helmet showed the main body of the ship slipping away to one side, fields flickering between the element she was looking from and the main body of the vessel. It was still elongatedly ellipsoidal, but each curved sliver of ship-element had separated slightly from the other, so that the ship looked like a fat throw-ball knifed open from tip to tail, segments teased apart. As she watched, the gap left by the departure of the part that she was in started to close up, the other sections pulling fractionally further away from each other. Then they reached the ship's outer field boundary and passed through opaque layers. Outside, the *Falling Outside The Normal Moral Constraints* was just a giant silver ellipsoid. It shimmered, disappeared.

The Demeisen figure was still there, seemingly floating in space. He turned to her. "Just you and me now, babe. And the ship-section sub-Mind, of course."

"Does it have a separate name?" she asked.

Demeisen shrugged. "Element twelve?"

"That'll have to do."

He crossed his arms, frowned. "Now; the good news first or the bad news?"

She frowned too. "Good," she said.

"We'll have you on Sichult in a few hours."

"What's the bad news?"

"This just in: Veppers might be already dead."

She stared at the image of the avatar. She hadn't expected this. "That it?" she said after a moment.

"Yup. You seem relatively unconcerned."

She shrugged. "I wanted him dead. If he's dead, good. Why only 'might'? What happened?"

"Someone nuked his aircraft as it was flying low over his estate. Some of his retinue killed, some injured; Veppers himself . . . mysteriously unaccounted for."

"Huh. I bet he's still alive. I'd want to see the body before I believe otherwise. And check it for neural laces or whatever."

Demeisen smiled at her. It was a strange, unsettling sort of smile. She wondered if this version of Demeisen would be different to the one controlled by the main ship. "Thought you wanted to kill him yourself," he said.

She looked at him for a moment. "I've never killed anyone before," she told him. "I don't really want to have to kill another person. I'm not . . . totally, completely sure that I can even kill Veppers. I think I can, and I've fantasised about it a hundred times, but . . . If he really was dead, maybe that would be a relief. Part of me would be angry he didn't die by my hand, but part of me would be grateful; I get out of finding whether I could really do it or not."

Demeisen raised an eyebrow. "How many times did he rape you?"

She let a couple of controlled, regular breaths pass before she answered. "I lost count."

"And then he murdered you."

"Yes," she said. "Though to give him his due, he only did that once." When the avatar didn't say anything, but simply kept looking at her, she added, "I'm not him, Demeisen. I'm not even like him. If I get close to him and have the gun or the knife in my hand but then find that I can't do it, then I'll be angry at myself for not being strong enough, for letting him get away with it, and for giving him the chance to rape and murder again." She took another breath. "But if I can do it, if I *do* do it, then on one level I'm no better than him, and he'll have won by making me behave like he does." She shrugged. "Don't get me wrong; I fully intend to put a bullet through his head or slit his throat if I get the chance, but I won't know if I can do it until the moment actually presents itself." Another shrug. "If it ever does."

Demeisen shook his head. "That is the sorriest, limpest, most self-defeating piece of self-motivating I have ever fucking heard. We should have talked about this before. I ought to have been giving you assassin lessons for the past umpteen days. How long we got now? Five hours?" Demeisen slapped one hand over his forehead and eyes, theatrically. "Oh fuck. You're going to die, kid."

Lededje's frown deepened. "Thanks for your confidence."

"Hey, you started it."

Twenty-six

"Veppers dead?" Yime Nsokyi said. "How?"

"In that explosion or the flier crash. Reports remain confused," Himerance said.

"Lededje Y'breq isn't back there already, is she?" Yime asked.

"Doubtful," Himerance said. "And I would doubt she could organise a nuke inside Veppers' estate either. She's just a kid with a grudge, not some super-powered SC agent. Not that a super-powered SC agent would use anything as inelegant as a bomb aimed at an aircraft. Or miss if they did."

"What if the Abominator's helping her?"

"I would prefer not to think about that," Himerance said with a sigh.

Yime frowned, looked about the palatial suite. "Can you hear that thumping noise?"

"That," the ship drone said, "is the hotel's general manager registering his disapproval at his pass-key codes not allowing him entry into his finest suite when there appears to be something 'going on' inside."

Himerance was frowning now. The ship's drone fell silent, hanging in the air for a moment.

"We need to conduct a small experiment," Himerance said.

"That statue," the drone announced, and Himerance turned to look at a three-quarters-sized statue of a buxom nymph carrying a stylised torch in one corner of the bedroom.

"What's going—?" Yime began, as a silvery ellipsoid flickered into existence around the statue, obscuring it. When the ellipsoid vanished with a small "pop", the statue was gone and where it had stood there was a fresh-looking patch of rug.

"What's happening?" Yime said, just starting to feel worried and looking from the humanoid avatar to the ship-drone.

The two machines seemed to hesitate, then the little drone said, "Uh-oh."

Himerance turned to Yime. "That was the ship attempting a Displace, back to it."

"The micro-singularity didn't arrive," the drone told her.

"What?" Yime said. "How—?"

Himerance stepped forward, took Yime by the elbow. "We need to go," he said, moving Yime towards the suite's entrance.

"Checking that tunnel again," the drone said, and flew quickly across the room, disappearing into the hole the circular bed had left.

"The ship's being instructed to quit the system by an NR vessel," Himerance told Yime as he hustled her into the suite's main drawing room. "In no uncertain terms. The NR think we're up to something and seem, by Reliquarian standards, extremely upset. They're intercepting any Displaces. The drone—" Then Himerance made a noise that was almost a yelp, and covered Yime's ears with his hands so fast it hurt. The explosion from the depths of the bedroom blew them both over, thudding into the floor. Himerance managed to twist in the air as they fell so that Yime landed on top of him. It still hurt and Yime's nose, which had thudded into his chin, started to bleed immediately. Every just-healed bone in her body ached in protest.

The avatar dragged her to her feet as clouds of smoke, dust and small floating scraps of debris came rolling out of the bedroom.

Yime started to cough. "—the fuck is going on?" she managed as Himerance walked her smartly towards the suite's vestibule.

"That was the tunnel being collapsed and sealed by the NR ship," Himerance said.

"What about the drone?" Yime asked, sniffing back blood as they approached the suite's double doors.

"Gone," Himerance told her.

"Can't we reason with the—?"

"The ship is reasoning as fast as it machinely can with the NR vessel," Himerance said. "To little avail thus far. It will have to flee or fight very soon. We are already effectively on our own." The avatar looked at the doors for a moment. They swung open to reveal a broad, plushly decorated corridor, a small man with a furious look on his face and three large men dressed in uniforms of what appeared to be a semi-military nature. The rolling cloud of smoke and dust flowed gently past Himerance and Yime, towards the people in the corridor. The small, furious-looking man stared in utter horror at the dust.

One of the large men levelled a thick-barrelled weapon of some sort at Himerance, who said, "I'm terribly sorry, I have no time for this right now," and – moving more quickly than Yime would have believed possible – was suddenly, smoothly, after a sort of liquidic, ducking motion, in the midst of the three large men, flicking the weapon out of the hand of the one pointing it while simultaneously, and – almost accidentally, it appeared – stabbing one elbow into the midriff of one of the other men, whose eyes nearly popped from his head as he collapsed with a whooshing noise of rapidly expelled air.

Yime barely had time to register this happening before the other two men went down too, one felled after the avatar pointed the weapon at him – there was a click and a hum, no more – while the other, who'd been holding the weapon, was sent flying backwards into the wall behind by a single thrust from Himerance's now-outstretched palm.

"Ah," Himerance said, taking the small man by the throat and pressing the gun against his temple. The small man looked more stunned and terrified than furious now. "Some sort of neural blaster." This remark seemed addressed to nobody in particular. His next was as squarely aimed at the hotel's general manager as the neural blaster. "Good day, sir. You will kindly help us to escape."

Himerance obviously took the man's subsequent strangled gurgle as indicating assent, because he smiled, relaxed his grip a fraction and, looking at Yime, nodded down the corridor. "This way, I think."

"What happens now?" Yime asked as they frog-marched the manager down the corridor. "How do we get off the planet?" She stopped and stared at the avatar. "*Do* we get off the planet?"

"No, we'll be safer here, just for now," Himerance told her, stopping at the lift doors and suggesting to the manager that he use his pass-key to priority-order an elevator car.

"We will?" Yime said.

The lift arrived; the avatar took the pass-keys off the manager, inserted them into the elevator car's control panel, pushed the manager out of the car and stunned him with the neural blaster as the doors closed. Himerance looked round the elevator car as they descended towards a sub-basement not usually accessible to non-staff. A small puff of smoke came out of the control panel through the grille of the emergency speaker. "Actually, no, we won't be safer here," Himerance said. "The ship will snap-Displace us off."

"'Snap-Displace'? That sounds—"

"Dangerous. Yes, I know. And it is, though we are assuming it'll be less dangerous than staying here."

"But if the ship can't Displace us now—?"

"It can't Displace us now because it and we are both effectively static, giving the NR time to intercept the Displacement. Whereas later it'll be coming through at very high speed, passing dangerously close to the planet, grazing its gravity well at high translight and attempting to fit the Displacement event into an ungenerous handful of pico-seconds."

The avatar sounded remarkably casual about all this, Yime thought. It watched the screen indicating the floors as it counted slowly down. The lift car's lighting, close overhead, made Himerance's bald head gleam. "Providing it's done at sufficiently high speed, that should leave the NR with insufficient time to arrange any interception of the Displacement singularity." The avatar smiled at her. "That's the real reason the ship is doing as the NR have demanded, and leaving; it'll power up the whole way out, execute a minimum-radius-to-power turn and come straight back in, still accelerating, snapping us off and then heading for Sichult. The whole procedure will take some hours, however, as the ship gathers speed, both to make it look like it really is leaving and to make sure that when it passes us it's going fast enough to confound the NR vessel or vessels. During that time we need to remain hidden from the NR."

"Will it work?"

"Probably. Ah." The car drew to a stop.

"'Probably'?" Yime found herself saying to an empty lift as the avatar moved swiftly between the opening doors.

She followed, to find they were in a deserted basement car park full of wheeled ground vehicles. Yime opened her mouth to speak but the avatar pirouetted, one finger to his lips as he moved towards a bulky-looking vehicle with six wheels and a body that appeared to be made from a single billet of black glass. "This'll do," he said. A gull-wing door sighed open. "Though . . ." he said, as they settled into their seats. "Oh, do put your seat-belt on, won't you? Thank you . . . Though the NR may well guess that the ship will attempt this manoeuvre and so either try to prevent or interfere with the Displacement. Or they might attack the ship itself, of course, though that would be rather extreme."

"They just destroyed the ship's drone and seem to be trying to kill us – isn't that fairly extreme already?"

"It is, rather," the avatar agreed reasonably, looking at the vehicle's controls until lights came on. "Though drones, avatars and even humans are one thing; the loss of any is not without moral and diplomatic import, of course, but might be dismissed as merely unfortunate and regrettable, something to be smoothed over through the usual channels. Attacking a *ship*, on the other hand, is an unambiguous act of war." A screen flashed on, filled with what looked like a city road map.

"Thank you," Yime said. "It is always salutary to be reminded of one's true place in the proper arrangement of matters."

Himerance nodded. "Yes, I know."

In the distance, up a short ramp, a large door to what appeared to be the outside was rising open. "Many of these are automatic too," Himerance muttered to himself. "That's useful."

Most of the other vehicles in the car park were turning their lights on; some were already moving, all heading for the ramp and the doorway.

"We'll leave in the middle, I think," he said, as their vehicle made a low, distant humming noise and moved smoothly off, joining the line of quickly moving cars. Judging by the ones she could see into, none of the others had any occupants.

"Are you doing this, or the ship?" Yime asked as they left the underground garage.

"Me," the avatar said. "The ship left some ninety seconds ago."

Outside, the enormous tunnel of the city was bright with artificial lights, the cupped spread of the place disappearing upwards and down into a faint haze. The far side of the city – a perpendicular jumble of mostly tall, variegated buildings – was only a kilometre or so distant but looked further away in the murk. Around them, the driverless vehicles the avatar had set in motion were all heading off in as many different directions as they could find amongst the city's jumbled network of streets. Above, little tethered aircraft flitted back and forth along the great cavern.

As Yime watched, one of the larger empty vehicles a short way in front of them in a side-lane slowed, met with some hanging cables and was hoisted rapidly into the air.

"We're going to do the same thing," Himerance said, shortly

before their vehicle followed the other one, though it then promptly headed off in the opposite direction.

Their vehicle rose quickly amongst the hundreds of cable-held craft.

They had reached a steady height and held it for about twenty seconds when the avatar sucked in a breath, the black glass around parted directly overhead then started to sink back into the sides of the vehicle. Before the retracting glass had reached shoulder level, Himerance's arm flicked almost too fast to see as he threw the stubby tube of the neural blaster out of the vehicle. Immediately, the glass moved back up around them.

Moments later there was a flash from behind, quickly followed by a great thudding bang which left the vehicle swinging back and forth, causing it to slow automatically, briefly, to correct the oscillation. Himerance and Yime looked back to see a blossoming cloud of smoke and debris rising from near the centre-line of the cavern city; pieces of a great bridge, sundered in the middle, were starting to fall slowly towards the river on the tunnel's floor. Directly above, more glowing pieces of wreckage and cinders were falling from a tiny, yellow-rimmed hole in the cavern ceiling. Echoes of the detonation slammed back and forth amongst the buildings, disappearing slowly down the tunnel city.

Himerance shook his head. "I beg your pardon. I should have thought they might trace that somehow. My mistake," he said, as they drew level with a tall stone tower. The glass around them flowed fully down into the sides of the vehicle. The vehicle was beeping irately, though it was almost drowned out by multitudinous echoing sirens starting to sound around the city. They bumped gently against the summit of the tower.

"We need to get out," the avatar said, rising, taking Yime's hand and together making the small jump onto the grass beyond the tower's parapet. The impact hurt her knees. The vehicle stopped beeping and swung away again, glass panels rising back into place as the cables above whisked it back to the heights.

Himerance hauled an old but stout-looking trap-door open in a flurry of earth and popping rivets. They hurried down an unlit spiral staircase and had descended about two complete turns – Yime following Himerance and trusting him to see in a darkness so profound even her moderately augmented eyes could register next to nothing – when there was a distant-sounding thud from outside. The tower shook, just a little.

"That was the vehicle we were just in, wasn't it?" she said.

"It was," the avatar agreed. "Whoever's coordinating this is thinking commendably quickly. NR, almost certainly." They thudded down more steps, spiralling downwards all the time, so fast Yime felt she was starting to get dizzy. It was hurting her knees and ankles and back, too. "Best not to tarry, then," the avatar said, putting on a burst of speed. She heard and vaguely sensed him disappearing round the curve of the winding stair.

"I can't go that fast!" she shouted.

"Of course not," he said, stopping; she thudded into him. "My apologies. Jump on my back; we'll go faster. Just keep your head down."

She was too breathless to argue. She climbed onto his back, legs round his waist, arms about his neck.

"Hold tight," the avatar said. She did. They set off, whirling down the steps so fast it was almost falling.

Those who had seen the first two incursions reported seeing a cerise beam destroy first the high bridge and then the wheeled, airborne cable-craft. In both cases the beam simply came angling down from the ceiling of the cavern having bored through many tens of metres of rock before transfixing its target.

The third and the last time the beam assaulted Iobe Cavern City, it hit an ancient ornamental stone tower, part of the original Central University buildings. The beam struck the old tower near its base, bringing the whole edifice tumbling down.

At first it was thought there had been no casualties, until, half a day later, the bodies of a man and a woman were discovered, still locked together, her legs round his waist, her arms round his neck, under the hundreds of tonnes of rubble.

*

There was a house which was the shape of the galaxy. It was a virtual house, of course, but it was very highly detailed and well imagined, and although the scale on which it modelled the galaxy could vary quite a lot from time to time and from place to place within it, the general effect was convincing for the beings who had brought the house into existence, and, at least as far as they were concerned, the surroundings felt agreeably familiar.

The beings concerned were Culture Minds: the very high-level AIs which were, by some distance, the most complicated and intelligent entities in the whole civilisation, and – arguably – amongst the most complicated and intelligent entities in the whole galaxy-wide meta-civilisation.

The house was used to indicate where the individual Minds were in the real galaxy, so that a Mind which existed within an Orbital Hub close to the galactic centre would be located in the great bulbous, multi-storeyed centre of the house, while a ship Mind in a vessel currently somewhere towards the wispy tip of one of the galaxy's arms would appear in one of the single-room tall outer wings. There were special arrangements for those Minds who didn't want their location known by all and sundry: they tended to inhabit pleasingly dilapidated outbuildings within what were effectively the grounds of the main construction, communicating at a remove.

The house itself manifested as an echoingly vast baroque edifice of extraordinary, ornamental richness, every room the size of a cathedral and full of intricately carved wooden walls and pierced screens, gleaming floors of inlaid wood and semi-precious stone, ceilings dripping with precious metals and minerals, and populated, usually quite sparsely, by the avatars of the Minds, which took on pretty much every form of being and object known.

Unrestricted by such tiresome three-dimensional constraints as the laws of perspective, every one of the many thousands of rooms was visible from every other, if not through doorways then through tiny icons/screens/apertures in the walls which, on sufficiently close inspection, let one see into those immensely distant rooms in some detail. Minds, of course, being used to existing within four dimensions as a matter of tedious day-to-day reality, had no problem dealing with this sort of topological sleight-of-hand.

The only reality-based restriction the galactic house modelled accurately was that produced by the deeply annoying fact that even hyperspacial light did not travel with infinite speed. To carry on a normal conversation with another Mind, one had to be in the same room and reasonably close to it. Even two Minds being within the same vast room but on opposite sides created a noticeable delay as they shouted back and forth.

Being any further away meant sending messages. These usually showed up as gently glowing symbols flickering disembodied in the air in front of the recipient, but – subject to the witheringly prodigious imaginations of Minds in general and the particular and quite possibly highly eccentric predilections of the sender in particular – could show up as almost anything. Swift-moving ballets consisting of multiply-limbed aliens, on fire and throwing shapes which just happened briefly to resemble Marain symbols (for example) were by no means unknown.

Vatueil had vaguely heard of this place. He'd always wondered what it actually looked like. He gazed around, astounded, wondering how you would describe it, how a poet might find the words to portray something of its bewildering richness and complexity. In appearance he was a pan-human male; tall and wearing the dress uniform of a Space Marshal. He stood in this vast room – shaped like the inside of a vast beach-shell to resemble the general volume of space called the Doplioid Spiral Fragment – and watched as what looked like a substantial chandelier lowered itself from the ceiling. Inspected closely, the ceiling was mostly composed of such chandeliers. When its lower-middle section got level with his head, the chandelier – a riot of fabulously intertwined multi-coloured glass spirals and corkscrew shapes – stopped.

"Space Marshal Vatueil, welcome," it said. Its voice had a sort of gentle, tinkling quality appropriate to its appearance. "My name is Zaive; I'm a Hub-mind with a special interest in the Quietus section. I'll let the others introduce themselves."

Vatueil turned to find that – without him having noticed them arriving – there were two humans, a large, hovering blue bird and what looked like a crudely carved, garishly painted ventriloquist's dummy sitting on a small multi-coloured balloon, all standing or floating around him.

"I'm the *Fixed Grin*," the first human told him; the avatar had silvery skin and looked vaguely female. "Representing Numina." It nodded/bowed.

"The *Scar Glamour*," the blue bird told him. "SC."

"*Beastly To The Animals*," the other humanoid avatar said, a thin-looking male. "I represent the interests of Restoria."

"*Labtebricolephile*," the dummy may have announced, having what sounded like trouble with the "L" sounds. "Civilian." It paused. "Eccentric," it added, needlessly.

"And that," the chandelier called Zaive said, as the others helpfully looked off to one side, "is the *Dressed Up To Party*."

The *Dressed Up To Party* was a small orange-red cloud hanging more or less over the hovering blue bird.

"The *Dressed Up To Party* is also non-aligned and is some non-specific distance away; its contributions will be sporadic," Zaive said.

"And probably beside the point, as well as trailing it," the blue bird representing the *Scar Glamour* said. It cocked its iridescently plumaged head to look up at the orange-red cloud, but there was no visible response.

"Together," Zaive said, "we make up the Specialist Agencies Prompt Response Committee, or at least the local chapter, as it were. A small number of other interested parties, each no less security-conscious than ourselves, will be listening in at greater removes and may contribute subsequently. Do you need any explanation regarding our titles or terminology?"

"No, thank you," Vatueil said.

"We understand that you represent the highest strategic level of command within the anti-Hell side in the current confliction regarding the Hells, is that right?"

"Yes," Vatueil confirmed.

"So, Space Marshal Vatueil," the bird said flapping its short wings lazily – too slowly for it to have truly hovered had this all been taking place in the Real. "You indicated this was both urgent and of the highest importance. What is it you wish to tell us?"

"It's about the war over the Hells," Vatueil said.

"That kind of came presupposed," the bird said.

Vatueil sighed. "Are you aware that the anti-Hell side is losing?"

"Of course," the bird said.

"And that we attempted to hack the substrates of the pro-Hell side?"

"We had guessed as much," the thin-looking male said.

"Those attempts failed," Vatueil said. "Therefore we decided to bring the war into the Real, to construct a fleet of ships which would destroy as many of the Hell-containing substrates as possible."

"So the entire decades-long confliction was for nothing," the blue bird said crisply, "putting it on the same level as the vows one assumes you must have taken at the start of the war renouncing resort to precisely the two courses you have just outlined."

"That's . . . a weighty thing to have done, Space Marshal," the dummy said, hinged jaws clicking as it spoke.

"It was not a step we took lightly," Vatueil agreed.

"Perhaps it was not a step you should have taken at all," the blue bird said.

"I am not here to justify my actions or decisions or those of my comrades or co-conspirators," Vatueil said. "I am here only to—"

"Try to implicate us?" the blue bird said. "Half the galaxy assumes we're behind the anti-Hell forces anyway. Perhaps by coming here – and being allowed audience despite the earnest entreaties of some of us – you intend to persuade the other half?" Directly above the bird's head, the little orange-red cloud had just started to rain, though no moisture seemed to reach the *Scar Glamour*'s avian avatar.

"I'm here to tell you that the anti-Hell forces came to an agreement with the GFCF and elements of the Sichultian Enablement

– behind the backs of the NR and their allies, the Flekke and the Jhlupians – to build us our fleet using the Tsungarial Disk. However, we have received intelligence that the NR thought that they too had an agreement with the Sichultia, promising that they – the Sichultia – would refuse to help the anti-Hell side and would do whatever the NR wanted them to do to stop any war fleet being built."

"The Sichultia sound as free with their agreements as you and your fellows are with your solemn undertakings, Space Marshal," the blue bird representing SC said.

"Must you be quite so unpleasant to our guest?" the silver-skinned avatar asked the *Scar Glamour*'s avatar. The bird bristled its feathers and said:

"Yes."

"We have also heard," Vatueil said, "that the NR, the Culture and the GFCF are currently in some way engaged in the Sichultian Enablement, especially around the Tsungarial Disk. Assuming this is the case, it was thought important that you were informed – at the highest level – that the Sichultia are on the side which everyone assumes you wish to win in the confliction."

"Difficult though it may be for you to imagine somebody keeping their word in any circumstances, Space Marshal," the blue bird said, "what makes you think that the Sichultia will stick to the agreement they made with you rather than the one they made with the NR?"

"The agreement made with the NR basically meant doing nothing. The agreement made with us meant becoming involved with a conspiracy that would be largely under the control of others and that would proceed regardless of the Sichultians' initial operational involvement, while exposing them to a substantial risk of being punished by the NR even if they changed their minds before their part in the conspiracy became crucial. It makes no sense for them to have entered into the agreement unless they were going to see it through."

"That does make sense," Zaive said, voice tinkling. "So," the thin male avatar said, "we should do nothing to stop the Sichultia from doing whatever it is they are doing in and around the Tsungarial Disk?"

Vatueil shrugged. "I can't tell you what to do. I'm not even going to make any suggestions. We just thought you should know what's going on."

"We understand," Zaive said.

"I have some intelligence," the blue bird announced.

Vatueil turned and looked levelly at it.

"My intelligence tells me that you are a traitor, Space Marshal Vatueil."

Vatueil continued to look at the bird as it flapped lazily in front of him. The orange-red cloud above the *Scar Glamour*'s avatar had stopped raining. Vatueil turned to address Zaive. "I have no more to report. If I may be excused . . ."

"Yes," the chandelier said. "Though there was no indication with the signal carrying you what was to be done with your mind-state following delivery of your message. I think we all assumed that you were to be returned to your war sim high command, but perhaps you had something else in mind?"

Vatueil smiled. "I'm to be deleted," he said. "To avoid any further unseemly hint at complicity with the anti-Hell forces on your part."

"How very thoughtful," the silver-skinned vaguely female avatar said. Vatueil chose to assume that she meant it.

"I'm sure we can offer you the processing space to be housed within a Virtuality," Zaive said. "Wouldn't you rather—?

"No, thank you. My original has been through more virtualities, downloads and re-incorporations than he cares to think about. Any selves he sends out such as myself are quite inured to the thought of personal deletion so long as we know our original persists somewhere." The Space Marshal smiled, and knew that he looked resigned as he did so. "And even if not . . . this has been a very long war, and I am very tired, in all my iterations. Death no longer seems so terrible a thing, on any level."

"That may," the blue bird said, "be just as well." For once though, its tone was less than cutting.

"Indeed," Vatueil said. He looked round them all. "Thank you for listening. Goodbye." He looked at the chandelier and nodded.

He winked out of existence.

"Well," Zaive said.

"Do we take this at face value?" the silver-skinned avatar asked.

"It fits well with what we know," the wooden dummy said. "Better than most sims."

"And do we trust the Space Marshal?" Zaive asked.

The bird made a snorting sound. "That errant, ramshackled ghost?" it said scornfully. "He's known of old; I doubt he even remembers who he used to be, let alone what he believes in or most recently promised."

"We don't need to trust it to incorporate the import of its information into our calculations," the silver-skinned female said.

The thin male avatar looked at the chandelier. "You need to tell your accident-prone agent to stop wasting time and get to where she's supposed to get to, preferably without, this time, getting any more innocent people killed. Stop the Y'breq woman killing Veppers." The man turned to the blue bird with the orange-red cloud hanging over it. "Though of course that won't be necessary if SC would just tell the *Falling Outside The Normal Moral Constraints* to stop indulging whatever bizarre fantasies of gallantry, vicarious revenge or just devilment it's currently revelling in."

"Don't look at me," the *Scar Glamour*'s avatar said, flapping indignantly. "That bastard excuse for a picket ship's got nothing to do with me." The bird cocked its head and looked up at the orange cloud. "You'd better be listening," it squawked. "You've got the contacts; *you* talk to the GSV that spawned that particular Abomination; get it to try and bang some sense into the bug-fuck shrapnel that makes up what passes for a Mind in that demented machine."

. . . good night, good night, good night.

A chill struck her skin. She wanted to shiver, but felt too lethargic; all swaddled, lost in a warm, baking fug.

What sounded like a real voice came clanging in, unwelcome. "Hello! Anybody in there?" it said. "Anybody alive?"

"Huh?" She heard herself say. Great; now she was hallucinating, hearing voices.

"Hello!"

"Yes? What? Hello to you too." She was talking, not sending, she realised. That was weird. It took a few moments, but she got her eyes open, unsticking them. She blinked, waited for everything to swim into focus. Light. There was light. Dim, but it looked real. Face plate of helmet; internal visor screen, currently showing just static, but enough to reveal that both her inner and outer suits seemed to have expanded around her, and chilly draughts of air were flowing over her exposed body, raising goose-bumps. She could breathe! She took some deep, satisfying breaths, luxuriating in the feel of the cold air entering her mouth and nostrils, and her rib cage being able to expand as far as it could.

"Auppi Unstril, that right?" the voice said.

"Umm, yes." Her mouth felt clogged, sticky; all gummed up like her eyes had been. She licked her lips; they felt puffy and over-sensitive. But just being able to lick them felt so good. "Who you?" She cleared her throat. "Who am I talking to?"

"I'm an element of the Culture Abominator-class picket ship *Falling Outside The Normal Moral Constraints.*"

"An element?"

"Element five."

"Are you now? Where did you come from?"

What Abominator class? she thought. Nobody had mentioned an Abominator-class ship. Was this real? She still wasn't sure that this wasn't just some very lucid dream. She found the nipple on the end of the helmet's flexible water tube, sucked on it. The water was cool, sweet, beautiful. Real, she told herself. Real water, real chill on the skin, real voice. Real real real. She felt the water coursing down inside her, chilling her throat, oesophagus and stomach as she swallowed.

"Is where I came from relevant?" the voice said. "My whole was pretending to be a Torturer class earlier, if that helps."

"Ah. Are you *rescuing* me, Element five?"

"I am. Currently I have Displaced nano-dust working to repair what I can of your Module. It should be ready to power up again in a few minutes. You *could* then make your way to the nearest base, which would be the near-planet monitoring unit five; however, in the light of the recent hostile actions I think it might be wiser and even safer if you join me, coming within my field enclosure. Your choice."

"What would you do if you were me?"

"Oh, I'd stick with me, but then I'm bound to say that, aren't I?"

"I suppose you are." She drank more of the precious, beautiful water. "But I will stick with you."

"Wise choice."

"How is everybody else? Are you rescuing the others? There were twenty-three other microship pilots and nearly forty others, plus the people on the *Hylozoist*. How are they?"

"The *Hylozoist* lost four crew, one person was killed when the near-planet monitoring unit five was damaged. Two of the Module/microship pilots were killed, one in a collision with a fabricary, the other burning up within the atmosphere of Razhir. The other pilots have been, are being or shortly will be rescued."

"Who were they? Who were the two pilots who died?"

"Lofgyr, Inhada was the one killed in the collision with a fabricary and Tersetier, Lanyares died when his ship burned up within the atmosphere of the gas giant."

Backed up, she thought. He was backed up. It's all right; he can come back. It will take time and even though he might not be exactly the same person, he'll be mostly the same person. Of course he'll still love you. He'd be a fool not to. Wouldn't he?

She found that she was crying.

"Bettlescroy. I understand you've been looking for me."

"Indeed I have, Veppers. You look well for a dead man."

The image of the GFCF Legislator-Admiral on the little flat-screen comms computer wavered a little. The signal was weak, multiply scrambled. Veppers sat with Jasken in a small room in one of his emergency safe houses in Ubruater city, a few blocks and the width of a ribbon-park away from the main town house.

The safe house – one of several prepared long ago, just in case the wrong politicians or judges got into positions of real power and started making things uncomfortable for creative, buccaneering business people who didn't always do things the conventional way – had shielded comms links to the systems in the town house. As soon as they'd arrived – both in the uniforms of paramedics – Veppers had taken a shower, scrubbing any remaining radioactive soot or ash out of his hair and skin, while Jasken had woken up the slightly archaic equipment in the study and started trawling the news channels and message systems. The series of urgent calls and messages from Legislator-Admiral Bettlescroy-Bisspe-Blispin III had been hard to ignore.

"Thank you," Veppers told the angelic-looking little alien. "You look as you always do. What's our situation?"

A wavering smile on the little alien's face might have been distorted or exaggerated by the lo-fi screen. "Your situation is that you need to tell me, *now*, Veppers, where our targets are. It is more than urgent; it is crucial. All we've planned and worked for now depends on this."

"I see. All right. I'll tell you."

"That comes as a great, if absurdly belated, relief."

"Though, first, I am – as you might imagine – quite interested in finding out who tried to blow me out of the skies on my own flier, over my own estate."

"Almost certainly the NR," Bettlescroy said quickly, waving one hand as though this was hardly worth mentioning.

"You've obviously given the subject considerable thought, ally," Veppers said quietly.

Bettlescroy looked exasperated. "The NR seem to feel you have betrayed them in some way. Though just possibly it was the Flekke, sub-contracting in some way, ever anxious to please. And the Jhlupians might feel wronged, too. Your friend Xingre seems to have disappeared, which probably means something. We will do all we can with all the resources we can afford to devote to the matter to find out who might have been responsible; however the *targets* are still – by far – the most important issue outstanding here."

"Agreed. But first, your situation. I've got a little out of touch here; what's happening?"

Bettlescroy seemed to be trying to control itself. "Perhaps," it said calmly, "I have not indicated as forcefully as I might that the target information is of vital importance *right now*!" it said, almost screaming the last two words.

"I take your point," Veppers said smoothly. "The targets will be with you very shortly. But I need to know what's happening."

"What's *happening*, Veppers," Bettlescroy hissed, sitting so close to the screen camera at its end that its face appeared distorted, almost ugly, "is that a fucking Culture *hyper-ship* that can split up to become a *fleet* of ships is laying waste to our fucking war fleet of ships even as we speak and even as you, unbelievably, continue to waste time. It's destroying thousands of them each *minute*! Within a day and a half there will be no more ships left! And this despite the fact that I took it upon myself to order that *all* the fabricaria able to do so start manufacturing ships, not just the proportion we originally agreed on."

Veppers assumed a look of pretended hurt. "Going back on our agree—?" he began.

"Shut up!" Bettlescroy shouted, one tiny fist thudding down on the desk beneath the screen. "The Culture vessel has also already worked out how to get the fabricaria-built ships to set about destroying each other, which might result in the ships annihilating themselves even quicker; within a matter of hours. It would appear only to be holding back from this course because it fears some of the ships might accidentally or mistakenly damage the fabricaria, a consequence it wishes to avoid if possible, to preserve the – and I quote – 'unique techno-cultural monument that is the Tsungarial Disk'. That's so thoughtful, don't you think that's so thoughtful? I think that's so fucking thoughtful." Bettlescroy stared out of the screen at them with a fierce, unnatural smile that held no humour whatsoever. "However, this *thing*, this wonderful super-powerful 'ally' that we suddenly discovered we had, now blithely tells us it will hold this tactic in reserve and meanwhile continue to target the ships itself for the sake of 'engagemental accuracy' and to 'minimise collateral damage', though frankly my fellow officers and myself strongly suspect it's really doing so because it's *enjoying* itself so much, just as it appeared quite heartily to enjoy disposing of nearly a third of our naval fleet on its approach to the Tsung system. I hope this is giving you some small, modest, indicationary idea of just how powerless we are out here at the moment, Veppers, old fellow, while we wait for your precious fucking targets.

"Meanwhile, we are continuing to deal with our pretend smatter outbreak, which has proved trickier than we anticipated, and are ourselves even having to destroy some of the fabricaria-built war fleet we worked so hard to create, just to make it look convincing to the Culture that we really are all just chums and allies fighting on the same jolly side.

"Oh! And I nearly forgot; an NR ship is causing havoc on/in/all over Vebezua! Yes! Another ship, possibly a Culture ship, possibly another Culture *war*ship, was last heard of high-tailing it out of the Vebezua system, possibly having delivered something or somebody, and possibly now departing there with the intention of joining in all the fun out here at the Disk and depleting our once-fine fleet of ships even quicker. And the NR themselves are making deeply suspicious noises, bordering on outright *hostile* noises, when it comes both to ourselves and you, Veppers, and are only not helping to destroy our short-lived war fleet because they want to see how fast and how ably the Culture vessel-fleet does so; valuable intelligence, we are given to understand. Though of course the presence and presumed hostility of the NR does mean that any of our ships that might escape from the vicinity of the Disk itself may well find themselves being picked off by the NR.

"There. *That* is the fucking situation. I face shame, humiliation, demotion, court martial and ruin, and – oh, *please* do believe me, *dear* Mr. Veppers – if such a fate befalls me I shall do *everything*

I possibly can to make sure that you fall with me, cherished ally and co-conspirator."

Bettlescroy took a deep breath, drew itself up and, collecting itself, it seemed, made a calm, expansive motion with its hands. "Now," it said. "I can't really imagine how many more of our ships have been laid waste while I have been speaking but I imagine the number comes to some several thousand. *Please*, Veppers, if we are to salvage anything, anything at all from what is increasingly looking like a calamitous venture and an utterly hopeless situation, tell us where the targets are. At least some of them, at least the nearest ones, given that we will have so few ships, so ill-equipped and so slow-moving, by the time you get round to finally telling us where . . ." Bettlescroy paused, ". . . the fucking . . ." it paused again, taking another deep breath, ". . . targets . . ." one last pause, ". . . are."

Veppers sighed. "Thank you, Bettlescroy. That was really all I wanted to know." He smiled. "One moment . . ." He clicked the sound off at the computer and turned to Jasken. On the screen, Bettlescroy appeared to be shouting, and striking the screen at its end with both hands. Jasken had to tear his gaze away.

"Sir?"

"Jasken, I'm absolutely famished. Would you mind seeing what we have in the kitchen here? Just a bite or two and some decent wine. Even water would do . . . but do look for some drinkable wine. Get something for yourself, too." Veppers grinned, nodded at the comms unit, where Bettlescroy appeared to be trying to bite the edge of the screen. "I can manage here."

"Sir," Jasken said, and left the room.

Veppers watched the study door close, then turned back to the screen and switched the sound back on.

". . . *Where*?" Bettlescroy shrieked.

"Ready?" Veppers asked calmly.

Bettlescroy sat staring at the screen, eyes wide, breathing hard. What might have been spittle disfigured its finely made chin.

"Good," Veppers said, smiling. "The most important targets – the only ones really worth bothering with now – are easily reached and close by; they're under the trackways on my estate of Espersium. In fact, come to think of it, somebody – possibly the NR, as you suggest – has already begun the task of destroying them, when they attacked my flier.

"Anyway, to reiterate: every trackway is underlain by what to the untutored eye looks like some sort of giant fungal structure. It isn't. It's substrate. Low-power, bio-based, not ultra-fast running, but high-efficiency, highly damage-resistant substrate; anything from ten to thirty metres thick under and amongst the roots, but adding up to over half a cubic kilometre of processing power spread throughout the estate. All the comms traffic to and from it is channelled through the phased array satellite links dotted round the mansion house itself. The ones that everyone still thinks just control the Virtualities and games.

"That's what you have to hit, Bettlescroy. The under-trackway substrates contain over seventy per cent of the Hells in the entire galaxy." He smiled again. "Of those we know of, anyway. Used to be slightly more, but very recently I sub-contracted the NR Hell, just to be on the safe side. I've been buying Hells up for over a century, Legislator-Admiral, taking the processing requirements and legal and jurisdictional implications off other peoples' hands for most of my business life. The majority of the Hells are right here, in system, on planet. That is why I have always felt able to be so relaxed regarding the targeting details. Think you can get enough ships to Sichult to lay waste to my estate?"

"Truly?" Bettlescroy said, gulping, still breathing deeply. "The targets are on your own *estates*? Why would you do that?"

"Deniability, Bettlescroy. You'll have to raze the trackways, wreck my lands, blast the satellite links and damage the house itself; maybe even destroy it. That house has been in my family for centuries; it and the estate are inestimably precious to me. Or at least so everybody assumes. Who's going to believe I brought all that destruction on myself?"

"And yet you . . . no, wait." The little alien shook its head. "I have to issue the relevant orders." The Legislator-Admiral bent over its desk, then looked up again. "That's all; the trackways of Espersium, centred on the house?"

"Yes," Veppers said. "Target away."

Bettlescroy took only seconds to issue the orders. When it came back it was after a blanked-out delay of a few more seconds during which, Veppers suspected, the Legislator-Admiral had composed itself, smoothed down its scalp scales and wiped its face. Bettlescroy certainly seemed much more like its old glossily imperturbable self when it switched back on.

"You would do this to yourself, Veppers? To your family's legacy?"

"If it keeps me alive to enjoy my spoils, of course. And the spoils promise to be fabulous; another order of magnitude greater than anything I'll be losing. The house can be rebuilt, the art treasures replaced, the trackways . . . well, I'd grown tired of them anyway, frankly, but they could be filled in and re-grown, I dare say. The energy weapons leave negligible radioactivity, hypervelocity kinetics leave even less, as I understand it, and the missile warheads are clean, aren't they?"

"Thermonuclear, but clean as possible. Designed to destroy, not contaminate," Bettlescroy agreed.

"There you are then; it's not as though I go camping in my estates at the best of times, so even if some areas are a bit radioactive I shan't be too heartbroken. Let's be honest; the grounds are mostly there to maintain a barrier between me and the proletarian hordes anyway. If the hills and fields do end up glowing in the dark they'll work even better as insulation against the milling masses. And, in the end, I can just buy another estate; another dozen if I like."

"And the people?"

"What people?"

"The people on the estate when it is laid waste."

"Oh. Yes. I assume I have a few hours before any attack takes place."

"Hmm." The little alien hesitated, peered at its screen. ". . . Yes. The quickest attack would come from a small squadron of the ships fitted with fleet-donated anti-matter for their warp engines; if they simply sped on past without attempting to draw to a stop first they could hit the targets within three and a half hours of now. But their on-board weaponry targeting accuracy would not be great at that speed; they would struggle to hit with less than a hundred-metre error-allowance, at best. Missiles and smart warheads would be more precise, though Sichult's own planetary defences would most likely intercept some of those. More pinpoint accuracy would need to come from ships that had slowed down almost to a stop. Again, your planet's own defences might exact a toll, though they would probably still arrive in such numbers that this would not matter. Say four to five hours for those to arrive. One might attack the trackways themselves with the first high-speed waves and target the satellite links near the house with the later-arriving vessels."

"So, bottom line: I'd have time to get a few people out," Veppers said. "Not too many, of course; it still has to look convincing. But I can always hire more *people*, Bettlescroy. Never a shortage of those, ever."

"Still, it is quite a toll you would ask of yourself."

"Sometimes you have to sacrifice small things in order to achieve great things, Bettlescroy," Veppers told the little alien. "Hosting the Hells has made me a great deal of money over the years, but they were bound to prove an embarrassment one day, or just be shut down, quite possibly with talk of law suits or reparations or whatever. All I have I can replace, and with the funds we have agreed on, and that wonderful ship . . . you haven't forgotten that wonderful ship, have you, Bettlescroy?"

"It is yours, Veppers," the Legislator-Admiral told him. "It is still being fitted out, to your instructions."

"Marvellous. Well, with all that, I'm sure I can console myself to the loss of a few trees and my country cottage. So; let's be clear. Nothing will happen for three and half hours, is that correct?"

The little alien looked at its screen again. "The first fly-by bombardment and missile launch targeting the trackways will take place in three point four-one hours from now. The missiles will impact between one and five minutes after the bombardment. The second wave of ships charged with carrying out the precision bombardment of the satellite links around the house will arrive between point five and one point zero hours later. We can't be any more accurate with the timing due to the inherent variability of warp-engine crash-stops, especially that far into the gravity wells of a star and planet. So sorry. I trust that will afford you the time to do what you need to do."

"Hmm. That will have to suffice, then, I suppose." Veppers made an expansive gesture. "Don't look so horrified, Bettlescroy! Onward and upward, don't you agree? Can't stand still; one has to embrace change, knock old stuff down to build bigger and better new stuff. Speculate to accumulate. All that sort of thing. I'm sure you have your own appropriate, culturally relevant clichés."

The Legislator-Admiral shook its small, perfectly formed head. "What a remarkable person you are, Veppers."

"I know. I amaze myself sometimes." He turned round as he heard the door behind him open. "Ah, Jasken; well done. Would you mind parcelling that stuff up to go, as a picnic? We're off on our travels again."

Twenty-seven

x*Labtebricolephile*

oLOU (Eccentric) *Me, I'm Counting*

Child, greetings. I enclose a recording of certain recent proceedings involving a mind-state representation of one Space Marshal Vatueil and a Specialist Agencies Prompt Response Committee. Please take note and act accordingly.

∞

xGSV *Dressed Up To Party*

oPS *Falling Outside the Normal Moral Constraints*

Take a look at this. SAPRC local franchise stuff; seems Space Marshal V. our son of a bitch.

∞

xPS *Falling Outside the Normal Moral Constraints*
oLOU (Eccentric) *Me, I'm Counting*

There was me about to call you Unknown Craft and wave a message beam vaguely in your direction, but now a degree of signal/identity regularity appears to be infecting the locality and I've been informed you are, after all, some sort of proper Culture ship. Hi. Me? Oh, I'm mostly kicking the living-dead shit out of the biggest sorta-smatter outbreak you ever did see in all the whole wide wonderful galaxy. What exactly are you up to? Do call; we're close enough – let's talk.

~Hello. I made a possibly foolish promise to a human on a mission and must discharge that before I am able to help you with the smatter outbreak, if that is what you would wish me to do and are hinting at. I appreciate you are being kept busy and might be able to use some assistance. I am seeing a remarkable amount of weapon blink from where I am.

~Which would appear to be on a very tight loop centred round sunny Vebezua, indulging in a translight comet impression. Well, there you are. I'm sure you have your reasons. But thank you. I am, as you say, keeping busy.

~I would hope to join you within a few hours.

~Heck, no rush. Aren't you the ship who took the image of Ms. Y'breq, few years ago?

~I am. Hence a feeling of responsibility for what has transpired.

~Decent of you. I have a presently soloing element carrying the revented Ms. Y towards Sichult even as we chat. You weren't thinking of trying to reunite her and the image at all, were you?

~No. The image remains stored, inanimate, and I intend to preserve it in that state. My promise was to get my human guest to where she wishes to go. Though my immediate concern is to avoid being attacked by the NR ship which seems aggressively interested either in whatever happens on Vebezua or in what I do. Or possibly what my guest does, or where the rescued Mind from the Quietus GCU *Bodhisattva* happens to be, which at the moment is within my field enclosure following the trashing of its ship by the Unfallen Bulbitian in the Semsarine Wisp. The offending NR vessel is reticent regarding divulging what precisely its priorities are, though they certainly seem to include threatening me. Much as I hate to add to your Do list, given your current preoccupation with clunking herds of near-mindless smatter vessels, there is nevertheless this highly capable NR craft giving a fellow Culture ship grief for no apparent good reason. I am a humble and rather elderly Limited Offensive Unit, by inclination and declaration devoutly Eccentric for many a century and hence long unused to the hurly-burly of even simulated battle and profoundly out of the circuit regarding recent advances in EqT ship weaponry and tactics; subjects in which I imagine you must excel. A thought, merely. When you have the time. Now, I must continue trying to arrange a high-speed Displace of two persons, including a non-lace-equipped human, from a planetary surface while an NR ship tries to stop me. Always assuming I can locate the two persons concerned; they appear to have vanished.

~Fascinating. You obviously have your fields full. I'll leave you to it. Do let's keep in touch.

"The *Me, I'm Counting*? The ship with Himerance?" Lededje asked. Suddenly she was back in her room in the town house, ten years earlier, listening in the darkness to the tall, stooped, bald old man as he talked softly about taking an image of her that was faithful and precise down to the individual atom.

"The very same," Demeisen said. Element twelve of the picket ship *Falling Outside The Normal Moral Constraints* was bearing down on the inner system of the Quyn system, heading straight for a region of space a few hundred kilometres above where the city of Ubruater on the planet Sichult would be in just a few minutes. The ship element was braking hard and negotiating even more strenuously with the relevant authorities on and around the planet. "It still has the image of you that it took when you were younger."

"What's it doing here?" Lededje asked. In a suspicious tone, Demeisen thought. They were stepped-back from full foamed-up ultra-alert, sitting in their seats on the module, Lededje's helmet visor lying opened so that she and the avatar could look at each other.

"I suspect it's carrying a person from Quietus called Yime Nsokyi," Demeisen told her. "Didn't mention her by name but a little research makes it highly likely it's her."

"And what's *she* doing here?"

"Quietus might be interested in you. As a revented little icicle they may feel that somehow you're their responsibility."

She looked at the avatar for a moment. "Are they always this . . . keen?"

Demeisen shook his head emphatically. "No. There's probably some other reason."

"Care to take a guess?"

"Who can say, doll? They may have some interest in the relationship between you and Mr. Veppers, especially as it might manifest itself in the near to medium future. They may not feel that your intentions towards him are entirely peaceful, and wish to forestall some untoward diplomatic incident."

"What about you; would you act to forestall this untoward diplomatic incident?"

"Might do. Depends on the likely consequences. You have my sympathies, goes without saying, but even I at least have to *look* like I'm taking account of the bigger picture. Consequences are everything." The avatar nodded at the screen. "Oh, look; we're here."

Sichult filled the screen; a fat hazy crescent of white cloud, grey-green land and streaks of glinting blue seas lay tipped and swollen across the screen. They were close enough for Lededje to see depth in the clear, thin wrapping of atmosphere and make out the shadows of individual storm cells throwing their dark, elongated shapes across the flat white plains of cloud levels extending beneath them.

"Home at last," Lededje breathed. She did not, the avatar

thought, sound all that pleased about it. He'd thought she would have shown more interest in the image of her held by the other Culture ship, too. He'd never understand humans.

"Ah, found him," Demeisen said, smiling.

Lededje stared at him. "Veppers?"

Demeisen nodded. "Veppers."

"Where?" she asked.

"Hmm, interesting," the avatar said. He looked at her. "You should dress for the occasion. Let's get you out of those cumbersome suits."

She frowned. "I like these suits. And they're not cumbersome."

Demeisen looked apologetic. "You won't need them where we're going. And they do constitute Culture tech. Sorry."

The seat around Lededje gently released her from its grip. Behind her, the module's bathroom had reformed.

Yime Nsokyi stood on the rim-rock of the shallow, jagged canyon carved into the karst. Above, the stars wheeled slowly. Some long, ragged lengths of clouds obscured patches of the sky, and in one place the cloud was lit up as though by an enormous searchlight, light spilling from an aperture above one of the outlying tributary tunnels of Iobe Cavern City. The resulting blob of uncannily glowing light, seemingly hovering just a couple of kilometres above the still-cooling desert, looked unsettlingly like a ship.

"There *were* people in that tower," Himerance said quietly at Yime's side. The avatar was monitoring signals from all over the planet while trying to establish contact with the *Me, I'm Counting*.

"There were?" Yime asked. She closed her eyes, shook her head.

They had commandeered five more vehicles on their way out of the city to this point, where finally the avatar felt they were safe. Himerance had commandeered them, anyway, using whatever Effector tech was built into the human-seeming body of a ship avatar; she felt like nothing more than his baggage, hauled along from place to place.

She remembered the stone tower, way back in the early evening, when she'd had to cling on to his back as they raced down the winding steps, dashing out through a thick door in the base – Himerance had muttered something about it being locked from the inside at the time – and then, with her once more on her own feet, running out across a courtyard, down some more steps and into a crowded pedestrian street just as a pink beam lanced from the cavern ceiling and struck the tower, bringing it down. She had wanted to keep her head down and keep on walking away, but of course that would have looked suspicious, so they had to stop and stare with everybody else for a while.

"How many?" she asked.

"Two," Himerance said. "Lovers, reading between the lines."

Yime sighed, looked down. The canyon floor held a dirt track, scribbled like dropped string between the jagged jumble of fallen rocks and scrawny, light-blasted scrub. "One of us is spreading destruction in their wake, Himerance," Yime said. "And I'm afraid that it's me."

"I wouldn't worry about it," the avatar said. It looked at her. "I'm afraid I am unable to contact the ship. Not without alerting the NR vessel, anyway."

"I see. What now, then?"

"We resort to a much older form of signalling," Himerance said, smiling. There was a hint of a glow on the horizon to one side, where the dawn would come soon. The avatar nodded in that direction. "We know which direction the ship is coming from. With luck and good timing, this will work. Excuse me." The avatar stepped in front of her, raising his hands, shallowly cupped, palms outwards, in front of his face, oriented towards the dim pre-dawn light-sliver over the distant hills. He looked round at her. "You would be advised to turn your back, put your hands over your eyes and close your eyelids."

Yime held his gaze for a moment, then complied.

Nothing happened for a few seconds.

"What are—?" she was asking, when a sudden flash distracted her. It was gone almost before she registered it happening.

"All clear," Himerance said quietly. She turned back to find the avatar waving his hands around. They were smoking. The flesh on the palms and fingers was blackened. He blew on them, smiled at her, then nodded at the ground. "We should assume the position," he told her.

They squatted, side by side, her knees and back protesting. *Oh shit*, she thought, as she clasped her hands round her shins and laid her head on her knees. *Here we go again.*

"Won't be for long," he said. "One way or the other, we'll know quite soo—"

"I don't *want* him to see me," Lededje said. "I don't want him to be able to identify me."

"Ah," Demeisen said, nodding. "So you might be able to surprise him later; of course."

She remained silent.

"So do something with your tattoo," Demeisen said. "Scroll it over your face so it obscures your features. May I?" The avatar gestured towards her face.

She was standing in the doorway of the module's bathroom area, dressed in the sort of casual clothes she'd been wearing and feeling perfectly happy and comfortable in ever since she'd been brought back to life, yet feeling oddly naked, vulnerable and exposed, now that she'd taken off both the outer armoured suit and gel suit within. Demeisen wore pale, loose, casual clothes.

She had thought of setting the tat to transparency, so that if Veppers saw her he wouldn't know she had it. She still had plans to use its – by Sichultian standards – unprecedented abilities to get close to him at some point in the future, when she'd have a weapon. Let him hear of some fabulous creature with a tattoo of unheard-of complexity and subtlety, better and more exclusive than anything he had ever possessed, and have him come calling, unsuspecting.

"All right," she said.

She watched in a reverser field as the tattoo rearranged itself on her face. In less than a second, she didn't recognise herself. The effect was astounding; all that had happened was that the lines bunched here and thickened there, became very fine here, hinted at shading there, at gradients that didn't really exist here and here and here, cast a sort of hinted-at ruddiness all over her skin . . . and just with that, with the suggestion of different planes and lines and altered surfaces, colours and textures, had easily done enough to make her face look quite completely different.

She moved her face this way and that, put the reverser onto mirror, all to check that the effect didn't just work from one angle or when lit only from one direction. The effect of disguise remained; her face looked broader and darker, her brows thicker, her nose flatter, her lips fuller and her cheekbones less prominent.

She nodded. "That is quite good," she conceded. She turned to the avatar. "Thank you."

"You're welcome," Demeisen said. "Now, can we go?"

"As though I have any choice."

"Sounds like a hearty affirmation to me."

"Wait; who do we say—?" she said, but then she was staring at the dim distorted reflection of her new, stranger's face for a moment, listening to the words "—I am?" sound loud and strange in her ears.

Before she knew it, she was standing blinking in the cool, pleasantly fragranced air of a large, bright room in what must be a tall building.

The view was of afternoon sky, puffy white clouds, and a city across a broad wooded park. The city looked like Ubruater. The room was very large and high ceilinged, with a large desk in one corner and some tall potted plants dotted about a gleaming wooden floor strewn with beautiful rugs. Those items aside, it was minimally furnished with large pieces in cream and grey. On one long seat, lounging, one arm flung over the back, the other holding a small cup, sat Joiler Veppers. To his side sat Jasken; on the other side of a low table sat a large, very straight-backed middle-aged woman Lededje half recognised. She had a child on her knee. A drone like a small smooth suitcase floated near the woman's shoulder. A wall screen, sound muted, was cycling through news channels; fuzzy images and clear graphics of dense fleets of ships filled the screen, interspersed by well-groomed, very serious-looking presenters.

The woman waved one arm languidly towards them. "Mr. Veppers, may I present Av Demeisen, representative of the Culture ship *Falling Outside The Normal Moral Constraints*, and guest. Ship: Mr. Joiler Veppers, Mr. Hibin Jasken, the drone Trachelmatis Olfes-Hresh Stidikren-tra Muoltz—"

"Though I answer to 'Olf'," the drone said, with a sort of sideways bow. "Too much spittle ruins these floors."

"And this is my son Liss," the woman continued, smiling, ruffling the blond hair of the young child on her knee. He was biting on a biscuit, but spared the time to wave. Then he patted his hair back down. "I'm Buoyte-Pfaldsa Kreit Lei Huen da' Motri," the woman went on. "Culture ambassador to the Enablement." She waved her arm again, towards a couch across from her, at right angles to the one that Veppers and Jasken sat on. "Please; sit down."

"Hello, all," Demeisen said loudly, radiating bonhomie.

Lededje watched Veppers watching her as she and the avatar approached the seating area. He looked pretty much as he had. Hair and skin as full and luxuriant as ever. Dressed more casually and soberly than he usually was when in the city; almost dully, as though he was trying to blend in for once. Nose a little pink and thin at the tip. She met his gaze only briefly, tried to look unconcerned. He was smiling at her. She recognised that particular smile. It was the one that acknowledged beauty but hinted at vulnerability, the one that was meant to say "I may be the richest man in the world but I can still be a little unsure of myself around beautiful women like yourself." She was aware that Jasken was also looking at her, but she ignored him.

She took a couple of quick steps just before they got to the seats, so that she sat closer to Veppers than Demeisen seemed to have intended. The avatar was to her right, Veppers at an angle, left and in front. The low table held what looked like the remains of a small picnic: pots, small trays, unfolded take-away plates, cups, saucers and some scattered cutlery.

"Won't you introduce your guest, Demeisen?" the ambassador said.

"Tsk!" the avatar said, slapping his forehead. "My manners, eh?" Demeisen waved one arm from Lededje to Veppers. "Doll, this is your rapist and murderer. Veppers, you ghastly cunt, this is Lededje Y'breq, back from the dead."

There was a tiny pause. Lededje took only that moment to register what had just happened. Then she bounced out of the couch she had barely sat down on, scooped up the sharpest-looking knife on the table and threw herself at Veppers.

It was only later she understood how little chance she'd really had. The knife disappeared from her grip, plucked away by Demeisen, despite the fact he was on her far side from Veppers.

Jasken moved less quickly, seeming almost to hesitate for a fraction of a second, but even as Lededje got one hand on Veppers' throat – he was shrinking back, eyes widening, as she threw herself forward – Jasken suddenly had her wrist in a grip like steel.

Meanwhile the drone Olfes-Hresh had snapped through the air to her other side, whipping a blue-glowing force field between her torso and Veppers' and gripping her left arm, keeping that hand held up and away. Lededje heard herself make an anguished, strangling noise as she tried to close her fingers round Veppers' throat.

She heard a brief, deep humming noise and experienced a sort of coldness wash over her, making her skin crawl, then – her hand still clutching at Veppers' throat as he thudded back into the back of the couch – she felt herself being grabbed round the waist. She tried to kick, but her legs seemed to have lost contact with her brain; she felt hopelessly, childishly dizzy, her hand was forced back, and she was pulled away across the low table in a further scatter of food, crockery and cutlery to be plonked down on the couch, not where she had been but with Demeisen between her and Veppers, who was sitting back up now and rubbing his throat.

Demeisen had an arm across Lededje's upper chest, pinning her against some flattened cushions. One of his legs was trapping both her legs under the couch.

"Gasslikunt!" said a small voice.

Kreit Huen glared at the avatar. "See what you've done?" she muttered. She cuddled the boy to her, patting the nape of his neck and back of his head with her hand.

"Motherf—!" Lededje began, struggling mightily to get out from under Demeisen's limbs, then trying to reach the avatar's face with her fingers, to tear his eyes out or scratch him or do anything at all to hurt him.

"Spirited little thing, isn't she?" Veppers said calmly, waving Jasken away as the other man tried to fuss over him.

"Behave," Demeisen said quietly, levelly to Lededje.

"I'll f . . . !" she spat, heaving herself towards him. She got her back about a centimetre away from the couch before she was thrown against it again.

"Led," the avatar said, a small smile on his face, "you were never going to get a clear shot at him. Now sit still and behave yourself or I will have to stun you again, and more than just your legs this time." He loosened his grip on her a little, tentatively.

She sat still, looked at him with an expression of cold loathing. "You unmitigated piece of ordure in human shape," she said, very quietly. "Why did you lead me on? Why did you give me any hope at all?"

"Things change, Lededje," the avatar told her, sounding reasonable. He withdrew the arm and leg that had been restraining her. "Circumstances, and likely consequences. That's just the way it is."

Lededje glanced at Huen and her child. "Go and stuprate yourself," she whispered to the avatar. He shook his head, made a *tsk* sound again.

Veppers looked at Huen. "Why is this psychotically rude man trying to convince me that this even more berserk young woman is the late, lamented Ms. Y'breq, and why are they even here?"

"He may believe that she *is* Ms. Y'breq," Huen told him. She turned to the drone, handing the child up to it. "Olf, please take Liss to the playroom. This was a mistake. I'm an idiot."

"Gasslikunt!" Liss repeated, cradled in ruby-red fields as the drone took the child and swept away towards the doors.

Huen smiled as she gazed after the boy, waving.

When the doors closed she turned back to Veppers. "I am not entirely sure why Av Demeisen thought to bring this young lady with him, but I wanted him here because he represents the most powerful vessel in the vicinity, with the power to overturn any agreement we might make if he doesn't concur. We need him on-side, Joiler."

Veppers had a sort of calculating look about him, Demeisen thought. He was also – going on heart-rate, capillary contraction and skin moisture readings – profoundly rattled, though hiding it extremely well. The man's gaze shifted, eyes hooded a little, from the ambassador to Lededje. "But I'm still being asked to believe that this person is some sort of reincarnated version of Ms. Y'breq," he said, as his gaze alighted on Demeisen, "and this . . . offensively rude, lying young man, allegedly representing a powerful Culture spacecraft, is allowed to make outrageous and obscene accusations without, I presume, being subject to any of the legal sanctions I would seek to impose on anybody else saying anything so utterly mendacious and, potentially – if anybody else was sufficiently demented to take his ravings seriously – so horrendously damaging to my reputation, is that right?"

"About the size of it," Demeisen agreed cheerily, clearing up some of the mess Lededje's lunge across the table had caused. Jasken, still with one wary eye on the girl, was sorting some of the debris on his side.

"You like to take your women from behind," Lededje said quietly, staring at Veppers. "Usually while facing a mirror. Sometimes, especially when you are drunk, you like to lean forward and bite the right shoulder blade of the woman you are fucking. Always the right, never the left. I have no idea why. You mutter, 'Ah, yesss, fucking take it,' sometimes, when you orgasm. You have a small black mole just under the fold of your right armpit, which is the only blemish you have allowed to remain on your body, purely for the purposes of identification. You scratch the right corner of your mouth when you are worried and trying to decide what course of action to take. You secretly despise Peschl, your lawyer, because he is gay, but keep him on because he is very good at his job and it is important to you to make people think that you are not homophobic. I think you may have had some sort of homosexual experience at school with your friend Sapultride. You think the screen director Kostrle is 'grotesquely over-rated', though you fund his works and advance him at every opportunity because he seems fashionable and you desire his—"

"Yes yes yes," Veppers said. "You've done your research; well done. Clever girl." (Still, Demeisen noticed, Veppers' involuntary stress signs had peaked again, and Jasken was suddenly trying hard not to stare at either his master or Lededje.) Veppers turned to Huen. "Madam. Can we get to the point of things here?"

Demeisen turned quickly to Lededje. "Are you mad?" he asked her quietly.

"Burning my boats, you treacherous fuck," she said, her voice sounding quiet and hollow. "If I can't kill the bastard maybe I can unsettle him a little. It's all you've left me." She barely looked at the avatar as she said this.

"Av Demeisen," the ambassador said, sitting up straight and brushing some crumbs from her fingers, "you need to listen to this." She nodded to Veppers.

Veppers looked at the avatar. He took in a breath, then expelled it, glanced at Huen. "This . . . person really does represent a Culture ship? You're sure?"

"Yes,"the ambassador said, watching Demeisen rather than looking at Veppers as she addressed him. "Get on with it."

Veppers shook his head. "Oh well." He smiled insincerely at the avatar, who smiled just as insincerely back. "The smatter is a diversion," Veppers told him. "I made one agreement with the Flekke and NR, to stay out of any conflict regarding the Hells. Smokescreen. I never intended to keep it. I made another agreement with the GFCF to provide them with targets for a fleet of ships they would build in the Tsungarial Disk while the Culture and anybody else who might have interfered was tied up with the smatter outbreak. That is the agreement that I intend to keep, so long as nothing untoward befalls me. Those targets are the Hells

– well, the substrates running them; the vast majority of them at any rate. All the important ones."

"And they are here," Huen said. "On Sichult, is that right?"

Veppers smiled at her. "Here or hereabouts."

Huen nodded slowly. "The latest reports I have indicate that a substantial number of the Disk- built ships have, surprisingly, escaped the confines of the Tsung system, possibly powered by unexpected amounts of power no one thought they might possess, and are headed this way," she said, glancing at Demeisen. "To Sichult."

"Sudden rush of anti-matter to the engines," the avatar said, nodding vigorously. "I've an element or two running them down, but a number will likely get through."

"Their targets are in or around Sichult," Veppers said. "I'll call in the exact locations when they're closer."

Demeisen's eyes narrowed. "Really? That's cutting it awfully fine, isn't it?"

"Timing is everything," Veppers said, smiling. "The point is," he said, sitting forward on his couch, towards Demeisen – who sensed Lededje tensing, and, without looking, put one arm out and behind him, across her chest, preventing her from moving – "that I'm on your side, sailor boy." Veppers directed another perfectly insincere smile at the avatar, who this time did not reciprocate. "On my say-so," Veppers continued, "if I'm around to give it, and enough ships get through to deliver the killer blows, all those nasty, horrible Hells will get wasted and all the poor tortured souls will be released from their torment." Veppers tipped his head to one side, interrogatively. "So what we need from you is some sort of guarantee that you won't interfere with any of this. Maybe you'll even help the ships get through, or at least stop anybody else – the NR, say – from interfering with them." Veppers glanced at Lededje before looking back to the avatar. "Deal?"

"Good grief, yes!" Demeisen said, reaching across the table to the Sichultian. "Deal!" He nodded vigorously. "Sorry for any earlier remarks! Nothing personal!" He kept his hand stuck out, and nodded at it. Veppers looked at Demeisen's open, waiting hand.

"You'll forgive me," he told the avatar. "I prefer not to shake hands. One never knows where other people's have been."

"Totally understand," Demeisen said, withdrawing his hand without any apparent self-consciousness.

"I have your word?" Veppers said, looking from Huen to Demeisen. "Both of you; I have your word, your personal and representational guarantee that I'll come to no harm, yes?"

"Absolutely," ambassador Huen said. "Given."

"A deal is a fucking deal!" Demeisen agreed. "You'll suffer no harm from me, I swear." The avatar looked round at Lededje, sitting simmering on the couch behind him. "Or my little pal here!" He took her by the shoulders with one arm, shook her.

She looked into his eyes. "Liar," she said softly.

Demeisen appeared not to hear. He sat back, grinning.

Veppers found some un-spilled infusion in an insulated pot, poured a little into his cup and sat back sipping it, gazing levelly at Lededje. He smiled at her, shrugged.

"Oh, come on, whoever you are. This is just how things are done. Those of us with advantage will always seek to increase it, and those wishing to make deals will always find somebody like me on the other side of the table. Who else would you expect?" Veppers gave a small, nasal laugh like a single half-snorted breath through his healing nose. "Life, frankly, is mostly meetings, young lady," he told her. He favoured her with a more relaxed smile. "Lededje, I should say, if that really is you." He frowned, looked at Huen. "Of course, if she really *is* who she says she is, she does rather belong to me."

Huen shook her head. "No, she doesn't," she said.

Veppers blew unnecessarily on his infusion. "Really, my dear ambassador? That may have to be settled through the courts, I'm afraid."

"No, it won't," Demeisen told him, grinning.

Veppers looked at Lededje. Before he could say whatever it was he had been going to say, Lededje said, "Your last words to me were, 'I was supposed to appear in public this evening.' Remember?"

Veppers' smile faltered only briefly. "Were they now?" He glanced at Jasken, who quickly looked down. "How amazing." He pulled an old-fashioned watch from one pocket. "Heavens, is that the time?"

"Those ships are just about upon us," Huen said.

"I know," Veppers said brightly. "And where better to be when they arrive than with the Culture ambassador, under the protection of a Culture warship?" He gestured from Huen to Demeisen, who nodded.

"Few hundred got through," Demeisen said. "Inner System and Outer Planetary defences somewhat struggling to cope. Modicum of panic amongst the clued-up societal strata, thinking this might be The End. Masses happily ignorant. Danger will have passed by the time they find out about it." Demeisen nodded, seemingly with approval. "Well," he said, "apart from that second wave of ships, obviously. That might cause some excitement later."

"Isn't it about time you told them where their targets are?" Huen said.

Veppers appeared to consider this. "There are two waves," he said.

"Sensing some rather premature glitterage from the city, there," Demeisen muttered, waving towards the buildings across the park. The wall screen was cycling through some blank, hazed, static-filled channels now. The rest were still concentrating on graphics and talking heads.

Displays of sparks like daylight fireworks, and some thin beams of light directed straight up, seemed to be issuing from the summits of some of the higher skyscrapers in Ubruater's Central Business District.

Huen looked sceptically at Demeisen. "'Glitterage'?" she asked.

The avatar shrugged.

Veppers looked at his antique watch again, then at Jasken, who nodded briefly. Veppers stood. "Well; things to do, time to go," he announced. "Madam," he said, nodding at the ambassador. "Fascinating to meet you," he said to Demeisen. He looked at

Lededje. "I wish you . . . peace, young lady." He smiled broadly. "At any rate; a pleasure."

He and Jasken, who nodded a trio of his own goodbyes, made their way to towards the doors. The drone Olfes-Hresh floated nearby, having reappeared earlier without anybody noticing. "Thing," Veppers said to it as he passed.

The two men passed beyond the doors.

Moments later sudden bursts of light stuttered in the evening sky beyond the city. The wall screen flickered, hazed, then went to stand-by.

"Hmm," Demeisen said. "His own estate." He looked at Huen. "Surprise to you too?"

"Profoundly," she said.

Demeisen glanced at Lededje. He flicked her nearest knee with one finger. "Snap out of it, babe. It's not about your little revenge trip; we're getting Hells destroyed. For free! Not even on our conscience! Seriously: who do you really think matters most, here? You, or a trillion people suffering? Fucking get grown-up about it, won't you? Your man Veppers skipping off with a jaunty smile on his admittedly eminently punchable face is a small price to pay."

A roar from overhead announced Veppers' flier departing. Demeisen looked round at Lededje.

"You lying, inconstant, philandering fuck," she told him.

The avatar shook his head, looked at the ambassador. "Kids, eh?"

Twenty-eight

She was in her sleeping pod, the aching fruit within its dark enfolding confinement, when whatever happened, happened.

She had been slowly stretching herself, extending one wing and then the other – creakingly, with much joint-grumbling and tendon-grating and what felt like even the leathery fabric of her wings protesting – then rotating her neck as best she could, against what felt like the gravel filling her vertebrae, then flexing first one leg and then the other, hanging by a single clawed talon each time.

Then, without warning, there was a sort of shiver in the air, as though the shock wave of a great explosion far away had just passed by.

The pod around her started to shake. Then it froze, somehow, as though the blow that had struck it had been cancelled from reality rather than allowed to ring on through the fabric of her great dark roost.

She knew immediately there was something odd and unprecedented about it, something that hinted at outside, at an existential change to her surroundings, maybe even to the Hell itself. She thought of the glitch, the silver mirror-barrier, the patch where the landscape had been deleted, smoothed over.

She had lost count of how many thousands she had dispatched since she had been brought back here. She had meant to keep count, but had baulked at scratching a mark for each death on the interior surface of her roost – she had considered this – because it just seemed so cold. She'd attempted to keep count in her head, but then lost it a few times, and then for a long time had thought that it didn't matter. The last figure she remembered was three thousand eight hundred and eighty-five, but that had been a long time ago. She had probably killed at least that number again since.

The pain grew each time, after each killing, each release, every day. She existed in a sort of continual haze of aching limbs and over-sensitive skin and grinding sinew and ever-cramping internal organs. She liked to think that she ignored it, but she couldn't really. It was there all the time, from when she woke to when she fell, moaning, grumbling, asleep. It was there in her dreams, too. She dreamed of bits of her body falling off or developing their own lives, tearing themselves off her and flying or falling or walking or slithering away, leaving her screaming, bereft, bleeding and raw.

Every day it was a struggle to let go of the upside-down perch, quit her roost pod and scour the blackened, pox-addled lands beneath for a fresh soul to release. She was getting later and later, these days.

Once she had flown for the joy of it; because flight was still flight, even in Hell, and felt like freedom for somebody who had grown up a devoutly ground-dwelling quadruped. Providing one got over one's fear of heights, of course, which somehow – since the long-ago days when she'd grown old within a convent perched on a rock – she had.

Once she had loved to go exploring, fascinated to find the parts of Hell she hadn't discovered before. She was almost invariably horrified by what she found, no matter where she looked, but she was fascinated nevertheless. Just the geography, then the logistics, then the hatefully sadistic inventiveness of it all was enough to captivate the inquiring mind, and she had made full use of her ability to fly over the ground that lesser unfortunates had to crawl, limp, stagger and fight over.

No longer. She rarely flew far from her roost to find somebody to kill and eat, and usually waited until she felt such pangs of hunger that she no longer had any real choice in the matter. It was a delicate balance and a tricky choice, trying to decide whether her grumbling, empty guts were causing her more discomfort as the day went on than the ever-present shoals and flocks of aches and pains that seemed to squall through her like some bizarre parasitic infection.

Her status as a soul-releasing angel had slipped, she suspected. People came from all around to be blessed by her, but there was not the same level of worship she had enjoyed before; she no longer appeared almost anywhere, to anyone. Now you had to be able to make your way to near where she lived. That changed things. She had become a localised service.

She suspected the demons had finally got wise and were arranging for certain individuals to be more or less presented to her for death and release. She did not want to think what unlikely favours or perverse rewards the demons exacted for this. And, frankly, she no longer cared. She was glad that it really did seem to release this or that particular soul from its suffering, but all the same, it was just what she did, what she had no choice but to do.

The last interesting thing had been when she'd gone to see the uber-demon. She'd been wondering about the glitch she'd discovered, the patch of hill and cliff and factory that had simply disappeared, and – after what had felt like weeks of mulling it over – had finally summoned up the strength to fly to where the vast demon sat and ask it what had happened.

"A failure," he'd roared at her, as she'd flapped painfully in front of him, still careful not to get too close to those terrible, body-crushing hands. "Something went wrong, wiped everything from that area. Landscape, buildings, demons, the tormented; all just ceased to be. Released more of the undeserving wretches in a blink of an eye than you've set free in all the time you've worked for me! Ha! Now fuck off and stop troubling me with matters even I have no control over!"

Now this.

She felt different. The pod she was hanging in felt different, and it was as though all the pain she had taken on was evaporating. A sort of back-surge of relief, well-being – almost sexual, nearly orgasmic in its contrasting intensity – washed through her, sloshing back and forth within her as though she was the hollow presence here, not the pod-roost. The sensation slowly lost energy and dampened down, leaving her feeling clean and good for the first time in longer than she could recall.

She found that she had let go of the perch, but was still hanging where she had been. Her body seemed different too; no longer so great and terrible and fierce; no longer Hell's dark angel of release. Trying to look at it, she realised she couldn't really see what she had become instead, either; it was as though everything about her had become pixelated, smoothed out. She had some sort of body, but it somehow contained all the possibilities of every sort of body: four-legged mammal, two-legged mammal, bird, fish, snake . . . and every other type of being, including ones she had no names for, as though she was some brand new embryo, cells so few and so fixated on simple, continual multiplication that they had not yet decided what to become.

She floated to the limit of the pod. It all looked and felt different: smaller, quieter – completely silent – and without the stink she realised had been in her nostrils for as long as she'd been back. The air in here now was probably completely neutral, odour-free, but that absence smelled like the sweetest, freshest mountain meadow breeze to her after what she'd been used to for so long.

There was, however, no exit, no way out of the pod, even where the hole at the foot had been. This troubled her less than she would have anticipated. The walls of the pod were neither soft nor hard; they were untouchable. She reached for them but it felt as though there was some perfectly clear glass between her and them. She struggled even to tell what colour the walls were.

Such relief, such relief, no longer to be in pain.

She closed her eyes, feeling things wind up, wind down, go into a sort of static, stored, steady state.

Something was happening; something had happened. She would not even start to think about what it might be or what it might imply or mean. Hope, she recalled, had to be resisted at all costs.

A sort of buzzing filled her body and her head. Behind her already closed eyes she felt herself starting to drift away.

If this was death, she had time to think – real, full, proper, no-waking-up-from death – then it was not so terrible.

After all that Hell had made her suffer and made her witness and made her complicit with, she might finally be getting to die in some sort of peace.

Too good to be true, she thought woozily. She'd believe it when . . . well . . .

xGSV *Dressed Up To Party*

oPS *Falling Outside the Normal Moral Constraints*

NR possibly labouring under all-too-accurate apprehension re YN's true mission. As was, anyway; YN since deactivated from our POV, traces removed, memories wiped (diaglyph details attached). Full deniability now possible. Try to get NR off *M,IC*'s case.

. . . I mean by using argument, absolutely not force.

∞

xPS *Falling Outside the Normal Moral Constraints*

oGSV *Dressed Up To Party*

And a fascinating link implied between NR and Bulbitians! Aloof!

∞

xGSV *Dressed Up To Party*

oPS *Falling Outside the Normal Moral Constraints*

That is not your business.

xPS *Falling Outside the Normal Moral Constraints*

o8401.00 *Partial Photic Boundary* (NR ship – assumed)

Greetings. Can't help noticing you've been combatively interested in some meatball on the good ship *Me, I'm Counting.* Imagining this isn't start of final applied stage of NR bio-disgust so there must be a specific reason. Care to share? I mean, I've very little time for the horrible, wasteful, bacteria-slathered, germ-infested, shit-filled squishy things myself, but I generally draw the line at trying to incinerate them – the effort/result equation is just *woeful.*

Smooches.

∞

x*401.00 Partial Photic Boundary* (NR Bismuth category ship)

oPS *Falling Outside the Normal Moral Constraints*

Reciprocated greetings. I am not free to discuss operational matters.

∞

xPS *Falling Outside the Normal Moral Constraints*

o*8401.00 Partial Photic Boundary*

Look, the only non-avatar on the tub is a not-even-neural-laced neuter-gendered human called Yime Nsokyi, of the Culture Quietus Section, currently slowly knitting herself back together after getting half crushed to death by an unhinged Bulbitian. What can you have against *her*?

∞

x*8401.00 Partial Photic Boundary*

oPS *Falling Outside the Normal Moral Constraints*

I remain unable to discuss operational matters of this nature.

∞

xPS *Falling Outside the Normal Moral Constraints*

o*8401.00 Partial Photic Boundary*

This is the bod who's famous in the Culture because she turned down SC. She is most certainly not part of SC. I should know; I *am* part of fucking SC. And – perhaps persuaded by your helpful and refreshing openness and infectious garrulousness – I am able and willing to reveal that she has been sent here specifically to stop what one might term a certain potential

loose cannon from interfering with your ally Joiler Veppers. So. From where comes the squabble?

∞

x*8401.00 Partial Photic Boundary*

oPS *Falling Outside the Normal Moral Constraints*

While I remain unable to discuss operational matters of this nature, your information will be both taken into account tactically and command up-chained.

∞

xPS *Falling Outside the Normal Moral Constraints*

o*8401.00 Partial Photic Boundary*

Right. Spiffing having this little talk. Want to come out to play? Help blow up some smatter?

∞

x*8401.00 Partial Photic Boundary*

oPS *Falling Outside the Normal Moral Constraints*

I am unfortunately unable to re-dispose myself in such an extemporisational manner, especially with regard to the overtures of a non-NR entity; however I am cognisant of the positive intention I deem to be behind said invitation.

∞

xPS *Falling Outside the Normal Moral Constraints*

o*8401.00 Partial Photic Boundary*

Steady.

"Bettlescroy. Happier?"

The little alien, shown in rather better definition on the main screen of Veppers' hired flier – though the amount of signal scrambling was still obvious – was back to looking as calm as usual.

"The first wave seems to have done what was required of it," the Legislator-Admiral conceded. "The pursuing element of the Culture capital ship has also continued on past Sichult and appears set on hunting down all the ships; they won't be returning." Bettlescroy shook its head, smiled. The image broke up a little, struggling to cope with such dynamism. "There is going to be a lot of space debris around the Quyn system, Veppers. Far less than in the Tsung system, of course, but more troublesome due to the higher amounts of day-to-day traffic around Sichult." The Legislator-Admiral glanced at another screen. "You've already lost numerous elements of your soletta, some important satellites – actually, almost all your satellites, both close and synchronous have had their orbits altered at least temporarily by the gravity wells of the passing ships – and at least two small manned space vehicles including one carrying a party of twenty-plus college students would seem to have been in the wrong place at the wrong time when the ships went past. I hope you've been watching the skies; should have been quite a pretty display."

Veppers smiled. "Happily I own most of the major space-debris-clearing, satellite- and ship-building and soletta-maintenance companies. I expect many lucrative government contracts."

"I imagine my sorrow for your loss will prove containable. Are you on your way to your estate house? The latest estimates have the second wave arriving between forty and fifty minutes from now."

"Nearly there," Veppers said. "Think we saw the last of the missiles landing, close in, a few minutes ago." He watched Jasken's side of the screen, where a dark, only half-familiar landscape was still unrolling towards them, slowing as the flier braked. On either side of the aircraft what looked like gigantic black hedges kilometres high rose up, still growing, into the evening sky. At their bases, spattered wavy lines of craters, some still glowing, were surrounded by the remains of smashed and burning trees, blackened, still smouldering fields of crops, smaller copses, woods and forests just catching alight, and the occasional wrecked and burning farm building. The smoke appeared to hem the flier in and rise even higher, the closer they got. They had seen various ground vehicles on the estate roads, all sensibly fleeing towards the perimeter. Veppers had thought he'd recognised at least one of them after catching a fleeting glimpse of a sleek yellow blob heading away fast along the estate's main access road.

"That's my fucking limited edition '36 Whiscord," he'd muttered, watching the slim shape disappear behind them through the smoke. "I don't even let myself drive it that fast. Thieving bastard. Somebody's in a lot of trouble."

On the comms, there was silence. Jasken had been trying to contact people at the house since they'd set out, but without success. Elsewhere, it was chaotic; a combination of the disturbed satellites, electromagnetic discharges and pulses associated with the energy weapons, hyper-velocity kinetics tearing through the atmosphere and nukes had left the area around Espersium in utter communicative disarray and sent a systems-deranging shock through the comms of the whole planet.

"Well, I wouldn't delay," Bettlescroy said. "The remaining ships of the second wave are being severely harried by the Culture ship-element following them and may not have as much time as we would like to carry out the most precise of attacks. I'd aim to be tens of kilometres away, along or up, when they drop by, just in case."

"Duly noted," Veppers said as, ahead, he caught the first glimpse of the mansion house in the distance, surrounded by walls of smoke. "I'll grab a few precious items, tell any remaining staff they're free to leave if they wish and be gone within half an hour." He glanced at Jasken as he cut the connection with Bettlescroy. "We've got that, have we?"

"Sir," Jasken said.

Veppers regarded his security chief for a moment. "I want you to know this is the hardest thing I've ever had to do, Jasken." He'd delayed telling Jasken what was going to happen to the estate until the last moment. He'd thought the man would accept this as just correct, standard, need-to-know security procedure, but – now he thought about it – he supposed even the ultra-professional Jasken might feel a little miffed he'd been kept in the dark for so long.

"These are your lands, sir," Jasken said. "Your house. Yours to dispose of as you wish." He glanced at Veppers. "Was there some warning for the people on the estate, sir?"

"None whatsoever," Veppers said. "That would have been idiotic. Anyway, who wanders the trackways? I've been keeping them as devoid of people as I can for over a century." Veppers sensed Jasken wanting to say something more, but holding back. "This was all I could do, Jasken," he told him.

"Sir," Jasken said tightly, not looking at him. Veppers could tell the other man was struggling to control his feelings.

He sighed. "Jasken, I was lucky to be able to off-load the NR Hell back to them. They're one of the few civs still willing to host their own and not care who knows it. Everybody else seems to have got cold feet. Nobody else I took them from would take them back. They were happy and relieved to get rid of them decades ago. That's why I got such lucrative deals in the first place; they were desperate. I even looked into placing them elsewhere, quite recently; GFCF put me in touch with something called a Bulbousian or something, but it refused. The GFCF said it would have been too unreliable anyway. I'd never have got the approval of the Hells' owners. You've no idea how tied my hands are here, Jasken. I can't even just close the substrates down. There are laws that our galactic betters have seen fit to pass regarding what they think of as living beings, and some people in the Hells are there voluntarily, believe it or not. And that's without taking into account the penalty clauses in the agreements I signed taking responsibility for the Hells, which are prohibitive, even punitive, believe me. And even if I *did* ignore all that, the substrates under the trackways can't be switched off; they're designed to keep going through almost anything. Even cutting down all the trees would only make them switch to the bio energy they've stored in the root systems; take decades to exhaust. You'd have to dig it all up, shred it and incinerate it."

"Or hit it with nukes, energy weapons and hyper-kinetics," Jasken said, sounding tired, as the flier rocked through a tumbling wall of smoke.

"Exactly," Veppers said. "What's happening here counts as *force majeure*; gets us off that contractual hook." He paused, reached over and touched Jasken on one shoulder. "I have thought all this through, Jasken. This is the only way."

They had avoided most of the slow-drifting smoke until now; it was rising almost straight up, shifted only a little by faint and fitful breezes, though the fires now starting to take hold were creating their own winds. Outside, beneath, this close to the house, it was almost midnight dark, here at the centre of all the destroyed and still flaming remains of the strewn, cratered trackways.

They crossed the circle of satellite plinths, where once domes had stood and now prone, stippled, phased array plates lay, processing the comms which linked the house and all that had been around it to the the rest of the world, the Enablement and everything beyond.

Part of himself, Veppers realised, wanted to call a halt now; enough damage had been done, the trackways and the substrates they had hidden were gone or going. The comms didn't matter without what they had to communicate. The Hells were erased, or so reduced they weren't worthy of the name any more.

But he knew that what had happened so far wouldn't be enough. It was all about perception. When the smoke cleared, figuratively as well as literally, he needed to look like the victim here. It wouldn't seem that way if the house got away unscathed and only the lands about it were hit. Some landscaping, bit of decontamination and then copious tree-planting; who'd give him any sympathy just for *that*?

"Still," Jasken said as they passed above game courts, lawns and the corner of the great maze – all mostly dark, lit only by a few bright embers that had drifted in from the burning lands all around – "they might have expected a little more, sir." Another glance. "The people, I mean, sir. Your people. They've given— "

"Yes, my people, Jasken," Veppers said, watching as the flier's landing legs deployed and the craft floated down through darkness, fire and confusion towards the flame-lit torus of Espersium house. "Who like you have always been well paid and looked after and known the kind of man I am."

"Yes, sir."

He watched Jasken as they passed over the roofs of the mansion. The cladding was dotted with scattered bits of flaming twigs and small branches which a few of the staff were running around trying to put out. Rather pointless, Veppers thought; the roof was fire-proof. Still, people needed to do something, he supposed.

The flier poised, ready to drop into the central courtyard of the house. "There isn't anyone special to you that I don't know about here, is there, Jasken?" Veppers asked. "On the estate, I mean. You've hidden it very well if there is."

"No, sir," Jasken said, as the flier descended into the empty heart of the torus-shaped building. "No one special."

"Well, that's as well." Veppers glanced at the antique watch as the skids touched the flagstones of the courtyard and the craft settled. "We need to be back aboard in twenty-five minutes." He pushed the seat restraints aside and stood. "Let's go."

"I'll stay with you if you want," Demeisen said.

"I don't want," Lededje told him. "Just go."

"Right. Guess I'd better. Stuff to shoot."

Ambassador Huen held up one hand. "Wait; you don't think we need any extra protection when that second wave comes through?" she asked, looking sceptical.

"I – another bit of me – might have run them all down before they can get here," Demeisen said. "I strongly suspect I'll account for a few myself in passing on the way back to the main event out at Tsung. Plus the Inner System and Planetary boys will be better prepared and have longer this time; this lot look like they're preparing to crash-stop. Which also implies greater accuracy from them. Should be safe enough." He nodded towards the city, where a little smoke was drifting, lessening all the time, from the summits of some of the towers and skyscrapers. "Last resort, that's what your glitterage is for." He looked quizzically at the ambassador, performed a curtsy. "By your leave, ma'am."

Huen nodded. "Thank you."

"Pleasure." Demeisen turned grinning to Lededje. He winked at her. "You'll get over it."

Then he was a silvery ovoid stood on its end. It vanished with a faint popping noise.

Lededje felt herself let out a breath.

Huen looked at the drone Olfes-Hresh, then closed her eyes for a moment as though tired. "Ah," she said. "Finally we get the official version." She looked at Lededje. "I'm told you are indeed Ms. Y'breq. In that case, I am glad to see you again, Lededje, though, given the circumstances of your death—"

"Murder," Lededje said, standing and going to the window looking over the park to the city, her back to the other woman and the drone floating at the ambassador's shoulder. Beyond the city, in the dimming evening light, more flashes lit up distant dark clouds that had not been there before.

"Murder, then," Huen said. "The rest of what Demeisen alleged . . ."

"All true."

Huen was silent for a few moments. "Then I am very sorry. I truly am, Lededje. I hope you realise we had little choice. To let Veppers go, I mean. And to treat with him."

Lededje stared at the distant buildings, watching the little wisps of smoke die, her eyes full of tears. She shrugged, flapped one hand in what she hoped looked like a sort of dismissal. She didn't trust herself to say anything.

In the reflection, she saw Huen turn her head fractionally towards the drone. "Olfes-Hresh," the ambassador said, "tells me you are in possession of considerable funds, controlled by a card in one of your pockets. "I was going to ask what you intended to do now, but . . ."

Then another silvery ovoid appeared, just where the one that had taken Demeisen had stood. It was gone in an instant, while Lededje was still turning round, and Demeisen was standing there again. Lededje almost yelped.

"Suddenly busy round here," Demeisen said to Huen. He spared

Lededje the briefest of nods. "You've more visitors. I'd better stick around for a few moments; say hi."

Huen looked at the drone.

"The ex-LOU*Me, I'm Counting*, of the Ulterior," Olfes-Hresh announced. "Just arrived."

Two more silvery ellipsoids came and went, revealing two tall, pan-human but most certainly not Sichultian people: a man and an androgynous figure that looked slightly more female than male. The man was bald, and dressed in severe-looking dark clothes. Lededje recognised him, though he looked more alien than the last time they'd met. The other person wore a sort of suit, even more formal-looking, in grey.

"Prebeign-Frultesa Yime Leutze Nsokyi dam Volsh," the drone announced, "and Av Himerance, of the ex-LOU *Me, I'm Counting*."

"Ms. Y'breq," Himerance said softly, bowing to her. "Good to see you again. Do you remember me?"

Lededje swallowed, wished she'd had time to dry her eyes, and did her best to smile. "I do. Good to see you, too."

Himerance and Demeisen exchanged looks, then nods.

Demeisen stared at Yime Nsokyi, gaze flicking over her from boot sole to high collar. "You know," he said, "I'm sure I've seen somebody else in Quietus wearing exactly the same clothes as you're wearing now."

"It's called a uniform, Av Demeisen," Yime told him patiently. "It is what we wear in Quietus."

"No!"

"We feel it shows respect for those on whose behalf we work."

"Really?" Demeisen looked thunderstruck. "Fuck me, I had no idea the dead could be so demanding."

Yime Nsokyi smiled the tolerant smile of those long-used to such remarks and executed a sort of nodding-bow to Lededje. "Ms. Y'breq. I have come a long way to meet with you. Are you well?"

Lededje shook her head. "Not great."

Demeisen clapped his hands. "Well, riotous fun though this is, I really need to be putting some heliopauses between me and here. See you all around. Ambassador."

Huen held up one hand, delaying Demeisen, to his obvious annoyance. "Do you think Veppers told the truth earlier?" she asked. "When he implied he had yet to reveal the targets for this second wave of ships?"

"Of course not. Can I go now? I mean, I'm going to go, but may I with your permission, given we seem to be observing excruciatingly correct protocol?"

Huen smiled and gave a small nod.

There was just about a delay between Huen nodding and the silvery ellipsoid forming and collapsing. The popping noise was more of a bang this time. Huen saw Lededje's shoulders relax again.

The girl shook her head, muttered, "Excuse me," and went back to looking out of the window.

"Are we clear, Olf?" Huen asked the drone.

"We are, ma'am," the machine told her.

"Ms. Nsokyi, Av Himerance," the ambassador said. "To what do we owe the honour?"

"I have been sent by Quietus to check on Ms. Y'breq, as she is a recent reventee," Yime Nsokyi said.

"And I promised to bring Ms. Nsokyi here," Himerance said. "Though I also thought it would be pleasant to pay my respects to Ms. Y'breq."

There was an anguished noise from near the window, where Lededje was staring at her reflection, her nose almost pressing against the glass, while the fingers of her right hand stabbed at the skin on the inside of her left wrist. They all looked.

She whirled round. "Now the fucking *tat's* stopped working!" She looked round all of them, meeting mostly blank looks.

Huen sighed, looked at the drone. "Olfes, would you?"

"Calling."

Demeisen's image appeared, translucent, on the polished wooden floor, just bright enough to throw a reflection.

"*Now* what?" the image said, waving its arms, gaze directed at Lededje. "I thought you couldn't wait to get rid of me?"

"What's happened to my tat?" she demanded.

"What are you talking about?"

"It's stopped working!"

The image appeared to squint, staring at her. "Hmm," it said. "See what you mean. Looks like it's frozen. Well, that will happen. Probably from when I had to half-stun you to stop you ripping Veppers' throat out; collateral damage. Sorry. My apologies."

"Well, fix it!"

"Can't. Heading fast for Tsung. Have to Displace you and the tat and I'm already too far away and getting further away too quickly. Ask the drone."

"Beyond my ken," Olfes-Hresh said. "I've had a quick look. I can't even see how it works."

"Come back!" Lededje wailed. "Fix it! It's stuck the way it was!"

The image nodded. "Okay. Will do. Not right now though. Day or two. Later."

The image had disappeared by the time the word "later" reached Lededje's ears. She buried her face in her hands and roared.

Huen looked at the drone, which made a shaking motion. "Not picking up," it said quietly.

"Is there anything I can do . . . we can do?" Yime said.

Lededje collapsed onto her haunches, face still hidden in her hands.

Huen looked thoughtfully at her, then raised her gaze to the Quietus agent and the avatar. "Perhaps," she said, "there is. Let me explain the situation."

"Before you do that," Demeisen's voice said from Huen's desk. "May I add something?"

"Oh, for fuck's sake," Lededje breathed, taking her hands away from her face and rolling backwards to lie on the floor, staring up at the ceiling. "Is there no getting away from this fucking machine?"

Huen was frowning at the drone. "I thought we were clear?" she said.

"As did I," the machine said, aura field purple-grey with embarrassment.

"Well, couldn't help overhearing," Demeisen's voice said.

"Liar," Huen muttered.

"And I thought you might like to hear this. Just dropped into my in-box, at it were. Theoretically anonymous, but it definitely came from my new best chum, the bright and breezy NR Bismuth category ship *8401.00 Partial Photic Boundary*. Slightly lo-fi after a lot of processing de-manglement, but I think you'll forgive it that. It's from about three hours ago, between Mr. V and Legislator-Admiral Bettlescroy-Bisspe-Blispin III, the bod in charge of the GFCF forces here in the Enablement. Here we go:"

"*Anyway*," Veppers' voice said, also coming from whatever comms gear was hidden in Huen's desk, "*to reiterate: every trackway is underlain by what to the untutored eye looks like some sort of giant fungal structure. It isn't. It's substrate. Low-power, bio-based, not ultra-fast running, but high-efficiency, highly damage-resistant substrate; anything from ten to thirty metres thick under and amongst the roots, but adding up to over half a cubic kilometre of processing power spread throughout the estate. All the comms traffic to and from is channelled through the phased array satellite links dotted round the mansion house itself.*

"*That's what you have to hit, Bettlescroy. The under-trackway substrates contain over seventy per cent of the Hells in the entire galaxy. Of those we know of, anyway. Used to be slightly more, but very recently I sub-contracted the NR Hell, just to be on the safe side. I've been buying Hells up for over a century, Legislator-Admiral, taking the processing requirements and legal and jurisdictional implications off other peoples' hands for most of my business life. The majority of the Hells are right here, in system, on planet. That is why I have always felt able to be so relaxed regarding the targeting details. Think you can get enough ships to Sichult to lay waste to my estate?*"

"*Truly?*" another voice said. "*The targets are on your own estates? Why would you do that?*"

"*Deniability, Bettlescroy. You'll have to raze the trackways, wreck my lands, blast the satellite links and damage the house itself; maybe even destroy it. That house has been in my family for centuries; it and the estate are inestimably precious to me. Or at least so everybody assumes. Who's going to believe I brought all that destruction on myself?"*

"And so on," Demeisen's voice told them. "Then there's this *really* good bit:"

"*And the people?*"

"*What people?*"

"*The people on the estate when it is laid waste.*"

"*Oh. Yes. I assume I have a few hours before any attack takes place.*"

"There's a bit of blah-blah-blah here from our boy Bettlescroy," Demeisen's voice said, "then:"

"*So, bottom line,*" they heard Veppers say, "*I'd have time to get a few people out. Not too many, of course; it still has to look convincing. But I can always hire more* people, *Bettlescroy. Never a shortage of those, ever.*"

". . . Fascinating, what?" Demeisen's voice said from Huen's desk. "Specially the bit about handing the NR's theme-park of woe over to somebody else before all the other Hells got wasted. Bet he thought that was being clever, getting the NR off his back. Just like the GFCF thought they were being clever swiping all that NR comms knowledge, back in the whenever-when, never thinking it might come with trap-doors the NR could tap into and copy their comms any time they wanted. Don't you think it's hilarious when people think they're being terribly clever? I know I do. Just as well some of us genuinely fucking are or we'd be in a hell of a fucking state. Well, my work here is done. Mostly, anyway; still more smatter-ships to smashify. Be seeing you!"

There was silence in the room for a while.

The drone Olfes-Hresh made a shaking motion. "Well," it said to Huen, "again, I think we're clear, and it's gone, but then I thought that the last time."

On the floor, lying loosely spread, shaking her head, Lededje sighed.

Huen looked up from her to Yime and Himerance.

"Obviously," she said, "there are things we ought not to be doing or taking part in here, either for first-principle moral reasons, or due to the regrettable exigencies of *realpolitik*." She paused. "However."

Twenty-nine

"The Scoudenfrast, I think. No, Jasken, that's a Scundrundri. The Scoudenfrast is the one alongside, the purple one with the yellow splodges. I always did think Scundrundri was overrated. Besides, with these gone, the rest I have in the town house will be worth more. Nolyen, give Mr. Jasken a hand with these out to the flier, would you?"

"Sir."

"Quickly, both of you."

"Sir," Jasken said. He lifted an armful of old masters and headed for the end of the long, curved gallery, followed by Nolyen, similarly laden. It was gloomy in the place; the house was relying on its emergency lighting, and not even all of that was functioning properly. Nolyen – a big, dim country lad from the kitchens – dropped one of the paintings he was carrying, and struggled to pick it up again; Jasken came back and used his foot to help lever the thing back up into the boy's hands. Veppers watched all this, sighing.

He was actually a little bit disappointed in his staff and their commitment. He'd expected to find more people here in the house, worried over the fate of their master – they still thought he might be dead, after all – and determined to help save the house from the surrounding and encroaching fires. Instead, he'd discovered that most of them had already fled the place.

They'd taken to the wheeled vehicles that the estate used on a day-to-day basis, and to those from Veppers' own collection of automotive exotica, stored and cared for in some of the mansion's underground garages. There were some fliers left dotted about the place but it looked like they'd fallen victim to the same stray radiation pulses that had knocked out the local comms.

Nolyen had greeted them joyfully as they'd left the flier and somebody had shouted a glad-you're-safe-sir or something similar from the roof as they'd walked across the courtyard, but that was about it. "Ingrates," Veppers had muttered as they made their way to the gallery with the most expensive paintings.

"Four minutes and I'll see you at the Number Three Strongroom!" Veppers called after Jasken, who, arms full of paintings, just turned and nodded. Veppers supposed they could have cut the paintings from the frames, like thieves did, but that had seemed wrong somehow.

Veppers jogged along the gallery, down a radial corridor towards some splendidly tall windows – my, there was a lot of smoke and even some flame out there, and it was far too dark for the time of evening – and let himself into his study. He sat at his desk.

The study was dark in the patchy emergency lighting. He allowed himself the poignant luxury of one last look round the place, thinking how sad, and yet also how oddly exciting it was that it might all soon be gone, then he started opening drawers and compartments. The desk – self-powered, identifying him by his smell as well as by his palm and fingerprints – made soft, sighing, snicking noises as it obeyed him; a little familiar oasis of calm and reassurance in all the chaos. He filled a small hide carry-bag with all the most precious and useful things he could think of. The last thing he lifted, after a slight hesitation, was a pair of knives, sheathed in skin-soft hide, that had belonged to his grandfather and, before that, to somebody else's.

A wind seemed to be getting up, judging from the way smoke was moving on the far side of the barely visible formal gardens; however, despite all the commotion outside, little sound got through the multiply glazed and bullet-proof windows. He was just closing the last drawer, ready to go, when he heard a noise like a faint "pop".

He looked up and saw a tall, dark alien figure standing looking at him from near the closed doors. For a moment he thought it might be ambassador Huen, but it was somebody else; thin, with a too-straight, contorted-looking back. Dressed in different shades of dark grey.

"Can I help you?" he said, putting the still-open hide bag down at his feet where he sat, and dipping one hand into it, feeling around. He made a waving, distracting gesture with his other hand. "For example, with your manners? We tend to knock first, here."

"Mr. Joiler Veppers, my name is Prebeign-Frultesa Yime Leutze Nsokyi dam Volsh," the figure said in an oddly accented voice that might have been female but that definitely didn't appear to be entirely in synch with its lip-movements. "I am a citizen of the Culture. I am here to apprehend you on suspicion of murder. Will you come with me?"

"How can I put this?" he said, raising and firing the alien-tech gun in the same movement. The gun made a loud snapping noise, light flared in the dim study and the alien disappeared in a silvery shimmer. The doors immediately behind where it had been standing burst open against their hinges, swinging broken and hanging into the corridor beyond in a flurry of black dust, a semicircular hole punched in each, circumferenced with glowing yellow-white sparks. Veppers looked at the gun – a present from the Jhlupian Xingre, long ago – then at the still-swinging, smoking doors, and finally at the patch of rug where the figure had been standing. "Hmm," he said.

He shrugged, stood, stuffed the gun into his waistband, snapped the hide bag shut and waved some of the noxious fumes away from his face as he exited through the wrecked doors, which were starting to burn.

"Jasken."

He heard the female voice pronounce his name behind him, and knew it was her. He placed the paintings carefully on the floor of the flier and turned. Nolyen had stopped in the doorway of the flier. He was staring over the top of the paintings he held at the young woman standing by the door to the flight deck. Perhaps he was intimidated by the scroll-work of faint, tattooed lines covering her face.

"Miss," Jasken said, nodding to her.

"It is me, Jasken."

"I know," he said. He turned his head deliberately, nodding to Nolyen. "Leave those, Nolyen; never mind anything else. Just leave; get well away from the house."

Nolyen set the paintings down. He hesitated.

"Get away, Nolyen," Jasken said.

"Sir," the young man said, then turned and left.

Lededje watched him go, then turned back to Jasken.

"You let him kill me, Hib."

Jasken sighed. "No, I tried to stop him. But, in the end, all right; I could have done more. And I suppose I could have killed him after he killed you. So I'm as bad as he is. Hate me if you like. I don't claim to be a particularly good person, Led. And there is such a thing as duty."

"I know. I thought you might feel some towards me."

"My first is towards him, whether either of us likes it or not."

"Because he pays your wages and all I did was let you fuck me?"

"No; because I pledged myself to his service. I never said anything to you that contradicted that."

"No, you didn't, did you?" She gave a wan smile. "I suppose I should have spotted that. How very correct of you, even while you were . . . despoiling his property. All those little whispered words of tenderness, about how much I meant, what we might hope for in the future. Were you always reviewing them as you said them? Running them past some lawyer bit in your brain, looking for inconsistencies?"

"Something like that," Jasken told her, meeting her gaze. He shook his head. "We never had a future, Led. Not the sort you wanted to imagine. More quick couplings while his back was turned, hidden from everyone, until one of us got bored, or he found out. You belonged to him for ever, didn't you ever understand that? We were never going to be able to run away together." He looked down, then back up into her eyes again. "Or are you going to tell me you loved me? Because I always thought you took me as a lover just to get back at him and have me on-side for the next time you tried to escape."

"Didn't fucking work, did it?" she said bitterly. "You helped him hunt me down."

"I had no choice. You didn't have to run. As— "

"Really? That's not how it felt to me."

"As soon as you did, I had to do what my duty to him demanded."

"So, none of it meant anything." She was crying a little now, but quickly wiped both cheeks with the back of her wrists, tears smeared across the tattoo lines. "More fool me. Because I didn't come back just to kill Veppers. I needed to ask how . . ." She stopped, swallowed. "Did it mean nothing to you?"

Jasken sighed. "Of course it meant something. A sweetness. Moments I'll never forget. It just couldn't mean what you wanted it to mean."

She laughed, without hope or humour. "Then I am a fool, am I not?" she said, shaking her head. "I really did think you might love me."

He gave the smallest of smiles. "Oh, I loved you with all my heart, from the very first."

She glared at him.

He stared at her, eyes bright. "It's just that love is not enough,

Led. Not always. Not these days; maybe not ever. And never around people like Joiler Veppers."

She looked down at the floor of the flier, brought her arms up and hugged herself. Jasken glanced at the time display on the flier's bulkhead.

"Could be as little as a quarter of an hour till the second wave arrives," he said. His tone was concerned, even kind. "You seemed to get here pretty fast. Can you get away again just as quickly?"

She nodded. She sniffed back her tears, wiped her cheeks and eyes again. "Do one thing for me," she said.

"What?" he asked.

"Go."

"Go? I can't just—"

"Now. Just leave. Take the flier and go. Save the servants and staff; all you can find. But leave him here, with me."

She looked into his eyes. Jasken hesitated, his jaw working. She shook her head. "He's finished, Hib," she said. "The NR – the Nauptre – they know. They can intercept whatever passes between him and the GFCF; they know about his agreement, about how he tricked them. The Culture know everything too. The Hells are gone, so he can't use those to save himself now. He won't be allowed to get away with all he's done. Even if the Enablement can turn a blind eye to something on this scale, he's got the NR and the Culture to answer to." She smiled a small, half-despairing smile. "He finally found people more powerful than he is to fall foul of." She shook her head again. "But the point is: you can't save him. All you can save now is yourself." She nodded towards the open door of the flier. "And anybody else you can find out there."

Jasken looked out through one of the high-level ports in the flier, at the skies above the dully lit mansion. A wall of smoke like the end of the world was lit from beneath by flames.

"What about you?" he asked.

"I don't know," she said. "I'll try to find him." Now it was her turn to hesitate. "I will kill him, if I can. Not pretending otherwise."

"He won't be an easy man to kill."

"I know." She shrugged. "Perhaps I won't have to. A condition of me getting this chance was that one of the Culture people went to confront him, give him the chance to turn himself in."

Jasken gave a small, snorting laugh. "Think that'll work?"

"No." She tried to smile; failed.

Jasken looked into her eyes for a little while. Then he reached behind his back and brought out a small gun, holding it by the barrel as he passed it to her. "Try the Number Three Strongroom."

She took the gun. "Thank you." Their hands hadn't touched as the weapon passed from him to her. She looked at the gun. "Will it still work?" she asked. "The ship was going to disable all the electronic weapons."

"Most are already fried," Jasken told her. "But that one'll work. "Just metal and chemicals. Ten shots. Safety catch is on the side facing you; move that little lever till you can see the red dot." He watched her take the safety off. He realised she'd probably never handled a gun in her life. "Take care," he told her. Another hesitation, as he seemed to think about coming towards her, hugging or holding or kissing her, but then she said:

"You too," and turned and left, walking out of the flier and across the courtyard.

Jasken looked at the floor for a moment, then along it to the paintings in their ornate frames.

Lededje found the young servant Nolyen in the archway leading to the main vestibule, crouched on his haunches. "You were supposed to leave, Nolyen,"she said.

"I know, miss," he said. He looked like he'd been crying too.

"Go back to the flier, Nolyen," she told him. "Mr. Jasken will need help looking for people to take to safety. Now, quickly; still time."

Nolyen ran back towards the flier and helped Jasken throw the paintings out before they took off to look for people to save.

He jogged down the stairs to the basement. The stairwell was poorly lit and he'd forgotten how far down the level holding the deepest strongrooms was. He'd rung for a lift up in the house, but even as he'd stood watching the floor-indicator display winking on and off with an error code, he'd realised he shouldn't step into an elevator car in the circumstances even if one did arrive.

He stopped on the last landing, above a pool of darkness beneath, and dug inside the hide bag, pulling out a pair of night-vision glasses; lighter, less bulky but also less sophisticated versions of the Oculenses Jasken had worn. They weren't working either; he threw them away. Next thing he tried was a torch, but the flash-light refused to work too. He smashed it against the wall. That felt good. At least the bag was getting lighter.

He felt his way down the last few stairs and opened the door to the better-lit corridor beyond. Pipes and conduits covered the ceiling, the floor was concrete and a few large metal doors were the only adornments to the rough-cast walls. A few very dim lights were on constantly; others were flickering. He was a little surprised Jasken wasn't here already. He supposed time seemed to move oddly when everything was getting this fraught. He checked the antique watch; at least twelve minutes to go.

The strongroom door was a massive circular metal plug as tall as a man and a metre thick. The display – he'd forgotten it even had a display – was blinking an error message.

"Cunt!" he screamed, smashing one fist on the door. He rolled the code in anyway, but the noises the mechanism made didn't even sound right and the display didn't alter. Certainly there was no series of reassuring clicks from umpteen places round the door's circumference, as there would have been if it was unlocking itself. He tried the levers and handles that then had to be moved, but they wouldn't budge.

He glimpsed movement further down the long curve of the corridor, near a set of doors leading to another stairwell.

"Jasken?" he called. It was hard to tell in the dim, inconstant light. Maybe it was the Culture lunatic who'd come to "apprehend" him again. He pulled the Jhlupian gun out. No; the figure moving towards him moved normally, looked Sichultian.

"Jasken?" he shouted.

The figure stopped, maybe thirty metres away. It raised its arms level in front of it, gripping something. A gun! he realised as something flashed. He started to fall into a crouch. There was a smack and a whine from somewhere way overhead and to his left, then a barking roar came ringing down the corridor. Crouched on one knee, he aimed the Jhlupian gun at the figure and pulled the trigger. Nothing happened. He tried again. The figure fired the gun once more and a bullet kicked off the top of the strongroom door, whining away behind him as another thunderclap of noise pulsed down the corridor. He could see smoke swirling round the figure. *Smoke*? What were they firing? A fucking *musket*? But at least their gun still worked, unlike the Jhlupian blaster. Like a knife would still work.

"Fuck fuck fuck," he said, throwing the useless gun away and scrabbling to his feet, holding the hide bag between him and the figure down the corridor as he ran for the doors he'd just come through.

There was something round lying on the floor of the first landing; he discovered this when he trod on it and his foot went out behind him, dropping him and banging his knee on the next step up. He howled in rage, limped on up the steps.

The fucking gun hadn't worked! It had worked before but it had stopped! Was it some fucking stupid ceremonial piece of junk that only had one fucking shot in it? Xingre, the bastard, had told him it could stop a tank, bring down aircraft and keep on firing till you grew old. Lying mother-fucking alien cunt!

He was one flight down from the ground floor when he heard the doors at the foot of the stairwell bang open and steps come hurrying up towards him. Fuck everything else, then; just get to Jasken, get to the flier. Cut and run. What fucker would dare fire a fucking gun at him anyway? Probably only the demented little bitch claiming to be Y'breq. She was about as good a shot as he'd have expected.

His lungs and throat felt like a blast furnace after running up all those steps; his knee was hurting really badly but he just had to ignore it. He threw open the door to the main ground-level corridor and ran for the nearest courtyard doors.

The flier wasn't there. He could see this twenty or more steps away from the doorway because there was a large open reception area with huge windows looking straight out at the courtyard, but he kept on running for the doors, not believing what he was seeing, and threw the doors open anyway, in time to see the flier pulling away overhead, as though it had just taken off from the roof of the mansion.

"*Jasken!*" he screamed, the force of it tearing at his throat.

He looked frantically round the circular courtyard. This couldn't be happening. The flier couldn't have gone. It just couldn't; he needed it, he needed it to be here, needed it so he could get away. That must have been another, similar flier he'd just seen above the rooftops. It couldn't have gone. It just wasn't possible. He was depending on it, so it had to be here. It couldn't disguise itself, could it? Go see-through or something freakish, could it? It was just a hired civilian flier; nothing military or alien. Best money could hire, built by one of his own companies, but it couldn't turn fucking *invisible*. He stared round the courtyard, willing the aircraft still to be there. But all that he could see was a half-collapsed pile of paintings; nothing and nobody else. He glimpsed movement through the windows to one side, in the corridor he'd just run down.

He ran for the nearest archway leading through the house to the grounds. A gun. He needed a gun. An old fashioned chemical-explosion gun. What had happened to Jasken? Jasken had a gun. He always carried several weapons. He had a little hand-gun that had no sight or screen or electrics in it at all, just as a last resort. Dear fuck, it wasn't *Jasken* chasing him, was it? He ran through the tall archway leading towards the outside, his steps echoing in the arch high overhead. He glanced back, saw the figure pursuing him, but stumbled and nearly fell as he did so. No, not Jasken. Too small and slim to be Jasken. And Jasken wouldn't have missed, not twice.

It had to be the little bitch claiming to be Y'breq. She must have tricked Jasken, had an accomplice; maybe the Culture maniac who'd tried to arrest him. They'd be flying the aircraft. The fucking

Culture! A gun. Where would he find a gun? He ran out onto the flagstone circle which encompassed the house.

The world was on fire; walls of smoke filled the sky, making a night lit up like hell, flames leaping from a hundred different places, trees and outbuildings all on fire or silhouetted against the fires beyond.

Gun. He needed a gun. There were old-fashioned, ancient, even antique guns splattered liberally over the walls of the house, just like there were swords and spears and shields, but none of them worked; none of them were any fucking *use*. Who the hell still used old-fashioned *guns* for fuck's sake? Gamekeepers? They used lasers like everybody else, didn't they? He wasn't even sure where the gamekeepers' cottages were; hadn't they been moved when he'd had the raceball court put in?

He limped on, breath wheezing, knee aching, wondering if he could hide in the maze; maybe jump out on whoever was pursuing him, slit their throat using one of the two knives he still had. He sort of remembered the layout of the maze, he thought. He looked at where the maze ought to be and saw its central tower, on fire, flames waving wildly like orange banners from its wooden superstructure. He looked desperately around, searching for the flier, or another aircraft. He should have headed for the garages, he thought. Maybe some of the cars were still there and working. He patted the pocket where his antique watch had been, but it was gone.

Tall, skinny towers and linked, soaring arches stood out black against a distant roaring wall of yellow-orange flame, off to one side.

The fucking battleships. They had chemical guns. There were explosives, rockets, grenades, bullets; all that stuff, there. He couldn't think of anything else. He ran for the battleship area. He looked back briefly. The figure sprinted out of the archway, heading towards him, then seemed to slow, looking about. Maybe they couldn't see him. He was wearing mostly dark clothes, thank fuck.

Throat on fire, legs like jelly, knee like a spike had been driven into it, he scrabbled around inside the hide bag, found a soft, double sheath, pulled it out and stuck it and the pair of knives it held into his jacket. He threw the bag and everything else away.

She had never fired a gun before, never even held one. She used both hands, hoping this was right. The noise of the old explosive-based weapon going off was so great, and the kick against her arms so hard, she thought it had blown up in her hands; she half expected to find she'd lost fingers. She didn't see where the bullet went, but now Veppers was on one knee, pointing something at her. The gun and her fingers were intact. She coughed on the acrid gas the gun had given off, fired it again. Another ear-ringing detonation. She couldn't believe it was meant to be this noisy.

She'd missed again. At least she saw where this shot hit: well above Veppers, near the top of the great circular door of the strongroom. She knew these old reaction weapons had significant recoil but she'd always assumed it happened after the bullet had left the barrel, on its way to wherever it had been aimed. Maybe it didn't work that way.

Veppers turned and ran, crashing through the doors to the stairs. She set off after him. When she got to the doors she kicked them open in case he was hiding just behind them. The stairwell was a little dimmer than the corridor, but she could see okay. Bits of a smashed-up torch were strewn across the first landing; on the first step up lay the antique watch Veppers had looked at in ambassador's Huen's office. She ran on up, seeing and hearing Veppers a handful of flights above.

Running along the corridor, she saw him hesitate in the courtyard, staring frantically about. Then he ran off through the main archway. And not running quite perfectly; limping.

Outside, once she'd exited the tall archway, she stopped for a moment, taken aback by the sheer apocalyptic scale of the fiery roaring chaos swirling around the mansion.

A ragged, tearing wind that seemed to have come out of nowhere howled beneath a cauldron of night-black, sky-obliterating smoke. Manically leaping, furiously rolling flames spilled everywhere; the air was full of whirling, burning debris, numerous as leaves in the first storm of autumn. The shock was almost physical, the heat on her face from the ubiquitous flames as strong as that from an equatorial sun; she slowed to a trot without realising.

She shook herself out of it, quickly looked around.

For a moment, she thought she'd lost him, then she saw him half running, half staggering in the direction of the water maze. He was silhouetted against flames for a moment and she aimed at him, nearly fired, but then decided he was too far away; the gun was for close range and she was anyway no marksman. Eight shots left.

Down a grassed bank, clattering against a chain-link fence, hidden from the mansion by the slope, running along the path, making for the gates that led to the network of channels around the lakes. The gates, the fucking gates; what if they were closed, locked? Then he saw something ahead, glinting in the flames, and running towards it found a crash-landed flier, one of the estate's runabouts, snouted into the path and the fence at one end of a trough of ploughed-up earth; the fence had tipped, fallen, lay flat on the ground just beyond the crumpled nose of the craft. He leapt onto the flier's stubby front canard, jumped over the fractured nose and was in the battleship ground, pumping and wheezing along the internal path beneath the towers and arches of the raised system of canals. The sheds where the ships were kept were on the far side of the grounds, away from the mansion, near the trees.

Crazy, crazy, crazy; what was he doing? The fucking sheds would be locked.

But maybe not. There were people there a lot of the time, and he'd been planning a battleship tournament in a few days, so the engineers and technicians would have been working on the vessels, testing them, readying them. It hadn't been night when all this chaos had kicked off, even though it felt like midnight now. It had been afternoon; people would have been in and around the ships and sheds, and what were the odds in the midst of all this mayhem that they'd carefully packed everything away and locked up everything they were meant to lock up? Not a chance.

See? He'd been vindicated. This had been the right place to come; his instinct had been smack on the money.

He – not this mad bitch running after him with a miniature cannon – would come out of this ahead; *he'd* survive, *he'd* win. He was the winner, he had the history of success, he was the one who knew how to triumph. Fuck; if it really was her he'd already killed her once. What did that tell you?

A burning tree, storeys high, already half uprooted, was slowly falling, thirty metres ahead of him. It came thudding through the fence, crashing and rolling off a flying buttress in a storm of sparks and splashing into a watery channel, smothering the path with flame. The buttress seemed to hesitate then started to crumple and fall, crashing down in a welter of stone and water, creating billows of steam.

The way ahead was blocked; he ran instead for the nearest wading point leading to the first of the islands. He could see the layout of the lakes and channels in his head, knew it better than the hedge maze because he'd looked down on it so many times. The wading points, surfaced with mesh-covered slabs under the water, were located in the middle of each island's shore line. They stretched as far as one island away from the pool in front of the maintenance area and the sheds. He could wade through the mud-bottomed pool or even swim the rest.

She saw him leap into the water maze over the front of the crashed flier, saw the great tree fall. She followed, vaulting the buckled nose of the flier, catching up as he took splashing to the water, wading from the mainland to the nearest island. Burning embers and curtains of smoke were blowing across the water maze, darkening and lighting the miniature landscape alternately, revealing and concealing the running, limping figure ahead of her as he headed for who knew where. Maybe he was thinking of the sheds where the ships were kept. Perhaps he saw himself jumping into one and firing all its pretend little guns at her. She followed via the wading point, the water in the channel cold round her legs, dragging at her, slowing her. It was like tying to run in a dream.

In the centre of the channel the water reached as far up as her hips before shallowing again.

Veppers had crossed the island beyond and was wading the next channel to one of the larger islands by the time she hauled her protesting legs out of the water. He disappeared as a dark, rolling cloud of smoke flowed between them.

When it cleared he'd gone.

She ran, panting, across the island, splashed across the next wading point and went stumbling up onto the next island. She looked all about, terrified that she'd lost him or that he might be lying in wait for her. She had to wave burning, floating scraps of twigs and leaves away from her face. A copse of trees forty metres away suddenly caught and flamed, casting a fierce yellow-orange glow over the whole low, hump-back island.

Something glinted down and to one side, in the reed bed close to her, and she turned.

He'd fallen, slipping on something as his knee had given way and his foot went out from under him, sending him skidding and plunging down the muddy slope into the reeds that lined the island. Wading the channels had taken the last of the strength from his legs; he doubted he'd be able to stand, let alone run any more. His back had hit some solid ground just before his feet and legs splashed into the dark water, and he was half winded, bouncing from the impact and turned onto his side. Behind, he saw a wall of black smoke just clearing and realised it had been between him and her as he'd slipped. She might not have seen him fall.

For an instant there he'd despaired, thinking he'd never get to where he was going and she'd catch him, but now he thought, No, I can use this to my advantage. She's the one who has to watch out. I'm going to win here, not her. Even upsets and what looked like misfortune could be turned to advantage if you had the right mind-set, the right attitude, if the universe was somehow always subtly on your side just because you fitted it better than anybody else, knew its true and secret workings better than anybody else.

He lay, partially concealed by the reeds around him, waiting for her. He dug inside his jacket, where the knives were, pulling one of them out of its sheath. When she came stumbling up onto the island, panting and dripping, he could see that she had lost him. He had his advantage. He raised himself up a little on one elbow, threw the knife with all his might.

Knife-throwing wasn't one of his skills, and the knives weren't throwing knives anyway. The weapon somersaulted a couple of times, flashing in the orange light from the fires that raged all around them. She must have caught a glimpse of it coming at her, because she started to duck and instinctively began to raise the hand nearest the knife's trajectory, to fend it off.

The handle of the knife caught her hard on one temple, grazing her, and the hand she'd raised to try and protect herself, the hand holding the gun, went on up past her head. An instant after the knife struck her head the gun roared, flashing in the night, its detonation flatter and less sharp than it had been in the tunnel beneath the house. He saw the gun fly from her hand as she staggered, stumbled and started to fall.

He'd seen where the gun had landed, though it had disappeared again after bouncing into some longer grass over the other side of the island. Still, he knew where it must be. He scrambled to his knees then his feet, finding renewed strength from somewhere, hands clawing at the mud and grass and earth until he was in a crouch, most of the way upright and could throw himself across the grass as the girl pirouetted nearby, staggering like a drunk, staring at him as he limped and hopped past a few metres away, heading for where the gun must be.

He should just have knifed her, he realised. He had the other knife. He'd fixated on getting a gun but that wasn't really what was important; what mattered was killing her before she killed him. The gun hadn't really mattered at all. What had he been thinking of? He was an idiot. Then he saw the gun, lying at the edge of the reed bed, a hand's breadth from the dark, glinting water.

He dived, hand outstretched, thudding into the ground, hand closing round the barrel of the gun, desperately slapping at it and trying to turn it as he brought his other hand up, finally grasping it properly. He rolled over, expecting to find her running towards him, leaping on top of him, clutching the knife he'd thrown at her or just with her clawed hands reaching for his throat.

She'd gone. He sat up as quickly as he could, legs quivering, chest heaving, breath whistling to and fro inside his throat. He stood, shakily, and saw her, down by the reeds a little way off, just starting to pull herself back out onto dry land.

Off to one side, more trees were catching fire, sending flames leaping and boiling into the darkness. They lit up the sheds where the miniature battleships were kept. He could see some of the vessels themselves: one on a wheeled cradle on the dockside, another floating in the water by the quay. Some of the sheds were surrounded by burning grass and fallen branches, flames starting to lick up their metal walls and curl over their shallow-pitched roofs. A burning bough fell from a tree and crashed through the roof of the nearest shed in a shower of sparks.

He walked, slowly, legs shaking, breath raw and ragged in the warm, fire-parched air, to where the girl was trying to pull herself out of the mud and the crushed, flattened reeds. Blood was running down her face from where the knife had hit her.

Part of him wanted to tell her he still didn't believe that she was who she said she was, but even if it was true, well tough. Winners won, the successful succeeded, aggression and predation and ruthlessness tended to win out – what a surprise. Just the way life was. Nothing personal. Well, actually, everything fucking personal.

But he didn't really have the breath for any of it. "Fuck you," he said at her as she crawled in front of him and he stood over her, pointing the gun at her straggle-haired head. He'd said it as loud as he could but it still came out as more of a wheeze than anything else. She swung at him, one arm and hand whirling round. She'd found the knife he'd thrown at her, had gone into the reed bed to find it. The blade whacked into his leg, into the calf just below his good knee, sending pain darting up his leg and spine and detonating in his head.

He screamed, staggered back, held the gun in both hands and nearly fell as the girl collapsed to one side, unbalanced by the need to wield the knife that was now sticking out of his leg. "Fucking little—!" he shrieked at her.

He steadied, straightened despite the pain, aimed the gun at her and squeezed the trigger.

The trigger was stuck. He heaved at it, tried again to pull it, but it just wasn't moving. Felt like his finger couldn't move. He tried to move the gun to the other hand, but even that was difficult. It was as though his hands were so cold they weren't obeying orders. He heard himself make a mewling, whimpering noise. He glanced at the side of the gun, looking for a safety catch, but it was already off. He tried the gun again, but it just wasn't happening. He tried to throw it away, but then it was as though it was stuck to his hand. Finally it sailed off into the darkness. He fumbled in his jacket for the second knife, then – staggering, feeling like he was about to black out – realised he could pull out the one sticking into his leg.

The girl was still on the ground near his feet. She seemed to be trying to get up again, then she collapsed back, thudding down onto her rump, one arm going behind to steady herself.

He found the second knife inside his jacket pocket, pulled it from its sheath. Somewhere off to one side there were lots of little explosions like fireworks. Light flickered everywhere. Stuff was whining and zipping overhead. He took a step towards her as she looked woozily up at him.

Then he was caught, steadied by something that wasn't him, rooted to the ground, unable to move, as though every part of him had seized up: muscles, skeleton, everything.

The girl looked up at him, and something changed in her face. It seemed to relax, and her shoulders and chest shook once, almost as though she was laughing.

"Ah," she said, and got her legs beneath her, pushing herself up until she was kneeling. She felt at the side of her head, where the blood was, looked at the darkness of it on her hand in the flickering orange light. She looked back to him.

He couldn't move. He simply could not move. He wasn't paralysed – he could feel his muscles straining, trying to move him – but he was stuck, as though enchanted, utterly immobile.

"Look at your hands, Veppers," the girl told him, over the noise of more explosions. Stuttering light flared against her mud-streaked face and wet, bedraggled hair.

He could still move his eyes. He looked down at his hands.

They were covered in fine silver lines, glinting in the firelight.

Where had—?

"Aye-aye," said a male voice nearby. "Pleasant evening for it, what?"

A tall, too-thin man in pale, loose clothes strolled past. When he glanced back, he saw that it was Demeisen. The avatar spared him a glance then went to stand by the girl.

"You okay?"

"Never better. Thought you'd left."

"Yup. That was the idea. Need a hand up?"

"Give me a moment."

"Happily." The man turned and looked at Veppers, folding his arms. "This isn't her doing this," he told him. "It's me."

Veppers couldn't get his mouth or jaw to work. Even his breathing was difficult. Then a thousand tiny fierce pains sprang up, as though hundreds of hair-fine wires were wrapping every centimetre of him, and were starting to shrink, cutting into every part of his body.

A bubbling, wheezing whine escaped his mouth.

The man glanced down at the girl again. "Unless you want to finish him, of course," he said to her. He looked back at Veppers, frowning a little. "I wouldn't though. Conscience can be a terrible thing." He smiled. "So I hear." He shrugged. "Unless you're something like me, of course," he murmured. "I don't give a fuck."

The girl looked up into Veppers' eyes as the wires of the tattoo device cut slowly into him. He had never known such pain, never guessed that anything could hurt so much.

"Quickly," she said, and coughed as more smoke and burning embers sailed past the three of them.

"What?" the avatar said.

"Quickly," she said. "Don't draw it out. Just—"

The avatar gazed into Veppers' eyes and nodded down at the girl. "See?" he said. "Good kid, really."

The pain, already intolerable, increased wildly, just around his neck and head.

The *coup de grâce* was Veppers' head twisting right round, an almost comical expression filling his already blood-flecked face as the tattoo lines flicked into a spiral, rose up and shrank inwards all at once, so that his head seemed to crumple and shrink into itself, becoming a far-too-thin tall cylinder that disappeared in a spray of blood.

Lededje had to look away. She heard what sounded like a whole big bowl full of rotten fruit being emptied onto the ground, then heard and felt the body thump into the grass beside her a moment later. She opened her eyes to see it twitch a couple of times, blood still pumping from the garrotted, twisted-open neck.

She felt she was going to faint. She put both arms out behind her. "Neat trick," she said, watching arcs of flame and little sprays of fire burst from the miniature docks and the sheds where the model battleships were kept, as they burned and blew up, shells and rockets whizzing everywhere.

"It moved over from you to him when you tried to strangle the fucker in ambassador Huen's office," Demeisen told her, going over to kick the body once, as though testing it was real. "Left you with nothing but a glorified sun tan."

She coughed again, looked around at the sheer lunatic devastation going on all around them.

"Other ships," she said. "Soon. Need to—"

"No, we don't," Demeisen said, stretching and yawning. "No second wave. None left." He stooped, plucking the knife out of the leg of the headless body, which had stopped twitching now. "Left the last handful for the planetary defence guys, to give them something to feel heroic about," he told her as he inspected the knife, weighing it in his hand, twirling it a couple of times. A furious whizzing noise, barely following a flash of light, was a shell from one of the stricken, fire-consumed battleships; the avatar's arm moved blurringly fast and he batted it away from his face without even looking, still admiring the knife. The fizzing shell slapped into the nearest reed bed and blew up in a tall fountain of water, orange-tinged white on grubby black. "I did think of letting just one through, or even stomping the relevant targets myself, just for the heck of it," Demeisen said, "and pretending. But in the end I thought not; better to leave more of the evidence on the ground. Plus some of the Hells have only gone dormant, still storing personalities. Might be able to save some, if there's anything sane left to save."

The avatar held one arm straight out and the tattoo – glinting, pristine – uncurled itself from Veppers' body, spiralling lazily up into the air like a twister-wind in a stubble field and wrapping itself round the avatar's hand like spun mercury, disappearing as it flowed over his skin and up his arm.

"Was that thing alive all the time?" she asked.

"Yup. Not just alive; intelligent. So fucking smart it's even got a name."

She held up one hand while he was drawing his next breath. "I'm sure it has," she said. "But . . . spare me."

Demeisen grinned. "Slap-drone, personal protection, weapon; all of the above," he said, stretching again, as though the tattoo had spread itself all over him and he was testing how it fitted his body.

He looked down at her.

"You ready to go back? If you're coming back?"

She sat, arms out behind her, blood in one eye, aching everywhere, feeling like shit. She nodded. "I suppose."

"Want this?" offering her the knife handle first.

"Better," she said, taking it, then struggling to her feet, helped by his other hand. "Family heirloom." She looked at the avatar, frowning. "There were two," she said.

He shook his head, *tsk*ed, stooped and pulled the other knife from where it had stuck in the ground. He took the double sheath from Veppers' jacket, presenting it and both blades to her with a bow.

A scale-model battleship, still tied-up to its quayside, on fire from stem to stern, lifted suddenly in the middle, breaking its back as it blew up, dispensing fire and flames, debris and shrapnel and angrily buzzing and whining shells and rockets all about. The first, keel-sundering gout of fire briefly lit up two silvery ovoids stood on their ends on a small low island nearby, before they vanished, almost as quickly as they had appeared.

Dramatis Personae

Ambassador Huen jumped before she was pushed, as was traditional. Even the very limited amount of interfering she'd suggested and sanctioned was somewhat more than was strictly allowable in the circumstances. She resigned her post, went home, spent the next few years raising her son and the following couple of centuries not regretting what she'd done at all.

The Abominator-class picket ship *Falling Outside The Normal Moral Constraints* manifested at the Board Of Inquiry Into The Recent Events Around The Sichultian Enablement as a fabulously tattooed limping albino dwarf with a speech impediment and double incontinence. Quickly cleared of all but the most allowable and – for an Abominator-class – expected malfeasance, it returned to its usual stand-by task of punctuated loneliness, sitting, generally in the middle of cold nowhere, waiting for stuff to happen and trying not to be too disappointed when nothing did.

It received from its fellow Abominator-class and other SC ships precisely the sort of congratulations and plaudits it might have expected for its actions around Tsung and Quyn; all deeply tinged with envy. It treasured them almost as much as the exquisitely rendered recordings of the engagements.

It spent quite a lot of time in or around the larger classes of GSVs, just for the company. Its avatar Demeisen continued to behave appallingly.

Joiler Veppers' reputation survived more or less intact for a few weeks, but then as the weeks became months and the months years, it all fell apart as stories of his cruelty, greed and selfishness, and the extent of his callousness towards his own people and even his own planet, became clear. It was over a decade before the first revisionist right-wing historian attempted to restore his reputation, and even then to no lasting effect.

Yime Nsokyi really had been an SC plant, deep within Quietus, for all that time, even if, in a sense, she hadn't known it herself after she'd both agreed to be so and then consented to have the memory of that agreement deleted. In any event, given that even in one of the most successful Specialist Agencies-led interventions in recent centuries she had been largely relegated to a supporting role, she resigned from the Quietudinal Service. More in frustration than disgust, but she resigned all the same.

She returned to her adopted home Orbital and began a successful political career, starting with the position of emergency drill supervisor on her home Plate and eventually becoming the representative for the entire Orbital. As with all hierarchic positions within the Culture it was almost entirely an honorary, figurehead role, but she found the achievement highly satisfying all the same.

Her personal life ended up consisting of a sort of cycle of being neuter, female and male in turn, each for a decade or so. She found that she was able to establish tender, meaningful relationships –

with an agreeable physical component when she was not neuter – at every stage, but would have been the first to admit that real passion and true love, if there was such a thing, always eluded her.

The ex-Limited Offensive Unit *Me, I'm Counting* returned briefly to the Forgotten GSV *Total Internal Reflection*, then resumed a life of galactic tramping. It found new hobbies.

Hibin Jasken served some time in prison for his complicity in a few of his late master's better-publicised crimes, though his efforts to pick up survivors from the firestorm around the Espersium mansion and his full cooperation with the authorities helped reduce his final sentence.

On his release he became a security consultant and successful businessman, living relatively modestly and contributing most of what he earned to charitable causes, especially those concerned with orphaned and disadvantaged children. He was instrumental in the Wheel *Halo VII* being turned into a mobile holiday home for the dependants of the bankrupt and destitute, and was an ardent supporter of the moves, eventually successful, to end the practice of Indented Intagliation.

The GCU *Bodhisattva*, its Mind re-housed in a new-build Escarpment class, remained attached to the Quietus section but subsequently spent a lot of time investigating – very carefully – Fallen and Unfallen Bulbitians, thinking to present a paper on the entities at some point in the future.

Auppi Unstril was reunited with a revented, slightly changed Lanyares Tersetier. It didn't last long.

Legislator-Admiral Bettlescroy-Bisspe-Blispin III came very close indeed to abject denunciation, demotion and utter ruin – both personal and familial – as the GFCF tried to decide whether all that had transpired regarding events within the Sichultian Enablement in general and the Tsungarial Disk in particular had been basically a thorough-going and unmitigated catastrophe or a sort of subtle triumph.

On the one hand the GFCF had lost influence and credibility, the Culture didn't want to be their friend any more, they had been humiliated in an unexpectedly and appallingly one-sided naval encounter, they'd had to hand back the supervisory role in the Disk – to the Culture, of all people – and they had been informed in no uncertain terms by the NR that a close eye was going to be kept on them in future.

On the other hand it could have been worse. And arguably one way of making it worse would be to admit just how badly things had actually gone.

Bettlescroy-Bisspe-Blispin III was duly promoted to Prime Legislator-Grand-Admiral-of-the-Combined-Fleets and presented with several terribly impressive medals. He was put in charge of finding new ways to impress, reassure and – ultimately – imitate the Culture.

Chayeleze Hifornsdaughter, saved from Hell and torment after many subjective decades and the best part of two lifetimes, found herself rescued from the dormant remains of one of the Hells that had existed beneath the trackways of the Espersium estate on Sichult and placed into a Temporary Recuperative Afterlife in a substrate on her home planet of Pavul. She met Prin twice thereafter: the first time when he came to see her during her convalescence, and once much later.

She had discovered that she had no desire to come back to the Real. She had become whatever the Virtual equivalent of institutionalised was, and there could be no returning. Another Chay already lived in the Real who had never been through all that she had, and in many ways that person was the real Chay; she herself had become something entirely different. She still felt something for Prin, and wished him well, but she had no need to be part of his life. Prin eventually established a happy, lasting relationship with Representative Filhyn and Chay was glad that he was content.

By then she'd found her new role. She would remain a creature of ending and release in the Virtual; the angel of death who came for people who lived in happy, congenial Afterlives and who – tired even of their many lifetimes lived after biological death – were ready to dissolve themselves into the generality of consciousness that underlay Heaven, or who were ready simply to cease to be altogether.

That was when she met Prin for the second time, subjective centuries later.

They barely recognised one another.

Surprisingly quickly, given the bizarre and volatile variety of peoples, beings and endemic moralities involved, the culture of Hells – already irredeemably reduced following the events on Sichult and the testimony of people like Prin – became something of an anathema pretty much throughout the civilised galaxy, and indeed within a single average bio-generation their very absence became accepted almost without question as part of what constituted being civilised in the first place.

This made the Culture very happy.

Lededje Y'breq – Quyn-Sichultsa Lededje Samwaf Y'breq d'Espersium, to give her the Full Name she assumed on becoming a properly established Culture citizen – took up residence first on the GSV *Sense Amid Madness, Wit Amidst Folly*, on what was in effect an extended cruise to see the galaxy, then, twenty years later, settled on the Orbital called Hursklip where, in her middle-to-old age, she built, largely by hand, a full-size replica of the battleship grounds that she had known as the water maze, complete with working miniature battleships. They could be human-powered, but each incorporated a well-armoured survival pod which kept their occupant safe no matter what. The feature became an enduring tourist attraction.

She never did return to Sichult, or meet Jasken again, though he tried to get in touch.

She had five children by as many different fathers and ended up with over thirty great-great-great-grandchildren, which by Culture standards was almost disgraceful.

Epilogue

Vatueil, revented once more and back to using what he liked to think of as his original name – even though it wasn't – sipped his aperitif on the restaurant terrace. He watched the sun set across the dark lake and listened to the crick and chirp of insects hidden in the bushes and vines nearby.

He checked the time. She was late, as usual. What was it about poets?

What a long, terrible war that had been, he thought, idly.

He really had been a traitor, of course. He'd been planted in the anti-Hell side long ago by those who wished to see the Hells continue for ever, a cause he'd supported at the time partly out of sheer contrarianism and partly out of that despair he felt sometimes, periodically – during this long, long life – at the sheer self-hurtful idiocy and destructiveness of so many types of sentient life, especially the meta-type known as pan-human, to which he had always had the dubious honour of belonging. You want suffering, pain and horror? I'll give you suffering, pain and horror . . .

But then, over time, fighting away, again and again, *yet* again, he'd changed his mind. Cruelty and the urge to dominate and oppress started to seem childish and pathetic once more, the way he'd accepted they were, long ago, but had somehow turned away from in the meantime.

So he'd spilled all the beans, implicated all those he knew about who deserved to be implicated, and had been quite pleased to see so much of what he had pledged to fight for crumble away into disgraced and piecemeal nothing. Hell mend them.

There would be people who would never forgive him for betraying them, but that was just too bad. They ought to have guessed, of course, but people never did.

That was the thing about traitors: they were people who'd already changed their minds at least once.

He made a mental note never again to insist on working his way up through the ranks He'd finally convinced himself he'd learned all the relevant lessons already, probably many times over, and the process was starting to smack too much of outright masochism.

The sun brightened slowly as it settled against the horizon, subsiding beneath a long sinuous line of intervening cloud to blaze through a channel of clear air with a languid, dying glory, hazy orange-red against a thin yellow arc of sky. He watched the star's disk as it started to fall behind a line of dark, distant hills, far across the plains. Closer to him, fringed by its still hush of trees, the lake had gone dark as ink.

He drank in the sunlight's slow dwindling.

From the first glint of dawn, and for the rest of the day, the sun was too bright to look at, he thought; you could only gaze steadily upon it, only truly see it, regard it, inspect and properly admire it, when it was at its most filtered – half hidden by the thickness of the atmosphere, with its cargo of the day's dust – and just about to slip away altogether. He must have experienced this on a hundred planets, but was only really noticing it now.

He wondered if this counted as a poetic insight. Probably not. Or if it did it had already occurred to countless poets. Still, he'd mention it to her when she arrived. Likely, she'd snort, though it would depend or her mood; instead she might assume that wry, amused expression that told him he was impinging, clumsily if charmingly, upon her territory. Tiny crinkles of skin formed under her eyes when she had that look. It would be worth it for that alone.

He heard steps. The maître d' crossed the terrace, arrived at his side, bowed fractionally and clicked his heels.

"Your table is ready, Mr. Zakalwe."